AND THEN WE HEARD THE THUNDER

John Oliver Killens

HOWARD UNIVERSITY PRESS
Washington, D.C.
1983

Third Printing 2004
Second Printing 1986

Digitally printed in Canada on acid-free paper by WEBCOM Ltd.
Production management and project consultation provided by Abram Hall Alternatives, Inc.

Library of Congress Cataloging-in-Publication Data

Killens, John Oliver, 1916–
And then we heard the thunder

I. World War, 1939–1945—Fiction. I. Title
PS3561.137A8 1983 813'.54 83–6174
ISBN 0-88258-115-5

"AND THEN WE SAW THE LIGHTNING, *and that was the guns. And then we heard the thunder and that was the big guns. And then we heard the rain falling and that was the drops of blood falling. And when we came to get in the crops, it was dead men that we reaped."*—HARRIET TUBMAN, *ex-slave, abolitionist, Union Scout, and Freedom Fighter (describing a battle of the Civil War which she witnessed)*

TO MY MOTHER

AND TO

HARRIET TUBMAN, ***who stands head***
and shoulders above most Americans
in my private Hall of Fame,

and to

MY BUDDIES, ***fallen and standing,***

and to

CHUCK AND BARBARA ***and to all***
young people everywhere.
May they never hear the man-made thunder
nor see the terrible lightning

INTRODUCTION

"How do you live in a white man's world? Do you live on your knees—do you live with your shoulders bent and your hat in your hand? Or do you live like a man is supposed to live—with your head straight up?" Joe Youngblood poses these questions in John Oliver Killens's first novel *Youngblood* (1954). In a review of that novel (*The New York Herald Tribune,* July 11, 1954), novelist Ann Petry quoted those lines and drew a perceptive conclusion: "This thematic question pervades the thinking, controls the action, dominates the conversation of all the characters—whether they be black or white."

The theme of the black man's struggle for dignity within a racist society is one that has, at the very least, influenced the work of black novelists from the time of William Welles Brown—author of the first novel published by an Afro-American, *Clotel, or The President's Daughter,* which was printed initially in London in 1853. Few novelists, however, have pursued the issue throughout their careers with as much determination and passion as John Killens. Therefore, Miss Petry's comments about *Youngblood* have proven not only accurate but prophetic.

Youngblood is a graphic, almost documentary tale of a black family struggling to survive in a racist, backwoods Georgia town. The story records the experiences of two generations of the Youngblood family. The author vividly portrays the grim reality of Jim Crow in the South. The brutal victimization of the Youngbloods and other blacks is counterpointed by the more optimistic portrayal of blacks' emerging awareness that resistance and confrontation are necessary despite the mortal risks involved. Still, Killens tended, as do many first novelists, to rely too heavily on the Manichaean principle of tension between good and evil for dramatic effect. From a structural standpoint, Killens diminished the oversimplified portraits of villainous whites and virtuous blacks by including the more subtly drawn character of Oscar Jefferson, a poor white farmer who gradually aligns himself with the Youngbloods. It is through Jefferson's agonizing psychic transformation that the novel achieves it greatest sense of moral depth and complexity.

Eight years after his first novel, John Killens published *And Then We Heard the Thunder* (1962). During the interim, he occupied himself with various pursuits, including writing for television and the movies. (Among his credits was the script for the highly praised 1959 film, *Odds Against Tomorrow.*) This hiatus from the rigors of fiction writing seemed to have worked to Killens's advantage. His second novel reflected a ripening of his talent and an expanded concept of the novel form. Although only slightly less insistently focused on the tragedy and irony of America's racial predicament, his second book displayed a breadth of thematic complexity and of setting that made *Youngblood* appear provincial.

Soon after the publication of *Youngblood,* Killens's work attracted criticism as "race" fiction that advocated a "separatist" ideology. When his second novel appeared, those judgments grew more insistent. But a close reading of *Youngblood* makes such reactions seem misdirected, even paranoiac. The novel has its faults, but these are weaknesses arising from the basic nature of its form. If published today, it would likely be categorized as a family saga—a naturalistic tale of one family's struggle to escape societal oppression. It is no more a race novel than Henry Roth's *Call It Sleep* (1934) or any of the numerous fictional sagas that document the horrors of the Holocaust. Like most of these novels, it suffers from excessive detail, repetition, stereotypical characters, and occasional sentimentality—weaknesses that generally result from an authors' glove-tight identification with the predicament of the group portrayed. Still, novels like *Youngblood* provide a passionately felt and literally detailed picture of a specific place and time. And in his first novel Killens created an indelible montage of the cruelty and injustice of black life in the Jim Crow South.

Because *And Then We Heard the Thunder* is also a long, sprawling, copiously peopled novel, it is not surprising that it has some of the same weaknesses as its predecessor. Set during World War II and focused on life in a black military company in basic training and on the battlefields of the South Pacific, it is full of gritty but extravagant detail and dialogue from barracks and foxholes. Thinly drawn characters abound and the repetitive manner Killens uses to drive home his antisegregationist, antiwar theme is often distracting.

Nonetheless, the book exhibits a marked extension of Killens's conception of the novel form. It shows the beginning of a stylistic stretching-out that would continue throughout his writing career. The story's setting also shows a fundamental conceptual enlargement. Instead of the rural southern background that had become commonplace for black fiction in the 1950s and 1960s, Killens chose a much larger canvas. The story begins in New York City, moves to a basic training camp in Georgia, and then on to the South Pacific campaign. It ends in Australia at the close of the war. This variegated background provides opportunity for wider narrative sweep and for comparisons of regional attitudes that bear on the novel's basic themes. Killens makes excellent use of this opportunity in his depiction of both the Filipinos's and Australians's reactions to black soldiers before and after they were exposed to the racist propaganda of white American soldiers.

Although the novel's hero, Solly Saunders, must contend with the same problem that plagued the Youngbloods ("Do you live like a man is supposed to live—with your head straight up?"), Killens has greatly extended the arena in which the protagonist grapples with his dilemma. In one sense, the Youngbloods's predicament was starkly simple: The issue was survival, attempting to salvage some scrap of dignity from an overtly brutal and hostile environment in which their adversaries were dead set on either destroying them or keeping them in their place. Solly Saunders's conundrum springs from the same racist societal distortions but is of an entirely different order.

Solly is an exceptionally talented and intelligent black

man—an employee of the New York City government with two years of law school. He is "handsome" and "articulate," which according to his bride Millie, "makes it much easier for *him* to be accepted in *their* world." Solly's problem emerges as one of the central themes in the novel: Does the spiritual cost of being accepted in *their* world outweigh the material benefits? Solly's ambivalence propels the narrative direction and plot in this story. "He wanted to be accepted in the world of white folks," Killens writes of Solly, "but wanted nobody to catch him working at it."

This shift in the fundamental predicament of Killens's protagonist is due, in part, to the eight-year gap between the publication of the two novels. When Killens's first novel was published in 1954 (the year the Supreme Court handed down the *Brown v. Board of Education* decision and ignited the Civil Rights movement), the proscriptions of Jim Crow America were not being opposed on a mass level. Despite black America's growing disenchantment, resistance to segregation was piecemeal. Attempts to alter the status quo were largely fought on an individual basis or through legal maneuvers directed by organizations like the NAACP. White America seemed deaf to complaints about the oppression of blacks, and social reform movements of any kind were rare. Indeed, there was sufficient reason for social critics to label this the "Silent Generation." But the seeds for the more volatile sixties were being planted. Shortly after the publication of *Youngblood*, Rosa Parks's confrontation with a Montgomery, Alabama, bus driver over the segregated seating policy of the bus company triggered a boycott that would transform black disenchantment into a mass protest movement. Martin Luther King, Jr.'s emergence as a national leader during the boycott and the continued push for school desegregation set in motion a series of events that made the sixties one of the most turbulent decades in American history.

By the time *And Then We Heard the Thunder* was published in 1962, America's black consciousness had been raised to a level that had been unimaginable a decade earlier. One result of that heightened awareness was the serious consideration of whether being completely integrated into the fabric of American society was the appropriate goal for blacks. Many leaders questioned the wisdom of joining a "sinking ship." Black nationalism was becoming a significant force. Blacks looked at Africa and other Third World countries as models for the newly emerging Afro-American nation.

The influence of this radical alteration of the main current of Afro-American thinking is clearly seen in the different attitudinal frameworks from which the protagonists of Killens's two early novels regard their environments. Although *And Then We Heard the Thunder* is set in the forties, its hero Solly Saunders is undoubtedly a character who functions with the awareness of a black consciousness that emerged in the sixties. It is an odd but intriguing combination of historical setting and an advanced sentient perspective—less extreme, certainly, but akin to placing a character with the racial perspective of Malcolm X in the fictional landscape of the antebellum South. This synthesis yields a novel that is far more advanced and complex than its predecessor.

Solly has moved beyond the fundamental consideration of racial injustice that preoccupied the Youngbloods. He is not merely concerned with whether one can "live with his head straight up"—that is an established priority. Solly must decide *how* to stand up, live with dignity, and avoid becoming a pawn used by whites to manipulate and control other blacks. He has moved from the preoccupation with *individual* survival that characterized the Youngbloods's struggle to a racial consciousness that is marked by an overriding concern for *black unity*.

Solly ponders the conflict between his sense of being an American (with its attendant emphasis on personal gain) and his awareness that such gain may well place him in direct opposition to the men in his all-black company. When he first enters the army, although he resents having been pulled away from his wife and what appears to be a promising career, he argues with fellow recruits who feel that the black man's fight is with white America, not with the Germans or the Japanese. Solly insists that the fight against Hitler is a "Democratic War." Early in the novel he says:

> "This is our country as much as anybody else's. You want the same rights and privileges of every other

American, don't you? All right then. When these rights are jeopardized, you have to fight just like everybody else."

Solly's insistent patriotism and idealism are eroded. He is forced into a situation where he must decide between allegiance to the army or his friends. He is hand-picked to be the company clerk after being praised for his "unusual qualifications for a Negro" and subsequently is used to convince other black soldiers to accept inferior treatment. When his closest friend, Bookworm, is beaten viciously by an MP, Solly persuades him not to go after the white soldier with a gun. Later he doubts both his good sense and the rightness of his position. ("You," he thinks to himself, "are the new-styled, slicked-up Uncle Tom.") When he is severely beaten and humiliated by local police and a high-ranking army officer outside the Georgia basic training camp, Solly's transformation is nearly completed. It is only the intrusion of orders for his company to be shipped to the South Pacific that forestalls his complete revolt against the army hierarchy.

Solly's internal struggle with the conflict between his perception of himself as a black man and as an American is the major theme of the novel. Killens clearly expresses his sentiments about this central issue in the final episode where black soldiers take up arms and engage in a bloody battle with white soldiers. Critic Addison Gayle, Jr., who has written perceptively about Killens's work, presents a lucid analysis of this point in *The Way of the New World—The Black Novel in America* (1975):

> Whatever happened to Saunders happened to him because he was black: position as Company Clerk, condescending respect from fellow officers, promotion to sergeant, exclusion from canteens and dance halls, and assaults upon his person by whites. Worse things did not happen to him as they did to others, only because of circumstances. Therefore, the war in which he enlists at the end of the novel, both metaphorically and actually, is not a personal but a collective one, and what is demanded of each warrior is not only valor and courage, but love and respect for one another. These are the qualities demanded by Killens of one black man for another, and the primary characteristic of com-

> rades-in-arms is love for each other. It is a first principle for the author. Men may be designated by race, by the uniforms they wear, by their status in a platoon, company or battalion. Black men may even be designated by the color of their skin; yet, to be a black man means to be cognizant of one's past, to opt for the collective 'we' over the individual 'I' and to love each black man as one loves himself.

Killens's feelings about the issue of black unity is indicated by his handling of the major theme in *And Then We Heard the Thunder* and in essays collected in *Black Man's Burden* (1965). His stand made his work central to the early seventies debate over a "Black Aesthetic." The proponents of this new aesthetic—most notably the late Hoyt Fuller (formerly editor of the Johnson Publications' *Black World*), poet Don L. Lee, Amiri Baraka and Addison Gayle, reacted to the weight given to form and technique as opposed to content in the evaluation of art. A reaction against art for art's sake and the ivory tower aesthetics of the literacy establishment, the movement proposed that since, as Baraka wrote, "All art is politics," black art, to be useful and viable, should reflect the positive black images growing out of the new black awareness. In an afterword to his *The Way of the New World,* Gayle suggested a criterion for assaying black art, and for that matter, any art: "How much better has the work of art made the life of a single human being upon this planet, and how functional has been the work of art in moving us toward the moment when an *ars poetica* is possible for all."

Few would argue the merits of this criterion as it relates to the spirit and intent of a work of art. But a problem arises when one tries to apply this idea as an aesthetic principle for literature. First, the judgment of whether a book has improved anyone's life is both subjective and temporal. It is a critical appraisal that must emanate from the personal experiences and biases that color a particular critic's perception. Moreover, any such appraisal is made from the limited perspective of a particular historical era and specific social context. It is open to the counter-criticism of subsequent generations. To regard any judgment of the relevancy of the spirit of a work of art as objective and timeless would, besides suggesting some belief in soothsaying, assume a kind of homogenized critical faculty or tyranny of ideas which the proponents of the new aesthetic would surely reject if applied to their own work.

Second, the criterion completely ignores the element of craft. Hardly any would contend that a well-executed work that proposed spurious or anti-human ideas should be hailed as great art. Conversely, few critics would argue that a vapid, crudely written book adhering to current estimates of the proper religious, political, or racial attitudes is anything more than well-intentioned.

Killens's novel, however, is texturally enriched by thematic threads that are developed simultaneously with Solly's struggle for racial identity and unity. The most significant is the antiwar aspect of the novel.

At the beginning of the novel, nearly all the attitudes expressed about the war by black men are linked to the characters' sense of racial injustice. The questions of whether they should fight and of *who* is their real enemy are voiced repeatedly in barracks banter. Killens misses little of the subtle irony of the black soldiers' predicament. "What you reckon I read in *your* paper last night?" Bookworm asks Solly as they march toward the ship to be dispatched to the South Pacific. "Some of *your* folks' leaders called on the President down in Washington and demanded that colored soldiers be allowed to die with dignity at the front rather than serve in the Quartermaster. Now ain't that a mother fer ya?" After the white regiments have boarded the ship to the tune of "God Bless America," the band begins playing "The Darktown Strutters' Ball" as black regiments go aboard. "I guess Charlie wants us to jitterbug onto his pretty white boat," Bookwoom says, "we ain't no soldiers. We ain't nothing but a bunch of goddam clowns." The black soldiers' alienation from the army and their skepticism about the righteousness of the American cause is a constant theme in Parts I and II.

In Part III, after Solly's regiment has stormed the beach of a South Pacific island, Killens begins to express doubts about the justification of war in general. Through Solly's meditations on his circumstance and graphic descriptions of the carnage and mutilation, Killens paints a grim picture of the lunacy and brutality of the fighting. He suggests that the underlying motives for the war effort are reprehensible.

"Does the damn war make any sense?" Solly asks himself. And later he provides his own answer. "I know one thing—when I get back home I don't want to see another uniform or another parade the longest day I live. . . . What are we doing in these people's country? No-damn-body sent for us. I mean the United States and Japanese Empire didn't ask these people, 'May we use your country for our little old battleground?' We rain down bombs on their cities and their homes and rice paddies, and we kill thousands of innocent people. . . . I want to know who really gets anything out of all this shooting and maiming and killing, all this so-called civilized madness?"

This idea parallels and complements Killens's major concern with black unity and the plight of the black soldiers. The sections of the novel dealing with combat contain some of the best writing in the book. In the depiction of Solly's encounter with a Japanese Kamikaze squad which attacked an American-held airstrip in the Phillipines, Killens evokes the sense of a near-fatal battle and the soldiers' cold terror. Throughout the descriptions of the American Army's occupation of the Pacific islands, Killens vividly conveys the initial horror of massive bombardment by heavy artillery, the fitful, sudden violence of surprise attacks, and the harsh reality of the steamy, insect-infested encampments. The narrative style is straighforward, nearly journalistic, and has the impact of some of the best of James Jones's writing about the same war.

In addition to the expanded setting, the more complex and subtle treatment of the racial issue, and the amplified thematic content, *And Then We Heard the Thunder* has another significant element that was generally absent in Killens's first novel. Although Killens is occasionally a ponderous writer, he has a formidable knowledge of black folk humor and a finely tuned sense of black dialect. In *Youngblood* these attributes were successfully employed in the novel's dialogue, but the narrator's voice lacked the irony that humor can provide. In his second novel, Killens made more frequent use of humor as a foil for the weighty issues that were his real concern: segregation, emasculation, and black awareness. In his next three novels, Killens continued to refine his work; as his writing developed, humor assumed even more import. But this lighter touch had already begun to emerge in his work.

In fact, there are two important comic characters in *And Then We Heard the Thunder* who are essential to the story's development. Both are black soldiers and both are introduced early in the novel. The way they are used to further the plot demonstrates some of the weaknesses and the strengths of Killens's work.

William Thomas Rogers is the company buffoon, an unconscionable sycophant who is ridiculed as an "Uncle Thomas" and "handkerchief-head" by the other men. It is Rogers's exorbitant eagerness, his insistent bucking for promotion and status, that provides context for most of the humorous repartee in the early sections of the novel. ("My man here been brown'nosing ever since he got inside the gate," Bookworm says of Rogers. "That's how come his breath smells so bad. I don't know what he's bucking for, but he's the original sepia Buck-damn-Rogers.") Structurally, Rogers's presence allows a more balanced view of Solly's ambivalence about opting for promotion and advancement or supporting the other black soldiers. Compared with Rogers's behavior, Solly's compromised leanings toward the military hierarchy seem insignificant. The difficulty is that the portrayal of Rogers is grossly exaggerated and one-dimensional. Rogers is a kind of vaudeville figure, a type of Kingfish against whose outlandish behavior the comportment of any other character would seem more humane and perceptive. In certain types of fiction, a burlesque character of Rogers's ilk is perfectly acceptable, but in a naturalistic novel such as this one, the presence is grating.

On the other hand, Jerry Scott, the company cook who habitually went AWOL, is a superb comic creation. Scotty, like Rogers, functions in the novel as a prod to Solly's eventual commitment to the other black soldiers. His comic demeanor is derived not from exaggeration but from the consistency of behavior within the novel's setting as well as from the validity of his reactions and observations. When first introduced, Scotty has been arrested for going AWOL; Solly has been charged with watching him. "Remember, you're responsible for him," a topkick has told Solly. "If the prisoner gets away, you do his time in the stockade." When the officer leaves, Scotty, as if he were Solly's alter ego, immediately zeroes in on the absurdity of the situation.

> "You look like a nice guy," Scotty said. "What you got against me?"
>
> "Nothing at all." Where did that question come from?
>
> Scotty laughed. "See what I mean? I ain't never done you nothing and you ain't never done nothing to me, but here I sit and I'm your prisoner and you got to hold me till they get ready to lock me up in the stock-damn-kade. . . . And look at you, a smart intelligent fellow. Should be using your own head about things and stuff, but look atcher. I'm under arrest in your charge. I get away, you have to do my time, and they didn't even give you a little biddy cap pistol to guard me with. Suppose I wanted to get away, what could you do to stop me? I could pick up something and knock you into the middle of next week. Now don't that make you feel like a fool? It sure do make you look like one."

On each of his infrequent appearances in the novel, Scotty brings the feel of ironic truth. He is perhaps the most memorable character in the book because his bizarre behavior is valid given the madness of the black soldiers' situation. Moreover, he is an example of the kind of ironically conceived and authentically rendered characters that would appear more and more frequently in Killens's work. This development would lead, eight years and three novels later, to publication of Killens's finest book, *The Cotillion* (1970). Killens is at his outrageous best in that novel. He has forsaken the blunt, occasionally melodramatic detailed presentation of racial injustice for an oblique, witty and more cutting and effective portrayal of the consequences of American racism.

In retrospect, it is difficult to deny that John Killens permitted his creativity and imagination to be too tightly reined in his earlier works. It is almost as if his passion to convey the literal horror of racism and of the resultant human condition overwhelmed his creative fictional instinct. As a result, those novels lacked the imaginative fullness and authorial risk-taking of some of his later work, despite their power and sincerity. (It is not incidental that

The Cotillion begins with a foreword in which Killens states: "I'm first, second and third person my own damn self. And I will intrude, protrude or exclude my point of view any time it suits my disposition. Dig that.")

Although he is not the most subtle contemporary black novelist and has generally eschewed experimentation in technique, John Killens has provided readers with novels that stand as chronicles, detailed documents of what Granville Hicks has called the "spectacular incidents of cruelty" that issue from "petty, mean-spirited, wanton discrimination." His novels provide an invaluable addendum to American social history. They dramatize and record the lives and experience of people too often ignored by historians. Moreover, he has peopled his fiction with characters who, in their refusal to capitulate to racist oppression, positively reflect the resiliency, integrity, and indomitability of the human spirit. John Killens's body of fictional work is as straightforward as an extended hand. It is as deeply felt as the work of any writer passionately concerned with man's inhumane treatment of his fellow man.

Mel Watkins
1983

Part I

THE PLANTING SEASON

CHAPTER

I

UNCLE SAM AIN'T NO WOMAN
BUT HE SURE CAN TAKE YOUR MAN—

That was the very very funny song some guitar-playing joker sang like Ledbelly at Solly's wedding reception just a few days ago when he was a newly wed civilian.

And then it was their honeymoon in the four-room apartment in Manhattan which one of their liberal white friends had loaned to them, and three whole days and nights of loving and sleeping and eating and talking and two Broadway plays and back to the loving and the naked mutual admiration and planning for after-the-war-is-over when Solly returned, and he would go back and finish law school, with this beautiful ambitious woman pushing him and shoving him onward and ever upward. They made love like desperadoes, as if there would be nothing left after the honeymoon was over. It frightened him. His married life and his honeymoon were too much the selfsame thing.

Their last night together they lay in bed in their birthday suits, taking a breather from the love they had been making. They talked about the job he was leaving in the City government. His eyes half closed, his nostrils sucked deep into his stomach the sharp sweet salty odor of the love already made. He told her he was the only one in his section of the Agency and things had gone nicely for him so far. He tried to disguise the pride in his voice because he was the modest type.

She played with the wild black grass on his chest. Her large light-brown eyes forever wide and knowing, and glowing now with obvious pride in him, her handsome brand-new husband. "Swell . . . Let's hope it stays that way when you get back," she said. "If too many of them get into your section, they'll make it hard for you. The way it is now, the white people treat you fine. Right? You get your promotions like you're supposed to. That's because you're the only one and you're handsome and agreeable. If you were black and ugly like some of them and talked like Amos and Andy, you wouldn't have it so good."

Millie moved her cool naked body close to him and kissed him behind his ear and he grew large and warm all over, and the him of him was quivering. "Slim and handsome and teasing-brown," she said, "and sensitive and intelligent and educated and ambitious." Like she was singing a love song to him. "You're lucky, darling. You're going to get ahead in this world. Nothing can ever stop you. You have all the equipment necessary."

It felt good to his happy ears and still it irritated him somehow. There was truth in what she said, he knew there was, and yet sometimes her brand of honesty rubbed against the grain like emery cloth. He hated to spoil this last night with her with a stupid argument which at the very most would be a desperate exercise in semantics, because Solly dreamed the same dream she dreamed for him. The great American story. An elegant woman at his side—opportunity—success—prominence—acceptance—affluence—home ownership—automobile—position. In one word, *Status*. But he wanted to write his own story in his own words with his own kind of sensitivity. He lived uneasily with an image of himself which evoked terms like "charlatan" and "rank opportunist." His dialogue would always be much subtler. In lieu of "success" his goal was "achievement." He was "militant" instead of "overly ambitious." He had spent two years in law school and also aspired to be a writer. Quiet-spoken in the main, he loved the play of words and the taste of metaphor. Words were the brick and cement, he liked to tell himself, for laying the foundation of his life's philosophy, and they must be used with exact precision. But this night he would ignore the subtleties. What difference did it really make? A rose was a rose was a rose, and a chicken was nothing but a bird. So drop the subject. God only knew when he would be with this gorgeous wonderful woman again. So speak to her of love, you fool. And love her, and to hell with rhetoric and all the phony subtleties.

Yet against his will he heard himself say, "But, Millie, I *am* black. What is this business? There's no possibility of me passing for anything else, unless I buy myself a turban. Face it —both of us are black. This surely isn't an interracial marriage." He tried to lighten things with: "If it is, I've got grounds for an annulment." He laughed and tried to kiss her.

She pulled slightly away from him and smiled her dimpled smile at him and she got out of bed and stood before him, proud in all her deliberately gleaming honey-colored nakedness. Like *Esquire* magazine for men. So lovely it was shameful. "Look at me, darling. Am I black?" She walked before him back and forth as if she were fully dressed and modeling for him.

He knew what she was saying to him. Ever since he graduated from the sullen slums of high school and went up the hill to the gleaming full-of-promise world of City College, things were suddenly different for him: the feminine glances of approval when he walked into a classroom and the masculine glares of white hostility. All at once he was handsome and articulate and his opinions oftentimes sought after and sometimes valued even, and in his senior year he was captain of the basketball team. And yet each evening, he remembered, after the shouting died away after the masquerade was over, he always went back home to Harlem, which was still home and always had been home since his mother brought him as a little boy all the way from Dry Creek, Georgia.

I'm a young deserving man, he thought, and I will one day do my dancing in the Empire Room at the Waldorf but at the same time keep in touch with my folks who will still be stomping at the Savoy.

She stood over him waiting now. Belligerent. "Well, am I black? Answer me." Her breasts stood firm and ripe and plump and autumn-colored and almond-nippled, her stomach smooth and roundish flat, and the slope of dark short hair curling sleepily between her thighs. "I didn't make myself the color I am, but I certainly don't wish I were different. If I were, I wouldn't be a secretary in a Wall Street law firm. I'm the only one down there, you know. And you're not black either and you know you're not. You're dark brown, and you have soft sensitive features, you're extremely handsome, and that makes a difference with white folks and you know it does. And it makes it much easier for us to be accepted in their world."

All right—all right! So he got ahead and they liked him at his office, because he was personable, and he was educated and he'd read all of the books they'd read, and he talked their language and laughed the way they laughed. In many ways he aped their style. So what? Sometimes Millie woke up all the contradictions sleeping lightly in the depths of him, and they pained him like a nerve in a tooth that was suddenly exposed.

And he shouted angrily, "Who in the hell wants to be accepted in their world?"

She came and sat on the side of the bed and took his face in her hands. "We do, darling. I love you so much! All of us educated Negroes do. That's why we go to college, isn't it?"

She was telling seventy-five per cent of the truth, maybe eighty-five or ninety, he knew it, and yet he shouted, "Hell no!" And then he said, "Forget it." She always pretended to be nakedly honest. And realistic. No one was completely honest. He knew that much about himself.

She said, "All right, darling," and lay beside him. And then they talked about the war. And she said, "I know you're not going into the Army with a chip on your shoulder. Forget about the race problem at least for the duration. Be an American instead of a Negro, and concentrate on winning the war, and while you're in the Army work for those promotions just like in civilian life."

He laughed and took her in his arms and kissed her eyes and kissed her nose and kissed her soft and eager mouth. "You don't have to worry about me, baby. I know the score. I know where and why I'm going, and I know what I'm going after."

Not even fools were completely honest. And Millie was nobody's fool. The thing was, she had always lived a taken-for-granted, sheltered, bourgeois colored life, while struggle struggle struggle had always been the blood of his existence. He took nothing for granted and he wanted everything.

When they fell asleep he dreamed about their conversation, and the dream was all mixed up and it seemed that the white couple whose apartment they were using came suddenly through the wall and the youngish crew-cut blond-haired man said. "Millie is absolutely right. Americans have to forget their differences now and stand together against the common enemy. A house divided—"

Solly turned upon the man and told him, "Mind your own damn business. I don't need anybody to school me on my patriotism."

But now the dream is ended.

The honeymoon is over.

Now I am a soldier. I'll be the best damn soldier in the Army of the United States of North America.

CHAPTER

2

"Saunders, Solomon, Junior—"

He stood there with the rest of the new recruits in a sandy area surrounded by strange white double-decked buildings. His first hour really in the Army and still in his civilian clothes. The old soldiers laughing and jeering at them from the windows of the double-decker barracks. But he was back home with his Millie. His heart and soul and mind back home with Millie. She was in his nostrils, in the taste in his mouth, in his arms close up against him. All around him and amongst him.

"SAUNDERS, SOLOMON, JUNIOR!" He did not hear the sergeant call his name. He was smiling sweetly with his Millie.

"SAUNDERS, SOLOMON, JUNIOR!" The sergeant shouting now at the top of his booming voice.

Solly jumped forward out of his daydream. "Right here! I mean here I am, sir!" He was in the Army now. He had to stay alert and stop daydreaming.

"Goddammit, you better wake up and soldier, soldier," the sergeant growled. "You been living long enough to know your name." The old soldiers howled. Even new recruits laughed nervously. Let them laugh. It would not take Solly long to acclimate. He had the proper slant on everything. He knew where he was going.

A soldier yelled from a window in the barracks, "Old Saunders Solomon standing up there daydreaming about his old lady and Jody Grinder already. Ain't even got on his Government Issue yet. After all, buddy boy, give the poor 4–F a break. Just remember he ain't got good health like you got." The old soldiers laughed and howled and hooted. Another one yelled, "I'll give a 4–F a break all right. I'll break Jody's mother-loving neck. I catch him kicking in my stall, goddammit."

"At ease, men!" A big black man with a stripe on his arm and a voice that sounded like coal sliding and tumbling down a coal shute stood before the new colored soldiers and started giving them orders. And they began to walk in a nightmare all day long in the blazing heat from place to place, and a shot in this arm and one in the other, six or seven times it seemed, and the biggest recruit of them all, Robert Lincoln, a six-foot-fiver, collapsed in a faint with the needle still in his arm. But that didn't help him. Ten minutes later he was back with Solly and the rest of them, walking around from place to place with a soldier with two stripes in charge and a soldier with three stripes and some with no stripes at all. And it seemed to Solly that the fewer stripes one of the old soldiers wore, the tougher he was on the brand-new men, so that he began to think that the fewer stripes you wore, the higher your rank. And: "Come on, soldier, get the lead outa your ass. You ain't on a Hundred and Twenty-fifth Street now."

That night he lay on his bunk less than a hundred miles from New York City in a strange new world of double-decked barracks and khaki uniformity and bars and stripes and follow-the-leader. He was too tired and excited to fall asleep. He heard the conversation of the other soldiers around him. "I don't believe it's going to be so bad. One sure thing, they feed you good."

It really wasn't as bad as he'd expected it might be. Solly felt a great relief that this was it, and he could make it easily.

"What I like about it," another soldier said, "everything is so efficient. Know what I mean? The mess hall, the dispensary, the this and the that and everything jumping. Know what I mean?" He snapped his fingers. He was big roundish brown-skinned, chubby almost, about five feet eleven, brown eyes popping out of his big round head. His name was William Rogers and he had an overanxious personality. Solly smiled. Rogers wanted to make good in a great big hurry. Well, Rogers wasn't by his lonesome. Solly had his own plans. For winning the Democratic War. Everything fitted into a groove—his attitude toward the war, his idealism, his qualifications, his over-all plans for moving ahead in this world. Past, present, future plans.

He sat up on the side of his bunk. A short squatty recruit across from him was reading in bed. Joe Taylor had been reading ever since he came into the Army, even on the train from New York and during the truck ride into Fort Dix from Trenton. Solly got some writing paper out of his bag and started to write a letter to Millie. He might as well write a letter. He couldn't go to sleep.

Darling Millie:
I miss you terribly. . . .

He paused and looked around him. How could he miss her terribly already? The Army had hardly given him time to have a comfortable bowel movement. Everything was done on the double. It was one mad scramble of efficiency. But he didn't cross out "I miss you terribly." It made him feel good to miss her terribly and it would make her feel even better.

One of the old soldiers walked noisily over to their side of the barracks.

"Howdy, men. Welcome to K Company. Glad to have you, yes indeed. Any loan sharks, crapshooters, or poker players in the crowd?" Nobody answered. "Anybody wanna get on any kind of time, want any kind of action, just look for me, Sergeant Kalloran. I'm the Action Kid." Kalloran looked around from recruit to recruit. Rogers got up from his bunk and stood eagerly at attention as if the Chief of Staff were in his presence. The sergeant stared at the round-headed bug-eyed man for a moment and finally told him to stand at ease. Rogers said, "Yes, sir!" The sergeant's devilish eyes shifted for a moment to Solly. "Dammit, soldier, you ain't got here yet before you writing a letter home. Ain't nobody move in on you that quick, I don't reckon. . . . I mean, Cheese and Crackers! Give poor Jody a chance!"

Solly didn't even look up at the sergeant, just kept staring at the letter he had started to write. The sergeant's eyes left Solly, as he silently considered the rest of the new recruits. He laughed out loud. "I got anything a soldier could want. Weekend passes, furloughs, Section 8's, discharges, brunettes and blondes and in-betweens. Is here all kinda girls. Fat girls, skinny girls, tall and short ones. Even got a few nice fat boys for them which taste runs in that direction. Know what I mean? Anything a poor Crute's heart could desire." A brutishly built contemptuous bastard, Solly thought, and hoped there were not many like him in the Army leadership. Kalloran laughed out loud at them and walked off toward the other end of the barracks. The new soldiers were tongue-tied for a moment.

Joe Taylor finally broke the silence. "Who let that mama-huncher loose?"

Rogers glared at Taylor. "You're so smart—tell me one thing. Who the hell is this Jody joker everybody's talking about?"

Joe Taylor looked up from his book. "Jody Grinder is a civilian—any lucky four-goddamn-F that's laying up with your old lady and grinding her all night long while you away in the service. In other words, Jody is the poor unfortunate bad-health stud that's doing your homework while you dying for your country."

Solly said, "A greater love hath no man." He liked the little husky soldier.

The brand-new soldiers laughed and chuckled, some of them uneasily. "Ain't nobody gon do my homework," Rogers said.

"Now there you go," Taylor said. "Any old fool can stop a bullet, but how many men can grind like Jody Grinder? And I think it's mighty nice of him to do a poor soldier's homework for him. It must be mighty hard too. But yet and still, no matter how weary he is, he's never too tired to take care of your old lady for you! I think we ought to give him a rising vote of thanks. It's a back-breaking job and Jody don't get no medals for it."

The men were laughing openly now. "Aw screw you, Shorty," Rogers said and walked away toward the stairway.

"Thatta be better pussy than you got back home," the chunky soldier called after him.

The lights in the barracks went off promptly at eleven, but Solly lay on top of his bunk long after midnight, staring at the darkness, his nose sucking in the sharp strange barracks odors of Army blankets and tobacco breaths and sleeping men and broken dreams and broken winds all rolled into one big overwhelming unfamiliar smell. And old-timers coming in all night long, undressing in the dark and cussing softly, and a soft-spoken flashlighted poker game on the other side of the barracks. He closed his eyes and tried to go home again. He would never get used to blindly following the leader if they were all like Sergeant Kalloran (that's why he had to be a leader himself damn quick), but it would take time for him to get used to having a B.M. in the chorus of six or seven other men, with still others waiting and standing over you laughing and chitchatting. Like today, he had had seven or eight B.M.s, with the latrine orderly standing there like he was giving church communion and every now and then chanting: "All right, soldier, let's cut it short and keep it moving. As these depart, let others come."

And yet somehow he really liked it. He *was* here, he *was* in the Army, and he especially liked the comradeship—he'd been lonely most of his life—and there *was* a war going on, and unlike World War I, this one was a Democratic War, and he would make the best of it. And he would aspire to be an officer and all the rest of it.

He fell asleep and went to New York to his Millie. They were taking a shower together, and he watched the water playing on her lovely sloping shoulders and on the very very softness and roundness and the nippled firmness of her breasts and dancing down her long supple body with the varying and varied shades and shadows of golden brown, warmly blending and clashing, and on the ample hips, and glistening like tiny icicles on the black triangle of curlish hair just beneath her belly, and he washing her back and she washing his, and back in the bedroom he put on his pajamas and went to bed and took them off again underneath the covers and lay there waiting impatiently for her, as she pinned up her brown hair and did all the other things that seemed so long and merciless and indifferent and overdramatic in the doing, and finally she came to bed to him and he reached out to her in a drunken ecstasy and . . .

It seemed that he had just fallen asleep when: "All right! All right! Every living ass! . . . Every living ass with a swinging dick!" He lay there at first, desperately trying to recapture his dream and reconstruct it. He sat up rubbing his eyes, wondering where the hell he was. And where was Millie? There were lights on all over the barracks, busy like Sixth Avenue and Twenty-third Street at five p.m., but outside the morning was still being muted by the stubborn darkness. And suddenly the big bulky sergeant came into hazy focus. "All right!" he yelled like a dozen foghorns blasting the mist. "Let me have it! Let me have it! Don't look at me with your eyes all red. . . . I don't want you, but release that bed!" And before Solly knew what was happening the cot had been upturned and he had been dumped onto the floor. "All right—all right—straighten your bed up, soldier. You must think you at home or some other junky place." Solly jumped up from the floor and moved angrily toward the sergeant. Kalloran turned and walked across the floor toward the round-headed Rogers, whose bed already looked like it hadn't been slept in and who had almost finished dressing. Rogers's big round eyes were popping with alertness and anxiety.

"You really on the ball, soldier, goddammit, what's your name?"

The soldier jumped to attention and saluted the sergeant, his eyelids batting like a bashful whore. "My name is Rogers, sir. William Thomas Rogers, Junior, sir." Talked fast and proper with the faintest trace of an acquired West Indian accent.

The sergeant laughed. "All right, Corporal Willie. See that these men in your squad make up their beds, wash up, and get dressed, and be downstairs in the next five minutes."

"Yes, sir!"

"You think you can do it, Corporal?"

"Yes, sir!"

The sergeant looked at his watch. "All right," he said. "It's exactly three and a half minutes to six. I want you to have every loving brother's sister's cousin's child downstairs and standing at attention at six o'clock. When the man toots his whistle I don't wanna see nothing but dust and statues. I want all of you moving your ass in double time and raising a cloud of dust when you come down these steps and out to the formation on the mother-loving two, and when the dust clears away I don't wanna see a goddamn thing but statutes standing at attention. Is that clear?"

"Yes, sir!" The sergeant walked away. Rogers turned toward the men screaming, "All right—all right—every living—every living! You, soldier, you, get the lead out your ass."

Rogers had the right attitude, Solly thought, but he tended to overdo it, and he was too obvious. Solly would get farther faster and would be calm and would not kiss any Government Issue backsides. He would learn quickly and carry himself in such a way as to win respect of men and officers alike.

"All right! All right! You, soldier, you!"

The little book-reading soldier looked up from his bunk at Rogers. He was about five feet four or five, but built solid up from the ground and a heavyweight from shoulder to shoulder. "Get up off it, Rogers. You came into Sam's Army the same minute I did. Don't let the sergeant's success go to your big ugly head. You ain't no corporal. You ain't even a private first-damn-class. You ain't hardly a buck-ass private."

Some men chuckled, some of them laughed.

The whistles blew and they ran and stumbled down the stairs half dressed and stood in formation like sleepy-eyed soldiers were doing all over camp. It was still dark outside, but over in the east the sun was slowly getting up and building a fire as if it had also heard the whistles sleepily. Solly figured they were loud enough. And there was Roll Call and Reveille and Chow Time in the Mess Hall and back to the barracks and two minutes later fall out again and Roll Call again, and after a while he lost all sense of time and space and chronology. Marching all over the world, it seemed, and getting everywhere in a hurry, but still in their civilian clothes and especially the thin-soled civilian shoes (he was anxious to get into his soldier suit), and taking this test and this examination, and Showdown Inspection with all of your equipment spread out before you to be checked by the pink-cheeked officers. Solly felt painfully self-conscious at the Short-arm Inspection with a dayroom cram-filled with naked men, black-skinned, brown-skinned men, varying shades and sizes, passing in review before a bald-headed pink-faced lieutenant with a placid face, and the sharp sweaty smell of the nervous bodies, and the loud angry odors of agitated maleness, and the serious faces and shamefaced faces. "All right, son," the lieutenant from the medics chided Rogers. "That's enough. You aren't supposed to play with it. You're a big boy now. Put your clothes back on.". . ."Yes, sir!" Rogers said, as the other soldiers howled with laughter.

And then there were aptitude tests and classifications and drilling all day long in the merciless sunlight. It was like something that went on and on without rhyme or rhythm and never ending. Solly's feet felt as if they were throbbing with a mouth crammed full of aching teeth. At about four o'clock on the second day they got their soldier suits and kissed their civilian clothes good-bye. And he was happy as they marched back toward their barracks, feeling a strange kind of anonymous security. No one could tell now whether they were raw recruits or just sloppy old-timers. They were really in the Army now.

That night at the Post Exchange, Solly met a fellow who used to live on his block back in the city, and he came to the barracks with Solly and sat on the side of his cot laughing and talking to the new recruits about Army life. "Man," Jim Jackson said to Solly, with some of the new men gathered around Solly's bunk, "you didn't know when you had it good. You shoulda stayed in law school. Sam's Army is just about the most."

"It isn't bad at all," Solly said. "I can make it standing on my head."

Rogers said seriously, "I think I'm going to like it too."

"That's cause you're in with the sergeant," the sawed-off soldier said. The men had already nicknamed him "Bookworm" Taylor. "You Sergeant Kalloran's right-hand ass-kisser."

"You better watch it, soldier," Rogers said. He was hot with anger. "I'll take you outside and kick your ass! I ain't playing!"

Jim Jackson laughed. "*Sergeant* Kalloran? Jesse Kalloran ain't no sergeant."

"What is he?" Rogers asked uneasily.

"He isn't anything but a buck private, just like the rest of us. He just came into the Army two or three weeks ago. He's *bucking* for sergeant or something all right, but he ain't nothing but a bullshitting buck private. Some of these studs are bucking just to stay at the Reception Center. Think they can B.S. around for the whole damn duration. Keep from going overseas."

All the men laughed now and Bookworm put his book aside and turned to Rogers. "If he ain't no sergeant you sure ain't no corporal, so get up off it, you bubble-eyed punk."

"Everybody's bucking around here," Jim told them. "You ought to see them cats stationed here permanently at the Reception Center. The privates are bucking for Pfc, the Pfc's bucking to be corporals to be sergeants and so forth and so on right up to the general. White and colored, everybody's nose is the same damn color."

Bookworm said, "My man here been brown-nosing ever since he got inside the gate. That's how come his breath smells so bad. I don't know what he's bucking for, but he's the original sepia Buck-damn-Rogers." All of the men were laughing excepting Bookworm and Rogers.

"Lay off that shit," Rogers told him, "before I fatten your lips for you."

"You sure ain't got them buck eyes for nothing," Bookworm said unsmilingly.

Solly said, "There'll be plenty of fighting where the man's going to send us. Don't waste your energy on each other."

"You got your big baby-blue eyes stuck in that goddamn Army book every chance you get," Rogers told the Bookworm. "You ain't doing that 'cause you like to read good literature. You getting ready to buck like a jackass."

"That's just what I'm going to buck like," Bookworm muttered half aloud. "Like a crazy jackass. Buck myself right out of this white man's Army."

Solly said to Bookworm, "That's the wrong approach completely."

"They don't give out many Section 8's around here," Jim said. "You got to be a raving lunatic to get one. They had a ofay stud over in the other area last week did everything crazy trying to get out. He met reveille in his underwear; he pissed in the middle of the mess hall every morning, he wore his trousers backwards. He did everything. It didn't make any difference. One of the captains saw him in the latrine taking a crap one day and walked over to him and pulled him up off the stool and told him, 'Prove to me you crazy, soldier. Eat that shit you just shitted and I'll personally see to it that you get a Section 8.' The soldier told the captain, 'You must think I'm a goddamn fool!' "

The men were stunned for a couple of seconds and then the laughter began to ooze out of them and they began to laugh and laugh and laugh some more at this fabulous place called the Army and at the soldier who came from Solly's block. Some of it was frightened laughter.

Solly said to Taylor, "That being the case, my friend, you better give up on the Section 8 and do like I'm going to do. Face the facts. You're a freedom-loving American citizen and Hitler is the enemy of everything we stand for." He really liked the little sawed-off heavyweight, but his attitude was ass-backwards.

"Who the hell is *we?*" Lincoln said.

"Are you for real?" Worm asked Solly. "Or is this your pitch for a Section 8? That's a smooth mother-loving curve you throwing. It might even fool the captain."

"You're in the Army," Solly said seriously, "so you might as well believe in what you're fighting for. I mean it. If Hitler conquered America, the Negro would be a hundred times worse off than he is now. Furthermore we're American citizens and the country is at war and they need us, and when we get back we won't let them forget that we fought like everybody else. This war is not like the last one. This is the real damn thing this time. Your commander-in-chief is the best damn president we've had since Abraham Lincoln."

Lanky stood tall with his six-feet-five and made like he was sawing on a violin. "Somebody sing 'The Star-Spangled Banner.' "

Solly argued, "What else can you do anyhow? You got to be in the Army. This is our country as much as anybody else's. It was built on the backs of our forefathers."

Worm said, "Any time Hitler wants to make a landing here, I'll damn sure be his guide. I'll point out all the high spots and hold the friggin' candle."

"Don't be an ass," Solly said. "You want the same right and privileges of every other American, don't you?"

Bookworm gazed wide-eyed at Solly. "Hell yes!" he said angrily. "But—"

Solly said, "All right then. When these rights are jeopardized, you have to fight just like everybody else. You don't think your Uncle is going to let you park your backside on the sidelines during the War, and after it's all over he's going to say, 'All right, you colored folks, you can have your freedom now, even though you didn't do a damn thing when we had to defend against the common enemy.' You don't think freedom is that easily won, do you? You don't think your Uncle is that big a fool?"

Bookworm stared at Solly and shook his head. "That's some weird shit you putting down."

"You better listen to somebody with some sense in his head," Rogers said. "You little sawed-off stupid-talking sapsucker."

Rogers came close to Solly and whispered with his brassy voice: "I dig you, pops. These other cats don't talk our language. They don't have the faintest notion what you putting down."

Solly stared blank-faced at Rogers. He could feel the soldier's breath on his cheek. "What're *you* putting down?"

Rogers said, "War or no war, you going to be a big colored

man in this white man's jungle. These squares around here ain't in your class. What I mean, I admire a cat like you that knows where he's going and got definite plans for getting there."

Solly thought angrily of Millie as he backed away from Rogers. "I haven't the faintest notion of what you're talking about." Thinking to himself, you know damn well what he's talking about, like you know what Millie's talking about.

Rogers laughed. "But I know what *you* talking about, sweet-talking pop-o. You better believe me when I say so. You may fool these other cats with all that hifalutin red-blooded patriotic bullshit, but I'm like you—I'm an opportunistic bastard my-own-damn-self. I just wish I had your polish."

Solly was overheated in his collar. This soldier very quickly grated on the tenderest part of his nerves. He turned to Jim Jackson. "Let's get some fresh air, buddy. I'll walk you back to your barracks."

He and Jim walked off together. Rogers laughed and laughed and laughed.

Next morning after breakfast they had a formation and a pink-complexioned man, with gleaming silver tracks on his shoulders and cap and an educated Southern accent that was almost disguised, called out some of their names, not including Solly or Buck or Bookworm or Lincoln. The men whose names were called were told to step out of line and to fall back into the barracks on the double and prepare immediately for Showdown Inspection of all their Government Issue, clothing and equipment, and out again with barracks bags and dressed to travel—destination undisclosed. And this kept happening all day long. And all the while in the back of his mind, and sometimes in the front of his mind, there was Millie and Mama and Mama and Millie, and what if his name were called and he had to leave for God-knows-where before seeing them again, and he wouldn't even have the chance to telephone them? Drill Drill Drill. He was the best driller amongst the new recruits. TO THE REAR MARCH! BY THE RIGHT FLANK MARCH! It came easy and felt good to him. He learned faster than the rest. But then there was formation again and more names called out, and lay everything out for Showdown Inspection and get ready to travel and drill drill drill in the burning sunshine, and later that morning Solly was put in charge of some recruits who had just come in wearing their strange-looking civilian clothes, and it seemed impossible to him that just a couple of days ago he had been in their same tissue-paper shoes. His feet ached for the new recruits. They sure did look peculiar.

HUNT TWO THREE FOUR . . . HUNT TWO THREE FOUR

It felt good to drill the new men. He was going places in a hurry. Rogers looked at him with envy.

That noontime at lunch Solly and Bookworm Taylor and Lanky Lincoln bought bogus passes from the bogus sergeant Kalloran, and they were going home that night AWOL, and nothing in the camp could hold them back. But right after lunch, it was: "Fall out—fall out—every living . . ." And the captain called his name, and all the rest of the men who had come the day he had come, and some who had come since his group, and even a few of the men who had just come yesterday. The medium-height chalk-faced captain looked up from the roster and into the eager faces of the men. "All right, boys, I want you to fall out and back into the barracks and be ready to roll in fifteen minutes." He spoke close-mouthed, and the words slid through his crooked teeth. His dark blue eyes roamed from face to silent anxious face. "Any questions?" The new recruits stood tall and silent for the captain. "You boys don't have any questions at all? Very well—"

Bookworm's hand went up, his large eyes wide and innocent-looking. "I'll show em how to buck," he mumbled to Solly, who stood next to him. "And I ain't gon eat nobody's shit either. Just watch my dust. Section 8, here I come."

"All right, boy, what's on your mind?" the captain said.

"I just want to know Captain, please, sir, are we in the Army?"

"What do you mean, 'Are—we—are you in the army?' "

"I mean, Captain, sir, are we in the Army? The United States Army?"

"You are *not* in the United States Army."

"I didn't think we were, sir. On the other hand—"

"You are not in the U.S. Army. You are in the Army of the United States."

Bookworm stared at the captain with an innocent and completely guileless look. "Wait a minute, Captain, sir. You getting us all confused now. You mean we are in the Army?"

The new recruits threw quick sly glances at one another. Buck Rogers nervously batted his big bug eyes. Solly fought hard to keep a straight face. The captain's cool chalky-white face turned redder and redder, warmer and warmer. "Of course you're in the Army, boy. You are not in the Regular United States Army—I told yer—you're in the Army of the United States. Where in the hell did you think you were? The goddamn Boy Scouts?"

Bookworm answered softly and sweetly as if he were licking an ice cream cone, "I *thought* we were in the Army, Captain, sir, with all these soldier suits and everything, all this 'Hunt, Hu, He, Ho,' and all that foolishness, marching up and down all day long, but you keep calling us *boys*, so I thought maybe we were somewhere else, cause I read in the *Daily News* where Mr. Roosevelt, the commander-in-chief his-self, said he wasn't going to bring nothing but men in the Army. Gonna leave the boys alone right long in here. So if I'm a boy, I just wondered if you could arrange it so I could go right back home to Mama and Papa, please, sir. I sure do miss em and I'm a heap too young to die on foreign soil. Khaki don't become me nohow. You understand—"

Laughter up and down the formation now—uncontrolled. Solly stopped laughing suddenly. Enough was enough. Bookworm was carrying it too far.

Worm stood still and silent and sweet-faced and at attention. He didn't move a muscle. Lincoln bent over, slapping his thighs and shaking all over. Soldiers passing the formation stopped and stared.

"I don't see nothing funny," Bookworm said aloud to no one in particular. "I really *don't* look good in khaki."

"At ease, men!" the captain shouted. "At ease, goddammit! Quiet! At-*ten*-chunt! Fall out of line, soldier, and report to me front and center."

Private Taylor stood straight, silent, serious.

"You, soldier! You! You hear me, soldier! Front and center on the double!"

Bookworm looked innocently at Solly standing next to him, and Solly felt an angry pain in his stomach as he struggled to keep from laughing aloud. At the same time he was scared for Taylor. Bookworm glanced at the soldier standing on the other side of him. There was an angelic look about the Worm, as if he might sprout wings any minute and go on to heaven where all the other angels dwell and study war no more.

"You, soldier, you!" the captain screamed. "Don't look at anybody else! I'm talking to you!"

"Me?" Worm pointed to himself. The captain could not

possibly be addressing Private Joseph Taylor. He was the only soldier who wasn't laughing.

"Yes, you! On the double!"

Bookworm stepped out of line and did a beautiful right face and put his two arms up in a fighter's pose and trotted toward the center of the formation like an old soldier and did a sharp left face which was a pleasure to behold, and he came to a halt in front of the captain, saluting him smartly. "Private Taylor reporting as ordered, sir."

The captain said, "Soldier, we're not going to toler—"

"Captain, please, sir, you forgot something. You really did." Sweet and gentle.

"Soldier, goddammit—"

"Captain! *Please,* Captain. You forgot to return my salute." The tenderest-hearted soldier in the Army of the United States of North America.

"You're in the presence of an officer, soldier. You—"

"Captain, *please*—"

The captain saluted, his forehead creased and bursting red like overripened pomegranate.

"That's more like it," Bookworm said. "I knew you had it in you." The soldiers laughing unrestrained. Lanky Lincoln bending his long body in half and howling.

The captain turned away from Taylor. "Take him away!" he screamed and motioned to two of the men. "Take him to the guardhouse. I'll teach him how to talk to an officer."

"Just treat me like a man, and I'll treat you like one, Captain, sir!" Bookworm shouted as they took him away.

They went back into the barracks to get ready to ride, Solly wondering what they would do to the Bookworm. He wanted the short squatty soldier to go with them. Even though he violently disagreed with Bookworm's campaign for a Section 8, there was something about this soldier, something real and warm and militant. Something enviable and honest.

The captain came up to the second floor and went from one man to another, taking their names as witnesses against the Bookworm. Solly's bunk was located in a corner farthest from the stairway, and he hoped the captain would have enough witnesses and stop before he came to him. He didn't want to be a witness against the spunky little soldier, and what kind of morale would a company have whose men were made to gang up on one of their comrades the first week in the Army? He cleared up the area around his bunk and put the last thing in his bag, and when he straightened up, the captain stood about four or five feet away from him.

"Your name and serial number, soldier."

You must get along with men like the captain if you're to get ahead in the Army, so give the man your name and number as if you don't know why he wants it, and later when it comes to bearing witness, you can cross that bridge when you come to it. You have a legal mind. You know damn well it makes no sense at all to snag your pants the first damn week. His face broke out in a nervous perspiration and a storm raged in his stomach. He needed another bowel movement.

"Is your hearing all right, soldier? I asked you for your name and serial number."

He stared at the red-faced captain and his tongue slipped noiselessly over his bottom lip and he cleared his scratchy throat. He could hear the other soldiers listening. "I think, sir, that to ask soldiers to testify against a fellow soldier, especially in their own outfit the first week they're in the Army, is just the worst thing that could happen in terms of morale. I think—"

Veins stood out like whipcord on the captain's forehead. "I don't *ask* you for anything, soldier. I *command* you. And I do *order* you now and forthwith to give me your name and serial number!"

Solly swallowed the stale air of the barracks. "My name is Solomon Saunders, Junior, and my serial number is 33–052–176, sir."

"Get one thing straight, boy—soldier," the captain said. "You were not brought into the Army because it needed your enormous brain power. Thinking is out of your jurisdiction. You're here to do what you are told to do, and nothing else. Is that clear?"

"Very clear, sir." He'd made a fool of himself. This was not the way to do it in the Army.

The captain turned and said to all of the soldiers: "All right, men, you have five more minutes." And walked angrily toward the stairway.

Solly stared after him, thinking if he is a typical Army officer, they are desperate for good officers. All the more reason to get promoted in a hurry.

After the men were ready to ride, a few of them came over to Solly's bunk. Lanky Lincoln said, "I'm with you, daddy-o.

I wouldn't testify against the Bookworm either. I dig it the most what you told the man. White folks ain't no goddamn good."

Solly said, "You can't lump all white folks together. I—"

Buck said, "Shame on the goddamn Worm. He should have known better than to be so stupid. And you better learn to keep your mouth shut," he said to Solly. "I'm surprised at you. I thought you had some sense in your head. You act like one of them bums in Union Square."

Clinton Moore, the soft-spoken soldier, said, "None of us are going to be a witness. Not in Fort Dix. We're going to be long gone in the next few minutes."

Clint is absolutely right, Solly thought. I let my stupid emotions lead me by the nose instead of my intelligence. That's the thing I've got to watch.

The whistles blew a half of an hour later, and they fell out downstairs in front of the barracks, kicking up dust and ready to travel, but they stood around for over fifteen minutes more before anything happened. Then a lieutenant came up and called the roll and the trucks pulled up. "All right, men, we're ready to go." He turned and talked to another lieutenant and got in a jeep and drove off again. Lanky Lincoln growling cheerfully, "Everything in this goddamn man's Army is hurry up and wait." And the men standing around grumbling and cussing and laughing and sweating in the midday sun that came down through the barracks and the bright green trees with a red-hot vengeance and set the day on fire. The lieutenant drove up about twenty minutes later, and the men were getting into the trucks now, Solly feeling angry and helpless about Millie and Mama and about leaving Bookworm behind, when the captain drove up in a jeep with the Worm, and Worm jumped out of the jeep and bounded upstairs, and in a few minutes he was back down again and into the truck and sitting next to Solly.

Solly laughed and said, "Bookworm Taylor, you're just about the most. Holding up the whole United States Army."

Bookworm said, "That ain't all I'm going to hold up before this foolishness is over."

"You're lucky they didn't keep you in the guardhouse."

Worm laughed angrily. "It wouldn't have made my business bad. I wouldn't mind staying in Dix for a while. I could *walk* to New York from this place. I asked the captain when he come for me, 'Ain't you gon keep me in guardhouse, please, sir?' He was so mad he wouldn't answer."

Solly laughed and leaned back in the truck. And now they were on their way out of the camp, just like they came a few days before, in a convoy of big Army trucks and whirlwinds of dust. It seemed like such a long time and so much had happened; yet he wondered if anything at all had happened, now that he was really in the Army now. And waving at the friendly white-faced civilians, a few of them colored. "Give em hell, boys!" And the big trucks bumped and bounced through the rough and rugged streets of old-fashioned Trenton, where another war was fought, the war of the great Revolution. It felt good to be part of this. He thought about home and Mama and Millie and Millie and Mama and the law school and love and career and future and success and—all of it seemed such a long ways away—farther and farther—maybe unimportant even. All of his future was a thing of the past. And everything merged madly into the present. And the present and the future was the Army and the Army life. And the War to Save Democracy. It was his war and he believed in it, and he would throw all of himself into it. And he would get promoted in a hurry and assume some leadership. He would have to talk to Bookworm. He had the wrong attitude completely.

Rogers's buck eyes looked worried for the very first time. "Wonder where we're going."

The men laughed nervously. Bookworm said, "If they send us all the way to Chittling Switch, Mississippi, it won't make Buck's business bad. He'd be like a rabbit in the briar patch. He comes from one of those towns down there so little, you can stand in the middle of town and piss a stream to the city limits. You can tell he's a down-home boy. Been up North just long enough to get big-city slick and pick up a brogue."

They all laughed a loosening-up laugh, even Buck, but all of them were worried-looking.

"I'm so glad I'm a British subject," Buck said.

"You a British subject all right," Bookworm said. "Them crackers down home subject to kick your big fat rusty-dusty."

This time they howled with laughter.

And now they were standing in the Trenton railroad station, and Solly looked around and looked at the two doors leading to the train platforms. He turned to Rogers and the Bookworm. "We'll all know in a few minutes which way we're going. If we go up to the platform through the door on the right, we'll know we're going to a camp up North, but if we go through that other door, it's shame on us."

A boy came through the station selling pop and hot dogs, and the men broke ranks and gathered around him. And suddenly Solly remembered and looked around him and started to run around in the station like it was a matter of life and death.

"It's over there," Bookworm said.

"I'm not looking for the latrine," Solly said, and he suddenly spied what he was looking for and he ran toward the newspaper stand to get some change and then to the telephone booth.

There was no air inside of the booth at all. He felt like meat being cooked in an oven. "Long Distance—" He didn't hear himself give the number to the operator. She'd better be home, he thought. Damn her sweet soul, she'd better be! It's Saturday and she'd better be home. He heard a faraway voice say, "New York City—" His heart beat angrily and his clothes stuck to him as if he'd been caught in a thunder shower. Why didn't she answer the phone in a hurry? The captain blew his whistle for the soldiers to assemble, and then he heard her voice come through like a piece of great uplifting music to him, and he started to laugh and talk at the same time and his face filling up, overflowing almost, and the captain's whistle blew again. She was so glad he called; if he had called two minutes later he wouldn't have caught her. She was getting ready to go to the grocery store. The whistles blew and she wasted the most valuable time in the world with chitchat about the grocery store, and there was so much to be said to each other, but it didn't matter, there was no time to say important things. "Take care of yourself, Solly. Don't worry about your mother and me. We'll be all right.". . ."I love you," he said. She said, "I know it, silly, and I love you too, and I know you're going to be all right in the Army and have a successful Army career.". . ."I love you, and don't you worry—I'm going to be the best damn soldier in my Uncle's Army and Schicklgruber's days are numbered. Just let me get my hands on him." Her presence in the booth with him was a physical thing that he could touch and smell and taste, and yet she felt so far away from him, farther and farther receding like the sands at Coney Island.

The whistles were blowing impatiently, and the telephone booth opened and Bookworm pulled at his arm. "Time to go, good kid. The man's looking for you." He told her, "I have to go now. Good-bye, I love you—love you—love you, dammit!" She said good-bye, and he listened in vain for her to hang up. "I have to go now," he repeated violently. Let her hang up first! She said, "I love you." The Bookworm tugged at his arm again. "Come on, man, before they put you in the guardhouse! I can see right now I'm gonna have to look after you and keep you outa trouble." Solly said once more to Millie, "I have to go now. Good-bye, sweetheart." And she said, "Good-bye, darling. Take care of yourself." And he put the receiver onto its hook and stood staring at it for a moment, and he felt like he had just said good-bye to the outside world and the Army was closing in on him forever.

The men had already picked up their bags and were following a lieutenant through the door on the right. And now they were up on the platform with the sun shining on their hot sweaty faces and most of them smiling nervously.

"We're going up North!" Buck Rogers shouted softly.

Yes, they were going up North, Solly thought smilingly, and maybe their camp wouldn't be so far from New York City and Millie and Mama, and the Army would be even greater than he ever dared to hope. They might be going to a camp even closer than Dix to the City and Millie and Mama. He was the luckiest soldier in the world. Look out, Hitler! Beware, Tojo! He felt like shouting "Hallelujah!" He thought his eyes had filled with tears of gladness.

But then another whistle blew from the platform across the way from them. And when Solly looked he saw the chalk-faced captain's silver bars blinking in the sunlight and the captain waving his arms to the lieutenant.

"Over on this platform, Lieutenant. Bring the men over here."

CHAPTER 3

"HELL AIN'T GOT A THING ON Georgia," Bookworm said the following day. And they got off the train and onto some trucks and rode over the red and flat terrain of southern Georgia amongst weird-looking multicolored camouflaged barracks till they reached the company area, and they stood in a red-clay field, ankle-deep in dust to meet their new commanding officer, a long tall red-necked thin-faced man, who walked back and forth in front of them, hitching up his trousers with his elbows. He didn't have any hips to hold them up. His feet were so tiny they seemed not up to the job of carrying his long body around.

"Men, I want to welcome you to H Company of the Fifty-fifth Quartermaster Regiment," he began. It was difficult to place his accent. Midwestern? No. Boston? No. Southern? Maybe. But not quite. "My name is First Lieutenant Charles J. Rutherford. I'm your commanding officer. Lieutenant Barnum here is your motor officer. Lieutenant Samuels is your executive officer. We're going to have the best damn outfit in the Fifty-fifth Quartermaster . . ."

The next few days things went so fast and looked so good they made Solly Saunders's head swim, and he had a hard time keeping sober and his feet upon the ground. Yet he had not had a drop of whiskey. The third evening he lay on his cot catching his breath and recapitulating the three days that had just galloped by. One of these days he would write it all down, he promised himself. The first night Worm and I met a pretty girl at the Post Exchange and Worm fell like a sack of bricks. She was pretty enough, and I could have gone for her myself, if I were not a married man. She wasn't pretty, hell naw, she was absolutely beautiful. Our eyes met once or twice or thrice, but I'm a solid married man. Forget it. And Worm is my best buddy.

SECOND MORNING we were interviewed one by one by the long-legged company commander. And then marched all day long in red-hot Georgia sunshine. That girl was pretty in the Post Exchange. Good luck, old buddy Bookworm. I was put in charge of drilling a squad of men. I'm not wasting any time.

SECOND EVENING I'm invited by the mess sergeant to eat with the non-commissioned officers at their table in the mess hall. I play it cool and nonchalant. But the big bruising gray-eyed motor sergeant gives me a bad time before I can sit down at the table and get myself together.

"What's your claim to fame, little old uppidy-looking Crute?"

"Beg pardon?"

"What is that you got, make the man think you so hot?"

I see smirks and hear some snickers. But I'm nonchalant. "I'm sorry, I don't follow you."

"Don't wantchoo to follow me nowhere. Just answer me my questions. You know anything about motors? Can you break down a two-and-a-half-ton truck with one hand tied behind your ass?" Laughter. I hear it and I'm hot but I keep cool. "You know anything about supplies? Can you make out a Morning Report? Know the Table of Organization? Army Regulations? Any kind of shit like that?"

"I—er—"

"What in the hell do you know?"

They laugh at me and loudly now. I start to get up from the table and tell the big bastard off. The first sergeant says something like, "He can read writing and write reading and that's more than can be said for half you ignorant bums." The men laugh but this time not at me. The first sergeant says, "And he's a lawyer too, so watch your step, and ain't no use to being jealous of him 'cause none of you didn't come within fifty points of the hundred-and-forty-two he made in his Classification test."

The gray-eyed motor sergeant says to me politely now, "Corporal Crute, you don't supposed to be in no dog-ass Quartermaster outfit. You sposed to be with the Judge Advocate's office or some kind of hifalutin shit like that. You too educated for us dumb-ass colored soldiers."

All of them are laughing now. I stand up and I'm mad enough to throw my plate at him. "Eating with you guys is no great big deal, you know. Especially you, you big—"

The first sergeant says quietly, "Sit down, Saunders, and eat your dinner. Get your hindparts off your shoulder."

Sergeant Perry, the mess sergeant, says, "Take it easy, greasy. You got a long ways to slide."

I sit down and pick up my fork. I got a long ways to slide all right, only I'm not going to slide. I'm going to climb and in a hurry.

Later. Same night. Worm tries to get me to go with him to the PX. I stay in the barracks and write to Millie. When Worm comes back he tells me, "Man, she asked about you."

"Who asked about me?"

"Fannie Mae Branton—the PX lady."

"Nice of her." I grow a little warm all over.

"She's got a friend almost as pretty as she is."

"So what, man? I'm not interested."

THIRD MORNING. I'm called to the orderly room, and Lieutenant Rutherford tells me that due to my qualifications I'm being appointed the company clerk, temporarily, of course. I'm getting ahead and fast. I'll climb right past those smirking noncoms. I thought about you Millie, as I listened to the company commander. I felt good—damn good! "You can go a long ways in the Army, Saunders, with your unusual qualifications for a colored man. Take my advice. All you got to do is have the right attitude and play ball by the rules of the game." I don't like the CO's accent which is only faintly Southern, disguised, but out of Texas, and I don't particularly like his kind of advice. But I will not be prejudiced. What the hell—

Same morning First Sergeant Anderson teaches me the Morning Report. "It's complicated," the Topkick says, "and you have to keep your mind on what you're doing when you're doing it, but you won't hardly have no trouble, a man with your ability." The Topkick is a real nice guy. The only trouble, this is his fifth year in the Army and yet he doesn't carry himself like a Regular Army man. He refuses to take the Army seriously. But that's his business.

This afternoon a session with Lieutenant Samuels, the officer I'll be working in the office with. He's the executive officer. Tan-faced white man from New York City where I come from. How lucky can you be? I know his type. I've had friends like him in New York City. A liberal. Maybe even pink. "You and I will get along," he tells me confidentially as he offers me a cigarette and gives me a light. "We're from the same background. City College—law school." I say to him, "Fine, Lieutenant." And why not? He could almost pass for colored with his Florida tan. Tells me he just came from Officer Candidate School three days before I came to the company. "You'll get to go to OCS," he says. "You're definitely officer material." How do you like that, darling Millie, and you, big-mouthed Buck Rogers? I'm not letting any grass grow under my feet. Worm can have the pretty PX lady. I haven't the inclination or the time. I'm a married man and I'm too busy going places. And winning the war.

It was nine o'clock in the morning, and the men were lined up outside in front of the barracks, getting ready to march to the motor pool. Topkick brought a little sawed-off heavily mustached brown-skinned soldier into the orderly room.

"You take care of this man, Corporal Saunders, till I get back from the motor pool. His name is Jerry Scott. Damnedest soldier in the Army. Been Absent Without Leave for more'n three weeks. He's under arrest in your charge."

"Yes, sir," Solly said, his entire body warm and tense, a million questions running around in his head and bumping up against each other. He knew of Scotty's reputation.

"We'll have to draw up the charges when I get back. He'll get a court-martial this time for sure. Sit down, Scotty."

"All right, Sergeant," Scotty said humbly.

"Remember," the first sergeant said to Solly, "you're responsible for him. If the prisoner gets away, you do his time in the stockade. The Army never loses." And the Topkick turned and walked out of the office and down the steps, as Solly stood looking at the little heavily built man, with the black shaggy bush over his lips and a sense of humor crinkling the corners of his mouth. There was something about the little soldier that reminded Solly of a lion. Maybe his massive head, maybe his angry orange-colored eyes, maybe the broad thick power in his shoulders and in his husky chest. Solly heard the Topkick as in a far-off distance—

"COMPANY—ATTEN-nn—CHUTT!" and footsteps of the men of H Company of the Fifty-fifth Quartermaster leaving him behind, heavily armed with pen and pencil and typewriter, with a prisoner for whom he was entirely responsible, because the Army never loses. He sat down at his table. He felt like running downstairs and catching up with the company. This was his fourth day at Camp Johnson Henry, and suddenly he felt his good luck running out.

He began to type the K.P. roster, glancing up now and then at the smiling harmless-looking prisoner. Solly's entire body was tense and rigid. Every time the little man cleared his throat or moved his feet, Solly jumped. He felt like a prisoner, and Scotty his guard, armed to the teeth. Why in the hell didn't guys like Scotty understand they could not beat the Army?

"If the prisoner gets away," the sergeant had said, "you do his time in the stockade." If the prisoner gets away, you do his time in the stockade. The Army never loses!

"You the new company clerk?" the prisoner asked.

"That's right," Solly said.

"I'm the best damn cook in the outfit," the prisoner said as a matter of fact. "In the whole damn mama-jabbing regiment. I just don't like the goddamn mama-jabbing Army, that's all. Too damn refining or whatever you call it. Like being in jail."

Solly said, "I like it fine in the Army. Not to make a career of course."

"You look like a nice guy," Scotty said. "What you got against me?"

"Nothing at all." Where did that question come from?

Scotty laughed. "See what I mean? I ain't never done you nothing and you ain't never done nothing to me, but here I sit and I'm your prisoner and you got to hold me till they get ready to lock me up in the stock-damn-kade." He shook his head. "The Army—the Army—the mama-jabbing Army—" He laughed. "All this HUP-HUP-HUP drilling and carrying on—for what? The Quartermaster ain't no Army. Didn't but one man get killed in the whole Quartermaster during World War I, and didn't no bullet kill him neither. A bag of potatoes fell on his head." He stared at Solly and roared with laughter, slapping his thighs, and Solly laughed in spite of himself. But he stayed nervously on guard even as he laughed, waiting for the lion to make his move. He'd heard of this cat's reputation.

"And look at you, a smart intelligent fellow, should be using your own head about things and stuff, but look atcher. I'm under arrest in your charge. I get away you have to do my time, and they didn't even given you a little biddy cap pistol to guard me with. Now ain't that a mama-jabber? Supposed I wanted to get away, what could you do to stop me? I could pick up something or other and knock you into the middle of next week. Now don't that make you feel like a fool? It sure do make you look like one." He laughed to himself. "I ain't got nothing against you, understand? But you just look so goddamn stupid, that's all. You look like Ned-in-the-First-damn-Reader." The lion stared at Solly and slapped his thighs and roared with laughter.

Solly felt his entire body burning with anger. He banged away at the typewriter, making mistake after mistake. He could imagine the stupid look on his face that Scotty had mentioned. He felt a sharp salty perspiration dripping from his forehead into his eyebrows into his eyes. Suddenly Scotty stopped talking and the typewriter sounded like pistol shots to Solly, but Solly's mind was on the little man grown suddenly quiet, and what would he do if Scotty suddenly made a run for it? Maybe he should turn his table around and make Scotty sit on the side of the room where he could keep an eye on him. He looked down at the paper and it wasn't the K.P. roster at all he was typing. It was FOUR SCORE AND THIRTY YEARS AGO. When he was first learning to type, he always used Lincoln's speech to practice his speed, instead of NOW IS THE TIME FOR ALL GOOD MEN . . . He continued to type the Gettysburg Address till Scotty cleared his throat and said, "Hey, Corporal Sandy, excuse me, but I got to go downstairs to the latrine. You wanna go along and keep me company?" He laughed to himself. "I gots to make wee-wee."

Solly didn't see a damn thing funny. The man was trying to make a fool of him and having a howling success. Maybe it was a trick!

"When I gots to go, I gots to go. Even the Army can't keep you from going when you really gots to go. Let's go, Corporal Sandy. I don't mean no harm."

Solly swore underneath his breath. He got up. "Okay, let's

go." And they went downstairs together. Solly stopped at the door. "I'll wait here."

"You better come inside. I might jump out of the window, and you'll have to do my time for me, and I sure would hate to see that happen. I wanna see you get promoted. You gon be a great big colored man in Charlie's Army."

Solly cussed softly and went inside with him and waited and they went back upstairs, and Scotty never did stop talking while Solly tried to drown out the sound of Scotty's voice by beating up the typewriter. He breathed heavily and looked up from the typewriter, his soft eyes growing dark with heat and anger. "Look, Corporal Scott, I have work to do. I want you to be a little quieter. After all, whatever trouble you're in, it's no fault of mine. This is the first time I ever saw you in all my life. So lay off, will you?"

"Okay, buddy boy. You and Charlie got the world in a jug." He was actually silent for a couple of seconds. And then on and on and on he talked and endlessly. About twenty minutes later, Scotty said, "Oops—I gots to go again. It's that damn lousy beer I drunk last night." And they went downstairs again, and up again, Solly getting angrier by the second. Ten minutes later Scotty had to go again. Solly looked up from his work and said, "Go ahead and come right back."

And as soon as Scotty left, Solly sat there wishing he had gone with him. It would be a simple matter for Scotty to continue out of the barracks and down the company street and be long gone, and he would be left to do Scotty's time. All his possibilities would go up in dust. It was unfair, it was stupid for the Army to leave him, nothing but a raw recruit, to guard a hardened criminal like Scotty and nothing to guard him with. But maybe they were testing him. To see if he really had the stuff in him—to be a non-com and, even more, to be a commissioned officer in the Army of the U.S.A. He tried to concentrate on the K.P. roster, but he couldn't help wondering what was keeping Scotty so long. . . . Perspiration broke out all over him; he got a sharp pain in his belly. Maybe he should go downstairs and see what was holding him. Just as he jumped up from his chair he heard footsteps coming up the stairs. He hoped it was Scotty. He prayed it was Scotty. He stood there waiting, out of breath, as Scotty came through the door again.

"What the hell were you doing down there so long?" he said to Scotty in angry relief.

"I was peeing, that's what. I'm a long-range pisser and ain't no law against it. Not even in Army Regulations. And thank God for that." Scotty started yacking all over again. "The Army is a mama-jabber. They put you to guard me. If I had wanted to run away, I wouldn't've come back to camp in the first damn place. Ain't that right? These people don't make no sense at all. The bad part about it is, everything one of these gray officers say, you have to do it, whether it make sense or it don't, and they got some stupid sapsuckers with that shining shit on their shoulders, you can believe me when I say so." He paused and Solly could feel his angry staring eyes poking fun at him. "Gots to go again, Corporal Sandy, I really gots to."

He went downstairs and Solly tried to push the uneasiness out of his mind and he banged away at the typewriter, making mistakes. This damn Scotty was messing him up, but good. He looked at his watch about ten minutes later. What the hell was Scotty doing down there so long? But he wasn't going to let Scotty run him crazy, and he was staring at his work, making himself concentrate, sweat dripping down into his eyes, his belly boiling, when the recruit in charge of the second-floor barracks ran into the orderly room with a broom in his hands.

"Corporal Solly! Corporal Solly! He's running away! He's running away!"

Solly scrambled from behind the table and ran out into the barracks, sweating all over now, his heart pounding in his forehead, and he could see Scotty's days and months and years in the stockade piling up on him, and oh Lordy—Lord! He would never get promoted!

"What? Where?"

"Your prisoner! I looked out of the window and saw him hauling ass across the field and disappearing into the woods. He's headed for the highway to Ebbensville!"

"Oh Lord!" Solly mumbled. "Goddammit!" He saw himself facing a court-martial, felt the stockade walls closing in around him and his tremendous expectations gone forever.

"I mean that stud was shaking ass!" Willie Johnson said. "You better do something and do it quick."

Solly started down the steps two at a time. Halfway down he turned around and came back into the orderly room. He couldn't catch Scotty with a ten-minute start on him. What the hell could he do? He heard footsteps coming up the steps from the first floor. The barracks were spinning around and around inside of his head. The Army had tested him and he had screwed up. He had disgraced himself completely.

"What's the matter, Corporal?" Lieutenant Samuels asked. "Where's your prisoner?"

"He—he ran away, sir—" He felt like the damnedest fool in the world and the angriest soldier.

"Ran away! You realize—"

"He went downstairs to take a leak and took off across the field and through the woods. How can I guard a man with a fountain pen?"

"All right—all right—you come with me. Maybe we can catch him in my jeep." They bounded down the stairs, taking them two and three at a time, and jumped in the jeep and took off down the road toward the highway leaving behind them tornadoes of red chalky dust.

"You should have never let him out of your sight, Corporal. You're responsible for him, you know that, don't you?"

"Yes, sir." He started to tell the lieutenant about how many times he had been downstairs with Scotty, and he had had his own work to do, but he didn't, because the whole story sounded ludicrous even to him, made him look ridiculous, or stupid, as Scotty had put it, and it wouldn't do Solly's case any good anyhow. He had been placed in charge of another soldier, a desperate prisoner, and had let him escape, and that was all there was to it, the way he figured the Army would figure. He had been given responsibility and he had goofed and he would suffer the consequences.

They turned onto the main highway going to Ebbensville. "How in the hell can they place a soldier in charge of a prisoner and not give him any kind of weapon?" the lieutenant muttered, mostly to himself. "What sense does that make?"

Solly said irritably, "That was *my* question—"

The lieutenant was silent for a moment. "There he is—there he is, Corporal." Solly had already spotted Scotty hoofing it down the road, kicking up trails of dust behind him.

They gained on him easily, and when they were almost upon him, he stopped running and threw up his arm, pointing with his thumb toward Ebbensville. He couldn't see who they were for the smoke screen of red chalky dust. They began to slow down, and as they passed, he shouted, "Hey there, how about a ride, com—rads?" They went past him a few feet and came to a stop. He started to trot toward them. "I sure do appreciate—" And then he recognized Solly and he halted in his tracks.

"Well, kiss my ass in Macy's window—I'll be a rotten mama-jabber!"

"All right, soldier," the lieutenant said matter-of-factly, "hop in and let's go."

"I don't believe I want to ride with you. I'd ruther walk. I ate too much this morning."

"Get into the jeep, soldier," the lieutenant said evenly, determined not to lose his poise.

"I am a corporal," Scotty said sharply. "Don't you see my stripes? Respect my rank if you don't respect me."

"Get into the jeep, soldier, goddammit. I guarantee you won't own those stripes much longer." The officer's tan face was red with anger, his small eyes getting smaller.

"That's all right, as long as I got em, I'm gonna demand goddammit you respect em, and don't cuss at me neither. Who the hell do you think you are anyhow?"

The lieutenant looked from Scotty to Solly to Scotty again. "Are you going to obey an order or are you?" A forty-five rested snugly in its holster on the officer's hip.

Solly said, "For your own good, Corporal Scott, get in the jeep like the lieutenant said."

Scotty got into the back of the jeep, muttering and swearing, and Solly turned the jeep around and started back toward the camp. Scotty kept up a steady fire of cusswords under his breath, but just loud enough for the lieutennant and Solly to hear. Solly didn't want to hear.

"I want you to shut up," the lieutenant finally said. "And right away."

"Who the hell do you think you are? Yelling at an American red-blooded soldier—you goddamn ninety-day wonder! I was in the Army when you were pissing in your mammy's lap."

Solly wished there was some way he could stuff his own ears with cotton and put a gag in Scotty's mouth. He didn't want to be a witness. It was a crazy nightmarish movie, and he was strapped in his seat and watching against his will. He wanted to tell Scott to shut his big mouth. Most of all he didn't want to be a part of whatever was developing at the rate of a hundred miles a minute.

When they came to the company he slowed up the jeep. "Don't stop," the lieutenant said. "Go on down to the battalion headquarters. I want to get some blank forms for a general court-martial."

"General court-martial?" Scotty repeated. "You talk like a damn jackass, Lieutenant. I ain't been gone but five or six days. How long I been gone, Corporal Sandy? Tell this fool something."

When they reached battalion headquarters, Lieutenant Samuels jumped from the jeep and started into the building. He turned and walked back to the jeep. "Corporal Scott, you stay in this jeep till I get back, you understand?"

"Don't yell at me," Scotty said. "Ain't nothing wrong with my ears. I wash em every morning."

"You're in charge of the prisoner, Corporal Saunders," the lieutenant said, and turned on his heels and walked quickly toward the headquarters building.

Before Solly could say, "Not again, Lieutenant!" the lieutenant had disappeared inside of the building. Twice in the same damn day! What could he do anyhow if Scotty took a notion in his head to jump out of the jeep and run up the road? He could run up the road after him like a fool and probably catch up with him and drag him back to battalion headquarters. He could—

Suddenly Scotty broke into a loud and boisterous laughter that startled Saunders. The little husky soldier laughed and laughed, pointing at Solly. "Boy—ha—ha-ha-ha—you're just about the most. Ha-ha-ha-ha." Tears streamed down Scotty's face as he shook with laughter. "You're the no-pistol totin-est policeman I ever did run into. You ain't even got a little short stick—ha-ha-ha-ha—oooh—haha-hahaha. Boy, this Army is just about a mama-jabber—er-he-hehehe—er-hahaha—" and slapping his thighs and shaking his head and pointing at Solly, whose face was growing hotter and hotter with anger at Scotty and the lieutenant and the soft-spoken first sergeant who had gotten him into this mess in the first place, and mad at the whole damn Army. All the while Scotty roared with laughter. Solly wanted to hit him in his mouth.

A white soldier pushed himself out from under a command car. Solly knew instantly from the maple leaf on the shoulder of his coveralls that he was a major and that he must be Major Davidson, battalion commander, the man who had a reputation for going to bat for the colored soldiers. He was a six-footer, powerfully constructed, swarthy complexioned, and his hair was a salt and pepper mixture of youth and middle age clashing and merging. "All right, soldier, not so loud. This is battalion headquarters. Men are at work inside. It couldn't be that funny." The major stood about twenty feet away.

Scotty stopped laughing and immediately launched his attack. He turned to Solly. "Why in the hell is all these white folks intercoursing with me today, Corporal?" Solly closed his eyes as if doing so would shut out the sound of Scotty's voice.

"You take it easy, Scotty," the major from Long Island advised, "and you'll keep out of trouble. Just lower your voice a little."

"You Georgia—" The rest of the sentence, the sonofabitch designation, was drowned out by Solly racing the motor of the jeep, making it groan and grumble and sputter, but sitting in the jeep with Scotty, he could still hear the corporal over the noise of the motor. "I ought to have you on a Hundred and Twenty-fifth Street. We'd string your peckerwood ass up on one of them lampposts in front of the Hotel Theresa."

Solly put the jeep in first and suddenly pulled away from the headquarters and started down the road. He couldn't explain his actions, except he wanted to get Scotty away from the major to keep him from getting both of them in deeper and deeper, as Scotty seemed determined to do. Ever since he enlisted Solly had been racing out of breath up the Army Road to Success, but thanks to Scotty he had hit a snag. His luck had run out suddenly.

"Where you going, daddy?" Scotty asked him pleasantly and unexcitedly, as if to pass the time of day. "You wanna go over to Ebbensville? You turn here at the next block, turn right at the next—I know a couple of fine dinners in that town. We can be there inside of fifteen minutes. We can have a ball—Hey, lordy mama!"

Solly didn't answer him. He just made a wide sweeping U-turn at the end of the street and came back toward the battalion headquarters. "Where are you going now, buddy? What's the matter? You done got chickenshit already? Boy, them chicks in Ebbensville is really ready. More pussy over there than you shake a dick at. Come on, buddy. You wouldn't turn me in to the man, now would you? I never thought you'd turn out to be an uncle tom."

Solly's voice trembled with his anger. "Goddammit, don't you call me an uncle tom. If you want to act the damn fool all the time, that's okay with me. But don't involve me in your stupidness. If everybody had your attitude there wouldn't be any Army."

Scotty smiled a wide smile knowingly. "*There* you go." And laughed aloud at Solly. "You sure do catch on quick. Your mama didn't raise no stupid children."

"You're nothing but a first-class fuck-up," Solly said. "But do me a favor. Stay out of my goddamn way. You hear?"

Solly came to battalion headquarters and made another sweeping U-turn and came to a halt right back where he had started from. He was fuming. The lieutenant came out of the headquarters building just as they drove up.

"Where'd you go, Saunders? You had me worried for a minute."

"Just took a ride down the block," Solly said, "to cool off the corporal a little bit."

"You were supposed to stay right here till I got back," Lieutenant Samuels said. Then he shook his head and said, "Never mind. I guess you've had enough for today as the unarmed representative of the Military Police." And he got into the jeep and they headed toward the company. Scotty was silent all the way home. The men were just coming back from the motor pool when they drove up. They watched Scotty and the lieutenant and Solly get out of the jeep and walk toward the building. The men had fallen out of ranks and had to go upstairs and get their mess gear for lunch, but most of them lingered around the entrance to the barracks and watched the trio enter, as if Scotty were a famous criminal like John Dillinger, and the other two were G-men. Solly felt ridiculous as he and the lieutenant walked into the barracks with the "dangerous" little big man strolling between them, at least a head shorter than either of them, with a smile on his face and a mixture in his light brown eyes of laughter and contempt.

When they got upstairs in the orderly room, the lieutenant turned to Solly Saunders and said, "Okay, Corporal. No more MP duty for you for the present. I'll take over from here. Go get your chow."

"All right, sir." And he felt a great overwhelming relief as he turned and went out of the orderly room toward his bunk to get his mess gear. The soldiers gathered around him and followed him all the way to the mess hall, asking him about

Corporal Scotty, the goddamnedest soldier of them all. If he saw him again a hundred years from then it would be too damn soon for Solly.

That afternoon, he and Samuels drew up the charges against Scotty. It isn't my fault, Solly told himself, that Scotty went AWOL for over twenty days. I have nothing to do with the court-martial. I'm just helping to draw up the charges. I'm in the Army following orders and doing a job and part of it is to draw up charges. Solly wished Lieutenant Samuels would stop looking over his shoulders. He didn't have a thing against Jerry Abraham Lincoln Scott (he hardly knew him) except that Scott was always working overtime at making a damn fool of himself and obviously thought he was a privileged character.

Solly's face broke out into a sweat as he worked himself into a clean violent rage against the soldier. He wished the lieutenant would stop breathing down his neck. His mind made a vivid picture of Scotty's face with the lionlike satirical expression. In the ear of his mind he heard Scotty's voice going on and on and everlastingly on. It seemed that he would always and forever hear him. It was Scotty's kind who made it hard for people like himself who really wanted to do a job to win the war and get the whole thing over with. Negroes like himself who understood the deeper meaning of the war. And had ambition.

When he finished, Samuels looked at the papers. "Good job, Corporal. Damn good job. Couldn't've done any better myself."

Solly said, "Thank you, sir." The one kind of person in the world he had no use for was a goof-off, a slacker, a goldbrick, who expected others to carry his weight. And that's exactly what Jerry Scott was. He was no hero, he was a shirker and a goldbrick. And Solly felt good about the part he played in drawing up the charges. He convinced himself he felt wonderful.

Samuels said, "Yes indeed. You and I have similar backgrounds. I was just two years out of law school when I came into the Army."

Solly said without enthusiasm, "I have one more year to do."

Samuels put his hand on Solly's shoulder. "We understand each other, Corporal. We're in this thing to make a better world for all of us to live in. I'm a Jew. I don't say I know what you folks are up against. I mean I don't know precisely, but—"

Samuels's hand was like an iron weight on Solly's shoulder. He got up and moved away.

Samuels said, "I know how it is, but don't feel guilty about Corporal Scott. He's the type that always stands in the way of progress."

Solly said quietly, "Don't worry about me, Lieutenant. I have no qualms whatever about typing up those charges. It's all in a day's work."

Samuels stared at him for a moment. "Good enough."

Solly said quietly, "I have the proper attitude about anything and everything."

CHAPTER

4

His ass was dragging the natural ground, in the poetry of his good friend, Bookworm Taylor. This was exactly how Solly felt. He was physically pooped and his head felt like it would pop wide open. All day long he had been getting out this report and that roster and the company payroll and running from battalion headquarters to regimental and back to the company, and then at about three-thirty in the afternoon, when his mind was so tired it felt like somebody had on roller skates and was jumping up and down on top of his brain, his boy, his buddy, Lieutenant Samuels, had remembered Solly saying he wanted to get out in the field with the men once in a while and not get piles from sitting on his behind in the orderly room all the time, and he had come into the office and told him here was the break he was looking for, and gave him permission to take the rest of the day off from the office and join the men on the obstacle course. And he had chinned-up and bitten his stiff upper lip and said, "Very well, sir," or "Thank you, sir," he didn't remember, and left the orderly room and put a pack on his back and an unloaded rifle in his hand and had gone with the rest of the men to jump ditches and crawl on his stomach and climb over ten-foot walls and under barbed wire and hurdle bars and fall in a creek and almost drown, which wasn't part of the drill of course. Everybody else jumped over the creek. He was out of condition. He, Solly Saunders, former track star and of college basketball fame.

He sat on his bunk and his mind made a tired hazy picture of Millie and New York City hundreds and hundreds of miles away, in another country, it seemed. Maybe it was in another world. He stretched out on his cot and closed his eyes and breathed heavily like he had been running up a long steep hill all the days of his life. He didn't feel like thinking and he didn't feel like talking to Bookworm or anybody else in Camp Johnson Henry.

"Man!" the Bookworm said, looking up from the newspaper he was reading. "You don't be can tell me nothing—Tojo is kicking gobs of crackers' asses! You hear what I say!"

Solly acted as if he were fast asleep, even though he knew the Bookworm would not be denied. He would keep talking to himself and moving around and rattling the newspaper and making a lot of other unnecessary noises until he got some kind of response out of Solly. He knew Solly wasn't asleep and Solly knew that Bookworm knew. Solly's tired mind wandered away in time and space, and he did not hear Worm's ranting and raving any longer. The letter from Millie on the day before, telling him she wasn't worried about him adjusting to Army life, and success and becoming an officer and onward and upward and all that . . . Sometimes she got on his nerves with the officer-success routine. She oversimplified the process. She was trying to keep herself occupied, so she wouldn't remember every minute of the day that he wasn't there. She had thought of doing either one of three things: some volunteer work for the Red Cross, be an air-raid warden, or work as a volunteer hostess at the Stage Door Canteen. She had decided that the last alternative was where she could do the most significant job for the war effort in terms of building the GI's morale. She was sure he would agree with her choice. She met so many lonesome soldiers down at the Canteen and every time she danced with one she thought of him. . . . It was damn sweet of her to think of him as she danced with another soldier. . . .

Against his will he wondered about Scotty, who had gotten thirty days in the stockade. What kind of a place was the post stockade? Whatever it was like, Scotty could blame nobody but himself. If anybody had begged for it, it was Abraham Lincoln Scott. He was a masochist—very sick character in his head.

"Them Japs are kicking asses and taking names. And what I mean, they don't play no favorites. Generals, colonels, sergeants, every living pinky hole is sucking wind! That's what I'm talking about!" Worm had worked himself into a sweating frenzy. He seemed to be waging a filibuster with the paper he held in his hand.

Sometimes Solly could stand in the midst of raging hell and not be there. His Army life so far . . . He was doing all right in the orderly room in spite of Scotty. By now he was doing all of the first sergeant's work. Solly did the Morning Report, the Sick Book, the K.P. roster, the Guard Duty roster, the payroll, the company files, and all of the other responsibilities the regimental commander delegated to the company commander, who delegated them to the first sergeant and the first sergeant on to Private (Acting Corporal) Solomon Saunders, and that was the end of the line. But he did not mind it really, and he liked the first sergeant, and he got along with Lieutenant Samuels. Even liked him maybe. Millie was forever nagging him about getting ahead and becoming a lieutenant and then a captain, there was no stopping a person with his good looks, his ability, his personality and education, she reminded him in every letter. And yet he was still an "acting" corporal instead of actual. Every day Lieutenant Samuels assured him he had nothing to worry about. "You just stick with me, my friend, and you and I will move mountains together even in Georgia. We'll have them singing 'Yankee Doodle.' " Samuels was all right. He just got on Solly's nerves sometimes.

Sometimes Samuels helped him with the office work, especially with the company records. Just the other day he told Solly he was doing a hell of a good job. He put his arms around Solly's shoulders. "Anything you want—name it."

Solly said he'd like to have his wife on the post just as the officers had their wives to go home to every night. . . . If Millie were here now—as tired as he was this weary night—if he could go home to her every night, she could caress his weary body, she could feed his physical hunger, she could soothe his tired mind. . . . He was lonesome. So damn lonesome.

"Old Tojo's feet must be glued to Mr. Charlie's pretty pink poopy!" Bookworm shouting like he just got religion.

"Are you blowing your stack? Over there raving like a

goddamn lunatic. Them Japs going to kick your big fat ass the same way if they catch up with you." Solly recognized Buck's voice like a brassy bass horn, and he closed his eyes even more tightly.

"The good Lord made em and the Japs don't pick em. Goddamn! Goddamn! Goddamn! They don't discriminate!" Bookworm acted as if he hadn't heard Buck Rogers say anything and was totally unaware of his existence. He laughed out loud to himself and slapped his knees. He was on stage with a soliloquy and having himself a ball.

"They'll pick *you* if they get hold of you, you stupid sapsucker. Your hindparts ain't made outa gold and it ain't built no different from the rest. Just bigger and fatter and makes a wider goddamn target." Buck laughed aloud, exaggerating his laughter and stomping his big fat feet like a prancing race horse. And other men were laughing now.

"Not me!" Bookworm finally looked around and acknowledged Buck. "I ain't mad with them Japs and I know good and well they ain't got nothing against me. I'm gonna tell the man, I love the Japanese people. But it do do your heart good—ain't that right, Solly? Every time you pick up the paper you see where the crackers are giving ground, running like hell with their shirttails out. And if you a deep thinker and a Race man like me and Solly and can read between the lines, you know it's really worser than they say it is. Tell him what I say, Solly. Tell this bubble-eyed fool something."

"They can put you in jail for that kind of talk," Buck said. "After all, you are an American soldier. I admit you're a poor damn excuse, but yet and still you wear the uniform, even if it does look like hell on you." Buck laughed and stomped his feet again.

If they would just take their crazy argument and carry it downstairs to the latrine or some other appropriate place, Solly thought. Anywhere—as long as they took it away from his bunk. He could make it easily in this Army if he could go home to Millie every night. Miss Branton reminded him so painfully of Millie it made his stomach hurt. . . . Scotty was a fool to think that he could beat the whole damn Army of the U.S.A.

"We ain't no soldiers, tell him, Corporal Solly. You a Race man. Talk to this antique fool. We're in the service department of the Army. Don't you know this regiment is a service outfit, ass? I thought you at least had that much sense. Any old fool knows that colored people join the service and white folks join the Army."

Laughing came from all over the second floor now, and Solly heaved a silent sigh. He knew he was in for a slight siege. That's all there was to it. The Bookworm had an audience and the show must go on and on and on. And the next time he went to the Post Exchange he was going over to the soda fountain and say, "Good evening, Miss Fannie Mae. You remind me so much of my wife. I declare you do. And how would you like to take her place while I'm in this lonesome place?"

He swallowed her deeply into his belly. Just thinking about it jokingly gave him warm chills and funny sensations. And it didn't do any harm just to think about her jokingly. Deep deep in him he missed Millie.

"They training us how to serve the white soldiers," Bookworm continued. "Course that suits you fine. Your first name should have been Uncle and I don't mean Sam."

"Harriet Beecher Stowe!" Lanky Lincoln yelled from across the barracks.

Solly stood up from his bunk and yawned and stretched till his whole body trembled in a nervous relaxation. He hadn't been over to the Post Exchange in a couple of weeks. Worm went every night like happily going home from work. Worm was hopelessly in love with the lady soda jerk.

Buck turned to him. "Will you kindly tell this sawed-off puddinghead he can't be walking around rah-rahing the Japs while they're killing our red-blooded American soldiers, threatening the land of the free and the V for Victory and the home of the brave and all that shit, and the Arsenal of Democracy? Maybe he'll listen to you, Corporal Solly."

"*Our* country—" The Bookworm laughed. "I bet goddammit you bet not let any of these Georgia pecks hear you claiming this country."

Solly stood tall and slim and straight and held his cap against his heart and closed his eyes— "That government of the people, for the people, and by the people shall not perish from the earth. . . . Amen—"

"Lanky Lincoln's great grandpappy—Abraham Lincoln," somebody shouted.

"Cut out the B.S., Corporal Solly, and tell this little jughead son-of-his-mother's-misbehavior something for his own good," Rogers insisted.

Solly said, "All jokes aside, Bookworm, you don't have a leg to stand on with that Japanese B.S. of yours. First of all, you are an American citizen, you're old enough to vote, and you're in good health and apparently you meet all the other draft requirements of the American male—"

"Apparently! Uh-uh. I ain't got nothing to do with that! *Apparently!*"

"Somebody musta seen Bookworm in the old swimmin' hole," Buckethead Baker said.

Lanky Lincoln said, "Leave it to a lawyer, boy. I sure am glad me and Solly good buddies. I'm going to write a poem for you, Solly. Don't get mad with me."

"Tell him about that mess, Corporal Solly," another soldier yelled.

Bookworm stood at attention and bowed his head in mock reverence. "All right, your honor, I confess everything. Go ahead and have me shot at sunrise."

"Furthermore," Solly continued, "there is no need of your Bee-Essing yourself about Tojo just because he's colored. Look at all the Chinese people he's killed. This is not a racial war. This is a war of democracy against fascism pure and simple, and if you're for Tojo, you're for Hitler. That's all there is to it. And Herr Schicklgruber says that a Negro is lower than an ape. Don't take my word for it, read *Mein Kampf.*"

"He must've known Bookworm personally," Buck said. "Course he's wrong about him being lower than an ape. Worm *is* an ape." He began to laugh and howl and stomp his feet and he lay down on Bookworm's bunk and rolled over onto the floor and kicked his feet like he was riding a bicycle and kept on laughing. Everybody was laughing now excepting Bookworm, who stared at Rogers in disgust and shook his angry head.

"It's dangerous to have a no-tail bear running around loose," he said to the hysterical Rogers. The laughter simmered down to a whimpering from Buck still lying on the floor. Worm stared at Rogers and looked around at the rest of the men. "Damn all this shit! Who started this stupid argument anyhow? Come on, Solly. Let's go over to the PX and see what's cooking. To hell with this clown!"

"I can tell you without moving a step. Nothing's cooking." Solly stretched out on his bunk again. "And you'd better stop rah-rahing Tojo or you're going to be cooking. You keep talking that crap in front of the good Corporal Buck and he'll have you up for a general court-martial." And I will have to write the charges.

Buck had gotten up from the floor and was sitting on the side of Bookworm's cot. "You damn right I'll have him court-martialed. I'll have him shot at three in the morning. Wait a minute—that would be too dark. Nobody would be able to see the target." Buck started to laugh and stomp again all by his lonesome.

"Aw, ain't nobody studying about smiling Buck Rogers. A handkerchief-head faggot, he volunteered so he could look at naked asses. That doctor at the Reception Center had his number. And he ain't got that nice fat round-eye for nothing either."

"Watch that shit, soldier," Buck said in the midst of the laughter.

"Come on, Solomon Saunders, Junior," Worm said. "I ain't never seen nobody like you in all my born days. Just sit on your dead ass on your fart-sack all the time, looking at the floor or up at the ceiling or writing letters. You better wake up and live. Let's go over to the PX and have a couple of short ones."

"All right already," Solly said. "But you might as well let the facts hit you in the face. Hitler and Tojo and the governor of Georgia are on the same damn team. All three of them're against you and me. And it makes no sense to root for one and throw brickbats at the others."

Rogers stared at Solly in open admiration and laughed and shook his head. "You're a smooth mother-lover with that Hitler-Tojo jive. I got to give you credit, poppa. Everything fits into the scheme of success of Solly Saunders—the education, the personality, the horse-shit propaganda. How long you been making everything fit everything else? The bullshit, the facts, the fiction, the ambition— You'd make a helluva psychoanalyst." He had come close up to Solly and was talking only for his ears to hear. Solly backed away disgusted.

"Get away from Solly, you queer," Worm said contemptuously. "He ain't no uncle tom like you. He's a Race man from way back. What I mean, he's proud of the Colored Race. All except one member of it."

Rogers did not take his eyes from Solly. "You're a Race man from way back, all right. And you been racing ahead of the field a long time. And you aim to keep your distance."

"Get the hell out of my face," Solly said to Rogers.

On the way over to the Post Exchange Solly felt he had to

explain his change of mind to his buddy. Every night for the last two weeks Worm had asked him to go the Post Exchange and Solly had refused. "Bookworm, doggone, boy, I sure was glad you suggested that we go to the PX tonight. Anything to get out of that lunatic asylum."

"The whole frigging Army is a booby hatch," Worm said. "The trouble with you, you're too damn serious. You better learn how to wear this world like a loose garment. You don't know how long this war gon last."

Solly didn't say another word till they reached the Post Exchange. He kept remembering what Buck Rogers said. There was one soldier who always made his flesh crawl.

When they got there they headed straight for the counter where the lady was, smiling her pretty dimples as beautiful as ever, and all kinds of soldiers hanging over the counter and skinning their jaws in her face. They stood there for a couple of minutes before the Bookworm gained her attention. She came over to them like they were long-lost friends or lovers.

The joint was leaping with GI desperadoes, and the jukebox blasting eardrums with "Blue Birds Over the White Cliffs of Dover."

"Oh," she said to the Bookworm while she stared at Solly Saunders, "I see your friend finally paid us another visit. We're deeply honored, Corporal Saunders."

He had only seen her a couple of times in all his life. "How've you been?" He smiled his crooked nervous smile and made much in his mind of the fact that she remembered his name.

"Just fine," she said laughingly. "Just fine." Her eyes were even warmer darker deeper than his image, and her full and curvy mouth was much too much and her soft breathing bosom against her blouse made him hot all over. And it was all because she reminded him of Millie.

"Yep," the Bookworm said boastfully. "He's the company clerk, my buddy is. Very very busy man. He's really the one in charge of the company. The Army couldn't make a move without him."

Solly said, "All right, Private Joseph (No-Middle-Name) Taylor, tell the lady what you want and stop taking up all of her time with the yackety-yack." Millie's mouth was smaller than Fannie Mae's and her eyes were not as black.

"The same as usual," Bookworm said, "and the same thing

for my buddy." And when the lady turned her back, he loud-talked: "She knows what I want, daddy. I'm here every night. One of these days she's gonna let me take her home."

Solly said jokingly, "Suppose I don't give you a pass. Those MPs at the gate will whip your head till their arms get weary."

Worm said, "The lady got an automobile, man. Her and her girl friend ride outa here every night all by their lonesome. Wake up and live."

They cut it short when the lady came back with the malteds and they stood there amidst the PX madness, sipping one right after another and talking about first one thing and then another, till it was time to close up the place. And Solly met her girl friend, Sally Anne Walters, who worked behind the tobacco counter. She was light brown-skinned with big gray eyes and dark brown hair flopping down around her roundish shoulders. She was slightly taller than Fannie Mae Branton. "Pleased to meet you, Corporal Saunders. Your partner talks about you so much, I almost feel like I already know you." Her eyes were wide and overanxious. He supposed she was a pretty girl.

And standing outside of the Post Exchange, Bookworm popped the question again. Could they escort the ladies home?

Fannie Mae laughed. "You don't discourage easily, Mr. Taylor. Indeed you don't." She turned to her girl friend. "What do you think, Sally Anne?" The whole thing was like it had been rehearsed.

Sally Anne said coyly, "I guess it's all right." But she did not disguise the eagerness in her voice nor in the side glance she gave Solly.

Bookworm said, "Sally and Solly—that's a good combination." And Solly could have killed him twice and once more for good measure.

Sally Anne laughed nervously. The four of them walked together to the area where Fannie Mae's car was parked, it being understood and taken for granted that Solly was going along to town with them to make an even number. They were standing in the parking area near her car now, and Worm was laying it on thick and heavy.

"Come on, man!" Bookworm said. "Don't be no chinch!

"I really wish I could make it, Joe. I mean I'm not kidding, I really do." He felt his face grow warm with anger. "I have to get back to the company and type up a roster for battalion. It has to be down there by eight in the morning," he lied. "You know I'd be glad to go if I could."

"Well, girls, I did the best I know how," Worm said, throwing up his arms. "Maybe you can make him change his mind."

"I don't think we ought to impose on Corporal Saunders. If he's busy, he's busy," Fannie Mae said, staring at Solly now and making him feel warm and silly.

"You understand, don't you?" he said. Without conviction.

They started to get into the car, and after a moment of embarrassed hesitation the Bookworm sat up front with Fannie Mae and Miss Walters sat in the back by herself. As they drove off both of the ladies said good-bye, and Bookworm said smugly, as if he were sliding into a nice warm bed and pulling the covers up around his neck, tucking himself in for the night, "See you back at the company, good kid. Don't work too hard."

Solly sat on his bunk back in the barracks and thought about Bookworm and Fannie Mae and Miss Walters, but mostly about Worm and Fannie Mae, and wondered what they were doing, and why in the hell should he care about what they were doing? His mind made all kinds of erotic images of Worm and Fannie Mae together. He didn't have any list to make up for battalion headquarters or any other headquarters, and now he wasn't sure why he hadn't gone with Worm and the ladies. Maybe it was because he was afraid the MPs might catch him off the post without a pass and he wanted to keep a clean record in the Army and to do nothing to jeopardize his possibilities. Maybe it was because he knew that Worm would sit in front with Fannie Mae and he in the back with Miss Walters, and maybe he was just a little bit jealous of Private Taylor—Private Joseph (N.M.I.) Taylor—not even acting corporal yet. All right, goddammit, maybe he *was* jealous. He thought about writing a letter to Millie, but he didn't feel like letter-writing tonight. She was probably at the Stage Door Canteen and at that very moment dancing in another soldier's arms and listening to his line and smiling in his face and maybe even making a date with him just to build up both of their morales.

He was still lying fully dressed on his back on top of his bunk when Bookworm returned. He closed his eyes and he heard the Worm moving around, taking off his shoes and maybe his shirt. He was the noisiest bastard in Uncle Sam's Army. Solly had an agonizing desire to move from the position he was in. He wanted to get up and pull off his clothes and get into bed, but what he didn't want was conversation, which he knew he would certainly get from Bookworm if he gave the slightest hint of being alive. He didn't feel like hearing about the great amorous exploits of one Private Joseph Bookworm Casanova Taylor.

"Hey, soldier, where the hell you been?" Solly heard Lanky's big bare feet flip-flapping across the floor toward the Bookworm's bunk.

"Where in the hell you think I been?"

He wished they would take their noise and carry it somewhere else.

"Come on, Worm, where was you? What you been up to?"

"I ain't been tending to none of your business. That's one sure thing."

Solly opened his eyes slowly and sat up on his cot. "Why don't you loud-mouth Bee-Essers let somebody sleep?"

"I knew good and well you were playing possum," Bookworm said delightedly. "You should've gone with me, good kid. I mean, they're fine as wine. You better believe me when I say so. Both of em—yours just as fine as mine is."

"What do you mean, yours?" Solly demanded.

"You been out with some bitches, man? You all right, Bookworm." Lanky sat down on the cot beside Solly.

"Two *fine de*licious dinners. Tried to get my cut-buddy here to go with me. He come talking about some damn company rooster or roster or whatever you call it. And boy that chick's weak for old Solly. I know what I'm talking about."

"Did you get any of the trim?" Lanky asked.

"That wouldn't hardly be any of your business, I don't think."

"Let me smell your hand. I can tell, you rotten bastard. Find out whether you been playing stink finger."

"You better get outa my face," Bookworm said, but it was obvious Worm was having the time of his life, and it made Solly hot against his will.

Lanky tried to grab Worm by the hand, but he pulled away from him.

"Get away from me, you faggot." Worm was getting on Solly's nerves with the big broad grin on his wide-open face.

"Old Bookworm playing stink finger."

There was an image in Solly's mind of sweet-faced Fannie Mae and he felt his anger mounting. She had more on the ball than both of these soldiers put together and multiplied.

"They got an NAACP in town, and my old lady is head of the Youth Council," Bookworm told Solly.

"Your old lady?" Solly couldn't help reacting.

"Sure it's his old lady," Lanky said. "Any time you get that trim, that's *you.* At least till another stud come along and beat your time."

"My old lady is the president," Bookworm repeated. "And I think Sally Anne is the secretary or some kinda shit like that. Miss Walters, I mean. I told them you'd be particularly interested in that kind of jive. Talking about some kinda Double-V for Victory, or something. That's their slogan. She's like you. She says she's an anti-fascist. Down here and over there."

"Damn all that jive, Worm. How was the pussy? Tell us about it. Ain't no need of keeping it to yourself."

Bookworm glanced at Solly and away again. He looked at Lanky and smiled sheepishly.

"I remember the first time me and my old lady got together," Lanky said. "It was in Central Park on a hot summer night. She'd been putting me off and putting me off. Before then, every time I asked her for some, she'd giggle me out of it or tell me she was scared or some other kind of old antiquated bullshit. But that night I told her she was going to get up off it, or else she wouldn't be seeing the kid no more."

"That's the way you have to put it down with some of these chicks," a new voice amened Lanky. Solly looked around him and saw that three other soldiers had joined the bull session. "You got to make em put up or shut up," Baker said. "If you don't, some other stud will. Ain't no goddamn lie." Baker had a big face and big handsome head and a big thick neck on a medium-sized body. "They used to call me Bashful Bill Baker from Jamaica, but now they call me Lover Boy."

Lanky Lincoln continued, "She commenced to crying and carrying on, and I just backed her up against one of them trees with a cool breeze blowing and pulled up her dress and hunched over my shoulders and got amongst her for a while—and ooh—goddamn— Got so good our legs commenced to tremble and our knees gave way and both of us fell to the ground without coming apart and I kept right on grinding!"

"Goddamn Old Rose!" a soldier shouted.

"Boy, they don't never forget a thing like that!"

"You ain't just a-bullshitting!"

Solly said, "Why don't you guys grow up? You act like a bunch of fifteen-year-old kids. What have you got against women?"

Baker said, "I got one big stiff eight-inch jab against them. That's what I got. And, man, they love it."

Little Clint Moore was the real bookworm in the outfit. He looked up from the book he was reading and said seriously, "You fellers forget your mothers are women."

Lincoln said, "Uh-uh! I didn't know College Boy played the mothers."

Clint stood up from his cot. He was about five feet five and slim and neat. He had a soft voice but when he spoke you heard him. "I have too much love and respect for women to play the mothers or the dozens or whatever you call it. And if any of you say anything disrespectful about my mother, I will pick up the first thing I can put my hand on and whale the hell out of you."

The men were silent for a moment. Then Lincoln said, "Aw to hell with College Boy. He don't know nothing about women-folks. If you bust that cherry, Jim, you got it made for life. I know what I'm talking about."

"You can go back there the longest day you live," Baker said. "Don't care if she gets married a million times, you'll always be the best damn man. They never forget."

"They never forget is right," Bookworm agreed, like an expert on the subject. Casanova incognito. "Not if you lay it on em like they like it."

Solly wanted to say, "Did you lay it on Fannie Mae, Mr. Bookworm? Tell us all about it, Mr. Bullshit Artist. Give us all the sordid details." But he didn't say a word. Maybe he was afraid of what Bookworm's answer might be, and what he might or might not do in reaction to Bookworm's answer. He felt his entire face fill up with anger and anger spreading through his shoulders and building a fire in his stomach. What was it to him anyhow?

"I used to have a old lady," Bookworm boasted. "She wasn't no more than sixteen years old. Lived way up in the Bronx. Boy, I didn't b'lieve in messing around in them days. I used to knock on her door and she would open the door, and when she saw me she used to grin he-he-he-he, and I'd say he-he-he-he-hell, let's fuck. I'm a busy man, I ain't got no time to mess around."

The men were howling and Solly was burning. He could not help it.

After the laughing and the foot-stomping and the thigh-slapping died away, Solly looked around at the serious faces of some of the men, their eyes riveted on Bookworm's face as if they were in Sunday School and Worm were the Sunday School teacher. Clint was reading his book again. Solly watched himself stand up and laugh out loud at Taylor. His own voice sounded strange to him. "You wouldn't know what to do with a woman if you had one, Bookworm Taylor—you virgin." He was staring down at the Bookworm now with an angry laugh on his lips and all over his face, and Worm looked up at him, his broad face wide open now in genuine amazement. He was speechless for a moment.

Solly said, "Why don't you just lay off the PX lady? You know good and damn well you didn't get anywhere near her. You didn't even swap any spit with the lady."

Worm answered weakly, "What's the matter, good kid? You jealous or something?"

"Jealous?" Solly repeated. "Jealous of a pissy-assed virgin? I'll bet you still got your cherry. I'll give you ten to one—like taking a cherry from a baby virgin." He looked around at the rest of the men. "Anybody wanna bet?"

The soldiers were laughing with Solly now and Worm was so surprised at the suddenness of the attack and especially coming from Solly Saunders, his bosom buddy, he couldn't get himself together. All he could say was: "What's the matter, good kid?"

"Just stop signifying about the PX lady, that's all. Just because the lady is nice and friendly, don't make a mountain out of a molehill."

Worm said weakly, "I ain't said nothing disrespectful about her."

"And *don't,* Mister Worm," Solly said and turned and walked the length of the barracks to the orderly room. And wrote letters to Millie and Mama.

He finished the letters and looked up from them, and there was the image of Fannie Mae staring at him from across the desk. He closed his eyes and he overflowed with loneliness. All through his face, all through his throat, his chest, his stomach, his loins, the cheeks of his aching buttocks, he longed for Millie. He heard the men out in the barracks still talking about women and laughing and stomping their feet. He opened his eyes again and Fannie Mae was still there staring with her large black eyes and a soft smile on her curving mouth, and at that moment a crazy thing happened. He heard music. He listened for a wild ecstatic moment, and then he picked up his pen and started to write. Ever since he could remember he'd had this fierce obsession to write, to put something down on paper, and he had started many novels many poems ever since he was ten or eleven or twelve years old and all by himself in a lonesome one-room kitchenette in lonely New York City while his mother made up hotel beds all day long in mid-Manhattan. He'd been published in his high school and his college magazines. He had a drawer full of rejection slips. His face filling up again and all through his shoulders and he wrote. His fingers trembled and he wrote:

This world is much too sad a place
For Fannie's warm and happy smile.
The feeling she feels far too deep
For the endless heartless guile
Of this unfriendly world.

He looked up at Fannie Mae. She was no longer smiling.

He wrote some more. He felt good when he was writing. He felt man. Whole. Complete. Fulfilled.

The tenderness that fills her face
Is unprepared for the awful bile
Of this world's great sophistication.
The true emotions of her heart
Are unprotected from the start—

He stopped and tore the paper up into little pieces. What did he know about her anyhow? And what did he know about writing? It was just that he was lonely, that was all. A lonesome one in a strange and loud and lonely place. She was lovely and he was lonesome. That was all there was to it. He could make it in this Army if he weren't so lonely most of the time. He had to get hold of himself. And maybe Worm was right. Maybe he took himself too seriously. He stayed wound up all the time. Maybe like Worm said—he should wear this world like a loose garment. He was too anxious about making good. Maybe he should—maybe he should go to the Post Exchange more often. And get himself some malteds. And a bit of recreation.

CHAPTER 5

Solly sat in the orderly room scanning OCS material. When Opportunity knocked, he intended to open the door. It was after midnight and he was getting sleepy and fighting sleep because he wanted to make sure Worm got back from town all right. Worm had escorted the PX lady home again and was out much later than he usually was. Solly heard him coming up the steps as noisily as usual. He knew Worm's walk by now. Solly dropped the book and jumped to his feet as Worm came through the door like a clumsy weapons carrier.

"What the hell happened to you?" Worm was like an accident looking for a place to happen—his lips cut and swollen and bleeding, his clothes torn and his necktie hanging down his back and his shirttail out all the way around. And he was hatless.

"You got a gun, Solly? You got a gun? I'm gonna kill me a sonofabitch tonight, if I have to hunt him all night long."

Solly took Worm by the arm and tried to sit him down. "What's the matter, soldier? What happened to you?"

He pulled away from Solly. "Never mind what happened. I just wanna get my hand on a gun and I'm going outa here and blow me a sonofabitch to hell!" His lips were quivering with anger. Tears streamed down his swollen face. He wiped his running nostrils with his shirt sleeves and the back of his trembling hand.

"Now wait a minute, Worm. Sit down and get yourself together." He put his hands on Bookworm's shoulders and tried to force him into the chair.

Worm pulled away from him again. "Ain't no whole lotta sit down. I wanna kill me a sonofabitch tonight. I mean that thing!"

"All right already. So you're going to kill you a sonofabitch. But just slow up a second and tell me what happened." He took a first-aid kit from the table and a bottle of iodine. When the iodine kissed Worm's broken lips he yelled bloody murder. "Now tell me what happened."

"You my buddy, ain't you, Solly?"

"Of course I'm your buddy."

"All right then, help me get a gun from somewhere, cause I just got to kill him."

"Kill who?" Maybe Worm ran into Fannie Mae's boy friend. He looked like he'd been battling a two-and-a-half-ton truck.

His eyes spilling over, his nose leaking— "After I took Fannie Mae home tonight I went by the Busy Bee Bar and Grill and got me a couple of sociable drinks. There wasn't a damn bit of disturbance in the Busy Bee at all, till them two cracker MPs come into the joint and started picking at the soldiers and pulling at the womenfolks. It's a good thing Fannie Mae wan't with me. I'da been a dead mother-lover if they'd started any stuff with her. So help me, I'da carried me a cracker away from here tonight just as sure as heaven's happy. They come over to where I was leaning on the bar and says to me, 'All right, boy, let's get going.' I says, 'Uncle Sam ain't got no boys in the Army.' He says, 'All right, don't get smart.' I says, 'Ain't nobody getting smart. You the one getting smart.' One of them says, 'Shut your goddamn mouth,' and I says, 'Why don't you bastards leave me alone?' That's when they started pushing me around. Took me out to their jeep and drove me off to the quiet spot and beat the shit outa me. I hit one of them bastards in the stomach so hard my arm went in up to my elbow."

"Did they hurt you anywhere else besides your face?"

"They hit me all over every damn where," Worm said, "and I'm gonna get em if it's the last damn thing I do."

"All right," Solly said. "But the thing for you to do right now is to take a shower and hit the sack and get some rest and get on sick call in the morning. Let the doctor examine you. You're going to be sore as a boil in the morning."

He was crying again. "You know where I can get me a gun? Solly, you're my buddy, aincha? Let's get us a gun and go outa here and kill us a few sonofabitching peckerwoods. Let's get us two or three guns." Bleary-eyed, swollen face, sniffling and crying and snuffing his nose, he was a sorry-looking mess.

Solly felt like crying himself. And felt like really getting a gun and blowing a few MP brains out. The Army working overtime to emphasize to the Negro soldier that he had no stake in the war. But dammit-to-hell *he* believed in the war. They couldn't stop him from believing. He was going to be a soldier, not a goof-off, and he was going to be an officer, in spite of the cracker MPs over in Ebbensville and the crackers in Camp Johnson Henry. In spite of Scotty and Bookworm too.

He said to the Worm, "All right—all right—"

Worm said, "This is the Army, ain't it? There oughta be a gun around here some damn where. It's supposed to be the Army."

"Let's get a good night's rest tonight, Bookworm. Take a nice hot bath. We can't even bring charges against the bastards, because you were wrong all the way. You were AWOL from the start."

"Solly, I hate like hell for a sonofabitch just to pick on me for nothing." He was crying like a baby. "Just cause I'm black—just cause they had guns and I didn't have none. And night sticks too, goddammit! I hate to see somebody take advantage of somebody else, especially a cracker. I don't like that shit, Solly. You know I don't never bother no goddamn body! Let's go kill both of the sonofabitches!"

"Okay, Bookworm, okay—but you wouldn't be much help to me tonight. You couldn't kill a gnat in your condition, let alone two pistol-toting crackers. Let's go downstairs now and take a warm shower."

"You can depend on me, Solly." He wiped his nose with the back of his shirt sleeves and put his arm around Solly's shoulders. "I wouldn't let you down. You the best friend I ever had in the world. I'll go over there with you right now and we can kill ourselfs gobs of peckerwoods. I'll die right by your side. I ain't never had a buddy like you before in all my life."

Solly tried to keep the heat from his voice. "First of all, we don't have any guns and nobody's going to give us any guns, and—"

"This is the Army, ain't it?"

"And secondly, if we went over there tonight, they would just whip hell out of both of us this time, and we would deserve it for not having any better sense. You were *A W O L*, absent without leave, and you're lucky they didn't ask you to show them a pass which you did not have."

Worm sucked the tears back up his nostrils and glared at his buddy. "So now I'm lucky? They beat the hell out of me, and I guess I'm lucky they didn't kill me. I should fall on my knees and thank the Lord."

Solly said, "You know damn well I didn't mean it that way." They were the best friend each of them ever had, and they stood there violently hating each other.

Worm said, "I think you're in love with this mama-hunching Army. You like it better'n you do me. You act like you a stockholder in this goddamn business."

Solly was hot now. "Jump to any conclusions you want to jump to. You're still in the Army and you got to be in the Army and you might as well stop fouling up and make the best of it."

"It's *my* fault my head ran into them MP nightsticks, I suppose. If they white everything they do is right, and I'm black and everything I do is wrong. I never thought I'd see the day you'd turn against me for the white man. I thought you was my bosom buddy—"

"I *am* your buddy," Solly said. "But when my buddy's wrong he's wrong even if he is my buddy. And when you go into that cracker town without a pass, you're asking for it."

He took Bookworm downstairs and made him take a nice hot shower and put him to bed. Worm went to sleep the minute he hit the sack and snored loud enough to wake the dead.

Solly lay on his cot next to Worm's cot staring up at the dark white ceiling. Maybe they *should* have gotten some guns and gone into town and shot up gobs of peckerwoods. Maybe the only way was to beat some sense into white people's heads. He thought he heard Rogers laughing at him through the silence of the sleeping barracks. And he heard crickets laughing outside. To hell with Rogers. Maybe Worm was right though. You, Solomon Saunders, Junior, are the new-styled slicked-up uncle tom—the only thing you have cast aside is the Amos-and-

Andy dialect. Face it. You value your Army prospects more than you do your buddy's friendship. You just don't want your buddy to catch you in the act. Why the hell not? Everybody's doing it. Dog eat dog eat dog eat dog. Millie knew him like a book. He wanted to be accepted in the World of White Folks, but wanted nobody to catch him working at it. He hoped Worm would not turn against him.

Who in the hell do you think you're kidding, Solly Saunders? You're not really worried about the Bookworm. With Worm you could almost fall in a stinking outhouse and come out smelling like perfume. By tomorrow Worm will realize it would have made no sense to return to town. He'll come to you and say, "You're my real bosom buddy. You didn't let me go back into that cracker town and tear my royal ass again. You saved my life." And he'll love you all the more for it. He's your best friend and much too close to see you as you really are. It's that handkerchief-head smiling Buck Rogers who jumps up and down like crazy on your tender nerves. You're scared he really knows you like a book. Just like you're scared that Millie knows you. At least Buck admits he's a first-class phony. But you dress yours up in the Race Man and the anti-fascist—in the Democratic War—"in the bullshit, in the facts, the fiction—" He heard Buck roaring with laughter this time, and stamping his feet. Solly leaped from his cot and moved swiftly toward Buck's bunk three cots away, and stared at the quietly sleeping round-faced soldier, sleeping like an innocent baby void of conscience. He wanted to dump the bastard onto the floor. He looked around him and down at the sleeping soldier again. He backed away embarrassed and moved toward the water cooler at the top of the stairs.

CHAPTER

6

Fall came late that year like it always does in Georgia, but when it came it fell in big and brown and golden-red. It started raining Thursday afternoon, and the men tracked red Georgia mud into the barracks all evening and half of the night. All night long it poured as if the sky would empty. It stopped the next morning around six o'clock, and the trees dripping with wetness seemed to be dying a thousand deaths, and in autumn death had a terrible beauty, as the dark green wet leaves crying and dying and turning golden-reddish-brown began to fall all over the camp, all over Georgia, and Scotty came home from the post stockade. Like a man come back from the dead.

Solly was in the CO's office getting him to sign the Morning Report when Scott marched in dragging his barracks bag behind him. He removed his cap and smartly saluted both of them and humbly requested that the CO grant him a ten-day furlough, and when the CO refused him and almost had a stroke in the process, Scott turned to Solly. "Tell him I need to see my old lady, Corporal Sandy. You his boy. He'll listen to you. I didn't go for that he-ing and he-ing stuff they was putting down in the post stockade. I'm a solid man and thank God for that."

Solly stood there silently sweating. Burning up. He stared at the soldier and shook his head. "I can't do you any good."

Later that night Scott cornered Solly, accused him of being an uncle tom. "Don't be scared of white folks. They ain't gon bite you."

Solly told him quietly, in a clean hot rage, "Whenever you want to act the fool, go right ahead, only leave me out of it. Have a ball. Blow your few brains out, for all I care, just don't ask me to lend you the pistol." He felt like punching the soldier in the mouth.

Scott said calmly, "All right—all right, Office Willie. You got the world in a job. I know you Cap'n Charlie's boy. And that's all right for you."

"On second thought, I'd lend you the pistol. *Stay away from me!*" Solly shouted softly to the angry-headed soldier.

Scott backed away from him and left him in the orderly room. Solly thought, all these bastards are getting on my nerves. Scott—Rogers—Bookworm. Everybody's trying to do me in. They're jealous. That's what it is. I'll show them—I'll show them. Then he thought, I've got to get hold of myself. I'm getting too jumpy. Worm had told him—wear the world like a loose garment. But Worm didn't have his potential. Solly felt like running outside and screaming.

Everything got on Solly's nerves. And almost everybody. Next morning Samuels came into the orderly room, looked over Solly's shoulders as he typed the K.P. roster, fumbled in the files, complimented him on the neatness and efficiency of the company records, and offered him a cigarette.

"What's the matter with the company, Corporal?" The lieutenant was seated behind the Topkick's desk.

"Lieutenant, I wish you would not call me 'Corporal.' " He felt a heat move around in his face. He took a long drag on the cigarette.

"You're acting corporal and you'll be corporal soon as the orders come from regimental. Just as soon as the colonel signs them. You typed them up. I recommended to Lieutenant Rutherford—"

"I typed the orders up and I was promoted to private first class. There were seven corporals made. Not one of them was Saunders."

The lieutenant's face flushed with his anger. He went to the files again and got a copy of the order. Solly went back to his typing. He heard the lieutenant swearing softly. The lieutenant stared at him again.

"Corporal, what in the hell is the matter with the outfit? We have good men in this company. They have high IQs in comparison with the rest of the men in the regiment. I checked at regimental this morning. But their morale is so goddamn low. They wouldn't extend themselves a half an inch more than they have to."

"Don't ask me, sir. I work in the office."

"Come on, Saunders. You're with the men in the evening. You're the company clerk. You're in a key position."

Solly thought, after all the jumping up and down, after all the hustling, Rogers is a corporal and I'm a private first-damn-class. And I'm an Army-loving stockholder and Cap'n Charlie's boy and the executive officer's confidante. Informer, if you please. He said, "I have no opinion on the subject." Heat moved through his body now. He wished every living thing would leave him alone.

Samuels said, "Colonel Williamson from post headquarters was in the company area yesterday. He's obviously a full colonel with eagle emblem and everything. He walked all over the area. Yet not one soldier called attention or saluted him. He heard one of our men on yard detail say to a couple of others, 'Look at that soldier with the chicken on his shoulder. If he ain't careful it'll shit all over him.' "

Solly suddenly erupted with laughter. He couldn't help himself, he tried to. All he could see was the picture of the soldiers and the self-important colonel with the shining eagle emblem on his shoulder. He laughed and laughed, as if he had been saving it up for years and years. Samuels stared at him and shook his head. Solly tried to stop. His eyes filled, his stomach hurt, but he could not stop laughing.

The high-pitched voice of the company commander came through the open window from down in the company area:

". . . NOT GOING TO STAND FOR ANY MORE FOOLISHNESS OUT OF NONE OF YOU. ALL THIS GOLDBRICKING AND GOOFING OFF ON DETAILS IS GOING TO STOP ELSE I'M GOING TO BURN EVERY

LAST DAMN ONE OF YOU. NEXT BOY MESS UP WHEN HE GOES TO TOWN I'M GOING TO PUT HIM IN THE STOCKADE AND THROW THE KEY AWAY!"

Solly stopped laughing and went to the window and looked down at Rutherford standing tall and red-faced and slim and chinless facing the company of silent men, hitching up his long-legged trousers with his elbows, walking back and forth shouting to the top of his tenor-sometimes-soprano voice, his Adam's apple moving up and down in his scrawny neck. Solly somehow felt free and loose like that garment Worm pretended always to wear. The CO must have gotten his ass eaten out up at regimental. His voice was strictly Southern now.

". . . THAT'S NO THREAT, GODDAMMIT, THAT'S A PROMISE!"

Solly turned from the window and moved back to the typewriter. He laughed a deep short laugh. "Lieutenant Charles Leander Rutherford—the greatest little old morale builder in the Army of the U.S.A."

Samuels stared at him and opened his mouth as if to say something of significance, changed his mind, and went out the door.

Rutherford came into the orderly room. "Saunders, I want you to find Sergeant Anderson wherever he is and tell him I want the entire company to go on a ten-mile hike this afternoon. Every last one of them including them on Kitchen Police and everywhere else, even including the mess and motor sergeants."

The men assembled in full field dress with pack and empty rifles and marched away from the company area. They marched with sullen angry faces and black and brown and sweaty faces till they reached the wooded area about a half a mile from the barracks. Lieutenant Samuels gave the order of Route Step, and the men immediately fell out of step with one another and began to talk. Laughing swearing mumbling grumbling. The day was scorching hot and the road was blazing red with heat and dust and Georgia sunlight, and the big heavy Army shoes kicked up clouds of red dust everywhere, and red dust on their sweaty faces.

The full field pack got heavier and heavier, as if Worm were riding Solly piggyback. Worm and Solly walked side by side, sweat and dust in their ears and eyes and in their mouths.

The pull of the pack on Solly's neck made him feel like his neck would snap any minute. Yet somehow he felt good this day. And very close to Bookworm Taylor and his other comrades.

Somebody up near the front of the formation started singing and everybody picked it up:

Glory, glory, Hallelujah,
Glory, glory, Hallelujah,
Glory, glory, Hallelujah,
His truth is marching on . . .

They lit up the green woods with their singing, some in tune, some way out, and almost imperceptibly they began to march with a free and careless cadence. For the first time since he'd been in the Army, Solly knew a warm and honest feeling of belonging, of being a part of whatever it was that the other men were a part of. He forgot the field pack on his back. Somewhere somehow the words got changed—contribution of Private Jerry Abraham Lincoln Scott.

"Glory, glory, Jody Grinder,
He's got your old lady and gone—

And then they sang:

They say this is a mechanized war,
Parlez-vous;
They say this is a mechanized war,
Parlez-vous;
They say this is a mechanized war,
Well what the hell are we walking for?
Hinky, dinky, parlez-vous—

Lieutenant Samuels and Topkick Anderson walked past them heading in the opposite direction. Worm said, "They must be trying to find Bucket-head Baker bringing up the rear. He's probably clean out of sight. That fathead sucker been trying to walk out of the Army with his bad feet ever since he got here."

The men were still singing "Parlez-vous." Solly looked back and saw Topkick and Samuels walking far behind the rear of the formation with Baker between them with his shoes tied together and hanging around his neck.

Somebody changed the lyrics of "Parlez-vous."

They say this is a white man's war,
Parlez-vous;
They say this is a white man's war,
Parlez-vous;
They say this is a white man's war,
Well what the hell are we fighting for?
Hinky, dinky, parlez-vous—

The men were laughing and shouting now. Solly laughed at first, but then he thought, this is not the white man's war. This war belongs to everybody.

The lyrics changed again.

Georgia is a helluva state,
Parlez-vous;
Georgia is a helluva state,
Parlez-vous;
Georgia is one helluva state,
The asshole of the forty-eight.
Hinky, dinky, parlez-vous—

The singing and the laughter ceased and suddenly he remembered again he was a beast of burden. He thought his back would break, his neck would surely snap this time. His mouth and throat were dry and dusty, caked with mud. He was ready to drop, when the Topkick caught up with them and called a halt, and the lieutenant told the men to fall out and take ten, take a smoke and anything else, so long as they didn't wander off out of sight. Some of the men dropped where they were on the side of the road, and some went a short distance into the bright green woods and stretched out on the glistening grass and leaned against the heavy trees. Bookworm sat with his head against a tall pine tree. Solly lay full length on the grass nearby as the sweat poured from him, gazing up through the top of the trees at the great vast empty blueness beyond. He took a long slow drag on a cigarette and it was delicious to his nostrils to his mouth to his throat and through his chest and shoulders to his stomach, and he was so tired he didn't think he'd ever get rested. Newly made Corporal Buck Rogers walked about amongst the men cautioning them to be careful with their cigarettes. Bucket-head Baker sat near Solly and Bookworm and pulled off his socks.

"Whew—" he sighed. "Goddammit, I just don't see how I'm

going to be able to make it in this man's Army—no shape, no form or fashion."

"Put your shoes on, man," Worm said. "You'll run all the snakes and lizards out the woods. And have some respect for me and Solly's tender nostrils. You must think you at home or some other funky place." Baker's shoes still hung about his neck.

Solly smiled. "He's telling you right, Bucket-head. If you and a skunk got cornered in a cave together, he'd come out with his hands in the air and proclaim you king of the pole kitties." The fellows near them chuckled. They were too tired to laugh aloud. Solly felt good. Damn good.

"You a real funny fellow, Office Boy," Bucket-head told him. "Funny as a broken crutch. Just cause you're the CO's pet you think your shit don't stink."

Solly said offhandedly, "I got your CO's pet." But he felt like Baker had kicked him in the stomach.

Rogers came over and sat down. "Ain't nothing the matter with Bucket-head's feet. His dogs ain't half as bad as mine. He's just trying to beat the rap. He thinks he can bullshit his great white Uncle. I went by the Service Club the other night and this bad-feet jitterbugging mother-huncher was outdancing everybody."

The men began to laugh and loosen up. "Old Bucket-head was dancing with one overgrown double-breasted chick, and the other cats stood around placing bets. They thought him and the hefty bitch was having a wrestling match."

"Watch that shit, you bubble-eyed bastard," Baker said.

Solly thought, so now I'm not only an intelligent stockholding Army-lover and Cap'n Charlie's boy. I'm also the CO's pet. I'm really getting up in the world. And everybody's got my number.

"You better watch the way you talk to a corporal. That's what you better watch," Buck Rogers said to Bucket-head.

"Listen to Barney Google," Bookworm said. "He thinks he's a goddamn officer already."

"You're another one better watch your step," Buck said to Worm.

"I got what it takes for a prissy-ass punk like you," Worm said casually. "You'll be a soldier before your dear old mother will—"

"Don't talk about his dear-old like that," Bucket-head said. "I understand she's a first sergeant in the Engineers and doing a jam-up job, bless her sweet soul."

"Shh—" somebody said. "Here comes the man."

Lieutenant Samuels came over to where they were sitting. "Will you help round up the men, Corporal? . . . Saunders, I meant, and tell them to gather in this vicinity. You may help too, Corporal." He nodded to Rogers.

The men gathered slowly. "All right, men," the lieutenant said. "You can sit down and relax, finish your cigarette or light another, anything, so long as you don't fall asleep."

Nobody laughed. The woods were heavy with a dark green smell and the leaves were falling golden brown.

The tan-faced white man, almost brown, stood looking down upon the company of evil- and good-natured colored men with all the complexions of the human race. He lit a cigarette and took a long slow drag, threw it down and started to mash it with his big nervous feet, picked it up again and stripped it down. Solly watched every move he made—Lieutenant Samuels, his buddy boy, the confidence man from New York City, the Ninety-day Wonder, always on the job. He liked the lieutenant sometimes against his better judgment. Maybe he didn't like him at all. Maybe it was only admiration.

"Men," the tan-skinned white lieutenant began, "I think I know a little about how you feel—"

Some of the men looked at each other and cleared their throats.

"None of us wants to be in the Army. Nobody likes war. Every one of us would rather be back in civilian life—"

Buck Rogers muttered under his breath, "Most of these mama-jabbers ain't never had it so good. You'd have to put a gun on them to make them get out of the Army. Some wouldn't go then. You'd have to shoot them first." He gazed attentively up into the lieutenant's face as some of the men lowered their heads in smothered laughter.

"—We have a job to do, so the quicker we get it done, the quicker we can all get back to civilian life. We didn't start this war, but we have to finish it. The forces who started this war are against everything we hold to be self-evident. If they should win, God help our democratic institutions. Hitler and Goebbels and Rosenberg have sold the German people a bill of goods called *'Herrenvolk,'* the master race, and are trying to impose this theory through war and destruction upon the rest of the human race. That's why we're fighting."

The lieutenant paused and his eyes went from one to the other of the men. "I know you men have a lot on your chest, so why don't you take this opportunity to get it off?"

Solly looked hopefully around him. Nobody bit. He felt a growing anger toward the men now—Buck Rogers and Lanky Lincoln and Clint Moore and especially Bookworm and Scotty. That's the way his people were—grumbling to themselves all the time, but when it was really time to speak up, all of a sudden they developed lockjaw.

"I want you fellers to open up. I really mean it. Ask any question on your mind. Let this be the bitching hour."

Some of them looked around at each other. A soft breeze blew through the green woods close to the ground, and the blades of grass did a crazy rhumba, and the leaves fell golden brown all around them, into their silent faces. Bucket-head Baker cleared his throat and faces strained and ears waited, but nothing happened. A grayish green squirrel raced down a pine tree, stood for a moment looking at the soldiers as if to hear what they had to say, and away he flew disgustedly through the tall green grass.

"An officer must be interested in the morale of his men. He must have the men's confidence, or else he's a failure as an officer. I know you men must have a million questions on your mind." He paused and waited. "How about you, Corporal Saunders?"

Solly looked down at the blades of grass dancing in the quiet breeze. His body grew even warmer. He felt the eyes of the other soldiers heavily upon him. He looked up into the officer's face. He stood up and stared out through the trees weighted down with a dark and heavy greenness toward the dusty road, and he felt a heaviness inside of him and all around him and leaning heavily against his slim shoulders. He was weary and exhausted.

"I don't have any questions, Lieutenant."

"Possibly you have a comment to make."

He stared at the friendly anxious face of the tan-complexioned white man and he looked around at the black and brown and light-brown faces. He cleared his nervous itchy throat. Why didn't this white commissioned officer leave him alone? Why didn't people leave him be? "I want to be entirely honest with you, Lieutenant, because that's the way I believe you want it." He wasn't even a non-commissioned officer. He was private-first-class acting corporal.

"Absolutely," Samuels said. "Otherwise we're wasting all of our valuable time and holding up the war."

"Well," Solly began, "I agree with you about Hitler and *Herrenvolk* and all of that stuff. I read *Mein Kampf,* and I hate what Hitler stands for as much as you do, but—but—but there's another angle to it. There're Americans who believe in *Herrenvolk.* The American Army is based on *Herrenvolk.*" He hadn't known what he was going to say. His voice trembled slightly as he took the clean green air of the forest into his dry and bitter throat. Yesterday he wouldn't have said a thing. "Still, even from the narrow standpoint of Negro Americans, I believe we have a stake in this war. I think if—I know if Hitler won, the Negro would lose the ground we've already struggled for."

"That's very true, Corporal. That is precisely the point."

"However, on the question of H Company in particular and the question of morale. We get all the dirty details. Somebody goes up to regimental and volunteers for us. At the same time we get fewer passes than any other company. And you know the story about how the MPs and Ebbensville's finest treat our men when they catch them in town, but nothing is done about it, except we go on ten-mile hikes, ostensibly to cool us off."

Some of the men laughed sarcastically. Solly paused.

"Continue, Corporal."

"That's all, Lieutenant. I'm with you, and I'm just as interested in the men's morale as you are, and anybody else for that matter." He sat down next to Bookworm and lay back full length upon the grass and the soft breeze blowing close to the ground caressed his sweaty face. He was a fool to shoot off his mouth like that. What would it get him?

"Thank you, Saunders. I want you to know I thoroughly appreciate your candor. Now we're getting down to cases!" He took off his glasses and glanced down and around at the men. "Anybody else?"

Bookworm raised his hand and Solly closed his eyes and held his breath. "How come we don't have colored officers in the Fifty-fifth Quartermaster?"

Samuels put his glasses on again and staired at Bookworm long and hard. Solly could feel the serious looks of the soldiers seated around him, and he could hear smothered laughing from a few of them. The laughter of derision. Why in the hell should he feel sorry for the officer? Samuels took an olive drab handkerchief from his back pocket and wiped his face. His voice had a strange muffled quality. "I don't know the answer to that one, soldier, except that many outfits don't have colored officers, and this happens to be one such outfit."

Some of the men laughed openly now, as Lanky Lincoln whispered loudly enough for all of them to hear, "No shit, Lieutenant?" and the lieutenant's face turned suddenly from tan to pinkish-red.

"At ease, men." He cleared his throat. "All right—all right —I know that what I just said is the understatement of the twentieth century, and it isn't really an answer to your question, soldier. All right—so it's true there is discrimination in the Army, a whole lot of it. And that song that you sang on the road a while ago that I didn't hear you singing—I didn't hear a thing, you understand—it's all true though. We all know it. But if you men help me to straighten up the outfit and help to build some pride in H Company, I'll promise you one thing—I'll do all in my power to see that you're treated as well as any outfit at Camp Johnson Henry." He paused. "Is it a deal, men?" He looked from face to face and he glanced at his watch. He waited but nobody cleared his throat. They were not in the market today. The sun was going down now, and dark ragged shadows cast themselves all over the dark green woods, settling softly now down through the trees and onto the faces and into the heavy silence.

Baker said, "We'll do the best we can, sir." Most of the soldiers laughed this time. Baker was the biggest goldbrick in the company.

"It's getting late, men," the lieutenant said. "Let's fall in out on the road and start back. Make sure you put your cigarettes out. And everything we said out here is strictly confidential between you and me, but don't forget what we talked about."

"How about a few furloughs and three-day passes? Everybody at Camp Johnson Henry gets passes and furloughs excepting us." Scotty's big voice boomed all over the forest.

"All right—all right," the lieutenant said. "I know that's a problem too. But that can also be straightened out. All I want from you men is a little co-operation."

"And all I want is a furlough," Scotty said. "And I'm gon

give myself one tonight," he mumbled underneath his angry breath.

That night Scotty kept his word and went AWOL again.

That night Solly followed his new "loose garment" policy, and instead of sitting in the orderly room reading a book or writing a letter, he hung out with the men in the barracks. He'd spent so much time by himself when he was a boy in New York City in those cold and lonesome railroad flats, sometimes he convinced himself he preferred his solitude. But it was never true of him. They were seated on Worm's and Solly's bunks, drinking whiskey straight from the bottle. Bucket-head put the pint whiskey bottle up to his lips and slowly tilted his head back and took a long and noisy swallow. "Where you get this bad-ass whiskey from?" he said. "If you don't have any good whiskey, I'd appreciate it if you didn't invite me to your party the next time."

"Ain't this a damn shame?" Buck Rogers said. "Before Uncle Sam called this jughead mama-lover he was out on the shorts snatching pocketbooks. When he came into the Army he didn't have nothing but his hat and his ass. Drank that goddamn sneaky-pete in Harlem all his life. Give me that bottle!" He grabbed the bottle from Baker's hand.

Some eager beaver downstairs yelled ATTENTION, and you could hear Rutherford's long strides coming up the steps from the first floor. Buck took a quick drink and put the whiskey bottle inside of his shirt. "Here comes Long Boy," he said out of the side of his mouth. "All right, all you sons-of-your-mothers'-misbehavior, let's make it look pretty for Captain Charlie. All except you, Corporal Solly. You already look pretty and you ain't no son-of-your— Never mind." He stood straight as a telegraph pole with his heels together and he opened his mouth and yelled like somebody was murdering him:

"AT-TEN-CHUN!"

Lieutenant Rutherford stood near the door to his office, his arrogant eyes roaming all over the barracks. He pulled up his trousers with his elbows and they slid back down on his hipless hips. "Come into my office, Saunders."

The lieutenant was seated with his tiny feet resting on top of his desk when Solly entered the office. He wore size 8–D shoes and they looked like a deformity in contrast with the six feet four inches of his lanky body. Solly started to salute him. Rutherford waved his hand. "At ease, Corporal." He stared at Solly. "How did you like the hike?"

"All right, sir."

"You think it was good for the men's morale?"

"I wouldn't know about that, sir."

"Aw, come on, Saunders. You can talk to your CO. After all, you *are* my company clerk."

"I wouldn't have any opinion, sir. None at all."

"I hear you all had a great big heart-to-heart talk out in the woods today."

Solly said nothing, his lips pressed together, his eyes narrowing.

"Is there anything at all you'd like to tell me, Corporal?"

"No, sir." The office was getting hot and sticky.

The lieutenant smiled his girlish smile. "You don't have to tell me, I know about it. I know all about the singing too—the 'Parlez-vous.' " He laughed. "I reckin all y'all New York boys just naturally stick together. They tell me New York City ain't made up of nothing but colored folks and Jews." He laughed again. "Did you and Lieutenant Samuels go to school together?"

Solly didn't answer. His stomach quivered with his anger. His fingernails bit into the palms of his hands.

The CO said nothing for a moment. He just sat there rearing back in his chair and smiling at Solly. "What I want you to do, Corporal, is get up a roster for Guard Duty right away. H Company goes on at four in the morning. That's a special assignment. We volunteered. We got such high morale."

"Yes, sir." Solly turned to leave.

"You doing a pretty good job, Saunders. Just a second. Lieutenant Samuels says you doing a damn good job." He paused as if he expected Solly to answer him.

"Yes indeed. And I got my eyes on you. There'll be a few more promotions coming up next week and I'm not going to forget you neither. You can put on your PFC stripes tomorrow." He paused again. "All the men will be restricted to quarters this week end, Saunders, but you can have a week-end pass if you want one. You and the first sergeant."

"No, sir, I'd rather stay at the camp this week end." And he was really the company commander's boy. It was true what Baker called him—Baker, Rogers, Scotty, Worm.

"You can have a pass. I just said you could have a pass.

You can go a long way in the Army, boy, with your education and your personality. I already told you. All you got to do is toe the mark!"

"No thank you, sir. Not this week end."

"What's the matter, boy? A sharp one like you must've had a whole lot of good-looking red-hot brown-skin mamas hot in behind you up in New York. You like womenfolks—don't you?"

Solly could feel the dampness over his lips, salty perspiration dripping from his forehead, his whole body wet and hot with anger. He told himself the CO was being friendly, in his own way. He wanted to make it in the Army, and the CO could be a big help or a hindrance. Make your choice. He swallowed hard and it lay whole and heavy in the bottom of his belly, a stomach-full of contradictions. "Sir, I don't care for a pass this time. I'd rather stay on the post this week end." He turned to go again.

"Wait a minute, Saunders."

Solly waited.

"We got the best company in the regiment and by God I'm going to prove it to them up at headquarters, if it's the last damn thing I do. And you put them stripes on Saunders, just as quick as you can and don't worry about nothing. All you got to do is play the Army game. Don't you worry."

"No, sir."

"You sure you don't want a pass?" the company commander insisted.

Maybe he should take the pass and then just fail to use it. Why antagonize the man?

"Yes, sir. I'm positive."

"Okay, Saunders, suit yourself," the lieutenant said. "But just remember one thing—I got my eyes on you. You're going to be all right in the Army."

Yes, sir, Captain Charlie.

CHAPTER

7

SUNDAY AFTERNOON. Lazy Southern October Sunday. Clear quiet sun-drenched like the middle of summertime. The living ain't easy, Solly thought. People giving up the ghost almost everywhere. The Germans rained bombs all night long on London town and the British with their chins up and Churchill with his cigar and his V for Victory and Stalin with his Moscow and his Stalingrad. And pretty Miss Fannie Mae Branton and her Double-V for victory.

He got off the bus in Ebbensville and went into the colored waiting room and found her number in the telephone directory. Why should he stay in camp on a day like this when the CO'd left a pass for him on his table in the orderly room? Just because Scott and Worm and Lincoln were confused about the war, it did not follow that he had to be. All right, pal of mine, you stay in camp with your Double-V and we'll pop in on your lady friend and see who wins the victory. Yuk-yuk.

The booth was hot and stuffy, and as he dialed her number a nervous sweat broke out all over him. Sitting on his cot in an empty barracks, the rest of them at the Post Exchange or the USO or somewhere, he'd been lonesome *period.* And way down deep down in the dumps. The phone ringing brought him back to now. At first he thought he was still calling New York City as he had done that morning in the Post Exchange and had found nobody home. But he was in Ebbensville in the hot booth and he thought, it's probably Fannie Mae's day to see her boy friend. So I'll just say I'm in town and thought I'd drop in for a hot minute and if she's busy, fine. The phone rang six or seven times and he started to hang up thinking nobody's home anywhere in the world, when he heard a woman's voice say, "Hello," but it wasn't Fannie Mae's. She said she was her mother and Fannie Mae was at the First A. M. E. Church at the N-double-A-C-P meeting. "You want to leave a message for her? You want to leave your name with me?"

"No thank you, ma'm. Never mind," he mumbled and stared at the receiver as he put it back on the hook. He felt a great relief, like a last-minute reprieve before the hour of execution.

He walked out of the bus station and stared across the empty plaza. What was there for him to do in a little cracker town like Ebbensville? To and fro across the plaza he saw Sunday-dressed people moving slow and easy in cadence with the dying summer day of autumn. Two days ago he'd thought fall was here, but it had been a false alarm. Not a colored person in sight. Beyond the plaza, a few automobiles crept along like they were going to the world's last funeral. He ached for New York City. Where were Ebbensville's colored people? If Millie had been home when he called her from the PX, he would not have come this day to Ebbensville. He would've talked to her and would have been fulfilled and would have gone back to the barracks and written her a letter. Damn the Bookworm.

He went back into the station and found the church's address in the directory, came outside again and caught a colored cab and took himself to church. To heck with Worm and Rogers too.

He thought her face did something pretty when he entered. Maybe he imagined it because his stomach acted up. He quickly sat down near the back. She was chairing the meeting and calling on another lady to give the last report. Most of the time he could not keep his eyes from her and did not pay attention to the serious young women who talked about a Thanksgiving party they were planning for some soldiers from Camp Johnson Henry as part of their Double-V-for-Victory program. Just before the meeting ended Fannie Mae introduced him and asked him to stand. He could hear the pride in her voice. She said she hoped the next time he would come much earlier and talk to them about NAACP work in New York City. She told the group he had been very active with the New York branch before he came into the service. "We want to assure you, Corporal Saunders, and the rest of your colleagues that we, the colored people of Ebbensville, have the boys out in Camp Johnson Henry very close to our hearts."

Later they sat in an ice cream parlor down the street from the church, and he stared at her and it was incredible how everything seemed to have happened before. Even back in the church he had an eerie feeling of strangeness and at-homeness clashing and merging. The stained-glass window with Mary's boy-child blinking softly in the dying sunlight. The people waving paper fans. The smell of soap, perfume, and perspiration. He'd almost known they'd end up at the ice cream parlor on the corner, as if he'd planned it all ahead of time. And her face was so familiar to him. He thought, maybe I knew her when I was a little boy in Georgia and she was a little biddy girl. He stared at her and away again and sipped his chocolate milk shake.

She said, "I'm so glad you came today. Where's Joe Taylor and your other buddies?" Her lovely face was all aglow. He felt deep stabs in his stomach.

"Were you born in Ebbensville?" he asked her. Maybe they grew up together in Dry Creek in the first years of their lives.

"Lived here every minute except the four years spent in college. You should've brought a few of the other fellers with you to the meeting."

"Who told you I was active in the N-double-A?" he asked her. Thinking he should have told her then and there, I'm the only one could get a pass. I'm Cap'n Charlie's favorite boy. That's why I'm here and the rest of them are back in camp. She made him feel he had been on a long long journey and had come back home at last. Get comfortable. Pull off your shoes. Get your pipe and rocking chair. And yet she made him feel a greater guilt than Millie, Worm, or Scotty or Rogers put together. She wanted to take him at face value. Nobody should take anybody at face value. Even Worm knew better. Good Lord this child was beautiful!

She looked up from her milk shake and her entire face was smiling. "Joe Taylor told me. You were a militant leader in the youth group up there. But he didn't have to tell me. Somehow I knew you would be."

"Not exactly a leader," he said. "Too busy working during the day and studying law at night." Too busy getting ready for the race. So I can outstrip the other rats.

"And active in the N-double-A somewhere in between. My goodness, that must have kept you humming!"

No matter what I say, he thought, she's bent on making me heroic. You want to burst her bubble, buddy? Just tell her you're a married man and you're Cap'n Charlie's special boy. Or maybe this was just her "be-good-to-the-colored-boys-in-the-service" personality. Little ol' morale builder. Maybe she made no distinction. Gave the same line to every soldier indiscriminately. Bookworm Taylor—Solly Saunders . . .

She said, "You folks have the Double-V in New York. Victory against the fascists overseas and against the crackers here at home."

He did not want to discuss the war or politics or Double-V or NAACP. He did not want to talk at all. He just wanted to sit and stare at her and feel good with her and be with her and wallow in good feelings, and let it go at that. Yet he heard himself say, "How can we win a war against the enemy if we fight amongst each other?"

She looked surprised at first and hurt almost. Her large eyes darkened quickly to black and lowered, and she sipped slowly on her milk shake. Then she said quietly, "Where is the enemy? Who is the enemy? Why should we discriminate? A fascist is a fascist and a cracker is a cracker. The war is everywhere we find it."

Arguing with her was like making love. It got him hot and bothered. He wanted to take her sweet face in his hands and keep it ever glowing the way it was this moment. At the same time he felt the need to fight with her, break down all her pious concepts, bring all her gods tumbling down around her, and let her worship only him. Blindly follow him everywhere with her face forever glowing like it was now this moment. All this and at the same time not to make her angry not to argue with her. Forget the war forget the Double-V. Smile again, my pretty baby. Smile, get angry, smile, be angry.

He said, "Look at it realistically. This is a house, and you and I are a family. We're having a family spat between us. A character very dangerous to both of us tries to break into the house and take it over. What do we do? Continue fighting each other and let him take over? Or do we stop and band together to fight him off and settle our family differences later?" He'd raised his voice at her unknowingly.

"Let him have the house," she said angrily. "What good is it? If you never let me breathe easy in it? Let him tear it down for all I care."

Her anger made him want her.

He said, "You don't mean that, darling." When he heard himself call her darling, he felt a tingling racing through his body that made him warm all over. "I'm sorry, I mean, Fannie Mae—I—" She must be aware that he was wild to be with her. Yet he told himself it was only intellectual attraction.

Her face flushed beautiful for him. "You'd better believe I mean it," she said. "Let the house go down and we can build another one." The perspiration on her nose.

She was teaming up with Worm and Scotty and all the rest against him. And he desperately needed somebody to agree with him, needed her, not cynical Buck or even Millie who had her own ax to grind. He needed pure agreement this day, this moment. He was a sixteen-karat phony and he needed her to believe he was the real thing with no strings attached. He had to have her on his side and close to him. He had to disagree with her and bring her to his point of view. And with no equivocation. He had to have her intellectually.

He said, "Face it. What if the working men of this country had the same attitude? There wouldn't be any no-strike pledges and there'd be strikes all over the place and we wouldn't be able to produce enough to win the war. The whole nation would be completely demoralized."

She shook her head. "A nation that can be so easily demoralized is pretty sick to begin with. Double-V could help to heal it and make it stronger for the battle." She was getting angry with him for not agreeing with her.

Stop fighting me! he almost shouted. How did he get into such a stupid argument? He had not come to town for this. He was perspiring now and getting angry and he realized what he was doing and why he was doing it. Doing his damnedest to rationalize his own position, his own being, his existence. And he wasn't being honest with her. He knew it, but it didn't stop him. He lowered his voice. "We have a stake in the outcome of this war. We are Americans who value freedom more than any other Americans. Maybe because we never had it."

She stared at him. He was so articulate and handsome and she had to admit that he made sense. She'd have to think about the sense he made, over and over, and digest it and see what the results were and have it out with him again. And she wanted there to be an again. Lots of them. He knew she was weakening and he touched her cheek gently with the tips of his fingers and drew them quickly away. He wanted to take her in his arms. He was a very foolish man.

Her face flushed. "In a way you're right of course," she said. "On the other hand—" But she liked him and did not want to make him angrier. He was such a moody fellow. He might never come to town again. So she did not pursue the "other hand." He was half right anyhow, and he was complicated and she wanted him to come again.

He said, "When our country is up against it, we cannot be opportunistic. We cannot take advantage of it."

She said, "Let's talk of something pleasanter. May I have another milk shake?"

He'd won but he did not feel good about his triumph. There was something phony about it. They got another milk shake each, and they changed the subject and talked of this and that and the other: music, books, sports, movies, and the like. He wanted desperately to capture the other mood they had begun with, but there it was between them, the Color Question and the war, and it stayed there till she drove him to the station for his bus.

The CO stood in the door staring at Solly's bowed head for a moment. Solly was busy with the Morning Report. He looked up finally and the CO gestured for him to carry on, the CO smiling friendly-like.

"Have a good time in town, Saunders?"

Solly said, "Yes, sir." He'd had a ball, fighting with the prettiest girl in Ebbensville.

"They tell me they got some real hot chocolate over there that just won't stop for the red light," the CO said. And he was really being friendly, but Solly's nerves were wearing thin.

He didn't say a word. He stared down at the Morning Report. The CO laughed. "I want you to make up an order tomorrow. I'm making another corporal." He paused and Solly waited. "I want you to make sure you spell his name right. His name is Solomon Saunders, Junior."

The CO paused again. Solly didn't know what to say, now that he was getting ahead in the Army. Finally he said, "Yes, sir." And that was that.

The CO said, "Keep your nose clean, boy, and you have nothing to worry about. Regimental says our paper work is the best in the whole damn regiment." He lowered his voice. "And another thing, between me and you, they're going to have a colored regiment on the post with colored officers and everything. Going to set it up sometime in March. Month after next they're going to send one man from each company in the Fifty-fifth to Officer Candidate School. But I haven't made up my mind whether I want to lose a good company clerk just so a new black regiment can get a fair-de-middling officer." He laughed his friendly laugh again. "What you think of that?" he asked.

Solly said, "Yes, sir." A good cool feeling rushed through his body. He was elated. There was no need to kid himself. He wanted to be an officer. He could not suppress a smile this time.

"Keep what I told you to yourself," Rutherford said, "and stay on the ball and keep your nose clean, and you haven't a thing to worry about from here on in." He stood for a while watching Saunders and turned and walked out of the door.

"All right, sir." He felt like shouting hallelujah.

Three days later he made corporal. He wrote Millie and his mother about his promotion and his great prospects. The Army wasn't so bad after all—after all. Fannie Mae Branton did not understand the complications. Maybe it was her Southern background. She was too beautiful to be so bitter. But what difference did it make to him whether she understood or not? She meant nothing in his young life. Who're you kidding, Solly Saunders? Who're you kidding, buddy boy?

CHAPTER

8

Rutherford also got promoted. He made full-fledged captain, and he really loved those silver tracks. He made everybody aware of them. He had a habit of sitting at his desk and rearing back in his swivel chair with a cigar in his mouth and his long legs propped up on the desk, and if he were talking to you about something, his eyes would shift from one shoulder to the other, glancing slyly at his gleaming bars. He reminded Solly of spectators at a tennis match. He was even trying to get a little more depth out of his voice, but the deepest he could go was a tenor that flirted dangerously with soprano. But he was Captain Rutherford, company commander, and he was the one that cracked the whip, and Solly was Corporal Solomon Saunders, Junior, the company clerk. The men of H Company had fondly nicknamed it Hell Company, but the men of the other companies of the regiment called it "Rutherford's Plantation," and the men of H Company had earned the title of "Rutherford's slaves."

He felt good, the brand-new corporal did. He had been over to regimental that morning and had come back to the barracks and up the steps to the second floor when he heard the soldier sounding off. Solly started to go back down again but something held him.

"I been home to fuck Miss Scotty. Where you think I been?"

They haven't seen you yet, even though the door is open. So go back downstairs and down to battalion and get those special orders. Get while the getting is good. Go! Go!

"What did you say?" the CO shouted, losing color.

Scotty roared like a lion. "I said I been home to fuck Miss Scotty—that's what I said. What you trying to do, Lieutenant, make a faggot outa me or something? You got your old lady here on the post with you. You fuck her every night, I reckon—that is if you ain't no punk or queer or something!"

The captain jumped from his chair shouting hysterically: "Shut up, Scott! That's enough, goddammit!"

"Shut up, Scotty!" Solly softly shouted, without knowing.

"One sure thing if you don't fuck your old lady, somebody else will do it for you. A woman gots to have it just as bad as a man. Ain't no two ways about it—"

Solly stood there transfixed.

"Get out of here, nigger! Goddammit! If I had my forty-five with me this morning I'd blow your goddamn black brains out!"

Scotty was jumping up and down. "Onh-honh! Onh-honh! Onh-honh! I knew it! I knew it! I knew it! I knew I would get you to tear your ass sooner or later! I knew I would get you to show your cracker, you peckerwood! You ought to be ashamed of yourself—a captain in the United States Army of Democrat America and President Roosevelt, and calling a poor little colored buck-ass private like me a nigger!"

"Get him out of here!" the captain screamed. "Somebody come get him!"

"Taking advantage of me just because you got me where you want me down here in Georgia. My feelings is hurt, Lieutenant! I really was deceived in you. I thought you was different—I—"

"Saunders! Saunders! Sergeant Anderson! Somebody! Anybody!"

Solly should have run like a thief back down the stairs, but it was too late, and he went into the captain's office on the double. "What's the matter, Captain Rutherford?"

The captain's face was like an overripened carrot, his breathing quick and short and hard. He could hardly talk now. His big Adam's apple seemed to have lodged in his narrow throat and choked off the words. "Ta-ta-ta-take this so-so-soldier inside and keep him there till I get back. Don't let him out of your sight." His face was losing color and even longer and thinner than it usually was. He looked like he had vomited his insides out and drained every drop of blood from his face. The veins in his forehead pushed against the pulled-tight surface and would pop out any minute.

"Yeah!" Scotty shouted softly. "I ain't gon tell no lie about it. Your old lady ain't no different from none of the rest. A queen gets bigged the same way a maid do. Tell him, Corporal. If you don't give it to her she going begging somewhere else cause she's bound to get it. She'll be fucking any and everybody—"

"Get him out of here!"

Solly stared at Scotty, paralyzed and speechless. He had an impulse to fall down laughing and roll all over the floor and kick up his heels and laugh and laugh and laugh some more and laugh and laugh like never before. At the same time he was afraid for Scotty. Especially for Solomon Saunders's expectations.

But Private Scott went on and on and on: "Goddamn if she won't be running after every brown-skin peter-pusher in Company H. Tell him what I say, Corporal Crute, goddammit!"

"I say shut up!" Solly shouted softly.

"Get him out of here! I gave you an order! Get him outa here before I kill him!"

The white-faced captain collapsed heavily back into his swivel chair. Maybe he was having a stroke. Solly started toward him.

The CO mumbled weakly, "Get him outa here!"

Solly turned to the little colored soldier with the bushy mustache. "Come on, Scotty."

Scotty said humbly, "Okay, Corporal Crute. I don't reckin you gon lead me wrong, beinst me and you both is colored." And followed Solly into the orderly room.

They stood for a moment looking each other over and listening for signs of life to come from the captain's office, but nothing came forth but a deafening roar of fearful silence.

Scotty smiled. "A cracker is a mama-jabbing motherhuncher."

Solly said, "Why don't you straighten up and fly right, soldier?" He went and sat down at his table and stared at the

Guard Roster. Maybe the captain had passed out for real! Maybe he should call the base hospital! Maybe he should get a jeep and take him there.

A few minutes later the captain came quietly into the orderly room. He was as white as an unsalted soda cracker, with long deep ridges in his apoplectic forehead. He didn't even glance in the direction of Scotty. "You keep the prisoner here. I'm late for a meeting at headquarters now," he said in a weak flat voice that didn't sound like the captain at all. "Don't you let him out your sight—not a single second. I'll get somebody to come over here and stand guard over him with a gun. Soon as the regimental meeting is over I'll be back here to draw up the charges. But until you're relieved you're responsible for him—understand?"

"Yes, sir."

The captain turned and walked out of the office and down the stairs.

They heard the door slam downstairs, and Scotty started to laugh and Solly said, "I don't know what the hell you're laughing about. You're really up the creek this time. They're going to throw the book at you, and I don't blame them. You begged him for it."

Scotty stopped laughing. "I don't give a shit about Long Boy. He tickles my royal hindparts. Boy, can I get under that mama-jabber's skin—" He laughed some more.

"He's going to get under *your* skin. I don't know what the hell your story is, but I wish you'd stop tearing your ass when I'm around."

"Man, Long Boy ain't scared of me—and I know good and well I ain't scared of Long Boy. They put me in this cracker Army against my will and had the nerve to put me under a peckerwood officer and send me to Georgia. Them Japs and Germans ain't done me nothing. These crackers is my natural enemy," Scotty said angrily. "And as long as I'm here I'm gonna fight em, goddammit. You take Texas Slim Rutherford frinstance. It would do me all the good in the world to make that mama-jabber blow his stack. I would figger I'd won the war. And I'm working hard at it day and night—you better believe me."

Solly stared at the little man. "You have the wrong slant on everything."

"Hell naw," Scotty told him. "I ain't crazy—not by a long

shot. And I ain't gon let these pink mama-jabbers get me down. If there's any getting down done, buddy boy, I'm gonna do it. And thank God for that," Scotty added as if he just remembered it.

Solly stared at the little man and almost admired him against his will, even though he was convinced that Scott was absolutely wrong. Foolish wrong. Stupid wrong. Crazy wrong. Scotty was Fannie Mae's Double-V taken to its ridiculous conclusion.

"Go ahead with your work," Scotty said. "I ain't going nowhere. You don't have to worry about nothing. I don't even have to pee this morning."

"And thank God for that," Solly said. And both of them laughed.

Scotty sat down in a chair near Solly and Solly looked at his Guard Duty Roster. He hoped Scotty would carry his spirit of cooperation one step further and keep quiet for a few minutes because he had to get his work done.

Scotty grinned and blinked his angry eyes. "Look at it this way. What the hell can Long Boy do to me?" He answered his own question before Solly could turn it over in his mind. "Not a goddamn thing. The baddest they can do is to throw my ass in the stockade. I ain't gon do enough for em to shoot me. I love *me* too much for that kinda shit. I don't never desert, I just go AWOL. I always come back before they catch me. So between the stockade and the Army, I mean, what's the big deal, McNeal? If I can get these fools to give me about two or three years straight at Leavenworth or some kinda shit like that, maybe by then the war'll be over. Dig? They know what I'm putting down, but ain't nothing they can do about it. When I came into the Army and they were giving me the oath, I was giving myself an oath. I was swearing to *me*, that I wasn't going nowhere where any shooting was, less it was in Mississippi or Georgia in the United Snakes of America. And I don't never go back on me."

Solly said, "You got everything ass-backwards. This may be a cracker Army but this is not a cracker war. This is a war *against* the crackers. I don't care what kind of war they think it is, this is *our* war goddammit!"

Scotty grinned. "All right—all right. Ain't no needa getting your bowels in an uproar. I see they finally made you corporal. And that's all right for you."

Solly said belligerently, "And that's not all I'm going to make, while you'll be making private-first-class fuck-up."

"I could be a mess sergeant with a master sergeant's rating, and I ain't got no education eetall. That's how come I can't understand a intelligent feller like you holding still for this peckerwood Army. Man! If I had as much up in my head as you got, I woulda got me a big civilian job behind a desk and kept that home fire burning. But I reckin the more education you get the more you look at things like white folks. You're like the slave that lived in the Big House. I'm a field hand."

Solly stood up and he was hot enough to start a full-scale war in the orderly room. He said, "Look, buddy, your opinions don't interest me in the least. And do me one small favor. Keep your mouth shut for the next few minutes till the MP comes. I've got work to do. That's your trouble anyhow. You run off at the mouth too much. And if the man throws the book at you, I don't blame him, and don't you blame me for typing up the charges. I only work here, I don't make the rules."

Scotty stared up at him smiling. "All right, Corporal Sandy. You and the white folks got everything."

Solly sat back down again and glared at the Guard Duty Roster. Scotty was deathly quiet for a moment, and then he said gratuitously, "I believe the MPs is almost as stupid as the officers."

Solly typed three more names on the Guard Duty Roster.

"I was on a train coming out of New York night before last with my first sergeant's stripes on and a great big lieutenant MP comes over to me—"

Solly hoped that Scotty wouldn't give him a bad time like before and run away again, and he laughed inwardly at the little soldier who was supposed to be dedicated to his contempt for the Army, and Army brass in particular, and yet outside of the camp, glorying in a Topkick's uniform. Scotty stood up and Solly looked up.

"Don't worry, Corporal Crute. I ain't going nowhere. I ain't gon get you in bad with Cap'n Charlie. I understand what you putting down. I just don't wanna pick up on it."

"I'm not worried about a thing," Solly lied.

"This MP lieutenant comes over to me," Scotty said, "and I'm telling you, man, I was scared shitless. He had a buck sergeant with him, understand? The MP pulled out his gun and I said to myself, 'Oh my Lordy Lord, this is it!' It got so quiet on that train you could have heard a rat pissing on cotton. He gave the gun to me and said, 'Sergeant, will you guard this soldier for just a few minutes? I got to go through the train and locate my girl friend.' " Scotty started to laugh and he couldn't contain himself. "Get the damn picture, Crute," he said. And he started to laugh again and finally Solly felt like laughing, but he brought himself up short. Maybe this was a trick—to get him to laughing and dash out of the door and leave him laughing.

"I didn't know what to think," Scotty continued. He laughed again involuntarily. "The MP said, 'This soldier has been AWOL a whole week. I'm taking him back to Dix.' I looked at the gun the MP was handing me, and I wanted to burst out laughing." Scotty started to laugh again.

"Get the picture, Corporal Sandy. I'm sitting there a colored buck-ass private in the rear-damn-ranks, been over the hill a whole damn month already—impersonating a first-damn-sergeant—and this white mother-hunching M-damn-P putting me on guard over a cracker buck sergeant who had only been gone over the hill a week." Scotty was laughing so hard that the tears spilled down his cheeks. "The Army is a bitch. I took the gun from the white boy and I said, 'All right, Lieutenant, sir, as a first sergeant in the great Army of the United States, and proud of my stripes and my responsibilities, I will guard this prisoner with my very life, till death do us separate.' " He sat down and started to laugh again. "I almost overdone it, understand? The lieutenant didn't know what to make of me. He said, 'Thank you, Topkick. If all the men in the Army had your spirit, the war wouldn't last very many more months.' And I said: 'Thank you, sir, it certainly wouldn't.' "

Scotty began to slap his thighs and laugh and laugh without restraint, and Solly could see the little soldier, who was a heavyweight from shoulder to shoulder, see him on the train with the first-sergeant stripes and with the bushy mustache that gave his big head a Stalin-like expression and the sarcasm in his light-brown eyes, and the white lieutenant MP and the white buck sergeant, and he looked at Scotty sitting in the chair and laughing like crazy, and he started to laugh; and both of them were howling with laughter when the armed MP sent by Texas Slim came striding into the orderly room.

Solly sobered quickly and turned the laughing soldier over to the Military Police.

Notwithstanding the captain's admonitions, it was hard to keep your nose clean. You couldn't live by yourself and only for yourself. You had to live with other people—especially in the Army. Somebody was always screwing up, somebody was always trying to involve you.

Sergeant Greer, the evil-eyed motor sergeant, went over into town one night with a pass and got roaring drunk and three white MPs tried to take his girl friend from him and he tried to whip all of them at once and he came back to the barracks about three in the morning, crying, bruised, cussing, bleeding. The next morning in the office, the CO accused the sergeant of disorderly conduct over in town and would not listen to Greer's version of what happened. The MP's report was enough for him. Greer, still drunk from alcohol and nightstick, cussed the captain and called him a liar to his face. Rutherford came from behind his desk and said, "Stand at attention, Sergeant!" And ripped the staff-sergeant stripes from his arm and said, "At ease, Private!" And ordered Solly to take Private Greer downstairs and give him a cold shower with all of his clothes on.

Next day Sergeant Anderson, the Topkick, led a group of non-coms in to see the captain on behalf of the broken motor sergeant, who was acknowledged to be the best motor man in the regiment. He insinuated Solly into being a part of the delegation. Solly tried to hedge at first. He told Solly quietly, "If non-coms don't stick together they are nothing to themselves or to the Army. Right?"

Solly said, "Yes—but—" He was sweating. Somebody was always putting him on the spot.

"I'm the easiest-going bastard in the world, but when my best soldier gets busted for being a man, I mean, the company will go to the frigging dogs, inside of a week, if something isn't done quick."

Solly said, "Maybe if you spoke to the captain by yourself. You're the first sergeant—maybe he'd listen to you." Every day he was put on the spot like this.

Topkick said quietly, "Well, I don't blame you for not sticking your neck out. I mean, after all, I'm just a jerk don't know any better. That's all right, the rest of the fellers agreed to go, excepting Rogers. That'll be enough I reckin. Probably won't do any good anyhow. I don't blame you. It ain't gon hardly ever happen to you. You don't ever go into town."

Solly went with the other NCOs. The reference to Rogers

helped to force his hand more than he or the Topkick realized. But just as he suspected, it did no one any good.

The CO would not talk with them. There were eight of them including Sergeant Perry, the mess sergeant. He told them they constituted a mob and he was going to forget they had come to see him like that. He said to Sergeant Anderson, "I'm surprised at you, an old Army man. You're my first sergeant. If you got anything on your mind you come and speak to me individually as my first sergeant, and not as part of an organized mob. And you too, Saunders, my company clerk. I should send the whole lot of you on a five-mile hike. Be dismissed and consider yourself lucky."

Later that afternoon the captain called Solly into his office and reprimanded him personally and individually and even maybe fatherly.

"You want to be an officer, Saunders?"

Solly swallowed hard and said, "Yes, sir."

"You sure got a funny way of showing it."

"Is my work unsatisfactory, sir?" His company-clerk work was the best in the regiment and he knew it.

"Your work is excellent, but that's not all of it, and you know it—I mean the attitude of an officer, and that's what I've been trying to teach you ever since you came into the company, but you'd rather listen to the Jewish lawyer. Ever time I turn around you all got your heads together. Well I sure can't make you, if it isn't in you. You can lead a horse to the water but you sure can't make him drink." He stopped to breathe and glanced at the captain bars on his shoulders. He looked again at Solly.

And Solly stared back at Rutherford, wondering who had the most sense, Scotty or Solly, and was the officer attitude really worth the horse's drinking? Or something.

"Have I treated you unfairly, Saunders?"

Solly looked the question in the face and on each side but did not look behind the question. And he said, "No, sir."

"Well, then, by God, you listen to me. There's no such thing as fair and unfair in the Army. There's only order and discipline. There're those who dish it out and those who take it. You have to make up your mind where you stand, one side or the other. You understand?"

Solly said, "Yes, sir." In a very special way the CO reminded him of Millie. Everything either this or that and oversimplified. But life was much more complicated. Life was much more than this or that, black or white. Life was grayish.

"And don't kid yourself, Saunders. You want to be an officer. I know you do. Any fool can be one of the mob. And I'm giving you an opportunity most colored boys don't ever get."

Solly had broken into an awful sweat now. There were many things he might have said and maybe even should have said, he knew what to do with words, but sometimes silence was the wisest course.

"I'm on your side. You understand that, don't you, Saunders?"

He almost lost his voice. "Yes, sir." And he hated his ambition. He was sick of saying yes sir.

That same night a few men sat in the orderly room with Solly talking about the Japanese giving ground in the South Pacific and the Germans catching hell on the Russian front and colored soldiers catching holy hell on the Southern front, particularly in Ebbensville and at Camp Johnson Henry and especially on Rutherford's plantation.

Bucket-head Baker said, "Man, a chicken ain't nuthin but a bird and a soldier ain't nuthin but a turd."

Bookworm said, "And a colored turd at that."

Solly said jokingly, "Maybe Scotty's got something after all. Take up residence in the post stockade. Come out again, go home, and return to camp and back to the stockade again. Maybe he's got something." But he didn't really mean it, not even jokingly. He was talking through his hat to impress the gang. He didn't really understand the man who could have been a master sergeant. He didn't want to understand him. He was afraid to.

Bookworm said, "Double-V for Victory. Tell em about it, Solly. Miss Fannie Mae Branton is the greatest."

Scotty was a damn fool pure and simple. Fannie Mae Branton was another question altogether. She was beautiful.

Buck Rogers came into the barracks with a bottle and he held it up to Worm's nose and Worm followed him out of the orderly room and the rest of the men followed the Bookworm.

Bucket-head said, "All you got to do to make a colored man happy is give him a drink of licker and a piece of hoecake."

They were seated around Solly's and Bookworm's living quarters and passing the bottle from one to the other. Worm got up and started to hum "Tea for Two" and did a soft-shoe routine.

He wasn't built like a dancer but he could really move. Smooth and graceful.

Buck Rogers said, "Man, it's a wonder the government don't charge you extra tax for building your ass so close to the sidewalk." The soldiers laughed.

"Jealous," Bookworm said, without breaking his stride. "This is how I used to win that damn amateur contest at the Apollo every Wednesday night."

Buck Rogers laughed and stomped his feet. "I knew I had seen you somewhere before. Goddamn, you're the jerk Puerto Rico used to have so much trouble getting off the stage."

The soldiers howled with laughter.

Bucket-head said, "They ought to do you colored folks like they do the Indians. Pass a law against selling whiskey to you."

The bottle was just about empty and the men were in their whiskey and the talk got around inevitably to Rutherford's infamous plantation. The whiskey had gone to Solly's head and he felt good. He saw Fannie's face before him.

Bucket-head said, "Yeah, Charlie's got a plantation and you all his slaves and ain't a damn thing you can do about it. You sure can't rise up against him and make a revolution."

Buck Rogers said, "Don't use that word around here. This is America, you stupid prick. Besides these fucking bunks might be wired for sound." He jumped up and turned one of the cots over and started to examine it.

The men laughed. Buck was forever clowning when the officers were absent. "Don't laugh," he said. "I like it here. By now I'm a red-blooded American. I don't want the man sending me back to Trinidad. I got enough of that British Subject shit."

Bookworm said seriously, "Double-V for Victory. Tell 'em, Solly!"

Bucket-head said, "Trinidad? Ain't no Trinidad in Mississippi."

Lanky said, "This is the white man's country and he can do you any way he wants to do you and ain't a damn thing you can do about it."

Bucket-head said, "When Charlie cracks his whip, all you can do is say, 'Mass'r, my back may be broken, but my spirit's undaunted!' "

Solly said, "And he'll pat you on the head and put a little more on your back." The men chuckled and laughed. He said,

"But remember, fellows, when the burden gets heavy and the going gets rough, just remember we're fighting a war for democracy." He felt good and big and comradely.

Bucket-head said, "Fighting who? *We* ain't fighting nobody. You think these crackers gon let you go over there and shoot at other crackers? They don't even give you a rifle to do Guard Duty. White sentries around here carry rifles and colored ones carry sticks. Man, a spook ain't nothing never was nothing and ain't never gon be nothing."

Bookworm turned on Bucket-head. "You bad-foot, handkerchief-head mother-huncher, you the kind that keeps the Race back!" He turned to Solly. "There ought to be something we could do to get this Texas peckerwood offa our backs. Maybe with that Double-V-for-Victory jive, we could take our case to the N-double-A-C-P. You ought talk to Fannie Mae Branton. That lady knows all about everything."

The bottle was empty and the Ebbensville White Lightning put a brand-new color on everything. And the image evoked at the mention of the PX lady—the church the ice cream parlor Fannie Mae. The comradeship he felt this moment with the men. Everything conspired against him. Without thinking deeply he said, "We could write a letter to the colored papers. Tell them how Negro soldiers are fighting these crackers for democracy down in Camp Johnson Henry in Ebbensville, Georgia. Blow the lid off of this goddamn camp. Tell the whole world about Charlie's plantation. So what could they do to us?" As soon as the stupid words were out of his mouth he was sorry he had said them. He was biting the hand that wanted to feed him.

"They could blow your heads off," Rogers said, sobering up immediately. "You ain't in no Boy Scouts of America. You're in the Army of the United States and your country is at war. You ain't even a second-class citizen any more. You're a second-class soldier."

"All right, Uncle Thomas," Worm said disgustedly.

Bucket-head said, "Colored folks ain't gon never stick together about nothing nohow. All the white man got to do is give one of you some cornbread and a drink of licker, and potlicker at that—"

Rogers said seriously, "I'm surprised at you, Corporal Solly. I'd expect something stupid from a fathead sucker like Bookworm, but you're an educated man. You know you can't start no stuff like that in the Army. Your whiskey must be talking to you."

Solly's mind cleared for a sober minute. He admitted, "That's some bad whiskey you were giving away."

Worm pulled at his arm. "Come on, Solly. Let's go get the letter written. Don't pay no attention to that uncle tom faggot."

Solly mumbled, "I drank too much—drank too much—"

Solly had gotten up off the cot. He sat down again. His head swam around. He was drunk, he told himself, Ebbensville-White-Lightning drunk, and unable to consider the pros and cons. And he was going to be an officer and he was drunk and going to be an officer. And Worm wasn't going anywhere. Fannie Mae knew the difference between him and Bookworm Taylor. You'd better believe she knew the difference.

Worm pulled at his arm again, almost pulled him to his feet. "Come on now. Don't get chicken. You supposed to be a stud that practice what you preach."

Bucket-head said, "Corporal Solly may be crazy but he ain't nobody's fool. He loves that company-clerk job—sitting on his pretty ass in a office all day long."

Rogers said, "You goddamn right! Me and Corporal Solly the only ones in the whole damn stupid outfit that have the intellectual capacity to be made officers in this mother-hunching Army. He's been through City College and I've been through Yale and all that kind of shit. I'm Ivy League."

Worm said disgustedly, "You been through Yale, you handkerchief-head mama-jabber, with a mop and pail. Went through the front door and came out the back."

The men were laughing now all over the top floor.

"Come on, Solly!" Worm put both arms around his shoulders.

Rogers said, "You run your big fat ignorant mouth and me and Professor Solly gon run our business. And we ain't thinking about doing nothing to jeopardize our potential for going upward and onward in this great Army of the United States of America, where every red-blooded citizen has a chance to be commander-in-chief."

Rogers had the stage now, and everybody on the top floor was listening, some of them moving in for a ringside seat. He was floor-showing and burlesquing and he was getting on Solly's tender nerves. He was stabbing where it really hurt.

"Me and Solly might get to be brigadier generals if this shit last long enough. You ain't seen no fucking bucking. Tell em what we gon do, Professor. We got our future to think about even after this is over."

The men at ringside were laughing and chuckling. Solly stared at Rogers in open disgust. He got to his feet. "You know what you can do for me."

Bookworm followed him across the barracks to the orderly room, leaving a roar of derisive laughter behind him.

They walked inside the orderly room and Bookworm closed the door. "All right, Solly, let's get the show on the road."

They stood there facing each other. Solly said, "Maybe we ought to sleep over it and wait until tomorrow evening." Millie was right. You could never trust your feelings. They betrayed you every time.

"Come on, old buddy." He tried to steer Solly to the chair in front of the typewriter. "You know tomorrow don't never come. If we don't do it tonight, it'll never get done."

Solly said, "I had too much to drink tonight. My head isn't clear." Why didn't Bookworm leave him alone? He had been feeling good and let his good feelings run away with him.

Worm repeated, "If we don't get it done tonight it'll never get written."

Solly pulled angrily away from Worm and turned to face him with a righteous unfelt indignation. "What the hell you mean, it'll never get written?"

"I mean, if our heads had been clear we wouldn've made the suggestion in the first damn place, and when our heads *do* clear up, Cap'n Charlie gon look bigger and badder than he ever did, and we gon start talking ourselves out of doing anything. That's the way educated thinkers always do. Anything they talk themselves into they can talk themselves out of without doing nothing."

"What makes you think you have a damn monopoly on being militant?" Solly demanded. He wanted to strike Bookworm on his wide-open signifying sanctimonious face. He heard Buck Rogers roaring out on the floor of the barracks. Rogers was a handkerchief-head opportunistic vulgar bastard!

"Don't get mad with me, good kid. After all it was *your* idea, and if you done let a uncle tom faggot like Buck Rogers talk you out of it, don't jump salty with me."

Solly said, almost shouting, "Get this straight. Neither you or Buck Rogers or any-damn-body else can talk me into anything or out of anything."

Worm said, "I reckin me and you is just different about this Army."

Solly said, "You're damn right. You're marking time and I'm marching."

Worm said, "Course I see your point. And I don't much blame you none. After all, Cap'n Charlie ain't gon send me to OCS. I ain't never gon be nothing but a buck-ass private, and that's all I wanna be till they make me a civilian."

Solly said, "Do me a favor, will you? Politely step to hell and be sure to tell them I sent you." He walked past Worm and out of the orderly room toward his bunk, where the bull session was still holding forth. Rogers had the floor. Solly stopped and turned and moved toward the stairs and went down them two and three at a time and out into the autumn dampness that chilled his hot and angry body.

It was almost time for the madhouse to close for the night, but the PX Commandos and desperadoes were still holding forth and the jukebox was giving out with Al Cooper's "How 'bout That Mess?" and two beer-drunken GIs were jitterbugging with each other over near the lady's counter in the midst of a circle of hand-clapping laughing hell-raising soldiers. Solly headed straight for the telephone booths. As he dialed the operator he felt the perspiration pour from all over his angry body. He saw the scene again in the orderly room with him and Bookworm and especially Rogers, and his stomach trembled with anger as he listened with a far-off corner of his mind to the cane-sugared voice of the Ebbensville long-distance operator as she made contact with New York City. Who in the hell was Bookworm Taylor to question his integrity? Let him do his own letter-writing. The voice of the New York operator was like home cooking and Far Rockaway and Seventh Avenue and Herald Square and "Stomping at the Savoy" and Delancey Street and "East Side, West Side, All Around the Town." He was as militant as any sonofabitch in Camp Johnson Henry. He was not like Rogers. It was just something Worm would never understand. He was for the war, and Worm and Scott were prejudiced against it. Everything was this or that to them. Couldn't see any further than their noses. He was an anti-fascist and the war was against fascism. He heard the New York operator repeat his number away up north in New York City, and brand-new perspiration broke out on his face as the phone began to ring. His heart began to make like a sledge hammer. Soon she would pick up the phone and they would be together again, he and Millie. But suddenly he realized he didn't really want to hear her voice tonight. He was in no shape this night to swallow the great American legend of upward and onward ad infinitum and ad nauseam. He didn't need that kind of dream tonight. Even as he heard her sleepy sensuous "hello," the receiver was already descending away from his face, and he placed it quietly onto its hook. Millie was an honest person, but he didn't need her brand of honesty at this particular moment in time and space.

He heard the telephone ringing urgently from the booth he had just left as he strode across the floor toward the lady's counter, and the jukebox blasting now with Duke Ellington Taking the A Train. She must have seen him as he left the booth. By the time he reached the counter she had almost finished making his chocolate malted. She smiled from the tenderest depths of her heart and it made his stomach hurt.

"That's what I call brown-skin service," he said with a nervous grin as she gave him his malted across the counter.

"We try to please the customers." She looked anxiously up into his face and away again. She looked at him once more and said, "Excuse me a minute," and went to wait on another soldier. It was the first time he had seen her since that Sunday over in Ebbensville.

He put the money beside the untasted malted and said, "Not tonight" under his breath, and turned away, just as she looked back again. He needed a sour taste tonight. He made his way to the beer counter and took some quick short ones just as fast as he could swallow them.

CHAPTER

9

But if you listened to Gabriel Heatter every night and his "good news today," you would think that the Russians would be in Berlin in two weeks' time and the war would surely be over by the end of the year. And all the romantic soldiers were dreaming of a white Christmas thanks to Bing Crosby and Irving Berlin.

Solly went over to the Post Exchange one evening to get himself a malted. That was the reason he gave himself. He had an irresistible taste in his mouth for one of Miss Fannie Mae's especially delicious chocolate malteds made especially by her and especially for him. And that particular evening he just had to have one. Couldn't possibly do without it. He hadn't been in the PX since he left the one untouched on the counter.

"Where's your friend?" she asked him. "I didn't know you went anywhere without your bodyguard."

"If you're referring to Private Joseph Taylor," Solly said, "he's on Guard Duty."

"Oh," she said. "How's he doing?"

"At the moment, Private Taylor is protecting the ammunition dump with a little biddy black stick."

She smiled and went to make his chocolate malted.

They talked about everything excepting the Army and the MPs and the NAACP, and she would leave him and wait on some lonesome soldier grinning in her face and insisting that she wait on him and nobody else, and she would come back to Solly and they would talk some more.

Once she came back to him and spoke to him from the depths of her dark black eyes. "There's so much I have to talk with you about," she said. His heart was swelling and filling up his chest and maybe it would burst wide open. The Post Exchange was ready to close now. He had drunk four of five chocolate malteds and tasted not a single one. Let's not talk about the Double-V. Let's never mention that again.

She looked up into his face into his eyes. Her own eyes were entirely black now and filled with seriousness. "Will you drive home with me tonight? My girl friend didn't come to work today."

"But Joe, he's my friend—" It was a stupid thing for him to say to her like that, and she was so beautiful and he was so susceptible. And during the past week Worm and he had seen very little of each other. After the letter that next day which they didn't write, they had hardly spoken to each other, even though their cots lay side by side.

"He's my friend too," she said. "Just a friend like you are. He's no more my friend than you're my friend. That is, I *think* you are my friend."

"I've got to—" It wouldn't do any harm just to ride home with her.

"It's all right," she said softly and quickly. "I can understand." She talked with her eyes as well as her lips and he should have known better.

As they drove toward the gate he saw the MPs and suddenly remembered he didn't have a pass. "Now how can I get out of the gate without a pass?" he said angrily to no one in particular. Everything he had striven for could be lost in the next damn minute. An anxious pretty face had smiled at him and he had lost his head completely.

"They know me. They know I work at the PX. They never stop me."

"It would be just my luck for this to be the first time," he said. "I forgot to tell you—I'm the luckiest guy in the world—and most of my luck is bad!"

As they came nearer to the gate one of the MPs motioned for her to stop. "Oh shoot!" she uttered softly. "I never saw this one before. He must be new on the job."

Solly did not open his mouth, but he felt his anger warmly mounting. Most of all he was angry with himself for being so stupid. Caught at the gate without a pass in a car alone with the Bookworm's girl, and conveniently Miss Walter, or whatever her name was, hadn't come to work that day. And the captain would know about it, as would Worm and the entire company, and it would be a mark against his record. He would be busted down to a private. No OCS—no nothing. It looked like a deliberate plot against Solomon Saunders, Junior. But he had himself to blame.

The big red-headed MP came toward them, throwing his flashlight into the car first on Fannie Mae's and then on Solly's angry sweating face. Just before he reached the automobile, the other MP let his flashlight play on the car. "It's all right, Mike," he shouted to the big red-headed one. "One of them PX broads." He smiled at Solly and Fannie Mae. "Go ahead," he shouted. "You're holding up the war."

Solly swore softly under his breath as Fannie Mae put the car in gear and pulled slowly away and onto the dark and dusty highway.

They reached the city and he stared out of the car at the small unpretentious and unprotected houses and then a section of brightly lighted streets and big impressive mansions with long white columns and dark majestic oak trees standing tall and awesome like mighty sentries in a staggered formation on the dark green lawns and the houses fifty to a hundred feet in from the sidewalk.

"This is where the real rich white people live," she said. "This is Kings Row Avenue. You're supposed to take off your hat and cut off the motor when you drive through here."

He laughed. "Which one of these houses does the *man* live in? Mr. Ebbensville, I mean."

She laughed. "We passed his house about a block or so back."

She made a couple of turns and was on the narrow dark streets again, the pavement bumpy, the houses much smaller and meek and timid and nondescript, and even the trees were scantily clad. Then suddenly they left the pavement and the car slowed down almost to a walk as it went carefully over the ruts and bumps of the red and dusty road.

"I know where I am now," Solly said. "You don't have to tell me."

"You're absolutely right," she said. "This is where the club members live. This is home sweet home."

Both of them laughed and he was aware of a great tension seizing hold of him and at the same time an almost forgotten relaxation. All the way from the camp they had avoided the Double-V like the plague. He should be back at the barracks writing a letter home. He was AWOL and he had put all his prospects on the line just to take this pretty lady home. He needed his head examined.

The car stopped in front of a snowy-white, wooden-frame, two-story house, with a white picket fence, and the flowers in the flower garden shone brightly in the moonlight. "This, kind sir, is home," she said. "Well you don't have to look like you're scared of the house. It isn't that ugly. And nothing inside of it is going to bite you."

He swallowed hard. "It's beautiful," he said with a far-away expression. "It really is."

No arguments tonight. No NAACP. No war. No politics. No Double-V.

They went through the gate and walked along the graveled walk toward the house together. Just warmth and friendship, that was all. She put her arm through his and he almost jumped, and he looked sideways down into her face, and he saw so much beauty and loveliness and happiness and contentment, it almost scared him to death. He would have to tell her tonight about Millie. Tell her he was a married man. It had gone far enough. Too damn far. She was so goddamn woman-ful—she and her Double-V. She was beauty, spunk, intelligence. She was—she was—He was a goddamn fool!

The front door opened onto a hall that ran the length of the house with rooms on both sides of it. She led him into the room on the left, the living room, and it was one of the most comfortable rooms he had ever been in, with large family portraits on the walls, of kinfolks past and present, and over the mantlepiece, a life-size picture of W. E. B. Du Bois, and an old-fashioned sofa in front of the fireplace and an easy chair on one side of the hearth and a rocking chair on the other.

"Sit down," she said. "You think we need a fire? Is it cold in here to you?"

He sat on the sofa and stared at the hearth. "Not at all. It's really quite comfortable," he lied. He was everything but comfortable, but it wasn't the chill that made him uneasy. It was the heat that he felt moving around in his collar and all through his body and the taste in his mouth and the tension moving around in his stomach and very much aware of his manhood now and the angry nearness of Fannie Mae. It was as if she had gotten all amongst him and inside of him.

She sat down beside him and she put her hand on his knee for the briefest second to attract his attention away from the fireplace that seemed to hold such a fascination for him, and he really jumped this time.

She said, "What's the matter, Solly?" Her large dark eyes entirely black now and full of deep concern.

He said, "No—nothing. I'm a little tired and jumpy, that's all. I suppose I'm just *nervous* in the service." He forced a shaky kind of laugh.

"Too much brain work," she said. "Joe Taylor told me. You do all the office work in the outfit. The first sergeant and the captain don't do anything at all. *You* run the company."

"Mr. Taylor is my friend and a good publicity man and a great exaggerator."

"Modesty will get you everywhere, young man," she said happily. And she got up and lit the fire in the fireplace, and came back and sat on the couch near him, facing the fire that was slowly catching on and crackling and spitting and moving into every corner of the hearth and coming alive and then all aglow, lazy and sleepy and comfortable. He could have fallen from the couch, he thought, and rolled up in the rug in front of the hearth and gone fast asleep.

He had the feeling she wanted to pursue the argument of the other Sunday evening, but neither of them wanted to risk it and spoil this night this moment. It was as if they had signed an unwritten and unspoken truce. No war tonight. Just peace. Only peace. And it was peaceful. The warmth in his face the taste in his mouth. He felt so at home in her home it was painful almost. Like the last time he was with her. It was strange the way he felt with her. A sweetish kind of nostalgia, as if he had traveled along this road once before in life—the same room, same fire in the fireplace, the same identical sweet-faced girl, same conversation—the warmth, the smell of the room identical. The same goateed Du Bois staring sternly at him from the mantel. He even knew what she would say next.

"We've had some mighty lovely weather for this time of the year."

He had come all the way into town to hear a comment on the weather. This was the important matter she wanted to talk with him about. At least it was not controversial.

"It's probably snowing back home," he said.

She looked up into his face and it was all in the deep deep blackness of her eyes and in every slight nervous movement she made. She wanted to fight him love him have him. Pushing softly against the bosom of her blouse and on her dark red misty lips he saw it, there the challenge was, and felt it running all through his own body, and now was the time to tell her about Millie, his Millie, whom he loved more than all else in the world, he told himself. He had to tell her because now was the moment. All he had to do was to reach out and take her into his arms and—great God almighty! She would either go into his arms eagerly and never let him go, never ever, or this pretty country girl might jump and run from him far far away, but she wanted him, and the shamefaced want was plain to see and feel and taste, and he was ashamed of his want for her. He had to tell this dear sweet child about Millie, but he hadn't the strength. He had too damn much manhood and he wasn't man enough.

Maybe the thing to do was to ask her what it was she wanted to talk to him about, and then they would be off to the wars again. And this would surely break the spell they had cast upon each other. He cleared his throat and started to speak and chickened out. He didn't have the heart to fight with her. He looked at his wrist watch nervously. "I guess I'd better be getting back."

She said, "Shoot! I meant to fix you coffee."

Before he could protest, she was gone just like that. A few minutes later she brought her parents in to meet him. The mother was a small woman who resembled Fannie Mae, her eyes, her mouth, her easygoing warmth, and the father, a medium-height, heavy-set man with a sense of purpose in the corners of his mouth and in the dark brown firmness of his narrow eyes. The father was principal of the Booker T. Washington High School, according to the Bookworm.

Mrs. Branton said, "We've heard so much about you, we feel we already know you. You seem like one of us. I declare you do."

"You must have me confused with the Book—I mean—Joseph Taylor."

"Oh no," she said mischievously. "You're Corporal Solomon Sanders and you're the company clerk and you're the brains of the outfit and you're a very nice person. And a handsome young man. An NAACP fighter from New York. I know you all right. Fannie Mae's been working at the camp about three months now, and there's been two or three of them that came to the front porch with her, but you're the first soldier ever to come in the house."

He stood awkwardly before them, and he felt like an impostor, a two-faced two-timer, with his ready nervous smile that made him look like the bashful kind and more genuine than any other kind. "I'm afraid somebody's been kidding you, Mrs. Branton."

Mrs. Branton smiled at him and said, "Oh, I don't think so," and Fannie made a sign to her and left the room. Mrs. Branton said to Solly, "Well, do come back to see us whenever you feel like it," and excused herself. "Going back in the kitchen to give Fannie Mae a hand."

Mr. Branton sat in the rocking chair. "I reckin our little town is a real comedown for a big-city man like you."

"I like the little I've seen of it," Solly lied. "I wasn't born in a big city, you know."

"New York's a fair-de-middling-sized town, I reckin."

"I was born in Dry Creek, Georgia."

Mr. Branton laughed and slapped his thigh. "Well I declare. You don't say so!"

"Yes, sir," Solly said, "Jacksonville County. Lived there the first seven years of my life."

"Well, I do declare. And I was fixing to ask you how you like these Southern-style crackers. But I reckin you're like the rabbit in the brier patch." He chuckled. "I don't care what anybody says, it's a doggone shame to send you boys to a cracker town like this here to teach you how to die for your country. I'd just as soon do my dying right here in Georgia."

Solly thought uneasily, there's that Double-V again.

"Watch it Father. Sometimes you forget the position you hold in the community. You keep talking like that, Booker T. will be looking for a new principal after all these years." Fannie Mae came back in the room with coffee and teacakes.

"After all these years, I'm too old to get down on my knees

to anybody but the good Lord. And sometimes I wonder maybe he's white."

They sat there drinking coffee. He could hear the mother moving around the kitchen. The father sat across from him, looking him over, sizing him up. All the comfort had disappeared.

The father said, "You have one more year in law school."

Solly felt like screaming, I'm married! I'm not after your daughter's hand. I'm not your future son-in-law. He said, "Yes, sir."

The father said, "Good. The Race needs some crackerjack lawyers."

Solly thought, there's the Race Question again. They'd been ducking it all night long. He said, "We certainly do." And let it go at that.

The father said, "Just telling the baby the other—she's no baby any more—just telling Fannie Mae. Colored man has to hit while the iron is hot. Can't be marking time while these white folks shooting at each other, else we'll have to start from scratch all over again when the shooting's over with."

Fannie Mae cleared her throat and started to collect the cups and saucers in a tray. She gave her father a look.

Solly thought, color color color! These people are obsessed with color. Don't they know the world is bigger than the colored race? The father expected a comment from him. Solly said evasively, "You've got something there, sir."

The father got another message from another look his daughter gave him, and he got up and said good night and followed her into the kitchen.

When she came back she sat down beside Solly and laughed nervously. "Don't pay Father any mind. The older he gets, the more radical he becomes. It's some kind of disease that gets progressively worse with him."

"I like your father," he said shakily. "And your mother too."

"I'm glad," she said in a quiet voice. "I'm very glad."

It was quiet in the house, and he heard her parents going up the hall up the stairs to their bedroom. He heard the father clear his throat loud and significantly. They stared at the fire in the fireplace, saying nothing for the moment. Then she said, "It *is* getting kind of late, I reckon. I wanted to talk to you about the Thanksgiving party we're giving for some of the boys."

"The men—" Thinking of Bookworm and the pink-faced

captain at the Fort Dix Reception Center. Such a long long time ago.

"The men," she agreed. "Especially those a long ways from home—" She stopped and turned to him "I *am* glad you liked my parents. Especially my father. He doesn't open up to everybody." She stopped, she hesitated, then she ventured, "I'm also glad you've thought about what we talked about—" She paused again, uncertain. "And you at least halfway agree with me—I mean, you see my point at least. You admitted to my father."

He grew warmer, and he stood and looked down into her anxious face. "I just did not want to argue with him."

And God have mercy, don't let her look at me like that!

She said, "I understand, Solly." It was almost a sob of ecstasy, pure and sweet and everlasting.

He said, "You do?" And had a weird impulse to run out of the room and up the hall and out of the house and up the walk and on and on and never stop running.

She said, "Yes—yes. I do! I do!" As if he'd asked her did she love him.

He sank back on the couch next to her. "I wish I did. Sometimes I think the thing for me to do is to take the chip off my shoulder and forget I'm a Negro and just look out for Number One and use to advantage the little education I'm lucky to have, and go onward and upward or wherever you go, on the ladder to success, and work on those promotions like mad till the war is over. I for one am sick and tired of the cry-babies in my outfit. There's a war against fascism or haven't they heard about it?"

She shook her head and a quiet cry slipped unwillingly from her wet lips, "No, Solly!"

He stood up again and stared down at her belligerently. "And why not? We're Americans first, aren't we? Americans first and Negroes incidentally."

"Are we, Solly?" He thought maybe she was going to cry but somehow knew she wouldn't. "Is that the N-double-A-CP's slogan up in New York City?"

"You better believe it is," he said. "And we Americans have a common enemy and we have no time for family squabbles. We can settle them later."

She shook her lovely angry head. "You can't believe that."

"What's wrong with me wanting to be an officer, I'd like to know. Is that a club for white folks only? And Negroes should not even try to break down the barriers? You think I wouldn't make as good an officer as some of these ofay ninety-day wonders?"

She shook her head as if it were in awful pain.

He chose to misunderstand her. "Thanks for the rousing vote of confidence."

"When you're an officer you're against the men," she accused him.

"Excuse me," he said, "I thought the idea was that the men and officers were together—a team—with a common goal, but one that needed followers and leadership."

She said, "Yes—all right, Solly. I don't know—you get me so mixed up. Of course, you should be an officer. I know it—I want you to be one—"

He said, "I know one thing—I'm sick and tired of people who are supposed to be my friends accusing me of every kind of opportunism in the book and for selling out the Race." He paused to catch his breath. "I know another thing—it's time I got back to dear old Camp Johnson Henry."

Then he looked down into her face and he said, "Fannie Mae" like a whisper, and suddenly he realized his mouth adored the taste of her name, just as his ears did love the simple music of her voice. His eyes drank in the deep sweet beauty of her face. Fannie Mae—Fannie Mae—Fannie Mae. It was not just the prettiness of her eyes, her mouth, her nose, the contours of her lovely face. It was far more than that. It was the deep and beautiful goodness greatness her beloved face exuded. He was a goddamn romantic, and he believed she was inside of her what her outside beauty said she was. He was a fool and he believed she was what she seemed to be. And he wanted her to believe in him. He wanted desperately for her to understand him the way he wanted to be understood.

She stood up. "All right, Solly. But about the Thanksgiving party, we especially want to invite the men who are far away from home, men like yourself. About fifty soldiers, and I want you to help me get up a list."

He said, "Okay, you can count on me." And they went out of the room and up the hall.

They were standing on the front porch now in the moonlight that was terribly disturbing, and he could smell the awful sweetness of the autumn flowers still in bloom and the nearness of her, dear Fannie Mae! There was a frown upon his face that was there without his knowing.

He said, "Swell, Fannie Mae. Fine. You know you can count on me."

He thought, all this talk about the war and the NAACP and OCS is the farthest thing from both our minds. And as they stood there in silence there was that same look about her, her sweet curved mouth slightly open, moist and eager, and the same movement, the nervousness, and now was the time to say good night and be on his way, and now he would tell her he was married. He made himself tell her. Not now—not now—not this moment. Tell her the next time. Don't spoil this precious unspoiled moment. He'd tell her right now. He'd make himself tell her about his Millie.

He said, "I feel very guilty about coming home with you. It isn't right because—"

"Listen," she said fiercely, "if you feel at all guilty, you shouldn't ever come again. Joe Taylor doesn't have any claim on me. He's a nice fellow and I like him very much, but that's as far as it goes. And it doesn't go any further no matter how much you might want it to go for some reason I can't understand."

Yes, a part of the great guilt *was* Joe Taylor, his noble incorruptible militant friend, on Guard Duty, and Solly was the man that made up the Guard Duty Roster, but that was not the important part. He had meant to tell her simply that he was married. "Fannie Mae—" The words were stuck like hardened glue inside his scratchy throat.

"You walk three blocks straight down Pine Street and turn right on Jessup Avenue and walk four more blocks straight down Jessup and you're at the bus station. Good night, Solly Saunders."

"I'm sorry, Fannie Mae."

"Good night, Corporal Saunders."

He said good night and turned to go, hating the weakness in him that he had so recently discovered.

"Solly!" she called softly to him. "Solly!" And he turned toward her again. "Be careful. Please be careful, and watch out for the police cars. They pick up our soldiers sometimes this time of night." He came back on the porch and they were standing very close to each other, the perspiration misty on her dark red lips, and her long-slung body sweet and round, yet slimmer than a sapling, in the soft moonlight that cast crazy shadows onto the porch, and her nervous bosom pushing her blouse, and just reach out and take her into your arms and kiss away the arguments, the misunderstandings, the great nervousness and the tears that stand just on the other side of her large black eyes, but you'd better not do that. You'd better not touch those wet eager lips and strike the match and set aflame the almighty fire. Because her kind of all-consuming fire might burn you alive—burn both of you. And yet it could happen in a split second, a slight movement a reaching out, and it would be on. It would be on and on and on—and Lordy Lord—

"Maybe I should drive you to the bus station. Wait just a minute. I'll get my keys."

"Oh no, no—Fannie Mae—that isn't necessary. I'll be okay. Don't worry about a thing. Hundreds of us come into Ebbensville every night."

"Are you sure? Please, Solly, let me drive you down there. I really want to!"

He shook his head.

"All right then," she said, "but do be careful."

"I will."

He meant to turn quickly and go back down the steps, but instead he held out his hands to her for some unknown reason and took both of hers and pressure against pressure, and he felt a tremble run the length of her body, and both of them flaming with the great desire, and even then he wished for strength to turn quickly and walk down the steps and run as fast as he could away from this place, but he could not release her. There was no such strength on earth for him. And before he knew it she was in his arms and his mouth against her mouth, and body against body in a sweet and mortal combat as they tried desperately to get even closer.

"Fannie Mae!"

"Solly—Solly—darling Solly!" A shouted whisper.

And away over somewhere in a far-off corner of his guilty conscience was a warning signal and an image of Millie at the very last moment, even as his hands moved over the soft tender places of Fannie Mae's throbbing body and he felt the love heat from all over her come through her clothing burning his hands, and a soft breeze blowing across the porch and the perspiration on his neck on his shoulders and the awful sweet wetness of her lips. Fannie Mae—Solly—her breath on his neck like a soft gentle whisper. It was much too late now for the guilty conscience. This was much too powerful for anything to stand in the way, as it overflowed now and spilled all over them. At that moment he knew no loneliness. Life was full and full and full. Life was love, and love was life.

The screen door opened noiselessly as she led the way back into the darkened house and they went quietly down the dark hall, and it was going to happen even as he had somehow known it would and had feebly fought against, and he was a fraud and it was going to happen and he couldn't feel sorry it was going to happen. They went into the dimly lighted living room, and everything was so quiet, their breathing sounded like the wind blowing through the fallen leaves of autumn. Fannie Mae. Dear Fannie Mae. I cannot spare you goddamn you! He stared at her as she turned toward him, her sweet face overflowing with love, her long body, her plump bosom breathing almost sobbing, and she was the most desirable woman who ever lived in all the world in the million million years of time. He opened his mouth to say Fannie Mae like a fervent prayer, but his face filled up and voice choked off, as they went into each other's arms again and lips against lips, body against body, he felt her knees buckle, and they almost went down to the floor.

He led her to the sofa and nothing else mattered in all the world except man and woman—this man, this woman. Solly and Fannie Mae. His clumsy hand unbuttoning her blouse and—

"No! Solly, no!" It was as if she said: Yes! Yes! Yes, my darling.

And now at last his glad hand held her swelling bosom, her bare breasts plump and soft and firm, and warmth and comfort, and sweetly brown-nippled and brown and dark brown and awfully tender to his touch. And bolder and bolder his hand became, a bold explorer, moving up her skirt now and over her feverish trembling body—

"Solly, please! Oh, God! Please, Solly! Stop! Stop! Stop! I mean it!" Dear Fannie Mae. Sweet Fannie Mae. Her thighs dark brown, long, roundish, warm. Varying shades of brown and black. Clashing and blending. And in between her thighs now the wet crotch of her panties told his happy hand how much she wanted him, even as she shouted angrily, "No, Solly, no! I don't want to! Please—Solly! I don't want to!" He heard her but it was all the same. He couldn't help her now, he could not even help himself. She struggled and she wrestled, but he was not strong enough to let her go. He kissed her voice away and he wouldn't be denied.

"Stop," she whispered angrily, "or else I'll call my father." Her protests were like spurs that urged him on and on and on. And finally her struggling ceased.

"Turn off the light, darling! Turn off the light!"

His hand went out almost automatically, as if he were at home and knew where everything was, and he clicked off the light and the house was so quiet it sounded like a pistol shot. And when he turned to her again, he could still see her happy frightened face as the light slowly left the room. And he took her into his arms and nothing else existed.

And now he sat there next to her with the love taste in his mouth and the love smell in his nostrils and her lovely head on his shoulders and Millie Saunders on his mind very very much, and he wanted to feel sorry about what he had just done, but it really was too close at hand to feel any sorrow or remorse. It was all inside of him and all around him and leaning against him. It was in his mouth. It was in his nostrils. It was all through his body. He tried to make a picture of Millie in his mind, but he couldn't quite make it. Each time it turned out Fannie Mae. Everywhere was Fannie Mae and everyone was Fannie Mae and Fannie Mae and Fannie Mae!

He was a boy again, a lonely boy, a long long time ago it seemed, and his mother a lonesome young woman in a big cold unfriendly city, in a two-room cold-water flat with patched linoleum on the floor. And he had been jealous of the man at first, when he started to come around to see his mother, but it wasn't too long before the man won him over—a union-organizer man, tall and handsome and as glib as they made them, and he and his mother would talk about the union this and the union that, and Mama's eyes would glow when he talked. The three of them would go to movies together and he would even help Solly with his homework sometimes. It was almost like having a father of his own. He even told some of his buddies on the block that Jack was his father returned from a trip to Africa. His father was a big-game hunter he told his buddies. But suddenly the great union-organizing man stopped coming around. And when Solly asked Mama what had become of Jack Benjamin, Mama said she didn't know, maybe he had gone on an organizing trip. But the next time he asked her, she told him simply and bluntly, "He's gone to Chicago—back to his family, his wife and three children, which I never knew he had till two weeks ago." And later that night she told him, "It's just menfolks in general, sugar pie. They're no doggone good. No good in the world—just like dogs—every last one of them." And the tears standing still in his mother's eyes. And as he listened to her he felt his own face filling up, and he wondered about the dead man who had been his real father and the hundreds of times he had heard his mother say what a good man his father had been, and he tried to make a life-size picture of the man who had been his father.

He had been a boy then and now he was a full-grown man—an adulterer. He stared into the heavy darkness of the room. An adulterer. A thing he had never been before.

"What's the matter, darling?"

"Nothing." He didn't want her to call him darling. He was an adulterer. He stared through the darkness at the fireplace where the fire had gone out long ago, but he imagined he saw shadows dancing on the hearth without any rhythm, like crazy little idiots dancing, and there was no comfort in them.

She clicked on the light and looked up into his troubled face and her own face full of dark eyes and sweet curving mouth partially open and white even teeth wet and glistening and love and love and love and maybe careless loveless love. The love already made gave her face a tranquil beauty he had never seen before. It was a qualitative transformation, softest sweetest face in all the world. And he wondered if it happened to every woman when she was really loved by the one she loved. He didn't remember Millie's face undergoing such a change.

"Solly—sweetheart! Tell me what's the matter!" Her voice was troubled, her eyes were worried, but he resented the innocent beauty of contentment still in her face. And he didn't want her to call him any sweet names, because he was a dirty dog.

He wanted to get up and get his garrison cap and be gone, but he wouldn't move.

"Do you love me, Solly?"

He saw Millie clearly before him now and he couldn't answer Fannie Mae.

"Do you, Solly, love me?"

He turned it over in his mind and deliberately made the question sound naïve and infantile to him. He thought of saying: Is that question necessary? Does a man have to love you to make love to you? Do you think you own me now—heart and soul and mind—just because you possessed my body for a few exciting moments? But instead he took her into his arms and kissed away her doubts and fears and she let herself believe that he had answered her. Yes! Yes! Yes! Yes! He kissed her mouth, her cheeks, her dark wet glistening eyes, and tasted her sweet salty tears, and he was a dirty low-down dog.

He looked at his watch, which he was unable to see in the dark. "I really have to go," he said. He had to get out of there as fast as his feet would carry him.

"Of course you have to go," she said. "If you don't, my father will throw you out." He hated the happiness he heard in her voice—the contentment and complacency.

And out on the porch with the full moon looking down on them he took her into his arms again for a quick desperate moment and kissed her briefly on her mouth and "Please be careful, Solly," and he turned quickly and went down the steps and "Good night, Fannie Mae," and he didn't look back and "Good night, Solly, do be careful," and he wouldn't look back. He couldn't.

CHAPTER

10

He could still taste sweet Fannie Mae in his mouth and feel her all inside of him and he could smell her special smell even as he thought about Millie away up north in New York City and Mama too. And here he was all by his lonesome walking through the darkness of a strange little cracker town called Ebbensville, Georgia. New York City and Ebbensville, Georgia. And he was a two-timer, a dirty low-down dog.

Street lights in the colored section were at every other corner. The alternate streets were a total blackout except for the moonlight soft and yellow. Solly's feet were like desperate eyes as he felt his way along the bumpy dusty sidewalks and stumbled over rocks and ruts in the road, and the moon went behind a big dark cloud and he could not see his hand in front of his face (and Fannie Mae was so damn sweet), and he was all alone and Ebbensville was a mean cracker town.

He was a kid about fourteen or fifteen or sixteen and he had just begun to smell himself and wrestle and play with girls again, the *opposite sex*, and get a kick out of it. The first time he noticed the little fuzz above his lips and under his arms and in other places even more private . . . and reading every book he could get a hold of on the *opposite sex*. . . . And the moving pictures and never fully understanding what he read. And girls started to get prettier and prettier to him—all the girls—and their mouths were pretty and their eyes were pretty and their arms and their shapely legs were pretty. And his first affair in a vacant lot in the early darkness of a brisk fall evening and the awful heat crazily sweet, and the overgrown girl and arms and breasts that he couldn't appreciate then and the thighs and legs and a ringing in his ears and Dora Mae moaning and groaning as if she were dying—he thought she might be—and then love's awful strange sweet smell and a brand-new taste of life in his mouth that never never would be forgotten, and all of a sudden a great big change and he thought he knew he was a man. He could never be a boy again. He had no idea where Dora Mae was or even if she were living or dead—or even if her name were Dora Mae. . . .

At the intersection he stepped off the sidewalk and he felt his feet go out from under him and abruptly back from the past to the present he came and off into a great black nothing and his heart leaped through his mouth and down he went into a ditch. He swore out loud and picked himself up and limped across the dusty street. He could feel his feet going in and out of the powdery dust now like walking on the deep plush carpet in a New York hotel where he worked one summer. But he didn't mind the bumpy road the dusty street the falling in the ditch the stinging bruises on his knees and arm, as long as he reached the bus station without being picked up by the MPs or Ebbensville's "finest." There was not an automobile in sight as he left the sidewalk and started to walk in the middle of the road in the middle of the total blackness. The whole world seemed to be fast asleep or playing possum. If he could just make it to the station. Just make it to the bus station. He would never get in this predicament again. He wouldn't have the occasion, because he was never going back to Fannie Mae Branton's, he promised himself.

Out of the colored section now and in the part of town where the not-much-better-off white people lived. The sound of his footsteps on the pavement was like an automobile backfiring, breaking the awful silence, and he wished for the dusty unpaved streets of the colored section. He tried to walk more softly but his footsteps seemed to get louder and louder, as if they were trying to wake up all the white people in Ebbensville,

Georgia. If they caught him in this section of town they could do anything they wanted with him. The local police wouldn't dare mess with him, he argued unconvincingly. He was a soldier in the U.S. Army. These crackers down here didn't give a good goddamn about the U.S. Army. He was GI, he was Government Issue. They wouldn't dare mess with him. But if the MPs picked him up, he could kiss OCS good-bye. The moon came out again and like a mighty floodlight it seemed to be aiming all of its beams on Solomon Saunders, Junior. There he is, white folks. There he is. He laughed bitterly aloud.

He froze in his tracks as he heard the growling sound of an automobile turning the corner behind him at the other end of the block and racing its motor. Sweat broke out all over his body. His feet took him without a conference from the middle of the road toward the sidewalk on the double. The worst they could do with him would be to turn him over to the post authorities at Camp Johnson Henry, and the worst he could be punished for was being AWOL for a couple of hours. Probably bust him down back to a private like the Bookworm and Scotty. And he could forget about his ambitions. He was an All-American goof. In Ebbensville, Georgia, they could do anything they wanted with him. They could kill him if it suited their pleasure. And yet he didn't really want to believe that they would dare touch a soldier of the U.S. Army. They wouldn't dare!

He jumped the hedges and landed into some white folks' backyard and he could feel the glare of the automobile headlights hot on his back. He tried to make his body smaller. A split second passed and he found himself behind a big tree standing tall and dark and throwing moonlit shadows all over the yard. He stood there waiting—waiting—waiting for what? He was a soldier and maybe this was how he would die for his country—killed in action, in the foreign country of his birth. Standing behind a persimmon tree in some white person's backyard like a common sneak thief. And they could give any alibi that came into their pure-white minds, or none at all. They could get him for burglary—they could get him for a peeping Tom. He stood there a million years sweating and waiting and hating violently hating the South and the Army for sending him way down South in the middle of nowhere to serve his country, and hating Fannie Mae for being whatever it was that she was and making him feel even more lonesome than ever before and being so warm and lovely and beautiful and militant, and hating himself especially for being so weak and susceptible to whatever it was that she was, and he should be back in the barracks, and it wasn't anybody's fault but his own. He heard the angry motor of the automobile distinctly now and his body drew up as stiff as a board, and he could hear his own breathing and feel his own breath. They had seen him and were playing a game. Goddamn them! He watched the arrogant police car drive up with flashlights sweeping both sides of the street, play briefly on the persimmon tree, hesitate, and his heart stopped beating and his hands tore angrily at the bark of the tree. The car continued up the street and turned at the next corner. And after they were gone he stood there shaking with helpless anger, the perspiration draining from him. He started to walk now, stumbling along, not giving a damn about the police car or the MPs or the Ebbensville police or anything else. He just wanted to get out of this foreign country where he was an alien, and never a citizen. A country where he was born and lived as a boy, but could never grow up to become a man. He heard another car coming up behind him. Well, let it come. He wasn't going to run and hide behind a tree. But his body grew tense and hot and rigid as he heard the automobile slow down and felt the lights of the car playing on him now and the blood in his body hot and cold like running water, but the lights were on him for only a moment as the car slowed down and turned into the driveway behind him. He breathed the night air strong and deeply. What the hell was he so nervous about? He walked two more blocks before he reached the street where the bus station was located. The bus would be leaving shortly, he thought, as the station came into sight across the broad plaza like an oasis on a vast desert. He saw the men lined up in two lines. He had to prevent himself from running. He was home safe. He was home safe!

He bought his ticket and stood at the foot of the colored line. He could breathe now. The Southern night was sweet to his nostrils and his throat. He wiped his face with an Army handkerchief, and he felt a great relief moving through his face and shoulders and down through his chest and into his stomach.

He was home safe! The perspiration drained from him. He would never goof like that again. Walking through that lonely town was the first time he really realized how desperately he wanted to get ahead in the Army, to be an officer and all the rest of it. And why not? The more Negro officers the more democratic the Army. Didn't that make sense? Isn't that what the war was all about?

The tall white bus driver said, "All aboard," and naturally the white soldiers got aboard first, and as the colored started to get aboard more white soldiers straggled in, some of them staggering in their whiskey and whooping it up, and as long as they came, the Negro soldiers had to wait their turn. Solly Saunders stood at the foot of the line fuming with a helpless anger, as he saw the white soldiers run up at the last minute, laughing and cussing and shouting and good-natured and Southern accents and Midwestern drawls and Brooklyn brogues and: "Boy, these Georgia peaches are killer-dillers!"

"The eating kind!"

A couple of white soldiers came toward the bus, medium-sized fellows, one serious-looking and one with a devilish smile on his face. They halted near the door and stared at the soldiers in the colored line and glanced at the motorman.

"All right, get aboard," the driver said.

"But these men were here before us," the serious-faced white soldier said.

"That's the colored line," the driver said. "They get on last. That's the law."

Solly found himself pulling for the white soldiers to stand up against the cracker. Stand up for your rights, goddammit!

Don't let that cracker push you around. Here were two white soldiers who knew what the war was all about. He felt a kinship with these men.

"It isn't fair," the white soldier said staring at his friendly-faced buddy.

Solly was almost glad he stood there, just to see and hear this happen.

"I don't make the laws, pardner," the driver said. He reminded Solly of Rutherford. Long, tall, and skinny and a big gun gleaming in its holster.

"You boys gon get on or gon get left?" the driver said to the two white soldiers.

They stared at each other and the smiling-faced soldier said, "What the hell. What can you do? We're in Rome, goddammit."

And they hesitated for a couple of moments longer and then got quietly on the bus.

And the white soldiers kept coming, while the mean-looking colored soldiers stood in line with chips on their shoulders, and finally the bus filled up to standing room only, and the motor sputtering and coughing and sounding off, and the door closing and the bus pulling out of the station now without any Negro soldiers aboard, and he felt that if he had a gun on him, he would shoot the tires full of holes and then just train the gun on the bus and pump holes in it from front to back and he wouldn't give a good goddamn who got hit or how damn many. It had happened the last time he was in town. As long as there were white soldiers to get on, he had had to stand there like a damn fool and see a couple of buses come in and fill up and pull out again heading for the camp. And each time he felt less and less a man, frustrated and helpless as they openly robbed him of his humanity and his manhood, him, Solly Saunders from New York City, a soldier in the Army of the United States. Who would one day be an officer.

He looked at the faces of the other Negro soldiers, angry and sullen. His ears picked up the grumbled cusswords under their breaths. Why in the hell didn't they do something about it? Why did they stand there night after night in the Army of the United States and let themselves be robbed of the dignity of being a soldier of serving their country of being a man? He summoned up the deepest kind of hatred and contempt for them and for himself. Why in the hell didn't he do something? He didn't even have a pass. He was Absent Without Leave, A-W-O-goddamn-L. He couldn't say a word. He even had to get off the bus at the stop before the camp was reached about a half a mile from the camp and walk the rest of the way and crawl under a barbed-wire fence, and make it through the woods. The second bus was half filled with white soldiers and no more of them around to get on, and why didn't the soldiers in his line get on? The cracker motorman looked around to see that no other white soldiers were getting on the bus. He came to the door and looked up and down the broad plaza to see if any more white soldiers were on the way, and now he would motion to the colored soldiers in a friendly fashion. "All right, boys, what are we waiting for?"

Up the plaza a block away Solly saw a police car slowly moving in their direction. Everything was slow in Ebbensville, slow and easy and nice and sweet as apple pie and sugar cane, but before you knew it lightning would strike and anything could happen. But he had nothing to worry about. Nothing at all.

The car came down the boulevard and slowed down almost to a stop, and turned in a driveway toward the station, creeping along. Solly could feel the anger of the other colored soldiers merging with his own, and the men up front started to board the bus without the usual signal or the words from the driver. He stood in the doorway, barring their progress, long and lank like Rutherford, with his hand resting carelessly on his forty-five and a friendly smile on his face. "Now wait a minute, boys. Ain't no hurry." He looked from them to the police car crawling up the driveway.

"All right, let's go, goddammit," a white soldier yelled from inside of the bus. "You holding up the fucking war."

The police car finally came up taking its time, and two of Ebbensville's finest got out and came over to the bus. One was a great big blond-headed cracker, big and tall and plug-ugly, with his police cap sitting back on his head and roosting on top of a big nest of hair. His feet were big and bad enough to be put in jail. He walked like he was stepping on hot coals. The other policeman was medium height with a soft pretty face and a long neck with a big Adam's apple and skinny as a broomstick.

"Howdy, boys," the bus driver said. "Y'all looking for any these boys, I got here? Anything happen in town tonight?"

"Naw," the skinny one said. "Just checking passes. That's all. We don't want nobody to be A-W-O-L. You know how it is."

"Go right ahead then and check them passes. You got here just in time. But don't take all night now. The boys inside want to get back to the camp."

Somebody inside of the bus shouted angrily, "Let's get going! You holding up the fucking war!"

The big cracker cop was already to the front of the line asking for passes. The colored soldiers were reaching into their pockets and bringing out their passes and showing them to the big cop who had no right to check them in the first damn place. And Solly Saunders reached into his own pockets searching for a pass that never existed and hoping that one of the soldiers before they got to him would challenge the cop, tell the cracker he had no right to look at their passes. They were not MPs. But not a single soldier challenged the white policeman as the big cracker came down from colored soldier to colored soldier. They just reached in their pockets and showed him their passes, some with blank expressions on their faces, some with anger, some faces frightened. The big bad-feet cracker was about five or six men away from Solly now and Solly's whole body was drenched with sweat and his poor nervous stomach turning over and over, and maybe the cracker would stop looking at passes before he got to the foot of the line. The little soft-faced cracker cop stood away from the men with his hand on his hip near his gleaming gun. Waiting to make himself a hero. This was the way they emasculated Negroes in Georgia every single day in the year. Solly imagined the plug-ugly one going down the line from man to man with a long white-handled razor and slicing brown and black testicles one at a time. The colored soldiers naked before the world and the two policemen. He could hear the testicles drop to the pavement with a horrible monotonous thud. The image was so powerfully real to him he felt a painful throbbing in his groins.

Three men away from Solly a little dark brown-skin soldier with big brown eyes like they should have belonged to a pretty girl put his hand in his pocket, but he didn't bring out a pass. He looked up at the big cracker and asked him, "Why didn't you inspect the passes of the men already inside of the bus?"

"That ain't none of your worry, boy. All you got to do is show me *your* pass. The only worry you got is if you ain't got no pass in your pocket."

The big bad-feet, plug-ugly cracker kept smiling, his face turning red, and the little cracker cop kept his hand on his pistol. The colored soldiers stood there worried-looking, angry and sullen, some of them scared. It was as if the whole town held its breath for a minute, and then breathed easily and went back to sleep, as the little dark soldier with the big brown eyes swallowed the night air and took his pass out of his pocket and showed it to the big cracker cop. And then the next soldier and the next, and now Solly Saunders, Corporal Saunders, candidate for Officers' School, company clerk, the brain of H Company. The man with the officer attitude.

He looked up at the big blond cracker and down at the ground. He didn't hardly have any choice. He had to challenge the cracker for the simple reason that he didn't have a pass to show him. Not even a bogus one. He looked up again and made himself stare the cracker in the face. Court was in session. The issue was joined.

He thought, I should tell them I'm a loyal American and I believe in the war, and tell them with a good old Southern "nigrah" accent. I'm such a trusted colored soldier I'm going to be an officer. Convince them that I'm neither agitator nor troublemaker. I have the proper attitude, and if they don't believe me, they can ask my captain. He's a Southern gentleman just like they are. The issue was not necessarily joined. It never was. Unless he joined it.

The big cop said (not unfriendly maybe), "All right, boy. Let's have it. We ain't got all night. Rest of these boys wanna get home to camp." He was doing a job was all he was doing.

Sometimes a good run is better than a bad stand and ten times more intelligent. Run away and live to fight another day. Solly felt the fresh sweat on his forehead, cleared his throat and moved his feet, and heard himself say, "I don't believe you have any right to be checking our passes. You're not the Military Police."

"Well, like I told the other boy while ago, don't worry too much about that. Thinking ain't good for you nohow. Make you git a awful bad headache. You let us do the thinking. Just show me your pass, boy, that is, if you got one."

"You don't have jurisdiction over a soldier in the Army, especially if he hasn't violated a civilian law."

The easy smile had left the big cracker's face now. He put his hand on his gun. "That's the trouble with niggers with a little education. They don't know when to use it and when to not."

Solly didn't say a word. He just stared at the cracker. He had started now and he couldn't turn back. The road was long and white and lonesome and narrow and no side roads—no bypasses, no detours—just straight ahead, and long and white.

"You gon show me your pass, boy, or you gon cut the goddamn fool?"

"I still say you don't have any jurisdiction."

The slow life of Ebbensville speeded up suddenly and things happened quickly. Both of the crackers pulled their guns on him.

"All right now, boy, you gon show us your pass?" And for a brief moment he wished he had told them from the beginning he didn't have a pass and had thrown himself on their white and tender mercy, their Southern hospitality. He wished desperately he had a pass to show them. But the way he figured, it wouldn't do any good to tell them anything. Not now. He had challenged their whiteness their jurisdiction their Godalmightiness, and he might as well stick by it for the good it would do him, and the taste in his mouth was better this way. He was scared, worried scared deep deep down in the pit of his belly and in the middle of his buttocks, and his body steamed with perspiration. But he had resisted the long white razor and his testicles were still intact. Ever since he came into the Army the war had raged around him. He'd been alert and agile, even as the bullets bounced around his feet, hitting Worm, Scotty, Sergeant Greer. With his fancy footwork and his ambition and his intelligence, he had avoided every issue. But now the issues were forever joined. With his education, his personality, he had thought They would surely spare him, but They had betrayed him.

"I'm a soldier and I have committed no crime against the civilian law and you have no jurisdiction over me." He tried desperately to keep his voice from trembling.

They had always betrayed him. He had betrayed himself from the beginning.

"All right, nigger, if that's the way you want it." And they pulled him roughly out of the line with their brave pistols gleaming in the tender moonlight and the bus driver shouted, "All aboard. Let's get going," as several of the soldiers stepped out of the line, including the little one with the big brown eyes and moved toward the policemen, the little fellow asking, "What's going on here?" Four or five other soldiers fell out behind them and crowded together.

The big cop turned on them with his forty-five. "Back up, goddammit, and git on the bus, or I blow every one of you to hell and back." His blue eyes wide and wild with fear on the borderline of panic.

"This is America—this isn't Germany," the little soldier said without flinching. "What are you going to do with that soldier?"

"Since you're so innerested," the big cracker said, "we'll take you along." He waved his gun. "The rest of y'all get the hell on the bus and I don't mean perhaps." The two policemen backed the rest of the men away toward the bus, cussing and grumbling, and the big cracker and the little cracker waving their guns courageously, and the brave bus driver with his gun in his hand, and the colored soldiers got aboard the bus, and the bus pulled out, leaving Solly and the little big-eyed soldier alone with the cracker policemen, and everything had started so slowly and happened so quickly. And at that moment in his short life he thought about Millie his Millie so many hundreds of miles away, and sleeping peacefully without any knowledge of the fix he was in, and Millie and Mama were sleeping soundly, and Fannie Mae too was probably asleep just a few blocks away, and it was all her fault but it wasn't her fault at all. He knew it wasn't. They took the two American soldiers over whom they had no jurisdiction whatever down to the Ebbensville police station, the City Hall, and as they sat in the back of the car together, Solly told the other soldier, "You shouldn't've gotten mixed up in this mess." His eyes filling up now with tears of admiration and a feeling of warmth and comradeship and coloredness moving all through his body. For the moment at least his own predicament was out of focus of his mind. And for the moment he felt better than he ever felt since he became a soldier in the Army of his Uncle Sam. He felt good deep down in the guts of him.

The little soldier whispered, "My name is James Larker. I'm in the Tenth Engineers—a hard work battalion. What's your name?"

"My name is Solly Saunders. I'm in H Company of the Fifty-fifth Quartermaster." He wanted to say something else to the soldier but he couldn't think of anything.

He sat there in the squad car in silence as he smiled at the bitter taste in his mouth. Damn them. They had caught him at last. They had been after him ever since he could remember almost, and one of his mother's greatest worries used to be that one day she would come home from work or they would call her on her job and tell her he was in trouble with the law and the police would have locked her baby up, but it had never happened in that great big city where a lonesome fatherless kid with a working mother could find so much trouble to get into. He had to wait till he came all the way down South in the land of cotton into the great democratic Army of the United States of America. His face filled up. He had bought the whole hogwash while pretending that he hadn't. It was a real funny joke. He remembered the first time They had actually chased him. . . .

It was right in the middle of the Great Depression and even Mama was unemployed. Out on the streets of Harlem he saw New York's Finest night after night break up street meetings and unemployment demonstrations and charge into crowds with their handsome horses and whip heads till their nightsticks looked like they were dipped in tomato ketchup, and dreaming about bloody heads all night long and the newspapers said it was the Communists stirring up trouble. And yet almost every afternoon Freddie and Jimmy and Lonnie and sometimes Joe MacBride and Solly would get together and one of them would say, "Wonder where one gon be tonight?" And they would wander all over Harlem till they found one. One night they were watching a meeting and a colored man was standing on a stepladder with the Stars and Stripes waving in the evening breeze and the little black man was shouting his lungs out about President Hoover and unemployment and discrimination, and suddenly the cops on their big proud handsome horses charged into the crowd, and Solly and his buddies threw marbles in the way of the poor unfortunate horses who slipped and skidded, and cops and horses fell all over the place. It was a trick they had learned from one of the men who ran the meeting. And before Solly knew it he was being chased by a big burly white cop shouting, "Goddamn little nigger!" and his back was exposed to the policeman's pistol and fright moved through him like an open wound, expecting to be shot down any second. Across Lenox Avenue and down to a Hundred and Twenty-second Street and back up to a Hundred and Twenty-fifth Street and "Stop that nigger!" Sweat draining from every pore of his frightened body. And on his street now and into his house and the door slammed locked behind him and the chain in place and—

"What's the matter, Solly? Where you been, baby?" And "Nothing, Mama—" And Mama shaking him till the tears spilled out. And BANG BANG BANG upon the door and "Open up in the name of the law!" And Mama to the door and Solly to the closet.

"What you want?" and "I want that boy! You know what I want!". . ."What boy?". . ."You know what boy!" And Mama and the policeman shouting at each other through the locked door, and the cop called Mama a Communist and Mama didn't even know what a Communist was. Finally the policeman walked away but he would be back, and he would find the little nigger if he had to burn down the goddamn block. And there wasn't time for Mama to ask any questions after the cop left. She gave him a nickel and sent him up to the Bronx to spend the night at a lady friend's of hers. He went out of the back window and across the yard littered with cans and broken bottles and trash and with a ragged black man standing in the middle of the yard singing, "Did Your Mother Come from Ireland?" and paper flying and the lines full of wet clothes shouting and flapping in the evening breeze.

He came back to the present when the little soldier seated next to him in the back of the car said, "I'm going to get out of Georgia even if I have to volunteer for overseas duty!"

Solly grunted. "You can say that again." He was still thinking about New York City and the fact that They had never caught up with him in his city and he had assumed They had given up the chase a long time ago. He had gone through high school, finished college, got a job, gone to law school, gone into the Army with great morale and tremendous expectations.

The squad car stopped. The little cop said, "All right, you niggers."

They escorted them into the Ebbensville police station and he was separated from the other soldier. They took Solly into a small musty room with a big bright light and the Chief of Police came in to take a look at him. The big cracker cop said, "Here that *bad* nigger is, Chief."

"You can't hold me here. I'm a soldier." And even as he said it he realized how ridiculous he sounded.

The Chief of Police, a great big handsome blue-eyed man with hair as white as cotton in the cottonfield, stood over Solly. "Goddammit, when we git through with you, old up-the-country nigger, you ain't gon never want to see no soldier suit the longest day you live."

Solly was scared now, with perspiration all over his body and draining from his armpits, and his crotch was wet with perspiration. They could beat him to death or blow his brains out and have his dead body locked up for resisting an officer. "Where's the telephone? I demand to call my first sergeant and my company commander."

At that moment a white man came through the door in a soldier uniform and a great hope formed and grew inside of Solly Saunders, almost popping out of his chest, as the tall white colonel came into the room. After all he was a soldier in the Army of the United States, and these civilians wouldn't give the colonel any stuff. They'd have to listen to him.

"What's going on here?" the colonel asked. The MPs were no bargain, but he would take his chances with them in preference to the Ebbensville police force. Maybe, Solly thought, maybe—they would have to listen to an Army colonel. Goddammit, maybe—the colonel did not sound like a Southerner.

"Got one of them monkeys from the camp in here, Colonel. Thinks he's a soldier cause they let him wear a soldier suit."

The long tall handsome colonel wore an MP insignia on his arm. "What did you lock him up for? What did he do?" They had to answer the colonel, because Solly was a soldier in the U.S. Army, and even the Georgia police could not supersede the U.S. Army.

"They have no right to arrest me. You're the head of the MPs in this town, sir. Will you kindly tell them they have no jurisdiction?"

The colonel turned and stared at Solly and Solly knew what a fool he had allowed himself to be for a couple of desperate minutes. "Did anybody ask you anything?" the colonel said. He turned to the chief again. "What's he been up to?"

The chief grinned. "Nothing much. He ain't got no pass and he was insubordinate to two of my officers. In other words, he's a sassy nigger, and we intend to teach him a thing or two. You know how it is."

The colonel said, "Must be one of them niggers from up my way. Let that uniform go to his head."

Solly heard his own stupid helpless voice shouting at the colonel: "Don't you call me a nigger! I'm a soldier in the Army of the United States. I'm a man, goddammit!"

The colonel walked over to Solly. "So you're a man?" He slapped Solly with his open hand with all of his might and white spots danced in front of Solly's eyes and his head swam around in an ocean of whiteness and he was temporarily deaf but he heard the colonel clearly.

"You are nothing but a nigger, nigger," the colonel said. "You are a nigger, your mammy is a nigger blacker than you, and your mammy's mammy is the blackest nigger that ever was a nigger."

Solly must have lost his mind temporarily as he broke away from the two cracker cops who held him and charged toward the colonel and knocked him halfway across the room. He walked up and down the colonel like he was doing a dance. Before the cops could move into action, Solly had the colonel by the throat and was bumping his head against the concrete floor, and might have killed him, had not the two cops pulled him off. They began to beat him around his shoulders and his arms and his hands with their nightsticks.

The chief shouted, "Kill that nigger! Y'all ain't doing nothing but playing with him."

A wild kind of panic seized hold of him as he realized they might really kill him then and there, he might be dead in the next five minutes, and he didn't want to die! He didn't want to die! He tried to shield his head with his hands, and his arms felt like they were pieces of iron. They meant to kill him! He tried to grab the nightstick from the little cracker cop. If he could make it to the door and run for it—but then they might take a notion to shoot him in the back.

"Don't kill him," the colonel said. "Just sit him in that chair and we'll teach him a lesson."

They forced him back into the chair and held him down. He had the colonel to thank for his life being spared.

The colonel said, "Pull his legs apart and keep them apart."

And through all of his pain and his desperate anguish Solly wondered helplessly why the colonel had told the Ebbensville cops to pull his legs apart. He didn't have long to ponder the question.

The colonel grabbed a nightstick from the big cracker cop, his gray eyes gleaming, and he began to beat Solly about his legs and thighs and in the direction of his groins, but Solly closed his legs and fell forward in self-defense. The fear was so great he thought his heart had stopped beating. The fear far greater than the pain. They forced him back into the chair again, and the colonel moved in with the nightstick and blow after blow fell upon Solly's thighs and almost in between his legs as he wrestled and struggled in a maddening kind of wild desperation and kept them from holding his legs apart. At the moment he feared for his manhood, and he had forgotten to fear for his life. White stabs of pain set his knees on fire, as the Army colonel kept swinging the nightstick like he was trying his best to break it in halves. But the colonel's age was not exactly in his favor, his strength was quickly spent, and the blows were as soft as a baby's now, but heavy as a sledge hammer to Solly's flaming thighs tenderized with throbbing pain. And everything began to go white around him, and he was sinking in an awful suck-hole of briny whiteness, sinking, sinking, and at that last moment he thought of Millie away off in New York City, sleeping peacefully and in her dreams pushing him onward and upward on the ladder to success, and Mama sleeping undisturbed, and only a few blocks away from this place Fannie Mae sleeping and Bookworm fast asleep on Guard Duty, and he had to keep these crackers from beating him in between his legs—he had to—had to—had to—even if they killed him. He had to—had to. . . .

The last thing he remembered was the little baby-faced sissified cracker cop going over in the corner and puking his guts. "Goddammit, colonel, sir, don't you think that's enough? I mean, after all, I ain't no nigger-lover, but he don't hardly know you hitting him now."

And Solly could hold on no longer, and save me! Save me! Somebody save me from sinking down—and everything completely white now as he fell forward to the floor.

And finally Solly Saunders slept.

CHAPTER

II

The next morning the Topkick and Lieutenant Samuels came to the jail for him and took him limping and smoldering with pain to one of the colored wards in the post hospital at Camp Johnson Henry.

As they left him, Topkick came back to the bed and said almost in a whisper, "Don't worry about the AWOL. I told the captain I know you had a pass because I made it out and he signed it with a batch of others. I told him you must have lost it in town, cause I know you had one when you left."

Solly said, "Thanks." He couldn't care less.

Topkick said, "Hurry back to the company before that office goes to the dogs. And the next time you get ready to whip all the white folks in Georgia, let the rest of Hell Company in on the party." And he smiled and left to catch up with Lieutenant Samuels.

And for the next two weeks Solly had loads and loads of time to himself. Lying there in his snowy-white bed with everything around him spick-and-span and gleamingly white, the walls the ceiling the bedpans all reminding him of MPs and

Army colonels, as did the nurses and doctors, everything and everybody pure-and-divine and everlastingly driven-snow white as the whitest dove and the whitest of the whitest angels. All was white excepting the patients in the colored wards, and the colored mop brigade. And he was sick and tired of whiteness.

He hated the Great White Democratic Army of the United States of America. They had taken one of their mighty cannons and placed it up against his forehead and blown away forever the brains of his grand illusion about the Army and the war. And now he hated everything about the Army. The individual asphyxiation, the principle of dumbly following-the-leader-who-never-knew-where-the-hell-he-was-going-or-why-he-was-going-and-what-he-was-going-to-do-when-he-got-there. K.P. and Guard Duty and Week-end Pass and saluting and drilling and bucking and passing-the-buck and apple-polishing and brown-nosing and Inspection, and more than anything else he hated the Dictatorship of the Brass and his own ambitions to join the Brass. His cup ran over with hate and spilled onto the ones he liked and loved.

Millie and her goddamn onward and upward philosophy he hated, and Bookworm because he was too damn uncomplicated and honest to be for real; Lieutenant Samuels and his phony Liberal Ethical Culture Brotherhood, and hated Rutherford who wanted to be his Great White Father. And Fannie Mae Branton most of all because she was too damn beautiful too militant too forthright too human and too much woman and too much in love with Solly and too damn sure he was in love with her.

The first time Worm visited him they were like strangers to each other, choosing their words carefully like fumbling with a foreign language. Finally Bookworm stood up to leave, and then Solly sat up in the bed with the pain shooting through him as if his entire body were a rotten tooth. Worm's good-natured face looked like the blessed angels had kissed him, and Solly wouldn't let him get away with it.

Solly said almost angrily, "You know why I was in town?"

Worm said quietly, "The cats in the company are salty as a barrel of mackerels. They want to go over into Ebbensville and turn that mother-huncher out once and for all. And they proud of you, man. I knew you had it in you all the time."

Solly said, "I took Fannie Mae home. That's why."

"It figures," Worm said without changing his expression.

"All the cats talking about the way you stood up to the man, and they—"

Solly said, "What do you mean, it figures?" He'd like to slap the complacency from Bookworm's face. Who in the hell did he think he was?

Worm said, "Course it figures. I was on Guard Duty and you were at the PX and she asked you to take her home and you were Johnny-on-the-Spot looking out for the Kid. I always knew you wan't no cracker-lover. I told that bucket-head bastard, Baker—"

"That is not the way it was," Solly said. "I wanted to take her home, and I wasn't thinking about looking out for you, my good cut buddy."

"So what's wrong with that? She like you a lot. Maybe she love you. How the hell do I know? When I'm with her all she talk about is Corporal Saunders, the company clerk. Anyhow, she ain't my broad."

"She ain't anybody's broad."

Worm said, "Anyhow, she's crazy about you. I've known it for the longest kind of time. I told Buck Rogers last night, I always knew you ain't never been no cracker-lover."

A shameful warmth ran through Solly's entire body, made him forget the throbbing pain he lived with. The only thing he could say was something stupid like, "You—you never told me —I mean—about Fannie Mae—"

"Why should I tell you anything? You're married. You're always telling me you're married. Besides, the Kid don't give up so easy—see?"

There was nothing for Solly to say. Just be silent and look stupid. "What did Rogers say about me and about what happened at the police station?"

Bookworm asked him, "Did you tell her you were married?"

"Why in the hell should I?" Solly could not keep the heat out of his voice or his face. "I just rode home with her. That's all there was to it." He was the biggest phony in the world.

"There's a heap more to it and you damn well know it. And if you don't know, you damn sight better ask somebody. She ain't the kinda girl to mess around with."

Solly almost lost his voice. "Don't worry about it, buddy boy."

"I ain't worried, but you better worry. She's the greatest—"

Solly said, "Do me a favor, Worm, and drop dead quietly

and unceremoniously." He lay down in his bed again and turned on his side with his back to the Worm and listened to his Army buddy as he walked angrily away from him toward the entrance to the colored ward and the pain moved in on him again, more than ever, his entire body flaming throbbing glowing with it. He could bite his lips no longer and he cried quietly to himself. Nobody heard.

Fannie Mae came to see him the second evening and she brought him fruit and flowers and a couple of books, and she came every evening afterwards during her hour off for supper. Each time she came she would kiss him briefly on his mouth and do the same before she left. And while she was with him he would feel whole again and alive and purposeful and know he was somebody. If Fannie Mae Branton loved him, he couldn't be the first-class phony he thought he was. After she left he would make up his mind and promise himself all day long to tell her on her next visit that he was a married man. This time for real he would tell her without fail, he would certainly tell her, he would give it to her straight.

When she came she never spoke directly about the incident.

During her second visit she said, "Well, the war will be over one of these days and things will be different for us, after all the sacrifices the colored soldiers are making over there and down here."

He knew she was trying desperately to wash the bitter taste from his mouth, but he would not be a party to it. "Don't bet your bottom dollar on it." His voice was trembling.

He heard the love in her own voice and the anxiety, and he also heard a brand-new thing—uncertainty. "You'll see," she said. "It'll have to be different. And that's why we say *Double-V*, so we don't mark time or lose any ground here in this place, even as we fight them over there." But her dear voice lacked the ring of conviction he had become accustomed to, had depended on, and he felt like crying because he wanted her always to have the strength of her convictions. He wanted her perfect, but he realized she was human. Angels did not copulate. He reached frantically around in his mind for words to encourage her, even as she tried to give him consolation. He wanted to take her into his arms and kiss her and love her, and at the same time he wanted to strike her hurt her deeply. Shake her up.

He laughed bitterly. "You actually can still believe in the war?"

She said shakily, "Yes—of course. Nothing has changed. I mean, darling—" He knew she was lying. He would always know when she was lying. She was not a lying expert—like him. He was an old pro.

He said, "Don't be sure too sure the war will ever end. And especially don't make any book on it being any different for us club members."

She put her hand in his and a soothing warmth went the length of his aching existence. She said with conviction this time, "One sure thing, it'll be different for you and me."

"Don't be sure about that either."

Her eyes widened with concern.

He should have told her then and there that even for her and him there was no afterward. Especially for her and him. But he was scared she would not come back to see him if he told her he was married, and if she didn't he would die. He would just lie there and stop breathing. He said, "I mean the war may never end for us. It happens to a thousand soldiers every day—in Europe and the South Pacific and Georgia and Mississippi."

She took his hand and squeezed it hard. "Don't say that, Solly! Hold on fast and never turn loose. We cannot let them get us down." Her eyes were terror-stricken. "Promise me—no matter what happens, you'll never die inside of you. Don't let them kill you off like that. I'm not saying it right, because I'm not sure of anything any more after what happened, except I'm sure of you and me—" Her voice choked off and she did not trust herself to speak. She did not want to cry in front of him. She had come to cheer him up, to give him strength and confidence in a better day somewhere sometime, and especially for him and her. She wanted it so desperately. He understood.

He shook his head from side to side.

She said almost in a whisper, "I don't know much, but one thing I do know with all my heart. You will come back. And you're going to be a great lawyer. And maybe I'll go to law school now, while you're in the service, and when you get back, we can be a team together. Saunders and Saunders." She was running way out in front a hundred miles ahead of him.

"I'm not going to be a lawyer!" he shouted softly. "If I ever do get back, I'm going to be a writer. I don't care what anybody else thinks about it."

She said, "Wonderful! Writers are the greatest people in

the world. They never die. They live on and on in their books and plays. And you will be a great one too. And when you're back and we're married, you can try everything out on me. Every page right after you write it, every chapter. Hot off the typewriter! And maybe you will teach me how to write—"

Take her into your arms and tell her she's the only one who understands; kiss her here and now from her head to her feet and especially her wide black eyes and especially her full sweet curving trembly mouth. He felt like crying in her arms and telling her everything he ever dreamed. At the same time blame her for his present condition, his being in the hospital, his Army expectations down the drain forever, and he wanted not to hear the great conviction in her voice nor see her face aglow with love. Because he loved her, and against his will he shouted softly at her, "Shut up!" And then he said, "I'm sorry, Fannie Mae. But I don't feel that way today. I'm sick and tired of everybody building me up so they can weight me down with obligations. I don't owe anybody anything but myself myself." Not even Millie, he thought. Everybody's got their eyes on me. Everybody with their ax to grind. But I don't owe a damn thing to Millie or to Fannie Mae or Bookworm or Samuels or Rutherford or Officer Candidate School. Or even to Mama. "If I choose to stop living at three o'clock tomorrow morning, it's no damn body's business if I do." He felt his face filling up but he wouldn't cry in front of her.

She said, "Be anything you want, my darling."

He said, "Don't try to tell me what to be! Don't try to arrange my life for me—"

She looked at her watch. He saw the deep hurt in her eyes. "I have to go now, Solly. But I hate to leave you in such a mood. We have everything to live for."

He said, "Don't do me any favors."

And the tears stood barely out of sight on the other side of her eyes now, and he thought, don't cry here! Don't cry here!

She kissed him on his angry open mouth, and he lived completely one more time, and she turned and hurried away from him.

He lay there breathing deeply now, as the pain and loneliness moved in on him, throbbing, thumping, stabbing, killing, in his loins, in between his legs, his arms, so painful he thought his heart would never stand it, and he could hear death with her cool white wings flapping, and he could smell death and he could feel it, and the clammy taste was in his mouth, and somehow he felt if death should come he would welcome her like a long-lost lover, and it would be peaceful, like a quiet rustling of golden leaves. He loved the fall of the year with everything dying, terribly dying, peacefully dying, goldenly dying, beautifully dying. Like everything else in life, death could be a thing of beauty. Especially in autumn. Some days he thought he wished that death would take him.

He got the sweetest letter from Millie. Congratulations on the promotion to corporal. When are you going to Officer Candidate School? You'll make the handsomest officer in the United States of America. Meanwhile she was doing her share on the home front, boosting morale at the Stage Door Canteen, and keeping her chin up, and trying not to worry too much about him, and she was putting aside as much money as she could, so that he could go back and finish his last year in law school, and they would have a little nest egg to fall back on when he put his shingle up. She loved him, oh God, she loved him. She would sacrifice everything for her great love for him.

Everybody had plans for him. Doing him favors which demanded obligations. Even Mama.

All of Mama's letters ended with: "Take care of yourself. Don't be a hero." He always laughed, but not at the very end which always said: "You're all I got in the world."

He remembered fragments from an ancient blues. Bessie Smith—Billy Holliday—

If I go and take a notion
To jump in the deep blue ocean
Ain' nobody's business if I do.

And that's exactly how he felt, Fannie, Millie, Mama, Bookworm, Samuels, Captain Rutherford—notwithstanding.

He heard the doctor at a bed nearby with his syrup-sweetened voice like a long-distance operator. Solly closed his book and waited. The doctor was probably a queer, he thought. Now they were at his bed, the doctor and the tired nurse, the dark-eyed sweet-faced one with the blue-black hair and: "How are you this evening, soldier?" And looking him over and probing him sadistically and temperature and pulse and nasty medicine and a needle in his tenderized buttock and the doctor's pale and stubby fingers and his face with the pallid smile of death. Go ahead, he thought, go ahead, do what you're big enough and white enough to do to me, you sadistic mama-jabbers.

They were leaving and he asked them in a trembly voice, "How long will I have to be in this place, Captain?"

"Oh, not so long. You'll be out of here before you can say Jack Robinson." He jabbed Solly in his ribs again playfully and Solly almost fainted. He wished for the strength to knock the smiling captain on his fat faggotty backside.

"The best thing in your favor, soldier, is your attitude. You're anxious to get out of here and help win the war."

Solly Saunders said, "Yeah, that's right. I'm anxious to get it over with. Just let me at them."

He lay there breathing deeply in his helpless hopeless anger for over an hour after they left. He laughed aloud and he thought, maybe I'm going crazy. Maybe this is what it feels like just before you lose contact with the real world, whatever that means. Images ran around in his head throwing hand grenades at each other. Was he still a man? Were his testicles intact? They ached as if they were being prodded with a red-hot poker. He had to hold his throbbing legs apart. He started to laugh again. If Millie Saunders were not pregnant she'd never be. Not with Solly Saunders's child. He thought, I'll cheer her up. I'll write her about my visit with the cops of Ebbensville and about the good times I'm having in this lovely white hospital. But he never wrote about it and she never ever knew.

Some hours he lay flat on his back scheming like a madman. If he acted crazy, maybe the Army would give him a Section 8, a medical discharge. He would love the Army then. His head was heavy, and every time somebody walked past his bed he thought they must be roller-skaters tap dancing on the inner layer of his skull. He thought, what would happen if I screamed and screamed to the top of my lungs? They would think I had blown my top, and they would be almost right. He thought, this must be somebody else's head. These are not my thoughts. My head was never this big or heavy. My mouth never tasted like the smell of dead bedbugs before. I lost my manhood and I'm losing my mind, and I hate the Army of the United States, and I hate Millie and Mama and Worm and Rutherford and Boy Wonder and Fannie Mae and all the rest of it, everything is phony, excepting Fannie Mae and Mama and Worm, and I'm mad at the whole damn world or maybe I'm just mad *period.*

He thought warmly of Jim Larker, the little big-eyed soft-spoken soldier from the work battalion. Had they beaten him up also? Was he somewhere in this white hospital all messed up in perpetuity, as they used to say in law school? Solly's eyes filled as he recalled the firm expression on the soldier's prettyish face and the way he had gotten out of line and stood with him, a total stranger. He remembered the ride to the police station. "My name is James Larker. Tenth Engineers—hard work battalion . . . going to get out of Georgia even if I have to volunteer for duty overseas."

Solly finally fell asleep and most of the night he dreamed of police stations and Jim Larker and police chiefs and Army colonels. He fought the bastards all night long. He and Larker. He did not know what woke him up but he was glad to be awake. It was about eight o'clock in the morning and he didn't even realize that Worm was standing at his bedside till Worm asked him, "What's the matter, good kid?"

The tears were streaming down Solly's face.

He looked up at Worm and he didn't even bother to wipe his eyes. "What in the hell do you think is the matter? These people pissing in our face every day of our lives and telling us it's raining outdoors and most of us believe it, and even so there isn't a damn thing we can do about it."

"We can write that letter," Bookworm said. As if he just happened to be standing there and just happened to have a letter to write.

"Write what letter?" He stared at Worm as if he thought the open-faced soldier was out of his mind.

"That letter you said you was going to write—to the colored papers and the NAACP and all that Double-V for Victory."

The pain halted, the tears dried up, maybe even his heart knocked off momentarily. The wheels turned over in his weary mind, and flares lit up and seemed to set his brain on fire. And he did not want to think about it or rationalize or talk about it; he wanted to do. He was sick and tired of introspection.

He said, "What have we got to lose?"

Worm said, "I ain't got a thing to lose. Depends on what you think is valuable."

Solly said, "Hold it a second. Let me think."

The wheels were turning, his brain was burning. Did he still live with illusions about this Army and the war? After all the dynamiting and the blasting, were ambition and illusion so indestructible? Yet he hemmed and hawed and hesitated.

He hated himself but he hesitated, as real world and dream world waged a deadly war inside of him. What was real and what was dream? He wanted to believe in something.

Worm said quietly, "If you still got to think about it, forget it. You just ain't ready yet."

Solly said, "Worm—I—" Somewhere in him he heard, Use your head, never ever trust emotions even if they're honest. And he heard another voice say Double-V for Victory—and what did he have to lose? What did he have to lose of value? The captain didn't know he was AWOL was one thing in his favor.

Worm said, "Forget it, good kid. When in the hell they gon let you out this place?"

Solly said, "You go to hell—you go to hell and tell them I sent you. You're so damn pious and self-righteous, I'll bet you used to be an altar boy."

Worm said, "I don't have to go because you send me, even if you are a corporal in these white folks' Army. That's one thing and that ain't two."

Solly said heatedly, "You smuggle the typewriter over here, and we'll do some letter-writing tonight."

Worm's voice was trembling. "Don't do me any favors, pardner. Don't let me talk you into anything you don't really want to do. Don't let your heart do nothing your ass can't stand behind."

Solly said angrily, "If you're scared to bring it, say so, and stop beating around the bush."

That night Worm sneaked the typewriter into the hospital and they wrote letters for two or three hours to all the Negro newspapers and Reverend Johnson Digby and Mrs. Bethune and to the President of the United States and to Eleanor Roosevelt Roosevelt.

Worm came for him the day he was released. Brought him his newly pressed uniform, brand-new necktie, shoes shined so you could see your face in them. He was grinning from ear to ear as he watched Solly get ready.

"Man, you are as sharp as a wedding dick. Don't you go round my old lady."

"Got good treatment in this place. I started to stay in here indefinitely."

Worm laughed. "The studs sure did miss you in the company. And the ladies in the PX."

Solly grunted. He was almost ready to go now. He adjusted his necktie, stuffed his shirttail into his trousers.

Worm said proudly, "Them letters we wrote to them people was a mama-huncher!"

Solly turned quickly toward the Bookworm. "You haven't heard anything from them, have you?"

"Hell naw." Worm laughed. "You'd be the first I'd tell about it. After all—you the ringleader."

"Yeah," Solly said. He was the ringleader. He was the master mind.

"Don't worry," Worm assured him, "we'll hear from them all right. When the shit hits the fan, boy—"

Solly looked long at his best buddy. Then he said to him quietly, "Meanwhile, let's drop the subject till something happens, honh? After all, they probably threw them in the wastebasket. We were pretty stupid to write them in the first place."

The Bookworm stared at him, no longer smiling, looking at his brand-new buddy.

CHAPTER

12

It was his first day back with the company. The captain sat silently at the Topkick's desk staring at the back of Solly's head as Solly banged away on the typewriter making out the company payroll.

Finally Rutherford said, "Saunders, I have done everything within my power to bring you forward in the Army, and I'm just about at the end of my rope."

Solly stopped typing and turned toward the captain.

"You can forget about OCS. That's down the drain, after all the trouble I went to. And if it wasn't for Sergeant Anderson, I would bust you down to a private, but he covered for you. I don't believe the lie he told me, but I can't disprove it. If I did, I'd have to break him too. So I'm letting you keep your stripes this time. But I'm warning you, Saunders, once and for all, I don't give a goddamn if you *are* the best company clerk in the regiment. I wouldn't even care if you were the best in the whole damn Army. The next time you get out of line or fuck up any shape, form, or fashion, I'm going to burn your ass, so help me. That is no threat, that's a promise. Is that clear?"

He said. "Yes. sir." From now on he would never let this

man know what his thoughts and feelings were. He would say yes, sir, no, sir, and under his breath say screw you, sir. His head was clearer now. He had no more illusions.

"The company records are in one holy mess. I want you to pitch right in and straighten them out. I don't care if you have to work at it twenty-four hours a day. We're going to have Regimental Inspection of company records next Friday morning, and if we don't pass it, it's going to be hell to pay, between me and you. If we pass it with flying colors I'm ready to wipe the slate clean. And I'll give you any temporary help you need. Is all that clear?"

He said, "Yes, sir." My Army IQ is twenty-three points higher. I'll outwit this peckerwood.

"This is your last chance, Saunders. If you got a personal problem, come to me, and I'll see what's what, but don't never come to see me as a member of a mob. You're my company clerk and your first loyalty is to me."

Solly had thought it was to God and Country. And he was remembering now the letter he and Worm had written, signed by others in the company. Romantic, idealistic, which were other words for stupid. Never again would he let his feelings run away with his common sense. What is a good mind for if not to be used to good advantage?

"You'll learn one of these days Samuels's kind doesn't mean you any good." The captain got up and sat down again. "I'm a Southerner, Saunders, and I know you New York colored folks are prejudiced against us. And I don't say like some hypocrites do, that some of my best friends are Negroes, and I didn't have a Negro mammy cause my family couldn't afford it. And I don't pronounce Negro 'nigrah' either. And I can say one thing in clear conscience—I am not prejudiced against the colored race. There's a place for everybody on this planet. Almighty God made all of us, and we ought to live in harmony, and I'm ready to meet you halfway any time any place."

Rutherford's voice was soft and low and he was almost out of breath, and Solly stared at him in amazement as he suddenly realized this man was serious in his convictions, and to that extent was honest.

"I don't know how I can make it plainer to you. I'm your commanding officer and you're my company clerk, and you're as good as any white one on the post, but if you give me another half a inch of trouble, I am going to do everything in my power to make you miserable the rest of your Army days. You understand?" His voice was trembling with his righteous anger. He had given this one colored boy every break in the goddamn book.

Solly thought, every man is honest if he does not deceive himself. He said, "Yes, sir." If those letters were ever published, then he had screwed up in perpetuity. What newspaper would be foolish enough to publish them at a time like this? From now on he would listen to his brain. He had gone way out on a limb and couldn't get back, and when and if the time came, all the man had to do was to saw it off. He had given Captain Charlie the rope to break his neck with. Never again, Millie baby.

He said, "If Private First-Class Moore could work with me till Friday, sir."

The CO said, "Tell his platoon sergeant I gave the order."

Clint and he worked like pack horses day and night, and Samuels helped them. And the colonel came and inspected. Friday night Rutherford called him into the office. He looked at him sternly. Finally he said, "Saunders, I don't know what I'm going to do with you, I swear before the Lord I don't. You've gone and fucked the dog again."

Solly thought, he's found out about the letters! And he realized then how scared he was about them. His heart was beating double-time. To hell with Scotty. He didn't want any part of the stockade. A sharp pain in between his buttocks. "We did our best, sir." Hating the sound of his own voice. "Private First-Class Moore and I—"

Rutherford cut him off. "You've done your level best all right. You just had the best damn records in the regiment, that's all." The CO smiling broadly now. "You just keep fucking up like that and you just might make sergeant one of these days."

The anger smoldered inside of him and he could not force himself to smile. He tried hard enough. This peckerwood bastard toying with him like he was a little boy. Well, he would give him smile for smile, even though he could not at the moment smile, and he would make sergeant and even maybe more than sergeant. And he remembered the letters and he was glad and sorry too. They would never see the light of day. No one would dare to publish them. No one would be so foolish.

Lieutenant Samuels had come to see him several times while he was in the hospital, and each time he had questioned Solly about the happenings in Ebbensville. His first Saturday morning out of the hospital, the lieutenant asked him to drive him into town on some business. It was a warm sun-washed day for the first of November even in Georgia, and a red dusty haze hung over the highway like an early-morning fog. If it were not knee-deep muddy in that part of Georgia, it was ankle-deep in dust. Take your choice.

As they reached the town the lieutenant asked Solly for the millionth time, "And you don't remember his name?"

"I don't remember that I ever heard them call his name," Solly answered nonchalantly. "His name was Colonel. Colonel Charlie Peckerwood the Third."

"Well," the lieutenant said his face turning red, "you know where the police station is. That's our first stop."

Solly stared ahead at the hot dusty road. He and his Great White Brother.

They were in the heart of the downtown district now, on one of the two streets in town that sported traffic lights, and it was Saturday and overalled crackers, some of them fat, most of them scrawny, and red-necked crackers and dressed-up crackers with brogan shoes in town from the country, and wagon-loads of crackers and cracker womenfolk and cracker children, and the stores and shops doing a thriving Saturday business, and the strong sharp smell in the air of horse dung freshly deposited, golden-brown and smoking, and slow-drag drawls and Southern accents and nickelodeons blasting away with hillbilly tunes and boisterous laughter, and all of it conjuring up memories, stowed away and long forgotten, of Dry Creek, Georgia, Lord Lord Lord, where he lived the first seven years of his life. He caught a brief glimpse of a lone black face and remembered another Saturday between ten and fifteen years ago—his mother and he walking all the way from Glenwood Bottom, where colored people lived, through Crackerville, through the downtown district, all the way to the train depot with three beat-up suitcases holding all the wealth they had in the world, and pink-faced red-necked crackers staring at them like they had just escaped from a circus cage, and waiting around on the colored bench for over an hour and catching the first thing smoking for 'way up North in New York City. A bittersweet nostalgia spread over the floor and roof of his mouth and he thought he smelled a sharp sweet fragrance of honeysuckles on the vine, and he stared at the strange familiar faces as if he longed to discover an old acquaintance. Samuels jarred him out of his romantics.

"This is it, Corporal."

Samuels got out of the jeep, and Solly got out and leaned against it. "So it is, Lieutenant." A worried expression settling over Samuels's face now that he had arrived at his destination. He took off his glasses and wiped them with an olive-drab handkerchief.

"You want me to stay out here and wait for you, Lieutenant? And keep the motor running?" He had no illusions now about himself or Samuels. If Samuels ordered him to accompany him, he'd go. Otherwise he did not need heroics today. He was no hero. He did not need to visit the scene of his degradation.

The lieutenant stared at him. "Suit yourself."

Solly snapped his heels to attention and saluted him with exaggeration, and Samuels turned and walked up the long walk to the courthouse. Halfway along the walk he stopped and turned and stopped again and then came back to the jeep.

Solly said maliciously, "Did you change your mind, Lieutenant? Scared of the big bad Chief of Police?" He did not want to go inside this place ever again.

"I think you should accompany me, Saunders."

"You give the orders. I'm just a soldier who doesn't need to be a hero."

Samuels forced a smile. "You're not scared yourself, are you, Corporal?"

Solly stood there hating the lieutenant. Maybe I am scared. Maybe it was *my* head they whipped and not my Great White Buddy's.

"Let's go, Corporal."

Solly thought, maybe these are *my* balls aching. Maybe that's why I am scared.

A young cop with a face full of red freckles was seated at the desk reading a Sunday funny paper and picking at his big pimply nose. The lieutenant cleared his nervous throat. The cracker policeman pretended not to hear. Finally he looked up from the paper and said, "You want us to keep this boy in jail overnight, Lieutenant? It's all right with us. We'll take good care of him." He looked at Solly and laughed.

Solly broke into a sweat. He glared at the cop. He stared at the lieutenant.

"I want to speak to the Chief of Police," the lieutenant said.

"Maybe I can help you."

The Chief came in from an adjoining room. Solly felt himself grow hot all over and his stomach turning upside down and his heart beating fiercely away up in his temples. He could hear his heart thumping through his ears. His thighs began to throb in pain. His entire body remembered. What the hell was he doing back in this place?

"What's going on in here?" the Chief of Police said. "Oh, it's you, Lieutenant," he said to Samuels. "What can I do for you? Why don't you let that boy stay outside till you get through with your business? Come on in and have a sitdown. It don't cost nothing. Or maybe you want us to lock him up again. We always happy to co-operate."

"I'm glad you want to co-operate, Chief Watson. I—"

"Don't be so formal," the friendly faced chief cop said. "Come on into the back room. Let your boy wait outside, lessen you want us to lock him up again." He stared at Solly and laughed.

The lieutenant was undecided, about going into the back room, that is, and Solly's heart beat double time and he was worried about his Great White Buddy, but was relieved when the lieutenant didn't move. "All I want to know, Chief, is the name of the Army colonel in here the night this soldier here was arrested. I won't bother you any further."

The friendly Southern hospitality vanished. "What colonel?"

"The colonel here the night this soldier was here." Suddenly the office got warmer and warmer and stuffier as the air got heavier.

"What you want with him?"

The throbs were painful and distinct now, the muscles in his thighs were dancing in fire to an off-time rhythm. He was weak all over.

"All I want is his name, and I'll look him up myself," the lieutenant said. "I want to have a little chat with him."

"What you want to talk to him about?"

"A few Army matters," the lieutenant said.

"What colonel?" the Chief said. Sharp and alert now, on

the ball. "I don't know nothing about no colonel." His face afire with Southern "white-folks" righteous anger.

"Corporal Saunders here says that there was an Army colonel here the night he was here."

"I wouldn't pay any attention to what that boy say, Lieutenant. He most probably don't rightly remember. Do you, boy?"

Solly didn't trust himself to speak. His legs began to ache and he thought maybe he was suddenly crazy with anger—maybe fear. He wasn't ready to be beaten up again. Well, but it wouldn't be so easy, since it was two of them this time, he and the lieutenant, or could he really count on the glib tan-faced New Yorker, when push came to shove? After all the lieutenant was a white man for all his Florida brownness, just like the rest of the crackers in the police station, and he was the only colored man, and blood and color were thicker than water. Two more cops came in from the back room. Perspiration drained from Solly, and he backed up without knowing.

"I say—do you, boy? You don't rightly remember, do you?"

Solly pretended the Chief wasn't talking to him.

"You see?" the Chief said to the lieutenant. "He ain't even got the nerve to repeat the same lie when he gets down here in front of us honest policemen. Most probably he'd been drinking some of the bad moonshine the nigrahs make around here outa snuff and piss and washing powder. You don't know these nigrahs like we do, Lieutenant."

"What about it, Corporal?" the lieutenant said.

"What about what?" Was this a trap? Was the lieutenant in cahoots with these cracker cops? He didn't want to believe it. Maybe he didn't actually believe it, and yet the question entered his mind and would not leave.

"What about the colonel?"

"What *about* him? I told you he was here. I told you what he looked like. I can't tell you his name for the simple reason I never knew it."

"Boy, you mean to stand up there and try to make me out a liar? Do you know who you talking to?" The Chief strode to within two or three feet of Solly.

Solly backed up a couple of steps and stared the white-haired cracker in his blue eyes. "I know whom you're *not* talking to. You're not talking to a boy. You're talking to a man who doesn't give a good goddamn about your white face or your white hair or your blue eyes or your Southern accent."

The Chief changed colors as he stared at him as if Solly had escaped from a lunatic asylum. After all that whipping they gave him last month he still thought he was a man.

"He's a crazy liar, Lieutenant," the Chief said. "I know you're not going to take his word before you would a white man's. I just know you ain't—"

There was a moment's silence as the lieutenant seemed to be pondering seriously the great momentous question of Southern Christian morality. The walls of the room seemed to hold their breaths and the ceiling descended. The lieutenant said, "Let's go, Corporal."

"Must be one of them New York Jews," one of the cracker policemen loud-talked. "He mess around with the colonel he won't be an officer many more days. Colonel got a heap of weight and I mean he pushes it around and he don't like no Jews to begin with nohow."

Solly laughed and Samuels burned.

It was a long long walk out of the office and down the hall, down the brick steps and along the walk and through the square, saying nothing to each other, looking neither behind nor to the sides, just walking together and erect like soldiers have a way of walking, Solly Saunders limping slightly, Robert Samuels burning greatly. And swarms and swarms of birds overhead coming South for the winter and going further South and keeping up an awful racket in this peaceful Southern town.

When they got to the jeep, Samuels had gotten himself together. "That wasn't too bad an ordeal for us, was it, Corporal? We shook them up a little even if we didn't accomplish our total objective."

Samuels was pleased with himself and Solly heard the Great-White-Father crap in the officer's voice. He was already angry with the lieutenant for ordering him to come to town and ordering him back to the scene of his debasement. Now he was enraged. He waited politely till the officer got into the jeep, like enlisted men were supposed to do, and then he leaped in and started the car and gunned the motor and took off up the street, scattering pigeons and some of the country crackers. Two blocks up he turn the corner on two wheels.

"What's the matter with you, Saunders? This isn't the way back to camp."

"I seem to remember hearing that the MP station for Ebbensville is out this road about a mile and a half."

"We're not going to the MP station."

Solly pulled suddenly into the curb and slammed on the brakes. "I figured that out there we might just be lucky enough to run into the colonel himself in person, and I could point him out to you. I mean we might even accomplish our total objective. That was our objective, wasn't it, Lieutenant?"

Samuels's tan face lost its color. "I have an officers' meeting back at the post, Corporal. Up at regimental."

Solly stared at him. "It wouldn't be too much of an ordeal for you, Lieutenant. The colonel couldn't be that much of a terror. And I'll stand by you one hundred per cent. I appreciate what you're trying to do for us colored folks." You phony bastard, he almost muttered aloud. I caught you with your pants down and you have nothing to brag about. What happened to your balls, Lieutenant?

"Let's get back to camp, Saunders. I must attend this special meeting at regimental." He was white as a soda cracker.

"You're giving the orders, Lieutenant, sir. I'm just your humble servant." He made a sweeping U-turn in the middle of the block and started back in the opposite direction. Thinking, this meeting must be very very special to be called on Saturday afternoon with half the officers already off on week-end passes.

CHAPTER

13

When he came out of the hospital he didn't go over to the PX until another week had passed. Not till she sent for him by the Bookworm.

She asked him how he had been and where he had been. He said, "Oh, just convalescing." And smiled a sickly smile at her.

"Are you all right now?" she asked anxiously, her dark eyes widened and deep with concern for him and especially him and no one but him, and she looked lovelier than ever to his eyes, and the memory of that night put a sweet and angry aching in the bottom of his stomach. But he said bluntly, "I'm okay."

"I wondered why you didn't come over to the PX. Nobody over here is going to bite you. I just wanted to talk to you about the N-double-A-C-P Thanksgiving party."

He said, "So here I am. Talk." That N-double-A-C-P covered a multitude of innuendoes.

They discussed the Thanksgiving party between intervals of her waiting on other soldiers, and he stood there till the PX closed, talking with her but never looking her fully in her lovely anxious face. Finally she asked him, "What's the matter, Solly?"

And he said, "Nothing's the matter. I told you already—I'm fine."

The Post Exchange was noisy as per usual, with the jukebox blasting eardrums with "Straighten Up and Fly Right" by the King Cole Trio.

"I don't mean that. I don't mean your health. You just act funny."

"Act funny? I don't know what you're talking about." People were always saying one thing and meaning something entirely different. "You mean you think I could make it as a comedian? I have comic potentials? Maybe the tragicomic, honh? That's an idea—laugh em cry em to death. Maybe I won't go back to law school after all. Maybe I'll go to a comedy school. That's me all right—Solomon Saunders, Junior, a Comedy of Errors. That's the story of my life. Maybe that's what I'll do—be a writer and the pen is mightier than the sword and I'll write the story of my life as a warning to every other human, but it won't do any good. Most human beings stink anyhow."

We could fly straight to the moon together—

Her dark eyes darkened larger, wider, blacker, deeper. "I mean—you've been out of the hospital over a week, but you didn't come by even to say hello."

"I've been very busy," he answered. "Very very busy." His voice was stronger now, but he couldn't look at her any more without growing warm all over. Warm and large. And maybe he would never look at her again without becoming warm and large.

"So I swallow my pride and send for you, and you come over against your will, and you act so funny and strange—like you never saw me before."

"I had to catch up with a lot of work that fell behind while I was in the hospital. You understand—" He wanted to add: And I'm married! And I'm sick of you and everything and everybody.

A big-headed large-framed light-brown complexioned soldier pounded on the counter. "Hey, Miss Pretty, will you give me a banana split please, mam?"

Be the new moon's first inhabitants—

"I understand," she said to Solly with a brand-new bittersweetness. "I understand that they've been holding up the war while you were in the hospital, General Solomon Saunders. Private Taylor told me."

"Lady—look—all I want is one little old banana split."

And now it was Harry James and his sweet seductive trumpet and his orchestra and his lady singer.

"Don't be like that, Fannie Mae."

"Maybe you're angry with me because I asked you to take me home that night. Maybe you're blaming me for what happened to you in town—" Solly thought:

—It seems I've dreamed this dream before—

"Don't be foolish," he told her. The Post Exchange was the noisiest place in the Army which was the noisiest place in the world.

"Excuse me, lady, I don't want to make anybody angry, but I've been standing here trying to get waited on for fifteen minutes. I don't want to be unreasonable, but—"

"Solly, I just don't know what to think. I—"

Many many moons ago—

"Give him a banana split before he splits a blood vessel," Solly said.

"Thank you, General, please, sir," the big soldier said and bowed to Solly.

—You and I together ever—

Soon after she came back to where he was standing it was time to close, and he walked with her and her girl friend to her struggle-buggy as she called it.

When they reached the car she turned to him, her mouth widening and curving and her eyes completely black now, black and shiny with the moonlight in them. "The one thing you can't allow this world to do to you, Solly, is to make you bitter. I mean about the Army and the war and everything. I know a little bit of how you feel. I hate it too—I hate it for you. But you just can't let it get you down. Not you, Solomon Saunders, Junior. That's all there is to it. You have much too much to give to this world."

He thought viciously, all I have to say to break up this romantic image is: I'm married, baby—and you will cloud up like an angry storm and the image will be blown to hell and back.

"We have to fight them every step of the way!" she said

fiercely. "In and out of the Army. That's the way things are for us."

"I'm fighting for me, baby, and nobody else but me, from now on in. I'm just about the most militant opportunist you ever saw in all your sweet life." Then he changed his tone and said, "Look, Fannie Mae. Maybe I conned myself into believing in this Army and the war, but now I know the whole damn setup is as phony as a nine-dollar bill. Don't talk to me about bitterness."

"I know—I know, sweetheart," she said. She had forgotten Sally Anne was there. "It's like we say in the N-double-A-C-P. Like I told you, we need a Double-V for Victory. Beat them at home and overseas." He didn't believe she believed it any more. Empty words that meant nothing to him or her.

He loved her, there was no denying it. More than anything else in the world. He said, "Fannie Mae—"

She reached out and took him by the hand. "I hate it all, my darling! Everything you hate I hate!" Without warning she put her arms around his neck and kissed him quickly fiercely on his mouth. "I promise never to let you down," she whispered. "Never ever. I'd rather die than let you down."

He hated to feel lower than a rattlesnake. He almost hissed at her. "Don't make me any promises. You owe me nothing and I don't owe you anything. I'm in great shape. I just don't have any more illusions. I don't need them. I'm happier without them."

She said, "There's no other promise worth the keeping. Nothing matters without you. Even if for you and me the war is phony, you just come back home to me, and we can build a life together."

Later that evening he lay on his sack and thought of Fannie Mae and Millie and held their faces close to him and away from him and he put his arms around them and felt their nearness to him and listened to their voices. How in the hell could he love two women? What was Fannie Mae to him, really? Realistically? She's just a gorgeous piece, that's all. A pretty woman whom he'd seen and wanted to have a thing with. That's all. And he'd had his thing and more than paid the price for it. So stop romanticizing the pretty little country wench. But he loved her, more than any other woman. Even and including Millie Saunders. He couldn't kid himself any longer. He loved her. He had messed around seriously with the idea of writing Millie and telling her about Fannie Mae and asking her for an annulment on whatever grounds were necessary. Millie was a sensible woman. But he would have to discuss it with Fannie Mae first and he had not found the strength in him to tell her he was married. He was an adulterous bastard and how did he rate two beautiful powerful women like Fannie Mae and Millie? Tomorrow evening he would write Millie and tell her about Fannie and then he would go over to the Post Exchange and tell Fannie Mae all about Millie. And he made up his mind he would do it tomorrow. He had put it off too long.

The next day at noon he got a letter from home. He came upstairs in the barracks and sat on his bunk, and Millie always wrote the same way she talked. He was afraid to open it at first.

> Dear Solly:
>
> I miss you so very much these days, no matter how hard I try to fill my life with other things. I work with the Red Cross, the air-raid wardens, and I still go down to the Stage Door Canteen. It doesn't do any good at all.

His face began to fill and he looked up and around.

> I suppose it is simply because you are my life, and without you there is very little left. I just don't seem to be able to grin and bear it like other wives I know. Some of my friends go to dances and go out on dates with the available men, but nothing like that interests me. I try awful hard to be brave and strong like you want me to be, but sometimes the tears just fill up my eyes no matter what. I wish you were here to kiss them away, my darling. My family doesn't understand me at all. They say, go out and have a good time. Don't be so serious. You're only young once. But where is the good time without you, sweetheart? I think your mother understands.

He stared at the letter, smiling bitterly. Your family is right. You should get yourself a solid 4–F citizen, and get it regularly. That way I wouldn't feel so damn guilty about Fannie Mae Branton.

> I spoke to my boss about you the other day. There is a possibility of your getting a job in our firm after you finish law school. I told them what a great brain you are.

Our firm! She thinks she's a partner in the firm already.

> Every move I make, darling, is with you in mind. Every plan, every thought is just for you.

Well, he wouldn't let this letter make any difference, he told himself belligerently. A letter was a letter—that's all—and nothing more. It didn't change him and it didn't change Millie, and it couldn't write Fannie Mae out of existence. He wouldn't wait a day longer. He'd write her tonight and tell her about Fannie Mae, and she would just have to be a sensible woman. She had her phony family in Crown Heights and all those colored society boys. She was beautiful and eligible and could marry easily again. She could call her shots.

> I love you so much my heart really aches sometimes with loneliness. There'll never be another man for me, my darling, even if the war should last a hundred years.

You don't even know the man I am now, he thought. I'm the bitterest bastard in the world. How in hell can anybody love me?

She had never written him a letter like this one. Damn her sweet time. It was as if she sensed the whole business between him and Fannie Mae and was trying to head it off. It was if she smelled the sordid mess all the way to New York City, all the way to the lily-white Wall Street law firm where she worked.

He put the letter aside and stared across the barracks. She didn't need him. Her family were bigshots and would be glad to shake her loose from him. She was the only daughter of one of the "first" families of Brooklyn, colored, that is. And proud of her light-skin bourgeois heritage. He knew all about her family's background. Her grandfather came from Virginia as a boy and worked in Wall Street in the Stock Exchange—with a broom and a mop and pail. His benevolent boss generously gave him tips on the Market and invested his savings wisely for him and made him "nigrah" rich, and Grandpa opened up a catering business. Catering to good rich white folks. One of the family's proudest moments and most often-used quotations was a famous compliment paid to Grandpa by his Wall Street boss. "Neal, boy, you are the whitest black man I ever met. If you'd been born white, you'd been a robber baron just like Vanderbilt or Morgan."

They were one of the *first* "families" to move into fashionable Crown Heights on President Street, before the grand white folks started running for their very lives. Grandpa worked himself to death and Grandma ruled the roost. Millie had had the cream of the crop of the young men of Negro society to choose from, but she had chosen Solly after three months' acquaintance. She met him at the Urban League. Solomon Saunders, Junior, who had neither pot nor window nor pedigree. He wasn't even a first-generation New Yorker. Well, she could go back to her colored society, her pretty light-skinned colored boys.

Solly remembered the Sunday evening he'd had to go to meet the family like they do in the corny novels about upper-upper-upper-class rich white folks. And they had stared down their skinny Nordic-type bourgeois noses at him suspiciously and superciliously. But Grandma liked him immediately. She said: "He's dark, but he's good-looking. And he reminds me of your grandpa, and he's got more get-up about him than all these trifling spoiled pantywaisted colored fraternity boys put together and multiplied."

He laughed, remembering. When they were courting and he wanted to get her goat or bring her down a couple of notches from her high and queenly horse, he would tease her to death about her family. He would tell her, "I keep forgetting your family are Black Irish, baby, and I sure don't want to get your Irish up, my wild Black Irish Rose!"

He would laugh and laugh and she would be angry and insulted and stop speaking to him. But now as he reconstructed it, he thought maybe he had not made her angry after all.

Her family was unbelievable. Her father was not a go-getter like his pa before him. His managing of the catering business was a holding operation. Her pretty, vivacious mother was a social climber, although no one seemed to know just where she was climbing or how far up. Millie's brother considered business a vulgar occupation. His name was Roderick and he called his grandpa "Papa" and he stuttered and stammered badly.

Once before Grandpa died he had a man-to-man talk with Roddy. "Rod, doggone, boy, you the last button on Jacob's coat-tail. You got to carry the family's name onward and upward, you know what I mean?" Roddy said, "All right, Pa-Pa-Pa-Pa-Pah—pa."

"Doggonit, boy, you been kicked outa some of the best schools in the country, colored and white. What you gonna do with yourself?"

"I don't know, Pa-Pa-Pa-Pa-Pahh—pa."

Grandpa said, "Well, I can see you ain't gon be no doctor or lawyer or chicken-eating preacher, and I'm glad you ain't gon be no schoolteacher. I'll tell you what I'll do. Maybe a change of environment would do you some good. I'll set you up in some little business anywhere you want to go—Cleveland, Ohio, or Dee-troit, Michigan, or Chicago, or something like that. Anything you want to do anywhere you want to go."

Roddy said, "I don't want to leave you, Pa-Pa-Pa-Pahh—pa."

Grandpa was swiftly losing patience with the last button on Jacob's coattail. "What in the hell you gon be in life, Roddy?"

"Nu-nu-nu-nu-noth-ing, Pa-Pa-Pa-Pahpa."

Grandpa had stared at the last button and broken into a loud and boisterous laughter, and all the rest of them had run into the room, and he had laughed till the tears streamed down his face and they had to bring him a Scotch and soda to calm his nerves. He dropped dead three weeks later.

Solly still didn't believe the Belford family actually existed. They were an old-fashioned novel he had read in a pocketbook edition.

Solly sat up on his bunk in the sun-washed barracks. One thing he had done with Millie was to make her move away from home and stay away. She was in *their* apartment with *his* mother. Well, she would go back to her people now. And everybody would be happy. He picked the letter up again.

> I have some good news for you, darling. We are going to have a baby.

His eyes stared at the written words unbelievingly, his stomach trembling. It was a false alarm—women were always having false alarms. He felt a chill move from the middle of his back fanlike out toward his shoulders and wave after wave after wave after wave. His face began to fill.

> The doctor says there's no doubt about it. Of course, I've known for some time now, but I did not want to bother you. You have enough on your mind—

He didn't read any further. He thought his heart would leap from his chest. He put the letter under his pillow and got up and walked across the barracks and down the stairs and out into the pouring rain. He was going to be a father. He did not realize it was raining. He was going to be a father—a thing he'd never been before.

The Thanksgiving party in Ebbensville was a great success. About fifty-five or sixty soldiers and thirty young courageous women. The dinner was served in the colored Pythian Temple. A big turkey dinner with every one of those Southern trimmings—turkey dressing and candied yams and potato salad and English peas and cranberry sauce and ice cream and cake and punch and lots of other things and plenty of everything, and afterwards a dance with a live dance band from Camp Johnson Henry, and Solly hardly spoke to Fannie Mae all afternoon and evening. He danced with her once near the beginning of the dance and then he went around dancing from Southern lady to Southern lady, and he watched six or seven other soldiers rushing Fannie Mae, and every now and then their eyes would meet, her large eyes full of questions unasked and unanswerable, and linger momentarily, and then look off into miles of emptiness. And Bookworm Taylor was having himself a natural ball.

Worm danced with Fannie Mae three or four rounds in succession and tried to bring her out of her distraction, as the music went around and around, and he tried to jitterbug with her, but she told him she didn't feel like it. Bookworm was a real gone bug. Like the cats at the Track on Lenox Avenue. Worm grabbed one lady and they bugged for a while. He threw her this way and that and cut all kinds of fancy steps, Savoy Ballroom style, and the lady refused to be confused. She kept right up with him to the tune of "One o'clock Jump," and the joint was leaping as people stopped dancing to make room for Worm and the swivel-hipped long-legged brown-skin lady who was time enough for him. The crowd made a circle and gathered around him and the lady, and they clapped their hands as the band played over and over again, the "One o'clock Jump," ad-libbing and off-jiving as they went along, and sneaking in portions of "Flying Home" and soaring way out and ending with the "Jump" again with the three trumpets blasting to the top of the roof, and the people shouting and clapping their hands. Bookworm was a natural bug.

The next time Solly glimpsed Worm he was dancing with the same young lady, doing a slow drag with his big head resting seriously upon her shoulder and cheek to cheek and his eyes closed to the awfully disturbing music of the "Stormy Monday Blues" and the vocalist making like Billy Eckstein.

It was Thanksgiving back in New York City, Solly thought, and already the stores have begun the great commercial push toward Christmas with lights and decorations and phony Santa Clauses, and what was Millie doing tonight on this, the first Thanksgiving of their marriage? She seemed a million years and miles away, unreachable in time and space. At the moment he could not even conjure up her face from out of his fickle memory. Lovely vivacious voluptuous Millie Saunders with their baby in her belly. With their baby in her belly.

"You look like you're lost," Solly heard her say, coming up behind him. "Aren't you having a good time? After all," she said with an exaggerated smile, "why do you think I went to all this trouble plotting and planning? It was all done just to make you happy. To raise your morale." She was in his arms now, dancing without any effort at all it seemed.

"I'll always be true, baby," the man sang in a voice that imitated Billy Eckstein. He had known what it would be like, dancing with her. She would be light as a soft summer breeze in his arms and so damn comfortable, he would feel at home as if he had a permanent residence in this place, and yet it was so upsetting and disturbingly sweet, her warm breath on his neck. She would remind him of Millie, and she *did* remind him painfully of Millie, as they danced their dance—Millie Saunders, his wife, with their baby in her belly and hundreds and hundreds of miles away, with his child in her swelling stomach—Millie Saunders. And at this moment Fannie Mae was more like Millie than Millie Saunders ever was.

Come back, pretty Mama.
Love me one more time . . .

He loved Millie Belford Saunders—nobody else—nobody else! But Fannie Mae was here and now and a bitter reality, sweet and tender, and at this moment he related to her from far far greater depths. The singer made up his own lyrics.

"All this conniving," Fannie Mae said teasingly, "just to get you to dance with me. Just to get you in my arms again. It's a sin and a shame." But he sounded just like Eckstein.

"You certainly went to an awful lot of trouble," he said in what he meant to be an offhand manner. "Not to mention the tremendous expense." He was warm from being close to her. And shamed.

"Why aren't you enjoying yourself?" she asked him almost angrily, looking up into his darkening eyes.

She was an armful—just right for him—and yet so goddamn wrong. "I am enjoying myself. What makes you think I'm not? And why wouldn't I be? I'm dancing with the loveliest girl in the State of Georgia. How do I sound?" How did he sound?

Come home, baby, need you all the time.

"But not in the State of New York—is that it?" He could feel her anxious nippled softness breathing against his angry chest and her heart beating violently against his ribs and her thighs against his aching thighs. And felt her throbbing in the him of him.

Now was the time to tell her he was married. Now that she had asked for it. But he couldn't spoil her party for her, not here on the dance floor. He would tell her tonight when it was all over, and then it would be all over between them. It had never really begun. It couldn't begin. "New York is a pretty large State you know. Gobs and gobs of people."

"That's what they tell me," she said. "But being a little naïve country girl, I wouldn't know anything about it at all."

The band had changed from "Stormy Monday" to "Good Night, Sweetheart," and the tempo had quickened and then the band drifted into "Home Sweet Home" and the tempo quickened. She looked up into his face and said, "Joe Taylor asked me to let him take me home."

"That's nice," he said. What else could he say? "A prince of a fellow is Joseph Taylor. The very best. I mean, he really is."

"I told him *you* were taking me home," she said.

"That's even nicer," Solly said absent-mindedly. "But you better beware of this fellow, Solomon Saunders. He's not as nice as Joseph Taylor."

"I figured there was things you and I might have to talk about—but maybe there isn't."

"There is," he whispered. "There definitely is." She misunderstood his meaning. Her face warmed up her dark eyes brightened.

Outside in the cool night air that bit into their warm nervous bodies, she walked close to him till they reached her car, and then she turned to him and said, "Do you want to drive?"

"Why not?"

And she gave him the keys and he got behind the steering wheel and she in beside him and close up against him and her innocent happy head up against his nervous shoulder. She reached toward his handsome somber face and caressed his cheeks. She gave him directions to get to her house and they didn't speak another word till they reached her house, and she said, "Do you want to go in for a while and sit on the porch? The full moon is out tonight."

He said, "I love full moons." And they went down the walk together hand in hand with the full moon bright and a ripened yellow and casting soft shadows onto the walk, into the flower gardens on each side of the walk, and the side of her slim nervous body walking against his agitated body. They came up on the porch and sat on a bench, and she turned toward him and said, "Solly! Solly!" And put her arms around his neck and his arms went around her waist, which was just an armful custom-made for arms like his, and at that moment he forgot everything else as his lips held her lips soft and firm as he remembered them, and her sweet breath against his cheeks and her active bosom softly against his chest, and after a moment there was a breathing spell in which she asked him, "What's the matter, Solly?"

The silky sweetness of her Southern accent got on his nerves. "It's getting late," he said. "We have to make reveille tomorrow morning, Thanksgiving party notwithstanding. Got to fight that war for democracy. Got to get that Double-V for Victory."

"I understand," she said quietly. "I understand." And she put her arms around his neck again, and he firmly and deliberately took them away from around his neck and placed them in her lap.

"What's the matter, Solly? What did I do? You couldn't be jealous of Joe Taylor—"

His mind deliberately played around with the question. In a way though he was jealous of Bookworm Taylor. "I am insanely jealous of the good Private Joseph No-Middle-Name Taylor. Yes I am." Bookworm could be completely honest with Fannie Mae, and that was a tremendous advantage. His own relationship with her was based on lies of commission and omission.

"Maybe," she said, "you still blame me for your being in

town the night the police picked you up. Maybe that's what the matter is." She said, "All the girls in the club were telling me tonight how handsome you are, as if I didn't already know you're the handsomest man in all the world, and the kindest and the most deeply feeling and the most intelligent, and I'm the luckiest woman in the world—" She stopped to catch her breath. "Don't blame me, Solly. Please don't blame me, darling, about that night. I'm so sorry about everything—"

He said violently, "I don't blame you!"

She put her arms around him again. "Thank you, darling!"

He was a lousy undeserving bastard. "Thank you, sweetheart! I know how you feel, and I hate it, the whole shooting match, as much as you do. I hate everything about it!" She kissed him on his mouth again. "I hate it! Hate it!" He took her arms away from around his neck.

"What's the mat—?"

"The matter is I'm married," he heard himself say in a voice he did not recognize. And at that moment he hated himself more than he had ever hated before in his entire life. Even more than he hated Army life. He felt a guilty aching in his head and a churning in his stomach.

She didn't utter a sound at first, and he wouldn't let himself look at her. There were a million easier ways to tell her, but after hemming and hawing and omitting and committing and running away and coming back again, he had finally chosen the most direct route—and maybe the crudest and cruelest or maybe the kindest after all. He was a mean sadistic masochistic sonofabitching bastard. He thought she was crying. He tried to put a consoling arm around her, but she moved quietly away from him. He put his hand into the thick blackness of her hair.

"No," she said. "That isn't necessary, Corporal Saunders."

"Fannie Mae, I'm—"

"And don't you go feeling sorry and guilty for the poor little country girl," she said sarcastically. "I saw you, I liked you, I thought you liked me, and I asked for it. You didn't encourage me one bit." He heard the bitter anger in her voice. He felt the sting like a driver's lash. "If anybody's to blame, it's me for being too—too—too forward—bolder than a lady's supposed to be. I was never like that before in my life, I can state you that. When I met you I just thought that all the roads of my life had led to you. It was a stupid sentimental thing. I never believed in fate before, but I remember saying to myself, 'Solly Saunders is the cause and the reason that you took a job in an Army Post Exchange.' I told myself that this was it. It looks like I was so wrong—I—I" Her voice broke off.

He shouted softly, "Stop it, Fannie Mae, goddammit!"

"The fact of the matter is, you tried to discourage me, but I thought you were being overly modest, or maybe loyal to Joe Taylor, and I loved you all the more for it. You know how those things are. And all the while I was just a little stupid naïve country girl to you—" Acid pouring fiercely from her. "I should have known that the smooth, suave, handsome gentleman from New York City couldn't possibly be so modest—" She choked off again. "Why didn't you tell me, Solly? Tell me—why didn't you? I can't understand how somebody as sensitive as you are could be so cruel and heartless. Or maybe I was something less than human to you? After all, I'm not totally naïve. I know how men are. But—but how could I have been so completely wrong about you? I mean, you are different. You are a sensitive person—"

"I wanted to tell you, Fannie Mae. I—"

"Are you in love with your wife, Solly?"

Was he in love with his wife? He didn't even know the answer to that any more.

"I am in love with my wife. I'm very much in love with my wife." Somehow the whole situation was unreal to him. How had he allowed himself to become so involved with another woman? He saw Millie's lovely face before him now, heard her sweet voice, held her in his arms and read her letters. Three months ago he would have thought it impossible that just a few months after their marriage any other woman could have had any attraction at all for him. When they kissed at Penn Station, he had thought the kiss could last till they were together again, no matter how long, for even a lifetime, because there was love. The morning in Penn Station felt like three hundred years ago to him. And Fannie was real and seated beside him and crying softly and the taste of her soft full mouth was on his lips. But how did it happen? And the strangest thing about it—he couldn't honestly say he wished the other night with Fannie Mae had never been. He couldn't wish that Fannie Mae had never happened to him.

"Why, Solly? Why? Was I just another chick to you that you could play around with? Was that it, Solly? Was that all it amounted to?"

Solly didn't answer. What other explanation was there?

"Was that it, Solly?"

He sounded like a stranger to himself. "You're a very lovely person, Fannie Mae, a tremendous person—the most wonderful woman I've ever known—and I was lonesome for New York and my wife and my mother. Maybe you don't know what it is to be lonesome. The Army is a lonely place. And you were warm and friendly and beautiful, and there was also an intellectual attraction, a mutuality, and I simply didn't have the strength to face up to what was happening. And suddenly I found myself relating to you like there was nobody else in all the world."

"Why didn't you just tell me you were married?"

"I think it was also because you reminded me so much of her."

He was caught completely by surprise when suddenly her hand went out and slapped him sharply up against his head and face and the sound of it breaking the awful stillness of the moonlit Thanksgiving night, and then sudden pain and the ringing in his head and the ache in his ears, and he sat there trying to make himself angry and self-righteous with her, but it didn't come off, and before he could get himself together she slapped him again and he thought he had lost his hearing completely.

And then she took his head in her hands. "I love you, Solly. I don't care. I love you! I love you! I can't help it! You're a dirty dog, but I love you! You're deceitful and you're no good and I hate you but I love you!" And she kissed his lips and his nose and his eyes and his cheek and his mouth again, her arms around his neck now, and his around her waist that was made for arms like his but never never for his arms. And he kissed her sweet and salty tears and he loved her he loved her he didn't give a damn he loved her! And he loved the ringing in his aching ears that would never ever stop. And then she moved away from him.

"All right then," she said. "It's all over, my darling. My handsome Lothario. But then I reckon it never really began—for you—did it? You just took advantage of the situation." She stood up and he stood up, and the full moon bathing the porch with golden yellow moonlight and crickets everywhere having a ball and a cool breeze blowing a sweet cool breeze over his damp face which was a mask of guilt and anguish. She spat the words at him. "I despise you! I hate the day I ever met you! You're nothing to me at all—nothing! Nothing! You're a phony! I see it all now."

In a way, he was glad she'd slapped him. He was actually relieved she'd slapped him, not once, not only in the heat of passion, but twice and hard and vicious and deliberately. And to hear her say she hated him gave him a perverse kind of satisfaction. He thought, you never really loved me. You just wanted to possess me for your own pleasure and self-aggrandizement, like a piece of property, and when you find you cannot possess me, you're ready to beat me up, destroy me. This is love? He started to say, It takes a phony to find another phony.

He said, "Go ahead—slap me again. You can't hurt me. Have a picnic." He was hurting her more and more, and he knew it, and he didn't want to hurt her but he couldn't help himself. He had taken her love and used it and abused it.

"I hate the sound of your voice," she shouted softly. "I hope I never hear your name again." Her black eyes wet and glistening in the soft cool autumn moonlight.

"Good night, Fannie Mae." He felt like crying, but he had to hold up the firm tradition of menfolks. He held out his hand to her, but she turned and walked into the house and closed the door in his face.

CHAPTER

14

Almost every day he got letters from Millie, but he couldn't get Fannie Mae off his mind, out of his guts. He'd be sitting on his cot reading a letter from Millie about the Red Cross work and the Stage Door Canteen or the progress of her pregnancy and he would find himself thinking of Fannie Mae, as if Fannie Mae were Millie or the other way around. And the days passed into weeks but time healed nothing. The PX lady lived in every corner of his consciousness. He would think of her and feel himself grow warm all over. And large sometimes. And guilty. And he remembered little things about her that he had not even noticed before. The way her face became alive when she talked, her full mouth curving and curling on one side more than the other, her eyes glowing dark brown to deep deep black. The way her heavy eyebrows raised when she was angry or concerned. The way she walked as if she always had important business to attend to. And sometimes he could hear her silken Southern voice and conjure up their conversation. And he remembered her NAACP and her Double-V for Victory. The only positive thing about the war to him was it had brought her and him together for the briefest sweetest moment. But most of all the thing he felt when he thought of her was the fire that burned inside of her and glimmered on the outside. Fannie Mae would never sit still and watch the world go by. And anything she touched would never be the same. You are my alter ego, Fannie Mae. You are the *I* that I aspire to be, but never have been yet. Never will be. My higher-level second self. Please do not despise me. He told himself he didn't care.

One night he was writing a letter to Millie when his Great White Brother came into the orderly room. They had seen very little of each other except strictly in the line of duty since the incident in town. They sat there for a few minutes, talking about this and that and mostly nothing, embarrassed by each other's company. Solly was more bored than embarrassed. He wanted to get on with his letter. There was nothing for them to talk about. They knew each other. They lived with no illusions.

"The war news today is terrific, Saunders. We got the enemy high-tailing on every front."

"Great" was all that Solly said.

Samuels said, "I can't wait to get over there. Those goddamn Nazi bastards!"

Solly said, "Me too."

The men were straggling back from the PX now. Baker came up the steps and when he reached the top he yelled, "Corporal Solly, you old-fashioned fist-fucker, why don't you come out of that orderly room and get some air in your ass sometimes?" He stuck his big head in the office doorway and said, "Ooops, excuse me, Lieutenant."

The lieutenant laughed. "That's all right, Baker. I fully agree with your sentiments."

Baker said, "Yes, sir," and kept going.

The lieutenant chuckled and somehow it angered Solly.

"You *should* get way from these barracks sometimes," Samuels said.

"Yeah," Solly said. "Take a furlough over in Ebbensville." And suddenly he was in the police station again and his thighs began to throb with pain, real pain, and he felt like screaming, his loins were alive and jumping, and only vaguely did he hear the captain's long legs coming up the steps and striding into the orderly room.

But he heard the captain's cultured-Southern tenor-soprano. "So we're having a little tea party, are we? Any outsiders invited to sit for a while? You-all New Yorkers sure do stick together, and a country boy like me wouldn't want to intrude. I expect you all speak the same language all right."

The lieutenant and Saunders got to their feet. The lieutenant said, "Come right in, Captain." His face was burning. The captain's entire face was smiling.

The captain said, "Thank you very much." And then he turned to Saunders. "You know how to spell my name, Saunders?"

"Yes, sir. I think so, sir."

The captain reached into the inside pocket of his coat and brought out some papers. "Why don't you do so then once in a while? The name is Rutherford R-U-T-H-E-R-F-O-R-D. Not Ruterford, the way you have it spelled on these orders." He threw the papers onto the desk.

"I'm sorry, sir. I had so many deadlines to make today. I had to get out the payroll."

"You're sorry?" The captain's voice was trembling now. He seemed to be deliberately working himself into a rage. "You're sorry? All I hear is a whole lot of excuses in this outfit. The question is, can you do the work or can't you? Maybe it's too much for you. Or maybe if you concentrated on your work more and spent less time spreading dissatisfaction amongst the men —and going over into town and making trouble."

"You have the wrong man, Captain. I haven't—"

There wasn't much space in the office but the long-legged Rutherford strode from one side of the room to the other and back to the center and he hitched up his trousers and glanced at the shining stuff on his shoulders. "I don't think I have you wrong, Saunders. I don't think so at all. I've had my eyes on you ever since you came into the company. You've been doing sloppy work and making trouble. That's the story of your Army life. I gave you a million chances to prove yourself, but you just keep on messing up. I talked to you like a father to his son, and now I'm going to take some disciplinary measures. I want you to go to your bunk and get ready for a hike with a full field pack on your back. I want you to be ready in five minutes for a five-mile hike. I don't mean tomorrow—I mean now, tonight. And just to make you honest I want the lieutenant to ride alongside of you in his jeep to check the mileage. I want you to take him out the Miller Field Road, Lieutenant Samuels. I want you to check the mileage on the jeep when he starts, and when it registers five more miles, I want you to turn around and start back. And when you get back, Saunders, I want you to write my full name correctly five hundred times and turn it in to the lieutenant and he'll turn it in to me."

The lieutenant's tan face was red like ripened pomegranate. Solly felt the heat move around in his own face like something alive and on the move. But he must control himself. He must keep his mouth shut or else he would lose complete control, which is exactly what Rutherford wanted him to do. He must use his head. He must not lose his temper now. The captain was just itching to make out court-martial papers for one Corporal Solomon Saunders, Junior, and charge him with insubordination. He stared the captain full in the face and for a moment they stood looking at each other eye to eye, till the captain shifted his eyes to Samuels and back to Solly again.

Then he said smilingly to Samuels, "By the way, Lieutenant, like I said last week, I know that MP colonel in town. We play golf together. Any time you want to meet him, I'd be tickled to give you an introduction."

The room was deafening with silence for a moment. Then Rutherford said, "Do you all have any questions about this moonlight hike?"

"No, sir," Solly said.

And Lieutenant Samuels said, "None at all, sir."

"Goddammit, you all can have a real exclusive time out there in the woods. You all are such good buddies. Just talking to each other to your hearts' content. Mutinizing one another. But I want you back here and my name written five hundred times before twelve o'clock. Is that clear?"

"Very clear, sir," Solly said.

He heard Bookworm's fat feet coming up the steps and he was singing as loud as he could:

> *Solomon Saunders,*
> *Solomon Saunders,*
> *Whatcha gon do when the world's on fire?*
> *Run like hell and holler fire—*
> *Run like hell and holler fire* . . .

He stopped at the top of the stairs and shouted: "Come out of that orderly room, Solomon Saunders. You work too damn hard on Rutherford's plantation. Goddammit, this ain't slavery time—"

Suddenly you could hear the great quiet that settled over

the second-floor barracks. Everybody heard it except Bookworm Taylor.

Bookworm had almost reached the doorway of the orderly room. "Goddammit, Solly, even slaves didn't work that hard when Cap'n Charlie wasn't looking at em. Besides, the PX lady is always asking about how you getting along. She—"

He didn't get any further. Rutherford's voice interrupted him. "Come on in, Taylor, and tell us all about the old plantation."

Bookworm stopped in the doorway, looking the situation over. His mouth was open but the words got caught in a traffic jam.

Rutherford was the only one in the office with a sense of humor, with a big smile on his skinny face. "Come on in, Taylor, and tell us all about it."

The words finally tumbled out of Bookworm's mouth. "No, sir, I'm kinda—you know what I mean—I'm in a little bit of a hurry right long in here. What I mean, I got to get to my bunk and catch up on a little—"

"You hear me talking to you, don't you, soldier? I gave you an order. Come on in and tell us about the old plantation."

Bookworm's face assumed an angelic blandness. He came through the doorway. "All right, sir. If you insist. On the plantation where my great-grandfather lived, the slaves loved old master so much he was scared to be caught down amongst the slave cabins after dark by himself. Scared one of them happy slaves would grab hold of him and hug the natural breath out of him."

Ten minutes later the men straggling into H-Company barracks stopped to stare at the peculiar sight of two angry soldiers with full field equipment on their backs standing in front of the company barracks and a white-faced lieutenant in his jeep giving them the order of "forward march." And they moved away from the company area.

"Goddamn Old Rose! Wonder what Solly and Worm been up to? They musta really torn their ass." Lanky Lincoln watched them till they turned the corner and went out of sight.

"When my namesake freed the slaves, he didn't know about Rutherford's plantation, I bet a great big fat man."

CHAPTER

15

He sat wearily on his cot after mail call and just before the call for supper. He read a letter from Millie describing in detail a great show at the Stage Door Canteen. Phil Silvers was there and Mrs. Roosevelt and Paul Robeson and Bette Davis and Lena Horne, and Ella Logan sang "My Bonnie Lies over the Ocean," and Hedy Lamarr cut a giant birthday cake and kissed six GIs whose birthday it was, including a light-skin colored soldier! Millie asked Solly when he was going to Officer Candidate School. Most of the letter was about the baby and the planning for his future. Solly smiled ironically. She always spoke of him as "he," and Solly hoped sarcastically and perversely it would turn out to be a girl. "We have to start now shaping his success. He will be handsome and we must prepare now to see that he gets every opportunity and teach him to take advantage of—" The heat stood in his angry eyes. "Education—doctor—lawyer—get ahead of the other fellow—" He got to his feet and looked around him. Sweat crept over his body like soldiers on reconnaissance. He knew a choking sensation that almost took his breath away. Goddammit, let him be born first, before you start strangling the life out of him!

He sat down again and lay the letter aside and picked up a copy of Johnson Digby's newspaper, *The People's Herald,* which his mother sent him every week. He turned the pages absently. "I promise you, little buddy, whether you be a boy or girl, if I get back from this madness, nobody is going to stuff your throat with success and get-ahead-of-the-other-fellow and opportunism and money money money goddamn money and all the rest of that bourgeois shit!"

Worm sat up on his cot. "What the hell are you mumbling to yourself about? You stay in that damn orderly room too much. You flipping your lid or something?"

He looked at Worm and back to the paper.

Worm lay on his cot and closed his eyes.

Solly's eyes and mind began to focus absent-mindedly on a letter to the Editor of *The People's Herald.* But he didn't really begin to pay attention until the end of the first paragraph.

"We Negro soldiers find ourselves in hostile country in a racist-type undemocratic Army preparing ourselves to go overseas to lay down our lives in a world struggle against Racism and Fascism and for the cause of Freedom and Democracy. This is a bitter pill to swallow."

Solly smiled and he swallowed hard and his face filled up and all through his shoulders. He looked at Worm again. "Some Negroes have written a letter to *The People's Herald* just like our letter."

Worm sat up quickly and turned to Solly. "What the hell are you talking about?"

Solly began to read aloud, chills racing up and down his back like the Penn Relays.

"We are Negro enlisted men but all of our officers are white and mostly Southern and mostly rabid Negro-haters. Our company commander is Southern to the core, and also of a Nazi mentality. The one thing he *has* to give Hitler credit for is his handling of the Jews. When we Negro soldiers go into town, we suffer all manner of indignities. We are looked upon with obvious contempt by the white people in the picturesque town of Ebbensville, beaten up with impunity by Ebbensville's finest and the Military Police. Our company commander intercedes in our behalf by sending us on a ten-mile hike." His voice began to tremble now.

Worm said, "Kiss my ass in Mississippi!"

"We are voices crying out in a wilderness of hostility and

un-democracy, victims of a cruel, sadistic, perverted, and hypocritical hoax. Some of us feel that we do not need to go four or five thousand miles away to do battle with the enemies of Democracy. They are present with us here and now and spitting in our faces . . ."

"That's our letter!" Bookworm shouted.

Solly's voice became a whisper, his throat becoming thick with fear.

". . . riding on our backs and breathing down our necks. God only knows why we haven't taken matters in our own hands, or when we might—"

His body was soaking wet by now, his voice trailed off, his breathing came in big fat gulps. He looked down to the end of the letter and saw the names of

PRIV. JOSEPH TAYLOR
CPL. SOLOMON SAUNDERS, JR.
PVT. RANDOLPH P. GREER . . .

He didn't get any farther. He heard the bugles calling for mess all over the camp and felt the movement of the men hurrying across the floor of the barracks and down the stairs and the noisy metallic sound of mess gear and the thumping of his heartbeat, and—

Worm said, "Great God almighty!"

Solly's hand shook as he put the paper under his pillow and reached for his mess gear and went with Bookworm toward the stairs. He had been scared about the letters, but till now he had not really let himself look squarely at the consequences. He had made himself believe they'd been thrown into wastebaskets and ignored. He'd almost made himself believe the letters had not been written. He had dreamed the whole thing up, lying up in the post hospital.

"FALL OUT FOR MESS! FALL OUT FOR MESS!" some big-mouthed sergeant yelled from the bottom floor of the barracks.

But now at this moment he was really scared, and he was angry at his fear. Deep aching stabs of emptiness had his belly in an uproar. He wasn't hungry, he felt the violent need of a bowel movement. His chest felt like a rotten tooth was aching in it. To hell with it, he wasn't scared! Why the hell should he be scared?

After supper, which he could not eat, he and Worm went back to *The People's Herald.* In another column they read the entire story. The Reverend Johnson Digby, Junior, had taken the letter and gone straight to the War Department, demanding an investigation. He'd held a press conference and denounced the treatment of Negro soldiers, North and South. The letter as well as the Reverend's actions appeared in all of the Negro newspapers and even in a few of the white.

Solly looked up from *The People's Herald* and stared at Worm and laughed a sickly kind of laugh.

Worm said, "All we can do now, my bosom boon, is wait till the shit hits the fan."

Solly's voice was gruff and thick. "That's one thing, old buddy, and that ain't two." He hated his fear.

The next night Worm brought him a note from Fannie Mae, which said, "I must see you, Solly. Please come over to the Post Exchange." He went to see her, needing to see her, wondering what it was she wanted.

When he reached her counter she looked up at him and away, and said quickly, "Will you ride into town with me tonight? There's something I must talk to you about."

Suddenly his heart exploded in his chest.

"I can't be caught in town again without a pass." All day long he had waited for the bomb to fall. Every time Captain Rutherford came into the orderly room, Solly thought, this is it —this is it. He thought, maybe he's playing cat and mouse. He knows all about the letters. Why doesn't he say so and get the battle started? But the day had passed and nothing had happened. And now she had another kind of bomb to drop. He thought of the night they made their love together.

She looked up at his anxious guilty face again with her large wide black eyes. Her curving mouth said, "Get one then." Like a captain giving orders. "You have plenty of time. It's an hour and a half before we close."

He tried to read the message in her face. Was it more bad news she had for him? When trouble comes it stays a month of Sundays. "All right, Fannie Mae."

She said, "Thank you, Solly." And turned away from him to wait on another homesick soldier.

It took him about forty-five minutes to track down Lieutenant Samuels, who signed his pass and told him he'd better be back by reveille.

All the way into town he wanted to ask her what it was she wanted. but he was scared of her answer. It could not be what he thought it was. It couldn't be that she was pregnant. It had better not be, lover boy. She wouldn't look so happy about it, would she? And triumphant? Well, whatever it was, she would tell him when she was good and ready. Maybe she intended to wait until she got him home. And then he began to worry about her parents. Had she told them he was married? How could he face them without knowing? And if he knew they knew, he could never face them.

When they reached the colored section his stomach knew a crazy giddy kind of panic. He said, "Your mother and father—do they? I mean—how can I—?"

She laughed. "Don't worry, darling. We're going to Sally Anne's."

He said, "Oh—" And felt a great relief. But then he thought, so Sally Anne is in on it too. Why don't we just publish it in *The Black Dispatch* and let the whole world know about it?

She said, "Sallie Anne and her family are out of town for the week end. She let me use her place this evening."

He said, "Oh—" Relax, you fool, and let whatever happens happen.

When they reached Sally Anne's, she fixed knickknacks and highballs, while he sat with his neck on the block, waiting for Madame Guillotine. Fannie Mae gave him a drink and came and sat beside him on the sofa and held her own drink out to him.

"Here's to you and me and freedom."

"And to friendship." What was she so glad about? You'd think the war had ended and she was the general who had won the final victory.

She took a swallow from her drink and put the glass on the coffee table and turned to him, and he thought, here it is, and his stomach did a somersault. Here it is. And you will never be the same.

"I'm so proud I could burst wide open." Her face was so aglow with beauty it made his stomach hurt. He felt like he was sinking in a whirlpool of her beauty and he wanted to grab hold of something before it was too late. Save me from sinking down. How could she be proud she was pregnant? Maybe she thought if she were with his child, he would leave his wife and marry her. It was a hell of a bitter joke, and he laughed and she said. "What's the matter?"

He was the last of the great goddamn baby-makers.

He said, "What are you so happy about?"

She said, "I'm proud of you and Worm and all the rest of them, and especially you, because Worm told me you wrote the letter, but he didn't have to tell me. I knew it when I read it in *The Courier*. That's why I had to see you tonight, to tell you, no matter how we feel about each other, I mean even if we never see each other again, I love you and I'm proud of you."

His heart cried out for joy. He laughed and took her in his arms and forgot himself completely. His hand moved up and down her back. For a second she forgot herself and then she moved away from him.

She shook her head. "No. We're not here for that." She got up and sat in a chair.

Maybe it was the other thing after all. Maybe this was just a build-up to the corniest dialogue in the world. The oldest script. "Do me a favor," he said. "Tell me—why *are* we here?" Is this the way we build to the climax? And now—the moment of truth. And he was sweating everywhere. The Army on the one hand and Fannie Mae on the other. He'd get both hands chopped off up to his neck. All because he let his emotions get the best of him.

She laughed. "Just to talk, sweetheart. Just to make sure we remember each other as friends—deep friends." She took another swallow of her drink. "I just felt—I mean I was so proud of you—I don't know—maybe I shouldn't've bothered you about coming into town."

He said, "Is this all you really wanted?"

She said, "Yes, friendship. Is that too much to ask? Do I mean so little to you? Do you feel your time is being wasted?" He heard the war-tone in her voice.

"No—doll baby." He got up and moved toward her.

She shook her head. "Just talk. And enjoy each other's friendship for the last time. That's all." He sat back down.

She took another swallow. "I can never drink more than one of these things. I felt so proud when I read your letter in the paper. It was almost as if I had something to do with it my own self. I know she's proud of you. Mrs. Saunders. She's a great woman."

Solly poured himself another drink and took a long swig and felt it hard and deep in his stomach, thinking Millie doesn't even know it happened. She doesn't read the colored papers.

My wife. And if she did know, she would raise hell about it. She would think me stupid. And she would be absolutely right. It was stupid. I am stupid. Past present future stupid. He stared at Fannie, saying nothing.

She had finished with her first drink and poured herself another. She held it toward him. "To our everlasting friendship, darling."

"To our everlasting friendship, darling."

She said, "Ten years from now I'll be a dried-up old-maid schoolteacher."

"You'll get married," he said. "Any intelligent man in his right mind would jump at the chance to marry you."

"I don't want *any* man. There's only one man for me and he's already spoken for and taken." She put the glass to her curving mouth and took a long gulp this time and she stared at him with hatred. "You're doggone right I'll get married. Don't you patronize me, Solomon Saunders, Junior. You think you're the only pebble on the beach, you got another thought coming to you. You—" She changed moods again midstream. "Solly, I understand—it's not your fault. I don't want you to despise me. I even know why you fell in love with me. Like you say, you were lonesome and I reminded you of her. Do you have a picture of her? Am I like her in temperament? In outlook? In—in personality? Am I as militant as she is? Am I half as pretty?"

He stared at her and shook his head from side to side.

She stood up and she glared at him. "Oh—so I'm not as good as she is, am I? Is that the reason you don't love me? I'm not pretty—"

He kept shaking his head.

"You said I reminded you of her. You told me—"

He stood up. "I lied to you."

She looked up into his eyes with her wide eyes. "You lied to me?" Her curving mouth trembling.

"You are nothing like her. You remind me of everything she isn't. You're the greatest woman in the world and I'm a damn fool and I love you."

Her black eyes asked him questions he could never answer. "I don't understand."

"You're the most beautiful women in the world, the most sensible and sensitive and craziest and maddest, and I shall never forget you a single moment that I live."

She was in his arms now. She said, "Solly—Solly—Solly! Don't do this to me, Solly. I can't stand it! It isn't fair! It isn't fair! Don't be cruel to me, darling!"

He kissed her eyes, he kissed her cheek, he kissed her forever curving lips.

"Damn the fairness," he said, "and damn the Army and damn me and my ambitions and everything but you."

She pulled away from him. She said, "Wait a minute. This is not the way I wanted it. Not why I asked you to come with me tonight. Just talk and reaffirm our friendship—this is all I had in mind. Don't get any ideas." She sat again in the chair across from him.

He sank down into the sofa. She was absolutely right. "All right. Let's talk then. I, Solomon Saunders, Junior, assert and hereby affirm that I value your friendship more than any friendship in the world. You've had a profound influence on me, and I'll never be the same. You have an outlook on life I am striving to achieve. You are my alter ego. You could be really truly my better half."

She sat there staring at him, her face aglow with love and beauty and fulfillment like he was making love to her. She couldn't stand it—couldn't stand it! "Stop, Solly, stop! You don't know what you're doing to me. You're sadistic."

He came and took her in his arms. She said, "No! I don't want your arms around me. You're mean and heartless and a liar just to have your way with me this time like the other time, I know you now. You mean nothing you say. You want to make a fool of me—" A hemorrhage of words flooding from her now.

He shouted, "Stop!"

She said, "I love you. Do you love me?"

"Yes! Yes! Yes! It gets us nowhere, but I love you."

He kissed her eyes her cheeks she went to pieces in his arms. He kissed her nose her open mouth eager for his kisses. "Be tender with me, Solly. Have mercy on me. With you I have no defenses."

"You can't mean that. Not you." She mustn't mean it.

"Yes, my darling. It's true, absolutely true. Everything else is false and phony."

He was speechless. She said, "And do you truly love me?"

"Yes! Yes!"

"Spare me this time. Let me go. Let's just talk and swear our friendship."

He said, "All right." And they sat down on the sofa together.

She said, "I have to get myself together. I shouldn't've taken the second drink. I'm not used to it." She picked up his glass and took a swallow. "The thing is, darling, don't ever let them get you down. Whatever happens as a consequence of the letter. This is what I really wanted to say, because I know there will be repercussions. Whatever happens, don't ever have any regrets about it. It was your real self, the truth of you, the deep things in you coming to the surface. It was the you of you. It was the you I always saw in you. That's why I love you and I'll always love you. Not just because you're beautiful. But because you demand your dignity and manhood. Manhood is more important than money or promotions. Please remember. Never sacrifice your manhood—never sacrifice your manhood. The one thing they will not stand for is for a black man to be a man. And everything else is worthless if a man can't be a man. My father has been principal of the public school for twenty years, but to any no-account cracker he is still a boy. They can insult your women in front of your face, and you either grin or hang your head or lose your life."

He tried to take her in his arms again, and she said shakily, "No—no." Then she said, "All right, one kiss then. Just one—"

And they kissed and she trembled and felt sweet delicious rivulets run all over her and drip from the middle of her like heated vapor cooling. She must be strong. She must not get confused or him confused. She moved away.

She said, "Maybe when you come back, if you still love me, I mean if you don't really love your wife—I mean a divorce—I mean, why shouldn't you?" She hated him for making her say it.

He was shaking his head. She said, "You're right. I have no pride. I should have waited for you to suggest it, if you wanted to, and besides, I wouldn't do it anyhow. I couldn't base my happiness on another woman's misery. But if you're ever without a wife—I mean—no, forget about it."

He said, "My wife is going to have a baby."

She looked into his eyes with her wide black troubled ones and the bright glow dying in them. He said, "All I can say is I love you and I'll always love you."

She almost lost her voice. "All right then." I won't cry. I will not cry. I must not cry. She felt the world move out from under her, and she reached desperately for him and he took her and he kissed her and her arms went up around his neck and her open mouth wet against his open mouth and she strained her entire body for him and felt like she was falling from the peak of some high mountaintop, and she felt like screaming: Save me, Solly! Save me! But she did not really want him to save her. Maybe just this time if she gave herself to him and let it never be again. She was burning up with wanting him.

She said, "Just this one time, darling. I mean just this one kiss. Nothing more." And she kissed him one more time and she moved away from him and straightened her dress and wiped her eyes.

She said speaking firmly now, "I'm strong now, Solly darling, and it's time for us to go."

He said, "It's early."

She said. "No—no—no—it's much too late."

CHAPTER

16

A few days later the regimental commander sent for Captain Rutherford.

The captain—every inch a soldier, all seventy-six inches and a half of him—strode across regimental headquarters to the colonel's private office. A tan-faced tech sergeant came out of the office.

"Go right in, Captain, sir. The colonel's expecting you."

Captain Rutherford hitched up his trousers with his elbows and walked through the door and closed it behind him. He sized up the situation with a quick glance. The colonel was seated behind his desk. The battalion commander, Major Davidson, was seated on one side of the desk and Captain Murdock, the regimental adjutant, was seated on the other. It must be something damn important! He almost smiled. But he was too much of a soldier to show his emotions. He saluted the colonel smartly.

"Have a seat, Captain," the Colonel said, and motioned to a chair in front of the desk.

The captain said, "Yes, sir," and sat down with a prideful dignity and looked the colonel in the face and glanced at the major and then at the captain and back to the colonel. It was one thing about his own make-up that really annoyed him—his eyes were always fidgety. Always had been. Almost anybody could outstare him, especially Colonel Spiggel-miser.

The colonel was a relaxed-faced well-fed man of about fifty years and of strong and medium proportions. Life was a stage and he seemed bored with the whole damn show. But Rutherford read an excitement in the colonel's expression which was unfamiliar, and he smiled deeply inside of himself. This must be damned important!

The colonel said, "How's H Company, Captain? Or is it Hell Company?" The colonel laughed a short dry laugh, which was like anybody else howling with laughter, Captain Rutherford thought.

"Just fine, sir. Couldn't be much better. Except that we're always working for perfection. That's our motto."

"And the morale of the men?"

"The best, sir. The very best. Best morale in the whole regiment." He glanced at Major Davidson's face, dark and brooding. That was the way with these New York Jews. Sly and not to be trusted and you could never read their faces. "I don't like to sound immodest, Colonel. The major can speak more objectively."

The major cleared his throat and spoke in a flat voice. "The captain has some very capable men in his company. His company clerk is one of the best in Camp Johnson Henry. And H Company also has the best motor-pool record in the battalion."

Captain Murdock coughed. He was an All-American boy, blond and clean-faced and blue-eyed and crew-cut and perfectly and precisely chiseled and looked just like a goddamn German to Captain Charlie Rutherford. "Best motor pool in the whole Fifty-fifth," Murdock said. "But you've been falling down in that department ever since you broke Sergeant Greer."

The Colonel leaned back in his chair and the springs squeaked and he leaned forward again. "Any troublemakers in the outfit? Any agitators? Any Communists?"

"No, sir. And nobody would listen to them if we did have one or two. We pride ourselves in our *esprit de corps*."

The colonel stared at Rutherford long and hard, as if he didn't believe what his ears heard or his eyes beheld, and a sudden warmth began to collect on the captain's neck and a redness moved into his face.

"You have an extraordinary outfit," the colonel said.

The captain said quietly, "Yes, sir. Thank you, sir."

The colonel said, "H Company has become famous without firing a shot. Haven't even been on the rifle range yet. Getting more publicity than Carlson's Raiders."

"We're due for the rifle range Monday after next, sir, and I have no doubt, sir, the men will make a name for themselves."

The colonel stared at him. "*You have no doubt*," he repeated after Rutherford slowly and quietly. "Do you know what the NAACP is, Captain?"

Rutherford pondered the question and debated his answer. If he answered in the affirmative the colonel might ask him for a definition. You couldn't trust Colonel Spiggel-miser. He was almost like a Jew. So he played it straight and said, "No, sir."

Well, you should. Every officer with colored troops should know about the NAACP. It's worse than the labor unions."

He almost lost his voice. "Yes, sir."

"Do you read the newspaper, Captain?"

"Yes, sir."

"Are you aware of this little tidbit in *The Afro-American*?" He picked up the paper from his desk and shoved it under the captain's nose and Rutherford broke out in a cool dampish sweat. He took the paper and stared at it and looked around at the adjutant and the major and back to the colonel.

The colonel said, "Direct your attention, if you please, to the little item in the center of the page regarding that famous outfit with the most outstanding *esprit de corps* and the greatest morale, to wit, Company H of the Fifty-fifth Quartermaster Regiment. Better known as Hell Company, on Captain Rutherford's old plantation."

Captain Rutherford was reading and sweating and changing colors like a chameleon. He finished the story but could not lift his eyes from the page to face the angry stare of Colonel Spiggel-miser. His mind went blank. He started to reread the story and his gaze wandered to another story entirely unrelated.

The colonel's voice blasted the agonizing quiet. "I think even you've digested the story by now, Captain."

The captain opened his little mouth but the words did not come easy now. Finally he said in a sickly voice, "Yes, sir."

The colonel said, "Of all the irresponsible unmitigated hypocritical liars I have ever met in my entire life, you undoubtedly take the cake."

"But, sir—"

"Do you take the important question of morale so lightly, Captain?"

"No, sir, but—"

"Here your men are two or three minutes away from mutiny, and you look me squarely in the face and tell me they have the greatest morale in the world. Of all the gall—" The colonel was working himself into a small volcano. His face was red and apoplectic. "I have a letter here from the War Department countersigned by the post commander calling our kind attention to the incredible morale of your outfit. It seems your men had such tremendous morale they wanted to tell the world about it, including the colored papers and the NAACP and the President of the United States."

"Sir, I think I can explain—"

"I've had enough of your explanations for one day, Rutherford. But don't worry. Your day will come again and damn quick. Meanwhile you get down to that outfit and get yourself some explanations. If there is an investigation by the War Department there's going to be hell to pay. I have to see the base commander at eleven-thirty. Now get down there and get to the bottom of things and damn quick. I want you back up here at thirteen hundred on the dot."

The captain jumped to his feet and saluted the colonel "Yes, sir!"

The colonel said, "Dismissed!"

Rutherford, carrying the newspaper, turned and went hurriedly out of the colonel's office and literally ran out of the headquarters building and jumped into his jeep and almost ran down everybody in his way, turning corners on two wheels in clouds of red dust, till he got to the company and jumped out of the jeep and long-legged it upstairs four steps at a time and strode into the orderly room, where Sergeant Anderson sat peaceably with his feet on the desk.

"Goddammit, Sergeant, look lively! Where the hell is Saunders?"

The sergeant jumped to his feet. "What's the matter, Captain Rutherford?"

"I asked you where the hell is Saunders?"

"He—he's down to battalion, tending to something or other."

"Something or other?" the captain shouted. "In the future

you're to know every time he moves out of this office exactly where he's going. Is that clear?"

"Yes, sir."

He threw *The Afro-American* newspaper on the desk in front of Anderson. "Here," the captain said. "Here, I want every one of these soldiers whose names are signed to this letter to report to my office in five minutes, including you, Sergeant Anderson. And I don't give a damn where they are or what they're doing!" The captain's long frame was shaking with anger.

"Wha-what's the matter, Captain?"

"You can read, can't you, Sergeant? I said I wanted every one of them and I want em right away, and I don't care how you get em in here, just so you do it in five damn minutes."

It took twelve minutes to round them up.

They sat there glancing nervously at one another. Topkick, Saunders, Bookworm Taylor, Baker, Lincoln, Moore, and Greer. Solly cleared his throat against his will. The captain's face had turned so white, it didn't seem to have any color at all. Rutherford stood up and hitched his trousers. He picked up *The Afro-American* newspaper and hit it with the back of his long skinny hand and he opened his mouth to talk but his tongue was tied momentarily. He put the paper back on his desk. Solly stared into space like the rest of the men and he heard the cadenced footsteps of a company of soldiers marching down on the company street below, and the shouted commands: "BY THE RIGHT FLANK MARCH! BY THE LEFT FLANK MARCH!" He could even hear the rhythmic rustle of their OD trousers. And it was so quiet in the captain's office he could hear a soft breeze roaring past his ears like listening to a seashell and at the same time there was no breeze blowing at all in the hot stuffy office, which was getting hotter and ready to blow apart any minute, the tension expanding expanding expanding . . .

The captain suddenly slapped his desk with all his might and a couple of the nervous soldiers jumped. "Goddammit, I'm getting damn sick and tired of all this plotting and scheming behind my back! And I'm going to get to the bottom of it this morning if I have to burn every damn last one of you. I'm going to find out what's behind it, too and who's behind it. Every time I go up to headquarters I catch hell about something H Company's done." He paused and looked from face to face. "All right now, what you boys got to say for yourself?"

Nobody spoke or even moved or even glanced or even

blinked or even breathed. The captain stood tall and lean and mean. He hitched his trousers and pulled an olive-drab handkerchief out of his pocket and wiped his face. "What happened to y'all tongues all of a sudden?" he demanded. "All this bitching behind my back and now you suddenly catch the lockjaw." He looked from one to the other of them, his high-pitched voice getting higher and higher. "What about you, Sergeant Anderson? What do you know about all this mess?"

The Topkick cleared his throat and his voice came out of it clear and clean. "I don't know what you're talking about, Captain Rutherford. I don't know what this is all about."

The captain spoke more softly now. "Now looka here, Topkick." He did not usually call him Topkick. "I ain't blaming you for all this mess. You're my first sergeant and I know you're loyal. If you been duped or misled or whatever you might want to call it, we want to know about it. That's the only way we can get to the bottom of this business. It's an awful mess, Sergeant, but me and you can straighten it out. We come from the same State and I know we can get along. And I know you want to do what's right. Now isn't that the truth?"

Solly listened harder than ever before but he didn't want to hear. He was afraid of what the Topkick's answer would be. Don't do it, Topkick!

The Topkick answered the company commander. "I really want to do what's right, Captain Rutherford. I always try to do the right thing."

Solly closed his eyes and wished for something to stuff up his ears. His respect for the Topkick was in serious jeopardy.

"All right then, Sergeant. Open up. Who're the trouble makers around here? Who're the letter writers? Who's doing all this plotting against the United States Army in time of war?"

Perspiration crawled all over Solly. Maybe I should tell the captain I'm the guilty one. Tell him I did it when I first went into the hospital.

"What plotting are you talking about, Captain, sir?" The sergeant's voice was soft and earnest.

Right after the beating, when I wasn't all there. That's when I wrote the letters, sir! Tell him—tell him. Tell the captain.

"Sergeant, don't I try to be a good commanding officer? Don't I try to do what I think is best for the men?"

Tell him I was sorry immediately afterward but it was too late then.

The sergeant cleared his throat again. "Yes, sir."

I was out of my head from the beating, or I never would have done it. It's all my fault, sir.

"Sergeant, you're a good man and I don't want you messed up in this business. It's real serious business too. This—this—this Communist plotting against the government of the United States at a time when our very life as a free nation is in danger. You understand that, don't you, Sergeant?"

Follow your head now, Solly Saunders. Don't let your feelings lead you wrong. Plead guilty, and throw yourself on the mercy of the court.

The serious faces became more serious and the men were worried now even more than before, and the captain's office got hotter and hotter. Solly smelled the awful heat in the room. He smelled the fear, including his own, even as he told himself he was not afraid. He was glad he'd written the letters, he told himself. He was glad.

"I understand, Captain, sir," the sergeant said.

"I told you once, Sergeant," the captain continued, his voice hardening. "I told you I didn't believe you had anything to do with the plot, but the only way you can make me absolutely sure of it, so I can stand up and testify in your behalf at the court-martial—the only way is to come clean. Tell me who was back of it. Tell me who duped you, who misled you."

"I don't know what you're talking about, Captain, sir," the sergeant repeated.

"Sergeant Anderson, I'm talking about all this goddamn N-A-C-P business—this—this—these letters to the colored newspapers—" He stirred up the papers on his desk. "This letter to the War Department—this letter to the goddamn President of the United States. What about it, Sergeant?"

"What about what? Sir?" he added.

"Who started this whole thing?"

"I haven't the slightest notion."

"Whose idea was it to send letters to the newspapers?"

"I do not know."

"You signed it, didn't you? Or did somebody forge your name?"

"I signed it my own self," the sergeant said with a tremble in his voice.

"I'm trying to help you, boy, cause we from the same State

and I know you didn't know what it was all about. But first you got to help your own self, and so far you haven't given me any co-operation at all."

The sergeant's silence rang in the room.

"This is serious business, Sergeant. This is conspiracy against the government of the United States. You aren't letting me help you, boy. You're tying my hands."

Use your head, Solomon Saunders. Outsmart the Texas peckerwood. Cop a plea of guilty and throw yourself upon the tender mercy of the court. With all the captain's Southern prejudices, he likes you in his own way, even though you despise the bastard. He wants to be your Great White Father.

He hated the thoughts he heard in his head, but they were there pleading their case, demanding to be heard.

The sergeant was silent and Solly could hear his own heart beating and he also heard the footsteps of some soldiers coming up the stairs to the second floor, and heard a jeep speeding past downstairs on the dusty street and somebody gunning its noisy motor. And smelled the stifling odor in the room of heat and fear and anger and felt the fire building in his stomach.

"What about the rest of you boys?" Captain Rutherford demanded. Nobody answered, and Solly was so nervous he could not have moved even if he had wanted to.

"What about you, Greer? I'm trying to help you."

The ex-motor sergeant stared at the captain with a scowl on his face. "Just like you helped me when them MPs beat me over in Ebbensville."

"How about you, Lincoln? You want to talk?" No answer—and Solly was sweating all over now and churning buttermilk in his stomach. Now is the time, he told himself. Now! If you have any guts you'll do it now. Outsmart the bastard!

"You, Taylor?"

Tell him you were not responsible at the time.

"I got nothing to say, Captain."

He turned to Solly, his small eyes aflame with anger. Solly looked up and stared at the captain and stared through him as if he didn't exist at all. He thought of Fannie Mae in the profoundest place where he was. Have no regrets she told him. But— And he looked like the calmest soldier in the world, but the perspiration all over his body and the fire in his boiling stomach and the aching in his buttocks told an altogether different story. He was scared. He felt her all around him, heard her tell him she was proud. And he was scared.

"How about you, Corporal? I even want to try to save your skin if I can."

Cop that plea now. Do it! Do it! It'll get all the others off the spot. They'll understand you did it just to get them off the spot. You'll be a hero. And yet he heard himself say calmly: "I cannot help you, Captain Rutherford."

"I know you're one of the ringleaders, Saunders. I've had my eyes on you ever since you came into the company. You been agitating like a goddamn Communist! And I'm gonna get every last one of you. I tried to be decent with *you,* particularly, I gave you the benefit of every doubt, cause you were educated and I thought you were different, but now I know don't any of you appreciate decent treatment. Education can't work magic with your kind. All of you're going to face a general court-martial for plotting against the government of the United States. Holding it up to ridicule before the whole damn world. Giving comfort to the enemy. I'll get every one of you shot at sunrise. This is war, goddamn you!"

Thank you, Fannie Mae. I feel much better, thank you.

"Just a minute, Captain!" Bucket-head shouted. "I ain't in this mess, I ain't in this mess at all. You ain't asked me yet. You ain't asked me nothing!"

"Well—?" the captain said, turning to Baker.

"Don't worry about a general court-martial," Solly heard himself tell Baker quietly. "The captain is just trying to scare us. He doesn't want you to be a man. Don't be his stoolie. Writing letters is not a crime."

"Shut your mouth, Saunders!"

"I don't know anything about nothing, Captain, please, sir. I wasn't in it at all." Baker got up and walked around shaking his big head.

"How do I know you're not lying through your teeth like the rest of these boys?"

Baker stood still. "No, sir. I wouldn't lie to you and I don't want to get into no trouble. I didn't know what I was signing. I just thought I—I—I don't rightly know what I thought. Maybe I thought it was the Guard Duty Roster." Solly thought any minute Bucket-head will fall on his knees in front of the tall cracker captain and maybe kiss his officer's shoes.

"Who gave it to you?"

"Corporal Solomon, please, sir. Or maybe Joe Taylor. I'm so nervous and upset I don't hardly know what I'm saying."

"Maybe it was both of them?" Captain Rutherford urged.

"Maybe it was, sir. Maybe it was?"

"Will you testify at the court-martial that these men concocted the whole scheme against the Army and the government?"

"I—I—I don't know about all that, sir. I don't want to testify at no court-martial. No, sir."

"Listen, Baker, I'm not going to stand for no crapping around. You either are or you aren't—understand? You either testify or face general court-martial along with the rest. That goes for you and the Topkick and Saunders and every last one of you."

"Yes, sir!" Bucket-head Baker said, shaking his big sweaty handsome head. "I'll testify. You don't have to worry about a thing, Captain, sir."

"I'm not worried," the captain said. "If you get up there and tell everything you know, *you* won't have to worry. And you, Sergeant Anderson?" He was eager for the Topkick to be on his side.

"I reckin I'm just as guilty as my company clerk, sir. I don't see where we did anything wrong anyhow. And furthermore I ain't no stool pigeon. I ain't never been and ain't gonna start now."

"Don't be no hero, Sergeant. Don't be a fall guy for a couple of no-good New York Communists."

"I ain't no hero, Captain Rutherford. But the way I look at it, if it comes to that, I'd rather be a hero or a Communist or whatever you want to call me, than be an uncle tom. I'm a first sergeant and that don't mean stooling on my men."

The captain turned back to Bucket-head Baker. "All right, Baker who told you to sign the letter?"

Baker looked furiously down at the floor. "The Bookworm," he mumbled.

"Who? Speak up, boy."

"Private Taylor, sir."

"Whose idea was it in the first place, Baker?"

"Sir?"

"You heard me."

"Corporal Saunders, sir."

Solly got to his feet, his intentions not entirely clear to him. But his feelings and his thinking were somehow co-ordinated.

The captain said, "Sit down, Saunders."

Solly said, "I can't stand much more of this, sir—"

The captain shouted, "Sit down! Do you hear me? You goddamn stinking Communist! Don't you hear an officer talking to you?"

"I am not going to sit here and watch you degrade a man—break his morale—make a man like Baker lose all of his self-respect." His voice was trembling. He stared at the red-faced apoplectic cracker and turned to go.

"I warn you, Saunders, if you leave this room, you'll be sorry. I'll throw the book at you, goddamn your black ungrateful soul!"

Solly turned toward the captain. But there was no turning back now. He was scared and soaking all over and nervous in the middle, and he saw the walls of Scotty's stockade closing in on him, and the Federal Penitentiary and a dishonorable discharge, but he had started and he would not turn back. And in a way he was glad the letters had brought things to a head. He was scared to death and glad. "You may do anything you think you're big and white enough to do, sir, but you're going to have a fight every step of the way." He watched himself wade further and further out into the angry ocean and at any minute it would be over his head. "All the way to Washington, and I'm not going to forget that you goddamned the President of the United States, the commander-in-chief, and you called Private Scott a goddamn nigger and you goddamned my black soul, and committed other acts unbecoming a commissioned officer of the United States Army, and my fondest hope is to meet you one day somewhere anywhere without those two bars you're hiding behind." Solly turned to leave again. He was trembling with rage.

The captain was speechless like everybody else. Before Solly reached the door, the first sergeant jumped up. "That isn't the way to do it, Corporal. Ain't no need of being foolish. Don't leave until it's over. We're all in this together."

Solly stared at the Topkick, the perspiration settling angrily into his eyebrows and over his forehead. He had let his emotions run away from him again instead of using his intellect. He'd let the captain make him blow his top. But the taste in his mouth was good to him. He was scared down in his stomach but he felt good up in his chest.

"You *better* talk to him, Sergeant," the captain said. "He's been listening to the New York lawyer. He's the one that got him in this mess."

"Nobody got me into a single thing, Captain Rutherford. Let us get clear on that. Whatever I did I'm man enough to stand by." That much was clean and clear to Solly. Manhood was important to him. He had not really lost his temper. His intelligence and his feelings were in close collaboration this time. Yes. Yes.

"Then you admit—?"

"I admit nothing. I merely said whatever I do, I do of my own free will and intelligence. Nobody masterminds me. I do my own thinking. I am my own counsel."

"You don't have to admit it," Rutherford said. "I know everything. I know all about it. I know about you and the lieutenant raising all that hell in town. I know about you attacking the colonel. I know who started all this NAACP mess here in the company, and I'm going to throw the damn book at every last one of you." He paused as if he had been running up a long steep hill and was out of breath. "And especially you—especially you!" He pulled his trousers up with his elbows. "And that ain't no threat, boy. That's a promise." He took all of them in with a sweeping glance full of scorn and hatred. The veins in his forehead seemed to be moving and breathing and pushing against the skin drawn tighter than a trap drum. He calmed himself. "I'm giving each and every one of you one last clear chance. Who wants to talk?"

The battle still raged inside of Solly. One last clear chance to cop a plea and save your ass and take the blame and alibi and be a hero. He opened his mouth but the words wouldn't come.

"I'm listening, boys."

He heard somebody breathing hard.

Bucket-head cleared his itchy throat.

CHAPTER

17

For the next few days nothing happened, except that a couple of nights later, Solly and Worm were seated in the orderly room Bee-Essing, when Bucket-head Baker came in from town and signed in for the night. Solly and Bookworm didn't say a word to Bucket-head. Baker checked in, then stood for a moment listening to Solly and Bookworm. He smiled good-naturedly and cleared his throat.

"Goddammit, why in the hell don't you two studs get off your dead asses and go into town sometimes and get your axles greased?"

"I mean I go for that Double-V-for-Victory jive," Worm said to Solly. "Especially against the Georgia peckerwoods."

Bucket-head laughed. "Boy, I did a mean wiggle with that broad tonight. You cats should have heard her groaning and grunting and calling my name. She can do more with a dick than a monkey with a peanut. Oooh goddamn!"

"I like *Mrs.* Roosevelt all right, you understand," Worm said, "but then when you take in consideration these Southern

Democrats, how can you go for the Democrat Party? I mean I'm a F.D.R. man, but them Southern Democrats got to go."

Solly said, "That's exactly what I was telling my Great White Buddy the other night."

"I thought about you when I was grinding, you fat-ass mother-huncher." Baker laughed again.

Solly looked up quickly. "What did you call me?"

The smile left Bucket-head's wide handsome face. "What you mean?" he asked.

Solly was standing now. "I say what did you call me?" All the happenings of the last months building in him like the flood tide.

"I said you cats ought to get into town one of these evenings."

"That's not what I'm asking you, man. I asked you what did you call me. You know what I'm talking about. You *are* a goddamn fool but you aren't crazy."

Baker laughed again uneasily. "I said I thought about you, you fat-ass mother-huncher—but I was talking to the Bookworm—"

He didn't get it out of his mouth before Solly's fist was in his mouth and Solly swarmed all over him. "Don't call me no mother-fucker, you handkerchief-head bastard!" Solly was as much taken by surprise as was Bucket-head, because he knew Baker had been addressing Bookworm. The realization made no difference. He was wild with rage. He clipped the big-headed soldier going and coming, as they battled all over the orderly room, knocking over chairs and tables, and Bucket-head picked up a chair and waved it over his head at Solly, blood streaming from Bucket-head's mouth and nostrils. "You better tell your buddy something," he pleaded to the Bookworm. "I'll break his goddamn neck—I'll kill him!" Solly moved in and threw his right fist at Bucket-head's big head as he swung the chair. He connected first and it sounded like something cracked, and the chair struck him a glancing blow on his neck and shoulder, and he went temporarily insane, it seemed. He hit the big-head soldier from every direction and went out of the door on top of his chest and combed him up and down, tears of unimaginable anger spilling down Solly's face as he worked him over. He battled Bucket-head all the way down the stairs, and halfway down, Bucket-head grabbed him in self-defense and they began to wrestle, and they stumbled and fell and rolled the rest of the way down the steep steps. And Worm ran down after them and soldiers came running from upstairs and down. "Kill that bucket-head sonofabitch!"

By the time Worm reached the bottom of the stairs, Bucket-head was getting up off the floor and Solly was lying there as still as death.

Bucket-head backed away from him. "I told that crazy mother-huncher to stop messing with me." Crying like a baby and his nostrils running and shaking all over.

"Somebody get the doctor!"

"He's dead already!"

Worm knelt over Solly and took Solly's wrist and couldn't feel anything happening at all. God have mercy! It had happened so quickly, but he could have stopped them if he really had wanted to badly enough. He took Solly's other wrist, and he thought he felt something happening, but he couldn't be sure that it wasn't his own heart pumping overtime. Somebody ran into the latrine and came out again with a bucket of water, and before Worm could say, "Hold it a second," or even think about it, the soldier dashed the whole bucketful, some of it on the Bookworm, the rest in Solly's sleeping face. Worm jumped and cursed.

"His eyes are opening!" one soldier shouted.

Worm looked back at Solly and Solly stirred and his eyes were open and blinking.

"Solly!" Worm cried.

Solly moved around and tried to sit up and Worm helped him gently. "What's going on here?" Solly finally asked.

"You're okay, Solly. Just take it easy. Your head hit the bottom step pretty hard."

"Where's that stool-pigeon?"

"Take it easy, Solly."

Solly pushed Worm away, struggled to his feet, and looked around him. "Turn me aloose, goddammit!" He staggered and swayed from side to side. "Where is he?"

Worm took hold of him again to keep him from falling, but Solly finally located Bucket-head and tried to pull away from Bookworm. "Turn me aloose, goddammit!"

Bucket-head trembling and crying and sucking his nose and backing away. He said, "You better talk to him. You better tell that crazy nigger something. I don't wanna have to kill him —I don't wanna—"

Solly wrested himself away from Bookworm and in the same motion made a lunge for Bucket-head, and Bucket-head broke out of the door and ran out into the chilly night. Before Solly could catch up with him he was long gone. Solly sat on the stoop in the cool night air. "I'll get that bastard if it's the last damn thing I do." He shook his head from side to side. He felt high as a Georgia pine. He touched the lump on the back of his head. Worm and Lanky took him upstairs and gave him some smelling salts and put some medication on the lump on his head that was growing by the second and put him to bed.

"You better get on sick call in the morning," Worm said, "and get a good examination."

"You're my cut-buddy, buddy," Solly said drunkenly. "My real bosom boon buddy-buddy."

Bookworm laughed. "If I'm not, I'll have to do till the real thing comes along."

CHAPTER

18

A few days later Captain Rutherford had them gather in his office again. He stood behind the desk with a beaming smile on his face. There were two additions to the gathering—Buck Rogers and Staff Sergeant Perry, the don't-give-a-damn mess sergeant.

He looked at them from face to anxious worried face. The air was close, the men were tense. "I got a little surprise for y'all. A nice little surprise. I think y'all gon like it."

Solly didn't look around but it sounded like the first sergeant clearing his throat.

"There's a cadre being made up to form a new regiment." He looked from face to face again.

Solly wasn't sure how to take the news. His stomach started acting up. Everything happened in his stomach.

"I'm recommending every last one of you to go out on the cadre. Every outfit in the Fifty-fifth is required to send eight men as cadre to form the basis of new companies in a brand-new special regiment being formed. You'll be leaving Camp Johnson Henry in the next few days." The captain was having himself a ball.

A wild thought started in Solly's mind and created a hope that made his heart beat fast and crazy. They would be heading North! And he would see Millie after all. . . .

"What you think of that, Corporal Saunders? Instead of a court-martial, I'm giving you a free train trip. You'll be leaving the dear old Southland."

To hell with Captain Charlie and Sam's Army, is what he thought, but he looked blank-faced at the captain and said, "Yes, sir." Whatever that meant. He already saw himself back at Dix, hitchhiking a ride to Trenton, or maybe all the way to the City—and Millie and Millie and Millie—and Mama too—and the theater with its long lines of soldiers not allowed to stand in the line ("Go right in, sir")—and the ride on the ferry to Staten Island, the subway, the elevated, the museum at Eighty-first Street—and the Savoy—and alone with Millie and the baby in her belly in the dark in the warm friendly darkness and in Millie's warm bed in her warm tender arms in her warm soft golden with-child body. He would miss Fannie Mae—that was the big knot in his chest now. He knew he would always miss her. She would always be a fullness in his face, a warmth in his shoulders. She would always be.

He heard the captain invading his dream with hand grenades. "Where you're going there's warm weather the year round. You won't be needing much winter equipment. And you won't be in California long anyhow. After a couple of months—probably not that long—you'll be bound for overseas and dying for your country. See how good I am to my bad boys?"

California was a million miles the other side of Nowhere. A chill moved over Solly's shoulders, and he stared at the smiling captain, and he knew an overwhelming sensation of helpless rage. And he understood what had happened. The brass had somehow managed to kill the story and avoid a court-martial, because, once it had gotten underway, heads might have rolled all along the line, even one or two among the brass. Even Captain Rutherford's little head. This way only colored heads would be offered for the sacrifice.

He vaguely heard the captain talking. "We're going to send eleven men from H Company. We're going to be very generous—L Company will only have to send five."

"Why you sending me with the rest of them?" Baker asked. "I been a good soldier."

"A cadre is made of two kinds of soldiers," the captain said.

"Number one—it's made up of fuck-ups and sad sacks like most of you soldiers—I'm not saying which. But you always have to throw in a couple of good ones in the lot to give it some kind of balance. After all, a cadre is supposed to be made up of top men. They supposed to give leadership and training to new recruits coming into the Army."

Solly almost said aloud, "The colored heads are on the block." He almost felt sorry for Bucket-head Baker.

He heard the captain like off in a distance. "Lieutenant Samuels is accompanying the cadre. I hope he likes the idea—he loves you boys so much. It woulda been a shame to leave him behind. And I'm going to get Scott out of the stockade to go along with you, to make sure you get some good home cooking." He laughed. "This is a whole heap better than court-martial, isn't it, Saunders?"

It was a victory for Rutherford all the way. That's what Samuels got for trying to pass for colored.

The next few days Camp Johnson Henry was a madder madhouse than ever to the ten cadre men of Hell Company and their somber-faced lieutenant. The eleventh man was Jim Larker of the Tenth Engineers. He got his CO to transfer him to H Company with the understanding that Rutherford would send him out on cadre. Larker was the pretty-faced boy who'd stepped out of line with Solly at the Ebbensville bus station. Solly and Jimmy had visited each other a couple of times since Solly came out of the hospital. They had hit it off with one another. The only trouble was, Jimmy was much too idealistic for Solly's present frame of mind. But they were buddies, and he was glad for Jim to come along to California.

It was almost like when they first came into the Army, with the shots-in-the-arms and the Short-arm Inspections and Show-down Inspections, two and three times a day, and Dental Inspections. A latrine rumor got started that they were being readied to be shipped overseas and directly to the front. Solly wouldn't put it past them. He thought very seriously about becoming a conscientious objector, but it was too late for that. The thought even entered his head to desert, but he was not a deserter, and he could never desert. He would go to California precisely as the other men were going to do, and spend a few days or weeks or months of training—special training, the captain said on the day following the initial announcement—and just like the others he would go overseas to God-knows-where, where civilized people were killing each other by the thousands every day.

One day over at the base hospital all of the men from all of the cadres from all of the companies in the regiment were standing in a poorly ventilated room in their birthday suits, with raincoats thrown around their shoulders for the sake of modesty and rubber boots on their feet for whatever reason. Bookworm said to Solly, "Let me out of this funky place before I suffocate." Solly told him, "This is a gas drill, buddy boy. Might as well die here as in the trenches." The medics came in and one of them, a major, told them, "Don't be bashful, men. Pull off your raincoats. Let's see what you're hiding." Some of the men chuckled nervously, they were all uneasy. When the major got to Buck Rogers he looked Buck up and down and sideways, as bashful Buck stood stiffly at attention, as naked as he came into the world. The major said, "All right, soldier, bend over and spread your cheeks." Buck said, "Yes, sir!" And he bent forward and made a perfect right angle from the waist and placed the middle fingers of both hands into his mouth and pulled it back almost up to his ears. Through the howling laughter of the cadre men you could hear the major. "No, no, soldier, I'm not the dentist. I'm strictly a back-door man."

After lunch, back to the hospital and the dental clinic. It was like climbing into an electric chair. Solly sat in a chair next to Bookworm. The dentist, a middle-aging gray-haired lieutenant, told Worm to open his mouth wide. Worm complied.

"Wider—" the lieutenant urged.

Worm said, "How's that?"

"Wider, a little wider."

Worm widened his mouth a little wider.

"You can do better than that," the lieutenant said. "Wider, boy."

Worm threw away his fear and caution and gave it all he had and stretched his mouth from ear to ear, and something went click like a purse snapping shut and Worm tried to close his mouth and couldn't, his jaws had unhinged, and he yelled bloody murder and grabbed one of the sharp dental instruments and went for the lieutenant, who danced quickly out of Worm's reach. It took five men to hold Worm down while the dentist put his jaws in line again. When Worm left the hospital his head was so bound with bandages, the men in the company thought he had been hit by an Army truck.

All during this time Captain Rutherford was in the best of spirits, pink-faced and smiling all of the time, and every time he met Solly in the office, on the stairs or the company street, he had something pleasant to say like, "I just know you and Lieutenant Samuels are just tickled to death to be leaving dear old Dixieland."

Two days later they left the regimental area in two-and-a-half-ton Army trucks with bags and baggage, along with cadre from the other companies, and went to the post railhead to be shipped across the country to California. They boarded the train and after an hour and a half of now-we're-leaving and not-yet-a-while, they finally pulled out of Camp Johnson Henry. They went through Ebbensville and Solly felt a pain tear into his stomach and move upwards through his body his chest and into his throat; he could not keep the image of Fannie Mae away from the eyes of his mind, nor could he get her out of his guts, and she seemed to be all inside of him and all around him, and he was a fool to feel this way, it was over and done with, he was a married man, and it was all over and done with, and in a few days he would be three thousand miles away and in a few months maybe six or seven thousand miles away, and he would never see Fannie Mae Branton again, and it was the best thing for all concerned. She would forget and he would forget, but it was easier said than done. He felt he was leaving an important part of himself in this little Southern town, but he was taking something with him he had never had before. So much had happened.

He was so different from the man he was four months ago. He had lived a thousand years since then. He had died a thousand times. He felt he'd been like an innocent virgin when he came into the service, and the Army had brutishly raped him of his youth, his faith, his idealism. His great ambition. He'd never believe in anything again. Never ever. He was old and disillusioned. He would never dream again. Millie was wonderful and loved him, but she did not know the Army. He thought of Fannie Mae again and thought his eyes were getting wet, and he had to get away from Worm and his yackety-yack that went on and on and everlastingly on. He'd never known anyone like Fannie Mae before Camp Johnson Henry. Thank you, Uncle Samuel. He got up out of his seat and walked to the end of the coach, and he met his Great White Buddy out on the platform between the coaches.

"I got good news for you, Corporal."

They were out of Ebbensville now and the train was reeling and rocking and the gleaming tracks were screeching and screaming and Fannie Mae and Fannie Mae and the earth lay green and red around them, as away off in the distance fall came raging out of the hills like forest fire.

Solly forced a mechanical laugh. "Don't tell me, Lieutenant, the war just ended."

"Better news than that, Corporal Saunders. Colonel Spiggelmiser thought we'd all be happier if our friend went along with us to make up the cadre. You'll find Captain Rutherford in the car up ahead. He's still our company commander."

Solly took a long protracted breath. "Now ain't that good news?" He did not really care about company commanders or lieutenants or executive officers. Screw them all.

He thought of Fannie Mae again and his face filled up and he turned his back to the lieutenant, as the train gave out a low and mournful wail, reeling and rocking and almost leaping from the tracks, dashing headlong out of Georgia through a dark-green jungle slowly turning golden brown.

Fall was finally here and he was leaving.

Good-by, Fannie Mae. Dearly beloved Fannie Mae.

With the large warm black eyes vast and deep and knowledge-seeking, and the misty lips curving sensuous soft and firm and saying everything profoundly of love and understanding, with the body warm and black and brown as dark-brown burnt toast and slim and sweet as sugar cane and sapling. You and your Double-V for Victory. By now you know it's all a fraud. The War, the Army, the Home Front, Democracy, ambition, the whole damn shooting match. Nothing's real but you and me. And I will have my manhood. Believe me when I say so.

His face was filling up now and almost spilling over. Fannie Mae, dear Fannie Mae, with the tough and tender strength.

Good-bye, beloved, good-bye.

Part II

CULTIVATION

CHAPTER

I

Solly relaxed for the very first time since he came into the Army.

They spent five hysterical days killing time in self-defense, doing nothing with a vengeance and seeing America first and chasing the dying days of autumn, he wore the world like a loose garment, and they arrived at Monterey, California, just as day gave up the ghost in a blaze of fire and brimstone away out over the wide Pacific at the edge of the Western world. Solly's face filled up and a chill danced madly over his shoulders as he watched the final Tuesday spasms, and he was not aware the train had stopped. How many million trillion days lay at the bottom of this mighty ocean?

Whistles blowing all around him. Rogers screaming: "All right! All right! Every living with a swinging!" Worm said, "You better wake up outa that daydream, Solly. Here come that bubble-eyed prissy-tail Field Sergeant Buck Rogers!" Buck was sounding off like a rusty foghorn. "Off the train and onto the trucks! Off the train and onto the trucks. Come on, soldier, take your finger outcha ass!" The holiday was over.

They got nervously off the train and onto the trucks and rode beside the rolling sea, which was frothing madly at the mouth and licking the salty edge of the continent and slapping the jutting rocks of ages and running out to sea and back again. The awesome beauty of the coastline cast a spell on the weary GI travelers that even took the Bookworm's voice away —temporarily of course. Even Scotty's. They followed the zig-zagging ocean for a short time, and then a wide sweeping curve took them out of sight of the bluish graying sea and onto a sweeping plateau, and off to the left on another level below them was God's most gorgeous countryside, green and yellow and orange and red and blue and purple and sexy and full of giving birth and peacefully restless was the land and unashamedly beautiful and growing under your very eyes. The grumbling trucks took them eastward from the sea to Fort Ord, California. And the next few weeks were fast and furious and many times more frenzied than the race across the continent.

The following day right after lunch more than fifteen hundred colored soldiers, black and dark-brown and medium and light-complexioned, tall and short and in-between, Northerners and Easterners and Southerners and not-so-many Westerners and sad sacks and GFUs and good soldiers and goldbricks and earnest soldiers and intelligent ones and even a few dedicated Section-8-ers, every living stood ill at ease on a wide green glittering field that sounded off like summertime. They were gathered there to listen to their new regimental commander, Lieutenant Colonel Robert Casanova Busby. He was a round stumpy nervous man of middle age and middle class, with overeager expectations. Standing on a wooden platform six feet off the ground, he reminded Solly of a few pampered middle-class bulldogs he had seen in life, strutting pompously along Central Park West and East at the end of milady's leash. His neck short and thick and fat and his voice thick and gravelly and as husky as a bulldog's. Every now and then throughout his speech he would remind the tired sweaty men of the importance of the task before them.

"You're special men,
Amphibi-ens—"

He told them they had to compress four months of amphibian training into a period of four or five weeks. Maybe less. "You people constitute the first colored amphibious regiment in the Army of the United States, and I hope you people realize the importance of the job that lies ahead of you. You're special men—Amphibi-ens."

Like he was huckstering soap on a radio commercial.

"In four or five weeks you have to become the best swimmers, the best marksmen, the best drivers, the best damn soldiers in the Army of the U.S.A." A soft-soap huckster for real.

He paused and mopped his brow and his juicy mouth with a large white handkerchief and let his hazel eyes rove nervously over the field of weary sweating restless soldiers. A grasshopper hedgehopped close to the ground like a P–38 past the bottom of Solly's trouser legs. The colonel really sounds like a bullfrog, Solly decided. A frog instead of a dog. A froggy-sounding frog at that.

"You're special men,
Amphibi—ens—"

They lived in the eastern section of Fort Ord in pyramid-shaped huts, five special men to a hut. There were twelve companies in the Fifteenth Amphibious Regiment. The first hut in each company was the orderly room, located at the top of a hill, and the other huts ran in twelve neat rows fanlike down to the bottom of the hill where a huge Post Exchange squatted amongst a grove of tall green swaying palms like a sprawling supermarket. With a background of heavy shining foliage it looked like a hopped-up Hollywood version of the South Pacific in a Bob Hope-Dorothy Lamour musical comedy. But at the crest of the hill beyond the company streets was a little hut, brown and unpretentious and humble and sincere, which was the Post Exchange for the special men of the Fifteenth Amphibious Regiment. The pretty one down at the bottom of the street was strictly for white folks only.

That evening they went to the Booker T. Washington Post Exchange, and it was so crowded they had to work their jaws up and down when they talked instead of sideways (Bookworm's description of it). It was like the IRT subway at five p.m. at Union Square and Fourteenth Street. You had to fight your way all the way to the counter where four young colored ladies, smiling and harassed, tried to cater to a couple of hundred soldiers, angry and laughing and evil and colored and some of them cussing and some of them sweet-talking, and by the time you got up to the counter they were out of what you wanted, if by then you remembered what you wanted. When Solly and Jimmy Larker and Bookworm finally pushed and shoved their way back out of the place, Solly felt like his sides had caved in on him. And he remembered vividly the jail in Georgia and the white-haired Army colonel and the nightsticks beating against his flaming thighs, and very very especially the feeling of hopeless helpless desperation.

They went without even thinking about it down the company street past the huts toward the supermarket Post Exchange, which was lit up like Times Square and almost empty with white soldiers, and a giant jukebox blasting the air with the Ink Spots *morale building* for the *Special Men.* And the palm trees doing a weird dance giving themselves completely and grotesquely to a cool breeze that was always blowing.

The MP at the entrance said, "Sorry, fellers, you're out of bounds." Solly wrote his own lyrics.

Listen to the pretty song.

"What you mean—out-of-bounds?" the Worm demanded. "I don't see no border lines."

This is what we're fighting for.

"I don't make the regulations, friend. I'm a soldier just like you. I'm just doing my job like they tell me to do."

A fire was building in his stomach. Solly said, "What is this anyhow? An exclusive country club or something?"

We must learn the reasons why.

"Look, boys, I don't have a thing against you people," the nervous MP said, "and I don't want no trouble. There's a PX right up the top of the hill." He's an amiable courageous bastard, Solly thought, with his nightstick on one hip and his forty-five on the other.

And be bitter never.

The Ink Spots sang inside the jukebox inside the supermarket Post Exchange where the blond-haired blue-eyed young ladies and the brunettes and the dark-eyed pale-faced ladies stood behind the counters doing nothing. There were not more than twenty soldiers in the place.

Solly said with heat in his voice, "This one right here doesn't seem to be doing much business at present. The ladies are falling asleep on their feet. . . . We figured we might do a good deed and patronize them a little. Liven things up just a little old biddy bit."

Jimmy said quietly, "We're soldiers, you know, and this would appear to be a Post Exchange."

The MP was rapidly losing his patience and the color in his freckled face. "But it's not for *you* soldiers," he said belligerently. "So why don't you wise guys beat it, honh? Why don't you just knock it off?"

Worm said, "Suppose we just want to stand right here and look at you? You a pretty handsome boy."

The freckle-faced MP stared at Bookworm and then at Solly and Jimmy and back to Worm. He put his hand on his nightstick and seemed to be debating with himself the knotty question of how to deal with these arrogant-acting colored soldiers who didn't have anything else to do but to give him a bad time and didn't have any better sense.

He said, "Suit yourself." He folded his arms and glared at them and they glared back and the heat collected in all of their faces and forgotten was the California evening breeze. Finally the MP gave them his back and placed his hands upon his hips. They stood there for a time, hot and frustrated, and then they turned about and went back up the company street, Worm saying aloud, "We oughta take that forty-five from Junior and whip his head till it rope like okry."

When they reached the top of the street they looked into the orderly room. Lieutenant Samuels was the Officer of the Day and was poring over some official papers. Solly started to say, "Excuse—" but Samuels said, "Come right in, fellers. I wasn't doing anything world-shaking." They hesitated at the door and he said, "I mean it. Come on in. I haven't had a stimulating discussion since we left good old Camp Johnson Henry."

They came into the hut. He said, "Well, men, tell me how do you like California, the land of sunshine and ocean breezes? Or is that Florida's slogan?"

"It don't seem to make much difference," Worm said.

"We just met a nice American gentleman about your complexion by the name of Mr. James Crow," Solly said. "And he gave us a little old orientation about what it is we're fighting for and with musical accompaniment. And now we're just about ready to lay down our lives for freedom and democracy."

The lieutenant looked from Solly to Jimmy to Worm and

back to Solly. "Mr. James Crow? What are you talking about?"

Solly told him in a restrained voice what had happened down at the superstructure. Samuels's tan face reddened, and he said it was a damn shame, and he was going to do something about it or know the goddamn reason why.

"Be sure to tell us the reason, Lieutenant, when you find it," Solly said sarcastically.

The next morning right after breakfast the entire 913 Amphibious Company of the Fifteenth Amphibious Regiment marched over to a wide sprawling motor pool where they saw their first amphibious vehicles. The motor officer, Lieutenant Graham, climbed into the Duck (officially named DUKW) and faced the men of 913. He was a sturdily built dark-haired officer who came from somewhere out of Jersey and sounded like he came from Joisey. He told them they were special men, and the Duck, "this very vehicle I'm standing in, has revolutionized the whole approach to island warfare. This Army truck with a boat built around it can come out of the water and run on land." He paused. "In a few weeks you have to master this vehicle on land and sea. You have to know it inside out and backwards and forwards, and we don't have a minute to waste. They don't need us tomorrow. They need us now, yesterday. That's why you're special men—Amphibians."

That's why they got a special PX for you, Solly thought. Because you're so goddamn extra special.

The motor officer seemed to be carried away by the sound of his salesmanship. "That's why 913 has to be on the ball," he shouted. "That's why you have to be the best damn company in the best damn regiment in the best damn division in the best Army in the whole damn world."

So now you know—that's why they treat you so damn special!

The next few weeks were ten times as frantic as the Reception Center at Fort Dix. Everything in a state of emergency. Everybody jumping up and down. From before daybreak to far into the night they were on the run from one thing to another. Duck convoys roaring along the lush coastline and into the foaming sea. Civilians scratching their backsides to see fifty black monsters come suddenly raging out of the ocean and tearing off down the highway. This was a particularly awesome experience at night, when they did their mock invasions and maneuvers. When they neared the shore with lights off and the

Duck motors and propellers kicking up the phosphorescent foam of the ocean's edge, and the Ducks themselves looking more like sea monsters than ever, and as they hit the beach the men would yell: "AH-GIBBI-DEE! AH-GIBBI-DOH!" whatever the hell that meant, and take off down the highway to the camp, lights dimmed and motors roaring to wake up the ever-sleeping dead.

The days raced by so fast, most of the time you didn't know what day it was. And they were so crammed filled with swimming lessons and rifle range and convoys and drilling and calisthenics and judo and infiltration course and orientation, there was hardly time to think of anything or anybody. Not even Fannie Mae or Millie. Latrine-rumored slogans flew thick and fast, a dime a dozen. Now we're going, now we're not. Get on the ball or on the boat. Don't be late for the Golden Gate. Alaska here we come. Fall in—fall out—forward march and on the double. Sometimes about three o'clock in the day, with the men's tongues hanging out and their hindparts dragging the ground and a couple of backs sprained by jujitsu, Sergeant Buck Rogers would tell his platoon, "Take ten, men. Take a break, take a smoke, take anything but a crap, we don't have that much time to ass around." He was the field sergeant with a sense of humor. When once in a while a poor soldier did stand up for his rights and wander or stumble into the latrine and fall asleep on the stool, he would inevitably dream another dream of embarkation to some faraway exotic land where all was peace and it was "Study War No More." More than half of the rumors were dreamed up in this warm and homelike atmosphere. Remember Pearl Harbor on the way to Honolulu. We're going to bust India wide open and look out for the Burma Road. One of the longest-lasting rumors was that they were going back across the nation and join a task force to open the Second Front in Paris. Every time a whistle blew another rumor hit the breeze. The Yanks were coming some damn where.

The first week at Fort Ord he got one letter from Mama, three from Millie, and not a scratch from Fannie Mae. In the second letter from Millie she suggested that she might come out to California to see him one last time before he took off for God-knew-where-or-how-long. In the third letter she told him she had inquired about train reservations and expenses, and she had made arragnements for a leave of absence from her job. He lay on his cot in his little brown hut and imagined how it would be to have her there for his last days. To have her to come home to each night at the end of his last weary days, crammed filled with obstacle courses and back-breaking judo and convoys and motor maintenance and office work and every damn thing else you could jam-pack into eighteen waking hours. Part of the time you were half asleep. He imagined her waiting for him each night over in Fort Ord Village, which was a temporary housing project for non-commissioned officers, located halfway between the camp and Monterey. Imagined her in her entirety, and a sweet warmth moved over the length of his body. And she was his wife and he had no right to fashion dreams with anyone but her. It would be a good thing to have Millie come out with their baby in her tummy. They said it was great to make love to a pregnant woman. And he would have one last chance to prove to her his love for her. What he desperately needed was to prove it to himself. But how in the hell could he send for her when he never knew from one day to the next when they would get their shipping orders? He got up off his bunk and put on his shirt and went to find his Great White Buddy.

Samuels was a big help. He told Solly that as a non-com he was entitled for his wife to travel to see him pullman-class at the expense of the Army of the U.S. His Great White Buddy would take care of the details the very next morning. But as to the question of when they would be moving out, nobody knew but God and maybe General Buford Jack. That was the risk he would have to take. Mrs. Saunders might come three thousand miles just for the long hot trip. By the time she arrived her soldier husband might be on the boat heading where? God only knew and General Jack.

Solly went back to his hut. He would write her tonight and tell her to catch the first thing smoking. It would be wonderful to have her. It would be— But suppose she got there and he was gone? He lay on his bunk and broke into a cool damp sweat. It would be hell for her to come all that distance just to find him gone, address unknown, just an Army Post Office number. He couldn't do this to her. Could not do it to himself. The thing to do was to wait till after tomorrow, after he and Samuels got the papers in order, and then he would sit down and write her and put it up to her, the pros and cons and the likelihoods, and she would make up her own mind, and he hoped she would come anyway. Maybe he would phone her tomorrow night. It would be good to be with her again, even via long-distance. He closed his eyes and fashioned her face. Fashioned her long slim autumn-golden body, the special taste of the breath from her lips, the particular smell of her body that was hers and only hers and hers and hers and hers—and suddenly everything in hell paid a visit to the company street.

He heard the shouting outside and footsteps running past his hut down toward the bottom of the street, and "Scotty!" and "Goddamn Old Rose!" and "Scotty!" A soldier stuck his head inside. "Come on, Corporal Solly. Your man is tearing his ass again!" Solly pretended he was asleep. To hell with Scotty. He wanted his image of Millie. Scotty was a private-first-class goof-off. Millie, darling, I want you to come and be with me. I want to hold you next to me. Someone ran into the hut.

"Come on, Solly!"

I want you, Millie—want you—

Bookworm jerked him to his feet.

Solly said, "To hell with Scotty! If he wants to act the damn fool, let him. I have more important things to think about."

Worm said, "Come on, Solly. Don't be chickenshit!" And pulled him toward the entrance of the hut, and he found himself against his will running downhill with the Bookworm, as the huts continued to empty. Some of the men with sticks in their hands and some with knives and one of them with a baseball bat. By the time Solly and Worm got down to the bottom, a crowd had gathered from other Duck companies as well as from the 913. And Technician Fifth-Grade Scott was sounding off in his inimitable style.

He was in the midst of the enlisted men along with two big hefty MPs and Captain Strausman, company commander of the 915th Duck Company, and regimental officer of the day. From the jukebox in the brightly neoned Post Exchange, Bing Crosby was singing pretty and outside leaves of trees were dancing, as Scotty sabotaged the setting. Everything so picturesque.

"Naw, we don't like it!" Scotty roared. "Hell naw! Here you goddamn people 'bout to send us somewhere south of west-hell to do your dying and you have the goddamn nerve to build a canteen in pissing distance from our tents and dare us to put our foot inside. . . . That ain't right, not worth a damn!"

"Tell em about that mess, Scotty!" Worm shouted as he shoved Solly through the crowd toward the lionhearted soldier.

Captain Strausman said, "Told you to shut your gawdamn

mouth, soldier." He was a little over six feet and looked like a college fullback. His voice was a curious mixture of German brogue and Southern accent.

"Don't raise your voice at me!" Scotty screamed. "Don't you raise your voice at me! We gon use this Post Exchange or rip the sonofabitch apart!"

Solly being shoved by Worm, they reached Scotty just as another white officer, a major, made his way from the other side of the mob of soldiers. Solly looked at the little angry-mad soldier and unwillingly felt a warmth of something indefinable. Almost without knowing he put his hand on Scotty's shoulder. Scotty turned quickly and then a smile broke over his face. "I know you with me, Corporal Sandy," he said calmly. He turned back to the red-faced captain and went into his rage again.

The major said, "Just a minute, soldier."

And Scotty swung around to do him in. "Who in the—?"

"All right, soldier," the quiet-voiced major said. "All right, I think I know what the problem is. I'm Major Stevens, and I'm from Boston, Massachusetts, and I am not prejudiced against your people."

Scotty stared at the major and stood at attention and pulled off his cap and saluted him. "All right, Cap'n, sir, I'll listen to you, but this Georgia mother-fucker is naturally got to go," Scotty said, pointing to the apoplectic Strausman no more than one arm's length away from him.

Strausman said, fuming, "Major, this soldier is guilty of insubordination and inciting a—"

The major said, "All right, Captain, we'll see what's what. The first thing to do is to disperse the mob."

Scotty said cagily, "You ain't gon trick me, are you, sir? You from Boston—"

"You have my word, soldier. You'll get nothing but fair play from me. Now let's go, fellows. Back to your company areas. Break it up now."

One of the MPs said, "Come on, break it up."

The men moved around and scraped their feet and grumbled but did not go anywhere.

Scotty said officiously, "Everything's under control now, com-rads. Colonel Stevens is a man of his word. He's a Northern stud. We'll be in the Canteen by tomorrow night." Some of the men cheered, others still grumbled, as they began to give ground slowly and move away.

The major said, "Now, Captain, you and I and the corporal can go over to post headquarters and see if we can't get to the bottom of things. I happen to be the base adjutant."

Strausman said, "I'm aware of that fact, sir, but—"

Scotty said in his humblest manner, "Can I make one last request, Major, sir?" It was the first time he called the major by his proper rank.

The major said, "What is it, soldier?"

"Can we take Corporal Sandy here with us? We in this thing together, and he can explain it heap better than me. He's an educated man like you, sir, and he's the company lawyer and the company clerk and all that kind of jive."

Solly thought angrily, how in the hell did I get into this mess? The major turned to him. "Are you a part of this disturbance, Corporal?"

He answered heatedly, "Yes, sir." What else could he say? Could he say: No sir, white folks, I ain't in this colored mess? He should have stayed in his tent like he'd wanted to. Should have stayed there with his Millie.

The major said, "All right then, but let's get going." The major was obviously anxious to get away from the mob of soldiers, who had not completely broken up, and as long as he stayed there with Scotty and Strausman, there was the chance they would collect again. When Solly and Scotty moved away with the officers, the Bookworm and a few of the soldiers followed. The major turned on them. "All right, men. As you were. Get back to your company area." Worm and Larker and the others halted. Worm looked to Solly. Solly's anger almost choked him as he said in a trembly husky voice, "Everything's under control." Worm's eyes asked Solly a million questions. Then he turned back and the others reluctantly followed suit.

They rode through the coolish night toward the other side of the camp with a full moon sifting golden through the palm trees. Scotty and he sat in the back of the jeep like they were being chauffeured.

Solly whispered angrily, "I told you before—next time you want to act the damn fool, leave me out of it!"

Scotty looked at Solly with an angel's innocence and said, "Beg pard-dron?"

Solly thought, if I had a gun, they'd lock me up for homicide. Justifiable.

As they walked into the major's office, Scotty whispered to Solly, "You do the talking for us, Corporal Sandy. I done tore my ass already."

"For *us!*" Solly almost shouted. A half an hour ago he had been lying on his sack in the quiet of his hut with Millie on his mind, his soul and body and minding his own business, and here he was thirty minutes later in the adjutant's office at post headquarters, and into something up to his ears and he didn't hardly know what it was he was into or the how-comes or the what-fors or the where-fores. The next time he heard Scotty's name called he was going to run like hell in the other direction. Ever since he came into the Army it had been he and Scotty, as if they were inevitably chained together and never for better, always for worse.

The major sat behind his desk. Captain Strausman said, "Major, this is really an affair of regimental jurisdiction. I think—"

The major said, "*I* think *I'm* qualified to determine the proper jurisdiction, Captain."

Strausman said, "Yes, sir, but this man here, Scott, is a notorious troublemaker. His record shows—"

Solly looked at Scotty standing there with his hat in his hand, the barest hint of a contemptuous smile on his lips. There was a madness in his eyes and an almost overstated purpose in the settle contours of his face. Scotty's truth was suddenly clear to Solly. This was where he lived, and he would not give an inch of ground to a living ass. You trespassed at your peril. This was his manhood.

"Why don't we hear from the men first, Captain? As fellow officers you and I can go over their stories after they're gone. Fine. Now then what's your story, Corporal?"

He was talking to Solly, and Solly thought, what is my story? He stared at the major and what right did Scotty have to put him on the spot like this? He wanted to say, I have no story. I'm just an innocent bystander, judge, your honor.

Captain Strausman said, "All right, boy, we don't have all night. This wasn't any business of yours anyhow, till you butted into it." The captain's voice was a red-hot poker digging into the smoldering ashes of his memory, stirring hot sparks into a flame, reminding him what his story was. He remembered painfully vividly the jail in Ebbensville and the muscles in his thighs began to dance. For us—for us. Scotty, you're goddamn right. For us! Thank you, Scotty! It's Worm's story, Clint's story, Jimmy Larker's and Buck's story, my story, even Bucket-head Baker's story.

"I beg your pardon, Captain," he said in a voice that camouflaged the anger raging in him. "I believe this is my business from the beginning to the end." My story whether I want it to be or not. I cannot duck it any longer.

The major said, "Go right ahead, Corporal."

"Yeah," Scotty said, "tell it like it was. Don't hold back nothing."

Solly said, "Major, sir, any day, any hour, any week, we men in the Fifteenth Regiment will be shipping out to some faraway place to fight and maybe die for our great country and for freedom and democracy." He could no longer smother the heat in his voice nor the fire building in his face and shoulders.

"We are called upon to die on foreign soil for something we're constantly denied right here at home in our own our native land."

Scotty sounded like a brother shouting deep from the Amen Corner. "Talk pretty for the people, Corporal Sandy."

"You will speak when you're called upon, soldier," the major said to Scotty.

Solly felt the angry coals being heaped onto the fire, building in his stomach now. At the same time he felt an overpowering frustration. "Here we are supposed to be fighting against the racist theories of Hitler and we find the same theories holding forth in our own so-called democratic Army. The wonder is that the Negro soldier is not a hundred times more bitter."

"Get to the point, soldier," Strausman said.

"I'm dealing precisely with the point, Captain, to the best of my ability." He breathed deeply and continued. "It is a cruel act, sir, to bring us three thousand miles from home to train us to die and to put that supermarket right in our backyard and tell us it's too good for us." His voice was trembling, his face perspiring but somehow dammit, he felt good.

"The point is," the captain said, "the Army is not based on sob stories. It is based on discipline, and you men are guilty of serious breaches—insubordination and inciting to mutiny and riot. These are the only points under consideration."

Scotty said to the major in a sweet disarming voice, "I don't know who's running this, sir, you or the captain. He keeps interrupting everybody."

The major said, "As you were," to Scotty, and he continued to stare at Solly.

Solly said, "Major, how would you feel if you were brought into your country's Army only to be treated as something filthy and unclean and to be spat upon contemptuously? Put yourself in our place."

The major looked at him long and hard then at Scotty and back to him. "Have you finished, soldier?"

"I am through, Major, sir."

"And you, Corporal er—er—"

"Technician Fifth-Grade Abraham Lincoln Scott. I'm the best cook—"

"And what have you go to say?"

"Nothing, sir," Scotty said with deep solemnity. "I'm not much of a talker, sir. I'm just naturally bashful, me, but we got Corporal Sandy here to speak for me and all the rest of the poor mistreated colored soldiers so far away from home, and thank God for that, sir, and I—"

"All right, soldier, that'll be enough. Just—"

"We just try to do the best we know how, sir, and ain't nobody can beat me cooking, and thank God for that, but these paddy officers—"

The major got to his feet. "All right, soldier! I said, all right, goddammit!"

"Yes, sir, Major, sir," Scotty said very very meekly.

The major turned to Solly. "Now you, Corporal. Take this man back to the company area and he is confined to quarters till further notice, and beginning tomorrow morning he is on permanent K.P. till your company leaves Fort Ord. I'll contact your commanding officer tomorrow morning." The major turned again to Scotty. "And you, soldier, are getting off extremely light, if you get no more punishment than this. You are undoubtedly the most insubordinate, the most undisciplined, the most mutinous soldier in the Army of the United States."

Scotty opened his angry mouth and Solly tried to head him off. Solly said, "Major—Major—" He had no idea what else he would say.

The major said, "And as to the questions you raised very—eloquently, Corporal, they are well taken, and will not go without immediate consideration." The major's voice hardened deliberately and he pounded his desk with his open hands. "Nevertheless, the Army cannot and will not tolerate any soldier taking matters into his own hands. I don't give a damn how righteous he may think his cause to be! That goes for both of you and anybody else, regardless of race or creed or color. Is that clear?"

"Very clear, sir," Solly said.

"Both of you are dismissed. Go immediately back to your company area."

"Who gon take us back, sir?" Scotty asked humbly, sweetly. "My feet are very tired."

"That's your problem soldier. Just get back to your area and get the hell out of here."

Solly said, "Yes, sir," and took Scotty by the arm. "Let's go, goddammit!" he whispered violently.

They started their long walk back to the East Garrison. They walked quietly, not speaking, through the soft California night. Solly knew that Scotty could feel the heat of Solly's anger, and he also knew that Scotty realized all of it was not directed against the white men they had left at post headquarters. This was one time Scotty must have figured that silence was purely golden. He would have made a great military tactician. At the same time the anger kept building up in Solly and he wanted the little mad soldier to give him some excuse to take it out on him. Just any little stupid comment. Any excuse at all. And he became even more furious when the biggest talker in the Amphibs suddenly clammed up on him. They rounded a sharp wide curve in the road and Solly was so hot he could not see straight. He turned suddenly upon the other soldier and grabbed him by his collar.

"Why is it ever since I've been in the Army I always find myself in some crazy fuck-up with you?"

Scotty looked up at him meekly, like a nice little baby lion with his feelings hurt. He smiled gently. "You took the words right out of my mouth, Corporal Sandy. I'm gon stay away from you from now on. You too hot tempered with the white man. You get a poor soldier in a whole heap of trouble."

Solly stared at him, controlling himself. The penalty for murder in California was the gas chamber. He released the soldier. "Why do you fuck with me so much, man? There are millions of other people in this Army."

Scott said sweetly, "Cause I like you the bestest. And

I'm gon stick to you like stink on shit. Make a man out you or break you."

Solly turned from him exasperated and they went walking up the road again. Solly said, "You're going to screw up once too often."

"So let them throw my ass in Leavenworth stead of putting me on the boat. You'll see me do some crying then."

Solly stopped and looked at Scott again and for the first time saw him clearly. It was one of the most lucid moments in Solly's life, with everything in focus. Scott was the only soldier in all of the United States of America that Solly knew of who had Uncle Sam over a barrel and could say, "All right, do me something!" He didn't seek to get ahead, he wanted no promotions, no extra-special privileges, no stripes, no nothing. He demanded nothing from the man but manhood.

The following night the supermarket Post Exchange was opened up to all American soldiers, excepting Scotty, who was confined to the company area and permanent K.P. duty and busted again from T–5 to private. And two days later the PX at the top of the hill closed down, and what happened to the colored clerks? They were transferred down to the supermarket.

A few nights later Solly came up from the PX and looked into the orderly room and saw his conscientious G.W.B. They talked till after midnight.

Samuels told Solly he had already spoken to the adjutant about the PX situation a couple of days before the flare-up. "He's a friend of mine from college days."

Solly said, "Big deal." A few beers that made Milwaukee famous did not bolster his enthusiasm. The one thing they never forgot when they were with each other was the Saturday they went to Ebbensville together in search of the MP colonel. It was always there between them.

Samuels said, "They had already decided to open it up to the regiment, based on my most vigorous recommendations."

Solly said, "Fine." And thought, he wants me to give him a citation.

"The adjutant is a liberal anyhow. Maybe even radical. He always has been."

"Makes me happy," Solly said. He also wants a citation for the major.

"It was just a matter of time and patience. All things are."

Solly stood up and exploded. "Don't you ask me to have any more patience than you would have, and don't be so damn happy-go-lucky with my life. I'm the one that's smothering. I've been a second-handed American all my life, but I damn sure haven't gotten used to it, you better believe I haven't. And I don't have any future plans for getting into the patience habit."

Samuels was speechless for a moment. "Corporal, I—"

"And if you're sitting there trying to take credit for opening up that Post Exchange, forget it! Everybody knows that Permanent K.P. Private Jerry Abraham Lincoln Scott is the responsible party and nobody else. Not you or your fraternity brother or any *body else!*"

"The adjutant was very impressed with your intelligence, Corporal." Give the lieutenant credit. He tries to keep his calm about him.

"And you openly insult my intelligence. Sir!" he added. He paused. "And now if I may go, Lieutenant, I have important matters to take care of of an extremely personal nature. And I really don't feel like hearing any more tonight about such revolutionary slogans as *Patience* and *Fortitude* and how great my liberal white friends are."

They stared into each other's face, Solly and his Great White Buddy.

"If I may leave, *sir—*"

"Good night, Corporal Saunders."

"Good night, Lieutenant—sir."

CHAPTER

2

The days raced by and there was never enough time to do anything, there was so much to be done. The records were a holy mess, but every man's file had to be in perfect order before he could be shipped out. Everything every man was required to do before embarking had to be entered on his record, whether he actually did it or not. Marksmanship, infiltration course, swimming, judo, amphibious training, obstacle course, dental history, medical history, shots taken, Short-arm Inspection, the works and nothing but the works. There was a man named Bell who refused to shoot his rifle on the rifle range. They faked the record. A nineteen-year-old boy named Banks who would never learn to swim. They faked his record. Captain's orders. Solly was responsible to the captain for every soldier's record, plus he had to go through all the frantic training the others went through, so that his own record would look just like the others. He was so tired at the end of each day he thought he'd never get rested in this life. Every evening about eight-thirty or nine o'clock he'd leave the orderly room and drag himself down to the PX and have a couple of beers and smile tiredly at the tired anxious sweet-faced lady across the bar and remember Fannie

Mae and go back up the hill to his hut and fall on his sack and find that he was too damn weary to fall asleep.

And yet somehow there was time to arrange for Millie to come—with the help of Samuels and even Captain Charlie Rutherford. The relationship between Rutherford and Solly had simmered down and cooled off, based as it was now on a realistic evaluation on both of their parts of the actual situation. Rutherford faced the fact that Solly was the best damn company clerk available. Rutherford's arrogance and ambition dictated that he have only the best. So if they had to work together they might as well bury the hatchet, at least superficially. Solly understood it, bought it. He was no longer a pouting boy. He was a man. He could not be *out* of it like Scotty. And since he would be in it, he might as well make the most of it.

Rutherford said, "Don't worry about anything, Saunders. You're my company clerk, and you just keep up the good work and stay out of mischief and I'm gon see if I can't get you a sergeant's rating." They had no illusions about each other's mutual love and admiration.

Solly called Millie the day before she caught the train, and that very night a full-blown rumor hit the breeze. They would be moving out in seven days. He heard it in the latrine where they all began and he paid it no mind. He heard it in the mess hall and got uneasy. He heard it at the Post Exchange, and by that time the seven days had changed to five. He left the PX and did not stop till he found the captain. The captain told him he'd heard the same rumor. He couldn't vouch for it, but what he did know was that everybody in the regiment had just been put on a twenty-four hour alert.

Solly said, "But my wife is coming out here. She's already on her way!"

The captain said, "There is nothing I can do about it. It might be three weeks before we move out, it might be three months, then again it might be three days. Man appoints, but God and the Army disappoints. That's what I've been trying to teach you every since I've known you, but you insist on acting like you think you're in the Boy Scouts."

Solly went down to the Post Exchange and called New York, even though he knew she had left already. It took fifty minutes to get through to the City, and when he did there was nobody home. He went over to the beer counter and drank beer till the place closed up. He went uphill to his hut with the knowledge that by the time she arrived he might be gone already. He lay on his sack with the meaningless chatter of the other soldiers swirling around him and the laughing and the kidding and the rumors flying thick and fast, and his head going around, and he thought he was in a madhouse, and he was crazy and the whole thing was a dream, a nightmare, and he would wake up any minute. His mind made an image of Millie. She was sitting on a train, beautiful and confident. He felt like crying, she looked so happy and alone, and gradually she began to fade and he could only see her face, and when he tried to look more closely, the face had changed to Fannie Mae's, and he was surely out of his mind.

All the men kept tight hindparts from hour to hour. It was now we're going, not yet awhile. And they were getting ready all the time. If a soldier sat in his hut and saw another soldier running down the street he wanted to know the reason why and when and where. Everybody busy as a dog scratching fleas and twice as nervous. In the middle of the third day the orders came. They would be moving out to the staging area at Camp Stoneman on the second day after Millie was due to arrive. Solly was slowly going mad with anger and frustration. He drank beer like it was going out of style. She was coming and he was going. Man appoints and the Army disappoints. Well, maybe he himself would do a little disappointing. Maybe when Millie got there he would fake some papers and steal a jeep and take off for Mexico and Guatemala and eventually South America. Sometimes he thought he still believed in the War against Fascism, which was being fought somewhere in some far-off place. He had a vague concern with its outcome. But he felt no loyalty toward this Army where he found himself.

He was serious enough to look at a map and trace the imagined journey. He took this idea around with him and at night he went to bed with it and dreamed about it. It was not entirely unrealistic. Every day he heard of soldiers, white and colored, stealing jeeps and command cars and taking off for destinations undetermined by military necessities. In his dream he and Millie drove along the gorgeous coast of Southern California and through the hills of Mexico and further south down down out of the hills from Mexico City, and her face changed gradually to Fannie Mae's, and he woke up on his sack, and he wasn't going to desert to any damn where, he didn't have the guts. He wasn't even going AWOL, as a couple of the men in the company had already done, including Scotty, who left two hours after the orders came. Before he left he told Solly he was just going to take about a month's vacation, he wasn't deserting, he was just allergic to big white boats, he didn't like any more water than you could get into a tub.

He stared at Solly and his voice got husky. "What you gon do in these white folks' Army without me here to look out for you?"

Solly knew a warm feeling in his shoulders. He laughed. "You'd better look out for your own self."

Scotty said, "So what can they do me when I come back? Put my ass in Leavenworth? That's better'n ducking bullets." Sometimes Solly wished fiercely he was Scotty. But he wasn't—he was educated. And had prospects for the future.

Solly borrowed the captain's jeep to meet Millie in Salinas. The train was more than two hours late, and he went into a tavern near the depot, and by the time it arrived he was almost drunk. Maybe it was the whiskey, but when he saw her get off the train and walk toward him he thought, great God almighty! She's more beautiful than I ever remembered! It's impossible! He took her into his arms and put his mouth against her eager lips, and maybe it was just another crazy dream of his—maybe she wasn't there at all.

"You're here—you're here," was all that he could think to say. I should put you in this jeep and head for Guatemala all the way down to South America. Venezuela—Argentina.

"Yes, I'm here, all in one piece, and everybody else in the station is aware that I am here."

"You——you're beautiful!"

"Now how could I be beautiful? I'm exhausted and you're prejudiced, and I wish the natives would stop staring."

He said, "And how's the baby?" Anxiously.

She said, "Which baby? Me or it?"

He took her around the corner from the station to a little country restaurant and they ordered a big dinner, but he ate nothing at all as he sat there, drinking her into all of his senses, oblivious to the food and the friendly-looking natives who openly stared at the handsome couple. Millie was starved and ate both of their dinners. He had not remembered her as a big eater. She's pregnant, you fool! The added weight just made more of her to be beautiful.

They drove along the countryside and the land made love

to her, the land which lay blossoming green and yellow and red and blue and violet and gleaming on each side of them and rolling all the way to the hills and rolling back from the hills, and blowing its breath sweetly, and complacently pregnant with the beauty of giving birth and growing—you could almost see and hear the growing of the fruit and shrubbery. But he wanted to talk about the City with a different kind of beauty, with a different kind of full-of-lifeness. The City, his City, ugly and loud and boisterous and violent and uncouth and cold and smelly and disinterested and gangster-controlled and minding-its-own-damn-business and everybody else's, going nowhere and going everywhere, and in the maddest kind of rage to get there in a hurry.

He took one hand off the wheel and put it around her waist and asked her, "How's the City?"

"It was snowing when I left, and you know how nasty it is when it snows in New York City. I was glad to get away."

She looked around at the teeming growth of the country-side and breathed the air permeated with the deep fragrance of its growth and growing. "I can't believe it. I just cannot believe it. Just four days ago I was in New York City, and it was ugly and cold and snowing, and look at all of this. The weather the land—"

"I mean how's the City?" he asked. "I don't mean the weather. I mean what's happening in the City?"

She stared intently at his profile. "Nothing," she said. "I told you—it's snowing. That's all."

He changed the subject. "How's the baby and how's Mama?"

"Your mother's in great shape. As healthy as a horse." His mother had never been that-kind-of-healthy. "She told me to tell you, 'Don't be no hero, doll baby. Just do everything he possibly kin to come back in one piece.' " She laughed. "Your mother is the most."

He clouded up. "And I'm going to do just that. You better believe me. I'm coming back in one whole piece. I'm concentrating on it. She will not be a gold-star mother, if her only son can help it."

They rode silently for a while, and when they reached the sea, her lovely face glowed as the awesome beauty of sea and surf and salty odor assaulted her senses and she was taken in completely, like a lover giving in at last at last. The sun in her face, the wind, the earth, the sea in her responsive body. She moved her leg against his leg and she stretched her trembling body, and her entire being seem to say, "Take me! Take me! Take all of me!" He felt a sweet salty taste in his own mouth and an aching in his loins and warmth throughout his body and a hurting in his stomach.

She said, "And to think I spent most of the time sitting at home and moping and feeling sorry for you, thinking you really had it tough, and all of the time you had all this." She waved her pretty well-kept hands at everything.

"I've been having a natural ball," he said.

They left the highway and turned abruptly from the sea as it licked its salty tongue against the continent, and a hundred feet away they entered Fort Ord Village, a place constructed and set aside for non-commissioned officers and their wives and children, with green lawns and white two-storied cottages. Solly had arranged for a room in a cottage on Monroe Street. He introduced Millie to the woman in charge of the cottage and she told them they were a beautiful couple and as a matter of fact they resembled each other enough to be brother and sister instead of man and wife. "Neither one of you nothing but children." She took them to their little back room, clean and spotless with its two iron cots and its dresser and its two chairs and its chest of drawers. "Just make yourself right at home. Anything you want, just call Miss Langford. I'm just at your beck and call."

The landlady gone, the door closed behind them, he went to her and put his arms around her and his hands on her and his lips against her lips and she pushed all of her body against him as if in terrible desperation, and for one brief moment she went to pieces in his arms, in a manner he had not remembered. But then she quickly got herself together.

He said, "What's the matter?"

She looked around at the glorified telephone booth of a room, and suddenly it looked cramped and inadequate and miserable, to him, the way she looked at it, whereas the day before, when Mrs. Langford had shown it to him, it had seemed idyllic and romantic and just the thing for unpretentious lovers like Millie and Solly Saunders. Their second honeymoon, their only honeymoon. Now he looked at it as it was. An act of desperation, pure and simple.

He said, "It isn't home, darling, but it's clean and cozy."

"It's cozy," she said. "There is that about it."

He took her into his arms again. "It's not as if we were leasing an apartment, baby, or buying a home. We're just buying a little time to be together. And the important thing is—we are together."

She held him tightly and she was like before again and he was warm again, but then she moved away again.

She said, "Do you have to go back to camp?"

He said, "I have to take the captain his jeep and do a K.P. Roster and get my night pass signed, and then I'll get somebody to drive me back."

She said, "Hurry back sweetheart. I'm tired from the trip and there's no need to stir me up and leave me."

He was shocked by her overtness. He remembered her as subtle, always subtle, and it was the way he wanted to remember her. Ladylike and subtle. He said, "I'll be back as soon as I can, and I'll bring some goodies for you and Junior."

A warm flush made her cheeks glow. She said, "And I'll catch a nap and dream about all the goodies you're going to bring me."

He stared at her and said jokingly, "Junior has made you even more beautiful than you already were and that just about makes you the prettiest pregnant woman in this whole wide world. And it's so wonderfully distributed." His face softened and so did his voice. "How's the baby been treating *my* baby? You don't even show a thing. I mean—not hardly."

The blood ran warm in her cheeks again. "Just fine. The baby's fine and I'm fine."

Solly said, "Did the doctor approve your trip way out here across the continent?"

She said, "You're the only medicine I need, darling. Better than anything the doctor could possibly prescribe."

He said, "And you're the freshest sassiest pregnant woman I ever came across."

She came to him and put her arms around him. "Hurry back and speak to me of love."

He ate her up and drank her down with his hungry eyes and mouth and shook his head from side to side.

She laughed at him and moved in closer. "Darling, I'm so glad to be here. It wouldn't matter if we were in a shack. I love you—I love you, and I missed you so much, and I hate for you to leave me. So please hurry back." She kissed his mouth his eyes his nose. "I just can't stand the suspense."

He became unbearably warm and prickly things raced across his back and he grew large against her pregnancy. He said, "I've got to go. I really must."

She said, "Go, silly, and hurry back. And don't worry about me. This place will be our castle for the next few weeks. That's the only thing that matters."

He should have told her then and there. She was so lovely and so happy, standing there, he didn't have the heart to tell her this was their first night in this place and tomorrow night would be their last. He held her close and squeezed her as if he would break her in two pieces, and then he left her hurriedly.

Buck Rogers drove him back from camp to the Village, and he knocked on the door and aroused her and introduced her with the sleep still in her face to Buck, and Buck stared at her and tears came to his eyes. She was so beautiful and nostalgic. When Buck left, Solly took her into his arms, and they lay on one of the cots and they kissed each other and felt each other and kissed each other and felt each other. And he smelled the kind of smell he half remembered, the special sweet moldish smell of her just after waking, mixed with the salty smell of her excitement. She caressed his ear with her delicious tongue and then she nibbled his cheek and tenderly bit his ear. And he lay on top of her, letting her feel the full weight of him, and he squeezed her till he heard her screaming softly in his ear and he felt her quivering in the middle of her and he put his mouth against her mouth and tongue to tongue, and when they came up for air, she said, "I feel so good I think I'm going to die!"

And he put his mouth to hers again and his hand beneath her clothes and he felt her quaking wetness and smelled her wetness, and she moved from under him and stood up, and he said angrily, "What the hell's the matter?" And then he said anxiously, "Did I lean too heavy on the baby?"

She said, "Silly—I just want to take a bath and freshen up. I was asleep when you came back."

He said, "Come on, you don't need a bath. Please—please." His head reeled and his stomach ached. He wanted her now and now and now and now.

She said, "It was a long trip, sweetie, and I need a good hot bath." She took her washrag, towel and soap and toilet water, her bathrobe and her nightgown, and she went up the hall to the bathroom.

It seemed like hours before she came back in her nightgown and her bathrobe, hours long and agonizing. And he was lying where she left him. Standing at attention. She stared at him and she took off her robe and stood before him, the pink sheer gown clinging to her profoundly beautiful body like it was hanging on in desperation and leaning against her wonderful breasts, honey-colored and cinnamon-nippled, and grabbing at her round slim thighs where they started from the dark V-crease beneath her slightly swelling pregnancy. He was hot all over and growing by the second and his head was getting giddy. Her gown went up over her head and she stood before him in all of her golden-olive loveliness. And great God almighty, her pregnancy was beautiful!—giving a subtle roundness to her belly that was never there before. He swallowed the funny taste in his mouth and got up and went to take her in his arms.

She said impatiently, "What were you waiting for? Undress!" And she began to unbutton his shirt and the fly of his trousers. "Off! Off! Everything off!"

And now they stood there in their birthday suits, and she looked him up and down. She said, "Beautiful! Just beautiful!" And why shouldn't she look at him like this? They were lovers, they were man and wife. She had just as much right to admire his body as he had hers. He was just a self-conscious old-fashioned mid-Victorian male-supremacist ass!

She said, "Take me up and carry me to bed."

He took her up into his arms and carried her to one of the little iron cots, and they lay there locked together in their nakedness, fitting one into the other's groove. There was not an nth of an nth of an inch between them. He wanted immediately to lose himself inside of her and escape the crazy world, but she said, "Not yet! Not yet! I want to just lie here next to you and feel you up against me and kiss your beautiful eyes and your sensitive mouth and your big ears and I want you to kiss me and kiss me here!" She cupped her breast. He kissed her sweet breast tenderly. She was breathing fast and furious and she stopped to catch her breath. And he looked at her and could not conceal his astonishment. He remembered her as forward and opinionated in other things, but in love-making she had always been the bourgeois lady. Coy and hard-to-get and always passive up until the final frantic moment when she went for all the marbles.

She said, "You think I'm acting like a common whore."

He almost shook his head off his body. His face was burning up with guilt. "Don't be silly."

She said, "Yes, you do. And I'm ashamed of the way I'm acting, but I've missed you so much, and when you're gone you'll be gone so long I want to enjoy every minute of you the next few weeks and let it last the next few years if necessary. And you're my husband and I'm not ashamed. Why should I be?"

He whispered, "Hush up, baby."

But she spilled over. "You hate me for acting like a whore, don't you? I can see it in your face. But I don't care. I love you love you love you." Her large eyes filled and overflowed.

And he was filled with love and pity and maleness and the nearness of her. He said, "I love you, goddammit." And really meant it.

She said, "No, you don't. I can tell by the way you look at me. I could tell by your letters. There's somebody else, I know there is! I knew before I came. That's why—that's why—that's why—" Her voice broke off and the tears spilled down her cheeks, and she was so lovely he couldn't stand to see her like this. He could never have imagined her like this. His image of her was complete with pride and haughtiness and unattainability, sometimes almost calculating. Sometimes he had thought her heart was a mansion filled with expensive furniture but uninhabited by people.

"There's nobody else!" he lied. "There never could be." Ever since he had met her at the station in Salinas he had struggled successfully to keep the Fannie Mae image out of his mind, but it had been there all the time, lurking just out of sight, just waiting for the chance to appear and to demand to be compared with Millie, but he wouldn't allow it—wouldn't allow it! I've forgotten you, Fannie Mae. I don't even remember your face. To hell with Fannie. I love Millie I love Millie Millie Millie!

Millie said between the sobbing, "I know there's somebody else. You're thinking about her now!"

He said, "I love you and only you!" And he sought to kiss away her doubts and fears, her insecurity. He kissed her eyes till they were dry of tears and wet with his kisses. He kissed her nose he kissed the corners of her mouth and then full on her lips and she stopped crying and put her arms around his neck, and he kissed the nipples of her gleaming breasts of autumn and the valley in between, and he kissed the slightly swelling mound of her pregnancy at the belly button and kissed her mouth again, and she was moaning with delight, and he put his hand all over her, and the lips at the mouth of her sex vibrating now underneath his tender touch, and she put her hand all over him and she was panting and moaning and groaning, and he thought her heart would surely stop beating. She said, "No! No! No!" And then she murmured, "Now, darling, now!" And he was more than ready now, and he sank himself inside of her and they were locked in a sweet mortal combat. And wave after wave after wave, the ocean tossed them up and down and all about, together and against together, together and against together, and then he thought he heard her scream like he was killing her, her eyes closed, her mouth open, as she went for the highest wave of all, but he could not reach it with her. At the very last moment he made the image of Fannie Mae, even as he tried desperately to erase the image and reach the crest with her, but it was all to no avail, and it left him high and dry. The ocean's edge receded now, wave after breathless wave, and she lay on the wet sand, breathing deeply, her eyes closed, her mouth open like she had eaten a sumptuous meal and sated her great appetite. She was somewhere all by herself now, lying in the shade of a swaying palm tree and purring like a motorboat. She opened her eyes and studied his face and put her arms around his neck.

"It was never like that before, darling. It was the greatest greatest greatest!"

He said, "Yes, it was truly great."

She said, "It was never like this ever before. Did the room spin around and around with you like you were on a carousel?"

He lied, "Yes, the room spun around and around with me like I was on a carousel."

She said, "Well, then now I know you love me." She sat up and looked around the room. She said, "I'll never forget this room. It is the nicest quietest loveliest soulfullest coziest sweetest tiniest profoundest sexiest room in all the whole wide world."

They got up and she put on her robe and he put on his trousers and they went down the hall and took a bath and came back and got dressed and walked down to the highway and caught the bus to Monterey, near the sea the open sea, and probably the loveliest quaintest town that ever was and ever would be. They had a snack in a small café and they walked around the town together and everything was lovely and romantic to her and she drank it in and ate it up with her enormous appetite. But every now and then against his will he would catch himself thinking of how it would be in Monterey with Fannie Mae and comparing her with Millie and he was a dirty low-down dog, and he would put his arms around his wife to reassure the both of them.

They caught the bus back to Ford Ord Village, and when they got off the bus, instead of going rightward up the road to the Village, they went across the highway to the edge of the world and watched the dark and foamy sea beneath the moonlight playing tag with California. They stood breathless side by side, with her head upon his shoulder and his arm around her waist.

She said, "I'm the happiest woman in the world."

He said, "And I'm the luckiest soldier."

"Do you really mean it, Solly?"

"That's the silliest question in the world."

She looked up into his face and kissed him briefly on his lips and turned and looked away to sea again, where the full moon was a mighty floodlight making a highway from the ocean to the stars. "You're not only the handsomest man in the company. I'll bet you have the highest Intelligence Quotient."

He laughed. "You're just prejudiced, is what."

"Well, aren't you? Haven't you? You're the company clerk —you've seen all the company records."

He said, "I plead guilty, your honor. Your most beautiful Grace. For some reason or other, mine happens to be the highest."

"I'll bet it's even higher than your captain's."

"Guilty again."

"And yet you're nothing but a corporal."

"Is that all I am?"

She said, "To me you're everything. You know you are. But why? Why?—Why haven't you followed the plan you had to get ahead in the Army? Why're you no higher than corporal? What happened to Officer Candidate School?"

"It seems I didn't have the proper attitude."

She said, "What're you talking about?"

"It's a long complicated story."

She said, "We have loads of time."

She didn't know how swiftly time was running out for them. And how could he explain to her in simple terms what had happened to his expectations? She had always lived a sheltered life, and he had contributed to the sheltering. He had not even told her of his one-night prison record or his visit in the hospital. How could he tell her about his CO, a man he hated and despised, yet almost clearly understood. A man who stood immovably between him and ambition and OCS and promotion and all the other U.S. Army ladders to success.

He said, "Some other time, my baby. Let's not spoil this precious moment."

He took her into his arms and kissed her as a sweet breeze came from off the ocean. And they turned their backs to the black sea with its white caps and went across the highway to the Village.

When they got back to their room they made love again and it happened all over again. The first act was the petting and building up the excitement and suspense, and Act Two was the delicious conflict, and in Act Three came the Moment of Truth and the Climax, but just as before, he imagined Fannie Mae, as hard as he tried not to, and just as before, at the very last millionth of a second he floundered and he foundered. It was as if you drank a cool glass of lemonade and felt it go down your mouth and throat but was robbed of its delicious taste. And afterwards, sated and contented, she talked greedily about it, and he agreed with her that it was the greatest ever ever.

And then she blew into his ear and said, "You know this is the first time I ever completely enjoyed it. This evening before we went out was the first time I ever reached an honest-to-goodness climax."

He sat up on the cot and studied her contented face. It was different from Fannie Mae's somehow. It was like the cat after she eats the canary, he thought, smug and arrogant. Fannie Mae's glowed with love, Millie's with a full stomach. He said, "You're kidding."

She said, "As God is my judge, this evening before we went out was the very first time." His eyes roved uneasily over her voluptuous body. She opened her eyes and closed them again and she seemed to be smiling all over herself.

He said, "I can't believe it."

Her mounds of nippled softness inhaling and exhaling, the roundish almost-flatness of her belly in and out and in and out. "It's all right, darling. It was well worth waiting for." She took his hand and he pulled away from her.

"Why didn't you tell me before?"

"Because you would have been angrier than you are now, and I wouldn't have known how to tell you anyhow. But there's no need to be angry, honey. You really made up for it today, and we have a lifetime before us. And you're the greatest lover of them all."

He said stubbornly, "I'm the same person I was then."

She said, "But I'm not. I used to be scared to death when you would have yours and nothing would happen to me. I would get right to the city gates but never reach the city. I thought that maybe it would always be like that, and I was scared to talk to you about it. I thought something was wrong with me."

Solly stood up and glowered at this gorgeous woman who was his wife, who was all at once a stranger to him. He was suddenly self-conscious and he stepped into his trousers.

She said, "Since you left New York I read every book I could lay hands on about the art of making love. The thing we were doing wrong was you weren't preparing me enough. It takes a woman longer to get excited."

He said disgustedly, "Good God! Do we have to talk it into the ground like this? I mean you're supposed to *make* love, not talk it to death."

She said, "Of course you have to talk about it. You sound like the nineteenth century."

The sweat poured from his angry body. "Keep quiet, will you?"

"You are absolutely reactionary, Solly Saunders, and you're supposed to be the great progressive." She held out her hands to him. "Come here, baby, and stop your silly pouting."

He went reluctantly to her and bent over her and she reached up and pulled him down till her sassy mouth grabbed his angry trembling lips.

Later he took off his pants again and started to get in the other bed. She had fallen asleep and was breathing deeply snoring slightly. He walked over to her and looked down into her lovely face and he tried to get into bed beside her, but there wasn't room, and he started to get out of bed again, but she moved in her sleep to the other edge of the bed, making room for him, and put her arms around his neck and her head upon his chest and it was only then that he realized she was crying quietly.

"What the devil's the matter with you?"

In the midst of tears and sobbing she said, "You think I'm just a sex thing. I mean nothing else to you. To you I'm brainless and heartless and—just a pretty piece—"

He said angrily, "It isn't true! You know it isn't!"

His chest was wet with her tears. "You think I'm stupid You don't talk to me about anything important."

"That isn't true!" he shouted softly.

"I know how you feel about the war, but you won't discuss it with me. I know it's antifascist and democratic. Even my boss discusses the issues with me more than you. And he's just as progressive and liberal as you are, and he doesn't think I'm beautiful but dumb."

Solly said out of his deepest anger, "I'll just bet he is and does!"

She sucked the tears back up her nostrils. "Its' a war we can't afford to lose. I agree with you. That's the main reason I wanted you to get promoted—be a leader—an officer—"

For the last few hours they had been as close as two persons could be and yet he suddenly realized she had made love to a stranger. She thought he was the same man he was four months ago. He sat up in the bed and took her by her sobbing shoulders.

He said, "Understand me clearly. I am not concerned about this madness called the Democratic War except to get it over with and get out of it. I used to believe in it. But I have had experiences in this democratic Army, and I no longer give a damn. I don't want to get ahead in here. I just want *out*."

She was shocked to silence for a moment. Finally she said, "You don't mean that—"

He said, "You'd better believe I mean it. And I don't want to discuss it any further." He got out of bed and got into the other one and lay there breathing angrily, as he listened to her whimper. She got up and came to him, and they lay naked in each other's arms.

She said, "Just tell me that you love me. It's the only thing that matters."

He said, "I love you—I love you—I love you—"

Everybody was on the run all day long the next day and well into the night. They were leaving for the staging area of the port of embarkation on the following morning at six o'clock. When he got back to their room they had a snack and they made love.

She had that same look of complacent satisfaction. She said, "Let's go to bed. It's getting late."

He said, "I have to go back to camp tonight. We're moving out tomorrow morning."

She said, "You're going on some sort of convoy?"

He should have told her when he met her at the depot in Salinas. He should have told her a thousand times before this time. "We're going to Camp Stoneman Staging Area up in Pittsburg, California. We'll be there for a few days getting ready to get on the boat."

She sat silently for a moment and then she looked around at the things in the room, one by one, the dresser, the chest of drawers, the chair, the other cot, the other chair, and then to him. "Why?" she said. "You—you should have told me. Why?"

"I didn't know myself till you were already on your way, and I didn't have the heart to tell you yesterday." He walked over to her and ran his hand through her hair. Her eyes were wide but not so knowing as per usual. Suddenly she looked lonely and betrayed and uncertain of herself. He had never imagined her this way, his proud and haughty one. She aroused in him the deepest compassion. He pulled her to her feet and into his arms. "Yesterday was such a beautiful happy day for us, I just couldn't—I mean I just didn't know how to tell you."

Her wide eyes filled and she told him she understood, it wasn't his fault. It really wasn't. She said, "I'll go with you to the staging point."

He told her they were going on a troop train and nothing but soldiers were allowed. She said she would catch a regular train then, because she was going, and she was going to be with him as long as he was in this country. He told her he didn't know how long they were going to be at the staging area, he didn't know if he could find a place for her stay in Pittsburg.

She said, "You don't want me to go. You're tired of me already."

He said, "Don't say that, Millie. Because you know it isn't true."

She said, "You don't love me—you don't love me, but I don't care. I'm coming up there anyway." She pulled away from him and sat on the bed and her eyes got wider and wider and the tears pushed out and spilled down her cheeks. He'd never seen her cry before she came to California. He went to her and sat beside her and took her into his arms and she tried to pull away, but he held her, he kissed her trembling mouth and her salty tears, and she put her arms around his neck and "Solly—Solly—Solly! You're all I got! You're all I love!"

He said stupidly, "Your family, they—"

She said, "I don't care about my phony family out in Brooklyn. You and your mother are all I have—all I give a damn about. You think they wanted me to marry you? You think they ever really forgave me?" She laughed bitterly. "You can't get out of it that easily. You're stuck with me for better or worse. I know you think it's mostly for the worst." And she held him desperately, as if she would never ever let him go, till death, not even then, and his body hard against the softness of her quivering body, and they made love, and this time love was good for both of them. They reached the city together, together together together! Like they had never done before. And she lay in his arms and laughed and cried at the same time, as if she were hysterical.

She came to Pittsburg two days later and they found a room in town in a private house. It was smaller than the room at Fort Ord Village, but every night for two weeks they lived desperately, loving fiercely, like they were trying to live and love a lifetime. And now all of that was over and the new thing lay ahead of him. The new thing was the big white boat.

His eyes searched frantically for Millie as he marched with the other soldiers up the long thoroughfare toward the boat. Women were running out to the line of march, crying and laughing and kissing the men good-bye, but where in the hell was his Millie?

Bookworm Taylor walked beside him, nibbling from a carton of Baby Ruth candy and keeping up a constant chatter. But Solly's eyes kept traveling up and down the line of civilians on either side of the street. She would be along here somewhere any second now and she would come calmly out of the throng and walk alongside him till they reached the ship. Solly's mind made a picture of her, and she looked the same as last night when he left her, as he had walked away from her, with the brisk California night air biting into his warm angry body, when he had turned for one last glimpse of her in the doorway, smiling and waving good-bye to him and looking desperately lost and helpless.

Last night they had sat on the side of the big iron bed which was almost as big as the two-by-four room, making conversation and half listening to a portable radio, acting like it was just any night and not their last night together. Play-acting like in the moving pictures. He looked into her lovely face and she thought about their baby lying quiet in her belly, and it was building up inside of him like tidewater in the time of flood. There they were, she and their baby, and he was going away from them, and he might be gone forever.

Suddenly he got to his feet. "Why the hell am I going overseas?" He wasn't asking her—she knew he wasn't asking her. And yet he wanted her to tell him.

"Every man has to go, dear heart," she said. "And I'm so proud of you, I don't know what to do."

He said angrily, wanting to hurt her now, for some sadistic masochistic reason he could not explain. Hurt her and hurt himself. "What are you so proud of? I didn't go upward and onward as you expected. I'm just a corporal, that's all, and that's just a couple of jumps ahead of a buck private."

She said in a quivering voice, "I'm proud of the fact that my husband is a soldier in the Army of the United States, and I'm not worrying about you coming back. I know you are, my darling. I—"

He said, "You're goddamn right I am. I'm going to look out for Solly and I'm not going to be a hero either. You can believe me when I say so."

She said, "Darling—"

He said, "The thing that I can't figure is why I didn't desert and go to Mexico or down in Central America somewhere like others did, till this damn stupidness is over."

She said, "Because you are an American, and your country is at war, and because I love you."

He said, "You tell me what a black American has to fight for."

He stared at her and could not help thinking of Fannie Mae. He had received a letter at the camp from her that very day. She'd been hearing from Bookworm all along. She told him she would never forget him, and she would never regret him, no matter how many times her heart broke every time the memory came, which was every hour every day. She couldn't stand the Post Exchange after he left. Seeing lonesome soldiers always made her think of him. So she had quit her job and she was thinking of joining the WAACs and serving her country in the battle for democracy. Maybe she would meet him somewhere sometime on some far-off battlefront. He read the letter after lunch. seated on his bunk in the barracks. read it two or three times and got angrier each time. He tore it into little pieces and let them drop on his bunk and picked them up again and put them in his pocket. He felt a wild and crazy rage. He sat back on his bunk and tried to write her a letter, but each time he got a page written, he would tear it up and put it in the wastebasket at the top of the barracks stairs.

Finally he went out of the barracks to the maddest wildest loudest Post Exchange in the world. He placed a call to Ebbensville, Georgia, and talked directly to her. He told her she must be out of her mind, volunteering into this cracker Army. She told him not to worry. She had already gone to the armory in Ebbensville to volunteer and had been turned down, because their colored quota was filled. Solly said, "Wonderful!" She said, "I love you, Solly." He said, "You didn't have any business trying to enlist in the first place." She said, "I'll always love you, even if I never see you again, cause I love you and I'm happy that I love you, and I'll never love another like I love you." He said, "I'll write you when I get where I'm going." She said, "I'll always remember you, Solly, and love you, and I'm glad that you love me, and I'm glad you called me to tell me you love me." He said angrily, "I did not call you to tell—" She said happily, "All right, darling, I understand." Then he said, "Yes, I love you." But how in the hell could he love two women? Another thing she said to him was, "I hate to say this, Solly, but there is nothing for us to fight for excepting freedom here at home. All the Negro soldiers should be conscientious objectors. They have no business in the Army." He tried to talk her out of her bitterness, tried to bolster his own shaky position.

When he came out of it, Millie was standing in his arms, her hand caressing the back of his neck. ". . . and for me," she was saying, "and for our future when it's over, and for your law career, and furthermore, you might as well make the best of it, there's nothing we can do about you. You can't be a deserter. You understand, dear heart?"

He put his hand on her roundish belly. "And for our child," he said gently. "For our quiet undemanding baby, who never kicks, no matter what, not even when the Army takes his dad away."

She looked away from his face and back again. "Do you love me, Solly? Do you truly love me?"

He said, "Of course I love you." Impatiently.

She said, "Do you love me more than anything else or anybody in all the world?"

Was she a mind reader?

"I love you and I'm in love with you. But that does not make me love the Army of my Uncle Sam."

She said, "I love you so much, Solly, it's really frightening. Back home I would wake up in the middle of the night, scared to death that you'd never come back to me, that you didn't love me any more—that—"

"Shut up!" he said. And kissed the words back into her mouth. "Hush your mouth, my baby."

She said, "Ever since I've known you, every thought has been for you. You don't think I really give a dime about this phony war. I don't care who wins, but as long as you have to be in it, I wanted you to make the most of it, but you never listened to me. Oh no—"

He stood away from her. "I have listened. I *am* listening. I didn't need to listen. I had the same idea as you had. I went you one better. I even believed in the war."

She wiped her eyes and blew her nose and sat down on the bed again. "Tell me where I'm wrong. You're a man with superior intelligence. You're a colored soldier."

"There is that last about me," he said drily.

"You have to be in the white folks' Army. You don't want to, but you have to be. What's wrong with hating it as fiercely as you can, but at the same time getting as much out of it as you can? You don't owe them any loyalty, but you do owe yourself a better life. That's all I ever wanted for you."

He went to her and sat down beside her and put his arms around her and kissed the fresh salty tears from her eyes. She was complicatedly uncomplicated. "I love you, Millie baby, I really do."

"What's wrong with getting as much out of the war as you can, even though you hate it? Answer me."

"Nothing. Nothing at all. And I don't even hate the war particularly." He just despised the Army.

"All the more reason why you should get the most out of it," she said. "Everybody is doing it. Look at all the big businesses. Everybody with brains is all out for the war effort to make as big a pile as possible."

He said, "Wave those flags and make that money, that's

America to me." He had a new respect for Millie. She was not naïve with her opportunism. She was awesomely realistic. And she was for him—first, last, and always. He understood this clearly. She was his woman.

She wiped her eyes again. "Then you agree?"

He said, "What's to disagree with? I never disagreed. I've made a few silly mistakes which stopped me temporarily, but no matter where they send me, I can work on those advancements, and I can make it, don't you worry. All I have to do is to put my mind to it."

She kissed his cheeks, his nose, the corners of his angry mouth. "I'm so happy, darling. My boss's son went to an American Officer Candidate School since he's been overseas in England. He's a captain already."

He said, "If it can be done, your husband will do it. Why should the bastards who *never* believed in the war make more out of it than me?"

She kissed his eyes. "And why should the Negro take a back seat? Especially a militant progressive Negro like yourself and with your superiority?"

He said, "Baby—"

She said, "My boss is a very liberal man, you know, Solly. He wants to talk with you as soon as you get back about a job in the firm as a legal clerk while you do your last year in law school. And if you come back home an officer, well the chances are—"

He said, "To hell with what your boss wants."

She nibbled and she tongued his ear and she was smiling happy through her tears. "This is our last night together. Let's not spend it all in talking." Then she turned from him and stretched out on the bed and began to cry and cry and cry.

He sat her up and took her into his arms. "What's the matter with you now?"

She put her head on his chest. "Nothing's the matter. I'm not crying." Her body shook with sobbing. She tried to laugh. "I'm just silly and stupid and happy and already I feel so lonesome." Her voice choked off again and she could not keep back the tears. "I feel like the world is moving out from under me."

"You have your family, you have my mother, and you'll have the baby. I'm the poor boob who'll be lonely."

She cried, "The baby! The baby! The baby!"

He said, "The baby'll be all right. I'll be back before he

misses me. Fathers are not that important anyhow. Now if you were going overseas and I were left to have the baby, that would be something really serious." He tried to laugh her out of it.

She stopped sobbing and she wiped her eyes. "This is our last night together, and I have to tell you something important."

Something scary in her voice alerted him. He felt a hard pain in his rectum, but he tried to be lighthearted. "Don't tell me at this late date I'm not the baby's father."

"Do you love me with or without the baby?"

"I love you *period!* What is this nonsense?"

And then she almost lost her voice. "There is no baby."

"I don't hear you. What *about* the baby?"

"I said there is no baby. There never was."

He said in a shaky voice, "That's a silly way to kid a man on his last night in this part of the world."

Her eyes were crying out for help in the flood of her angry tears. "There is no baby! There is no baby! There is no baby!"

He took her by the shoulders and shook her. "What the hell are you talking about?"

"I was never pregnant and I'm a deceitful bitch and I made it all up because I thought you didn't love me." Her voice choked and she cried and cried.

"Stop! Stop it!" he shouted. "You're upset because I'm leaving. You're hysterical—" He stood up and stared at her unbelievingly.

"I used to read your letters over and over again and I knew you didn't love me any more—I could tell there was somebody else—and—and I was scared to death of losing you. I didn't know what to do. So I thought, if he thinks I'm with his child he'll love me—" She lay on the bed and pushed her face into the pillow and cried like a motherless child.

He stopped breathing, his heart stopped beating, and he died and he was dead. Numbed-dead. Dead-dead. He wanted to go to her and say, "Yes, you're a lying deceitful bitching whore, yes, you are—you are—you are!" And slap her till his hand was dead, and slap her till she passed out, and keep on slapping her till she came to again. He hated her violently because she had deceived him, because she made him hate himself.

He stared at her. "Was it a miscarriage?"

She shook her head in anguish.

"Was it an abortion?"

"Go to hell!" she screamed.

He grabbed her shoulders and started to shake her. She was a murderer. She killed his child. "You're a monster, you know that? And I hate your goddamn soul!"

She said, "Go ahead! Beat me up! I don't care. That's what you want to do, isn't it? Kill me—I'm a monster!"

He turned her loose and walked across the room. He felt that everything was dead between them. And all was dead inside of him. And they had killed each other.

He thought his brains were burning up. He went back to the bed and put his hand on her shoulder. She shouted, "Don't touch me. Get out of my sight! I'm a no-good lying bitch! I know what you're thinking—I'm a lying bitch and a monster, but I'm not ashamed. And I don't ever want to see you again in all the days of my life. You're coldhearted and you're insensitive, and I'm so ashamed—I'm so ashamed! You're a brute—that's what you are!"

His head was like a Coney Island roller coaster. The war was raging in his stomach. His throat was dry, his brow was wet. He had no idea how he felt. He thought he was in a coma. He lived a hundred years this moment, and he could never be the same.

"I'll kill myself, that's what I'll do! I'll kill myself!"

He said, "No!" And he took her firmly by the shoulder and pulled her up from the bed and into his arms and said, "I love you!" But why did she do it! How could she make it all up like that! Why in the hell did she do it? He felt as if she had created their child and then murdered it willfully and maliciously. Just to get even with him.

She said, "No, you don't! You hate me! I'll kill myself, that's what I'll do. I know you hate me!" She was crying and talking and sobbing at the same time and she wet his shirt with her tears. And he was blind with hate and guilt and anger. His fault! His fault! His dirty low-down guilty fault. Goddamn her soul, it was his fault! He felt a great compassion for her.

He said, "Don't you tell me how I feel. I'm in love with you. I didn't *marry* your baby, did I? The only baby I married was a great big beautiful silly crybaby." He felt so guilty he felt like dying violently.

She took his handkerchief out of his back pocket and wiped her eyes and blew her nose. He said tonelessly, "Come on now —what kind of way is this to carry on on our last night together? We'll have plenty of time to make as many babies as we want just as soon as I get back. You can believe me when I tell you."

She laughed and her eyes filled up again, and he kissed away her salty tears. "It's all my fault," he said, "It's all my fault." And quietly he took off her dress and then her slip and then her brassière, he kissed the nipples of her gleaming breasts, took off her panties, stared at her roundish stomach. She said, "For the last two months I stuffed myself like a pig just to make my stomach fat." Her eyes filled up. He took her up in his arms and lay her naked on the bed. She shyly got beneath the sheets—tentatively, poised for flight, unsure. He pulled off his clothes and went to her and she was cold with fear at first, but he was warm, and he blamed her and he hated her, but he knew he was to blame, and he loved her, and he kissed away her doubts and fears, temporarily at least, and his body gave her body warmth, and they made desperation love together, and love was good and good and good. Love was good for both of them. And a little after midnight they kissed good night and he went wearily back to the barracks.

The soldiers were marching in full field dress, with packs on their backs, duffel bags on their shoulders, and carbines and rifles. They were talking and joke-cracking and nervously laughing as they approached the big white ship. They were the lead company in the regiment immediately following the last of the white troops. Even at route step there was a certain uniform cadence in the sound of their feet striking the asphalt road as they moved forward under the midday sun, through a long funnel of noisy people and quiet palm trees and gorgeous shrubbery. But Solly hadn't spotted Millie yet and he was getting sick from worry. Something must have happened to her!

Bookworm walking beside him, talking, laughing and grumbling, and eating candy. "Man, I'm telling you, these people a bitch on wheels. What you reckin I read in *your* Harlem paper last night? Some of *your* folks' leaders called on the President down in Washington and demanded that colored soldiers be allowed to die with dignity at the front rather than serving in the Quartermaster. Now ain't that a mother-fer-ya?"

Solly's eyes shifted distractedly from the line of people to the Bookworm and back to the people again.

Worm said, "Percy Black can have my uniform any day in the week, he wants to fight so damn bad. Them Japanese ain't done me nothing. I ain't mad at a living ass."

Solly could see the big ship plainly now and the white troops getting aboard, and the fear was almost overwhelming. Maybe he had already passed Millie and they hadn't seen each other for looking so damn hard. He opened his mouth and let the air go in and out to relieve the pressure in his chest and the griping in his belly. He thought of Fannie Mae and felt an awful guilt toward Millie. Maybe she had been so upset last night, she had become ill and something awful had happened to her, with no way to let him know, too sick to move. He could hear her crying: "I'll kill myself! That's what I'll do! I'll kill myself!" He felt weak all over. Maybe she—maybe she— A wave of panic swept over him, and wave after wave after wave. Maybe —maybe—she had seen through him completely, she had felt his hatred and his anger, even as they'd made their love together. And she had killed herself. He loved her! Yes he loved her!

And then he saw her up ahead, waving at him with the widest prettiest most confident smile that anybody ever smiled. He was so glad he could hardly move his lips to smile or laugh or anything else. He loved her, yes, he loved her. She came to him in all her raging beauty, and his ears burned as he heard the soldiers whistling and signifying.

"Hello, soldier boy, where do you think you're going?"

"Damn," he said finally in as calm a voice as he could manage. "I thought maybe you had forgotten what day it was. Thought you had forgotten to come to my going-away party."

"Now how do you sound?" She laughed at the funny look on his face and told him he looked cute with the dark sunglasses and needing a shave and the helmet on his handsome head and the pack on his poor back. She was at that very moment very very precious to him with their baby as yet unconceived and the way she submerged her own feelings for the sake of his, and he was an adulterous undeserving bastard! And a great guilt began to build inside of him mixed with an overwhelming tenderness. He couldn't keep the tears from coming to his eyes and spilling down his face.

He said, "You're so pretty you ought to be ashamed of yourself."

She pretended not to notice his tears and walked with

him, laughing and talking till they reached the last block. The women were not allowed to go any further. Looking at her, he wished somehow she would cry, just a little bit anyhow, and yet he was damn thankful she didn't. She reached up and kissed him quickly.

"Good-bye, darling, take care of yourself. And don't worry about me or Mama. I'll write every day, beginning this afternoon."

And he said, "Don't you worry about me, sweetheart. I'm going to take care of myself, and I'm going to get ahead in this Army, and I'm coming back to Millie."

She said, "Concentrate on the last item first and foremost, last and always and forever." And she kissed him and was gone.

The last of the white soldiers were boarding the beautiful white ship, and a band on board was playing "God Bless America." He felt a chill like a wave of electric current pass across his slim shoulders, and he wasn't sure whether it was from "God Bless America" or from leaving Millie behind. He hoped she could hear the band playing and that she would know how much it helped him to understand why Americans, no matter their color or condition, had to go to fight for their country so many thousands of miles away from home. "God bless America . . . God bless America . . . *I love this land* . . . He really loved this land.

They stopped in the middle of the block and stood waiting until the last white regiment was all aboard. He wanted to look back for one last glimpse of Millie.

I love you, Millie—I love this land—

He wanted desperately to look back, but he would not let himself. Then they started again, marching toward the ship, and it hit him like a vicious kick in the solar plexus, as suddenly the band stopped playing "God Bless America" and jumped into another tune—"The Darktown Strutters' Ball." . . .

He didn't want to believe his ears. He looked up heatedly at the ship and saw some of the white soldiers on deck, waving and smiling innocently and friendly-like at the Negro soldiers below, and yelling, "Yeah, man!" and popping their pinky-white fingers. A taste of gall crept from his stomach up into his mouth.

"Goddamn," he heard Worm say, "that's the kind of music I like." The husky little soldier cut a cute soft-shoe step. "I guess Charlie wants us to jitterbug onto his pretty white boat. Special men—we ain't no soldiers. We ain't nothing but a bunch of goddamn clowns."

Solly's stomach felt like he had been eating double-edged razor blades and an awful heat grew inside his collar. He hoped Millie was too far away to hear.

Worm grinned at him. "What's the matter, good kid? Mad about something? Damn—that's what I hate about you colored folks. Take the goddamn chip off your shoulder. They just trying to make you people feel at home. Don't you recognize the Negro National Anthem when you hear it?"

Solly didn't answer. He just felt his anger mounting and he wished he could walk right out of the line and to hell with everything. Nothing had changed though. He would still do what he had to do. He would take care of himself, he would get ahead in the Army, he would come home safe and sound to Millie. He would hate it and at the same time take advantage of it. There was nothing else that he could do. His face filled up, his eyes were warm and misty too. With "The Darktown Strutters' Ball" ringing in his ears he put up his head and threw his shoulders back, and he kept on marching toward the big white boat.

Part III

LIGHTNING— THUNDER— RAINFALL

CHAPTER

I

The big white boat took them to San Francisco, where four hours later they took another, an old Dutch liner, which had been converted hastily into a troop transport and renamed the *U.S.S. New Rotterdam,* and by the time the sun was about to sit down over the ocean, they moved under the Golden Gate Bridge and put out toward the open sea. Just as they were getting aboard, two MPs drove up with Scotty and put him onto the ship and into the brig.

Solly and Bookworm and Lanky Lincoln and Jimmy Larker stood on deck and watched the continent slip farther and farther away from them as they ploughed a long white foaming row through the middle of the grass-green ocean.

Ever since they left the docks in San Francisco, they had been looking for the rest of the ships to join the convoy. A Coast Guard cutter led the way and another brought up the rear. A big fat sluggish-looking blimp hovered above them like an ugly buzzard and these were their only obvious escorts. These three were giving them safe-conduct to a rendezvous with a large task force convoy consisting of other troopships and a couple of battleships and a couple of destroyers and mine sweepers and destroyer escorts. They would be well protected.

They pursued the sunset for over an hour and finally caught up with it at just about the time that their three escorts chickened out and turned back toward home, and darkness fell. Fell with a thud like black heavy drapes all over the ocean, far and wide all over the Western world.

The public address system blasted away at the dark and heavy silence:

NOW HEAR THIS—NOW HEAR THIS
NO SMOKING ON DECK OR STRIKING OF MATCHES.
LOCK THE PORTHOLES, SECURE THE HATCHES.
BLACKOUT REGULATIONS ARE NOW IN OPERATION.

And then a slight pause and then the deep brassy voice again said:

DUMP THE GARBAGE.

Buck Rogers pompously explained that the ships always dumped the garbage after dark, so that by daybreak they would be miles and miles away and a Japanese submarine would have a tough time picking up their trail.

"These people think of everything to protect your fine brown body."

Worm said, "Yeah—but what happened to the rendezvous? Them chickenshit escorts left us in this big black sea all by ourselves to root hog or die."

The silence was as thick and heavy and as awesome as the darkness. Solly staring with the rest of them over the side of the ship and seeing nothing but black space and great big white phosphorescent waves around the ship as it ploughed perpetually forward. It might have been a giant ghost ship sailing this side of an endless black wall, trying to come to the end of it and sail around, but never succeeding. Solly said he'd never heard of a troopship going overseas to the combat zone entirely unescorted.

Buck said, "Don't get scared, men. And don't be prejudiced. You know Uncle is going to look out for his colored nephews. Maybe the rendezvous is in Hawaii. Just because you're colored, you don't have to look on the dark side all the time. Wait till I get my life jacket on." He laughed nervously but nobody joined him.

The salty wet wind blew into their faces as the big ship

moved steadily and unafraid through the great big blackness, rocking deliberately from side to side, keeping time with the steady throbbing beat of the mighty diesel engine.

Worm said, "I got a good mind to jump overboard and make it back to San Francisco."

CHAPTER

2

Twelve days later Solly saw a ship on the horizon to the starboard. It blinked there for moment briefly in the sunlight and its sudden disappearance gave him an eerie kind of feeling, and after a while he thought perhaps it had been an optical illusion.

There was very little to do with his days. He spent many hours on topside, staring thousands of sparkling-blue miles into endlessness toward the edge of the world, where the sky and ocean came together and where his future lurked on the other side. If he could just see what lay ahead of him. But all he saw was the vast monotony of everything and nothingness.

Some of his hours he spent trying to get a novel started. He wrote pages, he tore up pages. He tried realism, naturalism, he tried streams of consciousness. He tried to remember Creative Writing courses he had had at City College. He sweated over pages, till finally he wrote five pages to his liking and he felt like celebrating. He drank beer with Worm and Lanky till all three of them were cockeyed. It was as if he had finished writing an entire book which a publisher had accepted. And he would be a novelist when he got back home and to hell with the legal profession.

It was the seventeenth day out when they saw the first thing faintly resembling land since leaving San Francisco. When they got an initial glimpse it looked like a dark shadow on the dazzling-bright horizon. Then it turned out to be a giant storm cloud, and then, as they came closer, it was obviously the Japanese fleet; then it was the convoy they had been catching up with since San Francisco, and as they came even closer they saw airplanes circling it, and they realized it was actually a Japanese aircraft carrier, and in Worm's expressed opinion, "Somebody should tell the stupid skipper of the *New Rottergoddamn-dam!*" who continued to head directly toward it as if it were a magnet or the point of debarkation. And then the airplanes changed before their eyes into sea gulls and the men laughed and the flattop changed into a huge desert rock jutting up out of the sea, away out there a million miles from nowhere. The *New Rotterdam* passed about two hundred yards to the left of the big black moss-covered mountain, and then there was the furious speculation that the Imperial Navy was hiding on the other side. And they laughed uneasily.

Between staring into the vast empty future and writing his novel about the Army and bull sessions with Moore and Worm and Rogers and Lanky Lincoln and Jimmy Larker, the time slipped past like the bottomless ocean beneath the ship. Some evenings he would sit in the hot and overcrowded hatch and watch the great and endless checkers duel between two of the oldest men in the outfit, Jackie Ray and Geoffrey Grant. The hatch smelled like a locker room—close and angry. Jackie was a tall lanky soldier from Cleveland, Ohio, and before that from Iberia, Louisiana, which he never mentioned. The men nicknamed him "Hopjack." In his youth he had been a professional tap dancer, according to him. And even now he was a fair-to-middling hoofer. Grant was a self-proclaimed Black Nationalist from New York City and Trinidad. The men nicknamed him, "General Grant." His face was always deep in thought and his forehead ever wrinkled. They had a checkers tournament going which began the day they put out to sea.

They played their games in a sweating deadly earnest and they argued the fate of the world. The General was pro-Japanese—he pictured the Japanese as the champions of the colored race. Hopjack was a Yankee-doodling flag-waving red-blooded American, who couldn't wait to get overseas and into the patriotic war.

Sometimes Solly would come from topside and walk over to them and ask them, "What's the score?" They always announced each other's score. The General would look up from the game and smile sheepishly and grudgingly admit, "White folks—228." And stare at the dark-faced Hopjack, whom he characterized positively as a white-folks' colored man, unworthy of human consideration. Yet they were the best of buddies.

And Hopjack would announce Grant's score triumphantly, "Japanese—221."

And the lead kept changing hands from day to day as the battle raged and the whole world hung in balance.

Solly would sit and watch and listen to them argue. One evening when the score was White Folks 356 and Japanese 359, Hopjack said, "Goddamn, you just as sneaky as them Japs."

Grant said, "Don't show your ignorance, mawn."

Hop said, "Your mama must've had a Jap insurance man."

Grant said indignantly, "The Japanese are not sneaky. They are an honorable race of people."

"How come that man was in Washington grinning in the President's face at the same time they snuck up on Pearl Harbor?"

Rogers came over. "You goddamn right they're sneaky. Remember Pearl Harbor, a day of infamy, so help us God, and chin up and V for Victory and we did it before and we can do it again, and all that kind of shit." He started to sing in his brassy bass:

> *"Land where my fathers died,*
> *Land of the Pilgrim's pride—"*

And Solly remembered Millie and Pittsburg and the day he left it all behind, and "The Darktown Strutters' Ball."

Hop got up and said, "I just wanna slap a dirty little Jap." And he did a fancy tap-dance step.

Other men had gathered around and were laughing at the floor show. General Grant was speechless with rage. He looked up and around at the laughing men and the wrinkles in his forehead seemed to be popping out of his tightened skin.

"You goddamn ignorant bawstards! The Japanese are fighting for your freedom and your dignity. The white man is the most deceitful, the most two-faced human being in all the world. But if he pissed in your face and told you it was raining outdoors, you damn fools would purchase umbrellas."

Solly felt a kind of vague uneasy sympathy with the General, and he was not one of those laughing, and neither was Clint or Jimmy Larker, whom the men had named the Quiet Man.

Solly said quietly, "I appreciate how you feel, and I don't blame you. But you have to face the facts. Both the Germans and the Japanese have fascist governments, and Hitler and Tojo *are* out to dominate the world."

Grant shouted, "Of course they are, mawn. That's what I been trying to tell these fools. Hitler and Tojo are going to conquer the whole damn world, and then after that, Tojo going to conquer Hitler, and the colored mawn going to rule the world. The bottom coming to the top."

Solly shook his head. He wanted Grant to tell him that Asia offered something different. Not just the bottom coming to the top. This was not enough for him.

Hopjack said, "They still the sneakiest people in the world and they snuck up on Pearl Harbor and you must be drinking jungle juice."

Solly wanted General Grant to say that Asia and Africa were the New World—the brand-new hope for all mankind. Because sometimes he himself harbored a sneaky suspicion that Western civilization was hopelessly hopeless. That it had had its chance and goofed it.

Grant said, "You got your facts all mis-screwed." Some of the soldiers laughed at him.

Solly said seriously, "But, General, the Japanese *did* make an unprovoked attack on Pearl Harbor. I mean, no matter what your sympathies may be—I mean—I may sympathize with you but—facts are facts—"

Grant screamed like a snake had bitten him. "Unprovoked? Unprovoked? I'm surprised at you, Corporal Solly. You supposed to be intelligent. You just like the rest of them—believe everything the white mawn say—"

Solly said, "But they did, didn't they? I mean, those are the facts."

Grant said, "What you think the American Navy was doing in Hawaii? What you think the Japanese ambassador was doing in Washington?"

Rogers said, "I'll bite—what was he doing?

"The white mawn in Washington didn't want to see the great proud Japanese people follow their destiny, which is to lead the colored people to rule the world. Africa and Asia gon come to the top."

Rogers burlesqued, "I don't want no goddamn spooks ruling over me. I know a couple of spook cops in Harlem. They get their nuts off whipping black heads. Course I don't blame them. They better not whip any of them pretty white folks' heads."

Grant said contemptuously to Rogers, "You have no dignity, Sergeant." He looked around at the rest of the men. "The United States was trying to choke the Japanese to death, cutting off all their trade with other countries and so, and the reason the Navy was in Hawaii, they were getting ready to attack the Japanese mainland, and the Japanese ambassador was in Washington talking peace and trying to head them off and trying to get a breathing spell for his great country and its mission. He thought he was dealing with gentlemen. He didn't know the white mawn. Washington turned him down flat, and although the Japanese were not ready yet to wage war against the United States, they had no alternative but to defend themselves."

"That is unadulterated horse manure," Solly said heatedly, and he stared at General Grant and felt like crying—crying for the misdirected bitterness erupting from this sensitive human being. And his country was responsible. His country was entirely culpable.

Rogers said, "You must have been one of those Japanese spies they rounded up in Harlem. How in the hell did you sneak into the Army?"

Grant glared at him. "Your pride is in your arse hole." And the General walked proudly toward the head.

It was just before noon on the twenty-fifth day when Solly saw a long huge strip of greenish earth begin to shape up out of the misty sea like a prehistoric monster and slowly but surely materialize. About a half an hour earlier, a reception committee of sea gulls had come out to meet them and guarantee them safe convoy to the biggest island in the Southern Seas. Between them and the big green monster were smaller islands, scattered over the translucent waters like lettuce leaves in a great and gorgeous salad. The tide was apparently in the flood because some of the smallest of the islands were entirely under water except for the tops of trees, which seemed to grow up from the ocean's depths. The *New Rotterdam* picked its way gingerly into the bay around the tiny uninhabitable islands and the coral atolls and lagoons and the dazzlingly beautiful but treacherous coral reefs toward the big granddaddy of the tropics. The job was made a little easier by the shattering radiance of the sun, which pierced the jeweled blue of the ocean's surface all the way to the bottom of the bay.

Solly stared off the side of the ship through the breathless heat and thought maybe this was where his body would be buried. Maybe tomorrow, maybe the day after that, maybe next month or even maybe this day now. Somewhere on this place, this island, were the men he had come thousands of miles from home and family to hunt down and encircle, to shoot down and to kill. Or be killed. Men like himself, born of woman, with frightened anxious families in their homeland. But it was all their damn fault. The little brown bastards! They let a bunch of power-hungry fanatics lead them down a highway to self-destruction. And misery for the rest of the world. They had made their choice and so must suffer the consequences. The color of their skin had nothing to do with it. He blamed them for fouling up his life in his short life's most important years, and he worked himself into a sweating fury. Maybe it was the heat, maybe the fear and anguish and frustration. Millie and Mama and Fannie Mae and career, writer, lawyer. Life was a tick-tock of infinity, and he was wasting his forever and forever and for what? And it was all their damn fault! These brown men somewhere hidden on this jungle of an island.

He said, "Worm, let's book the next passage back home. I don't believe I'm going to like this place."

Worm laughed his dry laugh. "This is home, buddy boy. We been on a long vacation. We ain't gon never leave again."

Grant's angry eyes were glowing. "Somewhere on this island is the heroes of the colored race!"

Solly said, "Stop kidding yourself, General Grant. We are Americans and these people are our enemies."

Hopjack cut a fancy step. "Let me at em! Let me at em!"

Buck said, "We know you aren't scared, old folks. Why in the hell don't you stop breaking wind? The heat is bad enough already."

Everybody is scared, Solly thought, and everybody is being brave. The big green glittering mystery ahead of them, rising quietly up out of the wide and deep blue water, was awe-inspiring. He was scared but at the same time nervously impatient. He was burning hot and boat-sick, and now that they had arrived he wanted to see what kind of country he had come to.

Far out in the bay the ship stopped suddenly, as if the white rays from the sun had dehydrated its engine. After a time it moved in toward the shore and then back out to the edge of the bay again, and back and forth three or four times, like it couldn't make up its mind, with frantic signaling to the shore and blinding signals in return. A couple of officers boarded the ship from a launch, stayed about fifteen or twenty minutes, and got off again and raced back to the island.

Worm said, "If we going ashore let's go, goddammit!"

General Grant said almost hopefully, "It sure would be funny if the Imperial Navy would slip up behind us at the mouth of the bay and sink every ship in the harbor. That's what you call a mouse trap—a masterful stroke of strategy!" As if he had just gotten word it was going to happen.

Rogers said, "Don't worry about nothing, fellers. Them Japs got better sense than to mess with Uncle Sam like that." He stopped. "Wait a minute—them bastards are just sneaky enough to try something like that. They don't know what cricket is." He cupped his hand around his mouth. His voice was like a muted foghorn. "All ashore that's going ashore! All ashore that's going ashore!"

Nobody laughed, and Solly wondered if it really mattered who won the war, even though he wanted to believe that it mattered desperately. To hell with it. He was in it and was going to make the most of it. Darling Millie. And don't you worry about it, Mama. Your boy is going to do his damnedest to come back home to you and Millie. He has no plans for heroism. Just get ahead and get it over and get back home and start life over.

Three hours later they still sat out in the blazing heat. Quiet Man Larker said, ironically, "Maybe they made a mistake. Maybe they're looking for us over in England to open up that Second Front."

General Grant almost took him seriously. "Then we could shoot up gobs of white men!"

But the impatience of the men notwithstanding, it was

almost dusk before they moved with deliberate purpose toward the zigzagging coastline of deep thick jungle standing breathless in the white heat even as the sun was leaving. Closer in you could see vehicles like giant cockroaches racing through the green thicket, and closer, thatch-roofed buildings and jeeps and trucks and dirt roads and people and "civilization." And finally the ship dropped anchor. A half an hour later the nervous men of 913 climbed, hot and sweaty, down the side of the ship on a swaying rope, carrying packs and duffel bags, and boarded a barge to take them ashore. The other companies in the regiment stayed with the ship and who knows why or what or when.

Bucket-head Baker stood on the barge alongside Solly and Rogers and Bookworm and the others. The barge rocked from side to side and it seemed a fifty-fifty chance that it would bump against the underside of the ship, which reached up out of the water to about a hundred feet above them. Even though no breeze was stirring, they felt a slight wet wind caress their nervous sweaty faces and it was good good good, and Buckethead opened his mouth to drink it in and smacked his lips. "The salty sea sure is delicious. Ain't nothing like it nowhere."

Solly looked up and around and his eyes discovered the source of the sweet breeze blowing. "Salty sea, your ass," he said triumphantly. "Somebody on board just took a piss and flushed the head." He pointed to a hole in the ship about thirty feet above them where the great salty flush had subsided to a feeble sprinkle.

The tension exploded in the heavy heat. The soldiers began to laugh and howl and stomp their feet like they were landing for a Sunday picnic, and the barge bumped heavily against the underside of the old *New Rotterdam*.

And now they stood at ease, ill at ease on the hot white sandy beach, near their packs and duffel bags and rifles, tired and sweaty and angry and nervous and slapping sand flies and mosquitoes. Solly felt he'd been baked in an oven and melted down. And the bugs were making a meal of him. Captain Rutherford told them, "Everything's under control. There's absolutely nothing to worry about. I just have to make a few arrangements. So y'all stay here near your gear till I get back. Take a smoke or anything else, but just don't move from the immediate area."

Scotty sang underneath his breath an old blues fragment.

"Gon grab me a freight train . . .
Take myself a ride. . . ."

The captain asked were there any questions and, before Scotty could open his mouth or raise his hand, called Saunders to accompany him in a jeep he had commandeered. Solly drove with the captain all over the strange and quiet terrain, with its majestic coconut palm trees and its great grass taller-than-tall-menfolk and almost thick enough to walk on top of, as the bright green color began to fade quickly into a dark green, almost black, and the daylight leaving and the sun setting somewhere way out on the Coral Sea. The sticky heat hung around for evening. The first stop was division headquarters and from there to corps, and then to base headquarters, the captain getting hotter by the second, but it did him no good. No place they went were they expected.

At the entrance to base headquarters a homemade sign read:

TIMES SQUARE TEN THOUSAND MILES AS THE CROW FLIES.

A round-faced major gave them a requisition to take to Quartermaster. "They'll give you some cots for tonight. At least your men'll have something to sleep on. Keeps happening all the time. Some promotion-happy lieutenant colonel hurries his outfit overseas before it's ready, just so he can make full colonel. I don't say it happened with you all, but it wouldn't be the first time."

The major must be kidding, Solly thought. Surely—I mean not even the Army! He was so hot and angry, he thought his head would pop wide open. Overseas to sweat and bleed and die ahead of schedule!

The twenty-five days at sea had given Rutherford a broiled-lobster-like expression sprinkled with sea salt, but he was boiling now and very much at sea.

"You're lucky to have something to sleep on," Captain Rutherford told the evil men about an hour later back at the beach. "Thanks to me and Corporal Saunders's loyalty and stubbornness and ingenuity."

But meanwhile night had fallen noisily and definitely and the ungrateful men did not feel lucky, neither did Solly, as the jungle got black dark and began to sound off with birds crying and lizards and frogs and other things whatever-they-were screeching and yelling and laughing and singing like the jungle was a madhouse or an all-night jamboree. And the night-fighters began their eternal blitzkreig. The anopheles mosquitoes came roaring out of the jungle in squadrons, in platoons, came in companies and in regiments, in divisions and in army corps. Came swooping down bloodthirsty and relentless and irresistible. It made no difference how many you killed, the brave mosquitoes kept coming on like a host of vicious vampires and they would not be denied.

The grumbling worried soldiers took up their cots and their gear and walked along a winding road into the screaming jungle. They went about two hundred yards and stopped in a small dark clearing. The captain told them, "This is it for tonight, men. Any questions? Have a nice meal and get some rest. Got a busy day tomorrow." And took off hurriedly in his commandeered jeep.

Solly laughed bitterly and looked around him. The air thick with buzzing mosquitoes and praying mantises, and the earth crawling with restless land crabs and centipedes and all kinds of things that had no "civilized" names as yet. Like the rest of the nervous men were doing, he unfolded his cot and sat on it and opened his rations and tried to eat some beans and hardtack, and every time he opened his mouth two or three mosquitoes went in on his fork or maybe they were praying mantises. Worm's cot was next to Solly's.

Worm said, "Ain't this a goddamn shame? And the man has the nerve to call us lucky—"

Solly said, "You're the luckiest bastards in the world." He was melting with perspiration and itching all over and imagined every bug on the island crawling underneath his clothes, up his legs in between his legs on his neck in his armpits—crawling crawling.

Worm said, "Thank you, Cap'n Charlie. I reckin we lucky you let us live, white folks."

Solly said, "Colored folks're the most ungrateful people the world has ever known. You're probably the first outfit in the war to come ten thousand miles over the biggest ocean in the world, through enemy waters completely unescorted, but you didn't get sunk to the bottom of the deep blue sea, and if that ain't luck I don't know the meaning of the word. And when you get over here you're not expected, nobody sent for you, nevertheless, the man at Quartermaster is kind enough to give you lodging for the night. But you are never satisfied."

Worm stared at Solly unbelievingly, and Solly started to laugh and swallowed four or five mosquitoes. He tried to spit them out and clapped his hands in front of his face and each time must have killed a dozen of them, but it made no dent in the population. His hand was red with mosquito blood and he felt like vomiting.

Worm lay on his cot and stared at the stars. Some of the men were telling jokes, some were playing the dozens. All of them were killing mosquitoes. Millions of them.

Worm said, "Why in the hell didn't we get off the ship when we first got here? At least we'd been able to set up light housekeeping before night came."

Solly said, "The man didn't want you to disembark in the heat of the day. He waited till the cool of the evening. Looking out for your comfort all the time."

Worm said, "You know what you can do for me in the cool of the mother-loving evening."

Hopjack was loud-talking to a group of the men about how it was going to be when the lights went on again—all over the world. "Man," he said, "I'm just waiting for the day this shit is over. I want to be one in that number in my full-dress uniform marching down Fifth Avenue with that white shit falling from them windows. Me and General Grant gon do ourself some strutting. We gon step higher than a mama-jabber." He threw back his head and marched a few proud spry steps toward the noisy jungle. The men looked at him as if they didn't believe it. Grant stared at him and shook his angry head. Solly thought, when I get back home I'm going to come into the house pulling off my uniform and never put it on again.

He heard Worm snoring on the cot next to him and he almost fell asleep himself despite the anger and the itching and the active perspiration, when suddenly the black emerald sky seemed to move in over them and lower the ceiling and black out the stars, and everything seemed to be holding its breath, even in the noisy jungle. Then Solly heard a deep rumbling building up somewhere on the island, culminating in an explosion that shook the island, and then another and then another and flash after flash of fiery comets racing madly across the lowered sky, and then the sky erupted and overflowed and emptied cascade after cascade onto this lonely South Sea island, as if it would wash it into the Coral Sea. Some of the men got up and started running through the rain toward the great trees in the jungle. A sharp flash of lightning streaked across the edge of the jungle, followed immediately by the loudest clap of thunder that ever thundered and one of the palm trees broke in two and coconuts fell as if the sky was raining them, and giant fruit bats (flying foxes) flying every which way. The men did a speedy "to the rear march" and sloshed quietly back to their cots.

Solly sat up on the side of his cot. Through it all, Bookworm remained where he was, drenched to the skin and lying on his cot with the back of his head in the palms of his hands. The harder it rained the louder he sang.

We're special men . . .
Am-phib-bi-ens.
We're special men . . .
Am-phib-bi-ens.

For almost an hour the black sky wept its bitter tears and suddenly dried them up again.

The next morning they took axes and buzz saws and machetes and sweat and elbow grease and moved the jungle back about fifty feet. The jungle residents gave ground before the onslaught of civilization—pythons, rats, dog-sized lizards, scurrying crawling flying screeching. The sleeping flying foxes hanging head down from the fruit trees. They were miserable-looking creatures, biggest bats in all the world, with a wing span of five to seven feet. Their faces looked like shrunken bears, and they were irritable and vicious when you disturbed them in the daytime. An apple-cheeked boy of the Third Platoon stood next to Solly, head-high in grass and bamboo, swinging his machete, when suddenly he fell as if chopped down by his own machete. Solly thought him victim of sunstroke, but when he died six hours later, the official rumor was typhus, infected by a rat flea. A couple of men were felled by sunstroke and one from a falling coconut. But nevertheless they beat back the jungle and its inhabitants, but where in the hell was World War II? And where were the Ducks for the Special men? The men were assigned to the waterfront, unloading ships, doing labor-battalion work.

The third evening he was summoned to the captain's tent for a conference with Rutherford and Lieutenant Samuels.

Rutherford stood up nervously and sat back down. "Here we are over here in the combat zone, and the Army wants us to have orientation courses. It seems they're worried we don't know how come we're over here."

Samuels said, "They might have something there, Captain."

And Solly wondered, why was I invited to this tête-à-tête?

Rutherford stood up again and sat back down. "Well, I think it's a waste of time, but orders are orders. It seems the base commander is specially worried about colored soldiers understanding why they fight. I told them over at base headquarters, the Negro was the most loyal American of them all. Am I right or wrong, Saunders?"

Solly said, "Yes, sir." He couldn't believe the man was joking at a time like this. Yet how could he be serious?

The captain said, "Well, we got to do it anyhow, and I'm putting you in charge of Information and Education, Lieutenant Samuels, and you'll be the non-com-in-charge, *Sergeant* Saunders. Y'all can work it out between you."

Solly answered without thinking, "No, sir—I mean I'd rather not, sir. I really would." The sticky heat, the mosquitoes, the crawling sweat, the fire burning in his stomach. And please don't call me *Sergeant* Saunders.

The captain said, "What's the matter, Saunders? All you have to do is to read this War Department propaganda and help Lieutenant Samuels break it down for the men." His face was flushed with heat and anger and yellowish from atabrine. He picked up pamphlets on his table. " 'Map Talk'—'Our Heroic Allies'—'Racial Prejudices, the Roadblock to Progress'—and 'After We Win the War, Can We Also Win the Peace?' I thought you would go for this kind of crap. What's the matter?"

Solly said, "Sir, I'm very busy getting the company records straight and helping the supply sergeant and—and like you say, why waste time on a lot of crap? I mean—"

The captain slapped the table and waved his arms. "That's your goddamn trouble, Saunders. You—you think you've got more sense than all the men who run this Army put together. You're too goddamn biggedy!"

Solly said, "But, sir, you're the one who called it crap. I'm just agreeing with you."

The captain's high voice trembling now. "Saunders, I could

have you up for insubordination. Don't push me too far. Don't depend too much on my good nature. The stockades over here are not like those Stateside."

"But, sir, you yourself said it was War Department crap. You yourself said there was no need for it, the Negro troops are the most loyal, you said—" He was playing with hand grenades that might go off in his face, but he felt a curious kind of satisfaction.

The captain said in a tired voice, "They *are having* a little trouble ever now and then over here with one or two agitators like you, goddammit, and we're not going to tolerate it in 913, and that's why we want you and the lieutenant to tell the men about patriotism and peace and freedom and stuff like that."

"Sir, I—"

Samuels said, "The morale of the men is primary, especially in the combat zone, and Corporal Saunders is the non-com for the job. No question about it."

Solly thought, yes, the men's morale is primary, but let somebody else explain it to them. Let Samuels find that MP colonel from Ebbensville and let them run the class together. I just want to do a job and get it over with and go home and forget it.

The captain said, "I don't have to ask you, Saunders, you know that. I can order you, and break you if you refuse, but it's a job you got to believe in or you'll mess it up, and I'm giving you one more chance to consider. You'll have a few additional duties and you'll get a T–4 rating. Now what's your answer? You gon be a private or a sergeant?"

Deep where his guts lived he wanted to say, Let me be a private—let me be a private! Let you and Samuels Bee-Ess the men about the Democratic War. But there was the other thing in him that wanted to be a sergeant and wanted to believe that the war time was not a total loss and that the War Department crap was not crap at all, but the truest meaning of the war. He had to hold on to something or go crazy in the jungle heat. When he spoke he hardly heard himself. "When do we have the first session, sir?"

"Friday." Solly heard the triumph in the captain's voice. "And you'll get your promotion tomorrow."

"May I have the material, sir, to look it over?" It had nothing to do with alternatives of promotion-or-demotion, he told himself, although that was part of it. And why not, goddammit, why not? The war was a great game and everybody with any sense was trying to run as far and as fast as he could until the game was over. And maybe if you shouted the slogans of the war loud enough and often enough, maybe it would help to make them come true. Maybe this was one of the ways to make sure to win the peace. Horseshit, Solly Saunders.

He hardly knew when the captain put his hand on his shoulder and handed him the material and left Samuels and him in the orderly room.

Samuels said, "We heard at headquarters today about a Negro outfit with Southern officers. They were in the first wave of a recent invasion and carried the fighting into the jungle, and when they stopped to count the cost, all of their white officers had been mysteriously killed, and even including their colored first sergeant."

Solly looked up at Samuels and started to laugh. "That was just to show that they weren't prejudiced. The Topkick must've been a white folks' colored man." He laughed and laughed till his stomach hurt, as Samuels stood there with his tan face turning red.

That Friday afternoon they had their first session. The topic was "Racial Prejudice, the Roadblock to Progress." The men listened to Samuels and Solly politely, but during the question period they tended to stray away from the topic. They wanted to know where were the Ducks, and how come they were brought way over here to do labor-battalion work at the waterfront. They were an evil angry unreasonable bunch, and Sergeant Saunders felt like a fool, and Worm and Scotty were among the foremost agitators.

But even Worm agreed and shook his big face up and down when Solly argued that there was nothing wrong with the War Department propaganda. The thing was, it was never put into practice.

"This is good stuff. This is how our country has never been, but this is how we want it to be. If we can use their propaganda to make things better for us—now—and after the war is over, what's wrong with that?"

Worm shouted from the Amen Corner: "Ain't nothing wrong with that."

Solly said, "We can say, 'Here it is in black and white—in your own words. Now let us practice what we preach!"

Worm said, "Ain't nothing wrong with that."

Later, after the session Buck Rogers said it was Communist propaganda. "I oughta know. I used to write that crap when I was president of the Young Stinkers League in Harlem."

Worm said, "You still stink."

Rogers said, "Watch that shit!"

Worm said, "I'm tired of looking at you."

Scotty said, "And I'm tired of that goddamn labor battalion."

That evening Hopjack strutted down the company street dressed to kill and sharp as a tack, going to play checkers with Grant in the mess tent. "Let me at em! Let me at em! Bring me way over here in the middle of nowhere to tote dat barge and lift dat bale. I'd ruther kick a Jap in the ass than go home on rotation!"

Somebody from one of the tents yelled, "Hopjack!" And he cut a quick fancy step and shouted, "Scat! Scat! Let me at them squeenchy-eyed mama-hunchers!"

But there were no Japanese to fight, there were no Ducks for the Special men; there was only the labor battalion at the waterfront. Tote dat barge and lift dat bale.

The next day a bulletin came across the captain's desk from the base Red Cross. Without reading it, Rutherford passed it onto Samuels, who read it and passed it on to Solly. It was an invitation to the enlisted men on the base (five to be selected from each Company) to attend a party at the Red Cross Recreation Center. Thirty beauties of the USO had come all the way from the U.S.A. the day before and would be present and hostessing and boosting the GI morale.

Solly asked his buddy, "How am I going to pick five men for such a detail?"

"I'll show you at supper," the lieutenant said.

In the middle of supper Samuels stood up from the officers' table and got the men's attention. "I want four volunteers for a special detail tonight."

Some of the men stared quietly at their plates; some looked sideways to see if any other poor fool would bite; some cleared their throats significantly and bit into the bully beef. But nobody bit. Not even eager-beaver Sergeant Rogers.

The lieutenant said, "I don't think you men understood me clearly. I said Sergeant Saunders needs four volunteers for special duty and not a single soldier stood up." He paused and looked from soldier to soldier. This time in addition to cleared throats and side glances and plate-staring, he got some significant moving of feet beneath the tables. Samuels said, "You men would sit there with your bare faces hanging out and suffer a soldier like Sergeant Saunders to go on a dangerous mission like this all by himself?"

There were uneasy looks on some of their faces now, and guilt and perspiration, as Worm got slowly to his feet, and then Lanky Lincoln, then Scotty, then the Quiet Man. Others started slowly to rise, but the lieutenant said, "Good enough. We have all that's necessary. Now, Sergeant Saunders, you read the orders." Solly got up and read the orders and the men who were standing laughed out loud, and most of the rest of them looked like they had been taking too many atabrine pills.

That night the five volunteers bathed in a creek near their camp and got GI-sharp and went with flashlights into the humid South Pacific night for about a mile and a half over a snakelike path through the noisy scary jungle. And with all the other noises, the particular screech of the flying foxes as they swooped down out of the fruit trees and hedgehopped along the flashlighted path like P–38's nightfighting, and the five special men ducked their heads so many times their necks got sore.

The Red Cross Recreation Center was lit up like Broadway with a real live band of colored musicians swinging like crazy "The One o'Clock Jump." The joint was leaping. The place was jammed with American soldiers with a few Australians dressed in their knee breeches. A gracious wide-smiling American middle-aged Red Cross lady met the Special men at the door. She had every tooth she ever had.

"The party for you boys is down the road about a mile past the gasoline dump and into the woods about a quarter of a mile over near the Quartermaster. You *cawnt* miss it."

Solly was numbed. Maybe not even surprised—just numbed. He felt a heat begin in his eyes and spread through his face and down through his shoulders and over his back. He heard Scotty grumbling behind him, "If these mama-jabbers don't want us over here, why don't they send us home?" He heard Worm mumble something about the Roadblock to Progress and the Darktown Strutters' Ball. He heard the colored band playing and saw the white folks balling. Sweat dripped down into his eyes and he could see nothing but the lady's smiling teeth which were probably false, come to think of it.

He said politely, "There must be some mistake, Miss. This

is the party we were invited to." He took the invitation out of his pocket and handed it toward her.

She looked at it as if it were a snake that would surely bite off her hand. Her beaming face was still benevolent and gracious though. She was a great white lady. "There *is* a mistake, Sergeant. That's what I'm trying to explain to you. The colored boys are—"

Worm said, "We are not interested in the Darktown Strutters' Ball."

The gracious lady said, "Beg pardon?"

Solly said, "Madam, we are not going over to the Quartermaster. We just arrived on the island a few days ago, and our commanding officer detailed us to spend the next couple of hours right here at this Red Cross Recreation Center. Are you going to supersede his order?" He hated her and her false teeth and her false face and her pretended civility. Hated her for making him come ten thousand miles to fight to come into a crummy crowded funky-smelling joint like this.

The lady took off her smiling mask and motioned to the MPs, and two large-sized handsome plug-uglies came over.

"All right, boys, we don't want no trouble and we ain't going to have none." The big broad dark-haired MP looked like a bouncer at a gangster shindig. "But if you're looking for it, I figure we can give you more than you can handle."

The blond one looked like a queer and sounded like one, cultured-like and Southern-fried. "My advice to you boys is to go quietly and don't start no rumpus." He was a big bastard. Him and his faggoty advice.

Before Solly could say, "We're not starting any rumpus. We just—" Scotty lowered his lionlike head and charged forward like a fullback into the midsection of the dark-haired MP and the MP ended up on the floor with Scotty on top of him. MPs came from everywhere. The pretty blond one cold-cocked Scotty with a blackjack before Solly could reach him. As Solly and Worm and Lanky and Jimmy moved toward their buddy, the MPs grabbed them and began to shove them around and jab them in the ribs with their nightsticks and twist their arms. Before they knew what was happening, they were lined up against the wall with their arms above their heads and frisked like the troublemaking criminals they were. It happened so quickly and efficiently, the party wasn't even interrupted. Only a few nearby were aware of it. The laughter and the dancing and the colored music went on and on. They brought Scotty to his senses and stood him up against the wall with the rest.

Jimmy Larker said angrily and quietly, on the verge of tears, "Are you people completely out of your mind? Do you have any idea what the war is about?"

Solly said, "Save your breath, Jimmy." He was hurting all over and panting like he had been running for a hundred years up a long steep mountainside. And he hated them all for what they were doing to him and Jimmy and the rest, especially to him and Jimmy, hated their goddamn unfeeling guts for pounding one more nail in the coffin of the war's morality.

The MP in charge said, "All right, get em outa here and over to the stockade."

A white corporal with a Southern accent came up to Solly as they were being hustled out of the place. "I saw everything, Sergeant. Who do you want me to notify?"

Solly's sides had that caved-in feeling again. He stared at the white soldier long and hard. The MP shoved him. Solly said, "We're with the 913th Amphibious. Look for Lieutenant Samuels and Sergeant Anderson and tell them what happened. We're on White Beach Road near Ordnance."

The big MP said, "Shut up and keep moving."

Solly said, "Sergeant Anderson and Lieutenant Samuels. 913 Amphibians."

The MPs hustled the volunteers off to the base stockade. Topkick and Samuels got them out a little after midnight.

Solly told Worm they were still lucky. "Lucky they didn't put us in the POW camp behind that barbed wire with the Japanese."

When he reached his tent he undressed in the darkness and got into bed and tucked his net and lay there for over an hour, but he could not fall asleep. His head felt so tight he thought it was going to burst wide open. He got up and lit a lantern and got pen and paper and sat on the side of the bed and wrote:

> I speak to you, America. I still think the most and hope for you the very best while there is still time. Yours was still is the greatest dream mankind has ever known. No land has ever had the potential that was yours still is yours.

Sweat crept all over his body like an army of insects on the march. His hand trembled. All the bugs on the island seemed to have come into his tent and flit and buzz around the lantern and into his face. He wrote:

> Take heed, America. Do not take my love for granted. I who have loved you most and betrayed you least. Unrequited love is always fraught with danger and destruction. Don't push me into saying: "goodie, goodie! I'll be glad when you're dead, you rascal you." My cheeks are wearing thin with slapping, they have been turned too often.

There was so much more he wanted to write to America the beautiful, so much to tell her in his heart, but his eyes began to ache and his hand shook now more than ever and the bugs were sitting all over the paper and on his hot face. He put out the lantern and tucked himself in and relived the evening at the Red Cross recreation center. He saw the woman's toothy smile, and Jimmy Larker's face and Scotty's and Worm's and the two MPs and the whole thing ganged up on him and his eyes were hot but he would not cry, and the trouble with him was, he still had not learned to wear this world like a loose damn garment. And finally he fell asleep.

The days came and lingered in the blue-white heat and passed into weeks and the men worked and melted on the waterfront and were eaten alive by mosquitoes at night and took atabrine and their skin turned to a greenish-yellow and half of them caught dengue and malaria fever and went to the hospital and came out again, and time went on and on and on. Malaria killed two of the Special men. And the great war seemed farther away to Solly than it had been in California.

Late at night in the sticky heat Solly sweated and struggled with his war novel, though he hadn't yet caught up with the fighting. He worked by a lantern light which attracted all the bugs on the island. And across the tent from him, Lanky Lincoln wrote lyrics about love. He was a man obsessed with tenderness in the midst of inhumanity.

During the second week Solly got eight letters from Millie and Worm got one from Fannie Mae. Worm told Solly, "She loves the ground you walk on, you lucky bastard."

One of Millie's letters made him feel like crying, but he held back the mighty flood. "When my menstrual period was late in coming, I got nervous and panicky. I told myself it was nothing to get up in the air about. It's been late before. It would probably come tomorrow or the day after. But after a considerably long time had passed, I went to see my doctor. I didn't dare let my hopes go up. But he said, 'Yes, Mrs. Saunders, it seems that you are definitely pregnant.' I was so happy I was trembling. It must have happened the last night we were together. Love was really in that room. I'm so happy I don't know what to do!"

He kissed the letter, he rubbed his face with it like it was a washcloth. His back and shoulders vibrated with warm feelings of love and exultation. He was really going to be a father this time. He would really be a father! Millie was beautiful and pregnant and his heart was beating too hard too fast and he felt fifteen feet tall and the he of him was throbbing like a heartbeat and when he got back he would make up everything to her. I promise you, my Millie darling. I love you and I promise you I love you and I promise you—I'll be back and make up everything to you. But even as he made his vow, he remembered Fannie Mae and the vow he made to her to never compromise his manhood.

One night about two-thirty in the morning Rutherford came into the tent. Solly had worked late on his novel and had just fallen asleep. The captain woke up the Topkick. "Come to the orderly room on the double." Sergeant Anderson stumbled around the tent trying to wake up and get dressed at the same time. He finally partially accomplished both and went out into the night. Solly drifted slowly back to sleep and dreamed about it. A few minutes later he was awakened by a commotion of hurried footsteps going up and down the company street and loud whispering voices. He thought hazily that everybody must be up excepting Solomon Saunders. Maybe the Japanese had counterattacked. At that moment a soldier's head appeared at the entrance to the tent. "Sergeant Saunders—Sergeant Saunders—report to orderly room on the two!"

When he got to the orderly room it was already a madhouse. Officers and non-commissioned officers and even just plain buck privates coming and going and conferring and whispering excitedly and running back and forth. He read the telegram on the captain's desk. It ordered the 913th to board planes at the Bay Airstrip at 0900 (9 a.m.) sharp and to proceed immediately to Charlie Bee. Ducks needed badly. Time of essence. It was signed by a brigadier general. They broke camp like a circus leaving town. At 0850 they were out at the airstrip, nervous and ready. For most of them, including Solly, it was their first flight. After standing around and hem-and-hawing, they boarded a dozen planes at about nine-thirty and flew two hundred and thirteen miles unescorted and unprotected up the Island to Calhoun Bay, which was just fourteen miles from the shooting and killing.

Lieutenant Graham, the motor officer, sat in the bucket next to him; pimples of perspiration stood at attention on his forehead. He confided his fear to Solly. "I'm pissing my pants," he said. "The first time I ever been up in a plane. These goddamn two-motor bully-beef bombers are rocky as a sonofabitch. Here we are, going toward the front unescorted. This thing doesn't have any guns in it anywhere. Two zeros could systematically knock every one of us out of the sky."

Solly was scared too, but he laughed at the lieutenant. "We're Uncle Sam's most expendable nephews. I thought you were hep to that, Lieutenant. They've made a colored man out of you." Solly laughed and the lieutenant stared at him and sweated more and broke wind way up in the air and didn't say excuse me.

The telegram made no difference at all. They got the same reception. Nobody expected them. Nobody knew what to do with them. They went through almost the same routine as before. Their supplies were being brought up by boat, and after running around like chickens with their necks off, the captain and Solly finally—just before dark and just before the anopheles went on the attack—got cots from the Quartermaster and found a clearing in the jungle, and the men got rained on all night long. The next day they were stevedores on the Calhoun waterfront. It was like a bad dream that you woke up from and then went back to sleep and put the pieces together. The bad dream became a nightmare, because the rain rained harder further north and the sun shone hotter and the mosquitoes grew bigger and the grass grew taller and the flying foxes twice as vicious. And malaria and dengue and yellow jaundice. And all day long and through the night you could hear the rumbling thunder of the war, which was just around the corner now, but as far away as ever.

One day Solly was down at the bay front, checking some supplies the men were unloading. It was so hot the grasshoppers didn't even move about. The sun was blazing red and yet when you got a chance to look at it, when it was looking at something else, it was actually a round silvery disk with a bursting shattering brilliance. It bounced off the glassy-blue water in the bay like a thousand sparkling jewels of all shapes, sizes, and denominations. Solly had already concluded that the equatorial imaginary line ran directly across the bay front, across the bare backs and faces of the Special men. Sweat drained from everywhere on Solly's body, dripped into his eyes, poured from his hair on top of his head. Talk about dehydration! He could feel himself drying up and losing poundage.

He was working near Scotty, when the lion-shouldered soldier stopped from loading for a moment to wipe his face and body (naked to waist) and under his arms, as the sweat continued to leak from him like the pores of his body were bleeding sweat. He did not hurry back to work. Nothing hurried. The sun beat down everything and everybody to the rhythm of a slow drag.

Staff Sergeant Buck Rogers walked toward Scotty and shouted at him in a husky sun-cooked voice, "All right, you little goldbricking mother-lover, let's get on the ball."

Scotty looked up at the sergeant and put his hand on the back of his hip and bent his body and went into one of his burlesques. "Yassa, old Cap'n. All right, Massa. I'sa comin', White Folks. My back may be broken but my spirit's undaunted."

The stage was set. The show would soon be on the road. The men nearby began to laugh and chuckle. Sometimes the sergeant enjoyed it as much as the men.

Buck said, "I suppose you're one of them smart ones."

Scotty scratched his head. "Nawsa, Cap'n. I ain't had no education and I ain't never been to school."

The men laughed louder. "All right, that's enough, all of you, let's get back to work. You, goddammit, you the big instigator." Buck waved his arm at the Bookworm.

Worm had just put onto the truck a piece of cargo that looked to be the size of a bale of cotton. "I ain't doing nothing, ol' Cap'n."

Buck was working himself up into a sweaty sunstroke. "That's the trouble. You don't never do nothing but signify and agitate like a goddamn Communist in Union Square!"

Buck was really angry now, but Worm was still floor-showing. He walked toward Buck, smiling angelically. "Just a minute, Sergeant. Don't be calling me outa my name. I don't play the dozens with *no* dear mother's bastard."

Everybody was watching the show by now. All labor battalion work had ceased. Buck shook his finger in the short soldier's face. "Watch how you talk to your superiors, mother-fucker!"

"Oh," Worm said smilingly, "so you were peeking, you sneaky bastard. You were peeking that night, and me and your dear old mama thought you were fast asleep—you naughty boy."

The men were laughing unrestrained and the sun was carrying out its scorched-earth policy systematically and Buck was hotter than South Sea Island beach sand at three o'clock in the afternoon.

Buck said, "All right, you little stupid sapsucker, are you going to get back to work or do you want to be charged with insubordination?" He turned and waved his arms. "And that goes for all of you bastards!"

Worm broke into a grin and started to do a soft-shoe dance. "Hehehehehe hehehehe—I was just teasing, boss. Please don't take me to the man. Please—" He moved away toward the stack of cargo at the water's edge, still dancing.

Hopjack shouted, "Scat! Scat! Everybody tryna get into the act."

The other men went snickering back to work.

It was hot hot hot.

"All right then, goddammit, I don't want no more trouble outa you else I'm going to have your dead ass put in the stockade and you'll be making little ones outa big ones."

Worm turned again and bowed. "All right, boss, ol' Cap'n. I told you I was just teasing. Please don't tell the man on me."

Buck said, "Just don't give me no more lip, that's all. Just get to hell back to work, else we'll reverse the procedure, goddamn. We'll give you some little ones and make you make big ones out of em."

Worm would have the last word or burst wide open. He picked up a heavy piece of cargo and maneuvered it up on his shoulder. "I told you I was just teasing, boss. I know you wasn't peeking that night, cause your mama stuck some cotton in the keyhole."

The men were laughing now, though working, and Buck

turned away, pretending not to hear the Worm. It was better that they laughed than grumbled while they worked in the hottest place on God's greener-than-green earth.

Lanky Lincoln shaded his eyes and looked up into the face of the sun and shouted, "Hey, looka there!"

Solly looked and now the sun was flinging silver pieces at the earth. The planes seemed to come directly out of the great white disk and glitter momentarily in its mighty beam and then streak toward the sweltering earth. Plane after plane peeled off from the sun and hurtled earthward.

Jack Titus a crackerjack mechanic and expert on airplanes, fighters, bombers, A-this, B-that, and P-the other. He knew them by names and numbers. He jumped up and down and laughed and shouted, "Look at them beautiful bastards! P–38's! Lockheed Lightnings! Fly mother-lovers! Fly! Fly!"

Solly didn't know what they were, but they were sleek and handsome and gleaming and streaking across the sky and heading toward Calhoun Bay. Lanky was also a plane expert. He said, "Those aren't P–38's, those are P–40's, man. Don't you see that gorgeous fuselage? I thought you knew something about airplanes."

The silver streaks got lower and lower (they moved like lightning, whatever their name) and they made a straight line for the Special men, and suddenly it was like the Fourth of July and thunder and lightning everywhere. Every ack-ack gun on the Island started sounding off and the sky was filled with tracer bullets exploding in the sky around the planes, as the silvery comets wiggled and ducked and dodged in and out of the bursting flak and kept coming on, and the Island trembled and the Special men dove under the trucks. One nervous soldier ran headlong into the sea. Watts was the only man in the outfit who never learned to swim.

From under the truck you could still see some of the silver stuff flashing across the brilliant sky and going into dives and pulling out again and laying their eggs of death and the earth beneath erupting, and one of the silvery buzzards swooped toward a ship in the bay and dropped its egg and climbed skyward again like a sea gull. It was a direct hit and the ship jumped fifty feet in the air with pieces flying everywhere and arms and legs and other debris and heads and bodies and settled back onto the water quietly and burning and disappearing into the bay.

General Grant got so carried away he came out from under the truck and started screaming like he was out of his mind.

"Gwan, Tojo! Gwan Tojo! Fly, black man! Show these white bawstards how you can fly!" He shook his fist at the planes ducking in and out of the flak and diving and laying eggs and climbing straight up again at ninety-degree angles. "Gwan, Tojo! Go on, mawn! Show these bawstards how to do it!"

Solly, along with Worm and Lincoln and about a dozen others, had been on his knees underneath the truck, and he had not been praying, but inside his stomach was like a volcano exploding and erupting. He had never been so scared before. He had never known the earth so scared that it quaked and trembled, he had never heard such thunder nor seen such awful lightning. He had caught up with the war, and his heart was pounding as loud as the ack-ack guns and he thought it would burst his chest wide open. He thought about home and Millie and the baby really in her belly this time and Mama and darling Fannie Mae in Ebbensville and all of it a million miles away from this madness. And he might not live to see them again, he might not live another minute. He was scared deep deep in his rectum scared. But suddenly the picture of General Grant standing there out in the open and cheering the Japanese struck him as the funniest thing that ever happened. He began to laugh and laugh and howl and his stomach griped with laughter. He fell on his back and held his stomach and laughed and laughed till the tears came down. Maybe he was crying. He almost rolled from under the truck.

"Gway, Tojo! Fly your arse off! Show them paddies, mawn! Show em! Show em!"

Solly could hear the shrapnel from the ack-ack jagged and deadly, falling back from the sky and raining onto the truck and beating up the dust around the General and he stayed out there in the open, yelling encouragement to Tojo. Solly wanted to warn him about the shrapnel but he could not stop laughing. His stomach hurt like he needed a B.M., but he couldn't stop laughing. He was crying too. Finally he heard Worm say to the General, "Get back under this truck, you stupid sapsucker, fore a piece of shrapnel fill up that hole in your head." But Grant kept screaming, "Gwan, Tojo!"

Suddenly without thinking Solly threw a diving tackle at the General and dragged him kicking and protesting underneath the truck.

And suddenly the storm ended as it began and the silver comets raced back toward the sun and disappeared, and the guns got quiet and the earth settled down in the awful heat. And the Special Men went back to work. And the war was far away again.

Every day the silver comets peeled off the sun and paid the island a brief exciting visit and always left their calling cards. The earth erupted and people died and life went on and on and on. Every day the Special Men unloaded the ships, and every night they were eaten alive by the mosquitoes. But one day about three months later the Ducks arrived and they became *real* Special Men.

CHAPTER

3

One evening about 1800, there was a special formation and Rutherford told them this was it. They would be a part of the second wave to hit the beach in a big important invasion. Their job would be to carry the anti-aircraft boys and their guns from the LST to the shore and help put up the gun emplacements. "We'll be about fifteen hundred miles from any American or Allied base or airstrip. We'll have to establish a beachhead and hold it under any and all circumstances. The only airplane protection will be from our Navy flattops. "At ease, Private Taylor!" The CO's tiny eyes went up and down the formation from man to man as if he were trying to look through them and inside of them and to read their thoughts their doubts their fears. The men stood tall and serious and silent for the captain. Even the mosquitoes stopped and listened. "From this minute on every man has to pitch in like a member of a team, like a member of a family. This is the most important task you ever had in all your life. This is why you were born."

Now my life makes sense, Solly thought. Now I know why I was born. Thank you, Captain. Now I can die in peace.

"I'm your commanding officer, but I also want you to look upon me as your friend."

There was a tremble in his captain's voice. His cockiness was gone. He wanted the men to love him. Really love him. Yeah, Solly thought, remembering the colored outfit who in the heat of the battle strangely lost their Southern officers and their colored Topkick. And the captain was remembering. Solly understood his captain. He wanted the boys of the 913th to regard him as their benevolent Great White Father. "Ain't nothing to be afraid of," he said shakily. "I'll be with you every step of the way. After the first few days everything'll be safe and sound. It'll be just like garrison. Just like it is here on this base." He paused and stared at the arrogant face of Private Joseph (NMI) Taylor. Two lady mosquitoes sat idling on Worm's forehead, but Worm didn't bat an eyelash. He stared back at the captain with a look on his face which seemed to his Great White Father to say: "You know what you can do for me and your just-like-garrison." The captain said, "All right, Taylor, any more guff out of you and I'll charge you with insubordination and throw the goddamn book at you." Taylor didn't move a muscle, not even in his face. Yet there was a subtle change in his expression which made him seem to be howling with laughter at the captain.

Rutherford shouted, "At ease, Taylor! That'll be enough outa you, goddammit!"

Rutherford hitched his trousers with his elbows. "Now I know we've had disagreements and sometimes some of you thought I was hard and strict, but I've always done what I thought was best for you. Everybody makes mistakes sometimes. That's how come they put rubbers on the tip of pencils. And now it's time for us to let bygones be bygones. Let's put our shoulders to the wheel cause we're in this thing together." He paused and stared at the earth and waved the mosquitoes from his face. "Lieutenant Graham got a few words for you." The captain walked away.

The lieutenant paced back and forth, white-faced and perspiring, and cleared his throat. "Men—speaking of morale and *esprit de corps* and all that stuff, I want to bring a question before you." He was sweating and uncertain. He was scared. Scary scared. "Men, I'm talking about respect for one another. Every time I walk up the company street I hear somebody calling somebody else a mother-fucker or a sonofabitch. This ain't nice, men." Most of the men stood tall and straight-faced. Sympathetic, understanding. "All over the place it's 'Good morning, mother-fucker' or 'Good evening, sonofabitch!' It's like you were saying to each other: 'Hello, sweetheart.' It's a goddamn shame and we got to put a stop to it." He could feel the men laughing at him behind their faces. "Goddammit, I ain't gonna have no more mother-fucking and sonofabitching in this outfit. All of you come from good Christian families, and we're going into combat and you should be praying stead of cussing, and I'm going to put a stop to it. It's not all of you. It's just rotten apples spoiling the barrel. And it's demoralizing. And I want my non-commissioned officers to help me in this determination." He searched their faces. They were colored and they should be especially scared of death and prayerful at this moment in their lives. He couldn't understand it. They were denying their culture. Maybe just to spite him and the U.S. Army.

"Sergeant Rogers!" he shouted gruffly.

Sergeant Rogers came briskly and smartly front and center and saluted the ruddy-faced lieutenant.

Buck said, "Sir, I want you to know that we non-commissioned officers are with you one hundred per cent in this noble determination, and we will discuss this question with the men and root it out of their systems."

Lieutenant Graham said gravely, "Thank you, Sergeant." He and Buck saluted and he walked away toward the officers' quarters.

Buck turned to the quiet men and by the time he thought Graham was out of earshot he shouted huskily, "I want every one of you mother-fuckers to stop saying mother-fucker."

The men broke up with howling laughter.

All week long they got ready for the Big Invasion. And it seemed like Hopjack finally was going to get the chance he had been begging for. Every evening he'd start down the company street shouting, "Let me at those buckteeth bastards!" All of the men laughed and joked as they got ready for the Big Day, but it was a grim and heartless laughter. Cleaning guns, checking gas masks and helmets and equipment, mounting guns into the Ducks, remembering home and cracking jokes and filling sandbags. Singing, laughing, letter-writing. Some praying. Some cussing. All of them scared, courageous too.

Captain Charlie said don't be scared, but he was scared himself. And Lieutenant Graham was scared to death and obvious. He drank jungle juice with the men and helped put sand into the sandbags and put his arm around their shoulders. He laughed and joked with them. Got roaring drunk with them. But nothing stopped the time from running out.

Lieutenant Samuels and Sergeant Saunders talked a lot but had very little to say to each other, as they grimly worked together getting the company records ready for the grand invasion. Once or twice Samuels tried to start a discussion about the war's morality, but Solly didn't want to hear it. One evening Worm and Quiet Man Larker were helping Samuels and Solly to pack the company files. Samuels started to talk about how different this war was from World War I and how things would have to be different when they got back home. But when he turned to Saunders for corroboration, Solly said, "Excuse me, Lieutenant, I have to go to the latrine." And he walked out into the night.

Nine days later they steamed out of Calhoun Bay on an LST and made off to another point where they would join a task force made up mostly of Landing Ship Tanks. Their Ducks were aboard the ship with them. Two days later they joined the rest of the convoy and put boldly and nervously out to sea. It was the biggest task force Solly ever dreamed of. As far as you could see in all directions were LSTs bobbing up and down on the vast Pacific with the curious rhythm of a prize fighter like hammering Henry Armstrong. Bobbing and weaving—weaving and bobbing. The LST was sturdy and seaworthy, they said, but she had no keel and her bottom was flat and shapeless, and when the waves were foamy she gave you many anxious moments.

And now it was the night before the great invasion morning. Solly stayed on deck till late. It was moonless. Not a single star up there. A perfect night for invasion. He stood gazing over the side of the ship. He had wanted to be with himself all by himself on this night that might very well be the last he'd ever know. He could see nothing but vast spaces of funereal blackness and white foamy waves around the ships as they ploughed grimly and perpetually forward.

He didn't know how many ships were in the task force. He estimated about a hundred and seventy-five LSTs, a complement of destroyers and mine sweepers and battleships and troopships and a couple of giant aircraft carriers, destroyer escorts, torpedo boats, and God and General Buford Jack only knew what others or how many others. This was it. Like the captain said, this is why your mama's baby boy was born.

He thought about home and his mother and Millie and their

baby forming slowly forming really forming in her belly pretty belly. He thought of their frantic love-making at Fort Ord and up in Pittsburg. The LST went *shromp shromp* from side to side and so did his poor nauseous belly. He hoped she believed he loved her, because he did love her. He loved her loved her. But his love for Fannie Mae was something altogether different. Maybe there were two kinds of love. Maybe three or four or five. You must not think of Fannie Mae. He should go downstairs and join the men. The cold salty sea whipped his hot face. He felt a nearness to death as never before, as if it were somewhere out there ahead of them, waiting for them, and they were moving calmly to the fatal rendezvous. His mouth was cold with the taste of death. His face filled as he thought again of the baby who was surely in Millie's belly this time and who might never see its father. He might be born an orphan just because his gutless daddy was on this particular ship in this particular task force and might be dead before day in the morning. My father died in the war to end all wars, and my child's father will die in the war to end all wars, and my child's child's father. And why and why and why goddammit! Why and why and why? Did it go on and on and never end? How could a few measly-minded men make decisions that committed the lives and deaths of millions? And the millions seemed to never mind. He tried to remember things about his childhood but they were vague now, like the ocean's blackness. He just had a feeling of his Time's great waste and Time squandered and Time pissed away and Time lost and never found, and now it never would be found. And Time as deep and fathomless as the waters underneath the boat. He wondered why men took life so seriously and yet gave it up so willingly on the altar of patriotism at the behest of high-priest politicians and high-priest ammunitions makers and high-priest newspaper publishers and all the other Bee-Essers and high-priest profiteers, and what do we ever really get out of it excepting death and destruction and widows and orphans and Tag Day for the Disabled Veterans? Times Square—won't you buy my poppy, Lady? Black clouds hanging separately in the sky like ragged shrouds, and the whole world was in mourning. If he had the guts he would go at this late hour of Time's great space, he would go below to the place where the loudspeaking system was and cold-cock the one in charge gently but firmly on the head with the butt of his carbine and wake up the ocean itself with this announcement, "Now hear this! Now hear this! Turn back you miserable fools before it is too late! Turn back all of you poor crazy bastards. If the bigshots are mad with each other let them fight their own battles, let them blow each other's few brains out!" He wished he had the nerve to do it!

You're thinking wrong now, buddy boy. Use your head and not your stomach. You're a sergeant and you're a little old morale builder, I & E man, and you have a great future ahead of you when you get home. You have looks and education and intelligence and personality. You are not like Worm and Scotty. You are positive.

The motion of the LST was getting to him now as the sea tossed it from side to side. A funny tumbling in his stomach and a swimming in his head. He wished he had the nerve to do it. But he was a coward like the rest of them. All of them were cowards excepting probably Private Jerry Abraham Lincoln Scott—maybe. He stared at the nearest LST as it bobbed and weaved from one side to the other. Its port side seemed to come up out of the water and reach vainly for the black sky, which seemed to reach for it, and then with the same rhythm it seemed to submerge beneath the ocean's black and foamy surface. Scott was the freest bravest meanest bastard in the world. He was glad he wasn't Scotty.

If only he believed like Samuels believed, that the war was being fought for something. For Freedom and Democracy. Let me believe! Great God almighty, let your doubting son believe. He wasn't even sure he believed in God who closed his eyes to so much injustice and his ears to so much weeping. Solly closed his own eyes and imagined a world after the war, in which he was walking everywhere in his country and through the whole world from Mississippi to Stalingrad to Calcutta to Johannesburg, with his eyes up and his shoulders back, a world in which his son could grow up knowing who he was and why he was, not cooking his hair or bleaching his face, but proud of the image in his mirror, and Millie and Mama proud and free and Fannie Mae in Ebbensville. And *me*, goddammit, *me!* In his vision he saw millions of people of all sizes and sexes and ages and colors and religions walking together everywhere, with the love of living glowing in their faces.

He said aloud, "Let me believe in this damn war. Let me believe things will be different. Let me believe it strong deep deep deep down in my bowels. Let me believe it's worth the dying and even worth my own damn death!"

The LST hit another heavy wave straight on and jumped up and down like it was doing a wild dance without musical accompaniment. It was completely at the mercy of the deep black sea, and it shook the vision out of him and brought him back to the here-and-now time.

Suddenly he felt sad and sorry for himself and for Mama and for Millie and the baby and Fannie Mae and Scotty and Samuels and Bookworm and Clint and Quiet Man and Hopjack and Lanky and Topkick, for all the poor helpless fools in the convoy riding toward a date with death and human destruction. He felt attack after attack of loneliness, wave after wave assaulting everything inside of him. Fannie Mae! Fannie Mae! You're with me tonight, my darling! My only darling! You know how I feel. You are the only one who knows! His aloneness was a black cloak wrapped around him like the night weighing him down and leaning heavily against him. Time was catching up with him, and he wanted to know what he was here for. He went below to look for Bookworm.

The stale air in the hatches hit him in the face with more force than the ocean wind on topside. The sultry closeness was mixed with the unsavory stink of sweaty humans, scared, brave, anxious and nervous and breaking wind, and soiled clothing and overused toilets. It was funny how the heads on troopships got fouled up so quickly. He thought of locker rooms and school and basketball and Rover Boys and better times and pure tremendous expectations.

Solly found Worm in Hatch Number 3, shooting crap with a group of white soldiers from a combat engineers' outfit. The game was going strong and right smack down in the middle of one of the aisles. The dice came around to the Bookworm and he winked his eye at Solly and went to work. He made seven passes in succession. Everything in the book. Nines, tens, fours, everything. Now he was sweating over a five. The skin stretched tight over his wide sweaty forehead.

"Fever, dice! Five when you stop!" he pleaded in soft earnest tones. He supplicated. He remonstrated. Finally the dice rolled three and two. Worm raked the green stuff in without a word.

A voice said softly, "Look at that little lucky black bastard!"

Pieces of breeze drifted quietly and determinedly through the funk of the stinking hatch. Somebody sneezed ferociously. Solly looked from face to face of the white men. Which one was it? Worm looked up and around, pulled out a handkerchief and wiped the perspiration from his face. He threw a four and said tonelessly, "Little Joe from Chicago. Be four when you stop, good dice." He immediately bucked it back again.

The same soft voice said, "Will you look at that little ol' lucky-ass nigger! Goddamn I reckin!"

Solly stood up and Worm stood up with the dice in his hand and looked down into the red-haired soldier's face. They were sure they had the right man. Worm said, "One more from you like that and one of us won't live to see the grand invasion! Cause I'll go to hell this very minute just to whip your ass good-fashion."

Solly said, "That goes for both of us. You better believe it."

The big soldier looked around at the rest of the men all of them white. He had a good mind to teach these black boys some manners, he seemed to be thinking. He might be killed tomorrow any-damn-how. Everything was quiet waiting for him to make his move. And he debated with himself. He could whip either one of them any day in the week fair and square, but they probably toted razors. All of them did. Goddamn their sneaky souls. Solly swallowed hard and the saliva stuck in his throat like glue. His nerves were sharp as a razor's edge double-edged. They were outnumbered twenty to one but he was ready. He didn't have to debate about this war right here and now.

The big red-headed bastard said in a husky voice, "Ain't no needa gitting all het up, fellers. I didn't mean no harm. After all, we in this thing together."

Solly said quietly, "All right now. We told you and we mean every damn word of it. We'd sooner die today as tomorrow morning."

A big blond soldier spoke with soft persuasion, "Don't pay my buddy no mind, mates. Overlook him. He's drunk, that's all, and he's scared of tomorrow's invasion. I swear to God he's drunk as a cooter."

Worm didn't look in the blond soldier's direction. "You better talk to him then. He bet not get so drunk he can't smell my whiskey. Cause I ain't most gon overlook him." He got down on his knees again and threw the dice. He threw six and then immediately threw a seven and gave up the dice and quit the game.

He stood up and said to Solly, "Let's get for home before we start us a private beachhead."

Solly said, "I'm with you, good buddy."

They went back to their own quarters where most of the men lay on their bunks wide awake in private conferences with themselves. The only man in the entire hatch who was fast asleep was Lanky Lincoln. Worm stood over the long rangy soldier who lay there with his mouth open and snoring evenly and calmly as if he were at home in bed dreaming about ice cream cones and apple pies and Coney Island and Nathan's hot dogs. Over on the other side of the hatch, a soldier was plunking on his old guitar and making like Josh White. Singing a chain-gang song:

Take this hammer—

Worm waved his hand close to Lanky's long eyelids. "This long tall mama-jabber would sleep through hell on Judgment Day."

Cair it to the captain—

A few of the men were gathered over by the Quiet Man's bunk, telling lies and laughing and talking nervously. Worm said, "You bastards better get right with God instead of all this lying and bullshitting and carrying on."

Take this hammer—Cair it to the cap'n . . .
Tell him I'm gone—

Bucket-head said, "Man, this was down in 'Bam where Worm and all them little Worms come from. This colored stud comes into town from the plantation riding one of old masser's big white horses and walks into the back of old masser's shop buck naked as a jaybird in whistling time. I mean this stud wasn't even wearing a G-string." The men began to chuckle. "Boss man told him, 'All right, I'm gon string your black ass up by the balls, but before I do, just tell me what the hell got into you?' Old Jim told the boss, 'Masser, I was coming into town minding my own business when this white woman rode up to me and gave me an order to follow her into the woods and I followed her orders. She went into the woods a piece and got down off her horse and pulled off all her clothes and laid down on the ground and told me to pull off mine. I followed her orders again and stood there naked and then she say come over to me, and I came over to her, and then she told me, all right, black boy, get in the saddle and go to town, and Boss Man, here I is!' "

If he asked you was I running . . .

The nervous men laughed long and loud, detonating the tension for the moment. They did not wake up Lanky Lincoln, but they disturbed Hopjack. He said, "You stupid sapsuckers keep up so much noise I can't hear myself think."

Tell him I was flying . . .

Bucket-head said, "Boy, I have gotten so much pussy in my day, of various races and nationalities, when I do die, they gon say, I died with my hammer in my hand."

Worm said, "Yeah goddammit, that's bout the only place you ever had your hammer. A woman would have to have a grudge on her cunt to give you some."

The men laughed louder than before.

Hopjack said, "I told you suckers to be quiet. They can hear you from here to Tokyo."

Solly said, "One thing is sure. Hopjack is going to get plenty opportunity to do a whole heap of ass-kicking instead of going home on rotation."

Hopjack laughed weakly and said, "Let me at the squeench-eyed mother-hunchers."

If he axe you . . . Was I laughin . . .
Tell him I was crying . . . .

The bull session broke up gradually. The men went to their separate bunks. Buck Rogers came over to Solly's bunk. His eyes were bigger than ever before. He said, "Move over, baby, I'm going to sleep with you tonight, you beautiful heffer."

Take this hammer . . . Cair it to the Cap'n . . .

Solly said, "Sorry, old buddy, but you ain't my type."

Worm looked down from the upper berth. He said, "Furthermore, you bubble-eyed punk, it's against Army Regulations for two men to sleep in the same bunk, but I guess that wouldn't include you nohow."

Tell him I'm gone . . .

Buck said, "All right then, baby, I'll settle for one sweet kiss, you gorgeous bitch." He sat on the bunk beside Solly and reached for him. Solly shoved him off the bunk. He had not made up his mind yet whether Buck was joking or really a queer.

Buck came toward him again. "Come on, you good pussy bitch, and give me your tongue, and I'll be satisfied. I'll go out of here in the morning and kill every Jap on that mother-hunching island." He stuck out his fat tongue.

Solly sat up on his bunk. "If you don't get the hell away from me I'll knock you on your big fat ass." He didn't feel like horsing around. He wanted to lie on his bunk and think and think and feel and feel and live and relive and live and think and think and live. It might be the last time. He had no way of knowing.

Worm said, "Sergeant Buck, are you really a queer? I mean if you ain't, you really do some good imitations."

Buck said, "Watch that shit, soldier. I'm only kidding." He looked around at the other listening soldiers. "Anybody don't believe I'm a man or think he's more of a man than me, just hit the goddamn deck and I'll meet them in the head."

Worm said, "Man, go on over to your bunk and beat your meat one more time. Ain't nobody gon say nothing about it."

The soldiers snickered.

Buck said, "That's the trouble with you ignorant bastards." His eyes were bigger than ever and he was angry and perspiring. "Can't treat you on the same level. Play with a dog he'll lick you in the mouth every goddamn time."

Worm leaped from his upper berth for Buck's neck. "Who in the hell you calling a dog, mother-huncher?" Buck moved just in time and Worm landed on the floor and was up in the same motion going for Buck. Both of them were raging mad. Solly jumped from his bunk and in between them and kept them from each other.

"There'll be plenty of fighting for everybody tomorrow morning. Both of you can give Hopjack a helping hand kicking asses and taking names."

Somehow this struck both of them funny, Worm and Buck, and they started to laugh and they laughed and they laughed. And Worm climbed back to his upper berth.

Buck spoke to all of them except the sleeping Lincoln. "That was just a little exhibition to loosen you men up. It's twelve-fifteen now and all of you better get some sleep, like Corporal Lincoln is doing, cause every living got to hit the deck at 0300. Because we expect every man in 913 to cover himself with courage and glory on tomorrow and all that kind of shit. Don't forget we're Special Men."

Scotty sang in his powerful rusty baritone:

"Oh say can you see
Any bedbugs on me . . ."

Billy "Baby-Face" (no-swimming) Banks shouted from his bunk, "No—no! No, goddammit, no! I don't wanna go on no invasion. I ain't mad with no damn body! I ain't mad with nobody!" He jumped down from his bunk and came toward Buck and Solly. "Why, Sergeant Rogers? Why? Tell me why I should be shooting at people tomorrow morning and ducking bullets? People I ain't got nothing against and ain't got nothing against me! People I ain't never seen and ain't never done me nothing!"

Buck said, "Take it easy, Baby-Face. You'll be all right tomorrow. You got more guts than you think you got. You the one soldier I'm not worried about." Banks was getting on everybody's nerves.

Baby-Face started to shake his head and cry, "No! No! It don't make no sense—don't make no sense atall!" Tears streamed down his babyish face unashamedly.

Buck's voice hardened, "Straighten up, soldier, goddammit. You a non-com. You're supposed to set an example for the men. So shut up that bawling or I'll throw your ass in the brig."

Baby-Face turned to Solly. He wiped his eyes with the back of his hand. "Does it make sense to you, Sergeant Solly? I'm scared, goddammit. Does this war make sense to a man like you?" He sank down on the bunk next to Solly. Buck Rogers moved quickly away from them.

What the hell could Solly tell him? "You're an intelligent educated man, Sergeant Solly. You tell me what it's all about. You're Information and Education."

Solly said in a husky voice, "You're not the only one scared, Baby-Face. I'm scared. Every man on this boat—every living ass in this task force is scared. A man who says he isn't scared in combat is either a fool or a liar. Officers, non-coms, enlisted men, every living is scared shitless unless he's a lunatic. But the things that divide the men from the boys, the brave ones from the cowards, is self-control." Baby-Face wiped his eyes and sucked the tears back up his nostrils and down into his throat, and what the hell could Solly tell him? "We owe it to ourselves and to the rest of the men to keep our fear under control." Even as he spoke Solly wondered how he himself would be on tomorrow with death exploding all around him. He almost wished the time would hurry up so the show could get on the road.

Baby-Face asked him, "Does this war make any sense to you, Sergeant? That's what I really want to know."

Solly felt like shutting up Baby-Face's mouth with his fist. He brought all of Solly's own misgivings to the surface. All his doubts and fears and trepidation. All his shitty idealism. He looked at Banks. What could he say to him? He felt his face filling up and through his shoulders. Let Banks find his own answers. He was only a few years younger than Solly. What could he tell this baby-faced man who probably never shaved nor ever even had a girl, hadn't had time to sow any oats. What could he say to Baby-Face Banks on the eve of the battle? Tell him the truth? What was the everlasting truth?

"Does it make sense to you, Sergeant Solly? That's all I want to know."

Solly swallowed the stale funky air of the hatches, and he was positive. "Yes. Yes, it makes a whole lot of sense," he said. What else could he tell him? "But let's talk about it after we get this particular job done. Right now we'd better get some sleep."

"All right, Sergeant Solly," the corporal said. Baby-Face went back and climbed up on his bunk and Solly lay on his, but nobody slept a wink excepting lanky Lanky Lincoln.

CHAPTER

4

And now it was a few minutes after 0400 and hell had been let loose on God's green earth. And fire and brimstone and thunder and lightning and Fourth of July and Judgment Day. There were from five to eight men in each of the Ducks on the decks of the LSTs. Most of them standing, watching the glorious colossal fireworks of this Hollywood production. Every warship in the bay was talking, yelling, barking, howling, screaming murder, bloody murder, as they moved closer and closer in toward the bleeding shore.

Schrruummpp—Schrruummpp—

Pow! Pow! Pow! Pow! BOOM! BOOM! BOOM! BOOM! BOOM!

The ocean quivered underneath them. The big guns the medium guns the little guns, all of them sounding off all at once and separately.

Does it make sense to you, Sergeant Solly?

The sky had changed from the night before, and it seemed like every star that ever was looked down on them that early morning. When the LST went into its rocking motion a sky full of winking stars seemed to dip downward toward the boats and up again and slide from side to side above them and down again and up and down and up and down, the heavens playing ring games with them.

Wheerrrrrrrrrr—BOOM—BOOM—BOOM—BOOM!

POW! POW! POW! POW! BOOM BOOM BOOM BOOM! BOOM!

Does this all make sense to you?

The entire world was thunder and lightning. Sound and fire. The bay exploding before his eyes. The battleships, the cruisers, the carriers, the destroyers and their escorts, big black prehistoric monsters belching fire and death and destruction onto the dark green island that lay helpless in the moonless night of early morning.

Solly looked at the serious faces of the other men in the Duck with him. Worm's face had a quiet humorous quality, as if he were chuckling at the world which had completely flipped its lid. Worm was frightened and amused. Baby-Face Banks was scared and sweating bullets, but when he caught Solly staring at him, he smiled a trembly smile as if to say, "Don't worry about me, Sarge. I'll make it this morning. I'm scared just like everybody else is, but I got everything under control even though it makes no sense to me." A couple of the men were from the Anti-Aircraft group. They were sweating like everybody else. The big friendly-faced dark-haired soldier closed his eyes every now and then to shut out the madness. The other one was blond and sad-faced and bluish-green-eyed and Irish and New York and slightly built and talkative.

"I've had twenty months of this fucking Island-hopping, and you supposed to be sent home on rotation at the end of eighteen goddamn months, and my papers were going through till they got all bollixed up. Another week and I'da been on my way. You'd think these bastards woulda left me back at the other base. It ain't fair. After all the invasions I already been in, to risk my life another time, after my time is already up. And I might get my head blown off this very morning."

Somehow the soldier's story made Solly hot and angry and helplessly sad, and he felt a crazy fullness in his face. The Army was heartless as well as senseless. The Army was a great big civilized beast.

But the war itself made sense, he argued with himself. You must always distinguish between the Army and the war. It is a war against the enemies of freedom and democracy. If you die today you die for freedom.

Over on shore he could see the planes like ghostly buzzards circling their targets and going into their dives and laying their death eggs and pulling straight up again as the earth below them erupted like a mad volcano. Circle and dive and drop the bomb and pull up again and set the goddamn world on fire. No anti-aircraft to challenge their rhythm. Solly watched the planes with a strange fascination, as if they were something detached from reality, a game the pilots were playing and a boring one-sided game at that. But they were on the side of Freedom and Democracy. You had to keep remembering. You had to be a true believer.

The battleships, the cruisers, the destroyers moving in closer and closer, the LCIs, the LSTs, the bombardment went on and on and on. Solly looked from face to face of the men again and back toward the shore which was closer now and clearer in its handsome rugged outline, as dawn barely began to lift itself from behind the mountain about a mile in from the coast. It was still dark but it wouldn't be long before day-break and day might never break for him again. This day in the year of Our Lord nineteen hundred and whatever-it-was (he couldn't even remember at the moment) he might cross that separating line and leave this world behind. But he would die for Freedom. He remembered all the old-fashioned songs his mother used to sing. Songs they used to sing down home at church on New Year's Eve at midnight. He couldn't have been more than three or four or five years old.

It may be the last time
It may be the last time
It may be the last *time*
It may be the last time
I don't know . . .

and

This time another year
I may be gone
In some lonesome graveyard
Oh Lord, how long?

and he remembered:

Stony the road we trod
Bitter the chastening rod

Thou who has brought us
Thus far on the way . . .

and he remembered:

Lift every voice and sing
Till earth and heaven ring
Ring with the harmonies of liberty . . .

His heart was one great sad and joyful song of hope and angry desperation. He wondered about the men hidden somewhere in the darkness on the island, dedicated to defend it with their flesh and blood. He mustn't think these kinds of thoughts, mustn't write this kind of novel. Men like himself, frightened and courageous men with eyes and mouths and teeth and hearts and souls and penises and bowel movements and ears and thoughts and feelings and dreams and hate and laughter and tears and religion and desires and aspiration and love and mothers and fathers and wives and children and bad guys and good guys. What the hell did he have against these men whom he had never gazed upon? He mustn't think like this. It isn't healthy at a time like this. But what the hell was the killing all about? He told himself it was for Freedom pure and simple. Nothing else. Nothing else, Billy Boy, but Freedom pure and simple. But he felt a raging anger chewing up his insides and filling up his face. He was part of the glorious patriotic flag-waving murderers, the most passionless, the most meaningless murderers the world had ever known. They were murderers for kicks and the bigshots' profiteering and for ticker-tape parades down the great Fifth Avenue. This was the damn wrong way for him to be thinking.

The sun was coming up from behind the silently suffering mountains now and splashing the land with soft pink colors clashing and tenderly blending with the dark green of the morning jungle. Things will be better when we get back home, somebody said somewhere some time. The new day was aborning now with all the subtle daybreak beauty and the first wave was hitting the beach now and the dying had begun in sweat and blood and in very very earnest. We are dying for a better world. From where he was out in the bay he could see the Ducks and the Higgenboats and all kinds of landing barges come up to the beach and the scared courageous men jumping out of the boats and moving forward, sideways and backwards like a host of desperate reptiles of all sizes and description.

SCHOOM-SCHOOM-SCHOOM-SCHOOM—WHEEEEERRREE—
BOOM BOOM BOOM BOOM BOOM POW POW POW POW!

It was almost 0600 now and they were letting the gate down on his LST, and he saw the first Duck of the 913th back out into the strange dark water and turn around and head toward the island and disappear in the morning mist. And for some stupid reason he remembered the face of a pretty girl when he was ten years old in elementary school. The sharp smell of the sea saturated all of his senses. He had never thought of her again since he left P.S. Whatchamacallit. The hard pain in his belly made him think his guts would burst wide open. She had a round scared face and big black eyes and that was easily thirteen years ago. Worm got quietly behind the wheel and took a deep breath and backed noiselessly into the water and turned toward the burning island. Solly thought, great God, if I must die this morning, let me lose my life for something.

And the PT boats chugging all over the place sending up their inevitable smoke screens and making their man-made fog.

Solly sat on the back end of the Duck, looking through the smoke and mist and fog at the backs of the other men, as the Duck ploughed silently through the water along with hundreds of others, kicking up a soapy phosphorescence into the new day that was borning. His face was calm but he was scared shitless and in a way glad of it, because he hoped he wouldn't mess himself and thereby lose his dignity. Yuk Yuk Yuk and triple Yuk. A destroyer escort went past them almost leaping out of the water as its pompom guns pumped fire toward the beach.

BOMP BOMP BOMP BOMP! BOMP BOMP BOMP BOMP!

Like somebody whipping the side of the widest wooden fence in the world with the biggest inner tube.

And he *was* scared. He kept thinking that within the next hour or so he would probably be lying on the sandy beach with a hole in his head and dead to the goddamn beautiful WORLD. And for what? The deep fear was that he would die for nothing, like most men did. He would never see his wife again or Mama or Fannie Mae or the baby in Millie's stomach. And why? He had a right to see his child at least one time in this one life of his. He had a right to hold him in his arms. He had a right to see one more baseball game, he had a right to life and law school and novelist and poet and Fannie Mae and Harlem and success and Coney Island and Harlem Y and Apollo Theater and

Dusty Fletcher and Pigmeat Markham and all the rest of it. Break it down to the least damn common denominator, he was plain scared for his own and worthless ass. He had a right to live goddammit! And die of old age, flu, or accident.

He wanted to live and taste the Freedom that the war was being fought for. And see his son grow up in the New World that was coming to him.

His mouth and throat ran wet and dry and cold and hot interchangeably. Crabs clawing at his insides made him need a bowel movement. His chest felt like iron weights were hanging from each nervous hair. Well, goddammit, he wouldn't mess up his pants, he hoped, and he damn sure wouldn't break down or up or where the hell it was you broke. I believe in the war—believe in the war. Believe—believe—believe—believe! In close to shore now he saw the palm trees, once undoubtedly handsome and stately, but now they were ragged, scorched and jagged, bent and headless, like victims of a firing squad. Dead men too damn proud to lie down in a sandy grave. Freedom-fighters everyone. Anti-fascists all of them.

He thought, with all that stuff they've been throwing onto this island since the invasion began, what the hell am I worried about? Nothing could stay on that beach and live after such a bombardment. Not even an anopheles mosquito. Everything was dead and dying and particularly everybody.

Yes, love, the world is waiting for the sunrise, he thought sweetly of the song. Precious darling with our baby. Dear loved ones, the sun may never rise again. Dearly beloveds . . .

My country, 'tis of thee . . .
From every mountain top
Let freedom ring . . .

A piece of water hit his cheek and then another and another. He opened his mouth and tasted the salty water drops and wondered if it were beginning to rain or whether the wind were blowing the water out of the sea. The rain began to come down harder. The sunrise had stopped rising. Day stopped breaking. God was weeping for mankind. Of all the things to happen! The first day everywhere they went they always met the rainy season. He laughed bitterly.

Worm said aloud without looking back, "Now wouldn't that tickle you grandma's puz-zerves? Them Mama-hunching foxholes gon be wet as a sonofabitch tonight. Miss Taylor's baby-boy child ain't gon have a dry spot to lay his weary head." Everybody in the Duck laughed like there'd be no tomorrow to laugh again—Solly harder than the rest. Even the little sad-faced Irish soldier who should have gone home on rotation laughed. Solly could have kissed the five-by-five Bookworm. It might be the last time they would ever laugh.

In a Duck nearby he heard the voice of the handsome gray-eyed evil-faced motor sergeant. Greer was singing to the top of his gravelly voice. Even Banks laughed.

It rained last night
And the night before.
Hope like hell
It don't rain no more.
Wanna see my baby one more time . . .

The rain stopped falling as suddenly as it started, just as the Ducks of the 913th hit the beach. The sun began to rise again. The world became alive again and good night sweetheart, till we meet whenever. What a stupid song to think about. And now he felt the ground underneath them even though they were not out of the water yet. It was the first time in his life that terra firma had not felt good to him. Now the water was completely out from under them, leaving them alone on the sandy beach with thousands of soldiers scared to death and stumbling over each other. It was a state of mass confusion and wholesale defecation. The only heartening thing about it was there was no fighting on the beach. The fanatical Japanese had taken down their tents and fled, which made more sense than anybody ever made since Solly came into the Army, or since the last time he talked with Fannie Mae. The Ducks moved nervously across the beach swarming with tenderhearted soldiers. It seemed to Solly that all of them had diarrhea and dysentery. It seemed every other soldier on the beach had his pants below his knees, squatting tentatively and fearfully and poised for flight. Or he was digging him a hole to crap in or he was covering it up or he was pulling down his pants or he was quickly pulling them up again. A panorama of bare backsides of all colors and descriptions. Flat, round, fat, skinny, white, black, pink, brown. Every living with a swinging.

A couple of the Ducks including Solly's moved to a road and down the road about a hundred and fifty yards, going past thickets of trees and bushes which might be teeming with Japanese for all the silent soldiers knew. They reached a clearing which seemed to be a gun emplacement the Japanese had left behind in a great big hurry. There were about ten or fifteen soldiers, some from the 913; the others were from Anti-Aircraft. They went quietly and nervously to work putting together the giant 90mm. Ack-Ack gun, which was a long slender black cannon that would hurl death miles into the sky. The little fellow who should have gone home on rotation dropped a bolt to the gun's tripod and it rolled just beyond the edge of the clearing. He went to look for it and he found it and stooped to pick it up and never straightened up again. And he would never go home on rotation or for any other reason. They would never piece him together again unless they did it in the next world that was swiftly coming to him. The explosion picked Solly up from the ground and threw him across the clearing almost to the bushes where other land mines undoubtedly lay quietly waiting for other boobs and boobies. He thought he was dead he thought he was dying he thought he was deaf and he would never hear again. He lay there on the trembling earth with bombs going off inside of his head. He was afraid to move for fear he wouldn't be able to move. Was he really dead? Maybe an arm was blown away and maybe a leg. He thought he heard other soldiers running gently up the road toward them. Japanese or Americans. He couldn't care. He had to move, he had to know. He had to move to know to move to know. Was his wet face wet with rain or blood or perspiration? BOOM boom boom boom, the bombs exploded in his head. He had to move. He moved his arms and then his right leg then his left, and then he worried about the Bookworm. He got up and looked around him. The men were stirring now except for a couple of them who would never stir again. Other men from 913 ran off the road with their M–1s and their carbines at-the-ready. Two Duck-loads of sandbags came up and the drivers jumped down at-the-ready.

He couldn't hear what they were saying at first. Finally he realized one of them was saying, "What happened, Sergeant Solly?"

"Booby trap," he thought he said. He couldn't be sure. He couldn't hear his own voice clearly.

He helped the Bookworm to his feet and the other men were coming to, excepting those two who lay over near where the bolt was lost. They lay so still and quiet black and white among the green growth of the bushes. They lay so quietly for Freedom. A few more Ack-Ack men came up, and the fresh men of the 913 pitched in, and they shakily continued to put the gun in place, and they surrounded the gun with walls of sandbags.

When they got back to the beach the sun was up and day had broken pretty for the people, and the seventh wave was coming in. Soldiers everywhere B.M.ing and covering it up like proud and shamefaced alley cats. The guns had almost ceased firing offshore and it was a quiet peaceful morning, like Sunday in a Jersey meadow. Soldiers eating and B.M.ing, putting it in and putting it out. "If Mama could see her brave boy now," the Bookworm said to Solly with his pants flopped down around his ankles. Worm looked so comfortable and sweet and angelic with the kindly sunlight shining warmly on his bare backside. The sun a great big ball of burning ice.

It was at this very moment when—in the words of the great authority on Army Regulations, Private Joseph Bookworm Taylor—it was at this very moment that "the shit did hit the natural fan."

SHOOOOSH SHOOOSH SHOOOSH—SHOOSH SHOOSHSHOOSH-SHOOSH—SHOOOOOOOOOSH-BOOOOOM! SHOOSH-SHOOSH-SHOOSH-SHOOSH—BOOOM! It sounded like somebody rattling shutters to wake up the world. Heads, arms, legs, torsos, ears, scattered all over the beach. At the first shooshing sound Solly hit the ground and then the explosion and eruption made the earth throw him up and knock him around. He scrambled around on hands and knees like the rest of them were doing, looking for a place to hide, but there was no hiding place. At first he thought, when he could think, our own Navy is firing on us. But when the shooshing sounds and the boom-boom-booms continued up and down the beach, he realized that the Japanese were throwing the stuff down on them from the hills where they had taken refuge during the before-day bombardment.

And through it all he thought he heard the voice of Billy Banks. Does it make sense? Does it make sense? Does it make sense? Does it make any sense at all?

And the waves of men kept coming in onto the beach and some were washed back out to sea with the ebbing of the tide.

SHOOSH SHOOSH SHOOSH SHOOSH BOOM
SHOOSH SHOOSH SHOOSH SHOOSH BOOM BOOM BOOM!

There was nothing to do but to lay on the beach and wet your pants and wait for death to take you kindly out of this madness. And hope that those honored dead would not have died in vain. He started to laugh. He was a long long ways from Gettysburg.

And then it was SCHOOM SCHOOM SCHOOM SCHOOM WHEEEEREE—REEE—BOOM BOOM BOOM BOOM! As the guns from the bay started talking again and this time for the hills to listen.

Right smack down in the middle of thunder and lightning and Judgment Day, all you could do is lay on the beach and get right with God and hope you didn't crap in your pants, for dignity's sake.

Solly pushed his body up a few inches and looked around him. Bodies were lying all over the place, whole ones and halves and in-betweens and blood everywhere. The beach was changing its pretty complexion from white to rosy red. The edge of the sea was red with blood like his Mama cleaning chicken in the kitchen sink. He didn't see Worm or Lanky or any of his buddies. He lay flat on his face again like he was in love with Mother Earth. An exhibitionist. Through all the noise, which was now one great big deafening roar, always building, never ending, he thought he heard somebody calling his name. Maybe he was asleep and dreaming.

He heard Sergeant Greer calling. He raised up and turned toward him. The motor sergeant was flat on his belly about a hundred and twenty feet away, wearing a big fat evil grin. The sweetest smile he ever wore. "Hey, Sergeant Crute, can I get me a week-end pass tonight? I needs me some poontang, *me*."

Solly turned away and started to laugh in the midst of raging hell and couldn't stop laughing. His eyes began to fill and he felt the laughter cramping his stomach and oozing through his entire body, he couldn't stop laughing, his stomach ached, and his eyes ran water, but he couldn't stop laughing—and—

SHOOSH SHOOSH SHOOSH SHOOSH BOOM!

After the earth stopped shaking him, he looked for the evil-grinning sergeant, but all he saw was a cloud of sand and a crater in the sandy earth where the sergeant lay a moment earlier. And he had had his last poontang.

They lay there off and on all day long between the two death-dealers, amidst the dead and dying and the mutilated.

Solly and Worm and Baby-Face went back and forth into the jungle and helped to put up five more Ack-Ack guns and came back to the beach to die a million times per minute.

They built themselves little shallow trenches to squat in and wait for death.

The guns offshore had stopped firing again, because the infantry had gone to the hills to carry the battle to the treacherous enemy, who would not come out and fight them fair and square. And by dark the guns from the hills had quieted down, and on the crimson beach things were peaceful for the moment. Solly and Worm and Lincoln and Baby-Face and Quiet Man sat chatting and snacking like they were back home at Coney Island. The only sounds were that of the monotonous waves lapping and licking the edge of the island. The men told jokes and sometimes laughed, but they could not drown out the muted sounds of the dying and moaning and the groaning all over everywhere. It seemed that all of the medics were stumbling drunk and you couldn't blame them either. It was one of the roughest jobs on a beachhead—tending to the maimed and the dying and the hopeless and the helpless, and always up to your elbows in blood. But Worm said nevertheless, "They sure do have a drinking good time. And they don't shit in their pants either and if they do they don't know the difference."

Solly thought he wished he was with the infantry. At least they were doing something—not just sitting on their backsides in little shallow graves awaiting death's convenience.

The gunfire in the hills was one continuous symphony all night long played by Thompson guns and carbines and M-1s and 50-calibers and 20mm.s and hand grenades and flamethrowers, a symphony of sad songs played by amateur musicians. Solly lay in the sand and closed his eyes and wrote his great American novel about the grand and glorious war. Played by boys who should be home playing baseball playing handball playing with themselves, smelling their pee and standing on the corner and looking at the girls with the long legs and pretty ankles and ripe tits, killing time instead of people, going to law school and to dances and to work and libraries and opportunity and planetariums and career and talking about the girls and imagining the girls and going to bed and having wet dreams instead of shamelessly wetting their pants in a nightmare staged in Hell and which went on and on and on and never ended.

He vaguely heard a voice reach into his inner consciousness. "Sergeant Saunders, we have to help the—"

"Help who?" Solly said angrily and sleepily.

He opened his eyes into the face of the motor officer. Lieutenant Graham was drunker than a medic on an early-morning beachhead. He was drunk and open-pored and his eyes were rimmed with crimson. He leaned toward Solly and almost fell on top of him. His face was rosy-red with alcohol and terror. "We have to round up some of the men and help the medics take the wounded out to the hospital ship in our Ducks."

Solly got up and looked around him. Lincoln and the Worm got up. And Quiet-Man Larker. The symphony still went on and on up in the bleeding hills.

Lieutenant Graham said, "You round em up, Sergeant, and meet me right back here, unshtand?" He leaned on Solly heavily and confidentially. "I'm not cracking up, Sergeant, I just had a few cocktails, and I don't mean Molotov. But I'm calm, cool, klected."

Solly rounded up some of the men, and they along with the medics began to round up those who would never be men again. Of course they only took the wounded. They left the dead for later consideration and the Graves Registration boys. Like the handsome blond head they saw lying on the sand without a body, with the deep blue pleading eyes staring up to where the stars lived as if they were watching his own soul ascending to the Hereafter. Like Sergeant Greer, who was nothing but a dog tag now, and like the Irish Ack-Ack soldier. Their first interest must necessarily have to be with the living, since they were a humanitarian Army, which no one would say for the sneaky *hordes* of *barbarians* who were the goddamn enemy. There was the blue-eyed black-haired soldier who would never walk again, not even hobble, he had nothing but patriotic stumps which once were legs, and his blood was very very red. They were red-blooded All Americans. And a colored chap named Jackson of the Third Platoon of the valiant 913th, the right side of his face caved in, and he would never wink his right eye at a girl again the way he used to do back home in Peekskill. He told Solly, "That's all right, buddy boy. I'm fine." His right eye had been pushed all the way into his face so that it was level with his ears. Solly took him by the shoulders and tried to keep from looking him in the face. And tried to keep from crying. Jackson's right eye seemed to have an existence all its own and stared sorrowfully at Solly as he helped him onto the litter. He said, "That's all right, Sergeant Solly. It ain't no fault of yours." Jackson's blood was the same color of the other soldier's. Blood-red and red blood. All American. His big black face was masked with blood. There were men whose arms hung on only by the bleeding skin of them. One soldier's leg was blown off all the way to his crotch and including his urinator. The poor vain handsome bastard kept yelling, "Shoot me! Kill me, you hard-hearted sonsabitches! You'd even have more mercy on a horse in my condition!" He begged Solly. "Please, Sergeant, please, blow my brains out!" He tried to hide his privates which he did not have to hide, and then he started to beat himself in the face with his fists till he was out of breath, but it did him no good. They were determined to save his life, for country, wife, and family and the Articles of War. You couldn't blame them. Solly understood the situation. In the American Army, life was very very precious. He worked with the detail three or four hours and vomited four or five times per hour, till there was nothing else to vomit and he began to vomit blood, which was messy pinkish blood and not as red as the blood that spilled all over the beach. When he was dry of vomit his face filled up and the tears flowed unashamedly. He was too damn chickenhearted.

All through the night all through the next few days the symphony in the hills, the Song of Death, went on and on and almost got monotonous. The 913 were up to their backsides in slit trenches of blood and salty sea and beach and air raids and wind and rain and friendly smiling Filipinos who sometimes turned out to be Japanese soldiers in disguise. It was an uncomfortable business making trip after trip after trip from the beach to the ships out in the bay with the bombs and shrapnel dropping all around you unconcernedly. You could get hurt, you really could get all messed up, as Worm continually complained. But it was better than just sitting on the beach with no place to go with nothing to do but crap your pants and wait for Death. And debate the war's morality, which, no matter how you looked at it, was academic at the moment. Day and night, the next few days they brought in hundreds and hundreds of infantry and anti-aircraft and engineers and other amphibians, and field artillery, and God-and-Jack knew what others, thousands of them, baby-faced ones and bearded ones and many of them clean-shaven boys scared to death, Negro, Jew, Gentile, Puerto Rican, Filipino, streaming onto the beach and dying on the bloody beach and pushing forward and onward courageously, mostly to the Jam Session in the hills and most of them too scared to think of being frightened. There wasn't time. There simply positively absolutely wasn't time. Solly thought, Death was a grim nervous impatient hand-rubbing gleeful sonofabitch.

The lucky 913 lost only twenty-three men that first very busy week, and after that things weren't so bad—after the infantry took the battlefront ten-fifteen-twenty miles away. Things weren't half bad. There were just the pesky air raids which went on and on, night and day and day and night: SHOOOSH-SHOOOSH-SHOOOSH-SHOOOSH SHSHOOSHSHOOOSH BOOMBOOM-BOOMBOOM and people got hurt, soldiers and civilians, some got killed, but all this was to be expected. *C'est la guerre,* as Solly had a way of saying. And everything for Freedom. Of course the men still suffered with the GIs, which was the Army's affectionate term for the plague of nausea and diarrhea and dysentery rolled into one.

The 913 set themselves up in a company area right there on Crimson Beach, and they built a latrine, the holy place for dreams and rumors, and a kitchen and foxholes, in which they lived most of the romantic moonlit bomb-dropping South Pacific nights. And they met the Philippine people who came into the company area in multitudes, they were always all over the place, and especially where the food was. They acted like they thought the beach belonged to them. But they were friendly for the most part—those who were not Japanese. You never knew. You never ever really knew.

And they met Rosita, who adopted them immediately. Beautiful Rosita. Skinny sweet-faced brownly sugared sloe-eyed Rosita with the heartbreaking smile. Six or seven years old and homeless and hungry and parentless and grandparentless and everythingless. "Americanos drop great big bomb go booom! And everybody dead dead dead!" Solly asked her, "How can you love us, little baby? How can you even smile for us? Why don't you spit on us as we deserve?" She stared at him and smiled. She was the mascot of the 913. Every time he saw her he thought his heart would break in two. How in the hell could this be right? How could this be a better world? Was the entire war a fake? Was he the biggest fake of all? With his frigging I and E? Teaching what he couldn't believe?

The men gave Rosita blankets and clothing, much of which she gave to others, and General Grant made drawers for her, cutting them from GI underwear, and she would proudly pull up her dress and show them to everybody who would look. She was Solly's tenderest moment in the war. He gave her everything he could lay hands on—food, candy, love, compassion—took her out in the bay in the Duck, which was against the regulations.

She loved the men of 913, one and all and indiscriminately, except that she was especially in love with Sergeant Solly and the long tall Lanky Lincoln, who in two weeks learned to speak in Tagalog and to make jokes with the people.

Among the Philippine people there were some gullible ones. Yes indeed. One day a pretty young woman came into Solly's tent and stood staring at him, shy and uncertain. They were the prettiest people in the world. Rosita asked her what she wanted—Rosita, seated on Solly's bunk and speaking like a housewife with authority to speak.

After a time Solly said, "Well, what can we do for you, Miss?"

The lady laughed and tittered, stood on one foot then the other, and Solly was growing warm in the collar. He said, "What is it you want?"

Rosita's little face was flushed with anger.

Finally the woman said, "Will you let me see it—please!"

"See what?"

She said, "*It*—" And she began to snicker again.

She was thin and had a soft brown face and wide brown slanting eyes too big for her face and shiny white teeth, and Solly didn't like to be laughed at, whatever the joke was. "What is it that you want to see?"

"White Yankee say black Yankee have tail tucked down in breeches."

Solly's face burned with his anger. He breathed hard and tried to calm himself before he spoke. "And you believe white Yankee, honh? And you want to see my tail? You believe your great white liberator?"

Her face was filled with fright now as she sensed his anger. She shook her head. "No—no—no—no! Me don't believe it. Me just want make sure me don't believe it." She bowed her head and backed away. "Thank you, good-bye," she said, and she went quickly out of the tent and ran up the company street.

He went to the entrance and called after her. "Come back and I'll show it to you."

Rosita came to him and put her arms around his legs. "Don't be angry, Sergeant Solly. Stupid girl no know no better!" He picked her up and held her close to him and she was all the children in the world.

All during this time Hopjack slackened his pace quickly down to a slow drag. All the zip was out of him. All the hop and all the jack. One day he dragged past Worm's and Solly's tent, and Worm said, "Hopjack! Hopjack! Scat! Scat!"

Hop shook his head. "Scat yourself, you little crazy sapsucker. These damn Japs got the old man in the go-long." His eyes were red like lanterns and sunken into his skull. He had hardly slept a full hour since they landed. The air raids all night long had given him insomnia. He volunteered as the permanent sergeant of the night guard. Told the CO he wasn't going to sleep anyhow.

Solly said, "You'd still rather kick them in the ass than to go home on rotation, wouldn't you, Hop?"

Hop shook his head. "That's a lie the old man could've helped from telling."

And to break the monotony of Bloody Red Beach there was the Philippine countryside with its tall palm trees and giant banana plants and its coconut trees and its abaca plants and its tobacco fields and its inevitable rice fields and its equally inevitable caribou, the rugged faithful water buffalo, the Filipino's very best friend. The sturdy menfolks in the fields behind their ploughs and their hard-working caribous and the women carrying babies on their backs and bending in the everlasting rice paddies with the water almost up to their knees. Solly thought of his own, the Negro people, standing deep in the corn and cotton fields of Georgia and Mississippi with nowhere to go and not a damn thing to look forward to. War or no war, it would make no difference to them, except for those who gave their sons up in noble sacrifice to the great bloodletting in the name of peace and freedom.

The countryside was drenched and splashed with every color known to man in the lowlands and the mountains. And there were mountains everywhere. Solly figured that's what the Philippines were. Millions of years ago, thousands of mountains came up out of the sea to catch their breaths and decided to keep their heads above water henceforth and forevermore.

And driving through the little villages, and watching the girls and the women sitting three or four or five in a row on the front steps of their huts with their heads in each other's laps, picking lice from the heads of long black hair with assembly-line efficiency. And in the evening lovely Philippine women in evening dresses squatting barefoot on their haunches on the street corners of the capital city. If you were romantic and idealistic you could almost love this country. And all through this time when he wasnt' B.M.ing or scared to death, he was asking himself, Why am I here? What am I doing in these people's country ten thousand miles away from home? Does the damn war make any sense? He felt they were not really wanted in this place, the great American liberators. And yet the war had to make sense to him or drive him crazy. He, Sergeant Solomon Saunders, Junior, Millie's husband, Mama's son, the get-aheader, the great morale builder of the Special Men of 913—the young man with a future, going places.

Two weeks after Liberation Morning, when things had really quieted down to two or three air raids a day and five or six per night and isolated instances of Japanese snipers sniping at you from the jungled mountains (a couple of men were wasted that way), the captain ordered another Orientation Session.

When Samuels spoke to Solly about it, Solly asked him to get another soldier for the job. Samuels persuaded and cajoled him. Finally Solly said, "Look, I mean it. I don't believe the War Department stuff any more. I don't understand it. I can't connect it with this madness we've gone through the last two weeks. I can't link it with the Red Cross—and all the rest of it—the killing the starvation and all the rest—" He stopped talking, he thought he might burst into tears. He was remembering the morning they came to this place.

Samuels said, "Sergeant, you are in the Army."

Solly said, "You know Rosita, don't you?"

Samuels said, "Rosita? What are you talking about?"

They stood outside the orderly room. Solly looked around them and away to the green-clad mountains from whence the brand-new day had come to drench the countryside with sunlight. He thought of Georgia—Sunday—summertime. A cow pasture in New Jersey summer Sunday. And in his mouth and in his throat the sick-sweet taste of nostalgia. He saw the crowded beach at Coney Island. He wanted to go home and damn the killing! Damn the suffering and starvation! Damn these poor-assed islands that had been poor before the war and poorer now and God knew what they would be like after the killing was over.

"Let me put it formally, Lieutenant. I hereby respectfully request that I be relieved of the duties of Non-Commissioned Officer in Charge of Information and Education. I'll put it in writing if you want me to."

The captain sent for him that evening.

He had taken a swim in the bay in the moonlight and refreshed himself with the memory of that first Liberation Morning. He got dressed up in khaki and went to the captain's quarters with the taste of death in his mouth and the stench of dying in his nostrils.

They stood outside the captain's tent. A piece of breeze came off the ocean like Millie blowing her hot breath on his sweating face. Millie pregnant with their child. Millie sweet and lovely Millie.

The captain hitched his trousers. "What's the matter, Sergeant Saunders?"

"Nothing, sir." Just sick and tired of everything. Especially your disguised Southern accent.

"You and Lieutenant Samuels 're doing a damn good job with that Orientation stuff, and I want you to know I appreciate the importance of the job you all are doing. Especially you. And there'll be other promotions too. The table of organization calls for two more staff sergeants in the company. And I heard today about an American Officer Candidate School being set up in Australia. You have nothing to worry about."

Millie blew her hot breath again upon his damp face from across the ocean. And she whispered, "Listen to your head and forget about emotions!" She cried, "Promotions! Promotions! Promotions!" It was his own voice he mistook for Millie's. Accidentally on purpose.

He said, "I don't know, sir. I—"

The captain said, "I've come to realize, Sergeant, there is nothing more important than a fighting man's morale. You can have all the planes and all the tanks and all the everything else in the world, it doesn't amount to a hill of beans, if the men don't know their cause is righteous. I was at a meeting at headquarters yesterday and this thing was brought home time and time again." He walked back and forth in front of Saunders. He stopped and hitched his trousers. "You and the lieutenant making preparations for the session Saturday morning?"

Solly's face was freshly sweating now and felt no breeze from off the ocean. He heard another voice inside him he could not identify.

"I think you ought to assign the job to somebody else, sir," he said. "Someone who understands it better—I mean the meaning of the war." He hated himself for beating around the bush like this. He should just tell this cracker to take the job and shove it.

"Lieutenant Samuels told me all about it, and I understand the way you feel. I know the Negro don't get all the breaks he's supposed to get, but I guarantee you—"

Solly said, "Sir, I prefer that somebody else—"

The captain was quickly losing his calm and patience. "You prefer! You don't have any preference in this Army. That's the whole damn trouble, I've been pampering this outfit too damn much, and especially you, goddammit! Now you listen to me. You're going to be promoted to staff sergeant and you know damn well you want to be. You don't fool me one goddamn minute. And you're going to still be in charge of I and E, and you're going to help lieutenant with that program Saturday morning. Is that clear?"

"Very clear, sir." If he didn't do it, somebody else would. He might as well get the promotion.

Rutherford put his hand on Solly's shoulder. "How come you and me always got to be fussing and fighting? I've always been fair and square with you." He sounded like a woman whining.

His hand on Solly's shoulder gave Solly a funny feeling, like he was going to be seasick on an LST. He pulled away from the captain and stood his ground. He wanted to go before he was ill in the captain's presence. He had agreed to do the job. There was nothing else to talk about.

The captain said, "This is top secret, Saunders. We'll probably move out next Tuesday to make another beachhead."

Solly almost laughed at first. This was why the captain was so anxious about the men's morale and the war's morality. Solly saw the first beachhead again, he smelled the blood of dead and dying and the wholesale defecation and knew the whole war raging in his stomach. He felt the GIs coming on him.

They had their session Saturday morning in the mess-hall tent. The topic was "Can We Achieve the Peace after We Win the War?" The subtopics were, "1. Can we put the Democracy we fight for into practice for all people?" and "2. Is War inevitable?"

Solly and Samuels labored and sweated in the morning heat. Samuels said the world would be different after the war. They would live to see a better world where all men would be free and equal regardless of race or creed or color of a man's skin or his religion. "This is exactly what the war is all about."

The men sat quiet in the stuffy heat and listened. Solly felt like a traitor and an uncle tom.

He said, "It's up to us, you and me, and all of us, to make sure we win the peace and freedom we are fighting and dying for. It's up to us to never let them forget the slogans of the war. If we do, shame on us!" He was trying desperately to reach them as the perspiration poured from him. He saw some of them shake their heads in agreement and heard one whisper, "Tell the truth!" Solly said, "Nobody is going to be more concerned with our freedom than we are. If we go back home and go to sleep, shame on us." He heard the Bookworm clearly this time. "That's what I'm talking about!" Solly said, "We all know what Fred Douglass said. 'Who would be free must themselves strike the blow.' "

During the question period, Lanky Lincoln said to Solly, "Man, don't you know these crackers going to revert to type? It's going to be just like it always was. I'm surprised at you. And as far as the inevitability of war is concerned, soon as this war is over with, before the powder gets dry, Russia and the United States going to be at each other's neck. There is no such thing as peace. It's always war. It just cools off every now and then."

An older soldier named Bell got really hot and bothered. He accused Solly and, by implication, Samuels and the entire War Department of being atheistic. "The Good Book says there'll be wars and rumors of wars and ain't nothing you can do about it."

Nevertheless Samuels and Solly thought that on the whole the session was a success, and Solly didn't feel quite as guilty as he had felt when it began. The captain came in near the end of it and congratulated them when it was over. But to hell with the captain's praises. Solly Saunders didn't need them. He had told the truth as he saw it and there was nothing to be ashamed of. And yet and yet and yet he did not like the taste in his mouth nor the feeling in his stomach. The question Lanky could have asked was: How can you fight a democratic war with an undemocratic army? It was the question Solly had asked himself many times.

The men's morale was not so low the following week. They were getting sort of used to the place and kind of comfortable. True, the air raids had not cooled off yet, and a few people lost little things like their lives each day, and some of the more sensitive soldiers still had not gotten over their first case of the GIs. Be that as it may, they were rewarded for a job well done by being chosen for a new invasion. Some of them were not appreciative.

But as Solly said, *"C'est la guerre."*

Worm said, "Say your ass. These crazy mother-hunchers gon keep farting around and get somebody all messed up."

Notwithstanding, early one pretty sun-washed morning they broke camp, three weeks and five days after they landed, and Rosita followed them laughing and screaming to the place where they left the beach and went out to the LSTs. And she hugged the men of 913, especially Solly and Lanky, she kissed the boys good-by, with tears streaming down her smiling face and some of their eyes filled up shamefacedly, as they left her standing on that lonely beach. Solly died a little that morning as they left her. Six years old and beautiful and parentless and grandparentless and homeless and crying smiling crying. Americanos drop great big bomb go boom! And everybody dead dead dead!

For what?

CHAPTER 5

They were in the fourth wave of the new invasion. And some of them got all messed up, but the way Solly figured, they never had it so good. The messed-up ones, they would lie up in some comfortable hospital or they would go home stateside or to Australia, and wouldn't have to worry any more about the GIs, which had you forever taking a crap or needing one, and your stomach full of cramps and wind, the goddamn miserable GIs, which went on and on till your excrement was blood and your hindparts were sore and very bloody and on and on and on and on, and don't forget at the other end, the vomiting, which always reaped a similar harvest. And Lieutenant Graham, the motor officer, who went stark raving mad, as did a half a hundred others on the beach that glorious victorious morning. The last Solly saw of him he dashed up the beach screaming, "The Japs are coming! Retreat! Retreat!" And before anybody could stop him he ran headlong into the water. He was fished out by the Navy, and a PT boat took him screaming and struggling out to the middle of the bay and Solly never saw him again. Of course those who would never go home were lucky too, the dead ones, because they had nothing to worry about. They didn't even have to worry about whether the war made sense or not or whether a better world would grow out of the embers of this old decrepit earth. They didn't have to worry whether the Red Cross would invite them to their parties. They had crossed over that River Jordan where all was peace and they could study war no more. No more I-and-E for them.

The same routine, the bombardment, the landings practically uncontested, and of course the GI fertilization of the beach and then the stuff screaming down from the burning hills and the moaning and groaning and blood and dying and further fertilization with blood and human excrement.

That morning on the once white but now crimson beach just before noon in the midst of the screaming thunder from the hills and the dying and the defecating and the moaning and the groaning and the great bloodletting, Billy Baby-Face Banks came up to Solly. There was a wildness in his eyes and a helpless anger in his face. "Sergeant Solly, how in the hell can you say it makes any sense?" He waved his arms. "It's crazy! Can't you see it? It's crazy! Crazy! Crazy! And it don't make a goddamn bit of sense!" William (no-swimming) Banks.

Solly stared long and hard at the baby-faced soldier—a boy the Army had not been able to make a man of. The tears were streaming down the soldier's face and Solly felt like crying too. He didn't trust himself to speak at first. But finally he said huskily, "You know it too?" And he turned and walked away, but Baby-Face followed him. "Sergeant Solly, I want out goddammit, and I'm going to get it the first damn chance I get. I mean it, Sarge!" During air raids he ran into the bay.

Solly said quietly, "Let me know and I'll go with you."

Why in the hell didn't Billy Banks understand that every American soldier had to fight in Freedom's cause? How could he bolster Billy's morale when his own was shot to hell? How could you make sense out of madness?

The first night on the newly invaded island they were air-raided all night long. Nobody slept but Lanky Lincoln. The next day they moved about fifty-five yards from the beach and set up camp in a small clearing surrounded on three sides by the jungle and on the other by the open road. A wild creek ran to the east of them and disappeared into the jungle. The second night they hit a streak of good luck. They were protected from the air raids by a ninety-nine-miles-per-hour typhoon. It blew down palm trees and bumped ships against each other out in the bay and turned some over and sank a few of the least seaworthy ones and turned over Ducks, and its over-all purpose seemed to be to wash and blow the island out into the deep black sea, and it pretty damn near succeeded. Solly and Jim Larker and Worm and Lanky and Scotty spent the earlier part of the evening digging an all-purpose family-type foxhole outside a tent they had thrown up hastily and which had even more hastily been blown away by the typhoon. So they ended up in the foxhole, which Solly said was the safest place after all, with trees blowing down all over the place. Sitting there in a hole in the ground the size of a grave, while the world blew away above their heads. The tall helpless palm trees stood moaning and groaning and sometimes screaming from the merciless whipping of rain and wind and hail the size of tennis balls. They sounded as eerie as the pom-pom guns and the shooshing shells of the Japanese mortars flung from the melancholy hills.

Solly said, "One consolation, Tojo won't be over tonight. Even he can't maneuver those Zeros in this kind of stuff."

You could look upward and see everything flying across the foxhole a mile a minute. Worm said, "Tents, clothes, shoes, tree branches, rifles, helmets, gas masks, now and then a skinny soldier, mess kits, cartridge belts, officers and monkeys and bull bats and banana bunches."

They sat there talking about home and comfort and a good hot dinner and a cool glass of lemonade and a hot cup of coffee and love and job and women, and finally they talked about the war, and Jimmy Larker said, "It's a war against fascism, and Negroes have as much a stake in it as anybody else."

Solly said bitterly, "That's like saying I'm just as rich as you are, when neither one of us has a pot to piss in. You should be in charge of I and E."

Worm said, "This is the kind of night when I could lay up with me some nice fat pom-pom. I love stormy-weather pom-pom. With the rain coming down and the wind blowing and your old lady moaning and groaning. Great-day-in-the-mama-hunching-morning!"

Jimmy said, "Forget about the Negro question for the moment. Who's the main enemy?"

Scotty said, "White folks. Captain Ratoff. Rat off his big white horse right on your big black ass."

Solly said, "Bilbo and Talmadge and Cap'n Charlie Rutherford and all of their cracker counterparts." Build that morale, Staff Sergeant Saunders. You're in charge of I and E.

Worm said, "A nice warm bed and some nice fat juicy pom-pom, with the rain rapping up against the windowpane but it can't come in. Great-day-in-the-mama-hunching-morning!" He was sweet-faced and nostalgic.

Solly said, "Still it's got to be better when we get back home this time. This is a war for Freedom." You had to believe or go raving mad. Run into the mountain jungle and forget it. "We'll make it better."

Lanky said, "Liberty, Egality, and Fraternity and all that other horseshit that these white folks don't believe in."

Solly said violently, "Goddammit! We got to believe in something! Tell them, Jimmy."

Scotty said, "Just cause you a staff sergeant you don't have to believe everything the man tells you. I thought they beat that shit out of your head in Ebbensville."

Lanky said, "You talk like one of those true believers, Solly. I'm really surprised at you. You really believe that crap you been teaching outa them Army magazines."

Scotty said, "You know what I believe in? I'm a true patriot. I believe in them dead American Presidents, every last damn one of 'em, I'm freakish for 'em, and I'm gonna collect just as many as I can when I get back in that other world after this shit is over. That's who I'm gon love and worship—George Washington—Abraham Lincoln—Alexander Hamilton—all them pretty pictures on them little biddy green pieces of paper coated with chlorophyll."

Solly said angrily, "If you don't believe in the war, why in the hell are you over here? Why didn't every damn one of you go AWOL?"

They had guards surrounding the edges of the camp and one of them sounded off so he could be heard by every living that was living, even if he wasn't swinging.

"Halt! Who goes there?"

The men in the foxhole reached for their wet guns.

It was Bucket-head Baker's frightened voice.

"Halt, gu-gug-goddammit! Who goes there? I ain't playing mother-fuckers! Sound off!"

The foxhole comrades could hear a rustling noise from the direction of the wild creek and then the rifle started talking.

"Pow! Pow! Pow! Pow! The Japs! The Japs! Pow! Pow! Pow! Pow! Pow! Pow!"

They were scared deep in their recta, but they leaped out of the foxhole and ran to the rescue, but by the time they got there Bucket-head had already stopped one of the enemy and the rest of them headed back upstream. Solly could only see their big broad leathery backsides. Wild hogs in the Philippines were huge and plentiful and vicious, with a reputation of anti-humanism, and they didn't do to mess with. The one Bucket-head had struck after emptying his rifle blindly into the creek stood bloody in water up to his black massive shoulders, staring wonderingly at Bucket-head and Solly and the rest of them with the lonesome eyes of a blind man selling pencils in the subway. The bleeding hog tried to turn around and join his buddies, but all he got for his efforts was a bloody watery grave. He sank like a ship going down at sea.

When they got back to their foxhole they tried to keep the weather out by covering it with tenting and nailing the tenting down with pegs. A half an hour later, Bucket-head slid under the tenting and joined them, as they sat there discussing wild hogs and carabous and pom-pom and the Democratic War against Fascism and debating whether or not it would be safer and more comfortable to leave the hole-in-the-ground and take refuge in one of the Ducks over on the other side of the area. The water which had been up to their hindparts had at this point crept up to their waists and was still creeping.

Solly said, "It's a good idea excepting that half of the Ducks have already been up-ended by the typhoon."

Quiet Jim Larker said, "The Ducks are the driest place on the island. All of them are covered by tarpaulins."

Worm said dreamily, "Them Filipino women are some pretty people, you hear me? And they're just about the most. Back in that other place, I was standing one day talking to one in her front yard, and don't you know, that chick took a whole bath with her dress on, she just kept talking and washing and she washed everything, and if I saw a little biddy bit of something, you did. I almost went blind from looking and I ain't seen hide nor mustache."

They laughed and chuckled. Bucket-head said, "Man! They really are something. They can stand straight up and hold their legs apart, and pull out their dress and piss without even wetting themselves."

Scotty said, "You're right about that. These chicks got bombsights on their pussy!"

They laughed and laughed.

Quiet Man suggested again that they go to the Ducks.

Bucket-head Baker said, "Hell naw. You cats crazy or something. It's raining out there if you didn't know it. We'd get wet as a sonofabitch tryna get to those Ducks."

They laughed with Baker. With the water up to their elbows they laughed. Somebody broke wind and the water bubbled and they laughed some more. Worm said, "Start across that wide-open area dark as it is, and one of them trigger-happy studs on guard duty'll blow you a brand-new asshole. You couldn't bomb me outa this hole till morning comes."

They laughed some more. Solly said, "We keep up this island hopping we'll be needing three or four assholes apiece. It'll be coming out of our ears and noses."

But when the water reached shoulder level, which was ear level for the Bookworm, Solly led the stalwarts across the area and into a warm and cozy Duck.

The next day was brilliantly and blindingly hot and almost totally without air raids, and they moved up the road and set up camp near the only American-operated airstrip in the entire Philippines excepting the one back on the other island. The Japanese had airstrips all over the place, on every island, even way up in the bleeding hills—in any place that they could clear away a little piece of area just big enough for one Zero to take off from, and tiny and obscure enough to be hidden from the eyes of Yank reconnaissance.

All along the countryside the air was filled with the sickening odor of rotting flesh. Dead Japanese fanatics stacked up like livestock in the ditches on each side of the dusty road—headless men, armless men, legless men, dead men every last one of them. The savage sunlight cooked their bodies, and dead homo sapiens give off a stench that make dead rats smell like an Evening in Paris some-damn-where. Solly thought, if we followed this madness through to its logical conclusion, we would jump off these Ducks right this minute and get ourselves some fresh meat for a change. Some nice juicy human ham hocks and shoulders and center cuts and heads and tenderloins and ears and jowls and rumps. Over in a field he saw powerful bulldozers, handsome and efficient, and digging shallow trenches and dumping hundreds of Japanese bodies altogether into their final resting places. The smell of death assaulted his nostrils, bloated his stomach, contracted his chest, stuck in his throat, and gagged his windpipe. He leaned over the side of the Duck and puked his insides out. The last thing he saw was a young Filipino woman way over in a field, squatting to make the earth more fertile.

In the midst of all the war's great ugliness he glimpsed one thing of beauty those first few days of the new invasion, like a lily of the valley growing proudly on a desert rock. He saw a woman's sweet face as she strutted through the new company area with a baby on her back and a bundle of GI clothing on her dark head. And a brown dog walked ahead of her with his mouth open and his red tongue busy in the heat. She made his stomach hurt, she was so lovely. Her skin like burnt brown toast and her eyes were black and shaped like almonds. Her graceful walk was pure and pretty poetry and a symphony of rhythms as she swung her hips from side to side. He got one brief quick glimpse of her, but the picture stayed with him as if he had shot it with a camera and it would be with him forever. He felt he had seen her face somewhere before, some time some place, felt it deeply in the essence of him. Her name was on the tip of his tongue, her face on the rim of his memory. He almost called out to her.

He was wide open for a women's face, her proud walk with her shoulders back, her womanliness sweetly disturbing to him. Millie was always with him now, as the days of her dear pregnancy came closer to their final sweet fulfillment. He had not heard from her in ten days, and he ached with loneliness and longing.

A few evenings later in their new camp area, they were standing in the chow line laughing and joking, and the mess sergeant shouting at them, "All right, come and get it in a hurry, goddammit! I got to go into town and get me some pom-pom! I'm sick and tired of round-eye!" The men were laughing but the mess sergeant was not even smiling. Sergeant Perry was dead serious. He was pom-pom happy. In-town might be overrun with Japanese, but he was going, he was going. Solly was daydreaming of his Filipino washerwoman. His dream was all mixed up with Millie and maybe even Fannie Mae. The men were breaking every rule of chowing under combat conditions, the main one being that they should have had a staggered chow line, three men at a time.

But there they were, at least fifty of them standing in line when suddenly the sky aglow with sunset hurled one of those silvery comets toward the earth. The Zero caught the entire island dozing and was almost down to a couple of hundred feet and heading inward when hell erupted from the earth. The Ack-Ack guns began to talk and trails of tracer bullets began to keep company with Tojo as he ducked in and out of the exploding flak like a lonesome halfback running broken-field. Most of the men in the chow line stood like they were mesmerized, and so did Solly, watching the fun and remembering Coney Island and Independence Day, maybe that's where he had seen her, Filipino washerwoman, impossible, as the tracers followed Tojo like a crazy rainbow getting larger by the second as more and more Ack-Ack guns picked up the merry desperate chase, and now the pretty-colored tracers came lower and lower near to the level of the trees and crisscrossing, and suddenly Tojo was not more than a hundred yards from the chow line of the 913 and less than treetop low and ducking and dodging the tracers which were too damn low for earth-bound people. Tojo began to strafe as he hedgehopped toward the chow line and the chow line emptied in two hundredths of a second. Even Lanky Lincoln moved.

"Tat-tat-tat-tat-tat-tat-tat-tat-tat," Tojo played a dot game down the company street. Solly ran toward his foxhole next to his tent and dove for it, but before he landed another soldier dove beneath him and just as he landed another fell on top of him and seconds later BOOOOOOOOOOOOOOOOOM! The loudest noise he ever heard. He lay there stone deaf and temporarily concussioned and sandwiched between two other soldiers, as the trembling earth shook them together like they were in a malted shaker. Finally they pulled themselves apart embarrassed, and before they could drag themselves out of the foxhole it was BOOM BOOM BOOM! BOOM!

After a time they saw that the boom-boom-booms came from the gasoline dump about a couple of hundred yards away. Tojo had laid his egg dead center. There must have been two or three hundred drums of gasoline in the gas dump, and all night long and every four or five minutes one would leap toward heaven and explode with sound and fury, with great flames licking the angry air to build a fire around the moon. It also was a lighted flare for Tojo, who came all night long that night at twenty-five- or thirty-minute intervals. He would come skipping up the island following the coast at tree level, so low you could shoot him with a rifle and even throw rocks at him ducking in and out of the Ack-Ack fire and laying eggs and playing dots.

There had not been time to build a latrine yet. They'd been too busy bringing fresh troops from out in the bay onto the beach, and arms and ammunition, and taking them to the front and coming back, ducking bullets, back and forth, and all day long into the night. But the Japanese had kindly left an open pit, 20′ by 30′ approximately, with a plank about ten inches wide that reached from one side to the other. It was about thirty feet from the back of Solly's tent and half filled with rain and urine and excrement and lighting up the neighborhood. That day they had sprayed oil upon the angry waters but it had not killed nor even stilled the awful stench.

Solly sat on his bunk waiting for Tojo's next visit, his stomach doubled up with cramps, exploding with cramps, and needing a bowel movement like he never did before and wanting desperately to go, afraid of disgracing his underwear. The problem was, what would he do if Tojo came in playing dots and caught him with his trousers down and squatting on that skinny plank? Would he dive into the cesspool? He'd die first, but if the man hit him he might be knocked alive into the moonlit pool and then he would surely die, a hundred thousand times. The stench of the cesspool lived in his nostrils.

Much of the night he spent seated on the edge of his sack with the cramps exploding in his stomach, waiting for Tojo's next visit. If Tojo's motive was harassment he was certainly succeeding. He had everybody rest-broken excepting Lanky, who slept through most of the night. He didn't even build himself a foxhole. The company lyricist said, "Frig it! If the man is going to get me, he'll get me. I sure ain't gon dig no grave for him to bury me in."

The chief bombing target was undoubtedly the airstrip, to render it unsuitable for planes to land or take off from. The second most important target was the Anti-Aircraft gun emplacement, which was only ninety-seven feet away from Solly's tent. The Anti-Aircraft group were a bunch of good-natured courageously frightened dark-haired and blond-haired boys, mostly from the bluegrass country of Kentucky. The dead Irish lad from Manhattan had been a member of their outfit. Worm and Solly and Jimmy got to know them on the comradely basis of drinking coffee with them late at night and talking with them about what the world was going to be like when the lights went on again all over. One of them, his name was Randy, was a friendly pessimistic bastard. He didn't believe he'd ever see the bluegrass country again. He said, "One of these nights, goddamn my sorry asshole, Tojo gonna drop one right into my mama-hunching lap." This was the second invasion he'd been on with the 913, and he had listened to Worm too carefully. And he prided himself on the fact that he could call as many mother-hunchers as the next mother-huncher.

It was funny how these blue-eyed bluegrass country boys seemed to have left their crackerism behind them in the blue fields of Kentucky. They had a natural ball with the mean bastards of the 913 without even trying hard. They didn't even appear to be self-conscious about it.

The night before, they had sat late at night in the 913 mess hall drinking coffee and batting the breeze. The one named Randy said, "Man, one of these days I'm gon bring my sorry ass to New York City, and I'm gon nacherl-born do my number with all kinds of peoples like they got up there. I'm gon be as free as the goddamn breeze—be happy as a possum up a 'simmon tree. When I get back, I don't reckon I'm gon take to country life any mother-hunching more."

Scotty said, "Goddamn, boy, you done just about got enough of Mister Ratoff's old mule farting in your face, ain't you, and not even saying, if you please."

All of them laughed including Randy. And when the laughter died away, he said, "I ain't never going home no more. I don't believe nobody ever goes home. I don't believe the war gon ever end."

Solly said, "Why're you in this war, Randy? What the hell is it all about?"

The big broad-shouldered mild-faced one named Harold said, "I'm in it cause I ain't been able to figure out how to get the hell out of the bastard."

Randy said, "I'll tell you like my daddy used to tell folks used to ask him did he fight in the First World War. He used to say, 'I fought and fought and fought and fought but they drafted me any-goddamn-how.' "

All of them laughed for Randy's sake.

Harold said, "If I could lose me something unimportant like a left arm or a leg or a left nut or something like that, maybe they'd let me outa this sonofabitch."

Solly said, "How about Freedom, Randy? Aren't you willing to fight for Freedom and Democracy?"

"And all that kind of shit," Worm added.

Solly was sick and tired of finding so many white soldiers who saw nothing for themselves in the anti-fascist Democratic War to save the World for Peace and Freedom.

Randy said, "I didn't have no goddamn freedom down on the farm where I come from. I worked from sunup to sundown and didn't never get nowhere. I ain't had no education or nuthin like that. And if I went back home right now, me and you couldn't go into town together. What kinda freedom is that? But y'all up there in New York City, y'all different, y'all got something to fight for in this war. They tell me up there freedom is a nacherl fact, and a man ain't nuthin but a nacherl man. If I was from New York City like y'all is, I wouldn't mind being in this mother-huncher."

Solly stared at Randy and started to laugh and couldn't stop laughing. Worm had a mouth full of coffee and it went down the wrong way and he got strangled and it came back through his nostrils and seemed to come from his eyes and ears, and he was laughing and crying at the same time, but Randy didn't see a goddamn thing to laugh about.

And now it was about 2347 o'clock and the full moon seemed to be aiming its special beam directly onto Solly's tent and into Solly's foxhole and on the pretty pool behind the tent. And where had he seen her face before? Worm sat on the other side of the tent on his cot and Jimmy sat on his, and they were discussing the stupidity of Lanky not building a foxhole and sleeping unbothered through the night and Solly trying hard to keep from crapping in his pants. Lanky was on a cot in the back of the tent with his net tucked in and actually snoring. Scotty shouting from the other side of the company street, "Hey, Sergeant Sandy, whatcha gonna do when the world's on fire—yah?"

Her face was like a baby's face. The Filipino washerwoman.

Solly shouted, "Run like hell and holler fire—yer."

She was not even five feet tall.

About midnight you could hear the faint rumblings of big guns down the other end of the island and you knew the man was on his way, and when they became louder and clearer, you knew a hot fear, as the guns picked up the chase nearer and nearer to the target, and you felt your face grow even hotter and the cramps in your stomach unbearable now and the very tip of the hole of your rectum nibbling angrily at the cot, and now you hear the Ack-Ack men in the gun emplacement ninety-seven feet away, telling you that Tojo is in at eleven o'clock at ten o'clock closer and closer, and the Anti-Aircraft louder and louder and nine o'clock and eight o'clock and when you hear the 90mm. gun in your own front yard begin to talk, you know the man is sitting on top of you. Sometimes he drops flares, sometimes bombs, and all the time he plays his deadly dot games.

The Ack-Ack man said "SIX O'CLOCK."

Randy from the bluegrass country said, "FIVE O'CLOCK." And all the island was sounding off and the sky was a pattern of red polka dots. And Solly went silently out of the side of the tent and slid into his foxhole, as did everyone but sleeping beauty. The big 90mm. was sounding off and the ground was trembling like an earthquake. Worm jumped in his hole and it sounded like he was diving into a swimming hole. The tide was in the flood and had paid his hole a visit. Solly and Jimmy began to laugh but Worm didn't see the humor of it. And Solly could see Tojo now coming in at three o'clock and heading for pay dirt, and how in the hell could they miss him with the earth quaking and coming apart from the giant Ack-Ack guns?

Suddenly General Grant emerged from the tent across the way and began to wave his arms and scream at the top of his voice.

"Gwan, Tojo! Gwan, Tojo! Fly your ass off! Fly your ass off! Fly, black man! Fly! Fly! Fly!"

As scared as Solly was, tears came to his eyes as he watched the General and thought about what a "freedom-loving" country had done to warp the values of this freedom-loving man. At that moment he hated everything in America that had pushed the General to this point in time and space.

Now the big gun ninety-seven feet away was talking and shaking the earth, beating out a rhythm like it was stomping at the Savoy.

SHU-LOOM-AH-SHU-LOOM-AH-SHU-LOOM-AH— SHU-LOOM-AH-SHU-LOOM—and every time it SHU-LOOMED it almost threw Solly from his foxhole. And Tojo almost sitting in their laps now and the General still standing in the middle of the company street with the full moon shining on his apoplectic face and screaming louder than ever and waving his arms.

"Flyyyyy! Flyyyyyyy! Fly, mother-fucker! Show these paddies how to fly!"

Scotty was in his foxhole outside of the tent next to the General's tent. And of all the people in 913, he stood up in his hole and aimed his rifle at the General. "If you don't get outa that street and shut your loud mouth I'm gon blow your ass up there so you can join Tojo!"

The spell was broken. Grant turned and looked disdainfully at Scotty and walked quickly into the tent with dignity. By that time Tojo had come and gone, but he left his calling card. He dropped his egg and—

SHOOSH-SHOOSH-SHOOSH-SHOOSH-SHOOSH-SHOOSH

Solly tried to make himself smaller underneath his helmet and held his breath and his anus bit the angry air and sucked the wind. He thought his race was run, his day was come, and it seemed like a century of waiting before—

BOOOOOOOOOOOOOOOOOOOOOOOOOOOM!

The good earth threw him five feet in the air and took him to her breast again and shook him like a sassy child, and suddenly everything was peace and quiet, as if there would never be noise again on earth. No sounds whatever. He would never hear a violin or a symphony or Jimmie Lunceford or a cricket laugh or Ellington or a baby crying or Lester Young or a mockingbird or his mother's voice or Fannie Mae's or Millie's voice or Beethoven or Benny Goodman or Anderson or Robeson or the screeching of a subway ride, or Lady Day or Ella. The earth would be nice and warm to him and still forevermore. And if he were dead it would hold him close to its bosom and keep him from ever growing cold as dead men had a way of doing.

The next morning he went about ninety yards from the camp to see what damage the bomb had wrought. And if they discovered a miracle drug that let him outlive old Methuselah, he would never forget the promise his guts made to his heart and soul and mind, and he would never be the same again. He would be quieter and more reflectful and older than he'd ever been. He was a grown man and he would put away childish things.

Worm and Lanky went with him, and when they got there, quiet men were passing the shack and looking in as if the bodies lay in state. Solly stood there with the helpless anger filling up his face and for a moment he could not look away.

Her face was so beautiful and sweetly calm in death, as she lay there on the floor of the shack with a big hole in the back of her head and a gaping canyon in her side and a hollow where her young breast used to match the other one and another huge chunk from the thigh of her left leg, and that was all the evidence. Do you know you died in Freedom's cause? The baby in her arms and the dog at her feet were serenely happy and unblemished by the bomb, but equally as dead as the mother. Madonna's face was soft dark brown burnt toast with soft brown-black eyes and her cuddly mouth relaxed and full with the appetite for life and living. Solly thought they'd probably been sleeping and never knew what hit them. She probably opened her eyes just in time to die with them open. It began to build up from the depths of his stomach and moved upward through his body through his chest and spreading over his shoulders. He thought he heard her silken voice softly screaming, "Where is God? Where is God? Where, Lord, is the Prince of Peace?" It was moving through his throat now. He remembered, "Now I lay me down to sleep, I pray the Lord—" And he couldn't remember the rest of it, and what is your name, beautiful Madonna, with the face of a gentle girl? He felt like he was her lover and had looked for her all these years, and he didn't even know her sweet sad name. When he was a boy in Georgia he had a dog just like the one that lay so quiet. It was choking in his throat now and filling up his face, and what was he becoming in the Army? A Private First-Class Pansy? He had never cried before so easily, every time he looked around. He turned shamefacedly from the shack and moved away, but he would never forget the woman's face. He would never forget the innocent baby and the dog with his tongue on the floor, who loved them and watched over them but could not protect them from the latest in civilized mass murder, made by man and named for a flower, the lovely bomb, the beautiful efficient deadly daisy-cutter. He would see Madonna's face in the face of every woman he ever met, past, present, and future. And in every Adam and in every Eve. And why not cry goddammit? The world was in a miserable mess and maybe tears would wash it clean, or destroy it like in Noah's time.

When he got back to the tent Jimmy was complacently brushing his teeth. Solly came in and sat down on his cot.

Jimmy said, "Lieutenant Samuels was here a couple of minutes ago. He says the captain wants you to come to his quarters."

Solly sat on his cot and stared at the floor and didn't trust himself to speak.

Jimmy said, "I said the lieutenant was—" He stopped and stared at Solly. "Well why in the hell did you go down there in the first damn place?" Jimmy was choking with rage. "What did you expect to find? Easter eggs?" The Army had made a man out of Jimmy. It had taught him how to cuss.

Solly stood up, his eyes bleary. "I don't know, Jimmy, but I know one thing—when I get back home I don't want to even *hear* rumors of another war. I don't want to see another uniform or another parade the longest day I live. I don't want to see any poverty either. I don't want to see any more misery or people suffering. I might run amuck if I do. And if a boy of mine puts on a scout uniform I'll break his damn legs off."

Jimmy said, "But—"

Solly said, "And I can't take that shit right now about the War against Fascism and the Arsenal of Democracy. *I don't want to hear it.* That baby-faced girl and her little baby and her dog, they hadn't done anything to anybody. What is it, Jimmy, when the world looks on while two big uncivilized civilized bullies—?" His voice choked off. He was crying and he could not help himself. "I'm a man, Jimmy, goddammit. I mean I hate this shit with all my heart! What are we doing in these people's country? No-damn-body sent for us. I mean the United States and the Japanese Empire didn't ask these people, 'May we use your country for our little old battleground?' We rain down bombs on their cities and their homes and rice paddies, and we kill thousands of innocent people. And what the hell do the Filipinos get out of it? Not a goddamn thing but death and starvation and degradation."

He sucked the tears back through his nostrils but they still streamed from his angry eyes. "I mean what's happened, Jimmy, to words we learned in school like liberty and justice and the Constitution and fair play and love thy neighbor and all that kind of—I mean, is it all a lot of bullshit? Is that all it is? What's happened to civilization?"

Jimmy said, "Lieutenant Samuels—he said it was—"

"Fuck Lieutenant Samuels. I don't need his brotherhood shit today. I want to know who really gets anything out of all this shooting and maiming and killing, all this so-called civilized madness. I—"

Jimmy said, "All of us need this brotherhood shit. If we had it, the world wouldn't be in the fix it's in."

Solly said, "Sometimes I wonder if General Grant is crazy

after all. Sometimes I think he's at least halfway on the ball. Maybe we are shooting at the wrong damn people. Maybe Western civilization has had its chance and flubbed it. It must be time for something else."

He stared bleary-eyed at the quiet soldier. "Jimmy," he said as he wiped his eyes with his shirttail, "you're one of the greatest guys I've ever known. I mean it. Let's be really good friends if we ever get back home again."

He felt foolish the moment the words were out of his mouth. He said, "Fuck it!" And he stuffed his shirttail in his pants and walked quickly from the tent.

He strode into the captain's tent and reported as ordered, and the captain said, "As you were." Rutherford was seated on the side of his cot in his underwear. He was pathetically undernourished.

Solly said, "I'll never be as I was."

The captain stared at him and got up and stepped into his trousers. "I got some more War Department literature, Sergeant. I want you to look it over when you get a chance. When things settle down here we're going to have sessions twice a month. Every man will have to attend. We'll teach them what this war is all about." He took some pamphlets from his table and handed them to Solly. Solly stood there with his hands to his sides as if he were not really there at all. And possibly he wasn't.

The captain said, "A couple of provocative ones. 'Our Soviet Ally in War and Peace.' And this one: 'Americanism versus Racial Hatred.' "

Solly still wasn't there. He was dead with his Madonna. Nothing from nothing left nothing.

The captain said, "Which one should we do first? What do you think?"

Solly licked his lips and swallowed. He was filled up like a swollen river but he would not overflow. He would not flood before Captain Charlie. The captain repeated, "Well, what do you think?"

"I really think it's a crock of shit, sir, if you'll pardon the expression. I think you ought to get yourself another boy."

The captain had sat down but jumped up again. "You don't know what you're saying, Saunders. This damn invasion's got the best of you. I'll overlook—"

"I'm saying that Bell was right the other day back in that

other place at that other session. That's what I'm saying." How long was it? Two weeks? Three weeks? It felt like years ago. "There'll be wars and rumors of wars just like he said the Bible said, as long as fools like me go out and kill each other and never know the reasons why. I'm also saying how in the hell are you going to fight a democratic war with a racist Army? That's what I'm saying."

The captain said, "As you were, Goddamit!"

"And you want your black boy, me, to give his buddies all the reasons for killing and for being killed. No thank you, Captain Charlie!"

The captain said, "After all I've done for you, this is your appreciation. It's all my fault though. I should have burned your ass a long time ago. But I thought you had it in you, damn you, to be somebody. I made you staff sergeant and just today I recommended you for OCS."

They stood there squared off like prize fighters. Onh-onh. It won't work this time, Cap'n Charlie. Take this hammer carry it to the captain tell him I'm gone. "Every white enlisted bastard I've met since I've been over here is looking for a lucky strike, a million-dollar purple heart, so he can go home and forget it. How in the hell you expect me to feel about it?"

Solly heard the three quick blasts of sirens signifying another air alert and three short roars from the Ack-Ack guns all over the miserable island and he saw Madonna's face and Millie with her swollen belly full of child. And Fannie Mae. And manhood. And everything goes on and on and on. And dying dying till you're dead.

The captain said, "Goddammit, Saunders, you've gone beyond redemption. Ain't nothing I can do for you. After all I tried to teach you." He had hurt the captain's feelings.

Solly felt good, speaking quietly. "I'm over here because I have to be. There is no other reason. No War to save Democracy —no nothing."

But the captain had not given up on his favorite student yet. He couldn't believe a black man could be so unappreciative. So lacking in humility. "You must have gotten hold of some of that jungle juice. You've done a good job, else I'd break you on the spot. I gave you them stripes and by God I can take them away from you just like that. Listen now, you take this literature and look it over and we'll talk it over tomorrow when you're to yourself." No black boy could be so arrogant.

He handed the pamphlets to Solly again. Solly stared at them as if they were a deadly dose of poison, as he held a heated hurried conference with himself. The Lord giveth, the Great White Father taketh away. Use your head, you damn fool! He's giving you another chance. He likes you. He really likes you. Use your head, forget your feelings! How badly do I want my stripes? And why shouldn't I be a staff sergeant and even be an officer? His chest burning his stomach churning his body leaking perspiration. Use your head and not your feelings. But he was tired of feeling bad. Darling pregnant Millie! Fannie Mae and sweet Madonna! Get ahead in the White Man's Army. Why the hell not? Why the hell not? But he was tired of feeling bad. And he was tired of making nonsense.

When he spoke his voice was trembling, "The war is over for me, Captain Rutherford. I'm just sweating it out from here on in. I'm just here because I have to be, and I'll do just what I have to do. I'm the worst man in the company you could get to do the job. If you order me to do it, I have no alternative but to go through the motions."

The captain walked up to him and ripped the stripes from Solly's shoulders. His high-pitched voice was hysterical with rage. "Private Solomon Saunders, you are permanent Charge-of-Quarters until I tell you otherwise."

Solly's voice no longer trembled. He said, "Thank you, Captain." The taste in his mouth was like when he was a little boy in Dry Creek, Georgia, and his mother gave him six cents to put in Sunday School, and he would always give a penny for Jesus and a nickel to the man who sold ice cream cones in the little ice cream parlor down the street from Mount Olive Baptist Church.

The captain dismissed him and he had turned and started out of the tent when he heard the captain mumble, "Too damn big for his goddamn britches!"

Solly smiled and kept moving out into the sunlight. He had burst out of his breeches because they were meant for boys to wear. And Solly Saunders was a man. He didn't need a Great White Father.

CHAPTER

6

The days rushed by with their air raids and Ack-Ack and bombardment and all the rest of it, death and destruction and starvation. The front moved on and on and ever forward and upward as the "fanatical" Japanese gave ground before the onslaught of the courageous Yankee liberators.

The Filipino people said, some of them unconvincingly, "Japanese—no! American—yes!" Waving their hands and bowing their heads.

The beautiful Filipino people who were always all over the 913 company area, friendly and hostile, looking just like the Japanese as far as American eyes could determine. And the proud Huks, men and women, guerrilla fighters, who came through the villages armed to the teeth, and so formidable that even some of the Filipinos would run from them, especially the collaborators who had lived with the Japanese and prospered. And the women, the beautiful women, petite and olive-complexioned and narrow-eyed and long black hair, and barefooted, and the children, many of them homeless and hungry and orphaned by the War of Liberation. And he looked for his Madonna in the eyes of every woman. The enterprising women who soon set up free-enterprise laundries all over the place to accommodate the wealthy Yankee liberators, who usually had other enterprising things on their minds for the women to do for them. And the men, many of them short of stature and handsome and proud of face and shoulders, and all of them wearing soldier suits and looking like the Japanese. But most of all the privation and the devastation, and the terrible degradation. The starving children who took their meals from the GI garbage cans and sometimes had to fight the poor starving rats over the delicious piles of GI slop.

The first week the girls who came for the laundry resisted the GI Casanovas with: "Filipino custom—do not touch." But by the third week the liberators, white and colored, had bought themselves into most of the homes with Yankee pesos and were touching everything and almost everybody. How long can you fight Them, from whence cometh the food-and-clothing things of life and which are never free? You can't even fight City Hall. The Americans had the bags of rice and the pesos and the blankets and the flour sacks for making lady's underthings and the black market and medicinal alcohol and sometimes even fresh meat, and the eternal cans of bully beef, and the Filipinos had nothing but their pride and their dignity and their ever-loving touchable selves. The white Yankees told the Filipinos not to sleep with the black Yankees because they would rape the women. The black Yankees told the Filipinos, "Them crackers ain't no goddamn good. We colored folks got to stick together."

An arrogant ungrateful Huk guerrilla told Solly, "The Japanese were here yesterday, you're here today, and we can't see no difference."

Solly didn't get around much any more, especially at night. He was permanent Charge-of-Quarters.

But it wasn't long before some of the gallant men of the 913 were making themselves at home and cementing international relations and loving their lady neighbors and shacking up. In spite of the fact that they put in long hours unloading ships and carrying men and cargo up to the front and ducking bullets and having the GIs and all the rest of it, they found time to fraternize. Worm left camp every evening like he was going home from work.

Life and living were ten cents a dozen. You were here today and gone today.

The 913 broke camp again and moved a couple of miles around the edge of the airstrip to another point on the other side, and this time they put up camp as if they would be there for the duration of the War of Liberation. They built flooring for the tents, they built a giant latrine high up on a windy hill for the dreamers and the rumormongers. They built a supply room and a mess hall. They set rat traps in each tent and killed a hundred rats a night, but the rats kept coming on and multiplying. They poured oil on the field bordering the company area and set off a fire and must have burned alive a million rats, and rats ran and screamed and scurried, but it didn't seem to make a dent in the rodent population. One night Solly and the supply sergeant put a rat trap in each of the tents, going from tent to tent, and when they finished they went back over their route and found a rat in every trap, and you could do this all night long and never find an empty trap.

Solly began to dream of rats, all sizes and descriptions and some of them in uniform. Every night when they went to bed and tucked their nets in and turned off the lanterns, the rats would invade the tents, foraging for edibles. Each rat would pick himself a likely tent. Solly would lie there some nights with the lights off and watch some big rat run around the ledges of the tent just eight or nine inches away, nothing between him and Solly but the flimsy netting. Sometimes the rat would stop and glare at Solly. Solly thought maybe this was another form of Japanese harassment.

One night his tentmates were all tucked in and Solly set the trap with a piece of bread and turned the lantern out, and before the tent got dark and before he got to his cot, the trap went off and jumped three feet and Solly must have jumped five feet.

The second night after they moved, Tojo laid an egg smack in the middle of the gun emplacement in the area they had just vacated and atomized everyone of Solly's coffee-drinking Ack-Ack buddies from the bluegrass country. And now they were nothing but images and memories and fading Southern accents and dog tags, and *c'est la guerre*. All's fair in love and fighting, and here today and gone today, and Stick-with-Jack-and-never-get-back. The Golden Gate in '48.

Solly sat in the orderly room a few weeks later, writing to Millie, who was expecting their baby the following month. He was still permanent Charge-of-Quarters and was back where he had started, at the bottom of the ladder. Private Solomon

Saunders, Junior. It was after midnight and they had already had a couple of air raids and the Black Widows were up, the nightfighters, and scouting the perimeter of the Philippine skies. The Black Widows were big black double-fuselaged pursuit bombers and highly efficient, and far deadlier than their namesake in the spider world. With them up there, there would be no more air alerts tonight. You could give odds on it. You could go to sleep and forget it. Calvin Potter stood in the entrance to the orderly room, looking like an apparition out of breath. He shook himself like a dog come in out of the rain, only it was dust that flew from him instead of water. He had been romeoing and had hitchhiked his way home on the road which was always ankle-deep in dust or mud, and he was covered from head to foot. He was old and gray with dust. He had been transferred to the Amphibs back on the other island.

He said, "Man, if that pom-pom wasn't so good, I'll be damn if my old lady wouldn't have to do without me most of these nights. That highway is just about a dusty mama-huncher."

Solly looked up from his letter. "There couldn't be much dust left on the road. You brought most of it with you."

Calvin said, "Man, her sister is prettier than she is, and she really got hot nuts for you. Always asking me, 'How's that Mexican beauty—how's Sergeant Solly?' "

Calvin was about as big as a half a minute lengthwise and otherwise. He looked like a good strong wind would blow him away. But he was the greatest lover who ever lived and ever loved, and that was a natural fact which you could prove by asking Calvin.

"These Filipino women gon kill me yet, and they are *pretty* women, you hear me, but they ain't no size at all. None of em. Don't weigh no more than forty-eight pounds soaking wet. But with Maria, that's forty-eight pounds of plump and juicy pom-pomming pussy. You hear me, Sergeant Solly?" Most of the men still called him Sergeant Solly even though he was a private.

Solly said, "I hear you. Now get the hell outa here so I can finish my letter." Solly remembered a previous night when Calvin, who had eyes almost as big as he was and bulging out of his head, and an over-all appearance reminding you of an undernourished Woody the Woodpecker, had told him about his amorous exploits back in Buffalo, New York, with Brenda Sutton, the internationally famous burlesque queen, who used to make the money and bring it to him cause she liked the way he grinded.

Cal sat down. "Whew! Man, Maria got forty-eight pounds of clean-cut tenderloin and she naturally knows what the Good Lord put it there for."

Solly said, "Look buddy boy, do me a favor. Spare me the details, I mean I really can do without them."

"Sergeant Solly, we grinded for a *while* tonight, and we used every position known to man and animals. OOoooooh-weee —we started out the old-fashioned way—"

Solly was getting warm in the collar. He said quietly to Calvin, "Fucking is very private and personal and sometimes even a sacred affair between a man and a woman and it is the concern of no other person. And I for one do not get kicks by hearing about how two other parties fucked each other. And if you had ever grown up or if you had any respect for Maria you wouldn't be shooting off your mouth like a—"

Calvin looked like a wounded woodpecker. "You're right, Sergeant Solly." He shook his head up and down. "I shouldn't be talking about her like this, cause she *is* a nice girl and I *do* respect her."

Solly said drily, "I'm glad to hear it."

Calvin said, "I sure am glad we liberated these people from the Japanese. These people so poor they make your heart hurt."

"Yeah," Solly said absently. "And we don't seem to have made them rich and we were here before the Japanese. A long long time before them."

Calvin said, "And, man, me and my old lady, whewee—we did a rear maneuver that made the moon start shining in the other direction, and then I backed into it, dog-paddling, and she moaned and groaned a while . . . and . . ."

Solly stared at the little man, half listening, and he wondered how it was possible to do all this fancy love-making in a one-room hut where the family slept and ate and lived—Maria's elderly mother and father and her grandmother and her brothers and all of her sisters. He shook his head and he realized that it did not matter whether he listened or not. Calvin was talking for himself to hear, reliving the entire scene for his own enjoyment.

"She propped one leg up on the wall and the other—"

Footsteps running past the orderly room. One excited soldier's voice dipped into the room. "Got three whores down in the Joint Motor Pool! Three whores down in the Joint Motor Pool!" The Joint Motor Pool was a joint one, shared by the Air Force mechanics and the 913 Amphibs, and they also used it jointly as a Joint for Whoremongering. Calvin jumped up and started out of the tent. He got to the entrance and ran back toward Solly.

"Lend me fifteen pesos, Sergeant Solly!"

Solly was almost frothing with anger but he laughed aloud at the soldier. "For—for what?"

"I want to get me some pom-pom down in the Joint Motor Pool! You heard the man!"

Solly bent over laughing at the soldier but he really felt like crying for him. "A lover like you doesn't need to buy any pom-pom. You just got through almost killing yourself."

"Come on, Sergeant Solly, you know I was just bull-jiving. How could anybody do all that kind of fucking with all them people in the house? Maria's a nice girl—I told you that."

Solly stared at him and laughed and laughed. "Buddy, you are the horse's ass. You just can't shit running."

Calvin said indignantly, "I thought you were a Race man, Sergeant. You gon let them white boys outbid us and beat our time down in the motor pool?"

Solly said, "You know what you can do for me and your Race man down in the motor pool."

Calvin stared at him and ran out of the tent.

Less than a half an hour later MPs swarmed all over the place. The Air Force and the Amphibs ran and scattered like thieves in the night. The thing the MPs wouldn't stand for was the Air Force and the Amphibs whoring interracially and interchangeably and socialistically. Jimmy, the Quiet Man, came into the orderly room out of breath.

"It was awful, Solly. It was really disgusting! And I didn't want to do it! I didn't want to do it! But they kidded me day and night—they said I was a queer or something. Said I didn't like women. But I didn't want to take advantage of those starving women!" He was crying now and he could not help himself. "I don't know what made me do it, Solly. I didn't want any whore pussy. I don't need it. They were lined up, white and colored, and climbing up on the Ducks, and as fast as one bastard would get up off of one of them, another would climb up and get on. They didn't even give the poor women time to straighten up or uncock their legs, let alone time to clean themselves. One of the women had her crying baby in the Duck with her."

Solly stared at Jimmy unbelievingly.

"I swear to God, Solly, I'm not like that. I'm not like that! We were like dogs! We were worse than dogs! Those pitiful goddamn women! Those goddamn pitiful women!"

The droning sound of the Black Widows roared into the orderly room. They were coming in from their reconnaisance and making twice as much noise as when they went out. Solly and Jimmy went to the door and stared out over the airstrip and watched the big black double-fuselaged bomber-pursuit planes leisurely soaring in for landing. They were big noisy bitches, Solly thought, and Jimmy was no animal. He was one of the few softhearted human beings that the Army had not made an animal out of.

Solly said, "Mothers and fathers, that's the biggest lie in World War Two, the coldest shit in town. The Army'll make a man out of your darling boy. The Army takes a human being and makes him into an animal."

All at once the Ack-Ack guns started sounding off about five miles down the island. One lonely Zero must have flown in at an altitude above the radar's sensitivity and cut off his motor and dropped down for a quiet visit. And now they had discovered him from all sides, as he headed farther down the coast, farther away from the strip. Jimmy and Solly looked back toward the strip where the noisy Widows were coming in, taking their time, unconcerned with the drama at the other end of the island.

Just as the last three planes were banking from out in the bay and turning in for a landing, the Ack-Ack started sounding off and crossing and crisscrossing and powerful searchlights flooding the sky, illuminating every nook and cranny and blazing pathways to the moon, and the ships in the bay barking and growling and roaring like monsters from another age.

Jimmy said, "The damn fools'll shoot down their own planes!" Which would not be the first time. Solly had seen the Anti-Aircraft crews get so scared and trigger-happy they shot down P–38's and even big birds who dared to think the sky belonged to them.

The planes came in lazily for a landing in spite of the Ack-Ack. The sky was a rainbow of tracer bullets and floods of searchlights. The phone rang sharply in the orderly room. Solly picked it up and the voice on the other end said excitedly, "Five American planes full of Kamikazes landed on the airstrip!"

Solly said, "What!"

"That's what I said, soldier. The orders are to defend at all costs. This is the only strip we have on the island. The sneaky bastards used five of our planes they'd previously shot down and came in under the radar on the tail of our night reconnaissance. Defend at all cost! We have to—" The voice cut off abruptly. Solly jiggled the phone. "Hello! Hello!" But it was no use. The line was dead.

He stood staring at the phone for a moment. He was inclined to laugh at first and would have laughed if it hadn't been a matter of life and death. His own life and his own death, especially. He ran to the entrance and blew his whistle. He said to Jimmy, "Round them all up, Jimmy, every living! The Japanese are taking the strip. Don't forget your rifle, Jimmy! Jimmy! Don't forget your rifle!"

He blew short quick blasts on the whistle as he dashed toward his tent to get his carbine. Where in the hell was he going and whom was he going to kill and why?

BOOM! BOOM! BOOM! BOOM! BOOM!

Already they were ripping up the airstrip.

BOOM! BOOM! BOOM! BOOM! BOOM! and

pow pow pow pow pow—Ziiiiiiiiiinnnnnng—Bop—

Solly fell headlong on his face as the bullets zoomed past his head and he thought they had ripped his ears off. He scrambled on hands and knees bruised and bleeding till he reached his tent.

Pow! pow! pow! pow! pow! BOOM! BOOM! BOOM! BOOM!

He fell into his tent and got his carbine and ran out again and fell on his face again as a bullet grazed the top of his skull, and he was hit this time. He felt his head and brought hot blood away on his hand. The baby would be born next month and he Solomon Saunders, Junior, would be lost in action ten thousand miles away from home. For what?

Pow! Pow! Pow! Pow! BOOM! BOOM! BOOM! BOOM!

They seemed to be everywhere, all over the place.

Tat-tat-tat-tat-tat-tat-tat-tat-tat—

Pow! Pow! Pow! pow! pow! Ziiiiiiiinnnnnnng—Bop—

He lay there quiet for a moment. Through all the thunder and the lightning he heard his mother's voice: "Don't be a hero! Come back to us! Son, you're all I got in the world." You got Millie, Mama! And Millie's got a baby live and kicking in her belly! And all I got is me—me—*me!* He crawled back inside the tent and lay there breathing loudly to himself. He would lie there till it was all over, and if his side won the skirmish they would think he was unconscious through it all. He had achieved a purple heart on top of his head already. There was no need to go to the airstrip looking for another one. And if the other side won, well, then he would be a Prisoner of War for the rest of the war's duration. And he would be alive and go home to his family. And he would really be a hero when all this shit was over. POW Saunders. His heartbeat was the sound of Ack-Ack guns thumping way up in the top of his head. Why not, goddammit? Why not play dead till it was over? The war was phony. Always phony. *Ipso facto* phony phony. It meant not a damn thing to him. He heard footsteps running past his tent toward the orderly room. He hoped they would not see him lying there. He heard the gunfire from the strip, heard the crying deep inside of him. He wished he felt like dying for his country's noble cause. He wished his country loved him like he could love his country. Like he even loved his country now. He was just scared, that's all, and he was letting his buddies down. After you cut through all the phony streams-of-consciousness, break it all down, and you're a coward and you'll always be a coward, and you're letting your buddies down. So blame it on Mama or Fannie Mae or the baby in Millie's stomach, or the war's morality, but you're fooling nobody but yourself. MY COUNTRY 'TIS OF THEE . . . SWEET LAND OF LIBERTY . . . He got up and staggered out of the tent and started running through the night. LAND WHERE MY FATHERS DIED . . .

He heard Lieutenant Samuels's voice off in the distance. "All right, men, let's spread out like a fan and move toward the northern end of the strip. That seems to be where most of them are concentrated."

He heard Topkick saying calmly, "Split up, fellers. Half of you spread out that way and half the other way."

And Samuels shouted, "Fod God's sake, don't shoot each other!"

Solly ran into the area near the orderly room just as his buddies moved away. He thought, why not kill each other? It makes as much sense as the other. Killing is killing. A chicken ain't nothing but a bird.

He thought he saw the Bookworm moving about fifty feet ahead of him. He said, "Watch out for yourself, buddy. We got things to do in that other world when all this shit is over."

And he thought he heard Worm answer, "This shit ain't never gon be over!"

Solly ran cautiously forward through the darkness now toward the sound and fury on the strip. He heard someone moving on his right and cussing softly to himself and he felt a wetness on his neck, and another soldier stumbling and running somewhere up ahead of him, and he remembered that the top of his head was bleeding. His heart beat all the way up in his temple and the blood hot all around his face, and he had a premonition this was it for him. He should have stayed in the tent like he had some sense. The air was warm and thick in his throat. The only other soldiers camped near the strip were a squad of Air Force maintenance men and a few Air Force Engineers and Anti-Aircrafters. The Infantry was at the front, which was miles away by now. And half of the 913 were taking soldiers to the front. The Field Artillery was miles away, and it was mainly up to about fifty men in the 913, and he had a strange calm feeling that this was the end of the war for Solomon Saunders, Junior. An armored group had moved out just yesterday, goddammit. It was mainly up to the less-than-half-strength of the Special Men.

BOOOOOOOOOM! BOOOM! BOOOM! BOOOM!

Tat-tat-tat-tat-tat-tat—tat-tat-tat-tat—

ZIIIINNNNNG-BOP—

He hit the ground again and the bullets hummed over his head and kicked up dust around his body and he scrambled forward and still he heard bullets singing Nearer My God to Thee. And fear grabbed him by the throat and strangled him and chilled his body and bombs exploded in his head and erupted in his stomach, and yet he had this feeling that within the next hour his worries would be over. He would never be frightened like this again. He would never argue with himself again the war's morality. He'd have his peace and freedom. Something said inside of him, "Come on, soldier, goddammit, get up off your ass and pay attention to what you're doing. You got people to go back home to. You got an airstrip to defend. You got buddies up there. You got Japanese to kill!" He knew that some of his buddies had already engaged the hari-kari fellows, he could hear the carbines and the M–1s talking back to the repeating rifles and hand grenades and the submachine guns. He got up and started to run again. "Hey, Worm!" He didn't hear footsteps any more. "Worm! Scotty! Where in the hell is everybody?"

Suddenly he sensed shadows to the left of him, almost imagined, and he turned quickly and saw them coming for him. He dropped to the ground and hesitated for a millionth of a second, thinking they might be men from the 913, but then they leaped for him and screamed and his heart leaped through his throat and still that last billionth of a second in which he hesitated to kill, but then the robust killer came alive and he squeezed the trigger and heard his own thunder and saw his lightning chop them down like bamboo grass. He was a killer! At long goddamn last his mother's baby was a killer! He moved forward now with a warm chill in his shoulders. He had taken life. You could only die once. Only cats had more than one life. Only cats—only cats—only cats. He moved hurriedly toward the shooting and the killing, toward Murder Unincorporated, and he would kill as many of them as possible, and if they killed him he would never know about it. Suddenly as if catapulted, he was out into the open strip where the entire world was going to hell with grandiose proportions.

BOOM! BOOM! BOOM! BOOM! BOOM! BOOM!

POW! POW! POW! POW! POW!—TAT TAT TAT TAT TAT TAT!

Wheeeeeeerrrreee—Ziiiiinnnnnggg—BOP!

Wheeeeeeeeeeeeeee—Ziiiiiinnnnnnnngggggg—BOP!

He dropped quickly and flat on the ground and hugged it tightly and desperately like he was he making love for the last time. The Kamikaze were everywhere blazing away with repeater rifles and submachine guns and hurling hand grenades. Solly's buddies were dropping like houseflies under spray gun attack, and bombs were going off in Solly's head and exploding in his stomach and erupting where his head lived so precariously, and he was scared scared hard scared aching scared way down deep between the cheeks of his quivering buttocks. And yet he felt a certain calm in the knowledge that he could have his cake and eat it too. If he were killed this very moment he would inherit swiftly that sweet peace of infinity. Thank you, Father. Peace, it's truly wonderful. Never again to feel the icy stabs of fear mixed with the heat of fear's great fiery furnace, and hell was cold and hell was hot and hell was here and death was peace. But if he should come through the gaping jaws of hell and live, he would be happy to be alive. For Millie and the baby and Mama and for Solly too. Like betting against the team you were rooting for. You couldn't lose. He laughed and ate the dirty dust.

TAT TAT TAT TAT TAT TAT TAT TAT!

Wheeeeerrrrr—Ziiiiiiinnnnnnggggg—BOP!

The deadly dot game kicked up dust around him and he hugged the good earth from head to foot, he rooted with his nose, he kissed it with his bruised and tender lips and he loved it with his aching loins, and he fought desperately and valiantly to control his body functions. Since he was a little boy he had always been nice-nasty.

Bop bop bop bop bop bop!

Ping! Ping! Ping! Ping! Ping! Ping!

The dot game left him alone for a moment and he was still alive. He was breathing and eating dirt and he thought he knew his heart was beating. Maybe they thought he was dead already. He lay there for God knows how long, digging into the dark earth cold and hot. And maybe if he lay still as death they would not bother him, they would fight all around him, and after it was all over he would be alive and the joke would be on them and he would be alive and breathing and smelling and working and talking and laughing and eating and screwing and he would be alive goddammit he would be alive. He thought the blood on the top of his throbbing head was caked up now. The world went to hell around him and the earth quaked underneath him. He thought about Millie and the baby who was already alive and kicking and getting ready to make his debut into the world next month, and about Mama and what was Fannie Mae doing this very moment? Where are you and what are you doing, my dearest darling, loving sweetheart deeply feeling baby-child? You were right. I *am* a conscientious objector. If I get through this one all in one piece, I'll take one of the Ducks and stock up on gasoline and rations and put out to sea one night and head for somewhere like Tahiti and sweat the war out with Gauguin's pretty people. Please! Great God Almighty, let this dying be something. Let My Country 'Tis of Thee really be a sweet land of liberty for me—for me—for me! The greatest fear that choked his heart was that he would die for nothing. Just be killed and die and no Sweet Land of Liberty. He didn't know whether he had fallen asleep or not, but suddenly he was aware again of the hell breaking loose around him. He pushed his body up a couple of inches and saw the belches of lightning all over the strip and volcanoes erupting everywhere and through the rainbows of tracer gunfire he saw Worm and Lanky, for one split second he saw the long and short of it, side by side, battling hand to hand with Kamikaze at the northern end of the strip with the forest as a backdrop. Solly got up on his haunches and turned around and scrambled back behind the Air Force Engineers building. The thing to do was to circle northward with the tents and buildings as protection and in a minute or two he could reach Worm and Lanky and the rest of his embattled buddies up near the tip of the strip, and they would kill as many of the other cats as possible, and if they were killed they would die together and would never disgrace their pants again, and Millie and the baby would have ten thousand dollars coming to them, and he would have peace forever more. That's all he wanted—PEACE! Peace! Peace and Freedom! And maybe he would die to get them.

He ran close to the earth like a fullback between the squatty Air Force Engineers building and the pyramidal tents on the other side. He had a feeling that the Japanese were everywhere all over the area, as if they were coming up out of the ground, he had a feeling he was being followed, but he was just about there now and all he had to do was to come around the next bend of tents and he'd be out on the strip and he would be with his battling buddies. And maybe he was wrong, he hoped with a maddening desperation. Maybe the world would be different, because they gave their lives this night. His country was the fairest land, the greatest potential of them all. His country would appreciate the life he was about to lay upon the altar.

He ran head down and close to the tents and in a couple of shakes he would be dying with his buddies. He could not get that sweet song out of his heart. FROM EVERY MOUNTAINSIDE LET FREEDOM RING . . . He was breathing deeply and he didn't want to die, he wanted to live, but *c'est la guerre,* and all the rest of the same horseshit in any language, and who in the hell was he to live when thousands of others were gasping their last on battlefields around the world this very second? I want to live—I want to live! Good Lord, I wouldn't mind dying if dying was for something. His mother said don't be a hero, Solly. He laughed, and he stumbled over ropes and tent pegs, and something or somebody sprang softly out of the shadows and landed on his back and they went down without a word. And Freedom's cause was here and now, and this was time. These were his chickens come to roost. Every goddamn cackling one of them. He felt the strange arm around his neck and the weight lean up off of him for the murmur of a second and Solly tried to straighten up quickly judo-style and throw his body from beneath the Kamikaze fellow. It was the last way Solly would choose to die. And yet he felt the cold steel stab cleanly in a place next to his shoulder blade and too close to his heart for comfort and felt the gush of his own hot blood and felt a sharp white hot pain near his heart and spreading fast throughout his chest, sharp, fast, white, hot, spreading-burning, he could not feel his poor heart beating, he only knew the beat of the pain, short, fast, white, hot, spreading, burning. Yet he knew the man's left hand had drawn back to stab again, and fright took priority over pain and he got strength from God or somewhere and struggled quickly to his feet, and he reached desperately over his shoulder and thank God for his Amphibious training and thank God Tojo wasn't heavy, and he grabbed the arm again descending and felt the cold steel pierce his own arm. But he held on, God only knows how or why, and he twisted his body lightning fast and threw the lightweight Kamikaze over his shoulder and fell upon him. The man was shouting from somewhere in his frightened throat and still striking out at Solly and striking home into his chest a couple of times before Solly could seize his arm, and then it was strength against strength, brute against brute, and his entire body crying and pleading with his muscles, and his heart his soul his mind, and he no longer heard anything else, the rest of the war did not exist for him. Nothing else ever was or ever would be. Suddenly everything in all his life boiled down to him and this hari-kari Japanese man-child born of woman breathing death and thunder in his face.

He held the man's wrist now and twisted his arm and he listened hard to hear it snap, both of them grunting and groaning and breaking wind, and he could see the young frightened face clearer now, much much clearer than any face he'd ever seen in all his life's brief span of time. And Solly seemed to be wallowing in blood, his own life's blood all over him and drenching the earth. Pow! The man's arm finally snapped at the elbow and the dagger dropped, and now Solomon Saunders held the dagger, and it was the worst way in the world to kill or be killed, and he felt his stomach erupting and scalding lava spilling over and eating up his insides as he raised his arm and hesitated, and the other soldier grabbed at him, and then Solly came down with a vengeance, and he felt the steel tear ruthlessly into human flesh like it was a chicken, and back and down, and he didn't hate this man beneath him. "I don't hate you, goddamn your hari-kari soul!" And down and back, down and back, and hot tears flooding Solly's cheeks and nausea in his nasty throat and down and back, the man's chest was a dark bloody geyser gushing blood, his pleading eyes his desperate eyes. "I don't hate you, Tojo, damn you. I don't hate you! I don't even know you—damn you!" The boyish soldier gave up the ghost just as Solly's steam gave out and he fell forward on top of this very very dead young stranger from the islands of Japan, and all was peace and all was quiet, and brotherhood and all that crap, even as the battle raged around the lucky living bastards who were dying on the strip for freedom.

Part IV

THE CROP

CHAPTER

I

He was dead and he was in Heaven where all good little boys went when they died, and big men too, and tiny girls and women, his mama said when he was a little biddy boy way down South in Dixieland, and his mama used to lay him down to sleep and pray the Lord his soul to keep, and when he believed most men were good and women too and went to Heaven when they died. And laughing was good and frowning was bad, and when you laughed the world laughed with you. And your mama is the Santy and your papa is the Clause, and both of em put together make a Santy Claus. And God made you and the stork brought you. But Solly was in Heaven now where the streets were paved with gold and flowed with milk and honey, he preferred syrup, personally, and hot biscuits oozing with butter, but he could not complain, he had crossed over Jordan and he had reached the Promised Land, where all was peace and the skies were not cloudy any day, and God was not a Great White Father. But why was he in Heaven? He was not good, he was a murderer and an adulterer, he had violated some of the Ten Commandments, maybe every one of them, but since they let him in the Gates, there must be a reason, there must be some goodness in him. Fannie Mae loved him, there must be goodness in him. Millie and Mama loved him too. His unborn baby loved him. He heard singing all around him. Singing to him.

Deep river
Your home is over Jordan
Deep river
You want to cross over into camp ground . . .

Why were they singing that song, when he was already over in Camp Ground? And where was the man in Charge of Quarters? He had a couple of things to say to him. Tell him he wasn't a murderer, tell him he never meant to be a murderer. I was fighting for democracy. And I just wasn't strong enough to fight all those bastards who made the war is what. I didn't even know who they were. I couldn't put my hand on them or single them out. They were omnipotent and omnipresent and omniscient and a whole lot of other omni-things, and I should have told them to go to hell and should've taken off for some faraway place at the other end of nowhere. But I wanted to fight for my country and for freedom. I was tricked, St. Peter, but the point is, I meant well. And I love life and I love people, and I guess you understand that, and that's why I'm up here where all is peace because I am a peaceful and a loving man. I love life and I love people more than anything else in the world. More than government more than success more than flags more than patriotism more than religion more than more than—more than family more than convention—more than dollars—more than bigshot—more than the great American Story—I love love and life and people. Can't you understand, St. Peter? If God is not country, not religion, not superpatriotism, if God is love and God is life, then that's why I'm here, St. Peter.

He was coming out of it again now slowly and with a rocking kind of a motion this time, back and forth, side to side, side to side and back and forth, and the rhythm strangely familiar and maybe not so Heavenly after all, and he heard "Deep River" faintly, growing fainter, and the water slapping against his boat, and everything made sense to him now, he knew where he was. He was on a boat, and that's why they were singing "Deep River." He was crossing the River Jordan and he would shortly be in Camp Ground. He felt his heart swell up with joy, but it was all mixed up with sorrow too. Where was Fannie Mae? Where was Millie and Mama? Where were Worm and Lanky and Scotty? And where was his newborn baby child? Where were Jimmy and Samuels and the rest? He didn't like the motion of the boat, he didn't like the rough waters of the Deep Deep peaceful River. God is love love love. He didn't hear "Deep River" clearly any longer. They seemed to be singing just barely out of his reach over on the other shore. Receding instead of coming closer.

He began to hear speaking voices strangely accented, and he picked up odors his nostrils remembered from it seemed years and years ago in another world, and memories crowded in on him invading all of his senses, white-odored memories and brown odors and brownish-yellow memories and Listerine and disinfectant and antiseptic memories and odors and flesh and medicinal and rubbing-alcoholic odors, and maybe he was still in Georgia and all the rest had been one great big bad dream or one great big good dream, and now he was waking up, but what about that rocking motion?

He was afraid to open his eyes at first, but finally he opened them and into the face of a white-uniformed pink-faced woman with dark brown eyes that had lived with pain and tenderness. Who are you, his own eyes asked. Who are you with the brooding eyes and hair the color of just-cooled ashes? You're no angel. Surely my angels are not your color. Take me back where I came from.

She smiled. "And how are you this afternoon, Sergeant?"

What a funny accent. It was un-American. Not even Southern-accentuated. But he was alive goddammit! He was alive! He was alive! Living! Living! He was breathing and smelling and hearing and tasting! And seeing! Seeing! He was seeing! He was feeling!

"The question is, 'Where am I?' " He had a talking voice. But why did she call him "Sergeant"? He was the buckest of buck privates.

"Well, you're on a hospital ship, and you were wounded rawther badly and I'm informed, rawther heroically, and they made you a staff sergeant, and you're on your way to Australia. Now how does that make you feel?"

"I feel much better, thank you." I'm a hero. Whaddayaknow—

"Dinky die?"

"I feel better," he repeated. I'm a staff sergeant. Going places—

She laughed. "You were supposed to say, 'Fair dinkum.' "

He said, "I feel fair dinkum."

She laughed and shook her head. "No, not quite—but you'll get the hang of it after a while. Fair dinkum you will." And she put the thermometer in his mouth and she took his wrist and looked at her watch, and he was alive, he was living! He had temperature and pulse and a burning pain in his chest and all around his heart, and the top of his head felt like hot lead was dropping onto the middle of it, and his left arm was like iron, but he was living. He opened his mouth to thank somebody, and she put her other hand on his mouth and brought his lips together again around the slender piece of glass.

When she took it out of his mouth she said, "You'll live, thanks to the miracle drugs and to your very strong determination."

He said "Dinky thingamigig?"

She smiled at him. "Dinky die—"

He said, "Dinky die?"

She said, "Fair dinkum, mate." She pronounced it "myte." She said, "Cheerio." She had other temperatures to take.

That night she came and she asked him to turn over on his stomach and he painfully complied and she pulled up his nightshirt.

"What are you doing?" he shouted weakly.

She said, "Now I know you're getting better." And she wet a cheek of his bashful backside and let him have the needle tenderly.

The next time he came out of it, she wasn't there, and he lay there for a couple of hours with the scorching agony around his heart glowing with the most frightening pain of all. He didn't know how his heart could stand such terrifying pain. Sometimes he thought someone had set fire to the hair on his chest.

She came late at night and took his temperature and his pulse and hoisted his smock and gave him a bird bath and gave him the needle, and he was helpless to resist. She knew everything he had.

Days passed in which he lived most of the time in that never-never twilight world between unconsciousness and reality and he could not tell the difference between dream world and real world, and sometimes he lived in the gone-by days of his boyhood and other times in New York playing handball and sometimes on the college basketball team and other times with Fannie Mae and at his desk in law school and with Millie and with his mother and a boy in Georgia again and in the Army overseas and a soldier in the Georgia jail many many times, and the scene at the Red Cross kept reappearing, reappearing, but he was never really in any of these places, excepting in the place wherever pain lived every minute—a throbbing head which seemed to have been converted into a busy rifle range, and a pounding heart in which blockbusters were continuously exploding. And his left arm always burning. He lived in fear of the veins in his head bursting open, of his heart muscles, which always felt like they were constricting or expanding like they were playing tug of war, and one day they would rip his chest wide open and tear his heart in two. His arm would never hold a woman.

One day the nurse came and took his temperature and pulse and then sat down awhile to talk. She told him she knew quite a bit about him, which he thought was an understatement. She had talked to a friend of his who was also wounded and on the ship.

He said, "Where is he?" He was scared to say, Who is he?

Boom! boom! boom! boom! His heart sounding off like thunder rumbling in the summer heat.

She said, "He's in another department. He was shot up pretty badly, but *you* were one of the critical cases. For four or five days we didn't know whether you would live or die. But you have vastly improved."

He said, "Dinkie die?"

She said, "Fair dinkum, myte."

He wanted to ask her who. What friend? But he was afraid she would say So-and-so died and So-and-so lost his leg and arm and So-and-so and So-and-so and So-and-so, and whatever she said, it would be final and irrevocable and everlasting. A sentence of capital punishment. A Supreme Court decision.

She said, "Lieutenant Samuels asks about you every day and so does Private Taylor and Corporal Larker and Private Scott and Banks."

He said, "How are they doing?" Thank God they were alive and asking.

She said, "Everybody's making progress. You were the worst off and you are mending nicely."

She stood up and held his hand for a quick brief moment and told him, "Cheerio," and she was gone.

Every time she came after that she would tell him something about Australia and she would also have something to say about Lieutenant Samuels, and her face would give out quick pink flushes, and he would feel little short stabs of loneliness. Solly told her about his family, his mother and his beautiful wife and the baby who was due in a few weeks' time. She said, "No wonder you fought so hard to live."

One afternoon she came and told him that they were off the coast of Queensland, which was her home state. They were in the Coral Sea and they were moving now through some of the most beautiful treacherous waters in the world. She wished he were able to go up on deck. They were passing between the Great Barrier Reef and the mainland. She had made the trip many times, a couple of times in glass-bottomed boats, but each time for her it was a brand-new experience. The perspiration above her mouth on the slightly mustached curve of her lip and the excitement in her voice as she told Solly about the thousands of fish of different families and denominations with so many hues they made a poor rainbow seem colorless. And likewise the coral, white, red, orange, and lemon-yellow, and the huge clams and the pearl oysters and octopi and color color color and everything color and motion and rhythm and the struggle for survival in the most beautiful most treacherous marine wilderness the world had ever known. An oceanic paradise and jungle rolled into one. She made it all come alive for him.

She stopped to catch her breath and then said, "You'll get a chance, to see it on your way back up north. There's so much to see, it's a bit of like they say of your New York. You could spend an entire lifetime seeing and seeing and being spellbound."

He said, laughing weakly. "You're a poet and don't know it, and I'm glad you showed it to me first with your eyes instead of mine."

She said, "I wish I were a poet. I've always wanted to be a writer more than anything else in the world."

He looked into her eyes and changed the subject, and they talked about Bainbridge, Australia, which was her home town, and ultimately the conversation got around to Lieutenant

Samuels, as it usually did, and she blushed painfully, and soon afterward she left him.

That night he wrote Millie a long letter telling her how much he loved her and how much he wished he could be with her as she approached her moment, which was *"their"* profoundest moment. He forgot the pain in his heart and he felt warm all over as he wrote her of his love for her. He described the Great Barrier Reef to her in all of its raging beauty and rhythm. And he loved her loved her loved her. With his purple heart he loved her.

A couple of mornings later Celia helped him to dress up in his khaki uniform and get ready to disembark. She gave him her address in Bainbridge.

"I want you and Lieutenant Samuels to visit with me after you're up and about."

He said, "Swell."

"Dinky die?" she demanded with a serious smile on her face and the perspiration always amidst the little peach-fuzzed mustache over her roundish mouth.

He said, "Fair dinkum." In a strange and husky voice.

She said, "Good-o. This is the last time I'll see you before we debark. Good-bye and get well quickly." And she kissed him briefly on his cheek and left the dew of her warm lips on him.

They disembarked around noon with bands playing from the docks and flags and banners waving and people warmly cheering, and even from his stretcher he could see some of the natural beauty of the harbor. This was Celia's home and he felt not exactly as a stranger.

They rode through the city on a train with him propped up and staring out of the window, and it was just as she had described it to him, with its forever shrubbery and its winding river and the wooden suburban houses built on stilts to keep the white ants from devouring them and with their inevitable verandas running around the fronts and sides of the houses like decks on an ocean liner. And forever again the flowers and parks and foliage and the trees of every nationality, every color, every aroma, and a long wooden fence bordering on a vacant lot with a large crude sign written in lime or whitewash

OPEN SECOND FRONT NOW!

His face filled up. He laughed and cried inside of him. The Second Front—Open the Second Front NOW! So many months ago the Second Front had opened. So many thousand men ago. So many thousand thousand boys . . .

He closed his eyes and he thought about Millie and he wondered how she was doing so close to her time. Maybe it had already happened. You always had to allow for miscalculations. It might be happening this very minute. Mama was there and she would look out for Millie, and she had her own family out in Brooklyn. She would not be alone. It was he who was the lonely one.

The train took them through Bainbridge to an Army hospital located at a famous race track which had been converted into an Army camp for the duration of the war.

The next morning he was visited first by Worm, then by Samuels, and late in the afternoon by Jimmy and Scotty and Baby-Face Banks. From what these disabled veterans told him he pieced the story together about the battle of the airstrip. They had captured ten of the Japanese soldiers, killed fourteen, and the rest had escaped into the village. The 913 had fought and died heroically for their country and democracy. The dog-tag fellows included Lanky Lincoln and Calvin "Lover Man" Potter and Hopjack and First Sergeant Anderson and seven others. Thirty-nine were wounded and most of them were in this same hospital. They were being recommended for the Distinguished Service Cross. They were heroes. They were bigshots of the colored race. Even Samuels.

He didn't sleep one restful hour that night. Against his will all night long he imagined Lanky and the Topkick dead forever more. He couldn't believe it. The versifier who loved life so much and feared fear so fearlessly, he would make no concessions with fear or death, not even build a foxhole to guard against them. He would never laugh again, bending his long body and slapping his thighs, and he would never write another lyric. A man who could learn a foreign language in two weeks! And Topkick dead! Easygoing Topkick who would not kill a mosquito if it were biting him on the tip of his nose. Buried in the cold white unfriendly earth so many thousand miles away from home. He saw them all night long and he saw Hopjack, scat! Scat! And Calvin Potter, and all the rest of them, and he felt guilty because he was glad he wasn't one in that number. He was glad and they were dead and he felt guilty and he was glad and they were dead and he was glad to be alive. And he felt sad and he felt guilty.

Two days later his mail caught up with him, and he got six letters from Millie and two from Mama. Millie's letters were so full of love and brimming over with happiness and plans for the future for them and Junior and missing him and wanting him and loving him and remembering Fort Ord and Pittsburg as the happiest times of her life. He read her letters and warm feelings moved through his body and soothed the burning pain in his chest, and he was glad to be alive, and when he went home to her he would make up for everything. For not being with her at this time when she needed him most of all and for the anxious times he'd given her when he'd given love to Fannie Mae. He would make it all up to her. He would give her so much love she would overflow with love and she would never doubt his love again.

He had everything to live for. Day by day the pains eased in his head and chest, his arm almost completely healed, and one day he could eat real food, and a couple of days later he could get up and walk around and go to the toilet and take a B.M. like it was supposed to be taken, and bathe himself and shave himself and look into a mirror. The first time he saw himself he did not recognize himself. He looked around and behind him and stared back at the mirror. He looked like a skeleton with skin stretched tight around it. His eyes were so deeply sunken he could hardly see them. His face was thin and long and gaunt. He looked like death A-W-O-L.

The fellows visited him every day and now he visited the fellows and the letters kept coming and he kept gaining strength. Then one week Worm and Samuels and Scotty and most of the rest of them left the hospital and were given thirty-day furloughs into Bainbridge, and Solly was as lonesome as a man could be.

Fannie Mae's letter finally caught up with him. She had a new job teaching school in the public school system of Ebbensville. She loved her job, she said she loved her job, but he could tell it was not enough for her. She was so very much more than an Ebbensville schoolteacher. She was a hundred times more than that, a hundred thousand more than that.

She told him that sometimes when she is sitting in the classroom feeling sorry for herself, she falls back on his love, and even though she knows it has come to nothing and will never come to anything, it helps her in her hours of deep despondency to say to herself, "I'm great—I feel good, and I must really be *somebody, because Solomon Saunders loves me.*" Her letter ended with: "Love you always, Fannie Mae" And made him feel a sense of greatness and at the same time like a lowly bastard.

Next day he received a book from Fannie Mae. *Twelve Million Black Voices,* by Richard Wright. And after he experienced this book, he knew he could never be the same. It was the most beautiful and the most lucid book he had ever experienced. The photography by Edwin Russkam together with Wright's awesome overpowering word images awoke inside of Solly emotions long asleep and almost forgotten. Sometimes he would be reading a passage, or sometimes a face would stare at him from the pages, and he would hear the voices, and he would feel a trembling in his stomach and a fullness in his own face, and he would feel his own blackness deeply, and be proud to be a black man.

One day he was reading the book and it suddenly came to him, and he said to himself, if I'm proud of me, I don't need to hate Mister Charlie's people. I don't want to. I don't need to. If I love me, I can also love the whole damn human race. Black, brown, yellow, white. Thank you, Richard. Thank you, Eddie. Thank you, darling Fannie Mae. He looked around at the other soldiers in his ward, most of them white, and he loved the whole damn miserable wonderful human race.

He ate well and began to put the pounds back, but he still had to carry around the extra weight of bandages on his chest. Each time he shaved he noted laughingly that more and more he was beginning to look like something, resemble somebody. The letters kept coming from Millie, but now it was time for them to stop and for the cablegram to come. It was four or five days late, and what the hell was the holdup? And surely she would remember to notify him. Mama would if Millie couldn't. Each day he told himself there was nothing to worry about and yet every day he worried. Maybe the cablegram got lost and the baby was already here and he didn't even know whether it was a boy or a girl, not that it mattered worth a damn.

One afternoon he was seated in a chair next to his bed reading a book, but his mind was thousands of miles away with Millie and the baby and Mama. He heard a voice say, "Well, we really have improved." He looked up into Celia's face, and he was truly glad to see her. She pecked him on his cheek and she stepped away from him and looked at him. "If I had met you on the street I would not have recognized you," she said. "I had no idea you were such a handsome boy."

He could hear the other soldiers on the ward watching and listening. Visitors were rarities. And such a visitor. He said, "How's Lieutenant Samuels?"

She said, "Bob's all right. He comes to see you, doesn't he?" With the perspiration and the peach fuzz above her mouth which was always rounding curves and going places.

Solly said, "Yes. He has to come out here every week for treatment and examination. I see them all once a week."

She said, "That's what he told me."

Solly said, "He told you right."

And she said, "What's the matter, Sergeant?"

He said, "Nothing's the matter." He was lonesome—very lonesome.

She said anxiously, "Have you heard from home? What about your wife and baby?"

He said, "I haven't heard. I don't know what the holdup is." He tried to laugh.

She said, "Don't let it worry you. Just a case of miscalculation. Happens all the time."

He saw the orderly coming toward him with the cablegram and he lost ten pounds of perspiration. He took it in his trembling hands and he opened it and he looked at everything else before he read the message. It had been sent six days before. It had been to the Red Cross. It had been to the Philippines. Finally his eyes went down to the message, and he would never be the same again. He was the father of an eight-pound five-ounce boy, but he was without a loving wife and his son without a mother. He read it again and again and again, but he could not change the wording. He thought, it's a typographical error. He thought, it's a practical joke. He thought, it's a goddamn lie! He thought, it can't be—can't be—can't be! But he knew it was. He knew it was—deep down in his bowels he knew it was! His mother wouldn't lie to him.

"Sergeant! What's the matter?"

But he could not hear her now as his heart began to swell, and all of the tension he had ever felt in all his life exploded in him and all of the fears and all of the sorrow and all of the love all of the hate and especially all of the guilt, everything in flood tide now. Nothing he could say, nothing he could do—nothing nothing nothing nothing could change the cablegram.

He stared at it and thought, maybe if I tear it into bits she will be alive again. The tide came in and the flood came up from the angry bitter depths and built through his shoulders into his throat and pushed out his cheeks and filled up his face. It was too much! It was too much to hold inside. The dam broke loose and Solly cried like a motherless child.

Celia took the cablegram from his hand and she read it and her own eyes filled for him, and she put her hand upon his shoulder and she wanted to say something to ease the deep pain, but she knew there were no such words—no such words in any language. The tears flowed down his cheeks, and he wiped them with the sheet, and still they flowed. When finally he was aware of her and her hand on his sobbing shoulder, he turned and stared at her as if he had never seen her before.

He whispered, "Please go. There's nothing anyone can say or do. Nothing can be changed."

She said, "All right, Sergeant. But I'll be back tomorrow."

He said, "All right." Why didn't she go? Now, go! Go now! And she put the cablegram on the bed and walked softly out of the ward. Something in a far-off corner of his feelings heard her walking away from him and wanted to call her back. But he would not, somehow could not.

All day long and all through the night he sat up in bed, staring into miles and miles of emptiness. Millie was at this moment in a cold box buried in the heartless earth. It was beyond his imagination. Outside his understanding. How could healthy beautiful, full-of-life, life-giving urgent Millie be no more of this world? He had just left her nine months ago in Pittsburg, California, full of hope and love and future. How could all of her be gone forevermore? A flock of beautiful birds fly across the sky and the hunter aims at them for sport and fires and life is gone for one of them. Is that all there is to it, Millie? Can it be like that for you? All of his images of her were of California vintage now. The cottage in Fort Ord Village and Millie, the walks they took at the ocean's edge at the rim of the continent and Millie, the small café in Monterey, the love that spilled over all over the place and the little telephone booth-of-a-room in Pittsburg and Millie and Millie and Millie, and the day he marched away from her. And how in the hell could they let her die? He blamed himself most of all. He should have had the courage to desert this goddamn man-made madness and should have taken her away to have their baby in an atmosphere of love and peace and quietness. She probably worried herself to death. He felt guilty about the anxious months when she thought he didn't love her. He would never be able to make it up to her. And never was a long long time.

He didn't eat anything until the following day at lunch and he immediately threw it up again. After lunch he got two letters from her written a couple of days before the baby was born. It was like hearing from the dead, and he pretended that the letters proved she wasn't dead. Her letters were full of love for him and for life and for their future together, for their child's and their children's future. He even let himself argue with some of the plans she was making for Junior. Wait till he is born, for Chrissakes! Let him catch his breath! Doctor—lawyer—who the hell needs it? He thought, I'm losing my mind, I'm arguing with a dead woman. She's dead and I must accept it. I must accept it. I can't believe it—can't believe it!

Celia came and stayed for a couple of hours, and they talked about it, and he was thankful, because he needed someone to talk to, or else he might have lost his mind, with the letters that kept coming from her day after day after day. It was a weird practical joke the Army Post Office played on him. Each letter always deepened and widened the gashes of his purplest of purple hearts. A few days later he got a letter from his mother. She told him the baby was fine and just like him, and Millie had had a very hard time and everything possible had been done to save her. It just wasn't meant to be. He tore up Mama's letter in little pieces, and then he knew that Millie was dead dead dead, he knew his Millie was dead.

Weeks and weeks of misery and loneliness and death-feelings and dreams of death passed by, and then another image began to make its way against his will to the surface of his consciousness. He was a dirty lowdown bastard! How could she even cross his mind so soon after his wife died giving birth to their child? She'd been dead only seventy-four days! How could he be so heartless? Damn you, Fannie Mae! And damn me! And damn our love and anything and everything that came between me and Millie Belford Saunders. And yet he could not help thinking about her and wondering about her, even though guilt hung around his bed like it was on guard duty. One day he thought to himself, he figured it all out, he said, Millie is dead for over a month and a half now, and she is dead forever more. I loved her and I still love her, but she is dead and gone and

I cannot bring her back, and our son needs a mother to love him and care for him as only a mother can. And Millie would understand this, and when the war is over, I will marry again, so the child will have a mother and so I will have a wife. Millie would want this for us. And when I get back I'll take my boy and we'll go to Ebbensville among other places, and if he falls in love with her and if she loves him, well then he'll have himself a mother and I will have a wife. And that's that, and I won't think about it any more. It's a long ways in the future, and besides the war might never end and I am a no-good bastard for thinking about another woman so soon after Millie's death. Millie my darling, forgive me—forgive me—forgive me.

Each weary day dragged by like a lonely month of Sundays, and yet the days were born and lived and died, giving birth to the next day and the next day and the next, till the days gave way to weeks and the weeks made way for the months, and he fought against the temptation of writing to Fannie Mae and telling her about the death of his wife and the birth of his son. He thought of just telling her this and nothing else, and letting the future take care of itself, but he never wrote the letter, because he felt guilty enough as it was. Oftentimes he blamed himself for Millie's death. He'd made her insecure with Fannie Mae, he'd made her pregnant and then had left her and gone away ten thousand miles to shoot at total strangers.

But time does pass, and wounds do heal, superficially at least, and his head and arm were healed completely now, and one day they took the bandages off his weary chest for good, and one day from his back, and weeks went by, and months went by, and now this day he was to finally leave the hospital and go on a thirty-day convalescent furlough. In the afternoon Celia would come and drive him into Bainbridge, where she had arranged a room for him not far from where she lived. His purple-hearted buddies were months since off their furlough and were attached to a Duck outfit at Worthington Farms, a camp on the other side of town.

All morning long he was nervous and impatient and thought that 1300 would never come. He got dressed early and shaved and packed, and now he wanted to be away from the hospital and everything else that even remotely suggested the Army. He wanted to go and be gone from this place. He wanted one p.m. to come, and for thirty days he would be a free man, and he didn't even want to hear about the Army or the war, which was still raging all over the world. He wanted to forget it ever existed. One of the things he would do once he got situated was to write Fannie Mae a long friendly letter. It wouldn't be a love letter, just a letter that told her where he was and how he was, and who he was—a widower and father. He had to relate to somebody back in that other world, besides his mother and his son.

Celia came and drove him back to the city, and on the ride he saw nothing and he said nothing. He was lost in his own thoughts of one day getting home again and putting the pieces together. She was making like a tourist guide on a Sight-Seeing bus on Fifth Avenue. This park and that river and this bridge and that historical significance, but he hardly heard a word she said. She said, "What's the matter, Solly?"

He said, "Nothing."

She said, "You act as if I'm taking you to prison instead of taking you out. You must have fallen in love with one of those pretty nurses at the hospital. Or maybe you liked the steak and eggs out there." She called them "styke" and "aigs." She asked him, "How do you like my car?"

He said, "Fair dinkum." And let her figure it out for herself.

She said, "It's just a bomb, but it gets me where I have to go."

She took him to her brother's house about three blocks from where she lived, in a section of town called Bensington. She introduced him to Betty, her brother's wife, and to Pamela, the sister of her brother's wife, and they showed him his room and helped him to unpack, as they talked to him and asked him questions about the United States and the American Negro and the CIO and Harry Bridges and Paul Robeson, and he wondered, who the hell are these people? And the sister of her brother's wife was particularly friendly, and finally Celia said, "He's crook. Let him take a nap and freshen up. Then I want to take him to my place for a spot of tea."

Pamela said impishly, "All right, but don't think because you saw him first you're going to have this beautiful man all to yourself, because you won't, and I will see to it that you don't. There is a male shortage, you know."

Celia laughed. "He'll be living in the same house as you, so you'll see more of him than I will. Besides he's not interested in Australian girls romantically."

She could certainly say that again.

He lay in his Australian room and looked behind him at his life and looked at the present mess his life was and tried to look into the future. He got up and looked in his bag and found the snapshots his mother had sent to him of Solomon the Third. He sat on the bed and looked them over. Fat as a pig and big as a house, and large dark eyes and head full of hair and high forehead; he had his daddy's mouth and mold of face, but the shape of his eyes were his mother's—large and wide and knowing. Solly's face began to fill. I promise you, little buddy, they'll never send you off to war—the Army'll never make you a man. I promise you hope and life and love and laughter and plenty to eat and Santa Claus and school and bubblegum and better world and bicycle and no-lonely-hours and peace-on-earth. And he was tired—he was weary. He stretched out on the bed again. Promise you school and opportunity . . . Sleep—sleep—please let me sleep! Come to me, sleep, and take me with you on that trip.

He could not sleep. He could hardly even close his eyes. And he realized he had not really accepted the fact of Millie's death. He had not accepted that in time and space the her of her was gone forever and forever. For the past year he had lived with death and died with death and cried with death and walked in death and wallowed in it. Waded in it. He had breathed it, he knew its smell, its taste, its clammy touch. He knew its color. How many times had he heard death's soft white flapping wings? So peaceful and seductive and deceitful, promising everything and giving what? But to imagine death had taken Millie, his wife Millie, whom he had lain close to and inside of and naked with and love-with and child-with and dreamed-with and future-with, to grow-old-with, to-change-the-world-with. His mind had half accepted it, but deep down in the guts of his guts he wouldn't believe it. It couldn't be! He was so many thousand miles away from the place where she lay for almost six months now, so still and cold and peaceful in death's dear everlasting sleep, and he told himself, maybe she is better off, all of her troubles over, all of her anxieties ended. She was secure at last in death. And with the son she left behind her she had immortality. She has conquered Father Time. Dear Millie—darling Millie. He got up and wiped the tears from his eyes. Had he been asleep? He heard voices of strange women.

Celia asking, "Has he been asleep?"

Pam answered, "Of course he has."

Celia asking, "How do you know?"

Pam laughed. "I put my ear to the keyhole and listened to his snoring."

Celia said, "He doesn't snore."

Pam said, "You seem to have rather intimate knowledge of his sleeping habits."

"I was his nurse, and don't be boorish. I already told you, he has no romantic interest in Australian women."

She could damn sure say that again.

He cleared his throat to let them know he was awake, and he came out of his room in his robe and said hello and went down the hall to the bathroom. He lay in a hot soapy bath and closed his eyes and felt a gnawing nagging emptiness. He tried to imagine his little son. What are you doing and whom do you favor and where are you going and when will I see you? When will I hold you in my arms? When? When? When will this civilized madness stop?

When they got to Celia's little white three-room cottage with the veranda that ran around three sides of it and the back porch with its latticework and red rosebushes, there were a couple of awkward moments in which they sat and stared at each other, alone for the first time, and for the first time she seemed to be fresh out of conversation.

Finally she said, "I have some slop if you'd care to have some."

He said, "Slop?"

She said, "Whiskey, I mean brandy. Would you care to give it a go?"

He said, "Fine." Exactly what he needed.

She came back from the kitchen with knick-knacks and brandy and they drank and stared at each other.

She asked him, "Would you care for a fag?" And she handed him a pack of cigarettes, and they lit up and sat there smoking and drinking and staring at each other, as if they were boxers or fencers sparring and feinting and looking for openings. Antagonists instead of friends.

She said finally, "These women will rush you off your feet, and I think I realize something of what you're going through. That's why I told Pam you were not romantically inclined at this point in your life."

He said, "Fair dinkum." Say it again and again and again.

"My sister-in-law is what you Yankees would call a wolf in a sheep's disguise."

He changed the subject. "How's the good lieutenant?"

Her face did a warm pink flush. "Bob's fine. He's out at Worthington Farms with the rest of your comrades. He's having dinner with us tonight."

Solly stared at the floor. She said, "Is that all right? And then we're going over to the Southern Cross. I'm not trying to plan your thirty days, but I thought at the outset—I mean you are a stranger in our—"

He said offhandedly, "Fine—fine—fine. Fair dinkum."

She said, "The Southern Cross is a serviceman's club for all United Nation soldiers, without regard to race or color or that sort of rot."

She saw his face grow warm and farawayish, and he got up and went toward the kitchen for another drink. He brought the bottle with him and came back and sank down into the chair. "Do me a favor. I don't want to hear about the war or the race question or any of that man-made stupidity for thirty days. All right?"

"Fair dinkum, Solly."

"Fair dinkum." Fair-damn-dinkum!

And he began to drink, like her whiskey was the last on earth, and the more he drank the quieter he became. Just drinking and staring morbidly at the bottles brought in from the kitchen as if they were really dead soldiers bleeding on some lonely beach, and every now and then he responded to a question from Celia, and every now and then staring at her thinking to himself, why in the hell am I here with you and why are you alive and healthy and Millie who had everything to live for is dead and buried in the cold earth and Fannie Mae is thousands of miles from this place, and Solomon Saunders Junior is dying dying always dying? Dying lonely by himself and frightened and eight-and-nine-and-ten-and-eleven years old in a cold-water flat in New York City, dying in a Georgia jail and Georgia hospital, dying on the bleached-red beachheads with Sergeant Greer and Calvin Potter and Sergeant Anderson and the little Irish soldier who should have gone home on rotation and the men of the 19th Anti-Aircraft and Lanky Lincoln and with homo sapiens dying everywhere on all the beachheads on all the far-flung battlefields, in the trenches in the cities and along the countryside all over the goddamn death-driven world.

Dying with his dead Madonna. Even Rosita might be dead. He wished he had died with Millie. He sometimes dreamed of having died with her and being buried in the ground with her, locked together forever in each other's arms.

What in the hell was this white wench doing here alive and arrogantly white and securely white, with Millie dead and Fannie Mae on the other side of the world somewhere, teaching children to dream, whose dreams were murdered long before they learned to dream?

He looked up and stared at Celia. What the hell is your excuse for living, pale-faced wench? Sitting there as if you have the world in a jug and the stopper in your anemic hands. You and your lieutenant make a wonderful pair with your ALL-MEN-ARE-BROTHERS crap, as you wallow in your brotherhood while the world around you goes to pot with song and fanfare and bands playing and flags waving. Boys dying, always dying—the boys are dying over there. He was really getting drunk. Drunk and angry with the world. He'd better not drink any more until after dinner or he would get as sick as a soldier on a beachhead. And he was already sick—sick of all the crap that went for Western civilization. This much he knew—man was born dying. And therefore man was born to die. He smiled. But man was born to die for something—a little tiny bit of something. Anything! But what?

And Celia was wondering. Is he always like this? Moody and noncommunicative and maybe even antagonistic? She'd gotten a different impression on the hospital ship. He'd been warm and friendly and articulate, and she'd looked forward to a growing relationship. Friendship only, nothing more. He was probably in a mild state of protracted shock and not entirely himself. His fight to live, his wife's death—the bloody war. The party at the Southern Cross would be just the thing for him. He pricked her curiosity. What was Solly Saunders really like? Who was this handsome somber black man?

Thoughts in his mind leaped about like grasshoppers in the hot sunlight. He was thinking about Jesus Christ and John Brown and Calvary and Harpers Ferry and Nat Turner at Southhampton in Virginia. All of them had died for something. Dying—dying—dying. He thought aloud, "Good Lord, I wouldn't mind dying if I died to free the people."

She said, "What did you say?"

He mumbled, "Man was born to change the world."

She said, "What?"

He said, "It was apropos of nothing."

She said, "What you need is a good stiff drink."

He was already soaring high as a P–38 and she had done herself some drinking.

He said, "Dinkie die and fair dinkum and you sure know what to say."

Millie died for something, he thought quietly. She died to give another life.

Celia said, "Good-o," and poured up two stiff drinks and began to open up. Her own life. She had wanted to be a creative writer, a poet, a novelist, but she was a nurse, but she would give up nursing as soon as the war was over if it ever ended. She had been married and her husband had been a union organizer, like her brother had been before the war, but when the war began her husband had volunteered, and before she knew what was happening to her he had been shipped overseas and thrown into battle and killed on the desert in Africa. She had been completely shattered.

Her eyes filled. "I didn't know what to do. I was lost. He was older than I was, but we were so good for each other. He was mature and he was sensitive to my needs as a woman and my aspirations. But he was a dedicated antifascist. When he died and so far from home, I was completely disoriented. I I didn't know what to do with myself. I didn't want to live at first. I thought I didn't want to live. But then I went to the Army School for Nursing. The—the—war was taking so many lives—I wanted to help to save a few—"

Her voice choked off. She wiped her eyes with a handkerchief. "I'm a fool for crying like this in front of you—embarrassing you. He was a man who hated war but he was the first to volunteer to fight. Can you understand?" Her dark eyes begged him.

He looked into her eyes and was stirred against his will by the deepest pity. Her face said that her heart had lived with stormy weather. A face above which storm clouds always hovered, and he knew now that her bluntness was a shield against the sharp edge of the world's brutality. Yet who in the hell was she to expect sympathy from him? She was white, and in this white world that insignificant fact gave her a head start on three quarters of its population.

She was crying now without restraint. "I don't know why

I'm acting like this. I don't usually—I haven't ever—I just somehow felt you were the only one I could open up my heart to. I feel close to you—like—like you were my brother—" She broke off again. "I'm sorry. I'm really sorry. The one thing I can't stand myself is a maudlin woman—" Her shoulders shook and she wiped her eyes and blew her nose, and she was sorry—she was sorry—

And he might have gotten up and gone to her and sat beside her and put his arms around her and said to her, "Cry, Celia, cry as much as you feel like crying. Just help yourself." He almost wanted to, but she was white, and he was angry with the world.

By the time Lieutenant Samuels came Celia had gotten herself together, and the lieutenant seemed genuinely glad to see his company clerk. He put his arms around Solly and laughed and stared at him.

"You look as good as a brand-new silver dollar."

Solly said, "You look pretty good yourself, Lieutenant."

Samuels said, "None of that lieutenant crap. This is Australia, and while we're off duty I'm Bob and you're Solly."

Solly said, "My mother didn't raise any backward children. You're Bob and I'm Solly." And then he noticed the double tracks on Samuels's collar. He said, "Well-well-well—so it's Captain Bob, is it?"

Samuels said, "In charge of a bunch of battle-scarred refugees from the fabulous 913th. They call us the 25th Amphib Platoon."

They went out for dinner to a small café and had steak and eggs and everybody seemed to be left-handed eaters, the way they held their knives and forks. The food was good as was the wine, and Solly began to loosen up.

Celia told him Australians ate with the fork in the left hand and the knife in the right.

He asked her, "Dinkie die?"

And she replied, "Fair dinkum."

When they left the restaurant they went to the Southern Cross where they ran into Worm and Jimmy and Scotty, who had come into town on five-hour passes. They grabbed each other and hugged each other like long-lost brothers a million miles away from home.

Worm said, "This is one of the few places don't many peckerwoods hang out."

Solly thought, here it goes again, but he was overjoyed to see his buddies.

Celia's brother said, "That's right, mate. We don't encourage them, and if they come they know they bloody well better behave themselves." He was a lanky carrot-headed rugged-looking extroverted bloke. "If they come here looking for trouble we throw them right out on their arses."

A tall stoutist balding man was playing on an old piano, Bomma-lomma-bomma-lomma, and people were dancing and some of the Aussie soldiers wore khaki shorts and a couple of the girls wore kilts of lively Scottish plaids.

The Southern Cross was dry as a chip, but Worm led Solly to the men's rest room and wet his whistle with apple brandy from his hip pocket.

"These Aussies are all right with me," he told Solly. "If it don't be for these Yankee mother-hunchers round this place we would almost have it made."

Solly said, "You're just prejudiced is what."

Worm said, "Studs out at the Farm say when they first came here a year ago, everybody was nice to them. They were heroes and color didn't mean a goddamn thing. Wined them and dined them and took em home to Mama. Treated them better than they were ever treated back home in Bam where they came from. But ever since about six months ago when them Southern peckerwood divisions came over here on the *Queen Mary* or *Elizabeth* or one of them Queens, they been putting places off limits to colored soldiers all over everywhere. The MPs worse than they are in Georgia. Man, a peckerwood ain't shit don't care where you take him. I hate the mother-hunchers."

Solly took another solid swig of the Bookworm's applejack. "I do not want to hear any of your colored folks' propaganda tonight. If you have an justifiable complaints, take them to the man himself down at headquarters on Adeline Street. General Bufford Jack, the GI's friend—the enlisted man's great white padre." He felt good. The applejack moved down through his chest and spread down into his stomach and slid around, and he was feeling good.

Worm stared at his buddy. Sometimes he couldn't tell whether Solly were serious or pulling his leg. "That head wound must've really messed you up."

Solly said, "White folks ain't so bad once you get to know

them better. Some of my best—" His voice wandered off absent-mindedly. He felt goddamn good.

And Worm was speechless.

Scotty floated into the rest room with an Australian soldier dressed in khaki shorts. His name was Dobbs. He had a bottle and some paper cups. He was as bowlegged as a bulldog. He poured up five drinks and passed them out and held his own cup out toward them.

"Here's looking up your kilts," he said.

Solly cracked up with laughter and particularly when Scotty returned the toast with, "Up your bloody kilts."

And Dobbs advised Scotty soberly in a drunken whisper to be careful whom he gave that toast to. "Some of the Sheilas might get the wrong impression."

Scotty told him, "Don't worry bout the mule going blind."

He and Scotty went out arm-in-arm.

Solly had been drinking since midafternoon and by now he had a heavy load. He smiled at Worm. "The trouble with you, you need some pom-pom. It would definitely change your disposition."

Worm shook his head in disbelief.

When they went back into the club room, the man named Danny was sweating at the piano and folks were gathered in a circle dancing the hokey-pokey.

Danny was playing and singing in a noisy baritone.

You put your right leg in,
You take your right leg out,
You do the hokey-pokey
And you turn yourself about . . .

And everybody was putting his right leg in and her right leg in and doing the hokey-pokey.

Celia's sister-in-law came over to Solly. "Come on, lovey, let's give it a go."

She led him by the hand to join the circle, just as they were putting their backsides in.

You take your backside out,
You do the hokey-pokey
And you turn yourself about . . .

And Worm and Solly went into the rest room for another wet one, and Scotty and Dobbs were in there downing brandy and "Looking up your bloody kilts." And when they came out again the folks were "Waltzing Matilda," and Pamela asked him again would he give it a go, and they danced, and she danced very closely with him, but it was just as if she were dancing with a man who wasn't there. Every now and then during the party Celia would come to him and ask him how he was doing, and then she would float all over the place, being saucily friendly with all of the GIs and the diggers, morale building, and especially with Captain Robert Samuels, and then back to Solly again, and Solly and Worm and Jimmy and Pam's brother killed a whole fifth in the rest room and helped Scotty and Dobbs with theirs, and Jimmy had been a teetotaler when he came into the outfit. The Army had made him a man.

Scotty had his arm around Hank Dobbs's shoulders like they were long-lost drunken booze buddies. He told Solly, "Man, I really dig this stud the most. And the first time I met him I started to put him out of his misery. Came over to me and said to me, 'Hello digger, welcome to the Southern Cross.' I misconscrewed this cat. I thought he'd called me the name they call your folks in Georgia. You dig me? After I found out what he was putting down, I told him he'd better learn how to talk plainer than that."

The rest room exploded with all of their laughter, including Dobbs and this time even Captain Samuels, who had just walked in and joined them.

When the laughter died away Dobbs said, "Here's looking up your kilts."

And Scott said, "Up your bloody kilts."

And they finished off the two dying soldiers and threw them into a waste basket and went back in to join the party.

They were dancing now and Celia was heavy in his arms, as if she'd also been hitting the bottle, and she asked Solly for the millionth time how he was doing and he said, "Fine. How're you doing?" And she said, "I'm having a bloody good time, but I'm knocked up, you know, so I'd better take it easy." He thought to himself, Captain Bob isn't letting any grass grow under his feet, and little Celia is on the air and broadcasting.

The last time Solly and Worm went to the rest room, Worm said, "These chicks are all right, but half of em pregnant, and what I mean, they don't mind telling the world about it."

Solly said, "Different culture different values, old buddy." His eyes and his tongue were getting heavier and heavier.

Worm said, "Here's looking up your kilts."

The next time he saw her she said, "I feel awfully crook. Will you please take me home? I'm knocked up, you know, I really mean it."

He said, "The captain—I mean Bob—"

"He has to go back to camp and it's in the opposite direction, but if the idea of taking me home is so distasteful to you—" She was pouting and angry and her sweaty mouth curved rounder and rounder and the peachy fuzz above her mouth, and he knew objectively she was the prettiest woman at the party, maybe even beautiful, and the diggers and the GIs had been shooting at her all night long, but like she kept telling her sister-in-law's sister, Solly wasn't remotely interested romantically, and furthermore she was Samuels's girl. And furthermore and furthermore—

Scotty and his buddy, Dobbs, sat in a booth sipping steaming hot tea and nibbling crumpets, and a couple of Yankee soldiers sat opposite them. One of them was drunk as an owl and red-faced and bald-pated and shiny-nosed and first sergeant. He kept reaching over the table and slapping Scotty on the arm and shouting, "You awright with me. Us Yankees got to stick together." It was a thick foggy Southern accent, and Scotty stared at the friendly drunken Topkick, whose head gleamed like the cue ball in a billiard game.

The other Yankee soldier kept mumbling, "My buddy is the greatest guy in the world. Know what I mean—old Army man—salt of goddamn earth—know what I mean?"

Scotty said, "Watch yer language—ladies all over the place—"

The Topkick said to Scotty, "That's all right, you can't fool me, I know you from down home just like me. Both of us peckerwoods together."

Scotty glared at the Topkick with a righteous indignation.

The Topkick got up for the third or fourth time and went stumblingly over to where Solly and Celia stood talking seriously, and each time he would unintentionally bump into Solly and Solly would accidentally shove him viciously with his shoulder and his elbow. "Can I have this dance this time, please Mam, Miss?" And she said, "I'm sorry, Sergeant. Not tonight. I'm knocked up—really I am."

Finally Solly told the sergeant, "Look, bub, by now even you should have gotten the idea the lady isn't dancing tonight with you." The sergeant stared at Solly unbelievingly. If the sergeant stood there any longer, Solly would punch him in his mouth. He was itching.

The sergeant went back to the table and fell into his seat. "Prettiest girl in Kangaroo-land," he mumbled. "Prettiest girl in Kangaroo-land, and she's bigged and she tells me so right in front of that goddamn sergeant. Whaddaya think of that?" he asked Scotty, yanking his arm. "You can't fool me—me and you both is Georgia peaches."

Scotty said, "Watch yer language."

Dobbs said drunkenly, "You're an awright peckerwood but watch yer bloody language!"

Danny, the piano man, was bomma-lomming:

Paper Doll. . . .

and singing loudly with his baritone that sometimes sounded like an Irish tenor, and the piano sounded like an old self-player pianola. And Solly and Celia were dancing again together, slowly dancing, with her head resting on his shoulder, and the Georgia Topkick could not keep his eyes on anything else for any length of time.

Celia said to Solly, "I'm so glad you're here with me tonight, my brother dear. I'm really knocked up and I don't feel like dancing with this one and the other. Especially the stinkos."

He said, "At your service, milady." Your brother is red-headed freckled-faced and is wearing khaki shorts and showing off his hairy legs.

She said, "Good-on you, myte." And leaned more heavily against him. And maybe he should let himself go with her and lose himself and forget it.

The Topkick's buddy said, "Greatest Topkick in the Army of the Newninety States. Ask anybody—"

The Georgia-talking Topkick patted Scotty on the arm. "I like you. You awright with me. Us Yankees got to stick together. Too many fu-fu-fu-foreigners round this place—" He stared away at Solly and Celia and muttered underneath his breath.

One of the ladies in plaid kilts came over to the table with tea and milk and sugar and refilled their cups, and the Topkick's buddy stared at her long legs and her roundish knees below her kilts, and he whistled wolfishly, and Scotty gave him a dirty look, and then Scotty stood up and bowed to the kilted lady with the green-blue eyes and the long light-brown pigtails, bowed like an honest-to-goodness gentleman and held his cup of steaming tea toward her as if about to give a toast.

And said, "Here's looking up—"

And Dobbs jumped up and put his hand over Scotty's mouth, and when he took his hand away, Scotty said, "Here's looking at you."

The lady smiled and said, "Oh—thank you."

The piano player kept bomma-lomming and singing loudly and the couples dancing, slowly dancing, and a group of diggers over in a corner making like a barbershop quartet, and Celia said, "Take me home, Sergeant Solomon Saunders, Junior," and the Topkick staring at Solly and Celia and mumbling underneath his breath and Scotty with his angry eyes on the baldpated first sergeant and Scotty's good buddy, Dobbs, chattering on and on and on about the bloody war and the blasted Army Regulations and the bloody brawss could you-know-what—

The baldheaded Topkick mumbled, "She's nothing but a foreign bitch, that's all she is! It's goddamn sin and a shame!" He looked from Celia and Solly down at his steaming tea and then to Scotty. "Ain't that right, buddy?"

Scotty's stare got dirtier and dirtier as he looked wordlessly at the Topkick through the steam from the cups of tea that were still too hot for mouth and throat.

The Topkick mumbled, "Dancing with that ugly bastard all night long—where I come from goddammit, he wouldn't get away with it—the good old Stars and Stripes forever—ahmo put a stop to it—" He had trouble getting to his feet. "In the Uniney States he wouldn't try it—"

And Scotty got up and took his cup of steaming tea-and-milk and poured it slowly and deliberately and drunkenly on the Topkick's bald pate and spreading it roundly like pouring pancake dough on a red-hot griddle. Scott said, "Shut your fat ass, you dirty-mouth peckerwood mother-fucker!"

The Topkick's buddy jumped to his feet, but no more quickly than Dobbs, who grabbed him by his collar and shouted quietly, "Break her down, myte—break her down!"

The Topkick looked dumbly up at Scotty who stood above him at-the-ready, hot tea spilling down the Topkick's steaming face and down his neck and drenching his shirt and the Topkick mumbling unintelligibly. He tried to get to his feet but Scotty shoved him back down in his seat.

"Don't vip a goddamn vop!" Scotty said.

Within a half of a minute the booth was surrounded by Australian diggers and a few of the Special Men.

Dobbs said to the diggers, "Put these peckerwoods out. Both of the Yankee bawstards're boiled, and we don't allow strong drinks in here."

"Yeah," Scotty shouted, "throw the Yankee bawstards out. They ain't got no couth and the mama-hunchers stinking from drinking. And cussing too."

"Righto!"

"Good-oh!"

"Out you go now—"

The diggers in the corner were singing:

Bless em all,
Bless em all,
The sergeants, the captains and all . . .
There'll be no promotions
This side of the ocean
And so fare well, bless em all . . .

The Yankee bawstards gone, Scotty and his buddy sat clinking their cups one against the other, and Dobbs said, "Up the rebels!"

Scotty said, "Yeah, up em."

Solly told his drunken buddies good-bye and left to take dear knocked-up Sister Celia home. When they got to the car she asked him to drive and he felt strangely that it had all happened before. Sometime somewhere. A girl, a car, a moonlight. Somebody had asked him to drive—some woman sat beside him—his buddy's girl—the whole damn scene . . . Everything always happened to him in triplicate, three or four times —five or six—

They drove through the city, subdued now by the quiet hours of early morning. They followed the winding Bainbridge River while the dim lights of the city bounced off its sleepy waters. Her head lay on his shoulder and she told him this was her city and she loved her city this time of night. This was her River City. They drove across the long majestic bridge, and she told him Bainbridge had started out as a penal colony. He was only half listening. His mind in Ebbensville with Fannie Mae. The night they came from the Thanksgiving party. A million experiences ago.

He said laughingly, "So your ancestors were jailbirds, eh?"

She said, "They bloody well were, and you're a damn snob, Solly Saunders, and my foreparents were the proudest diggers in the—" Her voice trailed off. She hiccuped. "Bless them all, the majors, captains, the colonels and generals and all." And she probably thought she was singing.

They went up a hill and down a hill and around another hill with trees everywhere and tree-lined streets and tunnels of trees and the smell of heavy greenness drunk with the dampish air of early morning, and they got to her house, and he walked with her to the door. She fumbled in her pocketbook and gave him the key. He unlocked the door and said good night.

She said, "How about a nightcap?"

He said, "No thanks. I want to get an early start. I want to see some of your River City. Before you know it my thirty-day reprieve will be over. And besides it's late and you, my darling Sister Celia, have to work tomorrow."

She said, "I *do not* have to work tomorrow. I have the whole week off to show you some of our little town, Banana City, and then the rest will be up to you. Unless you have other plans—"

He said, "All right then, I'll see you tomorrow." He started to say, "Don't forget—you're knocked up." But he just put his hands out to her and she went into his arms and put her arms around his neck. "Never ask a handsome digger to take you home and let him get away without a kiss. The Articles of War and Conquest." She put her misty peach-fuzzed mouth up toward his mouth and he kissed her mouth and said good night. Like the lady said, at this point in his old young weary life he was not romantically inclined. Neither of them were. Which made life so uncomplicated.

CHAPTER

2

All that week they went everywhere together, to the rainbow-colored countryside, to the jungle-clad mountains, to the coral-colored beaches, to the National Art Gallery, to the museum, to the beautiful University campus, scenic and sprawling, to the movies, to the George Washington Carver Servicemen's Club, to Mt Booth-tha Park, to the pastel-colored bay, to the Bainbridge docks. And he had always thought the phrase "purely platonic" to be the phoniest in the English language. But he had a ball that week with Celia, going everywhere talking about everything from coral reefs to politics, and he could be entirely relaxed with her because they both realized there were no romantic undertones. She warned every woman who came their way, "Don't waste your charms on handsome Solly. He simply is not interested." And when he took her home at night he could kiss her firmly briefly on her dewy lips, as she expected, and nothing else would be intended or expected. And that was that and for all that, and they were mature individuals, intelligent people, and they knew what they were doing.

Friday they went to the National Museum and carried lunch and spent the day, and when he got home he was pooped, and he did not feel like going to the party she had planned for him on Friday night. She dropped him off at her brother's house.

She told him, "You look crook. We've been going too much this week. I forget you're convalescing, and I'm your nurse, and you're supposed to be in my care. Maybe we ought to call the party off tonight."

He said, "Not at all. I'm fine." He thought the walls of him were caving in. "A party would be just the thing," he lied. At this point in his life he didn't like himself alone with himself. All he did was think think think, till his poor head ached with thinking.

She said, "Dinkie die?"

He said, "Fair dinkum."

She said, "Good-o then—but you have to promise me one thing."

He said, "What?"

"That you'll go in the house and keep Pam at arm's length and take a good nap and a nice hot bath and relax, before you come to my house for dinner before the party."

He said, "Fair dinkum," and she smiled and said, "Good-on-you."

He went into the house and fell on his bed and felt his tiredness moving in on him into every bone and muscle of his body. The burning pain throughout his chest, the throbbing in his head—he felt old before his time, a young man in an old man's body. He had a son he'd never seen except in snapshots, he was the father of a motherless child, and he felt like somebody's great-grandpa, and he loved Fannie Mae, he didn't care, he loved her, he couldn't help himself, he loved her, and he would write to her and ask her to be the mother of his child. And she would say yes—yes—yes—yes! And he would be healed and whole forever more. He smiled and felt a warmth move through his body like hot coffee in the wintertime. He would get up now and write to her—get up right now and write to her her—get up now and write to her—he was tired, too damn tired—pooped—pooped—and he would write to her tomorrow.

When he woke up he repeated, I'll write to her tomorrow. He lay in a hot bath soaking his body and writing the letter in his mind and he was with Fannie Mae again and held her in his arms and her dear face close to his face and she said, Solly!

Darling Solly! And he said, Dearest Fannie Mae! He got out of the tub and dried himself and put on his robe and took his dream with him to his bedroom and he got dressed, and when he went up the hall toward the door Pam met him and said, "Two letters came for you today."

She brought the letters to him, one from Mama and one from darling Fannie Mae. He went into his room with them. He read Mama's first, telling him about his son, who already had four teeth and looked just like his father, his spitting image, and big for his age and growing and smart as the devil, and a couple of snapshots of him in which he seemed to be yelling bloody murder and didn't favor anything. And then he opened Fannie Mae's and his hands began to tremble, and all over him warm rivulets of chills and thrills and perspiration. He read, "Dear Solly," and he put the letter back in the envelope, and he would read it later when he got home from the party. He was scared to read his letter. He laughed. After all the stuff he'd been through in the Army of the United States of North America, he let a little harmless letter from his very dearest friend make him panic. He put it on the bed and stared at it, as if it were a hand grenade that would go off any second. His whole body sweating, his heart pounding, he laughed and picked it up again and took it out of the envelope. It was not a booby trap.

She was well and confident he was the same. She had done a lot of thinking about him and her of late, and she saw now how silly it was of her to cling to something she could never ever really have and hold. So she had started to go out with an ex-GI, a veteran, injured in the European theater and honorably and medically discharged, who was teaching in the same school where she was teaching. Solly said aloud without knowing, "I'll put a stop to that. I'll get a letter off to her today—now! —AIR MAIL NONSTOP SPECIAL DELIVERY or maybe I'll send a cablegram." Take it easy, he told himself. Just act as if you never received her letter and just write to her and tell her how things are with you. Tell her Millie died in childbirth six months ago and you have a son without a mother. And what will be will be. He kept reading her letter with one part of his mind and scheming madly with the other. She said, "We're going to be married at the end of next month. I hope you get this letter in time so you can send me happy returns of the day." He read the lines again and again and again. That was how much she who loved him really loved him. She who would always love him no matter what. That's the greatest love in all the world, the love that weds another. Well, it was too damn deep for Solly. Fannie Mae was too profound. Maybe if he sent her a cablegram and told her he was now available, maybe she wouldn't go through with it. Maybe maybe—maybe not a goddamn thing—but maybe his darling Fannie Mae was a fickle-minded lover. But he knew it wasn't true. He knew the one thing Fannie wasn't was fickle-minded. She was just what she seemed to be—the most wonderful woman in the world—and she was going to be married to another man because she thought he loved another and could never be entirely hers, and he was going to send her many happy returns of the ever-loving day.

Usually when they built up in him he fought hard against the tears, but not this time. He wanted to open the floodgates and drown himself in his own helpless tears, and he sat down on his bed and tried every place where tears come from and he strained his insides out, but no tears came. He was so completely shattered he was numbed as if all of his senses were shot full with Novocaine. And what had he expected? What in the hell had he expected?

That she would wait a million years for a hopeless expectation? He'd read too many Brontë novels. He felt empty, he knew a great big nothingness spreading through his insides. He felt if somebody stuck pins in him all over him, he wouldn't feel a goddamn thing. And it's all your fault, you procrastinating bastard. You should have written to her months ago, and you have no one else to blame but you. Spending all your time with Celia. He closed his eyes and bit his lip and there was nothing, and everything was nothing and nothing was everything, and nothing from nothing left precisely not a goddamn thing. He remembered everything about her—her eyes, her mouth, her voice, her strength, her fire always burning fiercely bright. And the love they made together. And he died another time. For the love they made together.

And the party was a booze-up. Everybody brought his own slop with him. Celia's brother, Steve, and his wife, Betty, and Pamela and Captain Samuels and Hank Dobbs with his bowlegs in his khaki shorts and Maggie Sutton and a few others whose names Solly didn't remember. Everybody hit the bottle like dedicated alcoholics with a kind of morbid desperation and a grim determination to let the good times roll. What's these people's story? Solly had drunk brandy all through dinner and had a head start on the diggers and the sheilas and the Yankee Captain Bob.

Celia laid down the ground rules. "No politics, no romance, no war talk, no sincerity. Everything else goes. Wine, diggers, and song, and all is fair in love and war."

Solly said, "Dinkie die—fair dinkum."

A hundred drinks and about forty minutes later, Dobbs asked Solly, "How's the Party, mate?"

"What party?" Solly asked. "I'm having a ball."

Dobbs said, "The Communist Party. We don't like your fellow's *Victory and Awfter*. It might be awright for the U.S.A. but not for us. We're going to have Socialism here five years after the war is over."

Solly had had quite a few by then. "Which might be five years after hell freezes over." Whiskey usually made him brotherly and palsy-walsy, but tonight he felt beligerent even though he didn't want to be.

Steve said, "You're bloody well going to have fascism in your country. That's what you're going to have in your United States of America. Browder is a bloody fool."

Celia said, "Watch your language, Brother."

Solly didn't want to discuss politics with these people didn't want to get into a fight. He came to have a party. Enjoy himself. Forget the problem.

Samuels said heatedly, "I'm no Communist and I'm no fellow traveler, but Browder is nobody's damn fool either. And the U.S.A. is going to have progressive capitalism after the war. We're a highly industrialized country. We're the richest country in the world and our capitalists can afford to give our working people the highest standard of living in the world."

Dobbs said, "What can you afford to give your Negroes? That's what I bloody well would like to know."

Everybody all over the white world was an expert on the colored man. Solly groaned.

Maggie Sutton said, "Yes, what about the Negro question? That's one you can't answer so cavalierly." She was blonde. Her hair was white and flopping all over her white-white face and her eyes were the blue of the Coral Sea, green maybe, and her eyelashes were the color of her flopping hair. And she had had a few to drink.

He wished they'd talk of something else. It was a bloody bore, and he did not want an argument. He said: "Nobody is going to give me anything." Solly's tongue was like a sack of rocks. "I'm going to take what I get. Now let's change the subject, shall we?"

Steve said, "Hear—hear."

Hank Dobbs said, "Good-on you, myte."

Solly said, "And now let's drop the question, shall we? This is supposed to be a party."

Samuels said, "We'll work it out together when we get back. Isn't that right, Solly?"

Solly wanted to drink and lose himself. The phonograph was grinding out a Mills Brothers' recording that was all the rage in Bainbridge. *Paper Doll.* He recalled his silly poem.

This world is much too sad a place
For Fannie's happy smile.
Her feelings far too deep
For the endless guile. . . .

Solly thought his eyes were filling up. He was a fool. And Fanie Mae was a practical human being. Why should she wait for him? Who did he think he was anyhow?

Celia said, "Break up the politics, boys. Let's dance. This is a party, and I don't mean the Communist Party."

Solly said, "I'm on your side, Sister Celia."

Dobbs said to Celia, "And you, lovey, are a Trotskyite and a pacifist and that takes a lot of doing."

Steve said to Samuels, "You blokes carry your white supremacy everywhere. You swaggering bawstards, you come over here and try to impose your own sick policy on your allies."

Samuels said thickly, "Clean your own backyard. We'll clean ours after the war—right, Solly, old palsy-walsy?" Samuels got drunk very quickly. Very very very quickly.

"A Yankee colonel came to my house about three months ago and told me he heard we roomed niggers on furlough, and back in the States, he says, we don't socialize with them. They're all of them rapists. I told him you aren't back in the States, get out of my house, and he has had my house raided four or five times as a house of prostitution. That's your bloody progressive capitalism, and you know what you can do with it."

Solly wanted them to shut up with their Negro Question.

Dobbs said, "Up the rebels. Up the republic." And took another heavy swallow. He could drink a gallon of whiskey and still speak clearly.

Samuels said, "What about your White Paper? What about your own colored people?"

"That wasn't a race problem at all," Dobbs said. "That was a labor problem."

Steve said, "No personal offense intended, old boy, because I like you, and Celia likes you, but most of you white Yankees swagger like the Nazis. You yourself are different, but most of them act like they're occupying Australia. And if I were an American Negro I'd tell you all to go to blazes. No offense intended to you, old chap." Solly tried desperately to remember.

Tenderness fills her face
Unprepared for the bile
Of this old world's sophistication.
True emotions of her heart. . . .

Fannie Mae—Fannie Mae—what am I doing in this place, darling? And where are you?

Solly poured himself a stiff one and threw it down the hatch and felt it flaming in his stomach and moving upward toward his face. He was a red-hot fiery furnace. They were his friends and they meant well toward the colored people, so let them run off at the mouth. Why should he get into an argument? Frig em.

Dobbs said, "A Yankee chap told me the other day, comes from Mississippi, he says, 'I like your city, mate, I really do. Y'all all right. Y'all got electric lights and bathtubs.' He was a proper peckerwood and back home he was probably as poor as a bandicoot." Fannie, baby!

The true emotions of your heart
Are unprotected from the start . . .

Solly held his head in his hands. He felt like jumping up and down. The white storm raging all around him and grenades exploding in his stomach and bombs were bursting in his head. What the hell was he doing here? He felt like yelling help! help! help! I'm surrounded by white folks! Somebody come and save me quick! Fannie Mae! Bookworm! Jimmy! Scotty! Anybody!

He felt like standing up and shouting, "Shut up all of you! You're all white! You're all guilty sonsofbitches!"

Celia came and sat on the floor near his chair and looked up into his face. "What's the matter, Solly? You look like you're knocked up, and the party's just getting started."

He looked down into her face at the roundish mouth and the sweat on her sparse mustache like morning dew on a red rosy bush, her eyes full of deep concern and tender sensitivity. He said, "*I'm* knocked up?" And then it dawned on him about all the girls at the Southern Cross being knocked up, and now he was knocked up, and he began to laugh and he laughed and they stopped arguing to watch him laugh and he got up, and just wait till he told the Bookworm, who thought most of the women of Australia were in a permanent state of pregnancy, and he went stumbling toward the bathroom and he went inside and he puked his guts, and he flushed the toilet and pulled the lid down and sat on the stool and felt sick again and got up again and pulled up the lid and leaned his poor head over the stool.

And she said, "My poor darling is sick."

And he turned toward her and then toward the stool again, leaning his head over it and feeling dizzy, almost falling. She put her arms around him and he was embarrassed and appreciative, and leave him alone, goddammit! As he puked and puked and vomited, his stomach was a mad volcano.

She wet a soft washrag and wiped his forehead and his mouth and kissed his mouth. "Poor darling!" And wiped his mouth and kissed his lips and wiped his mouth and kissed his lips and wiped his mouth and kissed his unprotected lips. She got some mouthwash from the cabinet and he washed the insides of his mouth and gargled his throat, and she put her arms around his neck and kissed him and his head was dizzy and "My poor poor darling."

He thought maybe I should take this woman and escape this whole damn civilized jungle of madness.

He mumbled, "Baby, let's head for the wide and open bush beyond the mountains and stay there till the world comes to its senses."

"What are you mumbling, darling?"

He said, "Forget it."

They came out of the bathroom and Samuels met them

at the door, his tan face red with whiskey and embarrassment, or jealousy. "How's my boy doing? Can I help?"

Solly said thickly, *"I am not your boy,"* stressing every single word. *"I am my man."*

Samuels said, "I didn't mean it that way. You know I didn't."

"I know how you meant it. But don't you worry about it, Lieutenant, sir. I mean Captain. Miss Celia and I have no romantic inclinations whatsoever. We're strictly platonic. Brotherly and sisterly. You explain it to him, baby."

They were out of the bathroom now and starting down the narrow hall. Solly was in between the two of them and felt like yelling help! help! help! I'm surrounded by them! The whites got me! The whites got me! Save me! Save me! Samuels took him by the arm.

"For Christ sakes, Solly, we're friends, man!"

Solly pulled violently away from both of them and moved heavily toward the living room and sank down in an easy chair.

Dobbs said to Solly, "You're a thinking person, old boy. What do you see as the future of the Negro in America?"

Solly stared at Dobbs and he looked around, as they all sat there staring into his mouth as if it were dripping with pearls of infinite wisdom. Up your kilts—your bloody kilts. They did not really want to know his thoughts. They wanted affirmation of their own opinions. He'd been to these kind of things before, back in New York. The only Negro at a party—the center of attraction. The oddity. The noble savage.

He said, "Is this a party or is it a party? Will somebody play those Mills Brothers again? How about that 'Paper Doll'? That real live girl in Ebbens—"

Celia stared at him worriedly, and she got up and put "Paper Doll" on, and came back and sat on the floor near him. "Why don't all of you leave him alone? Can't you see he's knocked up? He gets enough of that back home and in the Army."

Knocked up—knocked up. He started to chuckle as if he were laughing at a joke he'd told himself. She put her hand on his knee and looked up into his face, her eyes anxious and asking him questions. Samuels said complacently, like he was sucking on an empty pipe, "American history has a way of unfolding in a progressive direction. We're an evolutionary country. We're sometimes slow but we get there just the same.

Americans believe in fair play. We are always for the underdog."

So talk that stupid crap, man. It doesn't bother me. Why should I get into a fight with these white folks? For what? This is suposed to be a party. They are bloody bores. He raised up slightly and looked around him as if he expected colored faces like Worm and Scott and Jimmy to materialize just by looking. Scotty would call these people some nowhere-mamma-jabbers. He sank down into the chair again. He would not get into their argument. It had nothing to do with him. We Americans are for the underdog so long as we can keep him under.

He got up again and pulled Celia to her feet and began to dance with her, just as Samuels repeated, "We're slow sometimes, I'll admit it, but we get there just the same."

Solly looked back over his shoulders and said, "We've only had three hundred years, fellers. You people have to give us time. Maybe in the next three hundred—I mean it takes a little time to evolve. Explain it to them, Captain Bob."

He danced her to the other side of the room away from the momentous debate. He felt Samuels's eyes heavily upon them and felt Celia's body heavily against him and heavy in his arms, and when the music stopped, she went to change the record, and he left her and got another drink and sank back into the easy chair.

Samuels was saying, "It's true. After the war it'll be the job of every decent-minded white person to do his share to see that the Negro becomes a part of the mainstream of American life."

Solly loud-talked, "Bainbridge's a great town, beautiful city, but I'd like to find out what Sydney's like."

Steve said to Samuels, "And your country is always spouting all that pious bourgeois hogwash about freedom and democracy, brotherhood and yet—it's hard to believe you could be so bloody schizophrenic—a bloody nation of schizophrenics. The way you treat your colored people—"

Solly loud-talked, "Maybe I'll spend the rest of my furlough down in Sydney. They say it's a great place—big city—"

Celia said angrily, "This is a party, not a debate—"

Solly said, "Why the hell not talk about it? You know anything more important?"

Dobbs said to Solly sympathetically, "I know how you feel, old chap, but—"

Samuels was still following his line of thought as if he had heard nothing that had been said within the last few minutes. "We owe it to the colored people. They've been the most loyal Americans of them all." He stared tenderly at Solly. "You've been kept out in the cold too doggone long. Like a stepchild looking into a warm house full of plenty."

This was too much. Solly got slowly to his feet. His head was going around and around as was his stomach. He said quietly, "I'm going to leave it with you people. I'm tired, sleepy, and frankly bored. But before I go, let me say this. Captain Bob, I don't want into your house of plenty. It may be plentiful with pimps and whores for all I know. On the other hand it may be a booby hatch plentiful with sick-in-the-heads, and who needs it? And you, Dobbsy, you don't know how I feel, since you don't look like a fuzzy-wuzzy." His voice was calm and he was angry enough now. "And you again, Captain Bob, I got a life-size picture of you battling for a better world for colored people. I remember how ferocious you were with that MP colonel over in Ebbensville. You were a raging tiger, weren't you? So you know it isn't likely that I'm betting too heavily on you. I'm putting my money on that large minority known as colored people, three quarters of the world's population. That's the basket I'm putting my eggs in. One more thing, Captain Bob—on loyalty. A slave's loyalty is always suspect unless he is a goddamn fool." Samuels's face was burning. He was speechless.

Steve said excitedly, "You're not a Socialist. You're nationalistic and you're anti-white and you're reactionary."

Solly said, "Just fine, thank you." And he turned to leave, but the room was spinning around and around much faster now, much much faster, and he had to hold on or he'd fall off the roller coaster, faster faster the room was whirling the ceiling descending. He reached desperately for the arm of the chair to brace himself but it impishly eluded him and he was falling falling falling. . . .

The men took him to a couch on the other side of the room and stretched him out, as he mumbled, "I'm all right—I'm all right—I'll be all right—don't worry about a thing—" Celia put a blanket over him.

They spent at least another hour drinking and arguing about the war-and-after and colored peoples and the labor movement and how about your own aborigines and your bloody White Paper and they talked about General Buford Jack whose headquarters were in Bainbridge on Adeline Street and the current prevalence of fairies, and they danced and Celia danced with Samuels and Pamela tried to awaken Solly, but Celia said to leave him alone.

Pam said, "Did he drink the same slop we drank? You must have been serving him some bloody plonk, that's what you must've given him."

Celia said, "He's a sensitive human being, that's all."

When the party broke up, Samuels stayed behind with Celia. He took her into his arms. He tried desperately to kiss her and finally she let him. Then she said, "I'm knocked up, Bob. I really am." And she moved away from him. And yet she did not look exhausted. She seemed leapingly alive.

Samuels glanced toward Solly asleep on the couch. "I'll help you sober him up and I'll drive him home in my jeep."

She said, "Don't bother, Bob. He can sleep there all night long, right where he is, so why disturb him?"

Bob stared at Solly again and back to Celia, his face burning from ear to ear. He tried to take her into his arms again. An act of halfhearted desperation.

She said, "He'll be all right. I shan't bother the dear boy at all. Please don't worry for him, he's really safe."

Bob was like a petulant five-year-old. "You never let me spend the night."

She laughed. "You never let me get you plastered. You're the most careful man in the world, you know."

He sat down again and stared at the floor in silence. He was making a fool of himself. Why didn't he just say good-bye and leave?

She said, "He's your friend. Could it be that you're jealous of him? The first thing you ever told me was about your sweet and loving wife back in the States and your dear dear darling children. My darling wife, Cora. My darling darling Cora." He didn't answer.

"Or maybe you're no better than the people he calls peckerwoods—maybe you're just smooth and sugar-coated. *He* thinks you're different. No matter what he said tonight, he thinks you're different." She was working herself up into a small-sized volcano and a very active one. "You're worried that he might be playing possum and as soon as you leave he'll leap up from the couch and rape me."

Bob looked up at her and shook his head. "Celia. Please—please—don't say that. I may be lots of things and I may even be jealous, but I'm no Mississippi cracker."

She didn't even hear him now. "Well, if he wanted me he wouldn't have to rape me. All he would have to do is take me, but he isn't even interested. And he's the most beautiful man I've ever known."

He was stunned and shaken. He got up and came toward her and put his arms around her. "Take care of yourself, Celia baby."

She said, "And he's presently unattached and that's more than we can say for you."

Samuels's voice was strange and gruff. "I think a great deal of both of you, I really do. You're my very best friends in this part of the world."

She said, "I love you too—you know I do—but I would give my life for him. He doesn't know. Or maybe he does know, but he isn't interested. And you, you keep being the human being you are, and don't start acting like a peckerwood."

He said, "You're beginning to sound like him already."

And he stared at her and it was true. He was jealous of the company clerk, even though he admired him. The black handsome bastard who lay sleeping on the couch, whom she preferred to him, *him*, HIM, Captain Robert W. Samuels, who was Free and White and Brass and American and over Twenty-one. How could she? She was intelligent, she was beautiful anyway you looked at her. Inside and outside. Superficial and profound. And this night this time he was way-down-under and thousands of miles away from home, and they were *really* his closest friends in this part of the bloody crazy world. Celia Blake and Solomon Saunders. They were his only friends here in this place. In divine desperation he tried to conjure up New York and home and dear Cora beloved Cora, and the rest of his family, his beautiful children, his mom and pop. He saw their faces, heard their voices. Saw them dimly, heard them vaguely. Celia's face and Solly's voice were more truthful to him now. They were real and here and now. But that wasn't it at all. It was just that he'd had too much to drink, he told himself, too goddamn much to drink, was why Cora's misty face began to disappear for Celia's. And he'd had too much to drink of life. So many things, too many things, he'd seen and done and felt and lived since he gave up his pretty family and got married to his Uncle Sam. Cora couldn't possibly know the him that he was now. A stranger to the man he used to be. The gentle bastard who had gone to war and killed to keep from being killed and for Country and Democracy, he'd lived through too much death and dying.

So now, here, this time, this place, he was at home with Celia and Solly. He had to go now and felt an empty aching loneliness deep in the guts of him. He put his hands on Celia's shoulders. She reached out and gently touched his troubled face and backed away.

"Good night, dear friend." Her warm voice and her lovely face were brimming over with emotions deeply felt.

And he said huskily, "Good night."

When he was gone she went over to Solly and looked down upon his sleeping face. She shook her head. He looked so sweet-faced and completely helpless with his lips barely parted and his arm from under the blanket hanging toward the floor. She knelt and traced the sweet curve of his mouth with her fingers and kissed him softly and she vibrated all the way down into the tunnel of her sex. She kissed his eyes, he stirred slightly, and she kissed his nose, she kissed his mouth with her lips that were sweating more than ever. Then she got up and pulled the blanket away and she started to undress him. "I won't wake you up, poor darling. I'm just going to make you comfortable and put you in a proper bed. I'm your nurse—I must take care of you." When she had undressed him, she stared at his unprotected unaffected nakedness, and she swallowed hard and her mouth was dry and she knew a sweetly weak and trembly feeling. And she kissed him tenderly. Then she struggled gently with him, half awoke him, and took him naked and stumbling to the bedroom (she was a nurse, it didn't matter—she was used to nakedness) and got him into the bed, half asleep and mumbling crazy mumblings, and she covered him up, and then she got undressed and went to the bathroom and washed her face and hands and cried and wiped her face and cried and brushed her teeth and got naked into bed beside him and she cried, and all up against him her arms around him and sharp currents of warm-cold thrills ran from the tip of her bottom to her brain and back and forth and back and forth along her spine, she shivered with excitement, her spinal cord a live conductor. Still asleep he put his arms around her and she felt him hard hard up against her even though he was asleep.

He was on the bloody beach—red beach again—and the thunder and the lightning and the dying and the bleeding and the moaning and the groaning, the guns in the hills and the guns in the bay and breathing death and wading in it up to his backside and the mortar from the burning hills—and all mixed up with a field of burning squealing scurrying rats—and

SHOOSH-SHOOSH-SHOOSH-SHOOSH-SHOOSH

"Drop, you crazy fool!" he shouted to Lanky Lincoln. "Take cover! Take cover! Goddammit! Take cover! Lanky! Lanky!"

He jumped out of bed, and where in the hell was he? She came into the room, and he stared at her in his naked confusion, and he had seen her somewhere before sometime in the whole eternity of time, and then he remembered where he was in space and time, and he dove for the sheet to clothe his body.

She went quickly back out of the room and after a while she called to him from the kitchen. "Get washed up, darling. Your things are on the chair. "I'm making breakfast."

At breakfast he said, "That was quite a night. I must've made a complete fool of myself. I don't remember—"

She said, "You were magnificent! Just beautifully magnificent!"

He said, "But how did, I mean how did I—?" And he nodded embarrassed toward the bedroom.

She blushed all over. "Bob—Bob Samuels helped you. He undressed you and put you to bed."

He said, "I must've really hung one on. I don't remember."

She said, "You hung a beauty right onto their chins, and they got just what they deserved."

He smiled, still very much embarrassed about passing out on the party and especially about her seeing him in his birthday suit with his penis full of urine and standing at attention. He smiled sheepishly and put his hand across the table and took her hand in a brief embrace. His embarrassment was silly, he thought. It wasn't the first time she had seen his nakedness. Besides, she was a nurse.

"I was having a bad dream—a terrible dream."

She said, "I understand. "I've had bad dreams."

He said, "Thank you." He had finished eating and stood up from the table and he felt a queasy something in his stomach and a dizziness, and he leaned against the chair.

And she said, "What's the matter, darling?" And came worriedly to him, and he turned from her and hurried toward the bathroom. And in the bathroom he threw up again and she wiped his face and gave him mouthwash and he washed his mouth and gargled his throat, and it was as if it had all been prerehearsed. He vaguely remembered. Except she did not kiss him this time, nor did she say, "My poor poor darling." This time she gave him something to settle his stomach.

They came back into the living room and she said, "Why don't you lie down again and get some rest? You're still quite shaky."

He said, "I have caused you enough trouble already."

She looked into his nervous face. "You could never cause me trouble. Not like that." She came and sat beside him and took his hand and looked again into his face. "Don't you know, Solly? Don't you know how much you mean to me?"

He said, "But—"

She said, "I care for nothing in the world excepting you. Nothing nothing—not a thing."

He said, "Celia—"

She put her hand on his mouth. She said, "Please! Don't say anything just now. I know how you feel. I remember the emptiness when I lost my Pat."

He said, "Celia, I mean—"

She said, "Hush—please! Don't say anything just now. Don't make me cry—not when I feel so happy."

He said, "I don't know how I feel about anything. I just don't know. I'm dead inside. I thought you knew. You told everybody—I have no romantic inclinations." He thought about Fannie Mae—he was dead inside and out. He would write to her this very day.

She said, "I told everybody but myself. I even told myself, but I wouldn't listen. I'm a fool. A stupid sheila! Maybe I'm just a common prostitute."

He shook his angry head. "You're none of those things and you bloody well know you're not." You're lily white, that's what you are. If you're white you're right. If you're black get back.

She laughed. "Listen to him—swearing like a blawsted digger." She stood up and took his hand. "Come now, lad. You must get yourself some rest. You're just out of the hospital a week, and I'm your nurse and I'm responsible for your health and welfare."

He got up and let her lead him to the bedroom. They stopped at the door and she told him to get undressed and catch a wink. "You'll have to sleep in the raw. I don't have any pajamas for you. I'm not used to overnight guests, especially of the male variety."

He went inside and she closed the door behind him, and she went and threw herself on the sofa. She thought, he's in there in my bedroom and he's undressing and I want him—I should be ashamed of myself—he's undressing in my bedroom and I want him! She felt alive and warm all over her restless body. She had never felt this way before. With Patrick it had been a thing of serenity. He had been older than she, and he had been husband, lover, father, teacher. He'd been her Rock of Gibralter, and when he had his arms around her she felt the world could never harm her. His love had been a shelter in a time of storm and stress. But Solly Saunders, slim and nervous, black and beautiful and growing-growing and arrogant and angry, excited every bone in her body. She wanted to take his black and beautiful anger into herself and wanted to know it inside of her and surround it and contain it and nourish it. And she could not weigh the consequences, never weigh the consequences. This was now and here and love and war and everything was fair, they said, and she would know him now and here, if he would have her here and now, she would know him now and here, or she would die forever more. She swallowed the morning air and knew a dark sweet taste in her mouth all the way to her trembling stomach.

She got up from the couch and she was quaking with excitement. Her breathing came in quick short gasps. She knew her want for him deep deep deep in that throbbing place where the people of the world are born. She tried to calm herself. She went to the bathroom and put cold water on her face. She patted her hair and rearranged her dress. She felt like a virgin and a whore simultaneously, and she wanted to know him now and now and now and here and now and forever now. This time it's now and now or never. She loved him and she wanted him, and love was its own justification.

She knocked on his door and knocked again. He said, "Yes?" sleepily.

She said, "May I come in? Are you undercover?"

He said, "I'm decent."

She came in and sat on the side of the bed. "How do you feel?"

He said, "Much much better."

And she put her hand on his forehead and she tried to keep it steady—keep it steady. She took his hand and felt his pulse. "You seem to be all right." She couldn't keep her hand from him. She put her hand on his forehead again and then on his arm, she rubbed his arm tenderly like massaging, and she became self-conscious and drew slightly away from him, and he said, "What's the matter?"

She said, "Nothing's the matter." I'm just melting with desire, that's all.

He said, "Dinkie die?" What the hell was she getting so serious about?

She said, "Do you like me, Solly?" Her voice, thick and throaty and her damp hand was on his arm again, and she tried to keep from trembling.

"What kind of a question is that?" he asked her.

"You don't hate me because I'm white?"

"I don't hate anybody because they're white. That's a waste of time and energy undeserved by white folks. I just don't like the ways of most white folks."

"You hate my evil ways?"

He said angrily, "I don't hate your ways. But why are you so serious this morning? Have I compromised milady's honor by getting drunk and spending the night in her bedroom?"

She said, "Take me in your arms for just one moment and tell me, 'I don't hate you, Celia dear.' "

He sat up in bed and the covers fell away from his naked shoulders and he took her in his arms and told her, "I do not hate you, Celia dear."

She put her arms around his neck and her mouth against his mouth and she murmured, "Love me! Love me! Love me then! Make love with me, for I'm lonely and in need of love!"

Her face was covered with perspiration, especially in the peach fuzz over her curving mouth which was open now and wanting to receive him. His hand caressed her shoulders and her back and down the middle of her back, and she kissed his eyes his nose his cheeks his ears his neck, and he shook his head and held her slightly away from him.

He said, "Darling Celia, I'm not ready for love again, I mean, not to be in love again. I'm scared of it. I'm too damn unlucky with it. I don't know how I feel about you. I don't know what I feel—" He should go into her arms and escape the whole damn miserable world. Forget it ever happened to him.

She got up from the bed. "I don't care—I don't care. I want you now—to make love to me—of me—with me—but now and now and please, my darling!"

He stared at her. She said, "I hate you! I hate you! You make me feel like a bloody whore, and I hate you, damn you, hate you! You make me feel all white and ugly and I hate you for it!"

He took her arm and pulled her to him as she struggled, weakly struggled. He kissed her trembling lips and he caressed her and he whispered, "I want you—I want you now—"

She said, "No, you don't! You have no feeling for me, you're just patronizing me. I don't want your blawsted kindness! You can bloody well go to hell for all I care—"

He said, "I want you now—I need you—I'm all alone—"

She pulled angrily away from him. "Tell me you want me then. Tell me you need me."

He said, "I want you and I need you."

She took off her clothes as fast as she could, every limb of her was trembling, and she got in bed beside him. And he was man and she was woman and he was big and hard and she was soft and small but pliant and they both were ready more than ready, and she was beneath him, holding all his weight, and she took his hard black fury into her hand and put it between her naked legs where the sweet mystery of life lived and always lived forever lived, and she at last contained his fury, increased his awful angry fury, furious and frenzied, and she lived and and lived and lived and lived, and up and down and up and down and up and down, they lived the maddest sweetest mystery, and faster faster faster faster. Her eyes closed her face losing color and covered with pimples of perspiration, her lips turning white and parted and pleading and moaning and groaning now, and straining every fiber in her body, and, "Oh, my darling, oh my darling, say you love me, say you love me, tell me that you'll always love me!" She demanded without knowing—hysterically demanded. And he said, "Yes-yes-yes, my dearest! Yes, my darling, yes!"

They fell asleep weary lovers and they woke up and they fell asleep and she woke up again. They lay naked on top of the bed, and she stared at him from head to foot and marveled at the beauty of his sleeping nakedness. A rosy color had come to her cheeks. She kissed his body and whispered softly, "I love you and I love your body, because it's beautiful and it smells good and special and it tastes delicious, and I love its varying shades of darkness and light going and coming, here black here brown here black here brown, I love your blessed face, your eyes which remember pain and loneliness and fear and disappointment and love and laughter, your eyes have cried, your eyes have laughed, your dear soft sensitive beautiful intelligent eyes. And your sweet mouth full mouth with the anger and the appetite for living and loving, and I hate the thin slits in the faces which most men have for mouths, and I love the lean nervous honest anger that your body talks about, and your profound compassion, and then I love I love I love I love your big bold dignified penis which is the blackest part about you and it gave me more love and more pleasure than I ever knew existed." He stirred restlessly still asleep, and her soliloquy had exhausted her and she was short of breath. "I love your mind in all its angry boldness, and I hope the anger never cools. I love the dark deep passion of your anger. Live it! Live it! Don't subdue it! I love and hate the way you make me feel the deep deep guilty feelings of being what the world calls white, but which your aborigines called more appropriately paleface—every time you look at me or even when I think of you—the painful shame for my race, which has lynched the races of the world. Can you forgive me for being white? Can you forget it? Can you ever really love me, darling? Am I living with illusion?"

He woke up and rubbed his eyes and stared at her and then remembered.

"Tell me, can you ever love me?" She didn't know he had awakened.

He said sleepily, "Promise me one thing."

She moved up against him and put her arms around his neck. "I'll promise you anything at all."

He said, "Promise you will not mention love again."

"I promise, Solly."

They got up and bathed and dressed and they had tea, and as they sat there eating, she said, "You hate me because I'm white, and I don't blame you, but it isn't fair—it just isn't fair!"

He looked at her with a painful smile. "First of all it isn't fair to say that I hate you, because it simply isn't true. But even so and furthermore, fairness is a thing no white has a right to ask of colored. I mean, look—who's been unfair to whom? Who's been unfair to my mother and her mother and my father and his father and who'll be unfair to my son and his children? 'Fairness' is a word that should choke in the white man's throat. I'm not asking any white man to be fair with Solly Saunders, baby. I live with no such false illusions."

She reached across the table, put her hand in his, and she said, "Solly, I—"

But he shook his head in anger. "Oh no, baby. 'Fair' is one of the most nothing words in Webster's dictionary, you better believe it. It is of no consequence whatever. It's a fool's paradise inhabited by idiots and dreamers."

"But I know you do hate me," she said. "I can feel the hatred. I felt it even as you loved me." She closed her eyes and shook her head. "No, it isn't true—it isn't true. How can I say you hate me when I know it isn't true?"

He said, "Dear Celia, I not only like you but I deeply deeply regard you. You are a warm sensitive beautiful human being, every last bit of you. And in another time we might have been Romeo and Juliet, for all I know, but we are in this time and here and now, and I am freshly out of being in love, so please don't look for love from me, because I care for you much too much to pretend. Let's just take what we have and let it do for the time being." His voice hardened. "And if we can't, let's break it off and here and now. I mean, forget it!"

She stared at him, her eyes filling up. His mood was always always changing.

He said, "And you have the cutest mustache. That's another thing about you."

She said, "You don't like my mustache." She was serious.

He laughed. "I adore your handsome mustache." You're not Fannie Mae. Let's face it. And you're white—let's face that too. And maybe I do hate you.

She smiled. "Then I shan't ever shave it. And maybe one

day you'll learn to love me, as much as you love my handsome mustache."

He said wearily, "You promised—"

"I'll never mention love again," she said, "until you mention love again."

She put her hand across the table and he took it in his hand this time. And he said, "Dinkie die?" It was a tender moment.

And she smiled and said, "Fair dinkum."

The next week he went all over the town by himself, he rode the trams, he rode the trains, he rode the buses. To the beaches, to the parks, to the outskirts of town, to the business district, to the quays. Several places there were the Yankee MPs who reminded him of the cops in Georgia. They told him the places were off limits even though he plainly saw white Yankee GIs already inside and could hear their boisterous laughter. He argued quietly with the MPs with their brave guns and courageous nightsticks. He argued even though he knew he argued vainly. He was so angry he thought his head might pop wide open. "All right, you looking for trouble, boy? Move along before we run you in."

He usually went where he hoped he would not run into Americans, and it was South Bainbridge and North Bainbridge and all around Banana City, and he liked the friendly Australian people with their warm and rugged manner and their idiom and accents.

He didn't see or hear from Celia for three days, and the evening of the third day she phoned him and asked him, "How about taking a walk with me?"

He said, "Sure—I'd love to." He was almost dead from walking and his dogs were barking, fiercely barking.

She said, "Good-o, meet me halfway. Come along the footpath on Alexander Street."

He said, "Footpath?"

She said, "What do you call it—sidewalk?"

They met as he walked along the paved footpath on Alexander Street, and they walked together through the soft Queensland night, they walked silently most of the time, hand in hand, lost in their separate thoughts. It was a time of the month when her life always stood precariously on the edge of a deep yawning abyss. She seemed to be walking forever on quicksand and she would never reach the solid ground. It was a couple of days before her menstrual period. They were the awful anxious irritable days when she died a thousand deaths a day and she lost her mind a million times and she was a stranger in an unfriendly world and nobody understood her, nobody loved her, and nobody gave a bloody damn. Nobody found any beauty in her and she hated the image she made for the world and felt sorry for herself, she who despised self-pity. She was young but overly concerned with growing old and dying old and leaving no footprints in the swiftly shifting sands of time. This night she could not take rejection, especially from Solly. Please! Love me—care about me—see some beauty in my life.

They sat down in a park and she leaned her happy head against his shoulder and they listened to the night wind singing love songs to the flamboyant eucalyptus trees and the poinsettias gleaming even in the darkness and the poincianas and hibiscus. She was aching with romantic feelings. She was leaping with them.

He was thinking of golden-brown leaves falling and he was a boy walking barefoot with the cool earth under him. Playing football and basketball, and squirrels running quietly through new fallen leaves in autumn time. And Mama with the tough and tender strength, and Solomon the Third, who was six months old already and who had never seen his mother and never known his father. His face filled up. One day I'll make it all up to you, my baby, and we will change this world together.

She said, "A tuppence for your thoughts."

He didn't even hear her. He was in Ebbensville with Fannie Mae. Holding her sweet face in his hand close to him now, and he was growing warm all over, and seeing her lying on the floor of a Philippine shack with the baby in her arms and man's best buddy at her feet, and Madonna's face was Fannie Mae's—her face—just like his Fannie Mae's.

He pulled his hand from Celia's without knowing, and to her it was like pushing her away from him, out of his thoughts, out of his sensitivity, out of his life, and she knew the awful feeling of it deep inside of her. She took his hand again and squeezed it. "All right then, a quid for your thoughts. How's that?" She laughed halfheartedly.

He came back for a moment and looked around and down into her face and took her face gently in his hands and he smiled for her, but she knew the thing was still there between them, always there, forever there and there and there and growing larger there, and she wanted him to love her, not to patronize or pity her. She pulled away from him and got up from the bench. "Let's go. It's getting late."

He said, "What's the matter, Celia?"

"Nothing. I'm just knocked up, that's all."

When they got to her door she turned to him. "Good night, Sergeant Solomon Saunders Junior, and good-bye and cheerio."

He said, "What's the matter? I mean, how about a night-cap? Unless of course you're fresh out of slop. I mean I'll go get some if you want—"

She looked up into his face and shook her head. "We'd better say aroo and cheerio."

He said, "But why?" If it were not for his overactive guilty conscience he could have himself a ball. If it were not for Fannie Mae.

She said, "And why not? Why not, as you Yankees say, why not have one for the everlasting road?"

They went inside and he sat wearily down and she got the slop and poured the drinks. He didn't need or want a drink. Why in the hell had he insisted? She held her glass toward his and said. "Here's to unrequited love, the bitterest wine in all the world. And here's to racial animosity. And here's to me, a stupid sheila—" She stopped. Her eyes were growing wide and glassy.

He shook his angry head. Don't bore me with this crap tonight!

"It's true, isn't it? That's what it's all about, isn't it? You have an edge against me because I'm white—that's it, isn't it, Sergeant Saunders?"

He should say, "You're mother-hunching right!"

He said, "No. It isn't true, and you know bloody well it isn't true."

She said, "You're lonely and you're a long ways from home and I'm just a good sort that you can put the hard word on whenever you feel the sexual hunger, but you despise me because I'm white!" Her voice choked off again.

He should have said, "You're goddamn right—so what?"

He went and sat beside her and put his arm around her shoulder. She put her head upon his chest and she wet his shirt with her tears. He said, "You know I don't despise you." He massaged her head and shoulder and the middle of her back.

"You make me feel like a lowheel—like—like a prostitute, like a thing for you to have your pleasure with, but you have no other feelings for me, and I offer you everything, all of me, but you hate all white people, and you make me hate all white people. You even make me hate myself. Sometimes it all crowds into my head and it grows and grows and grows and it collides and I feel my head is going to explode, and I feel like screaming, I think something is going to go pow and I'll go completely out of my mind and never return. You don't know—"

He massaged the middle of her back with tender strokes and she moved restlessly and restfully underneath his strong and gentle touch. Sometimes she really frightened him. "It's—it's—it's been more than six months since—since—" She lost her voice. She was treading on shifting sand and sinking sand and even maybe very quicksand. "It's been over six months, almost seven, since it happened and time enough for you to make your mind up. Time for you to live in the present and for the future."

He kneaded her skull with his fingers and it felt so good, so damn good, so bloody good, she almost grunted like a puppy. All through her it felt good good good. She was grateful. He said softly, "No, there hasn't been time enough yet."

Suddenly she pulled away from him and stood up over him. "You and your superiority! Your black smugness! Your righteous indignation. I'm sick and tired of feeling guilty and feeling white and dirty and responsible for every bloody evil the black man ever suffered at the hands of the whites since time began. I have nothing against your people—I never did anything against them—I—"

He got up and laughed and it was like spitting in her face. "I know, baby. One of your greatest lovers is a black man. It seems to me I've heard that song before. Well it's bloody tough, you know, and my heart bleeds for you. I mean you have it so much rougher than us colored folks, and you want this black man to make it easier for you. I told you once—I don't hate white people, Celia. Love and hate are profound emotions, and I'm stingy and particular. What is it? You want me to hate you? Would that make you feel better? Make you feel important? Is that the therapy you need?"

The hurt was there deep deep in her eyes and in the quivering roundness of her mouth. "Look," he said, "you want me to overlook entirely the fact that you are white. Can you overlook my color?"

She said, "Yes! Yes! Yes!"

"You're a liar," he said. He paused, breathing heavily, and then he said slowly, deliberately, "And besides, why should my color be overlooked?" He put his index finger on his face. "This is me. Black me. Proud me. Proud black American me, whose ancesters came from great Africa. Not arrogant, but just beginning to be proud of the specialness of black me. No bleaching powder no hair slick-em-up. No trying-to-be-like-you. Just the me I see in the mirror when I shave. So you would overlook the color of my skin? What else? How about my eyes? Do you know what color they are? And suppose my name were Dobbsy, would it be all the same to you? Suppose I were redheaded, bowlegged, Australian, would it be all the same to you? What about my height? It would be all the same to you if I were four feet tall or seven feet? Why is color suddenly of no significance? Do you ignore the color of a red rosebush? Would it be a rose if it were a greenish blue? Do you overlook all those colors out there at the Great Barrier Reef?" He walked over to her phonograph records and found the album he was looking for. "When you listen to him sing, do you forget he is a black man? Part of his strength and conviction is his blackness. Robeson, black man Afro-American." He thought of Richard Wright's *Twelve Million Black Voices*, the great black faces in that book, some weary faces, some without hope, most of them indestructible. He put the Robeson album back in its place and turned wearily toward her. He was tired of the whole damn business. It was time to go.

She said, "What I meant was, I don't hold your color against you. I love your color."

He said, "If the peoples of the world have to ignore each other's color in order to get along, then we *are* in a hell of a fix."

She said, "I don't want to ignore your color. I love your color. *I love your color.*"

He said wearily, "And you and I cannot solve the problems of the world just by loving each other's color."

She shouted softly, "But I don't want to solve the problems of the world. I just want to solve the problems of Solomon and Celia."

"But I definitely do," he said. "You'd better believe me. I can't live without wanting to solve them. I can't breathe without wanting a new dialogue in the place of all this goddamn clichéed obsolescence. If you don't understand this about me, then you know an image that has no relationship at all with Solomon Saunders, Junior."

She said, "I understand. I understand."

He said, "I wish I knew the words to make you see where I am in time and space. Your people are the mistreaters, mine are the mistreated. Your magnanimity comes a little late and easily, since yours is the guilty conscience. Your people are the malefactors, the offenders against the majority of the human race. It's easy for you to say, 'I forgive you for being black, and therefore you should forgive me for being white.' What are you forgiving me for? For living?"

She said, "Solly-Solly-Solly!"

He said, "So you personally haven't done anything against colored people, so you should be accepted by them. But almost every colored person in the world can say truthfully he's never done anything against white people. So what? Does this *ipso facto* wipe out white supremacy? Does it guarantee they won't lynch my boy in the state where I was born?"

She shook her head. And could not answer.

He put the glass to his mouth and took a long protracted swallow till every drop was gone.

He reached for his garrison cap. "And now that we've had one for the road, now that we understand each other, I'll be saying so long, it's been good to know you—"

She went to him again and put her arms around his neck. "Don't go, darling! Don't go yet! Please don't go!"

He said, "Celia—"

She said, "Do you like me?"

"Yes, I like you."

She said, "Did you like the love we made together?"

"All right—I liked the love we made together."

"But you would not waste your profound love on me? You would not even stoop to hate me?"

He said, "You are a lovely tender sensitive women, intelligent and—"

She laughed and took his cap from him. "Let's have just one more for the road, and maybe the road won't look so dim and bumpy. Let's have one for loveliness and tenderness and sensitivity."

She poured two more drinks and gave him one and took a sip of hers. "Tell me—what's wrong with me besides being a paleface? Do you not like my brown eyes? I've been told they're nice and warm."

"You have the nicest warmest eyes in all Australia."

"And how about my mouth? Is it not full and shapely? My lips are not thin and stingy like most Australians, are they? Pam says a spook must've put a hard word on my mother."

His hand went out automatically and sharply up against her mouth almost before the words came out, and he reached for his cap in her hands but she backed away from him.

"Why? Why?"

"You won't get another chance to insult this particular colored man," he said almost calmly, "you may rest assured."

She stood there shaking her head unbelievingly.

He said, "And now if you'll kindly give me my garrison cap, I'll be on my way. The first time I ever hit a woman in all my life. My most humble apologies. But then maybe you'll think twice the next time you feel the urge to call a Negro man a spook in order to put him in his place."

"But-bu-but we heard the soldiers call each other spooks many many times when they roomed at Steve's house. My-my brother's—the colored soldiers—we-we thought it was a term of affection."

He took his cap from her and went toward the door. She put her arms around his waist. "No, Solly, no! No, my darling. You know I didn't mean to hurt, you know I didn't mean to slur your people. I love you—love you. Oh my darling—"

He stood helpless with her arms around him and stared down into her face, and he didn't know how he felt or what he felt. He thought, why am I here? What am I here for? Why was I born in the first-damn-place?

She said, "Go ahead—slap me again. As many times as you want to slap me—slap me for all the times you've been insulted by the people of my race—slap me for all the times that you've been slapped. Slap me—slap me—I am guilty! I am guilty!" She broke off into sobs again as they erupted from the middle of her, her entire body shaking now. He took her tenderly to the couch and sat down with her.

"All right," he said, hating his softness. "All right—all right, I know you didn't mean to insult me, and I'm sorry I slapped you." He kneaded her skull and massaged her shoulders and her back as she writhed and whimpered like a purring puppy dog, and he hated himself for being so goddamn tenderhearted.

He said, "All right—all right, I'm sorry. What else can I tell you?"

She said, "You can tell me you love me."

He said to her out of his deep and tender feelings for her, "Fats Waller, used to sing a song back in the States—*Be sure,* I mean people *should* be sure before they say the word so damn glibly—I mean it's a hell of a commitment—I for one can't—I don't want to make it now. I told you in front—"

She said, "Yes, I remember, darling. But you do love me. In my heart of hearts I feel deeply that you love me. I know you love me. It's this thing that stands between us. It—it's the color of my skin."

He said wearily, "Listen to me, Celia. It would be easy for me to say, 'Yes, I love you—love you—love you,' and—"

She said, "Go ahead and say it and see what happens. See how it tastes and see how it feels."

He said, "I've seen too much pain and unhappiness and I've had enough myself to last a couple of lifetimes. The war will end one of these days we hope and then what happens to love? I go back to that other world where I have a son, and he and I will build a life together out of the ruins, and you'll build your own sweet life right here in Queensland."

"When you go back you can send for me."

"Look," he said, "I'm black and you're white. And Little Solly is black. The color of your skin *does* make a difference. Believe me."

She shouted softly, "It makes no difference—it makes no difference!"

He said harshly, "In my country you better believe it makes a difference. It makes all the goddamn difference in the world!"

"No! No! It doesn't—not with me!"

He said, "Let the facts hit you in the face, baby. The bloody MPs threw me out of two places today right here in your precious City of the Winding River. Not in Mississippi or Georgia —right here in dear old darling Queensland."

She said, "Solly! Solly! My dearest darling angry Solly!"

He got up quickly. "You're goddamn bloody right, I'm angry! But you're not angry, are you? You—you're just uncomfortable, that's all. You're not angry like I'm angry."

She said tonelessly, "I know how you feel. I don't blame you."

He said, "That's a lie you didn't have to tell. You can't know how I feel. And blaming or not blaming me makes no difference to me whatever. Don't give yourself so much importance!"

It would make things easier in his mind and heart and in his guts if everything were black or white—if tears, if blood were black or white, if dying, crying, poverty, or even death— And everything *was* black and white. He moved to the door and opened it and turned to her sitting lifeless on the couch. And said good night. She hardly heard him.

She didn't know that he had left. He knew she didn't.

Every day he rode the trams and buses all over Banana City. He didn't see her for a few days and he missed her, there was no doubt about it, he missed, he almost relished missing her. He enjoyed missing her, and he did not write to Fannie Mae, and whatever would be would bloody well be! Then one evening Celia came to her brother's for Solly and they went out on the town in her beat-up bomb with Solly driving, and a couple of places they went, the Yankee MPs put them out because the cafés were "off-limits" to American GIs. One of the "off-limit" places was a quiet sensitive cabaret off to itself and across the river into South Bainbridge, and as they left and got into the car and started to drive away they saw a gang of drunken GIs stagger gaily and boisterously into the club past the MPs, the Yankee MPs grinning at their drunken comrades.

Solly said, "You see—it's suddenly '*on* limits' again. That is the essence of Yankee morality. The American Way of Life, like hot dogs out at Coney Island and the KKK in Mississippi. And the spirit of Eugene Talmadge. That's what we're fighting and dying for."

She lay her head against his shoulder. Sometimes she was frightened by his overwhelming bitterness. "Things will be different after the war, darling. Don't you worry."

He turned and looked down into her face like she was a total stranger to him, and suddenly he started to laugh, loud and harshly, as if a geyser had erupted in him. She was frightened and she said, "Solly!"

"Things will be different after the war, darling, don't you worry," he mimicked her.

One of the MPs came over to the car. He was mild-faced and bowlegged and blue-eyed and medium-sized and corn-fed and Midwestern Yankee. A Minnesota gopher maybe. Nebraska cornhusker.

"What's the matter with you, boy?" He asked good-naturedly.

Solly tried to stop laughing. "Nothing, officer." Laughter still oozing out of him in bubbles.

"You all right, Miss?" the MP asked with real concern.

"I was never better," Celia said indignantly.

The MP said "All right then, boy, cut out the noise and get outa this neighborhood on the double. That's why you people ain't allowed in places like this. You don't know how to behave yourself."

Solly started to laugh again, quietly. "Yassah, Boss, but you schizophrenic Yankee paddies are the funniest people in God's creation. You're absolutely hysterically the ever-loving most—" He raced his motor and pulled away and left the MP standing there.

A few days later, Samuels drove into town for lunch with Solly. They sat in a little quiet restaurant not far from where Solly lived and looked each other over.

Solly said, "Thanks, Captain."

Samuels said, "You're not back in the Army yet. The name is Bob. And thanks for what?"

"For the other night at Celia's." His face grew warm with embarrassment. "Thanks for putting me to bed. It must have been a rugged—"

Samuels's face grew even warmer than Solly's, warm and red like pomegranate. And Solly knew. He covered up quickly. "Thanks for putting me on the couch and covering me up. Celia told me you—I mean—I must have been a mess. I've never been that drunk before in all my life." Thanks for nothing.

Samuels said, "It was nothing at all."

You're mother-loving right it was.

They had steak and eggs and coffee, and Samuels said, "A couple of days from now and you'll be back in the old routine."

Solly said, "I *can't* wait." And he got up and went to the jukebox and put a nickel in for the Mills Brothers' "Paper Doll," in respectful dedication to his girl in Ebbensville.

He came back and sat down and said, "My favorite song on the hit parade."

Samuels said, "I'd like to talk to you a little about your future in the service."

Solly smiled ironically. "I want a civilian first-class rating, if it isn't asking too much. I mean, if Uncle Sam can spare me."

I'll steal the doll in Ebbensville . . .

Samuels said, "You have two alternatives. You can go to a special Officer Candidate School right here in Bainbridge, and when you come out you would be assigned to the Duck outfit where the fellows and I are. It's pretty definite that we'll be here for the duration. We're so shot up, there's no place for a Japanese bullet."

Solly said, "Or?"

"Or what?"

"The other alternative?"

"If we tried hard enough we might be able to get you a medical discharge and you could go home and forget it."

Solly's voice was trembling. "What the hell are we waiting for? Let's plan the farewell party."

Samuels stared at him and said, "The farewell party might take about a month of red tape, whereas you could be in OCS next week."

From the purple-hearted soldier . . .

Solly said, "I'm not in that big a hurry."

Samuels discussed the pros and cons with Solly. If he went to OCS, with the recent institution of the point system for separation from the service, he might go home only seven or eight months later after all, and with an officer's status, more separation pay, more prestige, more this, more that, and more the other.

Solly said, "I can't hear a word you say. All the Army can do for me is give me *out*."

Samuels shook his head. "You're so bitter about the States, why're you in such a hurry to get back?"

Solly laughed. "I've got great big expectations including a son I've never seen." The wheels in his mind were turning like propellers on a P–38. Going home—Fannie Mae—going home—Fannie Mae—

Samuels said, "I think you're making a mistake."

Something deep in Solly began to argue with him quietly. Use your mind instead of your feelings. Why not become an officer? What the hell is six or seven more months? Especially in Australia—you can do six months standing on your head. No war—no problems. Your son is in good hands, your mother's. If you're going to go through life forever asserting the color of your skin, why in the hell did you go to college? Take advantage of your education, your personality, your intelligence, and submerge your asinine emotions. That's the trouble with colored people, even educated ones. More pay—more prestige—officers' quarters—and if you're an officer you can do more for the men—and get a better job when you get back home—and do much more for Junior when you get there just a few months later. Have more money to start civilian life with.

He said quietly and angrily, "I have to think about it."

Samuels said, "The men in the outfit would love to have you as an officer, and so would I."

He thought about Fannie Mae and he felt himself aging by the seconds and there was so little time, and he had wasted so much time, and he didn't want any part of the Army. He saw the bloody beach again and waves of men washed out with the tide, and he had to get home, had to get home. In the entire million million years of time he had only one half of a tick-tock left. He must get home and start the living. And yet a few more months—he must think of the advantage of going back an officer. He must think of Junior's future and his own. Fannie might be only a dream he was always dreaming. She was promised to another. Celia was here and now and willing. And why in the hell should he be in such a hurry to run home to the back seats of America?

Samuels stared at him and said, "How's Celia?"

He said, "Fine as sparkling burgundy, I imagine. When do we get my separation under way?" So little time—so little time. He was growing old so fast, so fast. There was no time to get ahead. He wanted to see his child so bad, it felt like rocks were in his stomach. See his child—teach him manhood.

"Tomorrow morning," Samuel said. His face grew warm and he stared down at the table. "How will Celia take the news?"

Solly said, "How're the fellows? And how is their everloving morale?"

A storm settled over the captain's face. He shook his head. "The worst—the very worst—and I know goddamn well I'm not to blame. It's the peckerwoods in this Jim Crow Army, turning Bainbridge into Georgia."

Solly laughed sarcastically. "You're beginning to sound like a colored man, a member of the Club, old Cap'n. You need a transfer, *quick*. You're getting nervous in the service."

"I've been all over everywhere protesting, from base headquarters to division to corps and even down to Adeline Street, and they all look at me as if I'm out of my mind."

Solly said, "You *are* out of your mind, if you think you're going to change this cracker Army. Your trouble is you always wanted to be an officer and a colored man too, and that's the ever-loving most impossible situation. That's exactly why I'm going home."

Samuels said, "They're complacently sitting on top of an ammo dump, and it might go off any minute."

Solly got up and motioned for the waiter. "Man, I do not want to hear your problems. Let's go somewhere and find a pub. I feel like celebrating. And I want you to sweet-talk me about how *we're* going to get me separated. Let's just hang a tiny one on, and then I'm going to my lonely room and write a letter to a lady and ask her not to sit under that apple tree with anyone else but me. And you and your colored problems can take a flying frig at the moon."

But when he left Samuels, he did not go to his lonely room. He went to town and sent a cablegram to his fickle-minded real live doll. All the way to Ebbensville.

CHAPTER

3

Red tape—white tape—blue-damn-tape. The first week back in the Army he spent most of his sweet precious time taking physicals and signing papers and waiting outside of offices. And like Samuels told him, it seemed that it would take at least a month to get him ready for the ship which would take him State-side back to that other-worldly world where brave red-blooded patriots bit their lips and counted their ration coupons and sacrificed and went without and stood in line for cigarettes and said V for victory valiantly. Meanwhile Samuels promoted him to a master sergeant and put him in charge of the 25th Amphib platoon for the short time he would spend with them. He was a Great White Buddy tried and true.

Also meanwhile, the tension built all over Banana City, all over Australia's eastern coast between the white and colored Yankees, which was mostly due to the hypersensitive arrogance of the colored. It was all their fault, Solly told Worm. Just because they were American soldiers ten thousand miles away from home, way down under over yonder, and just because many of them had risked their lives in the jungles of the South Pacific and left their black blood to smear the pretty white beaches on the sprawling far-flung islands, and left their black and brown and light-brown comrades to fertilize the land of strangers. Just because they were soldiers, tried and trusted, nephews of their Uncle Sam, they had the colossal nerve to want to go to all the places where the other soldiers went and to be treated free and equal. They were stinking opportunists. They wanted to take advantage of the situation; they wanted to be treated in Australia better than they were at home. What arrogance—what treachery—what unmitigated gall!

Solly shook his head at the Bookworm. He remembered Captain Rutherford. Solly said, "Colored folks are the most ungrateful people the world has ever known. The man was good enough to put some clothes on your back and give you a free trip abroad and give you a chance to die for your country in the Great War to save Democracy, and still you're not satisfied. You want the whole damn hog or none. You have the nerve to want to be free. That's arrogance, buddy boy. That's being downright biggedy."

Worm stared at his master sergeant. "Buddy, your head wound must have been a mama-jabber! You really need to go home bad!"

The Negro soldiers went into town every night all over town and went into all of the nicer places just to cause a disturbance and raise a row. Troublemakers pure and simple. They were looking for trouble and usually found just what they looked for. As fast as the MPs threw them out of one place, they would go into another. There must have been three thousand broken-down battle-scarred Negro soldiers in Camp Worthington Farms, which was situated in North Bainbridge out on the edge of the city, and each night just out of pure cussedness, almost half of them would empty across the river into South Bainbridge, most of which was "off limits" to them. And each night twenty-five or thirty of them would end up in an Army jail. The most famous jail in Australia was the Jones Street MP station. They had a reputation of whipping more heads per night than all the others put together. And they did their very damnedest to deserve their reputation.

It was not that all of the places in Bainbridge were off limits to the colored soldiers. They were welcomed by the Australians to the Southern Cross, and they could go to the Dirty Dipper and the George Washington Carver Service Club and the Greasy Spoon and the Bucket of Blood and to a few more of the lesser pubs.

But they had worn out their welcome even at the Southern Cross, which just went to prove the point once and for all. Every night there were all kinds of disturbances, fights and near fights, at the Cross, between white and colored Yankees, usually over who would dance with the sheilas or take up time with the shelias or take the sheilas home. Division headquarters finally had to issue orders placing the Southern Cross off limits to American soldiers one and all, without regard to race, color, or creed or previous condition of servitude. This was the last straw, and the Negro soldiers had better behave themselves from here on in, or face the consequences.

"We've been patient," the adjutant at division headquarters told Samuels, "but there are limits."

"Everywhere seemed to be off limits," Samuels punned bitterly. Sometimes he sounded like a colored soldier, even to himself. Sometimes he thought he even felt like a colored soldier.

"It's not as bad as you make it sound," the adjutant said quietly but firmly. "It's just the more exclusive clubs especially over in South Bainbridge. You know how it is. We want to maintain good relations with the people of Australia. You can understand that. Every American soldier must be a good-will ambassador."

Samuels said, "Colonel Davenport, I imagine you have received complaints from the Australian people about the Negro soldier's behavior? I mean especially the Negro soldiers?" He smothered the heat in his voice but could not keep it from his face.

The colonel batted his eyes and pulled on his unlighted pipe. "Not particularly," he said reflectively, "and that is what we mean to anticipate, and to head off, if we possibly can. We'd like to let them go wherever the other soldiers go, but we cannot afford to take too many chances. Question of public relations pure and simple. Has nothing to do with prejudice."

Samuels stared at the colonel. He thought of Solly, Master Sergeant Solomon Saunders, Junior, who was in the outer office waiting for him. For the last couple of days they had been all over town together, trying to find at least one sympathetic ear in the higher echelon. The colonel leaned back in his swivel chair and sucked on his Sherlock Holmesian pipe. He had the complacency of a fat filthy pig bathing himself in the noonday sun.

Samuels said, "Most of the complaints I've heard, sir, have had to do with white American soldiers. Why do we take it out on the Negroes? They have the best record, and yet white Americans can go anywhere in town—no place off limits to them—"

"That isn't true," the colonel said shrewdly. "There's this place we just put off limits. This Southern Cross, or whatever you call it. It's off limits to everybody."

"The Southern Cross," Samuels said heatedly. "I've been there myself, sir. It's—I mean, there's no cause for it to be off limits. They welcome the soldiers. Especially the colored—"

The colonel said softly and comfortably, as if he were talking only for himself to hear and was enrapt in what he had to say, "Well—it isn't as if they didn't have any place to go. Like I say, plenty of places are still not *off limits* to them." And he started to name a few of the dives still open to Negro soldiers, but Samuels had had enough colonels for one day, this was his third, and he said, "Thank you, sir." And turned to leave.

The colonel said, "Captain!"

Samuels turned again and said, "Sir, I— His face reddening like it always did when he was angry or frustrated.

The colonel leaned forward in his chair. "You were not dismissed, Captain. You seemed to have forgotten yourself."

Samuels said, "I'm sorry, sir, but somebody'd better listen before it's too late. Two of my men were beaten up last night in that Jones Street MP station. The Negro soldiers are angry, and I can't say that I blame them. There's going to be an explos—"

"No, Captain, you'd better listen. The colored soldiers will follow orders just like every-damn-body else. We'll make no exceptions just because they're colored, and if and when they get out of line, they'll be dealt with accordingly. And we'll make no exceptions with officers in charge of colored troops. When we issue orders, do us the courtesy to believe they have been given careful consideration. We don't suck them out of our thumbs. And we mean for them to be obeyed without any pouting or grumbling about them. This is the Army. You're not a den mother in the Girl Scouts. Get that clear!"

Samuels said, "But, Colonel—" The perspiration pouring from him, the anger mounting in him.

The colonel snapped, "That's all, Captain."

"But, sir—" He'd like to yank the arrogant bastard across the desk.

"I said—that's all, goddammit! You're dismissed." The colonel threw a salute across the desk at the captain trembling in his rage. Samuels returned the colonel's salute and turned to leave the office.

The colonel's voice softened. "Captain, I admire an officer who goes to bat for his men, but there's such a thing as going too far, and that's your tendency, which I will overlook this time."

Samuels said, "Thank you, sir."

Outside he and Solly got into their jeep, and Solly said, "And how was the chief boss-cocky?" He laughed. "I have a strange feeling, Captain Bob, of everything having been done before on some other stage at some other time, and—and—another boss-cocky—"

Samuels said, "Let's go somewhere to some goddamn pub, Solly Saunders, and get pissy-ass drunk."

Solly said, "You be the one, Cap'n Robert."

They found a pub over in North Bainbridge and they sat in a corner booth and signaled one of the publicans and told him to put a bottle on their table and figure out how much they owed him when they were finished with it.

The little sawed-off mustached publican said, "Who's shouting?"

Samuels said, "I'm shouting. You just bring the bottle, and when we're finished tell me the damage, and I'll shout bloody murder."

The publican said, "Fair dinkum."

They sat there downing drink after drink after drink.

Samuels said, "I am so goddamn mad I could bite a tenpenny nail in two."

Solly said, "I used to eat those delicious things for breakfast with condensed milk. Put lead in your pencil."

Samuels was just about half boiled already and his tongue was getting thick and heavy. "You're a real tough bastard, Master Sergeant Solomon Saunders, with your seemingly soft and easy ways, and most of the time you're right, goddammit—"

Solly laughed at his G.W.B. "And you *are not* the Second Coming of Abraham Lincoln in John Brown's body. Believe me when I say so."

Samuels's face was blood-red now with alcohol and anger which he tried to hide.

"You've been right about the whole goddamn thing. I admit it. You and your undemocratic cracker Army fighting the war for democracy and your Double-V for Victory. Every bit of it—all down the line. I admit it—"

Solly stared at Samuels and thought of Fannie Mae and his heart began to leap about and his body grew warm all over and a thick sweet taste was in his mouth, and he remembered her with all of him, and why in the hell didn't she answer his cablegram?

"I'm going to miss you, you arrogant so-and-so. How am I going to do without you?"

"Much better—probably," Solly answered absently. He thought sarcastically of Celia. "Much much better, I should think." And I'm going to do much better with Miss Fannie Mae. Maybe she's already married. Maybe she's in love with the lucky bastard with the billion-dollar purple heart.

"Will you promise to do me a favor when you get back? Will you go to see my folks for me soon as you get back to the city?"

"If you say so, Captain Buddy Boy. After I make my trip to Georgia."

"I'm going to give you their address right now. I want you to see them. I've mentioned you in my letters so many times, they know you by heart already."

"If you say so, Captain Buddy Boy." Any day now he would hear from her telling him she would wait for him.

"I do say so, you tough-hearted bastard, and I want you to go to see my wife and promise to give my two little boys a hug apiece for their lonesome bastard of a daddy." His eyes were filling, his face warm and glowing and slowly changing from tan to red.

Solly said, "If you say so, Captain buddy boy." He was a fool for sending the cablegram. She loved the purple-hearted bastard away back home in Ebbensville, teaching school with one another.

The captain said, "I do say so, and stop saying, 'If you say so,' with that bloody superior drunken smile on your bloody face. You're my friend, aren't you? Closest friend I have in this God-forsaken—"

He looked up into Samuels's face, which was carrot-red and open-pored. "If you say so, Buddy Boy."

Samuels raised his voice in anger. "You think I don't know how you feel, goddammit? I'm a Jew. When I was ten and eleven and twelve years old, pretty little blond American blue-eyed Ango-Saxon Protestant boys and girls used to gang up on me and beat my skinny ass every day on the way from school

—beat me up for something somebody's supposed to have done to another poor Jew two thousand years ago." He stared at Solly glassy-eyed and Solly hoped he wouldn't cry. Solly was fresh out of handkerchiefs. "I know how you feel!" Samuels shouted. "I know how you feel goddammit!"

Solly said slowly and heatedly, "*You don't know shit!* You know how I feel? You're a white man. Don't get carried away with that Florida tan. Only those who've paid the dues can know what it is to members of the Club."

"I do know! I do know!"

"You're a lying ass and a tinkling symbol," Solly said. "And you'd better stop talking so loud or you *will* know *precisely* how it feels. They'll mistake you for a colored man and throw you out of this high-class dump. And I won't know you from Adam's house cat."

The bottle was two thirds empty and they were three sheets in the wind and their eyes were almost four fourths shut, and Samuels shook his head. "You're a tough bloody bastard."

Solly said, "And you're a bloody phony boss-cocky, and you can't take colored criticism. That's what you are. And you want all the prerogatives of being white and want me to love and trust you like you're colored. I'm your buddy as long as I say das right boss, and yassa boss. Well that's the coldest shit in town!" He paused to catch his breath and then said, "I know one thing. You'd better call out to the Farm to the outfit like you had some sense and see what's happening and let them know where we are and how to get a hold of us if they need to. This is Saturday night and—"

"See what I mean? Always on the frigging ball." Samuels's face was burning up, but he tried to hide his anger. "How'm going do withou' you? You call em Sarge Solly, and speak to Charge Quarters and tell him give him Celia's number—and see if you can speak to Quiet Sergeant Larker—tell him keep things under control—"

Solly stood up and waved his fist at Samuels and laughed at him sardonically. "You're a first-class frigging phony, you know that, don't you? And you know I know it, don't you? But you're always in there pitching. That's what I like about you."

Samuels said, "Don't you wave your fist in my face. You just shut your mouth and call the platoon."

Solly said, "And don't you raise your voice at me. You're a peckerwood and you talk too bloody loud and when the chips are down you always show your color and you're a phony. Look at you. A white man always turns cracker red when a black man criticizes him. You should see your face right now."

"You just take your finger out your ass and make that phone call," Samuels said.

Solly said, "Blow it out you 'A' bag!" And turned from the booth and went drunkenly and overcarefully toward the public telephone.

CHAPTER

4

We shouldn't go into town tonight, he told himself. He knew they should not go to town. Deep in him Jimmy knew it, even as he showered and shaved and got GI sharp, like all the rest of the men were doing.

"Let's stay at the Farm tonight," he said as he stood near his bed on the second floor of the temporary barracks. He was adjusting his black necktie and Worm was sitting on the side of his cot brushing his shoes to a gloss he could see his wide face in. "Let's take in the movie out here at the Farm."

Worm looked up. "Who in the hell wanna see *Up in Mabel's Room?* Let's go into town and tear our ass. I wanna see what Maggie's room looks like. And if she comes to the Cross tonight, I'm gon put the hard word on that chick. You better believe me when I say so."

Stab after stab of nervousness in Jimmy's stomach. Every man in the 25th platoon felt he had to go to town and particularly to the Southern Cross, since the man had put it off limits to them. Even though most of them were as uneasy as Jimmy they had to go. Jimmy understood they had to go. Because they were soldiers who had been in battle and had seen men die like flies and mosquitoes and cockroaches, had seen their best buddies give up the ghost before their eyes and in their arms. And they themselves had fought and bled and almost died. Every one of them were purple-hearted. Their lives were as cheap as the sand on the beaches where they died, so many times they died. They had to up the price. It was time. Yes, it was time.

"What makes the Cross so special?" Jimmy said belligerently. Next to Solly he was the highest-ranking non-com in the 25th platoon.

Worm stood up and stared at his gleaming shoes, then he looked at Jimmy. "Cause that's where Maggie comes every Saturday night, and that's where you promised to meet your chick."

"We could call them and meet them somewhere else."

"Where?"

"Anywhere—I mean—anywhere."

"Maggie ain't got no phone, and ain't nowhere else that jumps like the Southern Cross. Where? Where?"

There was nowhere like the Southern Cross for the 25th platoon.

Worm said, "The main reason we got to go is cause the man say we can't go. Goddammit, this ain't Mississippi."

"We'll be deliberately looking for trouble, and most probably we will find it."

Most of the men were ready now and restless, and some of them had come over to where Jimmy and Worm were arguing. Jimmy Quiet Man Larker had the quietest strength in the 25th, and he could make his weight felt unobtrusively when he felt he was in the right. Tonight he was uncertain.

Worm said, "We got five jeeps requisitioned and waiting for us. What's the matter, you got shit in your blood since the man gave you them four stripes and made you the company-goddamn-clerk? Solly ain't letting no grass grow under his feet. And he's a master-goddamn-sergeant."

Jimmy said quietly and fiercely, "That has nothing to do with anything, and you know good and well it doesn't. It just doesn't make any sense for us to go into town looking for trouble. It's like begging the man to whip our heads."

Worm said, "You going, or are you gon get left?"

Jimmy said, "You're no braver than anybody else. But no matter how much we're in the right, we cannot buck the Army of the United States of America."

Worm said, "We got our passes. You gon pull rank and tear them up?"

Jimmy heard somebody mumble, "Chickenshit!"

And somebody else, "That's the way it is with them educated ones."

Worm said, "Are you with us or against us?"

Jimmy said, "Go to hell," and reached for his cap.

They drove five jeeps into town together like a convoy, and they stopped briefly at a liquor store and their next stop was the Southern Cross.

When they reached the Cross, Scotty and Worm and Quiet Man sought out Dobbs and Miss Daphne Walker, the lady in charge. Quiet Man was the spokesman. They went into her tiny office. Jimmy told Dobbs and Miss Walker they should know that the Army had put the Cross off limits to Government Issue regardless of race, color, religion, or previous condition.

Dobbsy said quietly, "We read the orders."

Scotty and Jimmy and Worm looked at each other and then to Dobbs and then to prim Miss Walker and back to Dobbs again.

She nodded her head. "We know all about it, boys." She was middle-aged and soft-faced and her hair had been jet black once, but was sprinkled with salt and pepper now.

Jimmy said, "We just don't want to make any trouble for you." The other men were quiet.

Dobbs said almost in anger, "This is still our country, I hope. And this is our club, and we don't give a tuppence about their orders. It's entirely up to you, mytes. You're the ones who'll suffer the consequences, if there be any."

They looked to Miss Walker. There was a subtle firmness in her dark blue eyes, in the soft but settled contours of her middle-aged middle-class face. She said quietly, "We're glad to have you. We feel at home with you, and we hope you feel at home with us. All of you—"

Jimmy persisted. "There may be trouble from the MPs." He almost wished that they would turn them out.

Dobbs said proudly, "Only the P.M.s can give us trouble. We're not answerable to your bloody MPs. Excuse me, Daphne," he said to Miss Walker. He turned to Jimmy and Scotty again. "If they come here looking for a rough up, we'll give em a bloody go! Excuse my language, Daphne."

They were standing in the door to the office now, which

was little larger than a phone booth. The piano playing pretty music and the shuffling sound of dancing feet. Daphne Walker smiled with all her built-in poise and her quiet dignity. "This is your home when you come into town, and we hope you know we mean it from the bottom of our hearts. Nothing your Military Police or your headquarters can do or say will change our opinion about the colored Yankees." The smile no longer on her face. "You have lived among us and we know who you are, and no amount of propaganda can change the living truth."

Jimmy heard the stubborn anger in her voice. He said thanks, and she went back into her little office, and as they went across the floor between the dancers, Dobbsy said, "She's aces, mytes, and she's full quid all the way." And he said, "How's about a little alleviation?" And they went with him to the men's room and he took a bottle from his hip pocket, and each of them took a long hard swallow down to their bellies and were properly alleviated.

Dobbsy said, "Up the Republic!"

Scotty said, "Up your bloody kilts!"

Quiet Man laughed and coughed and almost strangled and loosened up a tuppence worth.

Worm said, "Man, you worry too damn much. Wear it like a loose damn garment."

They went back inside where the party was going full swing now, with the big fellow, Danny, goosing the piano with his big fat fingers, playing loud and singing louder an old Australian folk song, and everybody dancing and the 25th Amphibs all over the place having a natural ball, as were a few other colored Yanks from out at the Farm. Toward midnight the place was jammed, the biggest crowd the Southern Cross had ever known. Diggers and Negro Yankees and women women everywhere. Blondes, brunettes, redheads, and in-betweens. All sizes and descriptions. Healthy ones, streamlined ones, stacked-up and built like there were no wartime shortages. The dancing had to be close-quartered, there was no room for rug-cutting and jitterbugging or Lindy-hopping. And yet somehow Worm, as usual, and his girl friend, Maggie, had themselves a little private space off in a corner of the room and were bugging like tomorrow was the end of it. She was sandy-haired and freckled-faced and swivel-hipped and very Australian, but she moved like Savoy Ballroom was her natural habitat.

Jimmy danced with one quiet soft-faced girl most of the

night, and he was warm and comfortable with her. They'd known each other since his first visit to the Cross and he had been to her house, met her parents. They had been a few places together. Back home he had always been one of the shyest guys in the neighborhood. The great war had relaxed him. The girls had always thought him cute.

Debby looked up into his face, and he smiled for her, but his eyes did not cooperate. She asked him, "What's the matter?"

He said, "Nothing. I'm having myself a ball."

She said, "You're so moody tonight. You seem a million miles away."

His hand pressed against the small of her back and he held her closer as they danced, and he laughed and said, "You're just imagining things." The hornets buzzing in his stomach. He thought, we shouldn't have come here tonight. We're asking for it. He'd always been the kind of guy who would go ten blocks out of the way to avoid a fight, if a fight could be avoided. Maybe we have to settle these kind of things after the war is over. Maybe Solly and Worm are dead wrong with their Double-V for Victory. Maybe maybe maybe maybe— Where in the hell was Solly Saunders?

Debby said anxiously, "You're not happy tonight. Did I do something to make you angry?"

He laughed and shook his head at her.

Worm and Dobbs and Scotty made frequent trips to the men's room and they had almost up-ended a bottle of plonk and a fifth of brandy.

Danny was playing Yankee boogie-woogie with an Australian beat, and the floor was crammed with dancers dancing, and in the middle of the floor Jimmy could actually feel the floor give way time and again, straining beneath the weight of the dancers. Laughing, talking, dancing, the joint was literally leaping. And over in a corner the inevitable group of diggers harmonizing to themselves, competing with Danny's boogie-woogie, along with a couple of drunken Amphibs. Eternally.

Bless em all.
Bless em all.
Sergeants, Captains
And all . . .

Off key, on key, who gave a bloody damn, the party went on and on and on till two p.m., when two carloads of MPs arrived, and then the picnic started. Dobbsy met them at the door.

He told the MP sergeant, "There must be some mistake, mytes."

The MPs shoved and pushed their way into the place already jammed and made it to the other side of the room toward the piano, shoving and pushing and being shoved and pushed in return. Everything was noisily quiet excepting Danny, who kept right on "Waltzing Matilda" loud and strong.

The MP sergeant said, "Will you kindly stop playing for a couple of minutes, mate?"

Danny played louder and louder and louder.

The MP standing next to the sergeant waved his gun at Danny. "Will you knock it off, feller? Or do we have to—?"

Danny was sweating bullets and the skin pulled tight over the ridges of his wide gleaming forehead. He stopped playing "Waltzing Matilda" and moved softly and swiftly into "Danny Boy."

Oh Danny boy,
The pipe, the pipes are calling . . .

The perspiration poured from him now, his shirt soaked at the armpits. The women and diggers began to applaud, as did most of the colored Yankees.

The MP sergeant was a powerfully chested man of medium height with a face like a belligerent bulldog, and his voice was like Jimmy knew it wouldn't be—a squeaky clarinet in need of tuning.

"All right—all right—that's enough of that."

Dobbsy came up to the sergeant. "Your bloody oath," he said quietly. "We've had enough of you already, and we'd like for you to leave—*now!*"

From glen to glen
And round the mountain side . . .

The Yankee sergeant stared at the little sawed-off Australian sergeant with his bowlegs bowing beneath his khaki shorts. He looked around at a hundred other angry and excited faces and back to Dobbsy.

"We have nothing against you Aussie people," he squeaked. "It's just that—I mean you know how it is. We have nothing against your Southern Cross. You're perfectly free to run it anyway you see fit. After all, it's your country, and—"

Dobbsy said, "Your bloody oath!"

The MP sergeant turned from Dobbsy. "All right—all right, all you GIs line up against the other wall. You're off limits every last one of you. Line up now and take out your passes. We want your names and serial numbers." Every MP had drawn his gun now.

Some of the colored Government Issue had slipped out of the back door, out of side windows, out into the alley, and taken off for points unknown. Some of them gave the MPs a wide berth, but most of them crowded in on the MPs along with the diggers. The MPs found themselves surrounded and jammed too close together for anybody's comfort. Their faces dripped with perspiration. Hypersensitive fellows, Jimmy thought anxiously, as he stood at the inner edge of the crowd. And some of them scared and dangerous with their courageous guns and nightsticks. You can't buck the Army of the United States, he had known you couldn't buck them. And they shouldn't have come to the Cross so soon after the order was handed down. The Army had to back it up and you couldn't buck the Army. He should have torn up the passes. Debby stood behind him, holding one of his hands and squeezing it and relaxing and squeezing and relaxing to the rhythm of her breathing, which came quick and short like she had been running up a hill. He felt her breathing on his neck. He was hemmed in by the other soldiers and diggers and the women, and he couldn't have lined up against the wall, even if he had wanted to obey the sergeant's orders. He couldn't say, "Make room, fellows, I want to line up against the wall like the sergeant says we should." He wished he could say something to this sergeant. Tell him these men meant no harm. The only thing they meant was to be men as all men must mean to be and were always meant to be. Debby squeezed his hand and he thought about home and wished he were home even if he had to be a little boy again, with his mother squeezing his hand and telling him to be careful. And when he was three and four years old, and his mother went to work to help his father make ends meet, and she would leave him with the older children, he used to say, "Mommy say everbody be cafful for me." And the older kids would laugh at him. But he was here and now and he was a man and Debby was behind him and the men were behind him and he was a man, and he should take charge here and now, and he wished he could find the words to tell this sergeant what it was all about, but as he stared into the sergeant's face, he knew there were no such words available. It was as if they came from opposite sides of the world and spoke different languages. He could not bridge the gap.

Oh come you back
When summer's in the meh-eh-dow . . .

"All right—all right now—give us room. Back up! Back up!"

The MPs began to shove and push again and pummel with their nightsticks, but they got nowhere in a hurry.

"Upya!" a digger shouted.

"Bash it upya!"

"Let's try to have some kind of understanding," Jimmy tried. "We can—we didn't—"

An MP standing next to the sergeant said, "Will you shut your big mouth and do as you're told?"

They pushed and nudged and prodded with their guns, and the crowd began to push back and one of the MPs lost his footing, and the MP sergeant lost his nonchalance.

"All right goddammit!"

Scotty roared, "Why don't you Yankee peckerwoods drop dead already?"

Quiet Man said quietly, "Let's talk this thing over—"

But things had gotten out of hand. The panicky MPs reached blindly into the crowd near Scotty and grabbed two soldiers. One of them was Jimmy, the Quiet Man. They put the soldiers in front of them and moved roughly toward the door.

Debby screamed.

Worm had been in the rest room for one last nip and was on the outer edge in the back of the crowd, and he pushed and shoved but could not get to the front. Scotty grabbed the MP nearest him and the MP shoved his nightstick into Scotty's stomach with all his might and Scotty doubled over and went down.

When the MPs reached the door the sergeant turned and announced with trembling rage, "We gave you folks a fair chance. Tomorrow we'll close you up and padlock you." They went hurriedly out into the night.

"Bash it upya!"

"Bloody bawstards!"

The MPs gone, the Amphibs piled out of the Southern Cross, Scotty and Dobbsy with them, and into their jeeps and headed for the Jones Street station. Worm was driving the front jeep with tears streaming down his face. "He didn't want to come into town," Worm said. He could hardly see where he was driving. "He knew what would happen—he knew what would happen. I talked him into it, and he didn't want to come, and they'll beat the hell outa him, and it's all my fault and he didn't want to come."

Dobbs sat next to Worm in the jeep. Dobbsy said, "It ain't your bloody fault, myte."

Somebody in the back of the jeep said, "Ain't no use of us going over there empty-handed. Them mother lovers armed to the teeth and they don't be jiving."

They went two more blocks down a dark and empty street.

"Them bastards got shooting shit and they don't mind using it."

Worm said, "So what, mother-huncher?" The tears had blurred his vision. He could barely see the road ahead.

"So let's go get us some shit—that's what. You sure can't get Quiet Man out with no much-oblige or if-you-please."

Worm put his foot on the brakes and pulled to the curb and signaled to the others, who followed suit. They jumped out of their jeeps and ran toward the front one.

"What's happening?"

"Nothing," Worm said. "We're just going to haul ass back to the Farm and get ourselves something to persuade these people with."

"Now you're talking like you had some sense," Private First-Class Billings said.

They discussed it for the briefest moment.

The Pfc said, "All right, let's stop shooting the shit and get on the ball."

They got back into their jeeps and went back in the other direction across the sleepy-headed town, leaving Dobbsy near the Cross.

When they got back to the Farm they aroused the entire platoon as well as a few in Engineers and in Ordnance and in Quartermaster, as quietly they ran through the darkness of before-day-in-the-morning, waking other sleeping Negro Yankees, and they got ammunition from Supply and quietly and desperately they worked, mounting 50-caliber machine guns on top of Ducks and trucks, and they got rifles and carbines, as they got ready for the combat zone.

Solly and Samuels had been at Celia's ever since dinner. They bought food and took it to Celia's and she cooked it for them while they drank cup after cup of coffee to sober up, and then they ate dinner and got drunk all over again. And they argued on the verge of fighting about everything under the sun and the moon and the stars, as she listened, and now it was late and time for them to go, and Samuels had passed out and was sleeping on the couch on the far side of the living room. And Solly and Celia were sitting in the kitchen drinking coffee and nibbling cold cuts.

And she said for the umteenth time, "So you're really going?"

He said, "Yes, I'm going home to my little family." His eyes were heavy very heavy.

She said bitterly, "And you're not going to send for me, you don't give a tuppence what happens to me, you're just going—"

He said quietly, "You'll be in good Yankee hands—at least for the time being." He nodded toward the living room.

She started laughing. "How can you be so cavalier about it? How can you give me to another man? How can you be so bloody inconsiderate of *me,* who loves you more than anybody ever loved you? You don't care a tuppence for me."

"I do care," he stated simply. "I care a million quids for you."

She wiped her eyes and blew her nose, and she laughed. "It's all very very cozy. You blithely leave me with your dear comrade. You leave one white friend in the hands of the other, and you go home to your insulated colored world and forget it ever happened."

She got up and came to him and put her arms around his neck and stood close to him, her legs between his knees. "Don't you want me tonight—at least?"

He looked up into her face, and he just sat there saying nothing.

She said, "Why don't you take him back to the Farm and come back and—and come back and talk to me?"

He said, "It's a long ways to the Farm and back." And was sorry that he'd said it in the manner he had said it.

She reached down and kissed his face. "How can you be so cruel?" She said, "Love me tonight. Take him home and come back to me."

He said, "I can't see how you can love me, I'm so goddamn cruel and heartless."

She said, "You're the sweetest man in the world, you're the most sensitive man in the world—to other people—and you're beautiful and you're tough and at the same time tenderhearted, and you're intelligent and you're good to all humanity, and you're only mean and cruel to me! And you're a bloody brute!" He felt her tears hot and salty on his cheeks and he tasted her sweet salty tears. He did not need her tears tonight.

He said, "There is something I must tell you—something about back home in the States."

"I don't want to know. I don't want to know! I already know! I already feel it in my heart!"

"I must tell—I must tell you. There's another girl back in the States. I've always loved her. There's—" She kissed the words back in his mouth.

"I know it and I don't want to know it. I can tell you. She's —she's beautiful, she's wonderful, and she's colored and there are no problems like with us!"

He said, "There is a problem—there is a problem. She's engaged to marry another man."

She wiped her eyes. "Then how? What?"

His anguished voice became a whisper. The one thing he did not want to do was to cause pain for anybody, especially one for whom he cared, like Celia.

"She became engaged before she knew I had lost my wife. I sent her a wire the other day about my present situation, but I haven't heard from her, and for all I know she might prefer the other fellow to such as me. She might be already married."

"Yes! Of course!" she said excitedly. But then she shook her head. "No—no she wouldn't. If she ever was in love with you, she wouldn't. And you know bloody well she wouldn't."

He said, "If it were not for her, Celia, I think maybe the other things wouldn't have a ghost of a chance to keep you and me apart. They just would not matter. I mean—"

She said, "Why didn't you tell me? How could—?"

He said, "I tried to—so help me—" And the telephone rang throughout the house and she did not move, and it rang again and again and again, and he started to get up and she said, "Let it ring. It's probably the wrong number. Nobody calls me this time of night."

It rang three or four more times and it stopped.

She said, "See, what did I tell you?"

And then it began to ring again and again and again, and he said, "I'd better get it."

She followed him as he went in the living room to the phone which was near where Samuels lay. The captain was trying to straighten up and was reaching for it. Solly picked up the receiver.

"Hello, Saunders here."

The other voice said, "Sarge?"

He said, "Yes—" His heart began to leap about.

The voice said, "This the Charge-of-Quarters, Corporal Jenkins." Solly felt the excitement in the corporal's voice. The corporal told him about the fracas at the Southern Cross and the men had come back to the Farm and had mounted 50-calibers on trucks and Ducks along with other colored soldiers and had taken off for town. They had made out phony papers for them going on before-day-in-the morning maneuvers. That's how they got out of the gate. Solly looked at his watch. "Great God almighty!" It was four-fifteen already!

"Why in the hell didn't you call me before they got started?"

The voice from the other end was suddenly weak. "I misplaced the phone number, Sergeant, I swear fore God!"

"All right," Solly said. "Now, where are they going, and which way're they going?"

"They're going to get the Quiet Man at the Jones Street MP station." The C.Q. added, "There won't be any shooting unless the MPs set it off."

When Solly hung up the captain was already sober.

Solly said, "Get yourself together. We got places to go." He said to Celia, "Get him some black coffee quick!"

Samuels said, "What—what happened?"

And he told them what Jenkins had told him, and she went for coffee, and he asked the captain, "Are you ready?"

"Ready for what?"

Solly tried to keep his voice from trembling. "I'm a master sergeant. That's supposed to make me a leader, and a leader is supposed to be with his men when they move against the enemy. I don't know what you're going to do, but I'm going to join them, just as fast as I can get to them." He reached for his field cap. She came back with two cups of coffee.

Samuels said, "Hold it a second, Sergeant. Let's not run off half-cocked."

Solly said, "What is there to talk about?"

"Why in the hell did Sergeant Larker let them do it? They listen to him. He could've stopped them."

Solly stared at Samuels and laughed bitterly. "Yeah—the only thing, I forgot to tell you, it's the Quiet Man they arrested." Solly remembered vividly the first time he saw Larker. "He always gets arrested." The Quiet Man with the big brown eyes.

Solly started for the door. He wished it had been someone else who'd got arrested. Why in the hell was Jimmy always the one to get out of line?

"I'm pulling rank," Samuels said. "I'm your superior officer and I order you to sit down at least for a minute and let's see what is to be done. At least until we drink the coffee."

Celia said, "Listen to him, Solly! Please listen to him!"

Solly sat back down and stared from one of them to the other. The captain drinking hot black steaming coffee.

"I'm sitting for a minute, Captain Samuels, sir, but I'll tell you right now, there's no rank in the Articles of War or Army Regulations, including General-the-Almighty-Buford Jack, can keep me from joining the 25th Amphib. *This* is *my* war, not that Murder Incorporated up on the islands. *This* is *my* beachhead, you better believe me!" He stood up again.

Samuels said, "There won't be any shooting. Surely you don't think—"

The phone rang again and Solly reached for it, and it was Corporal Jenkins again. "I forgot to tell you, Sarge, there's a cablegram came for you."

He thought he had imagined it at first, and then he felt a sudden giddiness, and felt a hard pain in his buttocks. Fear clogged up his throat and he thought he'd lost his voice, but he said, "Open it up and read it to me!"

"All right, Sarge. Just a minute." Then he read: "Will wait for you forever Fannie Mae Ebbensville Georgia U.S.A."

Solly said, "Thank you, Corporal," after he had put the phone back in its place. His head swam and he thought he might break down and cry for the joy his heart felt. He saw Fannie Mae's face before him now and heard her voice say,

"Will wait for you forever." He thought of Ebbensville, the house, the room, the fireplace. He forgot Celia and Samuels and Quiet Man and the Jones Street MP Station and all the rest of it. He was going home and Fannie Mae was waiting for him. Great God Almighty! How could any soldier be so lucky? He got up and walked around the room. Fannie, Junior, Mama, Solly—Fannie, Junior, Mama, Solly! Maybe he dreamed that last phone call.

Samuels brought him back to reality. "The phone call, Saunders—any new developments?"

Solly stared at Samuels as if he didn't recognize him at first. Finally he said, "No new developments." No new developments.

Samuels said shakily, "I'll go and you stay here with Celia. I'll head them off and talk them into going back to the Farm."

Fine! Fine—fine, Solly thought. His mind was a beachhead of contradictions. Now that Fannie would wait for him forever, he did not want to keep her waiting one minute longer than he had to. His head was like a carousel. He felt guilty about his buddies, but Fannie Mae—dear Fannie Mae—he didn't need to be a hero—he needed to be with Fannie Mae—and yet he heard himself say slowly, vaguely, "I'm going. I can't speak for you. I'm going and I'm going to join them, not to head them off. We're going to bring Jimmy away from Jones Street." He was Fannie Mae's man and he had to go.

Celia said, "No, Solly, no!"

Samuels said, "And all your plans will go up in smoke. They won't let you go home till the war is over, and even then they'll give you a dishonorable discharge. They'll send you up north to the front. They'll—"

Yes, he thought—he hadn't let himself think of the consequences until the cablegram from Fannie Mae. He didn't really give a damn about their dishonorable discharge, he told himself. But if he went outside this door and got in the man's jeep, this night of early-before-day-in-the-morning, he might never see his son in life nor Fannie Mae again nor Mama. Fannie Mae in Ebbensville, waiting for him forever. Because if he took this step, it would be the point of no return for him. After whatever happened happened, he could forget about his separation. He would probably be sent up north again island-hopping from beachhead to bloody beachhead till his number came up and his time ran out, and he felt his time was running out, as the perspiration ran from his head down and across his wide forehead into his eyebrows into his lashes into his dark and angry eyes and drained from his armpits now and down his thighs his legs, into his heavy Army shoes. He wanted to go home, goddammit he wanted to go home to Fannie Mae and Junior and Mama and forget it ever happened. He wanted to go home—go home—go home! The cablegram changed everything. And if he had not thought earlier that evening to suggest to Samuels to let the platoon know where they were, he would not have known about anything, and he would not have been involved, and he wanted to go home, but he couldn't go home, because he was who he was whoever the hell he was, he had to go join his buddies and be part of what they were a part of and die with them if it came to that. With them moving now at this moment to meet the enemy here and now in the profoundest battle for democracy that any Yankee Army fought on all the far-flung battlefronts of World War II. The Battle for the Quiet Man! There wouldn't be any shooting, the corporal had said, unless the MPs set it off. He heard Fannie Mae now, that last evening they spent together. "Never sacrifice your manhood. Never sacrifice your manhood."

Celia saw it in his eyes, he had to go, in the movement of his head and shoulders, he had to go, and she thought her heart would burst wide open for the love and fear she had for this slim nervous beautiful tough-and-tender black man who had to go. Nobody else existed in her right-here-now-world excepting him, not even she herself existed. She went to the floor and put her arms around his legs. The sobs came from the deepest and the softest places in her heart. She forgot Samuels ever existed.

"Don't go! Don't go! Don't go, darling! Don't go—don't go—don't go!" She saw him killed in the early misty sun-kissed Sunday morning on the streets of her beloved Bainbridge, she saw him lying still and calm in peaceful death, his dearest-face-in-all-the-world calm and still in dreadful crazy death. And he must not go, she wouldn't let him, she would not turn his legs loose, he would have to drag her with him if he went because she would not could not let him go. "No! No! No! My darling!"

He stared down at this sobbing woman whom seven or eight months ago he never knew existed, and he looked from her to Samuels, and he didn't want to go into battle again, Lord knows he didn't, he was sick of war and fighting, and he reached deep deep down inside of him in the foggy subterranean of his consciousness, he reached for anger against both of them. Didn't they know he wanted to go home to his family? He said, "Turn my leg loose. What the hell do you want me to do? Run and hide underneath your bed?" Fannie Mae had called him and he had to go to battle for his dignity and manhood.

"Don't be a hero, Solly darling! You don't have to be a hero!"

He thought of his mother's "Don't be a hero," and almost laughed. He reached down and pulled her up into his arms. He said gently roughtly, "I'm no hero, Celia. Listen to me. I'm scared, you hear me? I'm really scared but that has nothing to do with anything. I'm scared for me. I'm scared for Jimmy and all the rest. I don't want to be a hero. I don't need to be a hero. I wish I didn't know about it, but I do know, and I've got to go." He looked from the sobbing woman to the reddened tan-faced captain. "Goddammit, Robert Samuels, will you tell her why I have to go?" Solly said, "I want to go home, I'm no hero, I want to go home to my child and my family and my and my and my and my—Why in the hell don't you talk to this—this hysterical woman?"

Samuels's voice was low and husky. "He has to go, Celia."

She said, "No-no-no-no!"

Solly said in a strange gruff voice, "Celia," and breathing deep short gaspy breaths. "Celia, all my life, everything that ever happened to me has brought me to this very moment, every place I ever was, everything and everybody, every street I ever walked."

She sank to the couch as if he had slugged her. He leaned and kissed her gently on her cheek and said good-by. He turned to Samuels. "Now tell her why you also have to go, or be the phoniest bastard on God's green earth. Tell her those guys out there are the noblest comrades you'll ever know, and—and—and tell her that the Quiet Man is the finest of human beings—and—"

Samuels said in an almost whisper, "All right, Sergeant." And came and kissed her on the cheek.

And the two men left the house together.

Out on the porch Solly turned to Samuels. "I *have* to go, you know that, don't you? I have no choice. It's my own life I'm defending. That's my brother at the MP station. But you don't have to go. I mean, you can stay here with Celia and say you didn't know anything about it. Don't let me push you into—"

"I know what I can do, Solly Saunders. Don't be so goddamn high and mighty."

They stared at each other for a moment and Samuels was the first to turn and start walking down the steps toward the jeep. And Solly felt like crying. She was so close to him this moment. He held her in his arms almost, his Fannie Mae, but he might never ever hold her. Damn dignity and manhood, Fannie Mae, and damn you and your piety!

CHAPTER

5

The town was in a heavy sleep, and out in the Bay, and further, way out over the Coral Sea, the sun was stirring fitfully, as daybreak made its first beachhead against the nighttime in its final throes of dying. It was neither still-night nor yet-morning. The world a dark and gray and orange-pinkish thing, and the Ducks and trucks made awesome music humming down the King's Highway, as they headed swiftly toward the city which was softly drugged in slumber. The tall slim stalks of sugar cane stood delicately handsome and dancing in the fore-day-in-the-morning breeze. Beyond the cane fields were the mountains clad warmly in their jungle garments.

Seven Ducks and three trucks all with machine guns mounted, and fifty-some odd men standing beneath their combat helmets, armed with rifles and carbines. The men were wide awake and sleepyish and falsely brave, and angry men, nervous, scared, and trigger-happy . . .

At the Farm one of the guards at the gate was running to the phone in a little office the size of a tool shed. He called the base headquarters. After a couple of impatient minutes he heard a sleepy voice on the other end. He told the muffled voice about the big convoy of colored soldiers.

The voice said, "What? What are you talking about?"

And then the voice no longer sleepy: "What! Are you crazy? Niggers on maneuvers?"

The timid guard repeated his story and when the charge-of-quarters hung up the phone, he ran through the slowly lifting darkness to find the officer of the day who was asleep, but should have been awake, and the officer of the day ran to wake the base adjutant who was in bed with the wife of the base commander who was in town in bed with a young sweet boy in the Signal Corps.

"You'll find him there every Saturday night," the adjutant said indignantly. "He's a fucking degenerate of the lowest type."

A few minutes later the adjutant and the O.D. and a disagreeable master sergeant were in a jeep tearing down the highway in pursuit of the colored convoy. The sleepy-headed master sergeant thinking to himself, he should have gone into town the night before. He should be lying up with Mary Wilson in his arms with his legs wrapped around her hairy legs. He should be snoring in her face.

The convoy with its lead truck driven by Scotty had come to a two-way fork in the road and had taken the wrong one and had gone a few miles before it realized its mistake and had made a wide sweeping U-turn and was heading back for the big intersection.

The lead truck got back to the intersection five seconds after the adjutant's jeep. The adjutant, a handsome West-Pointed blondish dog-of-a-spitting-image of a slightly middle-aging All-American halfback, crew-cut and widow-peaked, Southern-born and bred and fed and thirty-fivish, straddled the middle of the road with his jeep and stood up in it and waved his field cap to halt the convoy. Scotty slammed on his brakes and swerved his Duck, barely missing the adjutant's jeep, and you could hear brakes squawking and squealing and crying and screeching loud enough to awake the sleeping fish way out in the Coral Sea.

Scotty shouted at the colonel, "What's the matter, mother-huncher? You tired of living? Oh, excuse me, Captain." He was always handing out demotions.

"Watch your language, soldier," the colonel said with dignity and Southern accent. "Who's in charge here?"

"What's it to you?"

The drivers in the other Ducks and trucks started blowing their horns.

"Let's get the show on the road, goddammit!"

Sergeant Henry Williams, a proper-talking soft-voiced soldier from Boston, was in the lead Duck. He was the ranking non-com. "You might very well say that I'm in charge, Colonel, sir, if you insist on being technical."

"What the hell do y'all think y'all up to, Sergeant?"

"We're not up to anything, sir. You might say we're going on a mission."

The horns began to sound off impatiently up and down the convoy.

"Let's get it on!"

"You're holding up the frigging war!"

"I order you Sergeant, to take these men back to the base."

"Come on! Let's go get the Quiet Man!"

"He's my mama-hunching boy!"

Some disrespectful soldier shouted from the second Duck, "I'd ruther kick a bloody MP's ass than go home on rotation!" And up and down the line of Ducks and trucks they yelled.

"Hopjack, here we come!"

"Scat! Scat! Scat!"

"Come on! Let's go if we going, goddammit!"

"What's the mama-jabbing holdup?"

The soldiers were whooping it up and the horns were blowing, and streaks of lightning flashed heavenly sparks out at the edge of the world where night and day were locked in bitter conflict. And the colonel was trying to shout above the noise and the sergeant said in a properly respectful tone, "Colonel, sir, even if I were disposed to follow your orders, I could not get these men to turn back now. They've been turned back too many times."

All three in the jeep were standing now, the colonel, captain, and the sleepy sergeant, and the colonel was waving his arms and shouting.

He said, "Now, men, I order you *now* to go immediately back to the base without further ado!" He was cracker-red with rage.

Scotty raced his motor and the Ducks behind him followed suit as likewise did the trucks behind the Ducks. Scotty said, "Move out of our way now, Colonel Peckerwood, please, sir. We got business to attend to."

The colonel pulled his gun, as did the captain, and they pointed them at Scotty in the lead Duck, and suddenly the shouting and honking died away, and a quiet came to the highway.

The colonel shouted, "You *will* order your men to return to the base, Sergeant, immediately, and you, Corporal-driver-whatever-your-name, you will proceed at once to lead this convoy back to Worthington Farms."

Corporal General Grant stood crouched behind the machine gun in the lead Duck. He turned it on its tripod and trained it on the helpless jeep. The sweat poured from the trenches in his angry wrinkled forehead. And how was the adjutant to know that the old man wasn't bluffing? How was he to even imagine that he was about to be blown unceremoniously into that other world where he would never have a care again?

It was so quiet you could hear the daybreak breaking, and Scotty leaped into the silence. "Colonel Peckerwood, whatever-your-name-is, sir—"

"My name is Colonel William Bradford the Third, Corporal," the adjutant said with dignity.

Scotty got out of the driver's seat and pulled off his helmet and stood at attention and saluted the colonel. The colonel had to return the salute.

"All right then, sir, Major Bad-fork, I'm going to follow your instructions. After all's said and done, every last man in this convoy is loyal-abiding Americans, and if all the other soldiers felt the way we feel about it, this war would end tomorrow."

The colonel was deeply moved by the simple honesty and childish patriotism in Scotty's words and in his guileless face. He put his gun back in its holster without knowing. "All right, Corporal, I—the name is Colonel Bradford. I appre—"

Scotty shouted, "Captain Bad-cock, sir, where you lead us we will follow. All you got to do is show us the way to go home. I'm from down home jus like you are." He saluted the colonel and the colonel stared at him and returned the salute.

Grant said angrily, "What the hell you doing, mawn?"

"Very well, Corporal. We shan't forget the part you're playing." The colonel sat down in his jeep and ordered his master sergeant to turn around and head back to the Farm. And Scotty pompously signaled the other drivers in the convoy to turn their motors over and get ready to ride.

The jeep took off and headed swiftly down the King's Highway back to the base, and the convoy followed suit, but when Scotty reached the three-way intersection, he said, "You close your eyes you lose sight on the world." And he roared his motor and made a sweeping U-turn, and this time he headed down the other highway which would take them to the Elizabeth Bridge and across it into South Bainbridge. Duck after Duck after Duck after truck came roaring into the intersection and made their sweeping turns, some on three wheels, and the men on the Ducks and trucks were yelling and whooping, and the dust was flying.

The jeep had gone almost a hundred feet before the colonel could bring himself to realize he had been taken by such a simple colored man as Scotty. The jeep turned around and came back to the intersection as the Ducks and trucks roared into their sweeping turns. The colonel was standing in his jeep, waving his gun and shouting for them to stop and eating dust, and the men as they swept into the turn were yelling shouting

"Blow it out your barracks bag!"
"Scat! Scat! Scat! Scat!"

"I'd ruther kick an MP in the ass than go home on rotation!"

It did not take the bright young colonel very long to realize that he looked foolish standing there airing his lungs needlessly and eating dust. He didn't like the taste of dust. It tasted dusty. He sat down again and swore aloud and the jeep turned around again and sped toward the Farm. It went a few hundred yards and stopped at an all-night diner, and the colonel leaped out of the jeep and ran inside to the telephone and called back to the Farm, and he called the base commander at his week-end rendezvous in town and he called division headquarters at Camp Bainbridge on the other side of town. He called this place and the other, and he called the Jones Street station.

The corporal at the Jones Street station said sleepily, "So what?"

"This is Colonel Bradford speaking to you, Corporal."

The corporal still not fully awake. "So some spooks went on maneuvers—so what? The fresh air's good this time of morning. You wouldn't begrudge them—"

The colonel said sharply, "Wake up, Corporal. This is Colonel William Bradford, base adjutant at Worthington Farms."

The corporal said, "Yes, sir! Yes, sir! Excuse me, sir!"

The colonel said, "Is Captain Westover there?"

The corporal said, "No, sir. Almost everybody's out making their final Saturday roundup. It's routine, sir."

The colonel snapped, "Let me speak to who's in charge."

As Scotty and his convoy reached the northern tip of Elizabeth Bridge, a truck of white soldiers approached it from another boulevard. The Amphibs got there first. They stopped and waited as the two-and-a-half-ton truck kept coming. Every Duck and truck in the convoy had its mounted guns trained on the truck. General Grant was itching. When the truck entered the last block before the bridge, Scotty sounded off a split second before the General would have.

"Halt, goddammit! Who goes there?" His great voice roared into the silence of the sleeping city.

And the truck kept coming, and Grant said to Scotty, "Don't worry about nothing, mawn. Just let em come a little bit closer, and I'll blow every last one of em some brand-new pinky holes."

Scotty roared louder than ever, "I said, 'Halt!' Who goes there, mother-fuckers?"

He heard a familiar voice shout, "It's me, goddammit! It's me—it's Dobbsy!" And the truck slowed down and stopped about fifty feet away. And Dobbsy jumped out and ran toward the lead Duck.

Scotty started laughing. "I thought so—goddammit—I thought so!" He tried to stop laughing. He stopped for a moment. "Hold your fire, men! These our comrades!" And he laughed and laughed and laughed.

When the bowlegged digger reached the lead Duck, Scotty told him, "Goddamn, buddy, you better learn how to talk quicker than that. We almost busted a cap in your ass." He laughed some more. "Goddammit, what you doing up this time of morning?"

Dobbs said, "The same thing you doing. We figured you bloody well might need a little support at the Jones Street station."

Scotty said, "Well good-on-ya, mytes. The more the more merrier."

Dobbs said, "What's the strategy and tactics?"

Scotty said to Sergeant Williams, "You tell him, Sarge."

The sergeant explained the plan was to go across the bridge and go three more blocks and then spread out and move toward the station from all sides and angles, and when they reached the station, a delegation would go inside and demand Jimmy's release, and that would be that. Of course, if the MPs refused to release him, they would take him by the sheer obvious force of their numbers. There would be no gunfire. Positively, there would be no shooting—unless it was absolutely necessary, in self-defense, as a very last resort.

Dobbs went back to his truck and the motors turned over and they started nervously across the bridge. Day had broken completely now out over the Coral Sea, and it was a soft and peaceful Sunday morning like Scotty remembered Sunday mornings back home where he came from. From Mississippi to Chicago to Harlem to Bainbridge. He had always been on the go ever since he could remember and Sunday mornings were Sunday mornings. The sky was a quiet ocean, deep and bluish and wide and far away and upside down. He'd seen Sunday skies before so many times. He was as nervous as a setting hen. His finest moment in the Army.

Worm was in the second Duck wondering at what lay ahead of them on the other side of the bridge and thinking of home and wondering would he ever get back to that other world which looked so pretty to him this morning. He was homesick, with the funny taste for home in his mouth and a home smell in his nostrils. It was Sunday morning and he could see his mother and his father. His mother, large in size and slow in movement but fast in her determination, getting ready for church. His father only went on Easter Sunday to cry for Jesus, and Worm went only when he could not get out of going. He could hear the sweet church music and he saw Harlem thronged with people in their Sunday-go-to-meetings. He saw the street-corner meetings. Think black! Buy black! Live black! The Apollo Theater. He laughed. He forgot the ugly side of it; he could only see the beauty. His Harlem, the city deep inside within a city. He forgot completely where he was and what he was doing. They were halfway across the bridge when he came to himself, and he thought about Solly. Where in the hell was Solly Saunders? Somehow he wished his friend were there in the Duck beside him, near him, or at least was somewhere in the convoy, and he would feel better about the whole damn thing. Solly Saunders, where are you in this sleepy river city ten thousand miles away from home? He and Solly had been through a gang of hells together and if he were going now to his death, he would like for Solly to at least know about it, and know the reasons why he had to go. His mouth was cold with the taste of fear. There won't be any shooting at all. We'll just go to the Jones Street MP station and demand that they release Quiet Man and tell them straight up and down what we will do if they don't release him, and as Williams said, we'll have them hopelessly outnumbered, and they'll realize they're outnumbered, and they'll release him, and that's all there'll be to it. They were across the bridge now. They would get Jimmy and go back to camp and face the music afterward. Court-martial and all the rest of it. Solly ought to be with them, goddammit! They went three blocks up the empty Sunday street and then they split up, half of them going to the right and half to the left, and the Ducks and trucks crept cautiously and almost noiselessly along the empty streets as if they were afraid of waking up the city, as they converged on the Jones Street station.

When they reached the front of the two-storied brick building fifteen or twenty minutes later, all the guns were trained upon the entrance, except the two trucks at the opposite ends of the convoy—which kept their guns trained up the wide and empty street. The delegation, each with rifle, leaped quietly from the Ducks and trucks and moved nervously and swiftly toward the entrance to the station. There were eight men in the delegation, including Worm and Baby-Face Banks and Dobbs and Sergeant Williams, who was more or less the spokesman. Scotty was in charge of the men outside.

The first cop they saw as they entered was a corporal seated dozing at his desk. Worm walked over to him quietly and prodded him with his rifle and he awakened instantly.

He said, "What the hell—?"

But as he spoke, four Amphibs had already moved swiftly to the back room where they found three other MPs shooting dice on a blanket in a corner of the room.

"Ada from Decatur!" a little sawed-off MP pleaded.

Baby-Face Banks said, "I got your Ada from Decatur."

The three cops almost jumped out of their skins.

They brought the three frightened crapshooters into the

front room to keep company with the sleepyhead corporal, who was wide awake by now.

Williams explained it to them briefly. "We're looking for a soldier by the name of Staff Sergeant James Larker. You brought him here tonight from the Southern Cross, and we intend to take him with us. That's about it in a nutshell."

The corporal said, "You—you can't do that. You have no papers. I mean, where's your order for release?"

Worm and Banks meanwhile had taken the MPs' guns and put them in a corner.

Sergeant Williams said quietly, "We have no papers, but we *will* do it, because we have guns and we have the drop on you and we have trucks outside with mounted guns and we have men outside to shoot them."

Worm said, "We ain't no hand to start no row, but we're hell when the row gets started."

The corporal flipped the pages of his record book. His hands were trembling.

Worm said nervously, "Take your fingers outcha ass and get on the ball before I blow your few brains out." He put his gun up against the corporal's head.

The corporal was sweating. He said, "We ain't got no record of your man in here."

Baby-Face said, "The redhead one there is one of the ones that was at the Cross tonight. I'll never forget that ugly face."

At that moment four more MPs came through the door, ushered in by five Amphibs. One of the MPs was the sergeant who had been at the Cross earlier and had taken Quiet Boy away. They had turned into the block from another street, and before they knew what was happening, they'd been surrounded by Amphibs.

Williams said, "I remember the sergeant. He knows where the Quiet Man is. Sergeant James Larker, that is."

The Jones Street station was hot and stuffy and getting hotter and stuffier, time weighed heavily on the Bookworm, and he knew the MPs were stalling for time, it being definitely on their side. The more time was wasted, the less chance the Amphibs had of getting Quiet Man out of the Jones Street MP station without shooting. He wanted to get Jimmy right away *now* and get the hell out of there while the getting was almost good.

He shoved his rifle viciously into the sergeant's belly. "Talk, mother-fucker, or I'll blow you a new one. Take me to Jimmy!"

Sweat poured from the sergeant's face. He led Worm and Williams out of the room and started up the stairway where the cells were.

Worm said, "You got the keys with you?"

The sergeant turned and went back into the room and went to the desk and opened a drawer and took a ring of keys, and they went out of the room and started up the stairs again. The sergeant moved too slowly for Corporal Joseph Taylor.

Worm prodded him with his rifle. "Get the lead outcha ass!" he shouted softly. "Or else I'm gon put more in your ass!"

It felt like a million years to Worm before they finally got to Jimmy's cell and unlocked the door. And now he had his arms around Quiet Man's shoulders. Worm's eyes filled up. "I'm sorry, Jimmy!"

"Let's get outa this sonofabitch," Baby-Face reminded them.

Worm said, "Watch your language, baby boy."

The other soldier who was arrested along with Jimmy was in the cell with him, and they all went down the stairs together. They took the MP guns and rifles with them, but did not take the telephones, and now the Amphibs were outside in the daylight again, moving toward the Ducks and Worm thought aloud, "It's too damn easy—too goddamn easy—" And for the first time that morning he was really scared all through his body and deep in his bowels and the perspiration drained from him and he could taste his fear and smell it. He began to run as did the rest of them toward the vehicles. One of the men running with a handful of MP rifles stumbled and fell and dropped the rifles, breaking the awful peace of the quiet morning. Worm ran back to the clumsy one and helped him pick the rifles up, and they headed toward the Ducks again.

"Let's get rolling!" Worm shouted softly.

A couple of the trucks had trouble starting and they wasted five or ten more minutes. But now they were in the Ducks and trucks, and Jimmy in the Duck with Worm—Worm's Duck with its Double-V insignia proudly stenciled in big letters on both sides and the back. The convoy was led by Worm this time, and his Double-V. And above the Double-V a larger "Fannie Mae" was stenciled. He started the motor and just before he took off he took a good full look at Jimmy. Jimmy's large soft eyes were pained and sunken, his face was drawn, at the same time his eyes and face were burning with the warmest fiercest feeling he ever felt in all his life.

Worm winked his eye. "How you doing, Quiet Man?"

Jimmy's voice was brimming with emotion. "Just fine," he said. "My right arm may be out of commission, but there's no use to complain. I got the best damn comrades in the world. I wouldn't even mind dying this pretty Sunday morning."

After the first block Worm picked up speed and the others followed suit, as the sky splashed tender sunlight onto the empty Sunday street, and the trees heavy with leaves and blossoms blooming cast soft shaky shadows and reached over the street and clasped each other forming a tunnel with more colors than the rainbow. They were moving at about fifty miles per hour, but Worm was conscious of everything. His senses were sharp as a double-edged razor blade. He wanted to go-go-go-go-go! If he could reach the bridge and get across it and get to the King's Highway he would have it made, he figured. He didn't worry about the court-martial which they would surely face. If they could just make it back to camp. The damn Duck seemed to be marking time instead of hauling ass. Uneasiness moved through his shoulders. Fear choked him in his throat and rumbled in his stomach. Yet there was also the good warm feeling of a great job done, the color of the trees and the sunlight sifting through the trees. He wished for Solly and remembered Fannie Mae and felt like shouting, "Double-V for Victory!" He looked sideways at the Quiet Man and stuck his fat foot further in the gas, and now they were going sixty miles an hour up the empty Sunday street. He saw the big bridge up ahead. They had it made! They had it made! And that was when their luck ran out.

Ziiiiiiiinnnnnnnngg—bop!

Ziiiiiiinnnnnngg—bop!

Tat-tat-tat-tat-tat-tat!

Ziiiiinnnnnnngg—bop!

From all sides came machine-gun music beating out a now familiar rhythm against the side of the Duck and into the Duck and ricocheting and peppering tiny holes into the windshield.

All of the men in the first Duck hit the floor excepting Worm, who put his head down and swerved into a sweeping U-turn and headed back down the wide and sun-splashed street, and Baby-Face, who crouched low behind his machine gun and played his own sweet deadly music. Other Ducks went into frantic U-turns and followed the Bookworn back up the street.

Tat-tat-tat-tat-tat-tat-tat—

Ziiiiinng—bop! Ziiiinnngg—bop!

Some of the trucks had trouble turning around and one of them got halfway around and stalled as the frightened driver panicked, clogging up the nervous traffic. Worm meanwhile moved two and a half blocks back up Jones Street on the double on the triple with death-talk talking behind his back. That was when he spied other trucks coming at them from three or four blocks up the street. And he could see the palefaces underneath the helmets and he saw rifles and machine guns mounted and they were Yankee trucks all right, but he thought they were not friendly faces. He put his head down even lower and gunned his motor and put his foot all the way into the gas and the Duck shot forward like a wild beast in the jungle. The men had come up off the floor all excepting one of them and they held their rifles at the ready. Whem Worm reached the next corner he turned into a narrow side street on two wheels, maybe one, tires screaming, brakes screeching, hell breaking loose all around them, he heard shooting everywhere. He slammed on his brakes and climbed quickly out of the driver's seat and told Baby-Face to take over as he leaped behind the gun.

"Let the mama-hunchers come!"

He noticed one man still lying face down on the floor of the Duck. He said, "Straighten up and fly right, buddy. We got important work to do." But the Amphib did not move, and a great fear grabbed Worm by the throat and filled his face and beat angrily where his heart lived. He got slowly from behind the gun and it couldn't be, it wouldn't be! Lord have mercy, Jesus Christ! He went to the soldier and knelt down and he turned the soldier over, but he knew before he turned him over, before he saw the hot hole in his forehead in between his heavy eyebrows. There was the same quiet smile on Jimmy's face, full of pride and love and dignity and deeply felt emotions. He had not had time to change his face to the proper fear of Death.

Worm could hear him now and evermore, 'No use complaining. I got the best damn comrades in the world." Worm smiled back at Jimmy's smiling face as the tears streamed down his own wide face. He turned him over gently, as anger almost ran him crazy. Guilt and anger. He went back behind his gun and yelled: "Let the mama-hunchers come!" Crying like a baby boy.

They were coming from all over Bainbridge and without Worm's special invitation. Coming particularly from the two camps on the opposite edges of the town. Most of them had already arrived. Thanks first of all to Colonel William Bradford the Third, the adjutant of Worthington Farms. He turned it on with phone calls, but after a while it got out of hand and he couldn't stop the patriots. Everybody wanted to wave the flag and crash the party and join the Sunday picnic. Up and down the downtown streets of South Bainbridge, the thunder and the lightning broke out all over everywhere. Worm could hear it all around him.

"Jimmy's dead!" he screamed to Baby-Face. "Quiet Man is dead!" he shouted now more quietly. And wiped the tears from his face and wiped his running nostrils.

They had almost reached the end of the block-long dead-end street, and Banks cussed and gunned the motor and when he reached the dead end he slammed on the brakes and backed up quickly and turned around, just as a truck of soldiers armed and helmeted entered the other end of the block—Eager-faced wild-eyed pale-faced Southern-accented men. Sweaty men. Pissy-scared and crazy-glad.

"There the niggers is!"

Handsome clean-cut all-American Jack Armstrongs.

"Git em! Git em!"

Some of the Amphibs on the Duck leaped with their rifles down to the street and ducked swiftly into the doorways, and their rifles started making speeches to the men with Southern accents from the little towns in Dixie. Some of them were chopped down and never made it to the doorways. Banks stepped on the gas and hurtled toward the Southern Yankees. Worm went crazy behind the machine gun, but went crazy with a vengeance. The first revenge he took was the baby-faced machine gunner and then he raked the truck from stem to stern as the bullets screamed around him. Quiet Man is dead—Quiet Man is really dead!

A few blocks away Scotty was hauling ass in his Duck up a long wide street, with his buddy, Corporal General Grant, to the rear of him seated behind the machine gun and making it talk sassy to the peckerwoods, as two Army trucks with machine guns mounted came after them down the Sunday-morning sun-washed street. General Grant combed the first truck from left to right and up and down, and it went crashing into the plate-glass window of a fancy clothing shop for men, Southern accents screaming and heavy plate glass flying and like a bloody reaper cutting, and blood was spilling everywhere. And Grant was laughing, harshly laughing.

"Get yourself some brand-new kilts free of charge, you peckerwood bawstards!" He laughed like a raging maniac. "I'm gon finish the job old Tojo started—this pretty Easter Sunday morning!" One blond-haired boyish-looking soldier climbed bleeding out of the ruins of the truck and ran around in circles and Grant took careful aim at him and put him forever out of his misery.

Scotty with his back to Grant thought, the bastard thinks it's Easter Sunday. He done flipped his fucking wig. Crazy as a Bowery bedbug and fifty times as blood-damn-thirsty. Scotty's lionlike shoulders hunched over the wheel as the the Duck leaped forward up the street. He was one of the best and craziest drivers in the outfit as well as the best and craziest cook. Two crazy bastards together, Scotty thought. Together two crazy mama-jabbing bastards—back to back—me and General-the-Goddamn-Grant.

Tat-tat-tat-tat-tat-tat-tat—

"This is Grant, you bawstards! General Grant, you white mudder-fuckers!"

Scotty laughed deep deep inside of him as he heard his General raving, but he really laughed to keep from crying. He heard the gunfire all around him and especially behind him and playing "The One O'Clock Jump" up against his Duck like Chick Webb used to play his traps at the Howard Theater in Washington, der Capital, and at the Apollo on One Hundred Twenty-fifth Street and "Drop me off uptown in Harlem." Great God Almighty, he'd love to be in Harlem now. Any minute he knew he would feel a little piece of deadly pointed metal come piercing in between his shoulder blades or in the back of his big head, he could almost feel it now, and he knew it had to come, and it would be all over with him, he was sure of this, and yet he felt no special pain or fear. He was fighting as he saw it, for that Freedom Democratic shit at long damn last and that Double-V for Victory! "You can't die but one damn time—you can't die but one damn time," he kept repeating to himself. It was funny even to himself, but he didn't feel any particular hate toward the paddies this morning. Just kill as many of them as we can, cause they're the goddamn enemy. They got eyes like me, got nose like me, got mouth and brains like me and ears like me and legs like me and they piss like me and shit like me, but they ain't no mama-jabbing good for me. Like Solly say, I don't hate them, I just hate their mother-hunching ways. And I don't mind dying if I'm dying kicking asses for my freedom.

He thought about Quiet Man and wondered had they beat him bad. Quiet was one of the nicest cats in all the crazy goddamn world . . .

Ping! Ping! Ping! Ping!

The little capsules of death beat it out against his windshield, and Jimmy was alive, that's one damn thing, but he hoped they hadn't beaten him bad. Cops were bastards everywhere the whole world over. Cops were bastards. He'd seen them in the Bowery and in Chicago and L.A. and in all the Skid Rows everywhere. He'd seen them up in Harlem, seen them on their handsome horses, seen them whip heads till their arms got weary. Seen them get their kicks kicking asses that could not defend themselves.

Jimmy's my man—he's my buddy! Jimmy and Worm and Solly—he would die for any one of them—and even batty General Grant. Jimmy'll be all right—goddamn—goddamn—he'll be all right.

Ping! Ping! Ping! Ping!

He thought, ain't this a bitch! Here I am worried about the Quiet Man and I'm getting ready to bust hell wide open in a few damn minutes. Getting ready just as fast as I can to attend my own damn funeral and worrying about the Quiet Man. Ain't this a mother-fer-ya? He started to laugh and he couldn't stop laughing and the tears rolled down his cheeks, he laughed and laughed, and the Duck began to swerve from one side of the street to the other as if it were trying to dodge the screaming bullets.

And General Grant in the rear of the Duck with his machine gun back-talking to Captain Charlie thought out loud, "That goddamn Scotty gone stark raving mad!"

Sergeant Henry Williams had gotten in another Duck instead of Scotty's when they left the jail, and now his Duck was being chased up a side street by two trucks with machine guns mounted and spitting fire and mayhem. Suddenly up ahead of them three White trucks turned into the street and came toward them from the opposite direction. And they were in the middle, with death hurled at them front and back. The Duck came to a halt and choked down and the trucks closed in. Within seconds every living on the Duck was dead excepting the sergeant and his driver.

"Niggers! Nigger! Niggers! Niggers!"

Hank Williams crouched on the floor of the Duck with death crisscrossing over his head and ricocheting. He decided to save his and his driver's life. He put a white handkerchief on the tip of his bayoneted rifle and held it up and waved it from side to side as the machine-gun fire continued to play its deadly music.

Finally and suddenly the music came to a stop.

Hank and his driver leaped quickly down from the Duck. Hank continued to wave his white handkerchief. They quite sensibly put their lives in the hands of the white men's tender mercy.

Hank shouted, "There's no sense in our killing each other like this. After all, we're all Americans."

"You're a nigger, nigger!" the gunner in the first truck shouted. And he opened fire on them and they fell dying in the sunlight near the shadow of the Duck. The last thought Sergeant Williams had on earth was what a goddamn fool he was to believe white folks knew what mercy meant. He wished he had died in the Duck with his buddies.

A sergeant in the first truck said to the gunner, "That wasn't necessary, you bloodthirsty sonofabitch."

The gunner laughed uneasily. "Ain't none of this goddamn shit necessary."

CHAPTER 6

By the time Solly and Samuels reached the north side of the bridge, the business in South Bainbridge sounded like a million typewriters going at the same time in all the office buildings in the world, typing out death notices to gold-starred patriotic mothers.

Tatatatatatatatatatatatatatatatatatat

ZINGZINGZINGZINGZINGZINGZINGZINGZING

bopbopbopbopbopbop!

Your sons were killed in action—

We commend your loving son for courageous service beyond the call of duty—

Tattattattattattattattattat

Zingzingzingzing

Bopbopbopbop!

A hundred thousand calculators adding up the casualties.

They all fell in the line of duty.

Tat-tat-tat-tat—tat-tat-tat—

Believe me, mothers—fathers—brothers—sisters—

Halfway across the bridge they stopped the jeep and they stood up in it and they could see the war in all its fury.

Amphibs racing desperately up and down the streets of a canyon deep somewhere in Hell, trying to blast their way out of a trap that was slowly closing in on them. Inch by inch the White armies moved in on the Amphibs and their Allies, foot by foot, street by street, drawing the noose tighter and tighter. Solly stood there helpless and crying. He knew it was true as surely as he knew his name, and yet he could not believe what his bleary eyes beheld. He couldn't wouldn't believe this was happening to the United States of America. His country and his mother's country and his father's country and his mother's mother's country and the country of his father's father. And what the hell could he do about it? He felt himself hardening all inside himself as if he were turning into cement, as the anger rose inside of him. He wiped his eyes and cried no more. And what could he do to help his buddies? Crying did no goddamn good. If they didn't surrender every one of them would be slaughtered.

Samuels stood beside him, shaking his head with the tears streaming down his own face as he watched the men being cut down like bamboo with machete knives. "I can't believe it! I just can't believe it!"

Solly said, "There's your goddamn democratic antifascist Army!"

"I can't believe it."

"You believe it all right. You'd better believe it. The question is—what the hell you're going to do about it?"

Samuels's voice was trembling. "Maybe if—maybe if I—went over there alone, maybe I could talk to some of the—I mean, whoever is in charge of the white men."

"No goddamn body's in charge. It's just a good old-fashioned lynching picnic. Red-blooded Americans getting their nuts off having a little clean innocent sport. It's open season."

"Maybe I can talk to some of them and get them to hold off at least long enough for me to get through to the fellows and get them to surrender."

Solly saw one of the Ducks go crashing crazily into the side of a building and bullets screaming and soldiers flying and winning purple hearts and some of them gold stars for their mothers.

He sat down in his jeep. He had to do something. He put the jeep in reverse and backed up swiftly in the direction he had come till he was off the bridge again. Australian people, dressed for church, some of them half dressed and sleepy-faced, all of them startled and unbelieving, had gathered at the northern end of the bridge, staring across the river at the sound and fury. Shocked and speechless.

When Solly and Samuels got back to the other side, people came toward the jeep and surrounded it.

"What's happening over there, mytes?"

"Bloody Yankees fighting Yankees!"

"The whole damn world is off its rocker!"

"Did the Japanese make a surprise attack?"

Solly asked somebody, "Where can I get to a telephone?"

A tall blondish man jumped into the jeep.

They took off down the street.

Samuels asked Solly, "What're you going to do?"

Solly said, "What do you think I'm going to do? I'm going to get some reinforcements here and I'm going in with them."

The Aussie said, "Turn right here, myte."

And they turned into a short street and they went two blocks and made another turn into an empty street and stopped halfway up the block in front of a little two-by-four café that semed to be just getting up for the morning.

Samuels said, "You're going to call Negro troops. You're going to turn it into a racial war."

Solly looked at Samuels and laughed bitterly as he jumped out of the jeep and ran into the café. He saw the telephone up against the wall and went toward it, and as he picked the receiver up, he heard the little radio on the counter.

Two people were seated at the counter drinking coffee and the owner was on the other side of the counter, leaning on it and staring at the radio, his sleepy eyes transfixed, as if it were the first he had ever gazed upon.

> . . . *People of Bainbridge were blasted out of their Sunday-morning complacency by the war which has finally come to our town. Down in the heart of the commercial district in South Bainbridge a full-scale battle is raging between Americans, blacks and whites. It is reported that a few of our own diggers are engaged on the side of the blacks.* . . .

Solly stared across the café at the radio as he phoned the first sergeant of some Combat Engineers out at the Farm, whom he was friendly with. Somebody finally answered at the other end, and when he asked for Sergeant Bailey, the other voice said, "Are you kidding? Every living is gone into town to help the 25th Amphibs!" He paused and then said: "I'm leaving in the next few minutes with the last of the Mohicans!"

Solly felt chill after chill race up his spine and spread out to his shoulders. He tried to get another number but stood there listening to the ring and nobody answered. The radio said:

> *Australian citizens are shocked at the display of racial animosity. . . . Other troops from both of the major camps are pouring into town and converging on the city toward the center of the tension. Unthinkable and shocking . . .*

One of the coffee drinkers said, "The bloody arrogant Yankee bawstards! Bad as the bloody Nazis!"

Samuels said, "Well?"

Solly said, "Everybody's getting into the act." He walked past Samuels out of the café and Samuels and the Aussie followed him. They got into the jeep and Samuels said, "Now what?"

Solly blew up. "Why in the hell do you keep asking me? You're a goddamn brilliant ninety-day wonder! You got the captain shit on your collar!" He started the jeep and headed back to the bridge. He stopped before he reached the corner, and he could hear the typewriters pounding out their death messages across the way and the calculators calculating and bolt after bolt of lightning flashing across the peaceful Sunday sky. The lanky Australian sat silently in the back of the jeep.

Solly turned to Samuels. "Before we go any further together, we have to decide who we are and where we are and why we are."

Samuels's tan face was red now and leaking nervous perspiration. "I don't get what you mean."

Solly said, "You know damn well what I mean. I know who I am—I'm a black man and I'm going to get to my buddies even if I have to wade through a goddamn river of white folks' blood."

They did not notice the Australian as he slipped quietly out of the back seat and ran toward the corner and went around it in the direction of the bridge.

Samuels argued earnestly, "This is your last chance to reconsider and turn back. One more soldier in South Bainbridge will not turn the tide one way or the other for our fellows. But you do have a chance to go home and forget about all this shit. You have a son whom you've never seen—you have a responsibility to him—you can go home and *not* forget this shit. You can do something about it."

Solly sat there listening to the thunder of his heart and the rumbling in his guts and collisions in his head, and all along he had tried not to think of his son, not to think of Fannie Mae, not to think of going home. He had had the picture of his buddies before him, especially the big-eyed Quiet Man who stepped out of line in the bus station in Ebbensville how many centuries ago? He wanted badly to go home, he wanted to hold his son and hear his son and see his son and know him know him know him. He wanted Fannie Mae to love her and to live with her. Samuels was right. Of course he was right. He didn't need to go across the bridge. He could say that he had a week-end pass and he spent the night at an Australian friend's house and he was drunk and he overslept, and by the time he got himself together, the war in Bainbridge was over and done with. Nobody would know the difference but Samuels and Celia and the charge-of-quarters and nobody else nobody else. Like Samuels said, he had a son, he had a responsibility to his son, greater than any loyalty he might feel he owed to Jimmy and the other poor bastards on the other side of the river, and he would be worth more to them, able to do more for them, and be missed more by his darling son than his buddies across the way. His son was motherless already. He didn't need to make him fatherless. He didn't need to prove himself to the men. He didn't need to be heroic. He had his purple heart already. Fannie Mae would never know.

Samuels saw Solly wavering and he moved in swiftly. "Furthermore, you're more valuable to everybody if you go back to the States and work like hell to build a better world. You owe it to those men over there. That's what Larker believes in. After all, you're educated."

Yeah, he thought, yeah. After all, I'm educated, and I owe it to the men not to die but to live and fight another day—for them—for Jimmy—for my son—and after all, I'm educated. He could go home next week to his son and Fannie Mae and his mother, and together with them he would build a life—writer —lawyer—prominence—leader—fighter— He could really be somebody. Fannie Mae and Solly Saunders. He had a responsibility to his son and his buddies and he hated himself. Use your head instead of your emotions, thank you, Millie. She was absolutely right!

Solly made a U-turn and headed back the other way, sweat draining from every pore in his body. He hated the very breath he took. But he was sensible.

Samuels said, "Where in the hell are you going now?"

"You're my captain, and I'm taking your advice. I'm going back to Celia's and back to the good old U.S.A. and live to fight another day. And there's my responsibility to my son to be considered, and—" His voice choked off.

They were driving now up a long wide thoroughfare bordered on each side by eucalyptus trees and hibiscus and jacaranda and poinciana and bougainvillaea. The street was drenched with sunlight and fragrance from the shrubbery. It was a day you could forget the war. And he would forget the war. They went up a long winding street, up and around and up and around. He didn't even hear the war any more. A tender breeze was blowing a wild sweet scent of blooms and blossoms and he breathed deeply and he opened his mouth and drank it all in. He never wanted to hear of war again. Nor feel the war, nor smell the war.

He stared sideways at Samuels, hating him for being white and for showing him a way to save his skin and for contraposing his son to his embattled buddies.

Solly finally got his voice again. "Which way're you going to jump?" he asked contemptuously. "Have you figured out what color you are this pretty Sabbath morning? And what are your responsibilities?" He could not make himself hate Samuels, he was just hot with him because he was here and now and he was one of the ones who would always know that Solly Saunders chickened out and deserted his buddies or whatever else you called it, a rose is a rose is a rose is a rose, and a chicken ain't nothing but a goddamn bird. He stopped the jeep and laughed harshly into Samuels's face.

Samuels said nervously, "I have conflicting responsibilities. I have a responsibility to my men, but I also have a responsibility to the Army of the United States."

Solly laughed again. "Your first and only responsibility you ever had is to you, Robert Samuels, you you you, nobody but you. To thine own self be true—William Shakespeare." And even as he said it and heard himself say it and watched Samuels's face flushing red with guilt and anger, he knew he had also found his own answer. If he were true to himself he could not be false to son or comrades or Fannie Mae or to people or to country, and if he chickened out or deserted now, he would know it and always and forever know it, and the charge-of-quarters didn't matter, nor did it really matter that Celia or Samuels would know, or even Jimmy, always and forever, as long as Solly Saunders knew it and he would never ever be able to forget. He turned the jeep about again and stepped on the gas and sped back in the opposite direction, down hills and around hills till he reached the King's Highway and headed toward the bridge. He could no longer smell the smell of jacarandas. Death invaded all of his senses. Maybe Death was driving him, luring him. He didn't say a word. He just drove madly till he reached the thoroughfare before the bridge.

His heart leaped about in a wild dance without rhythm, his body screaming perspiration. Now that he had made his decision he was sad and scared-to-death and happy. The front section of a convoy of gun-mounted trucks and Ducks with Negro soldiers was already halfway across the great bridge, the rear of the convoy extending back to two blocks this side of the bridge. The progress of the convoy had been halted by a steady vicious barrage coming from the southern tip at the foot of the bridge which was shaped like a rainbow. The front section of the convoy was at the tiptop middle of the rainbow and was naked and exposed. They were like targets on a rifle range. Across the river the sky was red, the war was raging.

Solly spied a Duck in a part of the convoy just off the bridge and started to aim his jeep at it, but then he stopped again and turned to Samuels. "All right, Cap'n, you'd better make up your mind in hurry what color you are, before my comrades mistake you for a bloody peckerwood."

Samuels said, "What do you mean?"

Solly said, "You know damn well what I mean. Are you with us or against us? You got one last clear chance to tuck your tail between your legs and show your damn true colors like you did in Ebbensville. You don't owe me a goddamn thing, and I'm going to leave the jeep right here. If this is not your fight, you can take it and go back home and forget it and hold hands with Celia and play the part of Nero."

Samuels said, "You are a bloody bastard!" His tan face was the color of an over-ripened carrot.

Solly said, "Don't do me any favors. Just tell me what your color is."

Samuels almost lost his voice. "I'm going with you, goddammit!"

Solly laughed.

He parked the jeep and he and Samuels ran across the wide thoroughfare toward a Duck about seventy-five yards from the foot of the bridge, with machine guns trained on him and Samuels all of the way. It seemed they would never get across to the Duck. The street seemed to widen every millionth of a second. They finally reached the Duck and grabbed the side and started to climb up, when the brown-faced sourpussed gunner said, "Hold it, both of you mother-fuckers!" And when Solly's head came up over the side of the Duck the gun was pointed down his throat.

He shouted feebly, "You hold it, goddammit! We're from the 25th Amphibs!"

The gunner said, "Talk like that then, cause I don't know you from Adam's house cat. You might be passing for colored this morning."

Solly fell over a wall of sandbags and into the Duck as did Samuels, and Solly said to the gunner and the other men in the Duck, with their rifles and their submachine guns ever at-the-ready, pointing to Samuels, "He's a light-complected colored man, and he's a member of the 25th." He was tired and breathing deeply. His heart was thumping in his forehead.

The gunner said distrustfully, "I didn't know y'all had no colored officers."

Solly said breathlessly, "He was passing for white just so he could be an officer in a colored platoon. He's a Race man from his heart."

Samuels face got redder and redder.

The gunner glowered suspiciously.

One of the other men in the Duck said dryly, "That's some real deep sophisticated shit. You have to be educated to dig that jive."

The Duck blew up with nervous laughter. And Solly felt at home—at home! He leaned back on a wall of heavy sandbags, which the men had stacked up two to three feet high around the inside of the Duck, and he closed his eyes and he was scared to death and happy. A corporal shoved rifles into his and Samuels's hands. as he leaned further and further back on the sandbags into the sandbags which seemed to suddenly soften, becoming plush, and he sank back back comfortably back, and he heard the thunder and lightning of the war all around him and he stared at Samuels seated across from him and all of Solly's weariness and nervousness and all of the sadness he felt for his country which he desperately loved in spite of not being able to love wholeheartedly—he loved his country angrily—made him glad Bob Samuels had chosen sides and Bob was his friend and Bob was his country, the best part of it, the healthiest portion, and he and Bob and Jimmy and Worm and Scotty and Lanky were the best part, and Bob was not a phony bastard, he wanted to believe, all white bastards were not bastards, and he remembered the two white soldiers at the Ebbensville bus station and the white soldier at the Red Cross Recreation Center, and Celia and Dobbsy and Steve and the dogtag fellows of the Anti-Aircraft, who were blown to hell up north in the Philippines. They were not bastardly bastards, he wanted to believe, and there were white folks back in the States who were not really bastard bastards, they meant well but did so poorly, he wanted desperately to believe, goddammit, it was his country as much as it was anybody else's, and he loved it angrily and critically, and he hated the phony patriots, the goddamn goose-stepping flag-waving patriots, who really loved the status quo more than they loved the country and its promises unfulfilled. Love love unrequited love loveless love—everything ganging up on him now. Love and sadness and gladness and sorrow and exhaustion and sleep and fear, as he sank further and further into the plushy softness of the hard sandbags and he went wearily to sleep, and he saw his mother saw his baby, and held his baby in his arms and laughed and cried, and he saw Fannie Mae who loved him loved him, believed in him and waited for him, and he attended his own wedding and the bride was Fannie Mae, and Samuels was at the wedding in his soldier's uniform, as were Worm and Jimmy and Scotty and Lanky Lincoln, and Solly said, "You're dead, old buddy," and was very very sad, deep deep sad, and the Duck moved forward jerkily and he woke up. And where was he? And how long had he been asleep?

He jumped up and looked around him as the Duck slowed down and stopped again. Solly said, "Where the hell are we?"

The gunner said, "You ain't missed nothing. We just a few feet closer to the bridge."

His head was clearing, his eyes discovered Samuels, and it came to him Who he was and Where he was and Why and When. His ears picked up the growing fury of the war.

He said, "Why don't we go across the bridge?"

The gunner said, "What the hell you think we been trying to do since I don't know when? The mother-fuckers at the other end don't like the idea."

Solly said, "Why don't we try another bridge?"

The gunner said, "Why don't you go back to sleep—?" He stopped and said, "Why *don't* we try another bridge?"

Solly said, "They have four other bridges across this river."

The gunner said, "Come with me." And they jumped down off the Duck and started running toward the bridge, where death was flying thick and fast. There seemed to be an endless number of gun-mounted White Army trucks at the other end of the bridge and they were spread out and scattered and aiming all of their fire up at the center of the rainbow. And now a couple of the trucks from the White Army had entered upon the other end of the bridge and were moving slowly toward them belching fire and dealing death. The world was one great deafening roar. Solly and the gunner ran head down toward the fifth truck from the front with the dot game kicking up dust around them, and finally they reached it and climbed aboard. It was the craziest time in the world for formalities with bullets beating against the trucks like a hailstorm.

"This is Master Sergeant Roger Jones," the gunner said. The master sergeant had black skin and cold-gray eyes and reminded Solly vaguely of Sergeant Greer.

Solly said, "I'm Solly Saunders of the 25th Amphibious, and my buddies are dying over there and I think we ought to try another bridge."

The other master sergeant stared at Solly long and hard. "Which other bridge?"

"How about the King George Bridge? It isn't very far from here."

Rogers said, "Get back to your Duck and let's get started."

They ran back to the Duck telling the drivers on their way about the change in tactics, and now the trucks already on the bridge were backing off again, some of them with dead and dying. The Army from the other side did not pursue them. Apparently thinking the Black Army had given up and chickened out, they backed off at the other end.

Before the Black Army started for the King George Bridge, they took the few dead and dying off the trucks and left a couple of the healthy soldiers with them to help a corps of shocked Australian volunteers take care of the poor bastards until the ambulances arrived.

And now they were approaching the King George Bridge, and Solly and Samuels were in the Duck which was second in line in the convoy now, and the sun was burning up the world almost like it used to do up on the torrid South Seas island. They moved onto the bridge behind the truck which led the convoy. Every man was crouching now with the perspiration on his forehead like tiny bullets standing at attention. Every man peering nervously over a parapet of sandbags, as over the river the war went on and on and on, and you could hear the steady beat of rifle fire and machine guns and submachine guns, and the whole thing like a great big human slaughter-house somewhere deep deep down in Hell.

They picked up speed after they reached the top of the incline at the middle of the bridge and it was downhill all the way. It was the first time Solly saw the gunner smile even though it was a nervous smile. His name was Johnson. He glanced at Solly and said, "Your brains should be in the White House, Sergeant. Goddamn if we hadda had you with us from the start, we'da been over there a long time ago. We'd most probably been dead and in Heaven already, or either busting Hell wide open." The men started to laugh and loosen up and Solly laughed and Samuels laughed and even the gunner slyly laughed. They were about three-quarters across King George and heading for paydirt and quietly laughing amongst themselves, when machine-gun bullets started bouncing off the trucks and Ducks like a wild tornado had worked itself up suddenly and was blowing fifty calibers onto nothing but the convoy. The first truck stopped and hesitated. The driver of the Duck nervously adjusted his helmet and put his head down and gunned his motor and pulled out from behind the truck and leaped the ridge which separated them from the other-way traffic lane and rammed against the railing at the edge of the bridge and almost went into the river, but he straightened up and took off like a Lockheed Lightning down the wrong lane in the face of screaming bullets toward the Fourth of July celebration. Every gun on the Duck was talking.

Solly looked behind at the rest of the convoy, and other Ducks and trucks were leaping the barrier over into the other lane and now the crazy convoy was tearing along two abreast.

Tat-tat-tat-tat-tat-tat-tat-tat

Ziiiiinnnng—bop! Ziiiinnnng—bop!

The stenos working overtime in the stenographic pool.

Pow-pow-pow-pow-pow-pow-pow!

Ping-ping-ping-ping-ping-ping-ping!

A ruthless hurricane of bullets batted Solly's Duck as it charged crazily forward like a bull enraged and bleeding. Solly crouched behind the sandbags behind a submachine gun from which one of the men had a couple of minutes before gained his purple heart and his everlasting peace. Solly had taken it quietly from the dead man. Now he was squeezing it lovingly and belching death at a group of trucks at the end of the bridge. As they came closer he concentrated on one particular big bastard-of-a-target who himself was pumping fire from a 50-caliber machine gun. Death bounced lively all around Solly. Ping! Ping! Ping! Ping! above his head and close to his ears, as merrily they rolled along. He wondered, where is Worm and Scotty? Are they living? Are they dead? What have the bastards done to Jimmy? I should have been with them in the first place. And love me, Fannie Mae! Love me! Love me! Love me, please, this Sunday morning—love me—love me! Understand me! And please don't marry another till you know that I am dead. Wait for me forever. Son—son—darling son! Mama, take care of my son!

He thought his heart would leap out of his chest, and his stomach thought his mouth had swallowed razor blades, and double-edged, but his teeth dug into his bottom lip and he tasted his own blood, and he put everything out of the ears and eyes of his mind and stared long and hard and deliberately at a particular big man whom he didn't know from Adam, the world was crazy, but there he was in a particular truck behind a very very particular gun, and then and then and finally Solly began to squeeze his own gun and talk his talk and listen to his own death music—tat-tat-tat-tat-tat-tat—the gun kicking his shoulder viciously and pow! pow! pow! pow! and tat-tat-tat—tat-tat-tat-tat, till he saw the big man go over backwards, his heels up over his head, and he turned his aim on another poor ignorant miserable anonymous bastard crouched behind another gun. A bastard whom he didn't know, had never known, would never know, and couldn't hate specifically, but kill and kill and kill and kill—and that's what makes the world go round and puts lead in your pencil.

The Ducks and trucks flew across the bridge like blind bats straight into the gaping jaws of Hell. He didn't know how they reached the end of the bridge (a couple of trucks crashed through the railing and plunged into the placid waters of the river), he didn't know how anybody stayed alive, but Great God Almighty, somehow they did, as the trucks poured off the foot of the bridge and through a blazing gap of Hell and brimstone on a peaceful Sunday morning which had already become afternoon racing madly toward the evening.

The truck he was in blasted its way up Mary Street, shooting at everything white that moved an eyelash and being shot at in return. Johnson crouched behind the sandbags behind his submachine gun with half-smile half-scowl on his face, like a man who had a job to do and was going about his business without any qualms or doubts or fears, as he policed one side of the street and left the other side to Solly. There were snipers all over the place, and he had the sharpest ears and eyes and nostrils in the world. They were three blocks up the street, which had suddenly become empty of trucks and gunfire and other people, when suddenly Johnson started raking a doorway on his side of the street before he came to it, before he could possibly see anybody in the doorway, but then came the screams and two men ran crazily out of hiding into the line of fire and they would never run or walk or scream again. Johnson saw to that. He grunted and mumbled, "Paddy bastards—"

On his side Solly knelt behind his machine gun, hoping he wouldn't have to use it again, even though he had already used it coming across the bridge and afterwards, and even as the bullets beat around his head and shoulders and up against the Duck, even as the men around him on the street and in his Duck fell in the battle. Even though he knew this was *his war*, his cause was just, he had no stomach for the killing. His face was filled, his insides were erupting, exploding like the street around him. He was pure-and-simple chickenshit. His mother had not prepared him for killing or for being killed. He vomited too easily.

Suddenly they plunged into another street where nothing was happening and he breathed more freely, sucking into his nostrils and his lungs the taste of gunsmoke and the smell of sunlight, and he breathed deeply and more easily. He was still alive and they had run out of the war. He didn't have very long to breathe though.

Up ahead of them a big truck turned the corner and came toward them. As they came closer he hoped and prayed they were colored comrades, and if not, please let them be Australians, but he knew in his heart they were red-blooded all Americans, and he aimed his machine gun at the cab of the truck, at the pale and frightened face which he saw clearly now, and they had begun to shoot at his Duck with rifle fire, and yet he hesitated, damn his chickenhearted soul, he hesitated, hoping that Johnson would open fire on them before he had a chance to. But when Johnson didn't, he thought even Johnson had had a stomachful, and he took his eyes off the other truck for a minute, and looked toward Johnson and his heart fell as he saw the great damn Johnson had fallen. He screamed, "Samuels! Bob! Samuels! What the hell did you come along for? Just for the ride?" His great White Buddy moved toward Johnson's gun, and Solly yelled, "Pick it up and shoot it!" But the Duck was already being peppered now and there was no time to let Bob do it. Solly turned his fury on the cab of the truck again and his dot game went from left to right and the pale-faced driver threw up his hands, and the truck swerved from the street onto the sidewalk and crashed into a shop window and turned over with a crazy sound and fury and glass flying and humans screaming like the jungle in the nighttime. The Duck began to swerve, their own driver had been hit and had slumped over the wheel, and Samuels jumped eagerly into the driver's seat and shoved the man aside, just in time to save the Duck from the same fate as the truck. Solly thought, the sonofabitch is glad to be in the driver's seat and not behind the gun. A big black soldier had the other machine gun now. There were only three of them breathing on the Duck now—he and Samuels and the other gunner. The rest had crossed the River Jordon. Samuels righted the Duck and went quickly up the silent street that was strangely quiet. You could hear the silence, even though you heard the thunder raging everywhere and all around you.

The other soldier shouted to Samuels. "Don't be in such a

hurry. I see some paddies crawling out from underneath the truck." And he raked his fire beneath the truck.

But Samuels kept moving up the empty street. And in a couple of minutes they were in the middle of the war again. Solly wondered where his buddies were. And if today was his dying day, he wanted to die with them this Sunday. Every overturned or empty Duck, every Negro standing or fallen that they came across, he searched in vain for a face from the 25th Amphib. Worm, Jimmy, Scotty—he never saw a one of them. They had been in the combat zone for two or three hours and no sign of one of his buddies.

They ran into another quiet street and when they were halfway up the block a soldier ran out from a doorway shouting:

"Sergeant Sandy! Sergeant Sandy!"

Solly's heart leaped about inside his chest and Samuels braked the Duck, and Solly shouted, "Scotty! Scotty! Damn your soul!"

The chunky soldier ran toward the Duck and climbed and scrambled in. His angry eyes were filled with tears of gladness and Solly could not help from crying. They put their arms around each other. They were speechless for a moment.

Finally Scotty said, "Goddamn, buddy, I'm more gladder to see you this morning than my old lady back on Edgecombe Avenue."

Solly did not trust himself to speak. He didn't want to break down and really cry in front of this lionhearted soldier, as he stood there remembering the first time he ever met this goddamn ornery bastard. "If the prisoner gets away, you do his time, the Army never loses." He understood Scotty at this moment, as he had never done before. Jerry Abraham Lincoln Scott was a dedicated patriot and Dignity was his country and Manhood was his government and Freedom was his land. This was where Scott lived. Or died. There wasn't that much difference. Solly remembered, "I been home to fuck Miss Scotty!" And he started to laugh and cry at the same time and he moved away from the other soldier and did not bother to wipe his eyes or blow his nose.

When he could finally speak he said, "Where're the rest of them?"

Scotty said, "They around here some-damn-where, dead or dying."

Solly said, "You're the first Amphib I've seen all day long."

Scotty said, "You shouldna strayed away so far from home. You almost missed every goddamn thing. Peoples is the craziest mama-jabbers in all the world. You shoulda seen that General-goddamn-Grant. He got his nuts off killing gobs of paddies this morning, and he's happy in Heaven this afternoon, or else he's busting Hell wide open."

Solly wiped his face with his sleeve and was scared to ask the next question. "How about Worm and Jimmy and the others?"

"Last time I seen Worm and Jimmy they was whaling, but that was early this morning. Maybe they got em back at the Jones Street station."

Solly said, "Maybe! Maybe!"

Scotty said, "That's a better *maybe* than a whole heapa maybe's I could maybe."

It was funny but for the last five or ten minutes Solly had not heard the thunder or seen or felt the lightning. He had stood in peace with Scotty. But now he heard it all anew. His heart began to explode again and hell was bursting in his belly and his whole body began to leak a brand-new perspiration. Maybe they were at the police station with Army colonels and cracker military cops, and it would be some place to go instead of roaming streets like bloodthirsty wolves. And they coud go and fight and live and hope. They were hemmed in anyhow.

He said, "Which way to the Jones Street station?"

Scotty said, "Tell that mama-jabbing driver to move over, I'll take you there." And when Samuels moved Scotty stared at him and started to laugh and laugh and laugh, and he climbed into the driver's seat as Samuels moved to let him in. He put his arms around the captain. "You all right with me, old buddy. You the first peckerwood I ever know who was a good peckerwood without being a dead peckerwood."

Samuels's face turned red as an overripened carrot, and Solly laughed inside of him till his stomach hurt. And he didn't know whether he was laughing or crying, as Scotty made a sweeping U-turn and moved back up the silent street toward the middle of the thunder and the lightning.

The fighting had broken out now all over South Bainbridge, even a few brief skirmishes in the residential section. All day long Celia had sat helpless near her wireless with the reports coming in of concentrated fighting in the commercial district and sporadic outbursts here and there and even now spilling over into North Bainbridge. And she could do nothing but sit and walk up and down and listen to the wireless and go crazy and cry and slowly die and die and die. A few times she went into the street and got into her bomb. The people in the streets were numbed and shellshocked. How in the hell could it possibly happen? How could it happen? A full-scale war in Bainbridge! American soldiers slaughtering each other on the streets of her Bainbridge. It wasn't true—it wasn't true. How could there be such bitterness? Where are you, Solly? Where are you, beloved Solly? Live, my darling, live! Kill if you have to, but please God, live, my bloody darling. Live for your child you've never seen. And live for Her and live for Me. Yes, yes, live for me. Live for all the times you loved me. And live for you—live for you you you! She tried to get through to the Elizabeth Bridge, but by evening the police and the provost marshals had roped off a section that reached six blocks square this side of the bridge and they would not let anybody through. A P.M. stopped her and she turned around and tried to go down another street and another and another, and she tried another bridge, but each time she was thwarted. She came back home after dark and she could hear the war over in the south of her city going on and on and on, and the reddened sky above the city looked like the entire world was burning down. Celia went back into her house and turned on the wireless and turned from station to station, and it was all about the "Battle of Bainbridge," they had already given it a title for posterity, the Battle of Bainbridge, which was still raging with a fury never witnessed before in the history of modern civilization.

This is the anatomy of hate, pure, clean and unadulterated. . . .

She turned to another station.

No wild men ever fought with more sheer ferocity nor with more hatred for the adversary. Both sides are . . .

She turned the dial.

As for the weather it was a balmy day in Bainbridge, made even warmer by the outbreak of hostilities. Bainbridgites are aghast and outraged and still cannot believe that . . .

She clicked off the wireless and went to the kitchen and got a drink, and she poured it down her throat and felt it spreading through her shoulders and burning up her stomach. How could it possibly be that people could be born in the same country and grow up together side by side and have such hatred for each other? It was the first time she could really even begin to appreciate the anger deep inside of Solly, the anger she had tried so hard to reach and to know and to understand and to feel and to hold and to caress and to soften into tenderness. Because he is a tender man. He is a tender human being. I have known his tenderness.

She went to the telephone for the fifteenth or twentieth time, and she tried to get through to the Farms, she tried to call the Jones Street station. Everywhere the lines were jammed. She finally got somebody to answer at General Jack's headquarters.

She said, "Why don't you people do something to stop the bloody massacre? Have all of you gone crazy?"

The polite American at the other end said, "Sorry, lady, we're doing everything we can." And he politely hung up, and she started to call him again, but she slammed the receiver onto the hook, and she sat on the couch, and she thought, maybe I'm the one who's crazy. Maybe I'm imagining the whole damn thing. It must be my imagination. It's just been too much for me, she tried to think soberly. Losing Pat so suddenly and now Solly is leaving me next week, but I just have to get hold of myself. She saw Solly now as plain as the moonlight, lying dead on a quiet street with his face his dear eyes staring sweetly at the moon, and she knew it was no dream she dreamed, she saw him dead, she saw him dead, and she would never see him alive again. She fell face down on the couch and she cried, "Don't be dead, Solly! Don't be dead! Don't be dead! Please, dear Solly, don't be dead!"

She reached out and turned the wireless on again.

. . . enraged Australian authorities are moving swiftly now to bring the Americans to their senses . . . an insult to the people of Australia . . . a slap in the face to the war against fascism . . .. Efforts to contact General Jack have so far been futile. The word is that he is up north where the other war is continuing. Our authorities have

reached all the way to Washington. . . . Meanwhile the Battle of Bainbridge continues unabated. . . .

It was after four in the morning and the Battle of Bainbridge was headed toward its second day, and they had battled every inch and every millionth of a second since they came across the King George Bridge, and Solly had lost track of time and space and he thought his back was breaking and his spine would snap in two and he would never sleep again and his eyes would never cry and his shoulder must be broken from the constant kicking of his rifle and the submachine gun, and his trigger hand was fast asleep it seemed, but he was wide awake. They had battled the others block for block, truck to truck, Duck to Duck and Duck to truck, building to building, house to house, hand to hand and man-to-goddamn-crazy-man. He'd seen dead and dying everywhere, but Solly had not gotten a glimpse of Bookworm or the Quiet Man. Scotty was killed near the Jones Street station.

They're all wiped out, he thought. All of them killed and dead and dead and dead, and maybe they were better off than he was, who had not received a single scratch. Worm and Scotty and Quiet Man and Worm and Scott and Quiet Man. They had paid their everlasting dues. He didn't know it, wasn't certain about Worm and Jimmy, but he felt in the pit of his stomach. All night long he and Samuels and the gunner had shot their way up one street and down the other, not knowing whom they killed or how damn many, and he didn't even know the gunner's name. The gunner was dead now and Scotty was dead, as were soldiers all over the place in every street in every doorway. All night long the guns were talking belching screaming one sweet tune of Peace Everlasting Found in Death's Eternal Tender Sleep. He thought, maybe it's all over now, the Battle of Bainbridge, because he couldn't hear the sound of war any more. His ears were deafened and maybe he would never hear again, or maybe he had also won that Everlasting Peace in Death. Maybe he was dead—he hoped—he almost hoped—

But he shouted to himself, "I'm still alive! I'm still alive! Fannie Mae, I'm still alive! Tell our son, I'm still alive!" as the crazy Duck dashed madly up a narrow street. They had changed vehicles three times through the night. From Duck to truck to Duck again. The Duck plunged suddenly out onto a broad plaza, made soft and mellow by an unfeeling unromantic orange-colored moonlight spilling all over it, and they had run completely out of the war. And it felt damn good to be alive and feel the cool fresh air like chilled wine rush into his weary lungs. He straightened up and looked around him and he opened his mouth and closed his eyes and drank the air in deeply all inside of him, and it was just like Scotty used to say, "You close your eyes you lose sight on the world, and you won't ever see again."

There was an almost imperceptible movement behind a park bench in the plaza as two M–1 rifles took careful aim at Solly, letting him come closer and closer so they could blow his head away. Closer closer closer—they could not miss him if they tried to. He should have never closed his eyes. *Closer-now!*

Samuels felt the movement more than heard it, and he did not hesitate for a why or where or who or by-your-leave. He combed the bench from end to end with a submachine gun he had inherited during an earlier part of the nightmare. Two brief shouts from the mourners' bench and all was peace and quiet there.

Solly hit the floor of the Duck like he was doing a belly-buster. When he finally got his voice again he said, "Thanks, my friend." *Time* was the only difference between life and death, and Time could wait and Time could also get impatient.

His friend said, "It's about time we called each other 'friend.' We've been working at it long enough."

Solly laughed weakly into the darkness. Just a hundredth of a second between his living and his dying. "You're a colored man tonight, old buddy. You have naturally earned your spurs. I'm going to vote you into the club." The driver softly laughed at them.

Samuels stood up and shouted angrily at Solly, "I am a white man and I am your friend, and you are a Negro man and you are my best friend, and we are both friends of the human race. Don't hand me any other kind of half-assed nationalistic shit!"

He stared at Samuels through the night, and he tried his best to laugh at Samuels. "Anything you say, old buddy boy."

The driver turned toward them and laughed again a kind of harsh and bitter laughter.

Their little tête-à-tête was rudely interrupted as they heard round after round of machine-gun fire sounding off about two blocks beyond the plaza. The driver made a swift U-turn and headed back toward the principal area of the fighting, which had quieted down considerably.

After a while Solly said, "Maybe everybody has just about run out of ammunition."

You could only hear sporadic outbursts now. "Or maybe they just ran out of steam."

They went wearily up a dark and narrow quiet street.

Samuels said, "Maybe everybody has reconsidered and realized what fools they've been. Maybe they've had a change of heart."

The driver said in a thick and dry and Southern voice, "You must be from up-the-country. A peckerwood is a peckerwood and he gon always be a peckerwood till he become a dead peckerwood."

Solly laughed and laughed and laughed and laughed. He remembered what Scotty had said a few hours earlier, and he laughed and cried and laughed and cried.

The lines were burning between Washington and Bainbridge, and ears were burning too. And heads of brass would surely roll.

Washington learned about the battle from Australian authorities and they in turn contacted Adeline Street, which was the Supreme Command of the South Pacific.

General Buford Jack was in the Philippines. One of his flunkies, Major General Benson, caught the full wrath of the Pentagon.

"No excuses, Benson! Just stop that goddamn race riot!"

"Sir—"

"Have all of you down there gone completely out of your mind? Don't you know what the war is being fought for?"

"But—"

"No buts, Benson. Stop it immediately, that's all, and get to the bottom of who's responsible, and I don't mean enlisted men. There'll be a full-scale investigation and court-martials and all the rest of it. This is a disgrace to America."

"Yes, sir—"

"And it better not get into the newspapers or else your head will roll along with the rest. That's no threat, that's a promise. It must get no publicity at all—you understand? I don't care what you have to do to prevent it."

When General Benson hung up he got in touch with the division commander and ranted and raved and swore at him and threatened. And the division commander called Brigadier General Jefferson Jamison, the base commander at Camp Worthington Farms, and on down the line till it reached the adjutant, Colonel William Bradford the Third.

"What the hell are you doing to stop this race riot?" the base commander asked him. General Jamison was a son of the South like his adjutant, and he was West Point and Regular Army and tall and blue-eyed and overly handsome and fiftyish and graying very hurriedly.

Bradford had just come into the office on the double and was almost out of breath. He said, "Nothing, sir. I mean we've tried but—"

The general said, "Nothing!" He stared at the colonel incredulously. "You mean you have done nothing at all?"

Bradford was not excited yet. As impressive an officer as the general undoubtedly was, it was almost impossible for Bradford to fully respect him, since he slept with the general's wife and knew that the general slept with every fat-assed boy he could lay hands on, even interracially, and from the general's wife he knew other intimate details about the great man.

"Sir, I telephoned you and I spoke to you about it when you got back to camp, and it didn't seem to—I mean I tried to keep them from—We did everything—"

"Listen carefully, Colonel Bradford," General Jamison said. "First of all, you had the first opportunity to stop the convoy from going into town—understand? That's when the whole thing should have been halted, but you let the niggers make a fool out of you by your own admission." The general paused and stared contemptuously at his adjutant. "Second—you're the one, again by your own admission, who triggered the riot with your idiotic phone calls. If you spent as much thought on Army matters as you do on the strategy and tactics of getting into the drawers of every whore from here to Melbourne, you'd be a military genius."

This bastard knows about me and his wife, the colonel thought, and he's ready to throw me to the pack. He ought to be thankful to me. I'm keeping Martha satisfied while he's running all over the place after every Tom, Dick, and Harry.

General Jamison said, "You were faced with a simple emergency situation, and instead of using your head, you panicked like a pregnant woman. And you are held entirely responsible for what has happened. Of all the stupid hysterical actions—"

The colonel was so angry he was trembling and his voice failed him temporarily, and he was scared now, because he saw the unveiled hatred in the general's face. And you got me where you want me, you limp-wristed bastard, and you'll feed me gladly to the wolves, and watch them pick me to the bone, and I have nowhere to pass the buck.

When he could talk he said, "Sir, I have to differ with you, sir, I don't—"

The general had worked himself into a rage. He slapped the desk with the palm of his hand. "I don't give a damn about your differing or who you're fucking or whose fucking you. Washington has sent the word down. You understand what that means? Somebody's ass is going to burn and it ain't going to be General Jamison's, understand? A race riot in Australia— When I get through with those black Amphibs they'll wish they'd never been born. And you, Colonel, you—"

"I won't be a scapegoat for anybody, General. Not even you. I'll—"

"You shut up and listen to me. I want every white man on this base who is not already over in South Bainbridge. I want them under your command. I want you to take them over the river and peaceably bring that idiocy you started to a halt. I want it done immediately. On second thought I'd better go with you. You might screw it up again. You let me know when you're ready."

Bradford stared at the general. He had the picture completely before him now. He was to be the scapegoat and the general would be the hero who put out the fire and saved the maiden's honor. And there was nothing he could do to change the story's ending. Nothing—not a goddamn thing—nothing he could do to save his own ass. He would be burned at the stake and General Jamison would get another citation. At the court-martial he could tell it like it happened and let the chips fall every damn where and bring the general down with him. He could do that, and he almost felt consoled by the realization that he had the power to destroy the general. He could pull the building down, even though he himself might be wiped out by the falling debris.

"Get going, Bradford!" the general shouted.

Bradford came to attention and saluted the general and went hurriedly out into the early morning darkness.

"When those damn Amphibs face my court-martial!" the general shouted to the early-morning darkness. "They want to fight, do they? I'll send the crippled black bastards up north to the goddamn front!"

For over a half an hour now they had left the Duck and walked the moonlit streets of South Bainbridge among the ruins of dead and dying, passing other Yankee soldiers, walking, riding, quiet soldiers, white and colored, and overturned trucks and Ducks upended and shattered plate glass, and everywhere it seemed that a combination of typhoon, tornado, hurricane, and earthquake had smashed and battered the business district. The shooting had died away completely. They had probably run out of ammunition, Solly figured. And run out of hatred, Samuels hoped. Solly and Samuels wearily patroled the streets with their empty rifles turning over bodies, looking for familiar faces. Looking in doorways and under Ducks and trucks. They stumbled over soldiers who had fallen asleep right where they were when the shooting ended. Solly remembered the men of the Bowery in the cold of New York winter. Day was about to break again as Solly and Samuels sat down on the edge of the sidewalk and all the fear and pain and horror and tiredness of the last twenty-four hours ganged up on them and moved in on them, and they stretched out and almost fell asleep, excepting they could not really fall asleep. Solly thought he would never be able to sleep again. He would always live with nightmares.

He said to Samuels, "Let's get going. We got to find Worm and Jimmy and get the hell out of this place." He tried to get up but could not make it. Why was he in such a big hurry? Where were they going anyhow? And what would happen when they got there? Court-martial—which would probably result in them being sent up north back to the front and join the other soldiers and complete the job of dying. Somehow now he envied Scotty.

Samuels said, "Just a few more minutes. Let's just sit here a few more minutes."

Solly said, "Come on now. Don't fall asleep. We have to get

the hell out of this place. Got to find—come on—come on. Don't fall asleep."

He struggled to his feet and managed to get Samuels to stand up, and they went stumbling down the street together.

"How do you get out of this place?" Samuels mumbled. "Which way is the bridge?"

They turned a corner and up ahead they saw a capsized Duck, and Solly broke into a run. He saw upside-down the Double-V, the Bookworm's famous trademark on the backside of the Duck. He shouted like a little boy on Christmas morning. He saw the big bright letters FANNIE MAE.

"It's Worm! It's Worm!"

They dragged the bodies from beneath the Duck. They were Worm and Baby-Face Banks and Jimmy.

Jimmy was smiling. Worm was angry. Banks's hardened baby face was no longer puzzled, as if he had at long last found a cause to die for.

Solly couldn't take his eyes from them—especially Jimmy, the Quiet Man. Smiling for eternity, caught for all infinity. As if he'd played a miserable joke on the whole damn world and made his exit. All three of them had found a cause worthy of their precious lives.

They laid them out on the sidewalk neatly side by side, and they sat down on the curb and cried. They didn't even bother to be ashamed of crying. They were filled up to the overflowing and they let the tears come down. They forgot that they were men and men were not supposed to cry.

Solly could think of nothing but they're dead and forever more they're dead, and Scotty is dead, and it didn't have to happen, and there's no earthly reason for it, and he remembered the first time he saw the big-eyed soft-spoken soldier from the work battalion that night in Ebbensville, but they're dead and dead and dead, and every time he thought he had stopped crying, it would keep building up in him, through his shoulders into his face, and he felt sick, and he thought the war is over for them, everything is over for them, and they're better off, goddammit, and I should be happy for them, and he cried and cried and he had to stop crying, it did no good, it would not bring Worm and Scotty and Jimmy and Billy back, but his eyes kept filling up and he could not help from crying. They had been babies once and their mothers and their fathers had looked at them and dreamed for them and they had been children on the streets of New York City and they had gone to school and they had dreamed and they had grown into manhood and had had hopes and aspirations to be somebody and success and families of their own, and here they were ten thousand miles away from home, fighting for their country and Democracy and Freedom and Manhood, and they were dead and dead and dead . . . And tomorrow they would still be dead and the day after that and after that and after that and they were forever ever dead. . . .

And there was no Freedom—no Democracy. And the world was sad—the whole damn world was the saddest place in all the universe.

Samuels said, "It doesn't make a goddamn bit of sense. It makes no—" His voice choked off.

Solly stood up and stared with wet eyes down at the bodies. "I promise you, my buddies, to never forget the way I feel this Monday morning. I will always hate war with all my heart and all my soul. I will always fight the men who beat the drums for war in the name of Holy Patriotism in any nation, any language. I will fight with all the strength that's in me the goddamn bloated buzzards who profit from this madness."

He sucked the tears back up his nostrils. He smiled at Bookworm. "And I promise you a Double-V."

His eyes and ears played tricks on him. He thought he saw Worm's lips break open and heard him speak as plain as day, "Where were you, Sergeant Solly? You shoulda been with us, cut buddy. We got our Double-V already."

Solly blinked his eyes. "Thank you, Bookworm."

And now he knew what he hoped he never would forget again. All his escape hatches from being Negro were more illusion than reality and did not give him dignity. All of his individual solutions and his personal assets. Looks, Personality, Education, Success, Acceptance, Security, the whole damn shooting match, was one great grand illusion, without dignity. Fannie Mae had called it manhood. Like something you keep reaching for that never was and never would be—without manhood. If he signed a separate treaty with Cap'n Charlie, would it guarantee him safe-conduct through the great white civilized jungle where the war was raging always raging? Would his son also get safe-passage? Anywhere any time any place? He had searched in all the wrong places.

"Thank you, Bookworm, buddy boy."

Samuels said, "What're you muttering about?"

"Thank you, Bookworm, buddy. Thank you, Baby-Face and Jimmy. Thank you, darling Fannie Mae. Thank you, Scotty!"

Never compromise your manhood, Fannie Mae had told him. Never sacrifice your manhood. He was a Negro and only with Worm and Jimmy and Baby-Face Banks could he achieve anything of lasting value. And Scotty and General Grant and Lanky. And Fannie Mae and Mama. And Junior. This was the ship to human dignity. All else was the open sea. Quiet Jimmy must have known this when he stepped out of line in Ebbensville.

His face was filling up again, kept filling up, and as he looked upon his buddies they seemed to be smiling at him, all three of them, all of the dead in South Bainbridge were smiling, all the fallen soldiers smiling smiling everywhere, and he turned his head from them, he tried to talk again, but no further words came now. He felt Samuels's arms around his shoulder. They sat down again and this time they did not cry. They had no more tears to shed.

Solly thought, Scotty and Worm and Banks and Quiet Man and all the rest—they are not crying. In death they've won their victory and left me here behind to cry for them, and die, and they are dead already and left me holding the bag. In a way he envied them. In another way he took strength from them, and felt guilty.

He stared at Worm and Banks once more and Quiet Man, and his face was filling up again. He felt a deep guilt that he was alive and only he was alive and all the rest were dead and felt even guiltier that he was so happy he was living. Why had his life been spared and for what purpose? His heart shouted for the joy of living. I'm so glad to be alive, Fannie Mae, I'm ashamed of myself, but I'm glad glad glad! A sweet cool morning breeze caressed his sweating forehead, and he promised himself and promised them that the world would know their story. If he lived, he would write it. He thought aloud unknowingly.

"If I get back home, my brothers, I'll tell the world about your battle here in Bainbridge. Maybe it's not too late yet, if I tell it to the whole wide world, tell them if they don't solve *this* question, the whole damn world will be like Bainbridge is this morning! The whole damn world will be like Bainbridge!"

He had forgotten Samuels altogether till he heard him

saying, "Maybe we'll really have peace this time. Maybe after the war is over."

Solly shook his angry head. "No peace—there is no peace—there is no peace till freedom. You can't make a man a slave and have him live in peace with you."

Two white soldiers came up the street toward them and stopped about ten feet from them. Solly and Samuels instinctively reached for their empty rifles.

One of the soldiers said in accent thick and scared and Dixiefied: "We ain't looking for no fight, mates. We just want to sit down and rest a little while." He was probably from Georgia. Or Texas or Louisiana or Alabama.

Solly jumped to his feet. "It's a trick! It's a lousy goddamn trick! They're up to something!" He almost fell on his face.

The bareheaded cracker soldier said, "Ain't no trick, mate. We just fagged out, beat down to the ground, and we ain't got nothing against nobody, and the whole damn thing don't make no sonofabitching sense." He spread his palms upward as if he were feeling for a raindrop. "Look, we ain't got no guns or nothing. We just sorry about the whole damn thing. Colored folks ain't never done us nothing. I didn't want to come into town. I swear before the living God, me and my buddy didn't want to come!" Solly stared at the pale-faced dark-haired bastard whose eyes were filling up with tears. The whole damn Army was nothing but a pack of pissy-assed cry-babies.

Solly said, "The only way to do it is to beat some sense into your heads." Maybe this way was the only way.

The soldier said, "You didn't see what we saw tonight. It was the awfulest thing in the world."

Solly sat back down, and the two men came and sat down near them but apart. The other white soldier said, "We ain't got nothing against nobody."

Solly mumbled, "Beat some sense into your heads. That's the only way to do it."

Trucks were coming up some highway some-damn-where, moaning and groaning, in his head he heard them coming, and dawn was breaking out in the bay, and way out in the Coral Sea the sun was making flames and torches to throw light on a brand-new day. And Solly thought, the world is waking up again. Let it stay awake forever.

He felt a heat all over him, consuming him. The whole damn world was burning down. He wanted to believe a new world would rise up from the smoking ruins. He wanted to believe whatever was left of the world would come to its senses and build something new and different and new and new and altogether different. He wanted to believe that East and West could meet somewhere sometime, and sometime soon, before it was too late to meet. Before the whole world was just like Bainbridge. And build something new that was neither East nor West nor North nor South, but something new, superior to anything that ever was. Like a new baby born of a particular man and a particular woman, with a part of each of them in it, but entirely different from either of them. He wanted to believe that Kipling's lie was obsolete. He wanted fiercely to believe—that all this dying was for something. Beat some sense into their heads. If they don't love you they'll respect you. He remembered General Grant and his pure and righteous anger. Maybe he was the wisest of them all. With his "bottom coming to the top." Perhaps the New World *would* come raging out of Africa and Asia, with a new and different dialogue that was people-oriented. What other hope was there?

Yes, Worm and Jimmy and Baby and Scott and Grant are dead, and the world is waking up again.

And we four soldiers sit here crying.

Five Negro soldiers stumbled up the street from somewhere.

"Which way to the bridge, mates?" one of them asked.

Solly stared up in their faces. Scared and lost and weary faces. He said, "Sit down, mates, and make yourself at home. This is the place where the New World is." They stared at Solly and the others. Another one came around the corner.

The talker said, "Well sure, why not? I mean, we ain't got no special place to go."

And they came and sat and waited. For what?

General Jamison's peace-mission trucks were now rolling into town.

The world is waking up again.

And we poor bastards sit here crying.

APPENDIX
Selected Reviews

From *Best Sellers*, February 1, 1963

The law school studies of Solomon Saunders are interrupted by his entrance into the army during World War II. Saunders is processed at Fort Dix and eventually sent to a base in Georgia. Saunders and the other non-commissioned officers in his unit are Negroes. Saunders thinks of the war as a struggle of democracy versus facism, but most of his fellow soldiers are critical of America's and the army's attitude toward the Negro. While visiting in a Georgia town near the military base, Saunders is seized by two policemen and taken to jail. When he appeals to a local army colonel for justice, he is savagely beaten by the colonel and the town policemen. Saunders becomes disillusioned and bitter; he realizes that the army is doing almost nothing to eliminate or control racial prejudice. Saunders and a few other soldiers write a critical letter which is published in several newspapers. As a result, Saunders and several of his fellow soldiers are transferred to an amphibious combat unit training in California. Prejudice is also encountered there. The Negro soldiers are allowed to use the Post Exchange only after staging a militant protest. The Negro amphibious group is shipped overseas to an island in the South Pacific. Soon Saunders and his unit are seeing violent action in the Philippines. Saunders is eventually wounded and sent to a hospital in Australia. There a white nurse falls in love with him. His wife had died in childbirth, but Saunders had previously found a Georgia girl named Fannie Mae who had attracted him. Saunders is again infuriated by the racial discrimination practiced in Australia by army authorities, although the Australians are free from prejudice. When the MP's continue their harassment of the Negroe [sic] soldiers, a full scale battle breaks out between white and Negro troops. Hundreds of men are slaughtered. Saunders and a few other survivors wait patiently for a new world to be born, a world free from hatred.

Several obvious faults are apparent in this novel. Some of the characters are simply mouthpieces for various viewpoints. Other figures are too consciously motivated by the author. The love scenes are routine—torrid, raw, and overdone in the popular fashion. The style is often too rhetorical, too hysterical, too shrill; and yet one tends to forgive most of these weaknesses because of the importance and validity of Mr. Killens's message. The author's earnestness and the obvious justice of his analysis and warning are particularly compelling and sobering. Mature and thoughtful readers who are not easily offended by unusual frankness of language might find it worth their while to reflect on the problems American Negro soldiers faced in World War II.

Paul A. Doyle, Ph.D.

From *The Critic*, "Education Shelf", February-March 1963

This is a difficult book to review, for a variety of reasons. There is no doubt, first, that it contains some of the rawest, crudest yet most real and convincing dialogue ever transferred from barracks-room Army life to print and paper. Ex-soldiers tell us that after a few months in the Army they don't even notice the continual vulgarity of their everyday language: after 200 pages of this novel the same thing happens. One becomes (for better or worse) inured to the language and then aware of its very real merits. This raises the second point of difficulty, for the subject matter—the life of a Negro soldier, an educated law student, from the time he is drafted into the Army early in World War II until the tragic events of race war between Americans in Australia near the end of the conflict—is, in some sense, dated. It is true that the real struggle still goes on, but the situations described here have to some extent been solved. So this story of discrimination in the armed forces is historical. Nonetheless it is terrifyingly real. The writer, who is gifted at writing dialogue while he often fails to create dimensioned characters, has raised a world for our inspection that is neither pretty nor pleasant to contemplate.

From *Herald Tribune Books*, April 14, 1963

You must put yourself in the skin of a man wearing the uniform of his country who does not dance at the U.S.O. the night white soldiers dance there, and sees German prisoners treated with more human dignity than he has ever received, and who is far freer in a strange land than at home. "You must consider," James Baldwin demands, "what happens to this citizen."

"I'm a young deserving man," the hero of Mr. Killens's second novel decides on his honeymoon, "I will one day do my dancing at the Waldorf but will at the same time keep in touch with my folks who will still be stomping at the Savoy."

Yet he resents his admiring bride's assurance that "You're going to get ahead in the world, darling." That's too explicit for Solomon Saunders. He isn't out for "success" but for "achievement." He isn't ambitious: merely militant. He doesn't talk to himself, but has interior monologues. And when he is inducted he resolves to be "the best damned soldier in the army."

The men who share his barracks don't share his resolution. "If Hitler wants to make a landing here I'll be his guide," one volunteers. It was no good explaining that, if Hitler conquered America, the Negro would be worse off. This party had done *all* his stomping at the Savoy.

Saunders's willingness to risk his life for his country is ultimately paralyzed by reluctance to serve a ruling class as secretly fascistic toward himself as is the enemy openly. His attempt to resolve this impossible predicament by adapting the Double-V-For-Victory sign—victory over white supremacists at home as well as abroad—works out no better than had his dancing schedule.

Although the author carries us through two years of warfare with a Jim Crow cast, complete with Cracker captain, he does not resolve the impossible predicament any more successfully than his hero. Yet he does reach for it:

"Perhaps the New World would come raging out of Africa and Asia," Saunders reflects, "with a new and different dialogue that was people-oriented. What other hope was there?"

Then he draws back. For while Mr. Baldwin's report of oppression derives first-hand from the suffering of the American Negro, Mr. Killens's report rings more like a program to which he is a conscientious subscriber. His novel so lacks the feel and smell of barracks and of the passion of men at war that we remain unmoved, at the close, by Saunders's wistful wish "that whatever was left of the world would come to its senses and build something new and different and new and new and altogether different. He wanted to believe that East and West could meet somewhere sometime and sometime soon, before it was too late to meet."

This rings as rhetorically as the Jewish lieutenant announcing in the midst of gunfire, "I am a white man, and I am your friend, and you are a Negro man and you are my best friend, and we are both friends of the human race." As Archie told Broadway-The-Lightning-Bug, "I don't hear no thunder."

Nelson Algren

From *Library Journal*, January 1, 1963

Eight years after "Youngblood," John Killens has written another novel of social protest, this time about Negro-American soldiers in World War II. It has its faults. Its style and diction are often amateurish and overmannered. It lacks taste, the instinct for using the right word. But it is powerful, passionate, and rises to a rip-roaring climax. The hero, Solomon Saunders, Jr., is a handsome, educated Negro with ideals, ambition, and the desire to "pass" as far as possible into a white world of prestige, power, and wealth. A mounting series of incidents of oppression, discrimination, unfairness, and police brutality which would try the patience of Job finally convinces him that the fight of all Negroes for equality and justice is his fight. The book contains graphic descriptions of his three love affairs, with his wife, Millie; with Fanny Mae, a Georgia canteen girl; and with the white Australian, Celia. Some minor characters are well drawn: Lt. Samuels, his Jewish lieutenant; Bookworm, the chronic AWOL and agitator. The battle scenes in the Pacific are vivid, as are those of a mutiny in Australia; and the language of the barracks and the field, accurately reported, is not for the Ladies' Aid Society. An earnest, immoderate, different war novel. For collections of modern fiction. —Lloyd W. Griffin, Asst. Ln. in charge of Humanities, Univ. of Wisconsin Lib., Madison, Wis.

From the *New York Post*, March 31, 1963

The blood-curdling climax of this novel is as inevitable in fiction as it was in real life in World War II. For what Killens depicts in his closing chapters actually happened: Negro and white soldiers, all wearing the same U.S. Army uniform, finally turned the weapons of modern warfare on each other, and the only badge of the enemy was the color of his skin. It happened in Brisbane, Australia, and it was one of the best kept secrets of the war.

"And Then We Heard The Thunder" is not a polemic on race relations nor an assembly of cardboard characters repeating the old litany of white man's inhumanity to black.

It is, as the leading trade magazine of the book industry told its subscribers during New York's newspaper blackout, "a fine job of writing which rises to true eloquence," and "has a cumulative impact that fairly rivets the reader to the pages." The hero is a Negro GI, Solly Saunders.

Fannie Mae is not necessarily the most eloquent of the three women—one white—who love the sensitive, college-bred Solly. But love only strengthens her conviction that the war provided an unrivaled opportunity for "Double V" —the wartime slogan of America's disadvantaged minority—victory at home and victory abroad.

To Millie, Solly's light-skinned sophisticate wife, World War II offered her husband a more cynical opportunity—officer-status, social prestige and a chance to lift them both above and away from the Harlem hordes.

To the pretty Australian nurse Celia, probably the least selfish of the three in her love, the war had brought Solly. But America defeated her too. For to Solly, she had the face—if not the body—of the enemy.

Solly is the chief protagonist, but he does not dwarf his fellow sufferers and associates. The panorama of Army prejudice could not be fully understood without Worm and Jimmy and Baby and Scott—not a Martin Luther King in the lot of them.

Equally vivid are the cracker Capt. Rutherford, the Jewish Lieut. Samuels (of whom Saunders demands more than he would of any Negro) and several other characters.

* * * * *

There are minor flaws in "And Then We Heard the Thunder." Solly probably has been portrayed as too handsome and too irresistible to women. For surely he is not this season's most lovable character. But this big, robust, readable novel more than fulfills the promise of Killens's "Youngblood."

Ted Poston

From the New York Post (March 31, 1963)

From *The New York Times*, April 7, 1963

An angry, uneven but often stirring book about a Negro amphibious regiment in World War II. Solly Saunders, a New York law student, enters Fort Dix determined to be "the best damn soldier in the Army of the United States of North America." But the pressures of Jim Crow force upon him the role of a "race man"—a militant battler for equality. From the red clay country of Georgia, where he is beaten by white police, to the Pacific theater where he is thrown out of a restricted Red Cross Club, Saunders is forced to make common cause with his race rather than with his army. In Australia, the hostilities that have been smouldering throughout the book finally erupt in a bloody race riot. Though Mr. Killens slides too easily into the platitudinous and the maudlin, pungent characterizations and a core of honest indignation make this an affecting novel.

From *Saturday Review*, January 26, 1963

In this big, polyphonic, violent novel about Negro soldiers in World War II, John Oliver Killens drags the reader into the fullness of the Negro's desolating experience. The author, formerly a member of the National Labor Relations Board in Washington and now a movie and television writer, served in the Amphibian Forces in the South Pacific. His novel, therefore, has the depth and complexity of lived experience. It calls James Jones to mind, though Killens writes with less technical control and more poetically. But his battle scenes have the same hallucinatory power; his characters live and speak the raw language of the streets and the barracks.

This non-Negro reader who served in the Pacific alongside Negro troops recognizes the events and characters of this novel; but he sees them with a sort of brain-twisting transformation of insights. He never gave much thought, for example, to the hideous irony of asking the Negro to fight (in segregated units) and die in order to preserve the very freedoms which he could not enjoy at home. Few non-Negroes knew the Negro soldier's common motto, the Double V for Victory: victory against Fascism overseas and victory against Fascism at home. Nor did it ruffle us to hear the band play "God Bless America" while we boarded troopships and then switch to "Darktown Strutters' Ball" when the Negro troops' turn came.

But here, living it through the Negro's reaction, we cannot believe our ears. We look up at the white soldiers on deck "waving and smiling innocently and friendly-like at the Negro soldiers below and yelling, 'Yeah, man!' and popping their pinky white fingers," and the same taste of gall creeps up from our stomachs into our mouths. And we hear a companion whisper, "We ain't no soldiers. We ain't nothing but a bunch of goddamn clowns."

The book's hero, Solly Saunders, is an educated Negro, a man of taste, position, and ability who went into the war with illusions about fighting to protect America from her enemies. He was confident he would advance, become a leader, do his part to democratize the army.

But he discovered, in those days before integration of the armed forces, that the Negro in uniform was even more harrowingly at the mercy of racists than in civilian life, particularly if the racist happened to be an officer. In order to advance he found he had to lick boots, turn against his own, "go white"—something he could not do.

The bitterness was compounded by rigid segregation even in overseas combat zones. Mimicking the attitudes of white officers, the hero explains:

> ". . . just because many of them [Negro soldiers] had left their black blood to smear the pretty white beaches . . . and left their black and brown comrades to fertilize the land of strangers. Just because they were soldiers, tried and trusted nephews of their Uncle Sam, they had the colossal nerve to want to go to all the places where the other soldiers went and to be treated free and equal. They were stinking opportunists. They wanted to be treated in Australia better than they were at home. What arrogance—what treachery—what . . . gall!"

If the Negro's bitterness and disillusion with his slave status in the old army were massive, he at least expected something better when he returned to America after fighting for democracy overseas. The reader, living all the indignities of the Negro soldier, sees clearly how it looked from the other side of the color line. Discrimination in the armed forces has been eliminated. But the deep wounds of Negro soldiers have not. This novel magnificiently illumines the reasons why. Their second victory—against Fascism at home—is slow in coming.

John Howard Griffin